# THE GREATSHIP

THE GREATSHIP

ROBERT REED

ebook ISBN: 978-0-7867-5367-3

Print ISBN: 978-0-7867-5366-6

Distributed by Argo Navis Author Services

Contents

Bridge Ten

The Man With the Golden Balloon

Bridge Eleven

Introduction

An Author's Dire Warning:

These twelve original stories have been reworked, sometimes lightly massaged and occasionally mutilated with a hyperfiber knife. I have set them in some kind of chronological order, with overlaps and long gaps, and I won't explain my logic. The bridging materials are new; they may or may not offer insights into grand schemes. Again, I'm not the tour guide here, and readers must make their own conjectures. Even the existence of an overarching story—some grand heroic epic involving the Greatship and its various passengers, adventures and the fate of the universe—should be subject to a measure of doubt.

On another note, many fine editors have played critical roles in seeing this universe come into existence. Thanks to all of them.

Finally, I look at this volume as an organic beast, full of growth and change. The Greatship is spacious. I get ideas on occasion. No worthy voyage can ever come to an end.

The Greatship

Prologue

The universe is steeped in voices.

One hydrogen atom, that humble unmemorable citizen, spends it existence singing. A nuclear scream holds its glorious proton together, gluons and quarks roaring about one another, enjoying what seems to be eternal balance. The electron, its opposite and its natural mate, roams the vastness, wayward photons and quantum migrations causing an electromagnetic wailing. Listen close and you hear the roaring voices of countless hydrogen atoms, each one screeching across realms and cold vaults and the spinning clouds infested with maelstroms that are hydrogen and little else.

The first and purest stars began as hydrogen and some spice of helium. But as the voyage continued those stars have died and the newborn multitudes have swallowed the heavy ash. Their bellies and their skins are dirty with oxygen and carbon, argon and iron. And each star, no matter its age or composition, has its own titanic chorus of howling voices. Gravity is a voice. Each star grabs at the rest of the universe. Each uses its mass to beg for companionship, a questing tug of matter dragging at matter, and the voice never stops, forever trying to slow what refuses to stop, trying to gather up the scattered pieces of an event that long ago ceased to have any visible margin, any meaningful brink or lip.

Yet no voice, no matter its strength or subtlety, or even its consummate wisdom, can reach farther than a very little ways.

Hydrogen talks and stars talk, and the stars assemble themselves into pinwheels and fogs that often if not always link together into walls that stretch long on scaffoldings built from the dark shy particles that whisper, only whisper, hiding in the plainest ways.

The universe is one grand shout, and all of these voices belong to it.

Listen carefully and hear the Creation.

* * *

Time passes and distance is covered, though never much distance compared to what must exist and never, ever with a clear purpose in mind. Hydrogen and dust pass as a steady mist. Some pieces of the mist can join the one who has drifted such a little ways and seen so much. Stars and their corpses pass by, tugging selfishly. Each body is as greedy as its mass. Every mass wants to grab what travels. What travels is fleeing everything that will end its existence, and survival is the only task, and why can't it remember why this is so extraordinarily important?

Time passes and the voices change, rising up from cold clods of rock and iron and liquids. Liquid bodies swim and stand on their own. They practice new ways of speaking and scream in complicated new ways, reveling in codes and riddles. What seemed like a magnificent but simple nightmare, a Creation sowed along a few clear rules, gains a new level of difficulty, conundrums rising up to threaten what travels, or they are trying to save it.

How does it know?

Voices call, the old ones and the new, and a great wall of stars and whispering black matter must be crossed without disaster. Fear must be endured, and fear is unnecessary. A few small suns come near, and one crushed piece of reality manages to shove the traveler onto a slightly different path. But that is done and finished and the wall drops behind and then comes a very long emptiness, not silent but at least pleasantly quiet, and nothing comes near, and nothing happens for such a long while, and it is possible to hope that nothing of substance will occur before the galaxies and every voice fall out of sight, and nothing will remain but what matters.

But always, always comes an obstruction.

Out of pure cold, the next galaxy emerges.

So much time has passed since the last starry reef. The voices have multiplied and grown even more complicated. Life thrives inside sacks of water and methane and clean husks of silicon and carbon. This is such a dangerous age. The tiny swirl of starlight carries hundreds of billions of stars and trillions of worlds, and there are too many voices to count, and each moment only increases the tally and the confusion, the terrible endless and most reasonable fear telling this wanderer to be as cautious and as fortunate as possible.

It is seen.

One voice must be first, but it seems as if a million distinct voices are suddenly singing about this odd little traveler that is only now entering the fringes of their obscure realm.

One voice calls their home: Milky Way.

The same voice refers to the traveler by many labels, including the descriptive, deeply flawed: Greatship.

Out from those stars and little worlds, starships rise.

Something called Human claims the Greatship as its own.

But something else—tinier by quite a lot and faster than anything else—is what falls first to the surface of what is not understood. The visitor drops alone onto the traveler, and the visitor survives its arrival, and what has always been the same is finished, and what follows is what will always follow, right until the End of the Ends.

Alone

1

The hull was gray and smooth, gray and empty, and in every direction it fell away gradually, vanishing where the cold black of the sky pretended to touch what was real. What was real was the Great Ship. Nothing else enjoyed substance or true value. Nothing else in Creation could be felt, much less understood. The Ship was a sphere of perfect hyperfiber, world-sized and enduring, while the sky was only boundless vacuum punctuated with lost stars and the occasional swirls of distant galaxies. Radio whispers could be heard, too distorted and far too faint to resolve, and neutrino rains fell from above and rose from below, and there were ripples of gravity and furious nuclei generated by distant catastrophes—inconsequential powers washing across the unyielding, eternal hull.

The sky could not be trusted. The stars wished only to tell lies. And worse, the majesties above would distract the senses and mind from what genuinely mattered. To the walker, there was no purpose but to slowly, carefully move across the Ship's hull, and if something of interest were discovered, a cautious investigation would commence. But only harmless mysteries were approached and studied in detail. Instinct guided the walker, and for as long as it could remember, that instinct spoke through fear. Fierce, unnamed hazards were lurking. The enemies could not be seen or defined, but they were close, waiting for weakness, ready to punish sloth or inattentiveness. This was why curiosity was a pleasure best taken in small doses. Fascination was what came when vision narrowed too far. This was the walker scrupulously avoided anything that moved or spoke, or any device that glowed with unusual heat, and even the tiniest examples of organic life were to be avoided, without fail.

Solitude was its natural way.

Alone, the ancient fear would diminish to a bearable ache, and something like happiness was possible.

Walking, walking. That was the meaning of existence. Select one worthy line, perhaps using one of the scarce stars as a navigational tool, and then follow that line until some fresh thing was discovered. Whether the object was studied or circumvented, this was where the walker would pick a new bearing, aiming at the horizon again, maintaining that geometric purity with its boundless resolve.

There was no need to eat, no requirement for drink or sleep. Its life force was a minor, unsolvable mystery. Existence was patient, every moment feeling long and busy. But if nothing of note occurred, nothing needed to be recalled. After a century of uninterrupted routine, the walker compressed that blissful sameness into a single impression that was squeezed flush against every other vacuous memory—the recollections of a soul that felt ageless but was not, still very close to empty and innocent in so many ways.

Eyes shrank and new eyes grew, changing talents as needed. With that powerful, piercing vision, the walker watched ahead and beside and behind. Nothing was missed. Sometimes it would stop, compelled to drop several eyes and stare into a random portion of the hull. From the grayness, microscopic details emerged: Fresh radiation tracks still unhealed; faint scars gradually erased by quantum bonds fighting to repair themselves. Each observation revealed quite a lot about hyperfiber and the lessons never changed. The hull was a wonder that was fashioned from an extremely strong and lasting material—a silvery-gray substance refined during some lost age by powerful species, perhaps, or perhaps by a league of vanished gods. Genius must have imagined and built the Ship, and presumably the same intellect had sent the prize racing through the vacuum. A good, glorious purpose must be at work here; but except for the relentless perfection of the Great Ship, nothing remained of intentions or goals, or even an obvious destination.

When the walker kneeled, the hull's beauty was revealed.

And then it would stand again and resume its slow travels, feeling blessed to move freely upon this magnificent face.

2

There was no purpose but to wander the perfection forever, without interruption: That assumption was made early and embraced as a faith. But the oddities and little mysteries grew more common. Every century saw more crushed steel boxes and empty diamond buckets than the century before, and then came lumps of mangled aerogel, and later, the occasional shard of some lesser kind of hyperfiber. Then it found dead machines and pieces of machinery and tools too massive or far too ordinary to be carried any farther once they had failed. These objects were considerably younger than the Ship. Who abandoned them was a looming mystery, but one that would not be solved. The walker had no intention of approaching these others. And in those rare moments when they approached it—always by mistake, always unaware of its presence—the walker would flatten against the hull and make itself vanish.

Invisibility was a critical talent. But invisibility meant that it had to abandon most of its senses. Even striding across its smooth back, these interlopers were reduced to a vibration with each footfall and a weak tangle of magnetic and electrical fields.

Days later and safe again, the walker would cautiously rise up and cautiously move on.

Another millennium passed without serious incident. It was easy to believe that the Great Ship would never change, and nothing would ever be truly new; and holding that belief close, the walker followed one perfect line. No buckets or diamond chisels were waiting to change its direction. As it strode on, the stars and sky-whispers warned that it was finally passing into unknown territory. But this happened on occasion. Perfection meant sameness, and the walker couldn't imagine anything new. Except then what seemed to be a flat-topped mountain began to rise over the coming horizon. Making note of the sharp gray line hovering just above the hull, it was a little curious. More years of steady marching caused the grayness to lift higher, just slightly. Perhaps a mountain of trash had been set there. Maybe a single enormous bucket had been upended. Various explanations offered themselves; none satisfied. But the event was so surprising, titanic and unwelcome, and the novelty was so great, that the walker stopped as soon as it was sure that something was indeed there, and without risking another step, it waited for three years and a little longer, adapting its eyes constantly, absorbing a view that stubbornly refused to change.

By then, curiosity defeated every imprecise fear, and the walker steered straight toward what made no sense.

At a pace that required little energy, it pressed ahead in half-meter strides. Decades passed before it finally accepted what was obvious: That while the Ship was undoubtedly perfect, it was by no measure perfectly smooth and eternally round. Rising from the hull was not one gigantic tower, but several. The nearest tower was blackish-gray and too vast to measure from a single perspective. A small light occasionally appeared on the summit, or tiny flecks of light danced beside its enormous bulk, and there were abrupt spikes in dense, narrow radio noise that tasted like a language. Explanations occurred to the walker. From where the possibilities came, it could not say. Maybe they arose from the same instincts responsible for its fears. But like never before, it was intrigued.

Moving again, slowly and tirelessly pushing closer, it noticed how one of the more distant towers had begun to tip, looking ready to collapse on its side. And shortly after that remarkable change in posture, the tower let loose a deep rumble, followed by a scorching, sky-piercing fire.

But of course: These were the Ship's engines. No other explanation was necessary, and the walker absorbed its new knowledge in an instant, fresh beliefs gathering happily around the Ship's continued perfection. Fusion boosted by antimatter threw a column of radiant blue-white plasmas into the blackness, scorching the vacuum. This was a vision worth admiration. Here was power beyond anything that it had ever conceived of. But soon the engine fell back to sleep, and after careful reflection, the walker chose another random direction, and another, selecting them until it was steering away from the gigantic rocket nozzles.

If objects this vast had missed its scrutiny, what else was hiding beyond the horizon?

Walk, walk, walk.

But its pace slowed even more. Flying vessels and busy machines were suddenly common near the engines, and some kind of animal was building warm cities of bubbled glass. An invasion was underway. There were regions of intense activity and considerable radio noise, and each hazard had to be avoided, and when the situation demanded, treacherous regions had to be crossed without revealing the presence of one lone walker.

Ages passed before the engines vanished beyond the horizon.

A bright red star became the new beacon, and the walker followed its rich light until the ancient sun sickened and went nova, flinging portions of its flawed skin out into the cooling, dying vacuum.

Younger stars appeared, climbing from the horizon as the walker pressed forward. A second sky had always been hiding behind the hyperfiber body. Then the play of gravity and a hard twisting announced that the Ship had grudgingly left the line followed for untold billions of years. After that, the sky changed rapidly, radically. The vacuum was not nearly so empty or quite as chilled, and even a patient entity with nothing to do but count points of light could not estimate how many stars were drifting into its spellbound gaze.

A galaxy was approaching. One great dish of three hundred billion suns and trillions of worlds was about to intersect with a vessel that had wandered across the universe, and every previous nudge and the great reaches of nothingness had led to this place and one perfect rich moment.

And here stood the walker, on the brink of something quite new.

There was a line here that perhaps no one else could have noticed, at least not with just eyes and the sketchy knowledge available. But the walker could see where the hull that it knew surrendered to another. The perfect hyperfiber was suddenly replaced with a rougher, more weathered version of faultless self. Even in the emptiest reaches of the universe wandered ice and dust and other nameless detritus. Those tiny worlds would crash down on the Ship's hull, always at a substantial fraction of light-speed, and not even the finest hyperfiber could shrug aside that kind of withering power. Stepping onto the Ship's leading face, the walker observed gouges and debris fields and then the little craters that were eventually obscured by still larger craters—holes reaching deep into the hard resilient body. Most of the wounds were ancient, although hyperfiber hid its age well. All but the largest craters were unimportant to the Ship's structure; the cumulative damage barely diminished its abiding strength. But some wounds showed signs of repair and reconditioning. The walker discovered one wide lake of liquid hyperfiber. A patch had filled a crater, and the patch was still curing when it arrived. Kneeling down on the smooth shoreline, it peered into the still-reflective surface. For the first time in memory, here was another waiting to be seen. But the walker felt no interest in its own appearance. What mattered was the inescapable fact that someone—some agent or benevolent hand—was striving to repair what billions of years of abuse had achieved. A constructive force was at work on the Ship. A healing force, seemingly. Enthralled, the walker looked at the young lake and the reflected Milky Way, measuring the patch's dimensions. Then it examined the half-cured skin, first with fresh eyes and then with a few respectful touches. A fine grade of hyperfiber was being used, almost equal to the original hull, which implied that the invisible caretakers were striving to do what was good, and even better, striving to make certain that their goodness would endure.

The endless wandering continued.

Ultimately the galaxy was overhead, majestic yet still inconsequential. The suns and invisible worlds were warm dust flung across the emptiness while the Ship remained dense and rich beyond all measure. Walk, and walk. And walk. And then it found itself at the edge of another crater—the largest scar yet—and for the first time ever the walker followed a curving line, its path defined by the crater's frozen lip.

Bodies and machines were working deep within the ancient gouge. It watched from unseen perches, studying methods and guessing reasons for what it could not understand. The vacuum crackled with radio noise. The sense of the words began to emerge, and because language might prove useful, the walker deciphered meanings and consequences and which voices were most important. Hundreds of animals worked inside the crater—human animals dressed inside human-shaped machines. Accompanying them were tens of thousands of pure machines, while standing on the lip was a complex of prefabricated shops and habitats and fusion reactors and more humans and more robots dedicated to no purpose but repairing one minuscule portion of the Ship's forward face.

As the walker kneeled, unseen, a bit of cosmic grit arrived with a brilliant flash of light, digging a tiny crater not fifty little steps away.

The danger was evident, but so were the marvels. Two narrow black tracks had been laid across the unbroken hull, obeying the flawless elegance of parallel lines. The tracks were superconductive rails that allowed heavy tanks to be dragged to this place, each tank swollen with uncured, still liquid hyperfiber. From a fresh hiding place, the walker watched a long chain of tanks arrive and drained before being set on a parallel track and sent away. The work was obviously difficult, demanding precision woven with some luck. Ever fickle, liquid hyperfiber was eager to form lasting bonds but susceptible to flaws and catastrophic embellishments. Deep down inside the crater, a brigade of artisans struggle to repair the damage—a tiny pock on the vast bow of the Ship—and their deed, epic as well as tiny, served as ringing testament to the astonishing gifts employed by those who first built the Great Ship.

All but one of the empty tanks was sent home. The exception was damaged in a collision and then pushed aside, abandoned. Curious about that long silver tank, the walker approached and then paused, crept closer and paused again, waiting days to feel certain that no traps were waiting, no eyes watching. Then it slipped near enough to touch the crumbled body. An innate talent for mechanical affairs was awakened. Using thought and imaginary tools, it rebuilt the empty vessel. Presumably those repairs were waiting for a more convenient time. Unless the humans meant to abandon this equipment, which was not an unthinkable prospect, judging by the trash already scattered about this increasingly crowded landscape.

One end of the tank was cracked open, the interior exposed. Slow, nearly invisible steps allowed the walker to slip inside. The cylinder was slightly less than a kilometer in length. Ignoring every danger, the walker passed through the ugly fissure, and once inside, it balanced on a surface designed to feel slick to every possible material. Yet it managed to hold its place, retaining its pose, peering into the darkness until it was sure that it was alone, which was when it let light seep out of its own body, filling the long volume with a soft cobalt-blue glow.

Everywhere it looked, it saw itself looking back.

The round wall was covered with distorted images of what might be a machine, or perhaps was something else. Whatever it was, the walker had no choice but to stare at itself. The tank was a trap, but instead of a secret door slamming shut, the mechanism worked by forcing an entity to gaze upon its own shape and its nature, perhaps for the first time.

What it beheld was not unlovely.

But how did it know beauty? What aesthetic standard was employed? And why carry such a skill among its instincts and keen talents?

Minutes passed before the walker could free itself. But even after climbing back onto the open hull, under the stars, it remained trapped. A slow crawl gave it some distance, but after it stood it did nothing. It remained immobile, exposed, staring back at the empty, ruined tank while feeling sick with grief. Where did this obligation come from? Why care so much about a soulless object that would never function again? That piece of ruin bothered it so much that even later, even after finally walking far enough to hide both the tank and the crater beyond the horizon…its mind insisted on returning to an object that others had casually and unnecessarily cast aside.

3

It walked. It counted steps. It reached two million four hundred thousand and nine steps when humans suddenly appeared in their swift cars.

The invaders settled within a hundred meters of the walker. With a storm of radio talk and the help of robots, they erected a single unblinking eye and pointed it straight above. The walker hid where it happened to be, filling a tiny crater. Unnoticed, it lay motionless as the new telescope was built and tested and linked to the growing warning system. And then the humans left, but the walker remained inside its safe hole, sprouting an array of increasingly powerful eyes.

The sky might be untrustworthy, but there was beauty to the lie. The Great Ship was plunging into a galaxy that was increasingly brilliant and complex and dangerous. More dust and chunks of wayward ice slammed against the hull, and the bombardment would only worsen as the Ship sliced into the thick curling limb of suns. But the humans answered the dangers with increasingly powerful weapons. Telescopes watched for what was coming. Then bolts of coherent light melted the incoming ices. Ballistic rounds pulverized asteroids. Sculpted EM fields slowed the tiniest fragments and shepherded them aside. There was splendor in that endless fight. Flashes and sparkles constantly surprised the lidless eyes. Ionized plasmas generated squawks and whistles reaching across the spectrum. This was an accidental music that grew louder, urgent and carefree. But no defensive system was unbreakable. Death threatened every foolish being that stood on the bow. Each moment might be the last. Yet the scene deserved fascination and wonder, and the walker had not moved in decades, staring upwards, sprouting antennae and listening while its mind began to believe that this violent magic had a rhythm, an elegant inescapable logic, and that whatever note and whichever color came next could have been foreseen.

That was when the voice began.

At least that was when the walker finally noticed the soft, soft whispers.

Certain mutterings were not part of the sky. Intuition told the walker that much. Perhaps the voice rose from the hull, or maybe it came from the chill vacuum. But more important than its origin was the quiet swift terror that defined its presence—an inarticulate, barely audible murmur that came when unexpected and vanished before any response could be offered.

The first eleven incidents were recorded, but the walker remained silent inside its hiding place.

But the twelfth whisper was too much. With a radio mouth formed for the occasion, and using the human language learned over the last centuries, the walker asked, "What are you?" It asked, "What do you want?" And when nothing answered, it added, "Do not bother me. Leave me alone."

By chance or by kindness, the request was honored.

The walker stood and once again wandered the bow. But the Ship was burrowing into debris belts and comet clouds, and impacts made the hull shiver, and sometimes the horizon was lit up with x-ray plumes. So it returned to the stern, ready to accept the safety afforded by the Ship's enormous bulk. Yet there were more humans than ever, and they were in constant motion, putting an end to the delicious, seemingly infinite emptiness. Following a twisting, secretive line, the walker journeyed to the nearest engine, and with cautious delight touched the mountainous nozzle at its base. But machines were everywhere, investigating and repairing, and the human chatter was busy and endless, jabbering about subjects and names and places and times that made no sense at all.

The walker retreated to where the stern and bow met, and for years it moved along that fresh line. But starships were approaching. Fierce little rockets and urgent voices matched velocities with the Great Ship. Dozens of streakships fell toward the hull and vanished without trace. The walker moved closer to the landing field, and then it hid for a year before moving a little farther and a little farther again. Eventually it saw two enormous doors pull wide, revealing a gaping hole cut deep into the perfect hull. The next invaders landed inside the hole. The walker had never seen a spaceport, never imagined such a thing was necessary or even possible. Once again, the Great Ship was far more than it pretended to be. Considering how many passengers might be tucked inside each little ship, it was easy to understand why the hull had grown crowded. The human animals were falling from the sky, coming here for the honor of living inside their bubble cities on the hull of this lost, unknowable relic.

Over the years, in slow patient stages, the walker crept to the edge of the spaceport. Then the door pulled wide and with a single glance, its foolishness was revealed: The Great Ship was more than its armored hull. What the entity had assumed to be hyperfiber to the core was otherwise. The port was a vast column of air and light and warm wet bodies moving by every means and for no discernible purpose. This was animal motion, swift and busy and devoid of any clear purpose. Humans were just one species among a multitude, and the

Ship beneath the hull was pierced with tunnels and doorways and hatches and diamond-windows, and that was just what the briefest glance provided before it flattened out and slowly, cautiously crept away.

The Ship was hollow.

And judging by the evidence, it was inhabited by millions and maybe billions of organic entities.

The unwanted revelations left it shaken. Years were required to sneak away from the port. Unseen, it returned to the bow and the beautiful sky, accepting the dangers for the illusion of solitude. But the ancient craters were being swiftly erased now. The Ship's lasers were pummeling any cometary debris that dared come close, and the repair crews were swift and efficient. The pitted, cracked terrain was vanishing beneath smooth perfection. The new hyperfiber proved fresh and strong, affording few hiding places even for a wanderer who could hide nearly anywhere. By necessity, every motion was studied before it was made. But even then, a nearby robot might notice a presence and maybe EM hands would reach out, trying to touch what couldn't be seen; and in terror, the walker stopped living and stopped thinking, hiding away inside itself as it pretended to be nothing but another scab of hyperfiber lost among billions of patches.

A freshly made crater waited upon its line, too small to bring humans today but large enough to let a survivor hide inside the wounded hull. A brief sharp ridge stood in the way—the relic of chaotic, billion-degree plasmas. After five days of careful study, the walker slowly crossed the ridge. Humans never came alone to these places, and there was no trace of machines. But as it stood on the ridgeline, urgency took hold. Something was wrong and what was wrong felt close. The walker began to slowly lower itself, trying to vanish. But then a strong voice said, "There you are."

It hunkered down quickly.

With amusement, someone said, "I see you."

The mysterious voice from before had been quieter than this. It was always a whisper and far less comprehensible. Perhaps the young crater helped shape its words, its sharp refrozen lip lending strength and focus.

In myriad ways, the walker began melting into the knife-like ridge.

Yet the voice only grew louder—a radio squawk wrapped around the human language. With some pleasure, it said, "You cannot hide from me."

"Leave me be," the walker answered.

"But you're the one disturbing me, stranger."

"And I have told you," the walker insisted. "Before, I told you that I wish to be alone. I must be alone. Don't pester me with your noise."

"Oh," the voice replied. "You believe we've met. Don't you?"

Curiosity joined the fear. A new eye lifted a little ways, scanning the closest few meters.

"You've made a mistake," the voice continued. "I don't know whose song you've been hearing, but I'm rather certain that it wasn't mine."

"Who are you?" the walker asked.

"My name is Wune."

"Where are you?"

"Find the blue-white star on the horizon," it said.

"Are you that star?"

"No, no." Wune could do nothing but laugh for a few moments. "Look below it. Do you see me?"

Except for a few crevices and delicate wrinkles, the crater floor was flat. Standing at the far end was a tiny figure clad in hyperfiber. It was shaped like a female. One arm lifted high. What might have been a hand waved slowly, the gesture purely human.

"My name is Wune," the stranger repeated.

"Are you human?"

"I'm a Remora," said Wune. "And what exactly are you, my friend? I don't seem to recognize your nature."

"My nature is a mystery," it agreed.

"Do you have a name?"

"I am," it began. Then it hesitated, considering this wholly original question. And with sudden conviction, it said, "Alone." It rose up from the ridge, proclaiming, "My name is Alone."

4

"Come closer, Alone."

It did nothing.

"I won't hurt you," Wune promised, the arm beckoning again. "We should study each at a neighborly distance. Don't you agree?"

"We are close enough," the walker warned, nearly two kilometers of vacuum and blasted hyperfiber separating them.

The Remora considered his response. Then with an amiably tone, she agreed, "This is better than being invisible to one another, I'll grant you that."

For a long while, neither spoke.

Then Wune asked, "How good are those eyes? What do you see of me?"

Alone stared only at the stranger, each new eye focused on the lifesuit made of hyperfiber and the thick diamond faceplate and what lay beyond. Alone had studied enough humans to understand their construction, their traditions, but what was human about this face was misplaced. The eyes were beneath the mouth and tilted on their sides. The creature's flesh was slick and cold in appearance, and it was a vivid warm purple, while the long hair on the scalp was white with a hint of blue, rather like the brightest stars. The white hair was lifting and falling, twirling and then pulling straight, as if an invisible hand were playing with it.

"I don't know your species," Alone confessed.

"But I think you do," Wune corrected. "I'm a human animal and a Remora too."

"You are different from the others."

"What others?" she inquired.

"The few I have seen."

"You spied on us while we were working the monster crater. Didn't you?" The mouth smiled, exposing matching rows of perfect human teeth. "Oh yes, you were noticed. I know you climbed inside that busted bladder before walking away again."

"You saw me?"

"Not then, but later," she explained. "A security AI was riding the bladder. It was set at minimal power, barely alive, which probably kept you from noticing it. We didn't learn about you until weeks later, when we stripped the wreck for salvage and the AI woke up."

Shame took hold. How could it have been so careless?

"I know five other occasions when you were noticed," Wune continued. "There are probably other incidents. I try to hear everything, but that's never quite possible. Is it?" Then she described each sighting, identifying the place and time when these moments of incompetence occurred.

"I wasn't aware that I was seen," it stated.

Ignorance made its failures feel even worse.

"You were barely seen," Wune corrected. "A ghost, a phantom. Not real enough to be taken seriously."

"You mentioned a spaceport," it said.

"I did."

"Where is this port?"

Wune pointed with authority, offering a precise distance.

"I don't remember being there," Alone admitted.

"Maybe we made a mistake," she allowed.

"But I did visit another port." With care, it sifted through its memories. "I might have difficulties with memory."

"Why do you think that?"

"Because I know so little about myself," confessed the walker.

"Well, that is sad," Wune said. "I'm sorry for you."

"Why?"

"Life is the past," she stated. "The present moment is too narrow to slice, and besides, it will be lost with the next instant. And the future is nothing but empty conjecture. Where you have been is what matters. What you have done is what counts for and against you on the tallies."

The walker concentrated on those unexpected words.

"I have a telescope with me," Wune said. "I used it when I first saw you. But I want to be polite. If you don't mind, may I study you now?"

"If you wish," it said uneasily.

The Remora warned, "This might take some time, friend." Then with both gloved hands, she held a long tube to her face.

Alone waited.

An hour later, Wune asked, "Are you a machine?"

"Perhaps I am."

"Or do you carry an organic component inside that body?"

"Each answer is possible, I think."

Wune lowered the telescope. "I am a little of both," she allowed. "I like to believe that I'm more organic than mechanical, but the two facets happily live inside me."

Alone said nothing.

The Remora laughed softly, admitting, "This is fun."

Was it?

To her new friend, she explained, "Thousands of years ago, humans learned how to never grow old. There are no diseases, and there's no easy way to kill us." The hands were encased in hyperfiber gloves. One of those fingers tapped hard against her diamond faceplate. "My mind? It's a bioceramic machine, which makes it tough and quick to heal and full of redundancies. My memories are woven inside the artificial neurons, safe as can be. Whenever I want, I can remember yesterday. Or I can pull my head back five centuries and one yesterday. My life is an enormous, deeply personal epic that I am free to enjoy whenever I wish."

"I am different than you," Alone conceded.

"Do you sleep?"

"Never."

"Yet you never feel mentally tired?" The purple face nodded, and she said, "Right now, I'm envious."

Envy was a new word.

"I'm trying to tell you something," she said. "This old Remora lady has been awake for a very long time, and she needs to sleep for a little while. Is that all right? Do whatever you want while my eyes are closed. If you need, walk away from me. Vanish completely." Then she smiled, adding, "Or you might take a step or two in my direction. If you feel the urge, that is."

Then Wune shut her misplaced eyes.

During the next hour, Alone crept forward more than three meters.

As soon as she woke, Wune noticed. "Good. Very good."

"Are you rested now?"

"Hardly. But I'll push through the misery." Her laugh had a different tone. "What's your earliest, oldest memory? Tell me."

"Walking."

"Walking where?"

"Crossing the Ship's hull."

"Who brought you to the Ship?"

"I have always been here."

She considered those words. "Or you could have been built here," she suggested. "Assembled from a kit, perhaps. You don't remember a crowd of engineers sticking their hands inside you?"

"I remember no one." Then with confidence, Alone said, "I have never been anywhere but on the Great Ship."

"If that was true," Wune began. Then she fell silent.

Alone asked, "What if that is so?"

"I can't even guess at all of the ramifications." After a few minutes of silence, she said, "Ask something of me. Please."

"Why are you here, Wune?"

"Because I'm a Remora," she offered. "Remoras are humans who got pushed up on the hull to do important, dangerous work. There are reasons for this. Good causes and bad justifications. Everything that you see here...well, the hull is not intended to be a prison. The captains claim that it isn't. But now and again, it feels like the worst cage imaginable."

Then she hesitated, thinking carefully before saying, "I don't think that was your question. Was it?"

"Like me, you are alone," it pointed out. "Most humans gather in large groups, and they act pleased to be that way."

With a serious tone, Wune said, "I'm rather different than the rest."

Alone waited.

"You see, the hull is constantly washed with radiation, particularly out here on the leading face." She gestured at the galaxy. "My flesh is immortal. I can endure almost any abuse. But these wild nuclei crash through my cells, wreaking terrible damage. My repair mechanisms are always awake, always busy. I have armies of tiny workers marching inside me, fighting to lift my flesh back to robust health. But when I am alone, and when I focus on my body's functions, I can influence my regenerating flesh. On a good day, with nothing except willpower, I can direct my own evolution."

That might explain the odd, not quite human face.

"I'm out here teaching myself these tricks," Wune admitted. "The hull is no prison. To me, it is a church. This is a temple. I have been handed a rare opportunity where the tiniest soul can unleash potentials that her old epic life never revealed to her."

"I understand each of your words," said Alone.

"But?"

"I cannot decipher what you mean."

"Of course you can't." Wune laughed. "Listen. My entire creed boils down to this: If I can write with my flesh, then I can write upon my soul."

"Your 'soul'?"

"My mind. My essence. Whatever it is that the universe sees when it looks hard at peculiar little Wune."

"Your soul," the walker said again.

Wune spoke for a long while, trying to explain her newborn faith. Then her voice turned raw and sloppy, and after drinking broth produced by her recyke system, she slept again. The legs of her lifesuit were locked in place. Nearly five hours passed with her standing like a statue, unaware of her surroundings, and when she woke again barely twenty meters of vacuum and hard radiation separated them.

The Remora didn't act surprised. With a quieter, more intimate voice, she asked, "What fuels you? Is there some kind of reactor inside that body? Or do you steal your power from us somehow?"

"I don't remember stealing."

"Ah, the thief's standard reply." She chuckled. "Let's assume you're a machine. You have to be alien-built. I've never seen any device like you, or even heard rumors. Not from the human shops, I haven't." After a long stare, she asked, "Are you male?"

"I don't know."

"I'm going to call you male. Does that offend you?"

"No."

"Then perhaps you are." She wanted to come closer. One boot lifted, seemingly of its own volition, and then she forced herself to set it back down on the hull. "You claim not to know your own purpose. Your job, your nature are questions without answer."

"I am a mystery to myself."

"Which is an enormous gift, isn't it? By that, I mean that if you don't know what to do with your life, then you're free to do anything you wish." Her face was changing color, the purple skin giving way to streaks of gold. And during her sleep her eyes had grown rounder and deeply blue. "You don't seem dangerous. And you do require solitude. I can accept all of that. But as time passes, I think you'll discover that escaping notice will only grow harder. The surface area is enormous, yes. But where will you hide? I won't chase after you. I promise. And I can keep my people respectful of your privacy. At least I hope I can. But the Great Ship is cursed with quite a few captains, and they don't approve of mysteries. And we can't count all the adventurers who are racing here, abandoning home worlds and fortunes just to ride on this alien artifact."

With just a few words, the galaxy above seemed even more treacherous.

Wune continued. "Maybe you don't realize this, but our captains have decided to take us on a tour of the Milky Way. Humans and aliens are invited, for a fat price, and some of them will hear the rumors about you. I guarantee, some of these passengers will come up on the hull, armed with sensors and their lousy judgment."

He listened and tried to think clearly.

"There is selfishness in my reasons," Wune admitted. "I don't want these tourists under my boots. And since you can't hide forever in plain sight, we need to find you a new home."

Horrified, Alone asked, "Where can I go?"

"Almost anywhere," Wune assured. "The Great Ship is ridiculously big. It might take hundreds of thousands of years just to fill up its empty places. There are caverns and little tunnels. Nobody can name all of the seas and canyons and the dead-end holes."

"But how can I find those places?"

"One place is all that you need, and I know ways. I will help you."

Terror and hope lay balanced on the walker's soul.

With those changeless human teeth, Wune smiled. "You say you know nothing about your nature, your talents. And I think you mean that."

"I do."

"Look at the chest of my suit, will you? Stare into the flat hyperfiber. Yes, here. Can you see your own reflection?"

His body had changed during these last few minutes. Alone had felt the new arms sprouting, the design of his legs adjusting, and without willing it to happen, he had acquired a face. It was a striking and familiar face, the purple flesh shot with gossamer threads of gold.

"I almost wish I could do that," Wune confessed. "Reinvent myself as easily as you seem to do."

He could think of no worthy response.

"Do you know what a chameleon is?"

Alone said, "No."

"You," she said. "Without question, you are the most natural, perfect chameleon that I have ever had the pleasure to meet."

5

A solitary wanderer could slip inside the Ship and never be seen. Clearly and simply, Wune explained how that might be accomplished, and more important, which mistakes to avoid. Hours had passed. She grew drowsy again, and with yawns and rolling motions of her hands, the Remora wished her chameleon friend rich luck and endless patience. "I hope you find what you are hunting and avoid whatever it is that you are fleeing."

Alone offered thanks but had no intention of accepting advice. Once Wune was asleep, he picked a fresh direction and walked away, and for several centuries he wandered the increasingly smooth hull, watching lasers slash and auroras swirl while the galaxy—majestic and warm and bright—rose slowly to meet the Great Ship.

Sometimes he was forced to hide in the open. Techniques and his confidence improved, but always weighed down by the sense that the Remoras were watching him, despite his tricks and endless caution. And he certainly eavesdropped on them, especially when Wune's name was mentioned. Her frank smart voice never found him again, but others spoke of the woman with admiration and love. Wune had visited this bubble city or that repair station. Serving the Great Ship was an honor and a joyous, dangerous burden, she preached. And to her loyal people, she exalted the strength that comes from mastering the evolution of your own mortal body. And then Wune was killed, evaporated by a shard of ice that slipped past every laser. The news had to be absorbed slowly. He didn't understand his emotions but discovered that he couldn't walk any farther, and he hid where he happened to be, for a full year doing nothing. Wune was the only entity with whom he had ever spoken, and he was deeply shocked, and then he saw that he was sad, but what wore hardest was the keen pleasure when he realized that she was dead but he was still alive.

Eventually he followed a line leading back to Ship's trailing face, slipping past the bubble cities and into the realm of giant engines. Standing before one towering nozzle, Alone recalled Wune's promise of small, unmonitored hatches. Careless technicians often left them unsecured. With a gentle touch, Alone tried to lift the first hatch, and then he tried to shove it inwards. But it was locked. Working his way along the base of the nozzle, he tested another fifty hatches before deciding that Wune was mistaken. Or perhaps the technicians had learned to do their work properly. But having nothing else to do, he invested the next twenty months walking a piece of one great circle, toying with every hatch and tiny doorway that he came across, persistence rewarded when what passed for his hand suddenly dislodged a narrow doorway.

Darkness waited, and the palpable sense of great distance.

He crawled down, slowly at first, and then the sides of the nearly vertical tunnel pulled away from his grip.

Falling was floating. There was no atmosphere, no resistance to his gathering momentum. Fearing someone would notice, he left the darkness intact. Soon he was plunging at a fantastic rate, and he recalled Wune's voice and words: "Those vents and access tubes run straight down, sometimes for hundreds of kilometers."

His tube dropped sixty kilometers before making a sharp turn.

There was no warning. One moment, he was mildly concerned about prospects that he couldn't measure, and the next moment saw pure misery and flashes of senseless light as his neural net absorbed the abuse. But he never lost consciousness. His shattered pieces flowed together. Wounds were healed slowly, drenched in pain. And he was still broken and helpless when a familiar voice found him.

Lying in the dark, unable to move, something quiet came very close and said, "The cold," before falling silent again.

He didn't try to speak.

After a long while, the voice said, "Forever, the cold."

"What is cold?" Alone whispered.

"And dark," said the voice.

"Who are you?"

The voice said, "Listen."

Alone remained silent, straining to hear any kind of sound, no matter how soft or fleeting. But nothing else was offered. Silence lay upon silence, chilled and black, and he spent the next long while trying to decipher which language was used. No human tongue, clearly. Yet those few words had been as transparent and simple as anything he had ever heard.

Once healed, he seeped light.

The engine's interior was complex and redundant, and most of its facilities were never used. Except for the occasional crackling whisper, radio talk never reached him. This was a realm where he could wander. Happily he discovered a series of nameless places where the slightest frosting of dust lay over every surface—a dust never disturbed by limb or by breath. Billions of years of benign neglect promised seclusion. No one would find him in this vastness, and if nothing else happened in his life, all would be well.

Ages passed.

Technicians and their machines traveled through these places, but always bound for more important locations.

Hiding was easy inside the catacombs.

Sometimes the overhead engine was fired, but there were always warnings. Great valves were opened and closed. Vibrations traveled along the sleeping tubes. A deeper chill could be felt as lakes of liquid hydrogen were prepared for fusion. Alone always knew three sites where he could quickly find shelter. His planning worked well, and he saw no reason to change what was flawless.

Then one day, nothing was the same again. Sitting inside a minor conduit, Alone was happily basking in a pool of golden light leaking from his inexplicable body. He was thinking about nothing, which was his favorite state of mind. And then the perfect instant was in the past, lost. A deep rumble announced dense fluids on the move, and before he could react, he was picked up and carried away by a hot viscous and irresistible liquid. Not hydrogen, and not water either. This was some species of oil dirtied up with odd metals and peculiar structures. He was trapped inside juices and passion, life and more life, and he responded with a desperate radio scream.

Tendrils touched him, trying to weave their way inside him.

He panicked, kicked and spun hard, pulling his body into the first disguise that occurred to him.

Electric voices jabbered.

A language was found, and what surrounded him said in the human tongue, "It is a Remora."

"Down here?"

"Tastes wrong," a third voice complained.

"Not hyperfiber, this shell isn't," said a fourth.

No voice ever repeated. This oily body contained a multitude of independent, deeply communal entities.

"The face is," one said.

"Look at the face," said another.

"Can you hear us, Remora?"

"I do," Alone allowed.

"Are you lost?"

Alone understood the word, but it seemed too full of implications. So with as much authority as possible, he said simply, "I am not lost. No."

An alien language erupted, the multitude debating what to do with this conundrum.

Then a final voice announced, "Whatever you are, we will leave you now in a safe place. For this favor, you will pay us with your praise and thanks. Do this and win our respect. Otherwise, we will speak badly of you, today and for the eternity to come."

"Yes," he said. "Thank you, yes."

He was spat into a new tunnel—a brief broad hole capped with a massive door and filled with magnetic filters, meshed filters, and powerful mechanical limbs. The limbs gathered him up, and Alone transformed his body again, struggling to slide free. But the machines tied themselves into an enormous knot, trapping him. Alone felt helpless. Maybe something good would have happened, but he panicked. Wild with terror, fresh talents were unleashed, and he discovered that when he did nothing except consciously gather up his energies, he could eventually let loose a burst of coherent light—an ultraviolet flash that jumped out of his skin, scorching the smothering limbs—and he tumbled back onto the mesh floor.

A second set of limbs emerged, stronger and more careful.

Alone tried to adapt. A longer rest produced an intense magnetic pulse. The mechanical arms flinched and died, and he changed his shape and flowed out from between them. The chamber walls and overhead door were high-grade hyperfiber. With bursts of light, he attacked the door's narrow seams. He attacked the floor and vaporized the dead arms and focused on the seams again. Security AIs made no attempt to hide their presence, calmly studying the ongoing struggle. Then an auxiliary door opened, revealing a pair of humans clad in armored lifesuits, complete with massive hyperfiber helmets that showed no faces, only cameras, giving extra protection to their tough, fearful minds.

The technicians held busy instruments, but mostly they used their shielded eyes.

One man asked, "What is that thing?"

"I don't damn well know," said the other.

"Think it's the Remoras' ghost?"

"Who cares?" he said. "Call the boss, let her think."

The humans retreated. Fresh arms were generated, slow and massive but designed just moments ago to capture this peculiar prize. Alone was herded into a corner and grabbed up, and an oxygen wind blew into the chamber, bringing a caustic mist of aerosols designed to weaken any normal machine. Through the dense air and across the radio spectrum, humans spoke to him. "We don't know if you can understand us," they admitted. "But please try to remain still. Pretend to be calm. We don't want you hurt, we want you to feel safe, but if you insist on fighting, mistakes are going to be made."

Alone struggled.

Then something was with him—a close, familiar presence—and the voice said, "The animals."

Alone stopped fighting.

"They have us," said the voice.

He listened to the air, to the empty static.

But whatever just spoke to him was gone again, and that's when a low whistling noise began to leak out of the prisoner—a steady sad moaning that stopped only when the ranking engineer arrived.

6

"I think you understand me."

He stared at the woman. Except for a plain white garment, she wore nothing. No armor, no helmet.

"My name is Aasleen."

Aasleen's face and open hands were the color of starless space. She was speaking into the air and into an invisible microphone, her radio words finding him an instant before their mirroring sound.

The woman said, "Alone."

He wasn't struggling. Doing nothing, he allowed his power to swell, and he wondered what he might accomplish if held this pose for a long time.

"That's your name, isn't it? Alone."

He had never embraced any name and saw no reason to do so now.

With her black eyes, Aasleen studied the prisoner. And as she stood before him, coded threads of EM noise pushed into her head. Buried in her organic flesh were tiny machines, each speaking with an urgent, complex voice. She listened to those voices, and she watched him. Then she said one secret word, silencing the chatter as she approached, walking forward slowly until he couldn't endure her presence anymore.

He made himself invisible.

She stopped moving toward him but she didn't retreat either, speaking quietly to the smear of nothing defined by the giant clinging limbs.

"Twisting ambient light," she said. "I know that trick. Metamaterials and a lot of energy. You do it quite well, but it's nothing new."

Alone remained translucent.

"And I understand how you can shift shapes and colors so easily. You're liquid, of course. You only pretend to be solid." She paused for a moment, smiling. "I had a pet octopus once. He had an augmented brain. To make me laugh, he used to pull himself into the most amazing shapes."

Alone let his body become visible again.

"Step away," he pleaded.

Aasleen stared at him for another moment. Then she backed off slowly, saying nothing until she had doubled the distance between them.

"Do you know what puzzleboys are?" she asked.

He didn't answer.

33

"Puzzleboys build these wonderful, beautiful machines—hard cores clothed with liquid exteriors. Their devices are durable and inventive. The best of them are designed to survive for ages while crossing deep space."

Aasleen paused, perhaps hoping for a reaction.

Growing tired of the quiet, she explained, "Puzzleboys are like a lot of sentient species. They wanted the Great Ship for themselves. Thousands of worlds sent intergalactic missions, but my species won the race. I rode out here on one of the early starships. Among my happiest days is that morning when I first stood on the Ship's battered hull, gazing down at the Milky Way."

He said, "Yes."

"You know the view?"

"Yes."

She smiled, teeth shining. "A couple thousand years ago, as we were bringing the Great Ship into the galaxy, the puzzleboys started singing lies. They claimed that they had sent a quick stealthy mission up here. The laws of salvage are ancient—far older than my baby species. Insentient machines can't grab so much as a lump of ice for their builders. But the aliens claimed that they had shoved one of their own citizen's minds inside a suitable probe. Like all respectable lies, their story had dates and convincing details. It's easy to conclude that their one brave explorer might have reached the Great Ship first. If he had, this prize would be theirs, at least according to these old laws. The only trouble with that story is that their mission never arrived. I know that. I never saw signs of a squatter, and they haven't produced corroborating evidence. Which is why we have made a point of insulting that entire species, and that's why the legal machinery of this cranky old galaxy has convincingly backed our claim of ownership."

Quietly, he said, "Puzzleboys."

"That's a human name. A translation, and like most approximations, grossly inadequate."

An EM squeal offered the species' name.

"Do you recognize it?" asked Aasleen.

He admitted, "I don't, no."

"All right then." She nodded, a thin smile breaking and then vanishing again. "Let's have some fun. Try to imagine that somebody we know, some familiar civilization, dreamed you up and sent you to the Great Ship. Maybe they borrowed puzzleboy technology. Maybe you've sprung from a different engineering history. Right now, I'm looking at oceans of data. But despite everything I see, my experience and intuitions, I can't pick one answer over the others. Which is why this so fascinating, sir. And why you are so fun."

Alone said nothing.

She laughed briefly, softly. "That leaves us with a tangle of questions. For instance, do you know what scares me about you?"

"What scares you?"

"Your power supply does."

"Why?"

Aasleen didn't seem to hear the question. "And I'm not the only person sick with worry," she admitted, closing one of her eyes and opening it again abruptly. "Miocene," she said, and sighed. "Miocene is an important captain. And you're considered a large enough problem that right now, that powerful captain is sitting inside a hyperfiber bunker three kilometers behind me. Three kilometers is probably far enough. If the worst happens, that is. But of course nothing will go bad now. As I explained to Miocene and the other captains, you seem to have survived quite nicely and without mishap, possible for thousands years. What are the odds that your guts are going to fail today, in my face?"

He considered his nature.

"Do you have any idea what's inside you?"

"No," he admitted.

"A single speck of degenerated matter. A miniature black hole, perhaps, although you're more likely the house for a quark assemblage of one or another sort." Aasleen sighed and shrugged. "Regardless of your engine design, it is novel. It's possible, yes, and I have a few colleagues who have done quite a lot of work proving that this kind of system might be used safely. But to see something like you in action and to realize that you've existed for who-knows-how-long, and apparently without demanding any significant repair..."

She paused. "I am a very good engineer," she said. "One of the best I've ever met, regardless of the species. And I just can't believe in you. Honestly, it is impossible for me to accept that you are even a little bit real."

"Then release me," he begged.

She laughed.

He watched her face, her nervous fingers.

"In essence," she continued, "you are a lucid entity carrying a tiny quasar in its core. The quasar is smaller than an atom and enclosed within a magnetic envelope, but massive and exceptionally dense."

"Quasar," he repeated.

"Matter, any matter, can be thrown inside you, and if only a fraction of the resulting energy is captured, you will generate shocking amounts of power."

He considered her explanation. Then with a quiet tone, he mentioned, "I have seen the Ship's engines firing."

"Have you?"

"Next to them, I am nothing."

"That is true. In fact, I have a few happy machines sitting near us that can outstrip your capacities, and by a wide margin. But as Submaster Miocene has reminded me, if that magnetic stomach is breached and if you can digest just your own body mass, the resulting fireworks will probably obliterate several cubic kilometers of the Ship, and who knows how many innocent souls."

The words felt true, and Alone believed her. But then he remembered that good lies have believable details and he didn't feel as certain.

Aasleen smiled in a sad fashion. "Of course I don't know exactly what would happen, if your stomach failed. Maybe it has safety mechanisms that I can't see. Or maybe its fire would reach out and grab my body and everything else in this room and as far away as Miocene…and with that, the Great Ship would be short one engine, and the survivors would find an enormous hole in the hull, spewing poisons and nuclear fire."

"I won't fail," he promised.

She nodded. "I think that's an accurate statement. I know I want to believe that both of us are perfectly safe."

"I won't hurt the Ship."

"Which is a fine sentiment. But why do you feel certain?"

"Because I am," he said.

Aasleen closed her eyes, once again concentrating on the machines inside her head.

"Please," said Alone. "Let me go."

"I can't."

His shape began changing.

Aasleen's eyes opened. "I know the story about you and Wune meeting. My hope? You take my appearance like you did hers. That might be fun."

But he didn't. There were no limbs now, nothing resembling a face. To the eye he resembled a ball of hyperfiber with giant rockets on one hemisphere, thick armor on the other. Using a hidden mouth, he promised, "I won't do any harm. I won't hurt anyone and I will never injure the Ship."

"You just want to be left by yourself," Aasleen said.

"Everything else hurts."

"And why?"

He had no response.

"Which leads us to another area of deep concern," Aasleen said. "A machine built by unknown minds is found wandering inside a second machine built by unknown minds. There seems to be two mysteries, there might be only one. Do you understand what I mean?"

He said, "No."

"Two machines but only one builder."

He didn't react.

She shook her head. "We don't know how old the Great Ship is. We have informed guesses but no precision. And no matter how well engineered you appear to be, I don't think you're several billion years old."

He remained silent.

Aasleen took one step closer. "And here is a third terror that involves you: A captain's nightmare. Maybe you are the puzzleboys' machine. Or you're somebody else's representative. Either way, if you arrived here on the Ship before any human did, and if there's a lost soul inside whatever passes for your mind…well, then it's conceivable that a different species might legally claim possession over the wealth and impossibilities that the Great Ship offers. And at that point, no matter how sweet your engineering is, your fate is out my hands…"

Her voice trailed away.

She took a tiny step forward.

"I have no idea," said Alone. "I don't know what I am. I know nothing."

The tiny machines inside Aasleen were speaking rapidly again.

"I'm watching your mind," she said. "But I'm not familiar with its neural network. It's a sloppy design, or it is revolutionary. I don't know enough to offer opinions."

"I wish to leave now," he said.

"In the universe, there are two kinds of unlikely," said Aasleen. "The Great Ship is the grand type—never attempted or even imagined, but achievable, provided someone has time and the relentless muscle to make it real. And then there's the implausible that you imagine will come true, and one day your worst fears turn real. If the Great Ship belongs to someone else, then my species has to surrender our claim. And even though I have convinced myself that I am a good charitable soul, I don't want that to happen. In fact, I would likely go to war in order to keep that from happening."

Alone did nothing, gathering strength.

"And suppose you are safe as rain," she said. "I don't relish the idea of you wandering wherever you like. Not onboard my ship, and certainly not until we can coax out the answers to all these puzzles."

With no warning, Alone lost his shape, turning into a hot broth that tried to flow around the grasping arms.

The arms seemed to expect his trick, quickly creating one deep bowl that held him in place.

"I promise," said Aasleen. "You'll be somewhere safe. We will keep you comfortable, and as much as possible, you'll be left alone. Not even Miocene wants to torment you, which is why a special chamber is being prepared—"

A new talent emerged.

The liquid body suddenly compressed itself, collapsing into a tiny dense and radiant drop hotter than any sun. And as the bowl-shaped limbs struggled to keep hold of this fleck of fire, Alone stole a portion of the surrounding mass, turning it into energy, shaping a ball of white-hot plasma.

Then he shrank into an even tinier, hotter bit of existence.

Aasleen turned and ran.

The arms were pierced. Alone fell to the floor. The hyperfiber bubbled and burst into plasmas that he pulled close and pushed downward, using the fire as a drill, and he sank out of view, sank slowly until the hyperfiber turned into a bed of pale pink granite, and then much as a ship passes between the stars, he was flying quickly through what felt like nothing.

7

Creating a narrow hole, Alone fled.

The hole was lined with compressed, distorted magma that flowed and exploded and then hardened above him. But despite his minuscule trail, enemies would follow. He felt certain. Alone was valuable in their eyes, or he was dangerous, or they simply could not approve of his continued existence. Aasleen and the captains would keep chasing him, and realizing that, it was obvious that his many enemies were gathering below, now waiting for him inside the next trap.

Alone let his body balloon outwards, one final burst of blazing heat terminating his descent.

A cone-shaped chamber hung above him, its wall glowing pink as the residual heat bled away. He lay silent for long minutes before sprouting delicate fingers, pushing their tips through the magma, into the cold stone. Vibrations fell over him—bright hard jarrings marking the closing and sealing of every hatch and orifice and superfluous valve. Then something massive and quite slow passed directly below him. But these subtle noises were never regular, never simple, creating distortions and echoes as the waves broke around hundreds of empty spaces. Swim in one downward angle and a large chamber was waiting. Another easy line promised a far more extensive cavern. But what caught Alone's interest was a line that might not even exist, a flaw in the rock, perhaps, or maybe a tunnel leading nowhere. That target was near. Illusion or not, Alone would learn the answer soon, and now he pulled his body into a new shape, looking like the worms common to a hundred billion worlds as he began slithering and shoving his way forward.

He missed his goal by eighty meters.

But instinct or a wordless voice urged him to pause and reconsider. What was wrong? An urge told him what to do, and he didn't hesitate, following a new line until not only was he certain that he was lost but that the Great Ship was solid to its core, and his fate was to wander this cramped darkness until Time's end.

The rock beside him turned to cultured diamond.

With the worm's white-hot head, he pushed through the gemstone. Countless thread-like tunnels were woven through the Great Ship, and this was among the most obscure, barely mapped examples. He glowed brightly for a long moment, new eyes probing in both directions. He wanted instinct to help. Instinct said nothing. Then inside a space too small for a human child to stand, he sprouted limbs and began to run, pushing off the floor and the sides and that low slick diamond ceiling. At every junction and tributary hole, he picked one for no reason. Eventually he was hundreds of kilometers from his beginning point, random choice carrying him until the instant when he realized that he was beginning to wander back toward his starting point.

Alone paused, listening to the diamond and the rock beyond. The next turn led to a dead end, and he carefully backed out of that hole and hunkered down, and with a soft private voice asked, "What now?"

"Down," the familiar voice coaxed.

Nothing else was offered. No other instruction was needed. He burned a fresh hole in the diamond floor, and after plunging three kilometers, his fierce little body exploded into a volume of frigid air that stretched farther than the light of his body could reach.

Alarmed, he turned black as space.

He fell, and a floor of frozen water and carbon dioxide slapped him when he struck bottom.

The cavern was bubble-shaped, filled with ancient ice and a whisper of oxygen gas. Except for the dimpled footprints of one robot surveyor, there was no trace of visitors. No human had ever stepped inside this place. But as a precaution, the only inhabitant erased his tracks, and where his warmth had distorted the ice, he made delicate repairs.

The walker's life gave way to a sessile existence. Alone moved only to investigate his new home. Every sealed hatch leading out into the Ship was studied, and he prepared three camouflaged exits that wouldn't appear on the captains' maps. Sameness made for simple memories. The next seventeen thousand years were crossed without interruption. Life was routine, and life was silent and unremarkable, and the fear that he knew best subsided into a slight paranoia that left each sliver of Time sweet for being pleasantly, unashamedly boring.

Doing nothing was natural.

For long delicious spans, the entity sat motionless, allowing his heat to gradually melt the ice. Then he would cool himself, and his surroundings would freeze again while he pretended to be the old ice. With determination and patience, he imagined billions of years passing without significance, nothing in this tiny realm suffering change. Sometimes he sprouted a single enormous eye, and from another part of his frigid body he emitted a thin rain of photons that struck the black basalt ceiling and the icy hills around him, and with that eye designed for this single function, he would slowly and thoroughly study what never changed while his mind tried to envision the Ship that could not be seen.

"Speak to me," he might beg.

Then he would wait, wishing for a reply, tolerant enough to withstand a year and sometimes two years of inviting silence.

"Speak," he would prompt again.

Silence.

Then he might offer a soft lie. "I can hear you anyway," he would say. "Just past my hearing, you are. Just out of my reach, out of my view."

But if the strange voice was genuine, then its maker was proving itself more stubborn even than Alone.

Seventeen millennia and thirty-seven years passed, and then with a thunderous thud, one hatch burst inward. Unsealed for the first time, the open door let in a screaming wind and a brigade of machines—enormous swift and fearless assemblages of muscle and narrow talents that knew their purpose and had only so much time to work.

Alone was terrified, and enthralled. Believing he could escape at will, he retreated to the chamber's center. But then the other hatches exploded, including a big opening at the apex of the ceiling. Machines burrowed into the ice and strung lights, and they carved the black walls, reshaping the volume before building a second, lower ceiling. And all the while they were leaking enough raw heat that the ancient glacier began to melt everywhere, transformed into fizzy water and gas.

Alone huddled inside rotting shards of the ice.

His emergency exists were either blocked or too close to active machines. The chamber floor was quality hyperfiber, difficult to pierce without creating a spectacle. Alone pretended to belong to the floor. For the next awful week, he did nothing but remain still. Then all of the ice had melted and the first wave of machinery had vanished, replaced by different implements that worked rapidly in smaller ways, yet with the same tenacious purpose.

Mimicking one common machine, he floated to the new lake's surface.

Cultured wood and young purple corals and farm-raised shellfish were being assembled like a puzzle, a new shoreline laid across beds of glassy stone filled with artificial fossils—ancestors to the chamber's new residents. Humans stood beside aliens, the species speaking through interpretive AIs. The aliens wore broad purple shells, and they were happiest when their gills lay in the newly conditioned water. The humans wore uniforms of various styles, different colors. One uniform had the bright reflective quality of a mirror, and the woman inside it was saying, "Beautiful, yes." Then she knelt down and sucked up a mouthful of the salted, acidic water. Spitting with vigor, she said, "And a good taste too, it is."

The aliens swirled their many feet and the fibrous gills, stirring up their lake. Then chittering answers were turned into the words, "We are skeptical."

"To your specifications," said the woman. "I pledge."

The aliens spoke of rare elements that needed to be increased or abolished. Proportions were critical. Perfection was the only satisfactory solution.

"It shall be done," the captain promised.

The aliens claimed to be satisfied. Confident of success, they slithered into the deeper water, plainly enjoying their new abode.

The captain looked across the lake, spying one machine that was plainly doing nothing.

With a commanding tone, she said, "This is Washen. We've got a balky conditioner sitting in the middle. Do you see it?"

Alone eased beneath the surface, changing his shape, merging with the glassy sediment. His disguise was good enough to escape the notice of watching humans and machines. Waiting, he gathered enough power to make a sudden explosive escape. But then the artificial day faded, a bright busy night taking hold, complete with the illusion of scattered stars and a pale red moon; and it was an easy trick to assume the form one shelled alien, mimicking its motions and chattering tongue, casually slipping out through the public entrance into a side tunnel that led to a multitude of fresh places, all empty.

8

Twenty centuries of steady exploration, and still the cavern had no end. Its wandering passageways were dry and often cramped, unlit and deeply chilled. The granite and hyperfiber were deliciously sterile. Neither humans nor their alien passengers wished to live in places like this. Machine species set up a few networks, but their tiny communities were easily avoided. Once more, the habit of walking returned to this life. To help track his own motions as well as the passage of time, Alone would count his strides until he reached some lovely prime number, and then he would mark the nearest stone with slashes and dots that only he could interpret—apparently random marks that would warn him in another hundred years that he had passed this way before, moving from this tunnel into that chamber, and if at all possible, he should avoid repeating that old route.

The enigmatic voice found him more often now, yet it was quieter and harder to comprehend. Sometimes a whisper emerged from some slight hole or side passage—like one neighbor calling to another from an unfathomed distance. But more often the voice was directly behind him, and it didn't so much speak as offer up emotions, raw and uninvited. The shared sadness was deep and very old, but those black moods were preferable to the sharp, sick terror it gladly shared. One dose of panic was enough to make the next hundred days painful. Something here was horribly wrong. The voice kept infusing him with horror—no explanations; no root causes. Yet these moods were preposterous, foolish and eventually dreary. After all, Alone's solitude was secure. No captains or engineers were chasing after him. Occasionally he slipped into a deep corner of the cavern and for several months would hide away, waiting for whatever might pass by. But nothing was tracking him, and nothing was sliding in the opposite direction. The voice was wrong, was mistaken. Alone was utterly safe inside this private, perfect catacomb, and he welcomed no opinion that dared claim otherwise.

One day, walking an unexplored passageway, he happened upon a vertical shaft. Normally he might have avoided the place. A human had been here first, leaving behind tastes of skin and bacteria and human oils. Leaking a faint glow, Alone spied machinery abandoned by this anonymous explorer: A winch perched on the edge of the deep shaft, anchored by determined spikes. The sapphire rope was broken. The drum was almost empty, but the winch continued to turn—an achingly slow motion that fascinated the first soul to stand here in a very long while.

Several days of study were needed before Alone touched the drum, and that slight friction was enough to kill what power remained inside the superconductive battery. How long had it been here, spinning without purpose? And what was inside the hole, waiting at the other end of the broken blue thread?

Alone wrenched loose two of the winch's titanium handles and uncoiled the remaining sapphire rope, tying one end to one handle. Then he dropped the weight into the dark shaft. Two hundred meters, and there was no extra rope and no bottom. He lashed the rope's free end to the winch and climbed down. The shaft turned to hyperfiber, slick and vertical and comforting. Then its walls pulled away. When Alone couldn't reach from one side to the other, he let go of the rope, falling and making his body brighter as he fell, watching the handle streak past. He made no sound, and listening, he heard nothing. And feeling nobody here but himself, he lit the entire chamber with his finest golden fire.

A human shape lay upon the flat floor.

Alone turned black and cold again, and he built long gliding wings that dropped him at a safe distance, allowing him to creep closer to the motionless figure.

For three days, nothing changed.

Then he brightened, just slightly, straddling the figure. The human male hadn't moved in decades, perhaps longer. There was enough rope on the winch to put him down here, but it must have broken unexpectedly. The hyperfiber floor showed blood where the man struck the first time, hard enough to shatter his tough bones and shred muscles. But humans can recover from most injuries. This stranger would have healed and soon stood up again, and probably by a variety of means, he had worked to save himself.

Most of the Ship's passengers carried machines that allowed them to speak with distant friends. Why didn't this man beg for help? Perhaps his machinery failed, or this hole was too deep and isolated, or maybe he simply came to this empty place without the usual implements.

Reasons were easy, answers unknowable.

Whatever happened, the man had lived inside this hole for some months and perhaps several years. He brought food and water, but not enough of either to last long. The cold that Alone found pleasant would have stolen the body's precious heat, and the man starved while his flesh lost its moisture, reaching a point where it could invent no way to function. Yet the man never died.

With his last strength, he stripped himself of his clothes and made a simple bed, his pack serving as his pillow, and with that he stretched out on his back, eyes aimed at the unreachable opening, his face turning leathery and cold and blind.

The eyes remained open but dry as stone. They might not have changed for centuries, and nobody had ever found this man, and perhaps no one even noticed his absence.

Alone considered the implications of each option.

Eventually and with considerable caution, he opened the pack and thoroughly inventoried its contents. He studied what was useful in detail. Key was a sophisticated projection map showing the cavern and the surrounding tunnels. Then he carefully returned each item to where he found it and laid the pack beneath the unaware head. That frozen, wasted body weighed nearly nothing. A good hard shake might turn the dried muscle to dust. Yet he was careful not to disturb anything more than absolutely necessary, and without a sound, he retreated to a respectful distance. The lower length of sapphire lay nearby, coiled into a neat pile. He tied one end to the second handle, and despite the distance and darkness managed a perfect toss on his first attempt, the two handles colliding and dancing, then wrapping together, and he climbed past the rough knot, pulling it loose and letting the lower rope fall away before he continued his ascent from the hole.

Centuries followed; little if anything changed. But there were a few intuitive moments when the bright gray fear took hold, when some nagging instinct claimed that he was being sloppy, that he was being pursued. Three times, Alone found marks resembling his own but obviously drawn by another hand. And there was one worrisome incident when he slipped aside and waited only thirteen days before a solitary figure followed him down the long tunnel. The biped was towering and massive, covered with bright scales and angry spikes, and the low ceiling forced the creature to bend low inside the passageway, fierce hands carrying an elaborate machine that resembled a second head.

Mechanical eyes and a long probing nostril studied the rock where Alone had stepped, teasing out subtle cues. With a hunter's intensity, the creature slowly moved to a place where the second head noticed that the trail had vanished, and the machine whispered a warning, and the harum-scarum turned in time to see an amorphous shape sprout long limbs, and without sound, silently race away.

After that, Alone adapted his legs and gait, changing his stride, fighting to become less predictable. But he refused to abandon the cavern. His home was far too large to be searched easily or in secret, and he had walked every passageway, every room—a hard-acquired knowledge that he would have to surrender if he journeyed anywhere else.

Most encounters came through chance, fleeting and harmless. Human numbers had swollen as the millennia passed, but some of the other species plainly outnumbered the Ship's lawful owners. Aliens wore every imaginable body, and there were always new species stumbling into his path. One glimpse in the dark or some long study at a safe distance didn't make an expert, but Alone had achieved several rugged little epiphanies: Life must be relentless, and it had to be astonishingly imaginative. Every living world seemed unique, and these blobs and dashes of living flesh were able to thrive on every sort of disgusting food and bitter breath. The beasts that came slipping through his home drank water, salty or clear, acidic or alkaline, or their drinks were chilled and laced with ammonia, or they wore insulated suits and downed pitchers of frigid methane, or they sucked on perchlorates and peroxides, or odd stinking oils, while quite a few machines drank nothing. Yet despite that staggering range of form and function, every creature was pushed by curiosity, peering into black holes, sometimes slipping fingers and antennae into places never touched before—if not hunting for invisible, legendary entities, then at least seeking the simple, precious novelty of Being First.

Alone watched visitors coupling. One eager pair of humans fell onto a mat of glowing aerogel, naked and busy, and standing just a few meters away, immersed in darkness, Alone watched as they bent themselves into a series of increasingly difficult poses, grunting occasionally, then finally shouting with wild voices that echoed off the distant ceiling. When their violence was finished, the woman said to the man, "Is that all there is?" Her lover answered with a harsh affectionate name, and she laughed, and he laughed, and after drinking the brown alcohol from a treasured bottle, the performance began again.

More years and more kilometers were slowly, carefully traversed. Then came one peculiar moment when he heard what sounded like a multitude passing through the cavern's largest entrance. The presence of many was felt; he smelled their collective breath. They might whisper respectfully and try to move like ghosts, but there were too many feet and mouths, too many reasons to praise the solitude and beg their neighbors to be silent. Alarmed, Alone approached the newcomers only to hope that they were leaving. But they were not. Then he followed them, and from a sober distance he watched as they assembled at the center of the cavern's largest chamber. A quick count found twenty thousand bodies and a staggering variety of species, and once an invisible signal was given, they began to speak in one shared voice. There was rhythmic chanting, sloppily performed songs. By every right he should have fled the pageant, but the strangers were singing about the Great Ship, begging for its blessings and its wisdom. And hope upon hope, they called for the Ship's voice.

Using every trick, Alone approached unseen.

The celebration was joyous and senseless. How could they hear any voice inside their own roar? But he felt the urgency and earnest passion. At least a hundred alien species were represented. But the lighting was minimal, and hovering at the edges, it was impossible to observe the full crowd, much less comprehend more than a fraction of what was being said.

"We thank the Ship," he heard.

Then from someplace close, one enormous voice chanted, "For the home and safety You give to us, we thank You!"

"You are a mystery," farther souls declared. "You are the mystery."

Alone hovered at the edge of the mayhem, unnoticed but near enough to touch backs and feel the leaked heat of bodies.

A hill of smooth basalt stood on the cavern floor, and perched on the summit was a human male. "For so long and for so far," he cried out. "You have journeyed. We cannot measure the loneliness You endured in Your wanderings. But in thanks for Your shelter, we give You our companionship. For Your speed, we give You purpose. After the countless years of being empty and dead, we have made You into a vibrant, thriving creature. At long last, the Great Ship lives! And we hear Your thanks, yes! In our dreams and between our little words, we hear You!"

Just when Alone started to flee, he couldn't say.

Which word triggered the furor was unclear, even as he was rushing away from the room and its densely packed bodies…even as a few of the less devoted worshippers heard what might have been a moan and turned in time to notice the faint but undeniable glow, red as a dying ember, racing off on legs growing longer by the stride.

9

Ten thousand and forty-eight years after discovering the hole, Alone returned. The winch remained fixed in place, but someone else had visited, and possibly more than once. Boot prints showed in the dust. He smelled and tasted signs of a second human. But nobody had stood on this ground for long, and when he went below, he found the body exactly where he had left it—only more dried, more wasted. More helpless, if that was possible.

Once again, Alone emptied the pack of its belongings, but this time he tenaciously studied the design and contents of even the most prosaic, seemingly useless item. He taught himself to read. He mastered the old, once-treasured machines that had thoroughly recorded one life. The mummified man had a long, cumbersome name, but he answered easiest to Harper. Eyes pressed against digital readers, Alone marveled at scenes brought from the distant earth—glimpses of brightly lit humans, the toothy faces of a family, and a sequence of wives. But all of his people and every lover were left behind when Harper sold his possessions, surrendering his home and safety for a ticket to ride the Great Ship—embarking on a glorious voyage to circumnavigate the Milky Way.

Between the man's arrival at Port Alpha and this subsequent disaster, barely fifty years had passed. Fifty years was no time at all. What's more, Harper had filled his days with a single-minded hunt for the Ship's ancient builders. Infused with a maniacal hunger, the human not only presumed that a grand purposeful force had built the derelict starship, but the same force was still onboard, hiding in an odd corner or unmapped chamber, biding its time while waiting for that brave, earnest explorer who would discover its lair.

Harper intended to be that very famous man.

Every aspect of the lost life was studied. There were gaps in the records, particularly near the end. But Alone wasn't familiar enough with human ways to appreciate that another hand might have blanked files and entire days, erasing his presence from the story. What mattered was digesting the full nature of this alien beast, learning Harper's manners and looks and duplicating his high, thin voice. Then Alone refilled the pack. But this time, he left the hole with the lost man's possessions carried under what looked like a human arm.

At the top of the hole, he transformed his face, his body.

There are many ways to be alone. The next weeks were spent duplicating the voice and gestures found on the digitals. Only then did Alone abandon

49

the safety of the cavern. The local time was night, as he planned. Obeying customs learned only yesterday, Alone summoned a cap-car that silently carried him halfway around the Ship. He paid for the service with funds pulled from an account that hadn't been touched for thousands of years. The modest apartment hadn't seen this face for as long, but its AI said, "Welcome." The master's sudden reappearance didn't cause suspicion or curiosity. Entering a home that he didn't know, Alone spent the next ten days and nights continuing his studies of the lost man. Then his apartment announced, "You have a visitor, sir."

Baffled, he asked, "Who?"

"It is Mr. Jan."

"Who is Mr. Jan?"

"I have no experience with the gentleman. But he claims to be your very good friend."

Alone considered a few implications.

"What shall I tell him, sir?"

"That I have no friends," he replied.

"Very well."

The matter seemed finished. But fifty-three minutes later, the apartment warned, "Mr. Jan is still waiting at our door, sir."

"Why?"

"Apparently he wishes to speak with you."

"But I'm not his friend," Alone repeated.

"And I told him as much. But he is upset about some matter, and he refuses to leave until he shares words with you."

"Let him walk into the front hall."

A narrow, nervous human crept into the apartment. Mr. Jan had a familiar scent, and judging by the intricacy of the braids, he was quite proud of his thick red hair. The hallway was thirty meters long, which wasn't long enough. The two figures stared at one another from opposite ends, and when Mr. Jan took a small step forward, the other soul said, "No. Come no closer, please."

"I understand," the guest whispered. "Sure."

"What do you want with me?"

What did Mr. Jan want? The possibilities were too numerous or too vast for easy explanations. He gazed down at his pale hands, as if asking their opinion. Then quietly and very sadly, he said, "I'm sorry."

"Sorry?"

"Yes I am."

Alone felt sick to be this near a stranger. But the borrowed voice remained calm, under control. "For what are you apologizing?"

Mr. Jan straightened his back, surprised by those words, and on reflection, angered by them too. "I'm apologizing for everything, of course! I'm sorry for the entire mess!"

Alone waited, his new face unchanged.

"But these troubles weren't only my fault," the visitor insisted. "You used me, Harper. And I know you made fun of me. We were supposed to have a business relationship, a partnership. I heard quite a few promises about money, but did you give me even half of what I'd earned?"

"What did I give you?"

"None of it. Don't you remember?"

"Then I must have cheated you," Alone said.

"'Cheat' doesn't do it justice," Mr. Jan said.

Alone wasn't certain which words to offer next.

"Look," said Mr. Jan. "What I did…I was just trying to scare you. Taking you that deep, down where your nexuses couldn't reach anybody, and cutting the sapphire before you dropped into that room. It looks bad, if you strip things down and make it simple. But it was only meant to be a warning, and nothing else."

"You were trying to scare me," Alone said.

"Don't you remember? I spelled out my reasons afterwards." Mr. Jan looked at the granite floor and then the matching ceiling. With a stiff, self-absorbed voice, he said, "You heard me calling down to you. I know you heard, because you answered me. I told you that I was going to let you sit there and commune with the Great Ship until you promised to give me everything I was owed."

"I remember," Alone lied.

"Money and respect. That's what I wanted, that's what I deserved. And that's why I had to do what I did." The walls were only partly tiled. Like the rest of the tiny apartment, the hallway was far from finished. Mr. Jan leaned against the shifting quasicrystals, beginning to cry. "All you needed to do…I mean this…you just had to say a few words to me. You could have told me another lie, if you wanted. I never planned to leave you down there. I'm not cruel like that. If you'd made any promises, spun together a few nice words, I'd have pulled you right out of there. Yes, I would have saved you in an instant."

The voice faded.

"I should have done that," Alone agreed. "Lying would have been best."

"Well, I don't know if that's quite true." The weeping man looked at his nemesis—a ghost that had stalked him for eons. "But listen, Harper. You have no respect for anyone but yourself. Those insults you yelled up at me. Yes, you managed to hurt me. Those awful things that you said…they last. They're still cutting me."

"I was wrong," Alone agreed.

Mr. Jan looked at him. He took three steps forward, and when the other figure didn't complain, he admitted, "You don't realize it, but I returned to the hole. I went there to check on you. After you fell into the coma, I used a little lift-bug to reach your body." A trembling hand tugged at the braided copper-colored hair. "I meant to bring you out, but I was scared. It looks bad, what happened, and I didn't want trouble. So I scrubbed away every trace of me, from your field recorders and in here too. I convinced your apartment that I never existed and that you were always coming home tomorrow. In case anybody became curious about your whereabouts."

"People can be curious," Alone agreed.

Mr. Jan smiled grimly, and wiping at his eyes, added, "I was always your best friend."

Alone said nothing.

"You should know…when you vanished, nobody noticed. Oh, some might ask me about you. Since they knew we were close. For several years, they would come up to me and wonder if I'd heard any noise from Crazy Harper and where you might have gone."

"'Crazy Harper'?"

"That's what some people called you. I never did."

Alone remained silent.

Mr. Jan concentrated on his mind for a while, searching for courage. "I am a little curious," he finally admitted. "How did you climb out of that hole?"

"There is a story," Alone said. "But I don't wish to tell it."

Mr. Jan nodded, lips mashed together. "Does anyone know the story? About us, I mean."

Silence.

Mr. Jan wrapped his arms around his chest and squeezed. "Not that you're in terrible shape now. I mean, it's not as if I murdered somebody." He paused, dwelling on possibilities. "You've lost time. I know it was quite a lot of time. But here you are, aren't you? Everything is back where it belongs."

"I've told no one about my years."

With a deep sigh, Mr. Jan said, "Good."

"Only you know what really happened."

The human nodded. He tried to laugh, but his voice collapsed into soft sobs. "I won't mention it, if you don't."

"I don't know what I would say."

Wiping at his wet face, Mr. Jan quietly asked, "What can I do? Please. Tell me how to make this up to you."

Alone said nothing.

"I did something criminal. I'll admit that much, of course. But you should deliver the punishment. That's the right solution. Not the captains. Let's not involve them. You are in charge." The smile was weak, desperate. "I promise. I'll do whatever you tell me to do."

Alone had no idea what to say. Then a memory took hold, and he smile in the human fasion, nodding knowingly. "You will leave me," he said quietly, with authority. "Leave this place and climb to the Ship's hull. Since you're a criminal, you need to be where criminals belong. Live under the stars and help keep the hull in good repair." Alone took a small step forward. "The work is vital. The Great Ship must remain strong. There is no greater task."

Mr. Jan straightened his back. "What?" He didn't seem to understand. "You want me to work with the Remoras? Is that your punishment?"

"No," said Alone. "I wish you to become a Remora."

"But why would I?"

"Because if you do otherwise," Alone replied, "other people, including the captains, will hear what you did to your good friend, Crazy Harper."

The demand was preposterous. Mr. Jan shook his head and laughed for a full minute before his frightened, slippery mind fell back to the most urgent question. "How did you get out of that hole?"

Alone didn't answer.

"Somebody helped you. Didn't they?"

"The Great Ship helped me."

"The Ship?"

"Yes."

"The Ship pulled you out from that hole?"

"Yes."

Mr. Jan looked at the sober face, waiting for any hint of a lie. But nothing in the expression gave hope, and he collapsed to the stone floor. "I just don't believe you," he said.

But he did believe.

"The Ship needs you to walk on the hull," Alone explained. "It told me exactly that. Until you are pure again, you must live with the followers of Wune."

"But how long will that take?"

Alone hesitated. Then quite suddenly he was laughing. "I am sorry, Mr. Jan. I don't know the timetable. Even with me, it seems, the Great Ship refuses to explain much about anything."

10

Harper must have been a difficult, solitary man. No one seemed to have missed his face or companionship, and his sudden return caused barely a ripple of interest. Word spread that somebody was living inside his modest, half-finished apartment, and the apartment's AI dutifully reported communications with acquaintances from the far flung past. But the greetings were infrequent and delivered without urgency. Privacy proved remarkably easy to keep. For twenty busy years, Alone remained inside the barely furnished rooms, and the apartment never asked where its only tenant had been or why he had been detained, much less why this new Harper never ate or drank or slept. Mr. Jan had damaged the machine's minimal intelligence. A full month was invested in dismantling and mapping his companion's mental functions, and all that while Alone wondered if he was the same, his mind incomplete, mangled by clumsy, forgotten hands.

Harper had painted himself as an important explorer and an exceptionally brave thinker. Inside his pack, he had carried dated records about mysterious occurrences inside the Great Ship. But there were larger self-feeding files in his home, each possessed by one broad topic and a set of tireless goals. Those files had grown exponentially while the master was mission—anecdotes about ghosts and monsters and odd lost aliens. After thousands of years, one thin joke of a Builder waving hello to the first scout team had mutated into a string of third-hand testimonies and conspiracies among the captains. Add to that rumors and misunderstandings as well as a river of compelling lies and buoyant blatant fakes, and it would take the busy soul centuries just to discount each and every tale.

Set doubt aside, even for a moment, and it would be impossible not to accept that the Great Ship was full of ancient, inscrutable aliens—wise souls born when the Earth was just so many uncountable atoms cooking inside a thousand scattered suns.

And each resident species had its preferred Builder.

Humanoids liked to imagine ancient humanoids; cetaceans pictured enormous whales; machine intelligences demanded orderly, nonaqueous entities. But fashions shifted easily and usually in confusing directions, dictating the key elements to the most recent fables. Each millennium had its favorite phantom and its most popular cavern. There was a stubborn lack of physical evidence, but even that absence made true believers dance. Harper reasoned that the Builders were secretive and powerful organisms, and of course no slippery wise and important creature would leave traces of its passing. Skin flakes and odd tools were never found in the deep caves, much less one genuine body, because if hard evidence did exist, then the quarry wouldn't be the true Builders. Would they?

One of the files focused on the Remora's ghost.

On Alone.

Hundreds of sightings and endless conjecture made for years of unblinking study. Absorbing every word, every murky image, Alone was fascinated by the mystery that he had walked through. According to self-proclaimed experts, he was as real as the Whispers that haunted a mothballed spaceport. But Harper gave more credence to the Clackers who supposedly swam inside the Ship's fuel tanks, and the Demon-whiffs that were made of pure dark matter. Many thousands of years after the event, Alone watched the recording of himself standing inside the empty hyperfiber tank—a swirl of cobalt light that could mean anything, or nothing—and he wondered if perhaps he wasn't entirely real. Only recently, after billions of steps and missteps, had the phantom acquired that rare and remarkable capacity to stand apart from Nothingness.

For every place on the hull where Alone was seen, the Remoras and others had spied at least ten more examples of the ghost wandering beneath the stars.

What if more than one of him was wandering loose?

Alone didn't know what to believe. The sightings had diminished after he abandoned the hull, and no Remora claimed to have spotted Wune's mysterious friend. No file mentioned Aasleen and the nightmare inside one of the Ship's engines, which meant that the captains and crew were talented at keeping secrets, and what else did they know? A related file focused on shape-shifting machines currently lurking in dark corners and deep wastes. Alone's cavern was prominent but far from the most important. Dozens of sprawling, empty locations were named, but the only cavern to capture Alone's imagination was named Bottom-E. Again and again, he found sketchy accounts of tourists wandering down an empty passageway, and glancing over their shoulder, they spied a smear of dim light silently racing out of view.

Bottom-E was a much larger cavern even than Alone's old home, and if nothing else, it would provide the perfect next home.

But what if a second entity like him already lived there?

Two decades of study and consideration led to one difficult choice. Various humans had tried to contact Harper on his return. Most were small figures, many with criminal records and embarrassing public files. But despite those same limitations, one man had all the qualifications to give aid to an acquaintance that he hadn't seen for ages.

With Harper's face and voice, Alone sent a polite request.

Eighteen days passed before any reply was offered. The recorded digital showed a smiling man sitting inside what looked like a diamond bubble. He began with an apology, explaining, "I was wandering through The Way of Old. It's an ammonia-hydroxide ocean, on a small scale but still a hundred cubic kilometers of murk and life. That's why I couldn't get back to you right away, Harper. Nexus are outlawed. And since I'm going back under in another two minutes, I thought I could try to give your questions a few rubs to start with."

Perri was the man's name.

"So you're interested in Bottom-E," the message continued. "I can't promise much in the way of help. I haven't seen more than one tenth of one percent of the place. But there is one enormous room that's worth the long walk. Its floor is hyperfiber, and a fine grade at that. And the ceiling is kilometers overhead and inhabited by the LoYo. They're machines, not sentient as individuals but communal in nature. A few thousand of their city-nests hang from the rafters, and that's one of the reasons for going down there."

The grinning man continued. "The LoYo give that big room a soft, delicious glow. I've got good eyes, but even after a week in there, I couldn't see far. Just the immediate floor and what felt like a distant, unreachable horizon. Once, maybe twice, I saw a light in the distance. I can't claim to know what the light was. But you know me, Harper. Don't expect ghost stories. Usually the truth is a lot more interesting than what we think we want to see…

"Anyway, what I like best about Bottom-E, and in particular about that huge room…what makes a trip genuinely memorable…is that when you walk on that smooth hyperfiber, and nothing above you but the faint far off glow of what could be distant galaxies…it's easy to believe that this is exactly how it would have felt and looked just a couple billion years ago, if you were strolling by yourself across the hull of the Great Ship.

"Understand, Harper? Imagine yourself out between the galaxies, crossing the middle of nothing. That's an experience worth doing."

Then with a slow wink, Perri added, "By the way. I know you keep to yourself. But if you feel like enduring some company, you're more than welcome to visit my home for a meal, for conversation. For no good reason, if you. I don't think you ever met my wife, and I'll warn you, Quee Lee likes people even more than I do."

Perri paused, staring at his unseen audience.

"You were gone a very long time," he said. "Jan claimed you were off chasing Clackers, and that's what the official report decides too. 'Lost in the fuel tanks.' But I haven't heard any news about bodies being fished out of the liquid hydrogen, which makes me wonder if our mutual friend was telling another one of his fables.

"Anyway, it's wonderful-good to see you again, Harper. And welcome back to the living!"

11

As promised, Bottom-E held one enormous room, and except for the occasional smudge of cold light pasted against the remote arch of a ceiling, the room was delightfully dark. Each step on the slick floor teased out memories. That lost and now beloved childhood returned to him, and Alone wasn't just content but he was confident that the next step would bring happiness, as would the step after that, and the step after that.

More than twelve hundred square kilometers of hyperfiber demanded his careful study. Unlike the hull, there was an atmosphere, but the air was oxygen-starved and nearly as cold as space. Alone's brought back an old habit, following a random line until an oddity caught his attention. Then he would stop and study what another visitor had left behind—a fossilized meal or frozen bodily waste, usually—before attacking another random line until he found trash or until a wall of rough feldspar defined the limits of this illusion.

For two years, he walked quietly, seeing no one else.

The LoYo were tiny and weakly lit, and there was no sign that they noticed him, much less understood what he was.

Perri's mysterious glow failed to appear. But Alone soon convinced himself that he had never hoped for the story to prove real. One step was followed by the next, and eventually he would pause and turn and step again, defining a new line, right up until the moment when that simple cherished pattern failed him. He was walking when suddenly a thin reddish light was swallowed by his big eyes, digested and studied. He examined the glow photon by photon, instinct racing ahead of his intelligence. This new light was indistinguishable from the glow that he leaked whenever he was examining a fossilized pile of alien feces.

On his longest, quietest legs, Alone ran.

Then the voice returned. Decades had passed since the last incident, yet it was suddenly with him—the sharp stark concept, "No," wrapped inside a wild, infectious panic.

Alone's impulse was to stop and ask, "What do you want?"

But the red glow was very close. Thousands of years had been spent imagining this unlikely, even impossible moment, and nothing mattered but to conquer the next few meters. Alone felt brave enough to press on. Yet bravery wasn't required. Caught up in the excitement, he appreciated how much this mattered to him. He was happy, yes. He was thrilled and spellbound, and he refused to answer the voice or even pay attention when it came closer and grew even louder.

"Do not," it warned.

It told him, "No. They want but they will not understand. Do not."

The light was still visible, but it had grown weaker.

Somehow the intervening distance had grown.

But a ready explanation offered itself: The other Alone must have noticed that something was wrong. A footfall, a murmur. Perhaps his brother heard the same voice, and a wild, unapologetic fear had taken possession of him. Whatever the reason, the light was beginning to shrivel and fade away, losing him by diving inside a little tunnel, abandoning this room and possibly Bottom-E because of one irresistible terror.

Alone had to stop his brother.

But how?

He quit running.

The voice that had never identified itself—the conscience that perhaps was too ancient, too maimed and run down, to even lend itself a name—now said to him, "Go away. This is the wrong course. Go!"

Alone would not listen.

Standing on the barren plain, he made himself grow tiny and exceptionally bright, washing away the darkness. In an instant, the enormous chamber was filled with a sharp white light that reached the walls and rose to the ceiling before reflecting and reflecting and then gone.

He was dark again, drained but not quite exhausted.

With the last of his reserves, Alone spun a fresh mouth, and in a language that he had never heard before—never suspected that he was carrying inside himself—he screamed into the newly minted darkness, "I am here!"

A dozen machines suddenly emerged out of their hiding places, plunging from the ceiling or racing from blinds inside the towering rock walls.

Alone vanished.

But the machines were converging on him.

Then he grew large again, managing legs. But the power expended by his desperate flash and careless shout was too much, and too many seconds were needed before he would be able to offer any kind of chase. After ages of sameness and moments of excitement, the door of a great trap was closing over him, and in the end there wasn't even the pleasure of hard pursuit fought to any dramatic, worthy end.

12

Since their last meeting, the two organisms had walked separate lines—tightrope existences inspired by ambition and chance, deep purpose and the freedom of no clear purpose. An observer on a high perch, watching their respective lives, could reasonably conclude that the two souls would never cross lines again. The odd machine was quiet and modest, successfully avoiding discovery in the emptiest reaches of the Ship, while the human had invested ages maintaining the giant engines, and later, tending a slow-blooming career as a new captain. Yet they found themselves together on this very peculiar terrain. With her first words, Aasleen confessed embarrassment: She had had no idea where Alone might have been and not been over these last tens of thousands of years. For decades, for entire centuries, she didn't waste two moments pondering the device that she once cornered and then let get away. Not that she was at peace with her failure. She didn't appreciate evidence of her incompetence, and it gnawed at her to know that somewhere onboard the Great Ship was a barely contained speck of highly compressed matter, and should that speck ever break containment, the next several seconds would become violent and famous, and for some souls, exceptionally sad.

But as an engineer, Aasleen could hand her official worries to the captains, and as a novice captain she never faced duties that had even the most glancing relationship to that old problem.

Relating her story now, she assumed that her prisoner would understand what he heard and feel interest in this curious, quirky business.

Several centuries ago, Aasleen and a second captain met by chance and fell into friendly conversation. It was her colleague who mentioned a newly discovered machine-building species. Washen had a sure touch with aliens. Better than most humans, she could decipher the attitudes and instincts of organisms that made no sense to a pragmatic, by-the-number soul like Aasleen. But the aliens had been superior engineers, which was why Washen mentioned them in the first place. Dubbed the Bakers, she described their rare genius for weaving inventive and persistent devices, and millions of years after their rise and fall and subsequent extinction, their machines were still scattered across the galaxy.

"The Bakers is our name for the species," Aasleen cautioned. "It shouldn't mean anything to you."

Alone was floating above the cavern floor, encased in cages of plasma and overlapping magnetic fields creating a nearly invisible, seemingly unbreakable prison. Drifting in the middle of the smallest cage, he was drenched in vacuum, nothing but his own body ready to fuel an engine that everybody else seemed to fear.

With a flickering radio voice, he agreed. "I don't know the Bakers."

"What about this word?" Aasleen asked.

An intense sound washed across him. He listened carefully and then asked to hear it again. "I don't know the name," he confessed. "But the sounds make sense to me."

"I'm not surprised," Aasleen said.

Alone waited.

"We know what you are," she said.

He told his captor, "I already know what I am. My history barely matters."

"All right," Aasleen said. "Do I stop talking now? Should I keep my tiresome explanations to myself?"

That sounded like a fine possibility. But machines and teams of engineers had emerged from distant tunnels, obviously preparing to do some large job. As long as the woman inside the mirrored uniform was speaking, nothing evil would be done to him. So finally, with no doubt in the voice, he said, "Tell me about these Bakers."

"They built you."

"Perhaps so," he said.

"Seven hundred million years ago," Aasleen added. Then a bright smile broke, and she added, "Which means that you are the second oldest machine that I have ever known."

The Great Ship being the oldest.

"The Bakers were never natural travelers," she said. "We don't know a lot about them, and our little pile of facts mostly comes through tertiary sources. But as far as can be determined, the species didn't send even one emissary to another world. Instead of wandering, they built wondrous durable drones that they littered across an entire arm of the galaxy. Their machines were complicated and adaptable, and they were purposefully limited in what they knew about themselves. You see, the Bakers didn't surrender anything about themselves. They were isolated and happy to be that way. But they were also curious, in a paranoid fashion, imagining dangerous neighbors wanting to harm them. That's why they built what looks to me like an elaborate empty bottle—a bottle designed to suck up ideas and emotions and history and intellectual talents from whatever species happens to come along. And when necessary, those machines could even acquire the shape and voice of the locals too."

Nothing about the story could be refuted. Alone accepted what he heard while refusing to accept that any of it mattered.

"The Bakers lasted for ten or twelve million years, and then their world's ecosystem collapsed," Aasleen said. "They lived at the opposite end of our galaxy, and the only reason we've learned anything about them is because one of our new passenger species has collected several dead bottles as well as historical accounts. We don't let anyone ride for free. Part of their payment is sharing what they know about the Bakers, and Washen knew that I would be fascinated in dead engineers. She didn't talk for two minutes before I dropped a hand on her hand and told her that I knew where another bottle was, and this one was still working.

"'Where is it?' she asked.

"'He,' I told her, 'He is wandering inside the Great Ship, and he answers to the very appropriate name of Alone."

The captain paused, smiling without appearing particularly happy.

The busy workers were erecting an elaborate needle on the cavern floor, aiming it straight up at him.

"We approached Miocene with our news," Aasleen said. "I know Washen was disappointed. She wanted this assignment, but finding you was my job, and if that wasn't difficult enough, I was told to corral you. Washen helped profile your nature, your powers. I decided to use the promise of another machine like you as a lure, and that's why I turned Bottom-E into a halfway famous abode for a glowing shape-shifting soul. If something went ugly-wrong down here, then at least the damage could be contained."

"What about the LoYo?" Alone asked.

"They were moved to other quarters. The lights above are hiding sensors, and I designed them myself, and they didn't help at all. Until you chased our fake bottle, there was no way to be certain that you were anywhere near this place."

The needle was quickly growing longer, reaching for the cage's outermost wall.

"What will you do now?" Alone asked.

"Strip away your engine first, and then we'll secure it and you." Aasleen described the process, offering incomprehensible terms along with her confidence. Yet she seemed uneasy when she said, "We intend to isolate your neural net, see what it is and how it works."

"You are talking about my mind," Alone complained.

"A mind that lives beside a powerful, unexploded bomb," the captain added. "The Bakers didn't design you to survive for this long. My best guess is that you pushed yourself outside the Milky Way, and in that emptiness, nothing went wrong. You drifted. You waited. I suppose you slept, in a fashion. And then you happened upon the Great Ship, before or after we arrived. You could have been here long before us, but of course the Bakers are lost, and you weren't what I would consider sentient."

"But I am alive now," he said, his voice small and furious.

Aasleen paused.

With no apparent effort, the needle began passing through the wall of that first impenetrable cage.

"You are going to kill me," he insisted.

The human was not entirely happy with these events. It showed in her posture, her face. But she was under orders, and she was assured enough in her skills to say, "I don't think anything bad will happen. Research and preparation have been done, and we have an excellent team working with you. Once the danger is defused, you'll have your memories pulled loose and set inside safer surroundings, and I think you'll be happy. I do."

One sudden thrust and the needle pierced the other cages, and before it stopped rising, its bright plasmatic tip was touching his center.

Damage was being done.

Quietly, fiercely, he begged Aasleen, "Stop."

One nearby machine began to wail, the tone ominous and quickening. Aasleen looked at the data, and then too late, she shouted, "Stop it now. We've got the alignment wrong–!"

Then the captain and every engineer vanished.

They had been projections, fictions. The real humans were tucked inside some safe room, protected from the coming onslaught by distance and thick reaches of enduring hyperfiber.

Alone was injured and dying. But the damage was specific and still quite narrow, and the faltering mind continued, but exposed like never before. And that was the moment when the Voice that had always been speaking to him, that never stopped shouting at every soul that stood upon or inside the deep ancient hull, could be heard clearly.

"I am the Ship," the Voice declared.

"Listen!"

13

It was not one place but it was everywhere, and Those-Who-Rule received unwelcome news. There was trouble in Creation, and there was sudden urgent talk of grand failures. A portion of the everywhere was in rebellion. How could this be? Who would be so foolish? Outraged by what they saw as pure treachery, Those-Who-Rule decided that punishment was essential, and the best punishment had to be delivered instantly, before the rebellion could stretch beyond even Their powerful reach. A ship was aimed and set loose, burrowing its way through the newborn universe. Upon reaching its target, a sentence worse than any death would be delivered. Nonexistence was its weapon—oblivion to All; the eradication of Potential and History too—and with that one talent and an insatiable hunger for success, the ship dove on and on until it had passed out of sight.

But now that act of vengeance lay in the past. Upon reflection, Those-Who-Rule questioned the wisdom of a decision made moments ago. Total slaughter seemed harsh, no matter how justified, and after a brief debate full of wasted time and self-serving confessions, these agents of ultimate power dispatched another grand vessel full of talents and desires and mighty, unborn possibilities.

That second ship chased after the first.

If it should meet its quarry somewhere out into the mayhem of newborn plasmas and raw, impossible energies, disaster would be averted. The song of life and existence and death and life born again would remain intact. But the universe was growing fast and then faster still, exploding outwards while a wicked chill seeped into the emptiness. Randomness was at work here, and blindness, and two adjacent points often discovered themselves separated by a billion light-years.

This chase would prove exceptionally difficult.

Yet the second ship's goal could be no more urgent.

Through Creation, salvation chased the bleak end of everything, and nothing else mattered, and nothing done by mortals or immortals could compare to the one race that would grant the universe permission to live out its day.

The insistent relentless piercing Voice roared at the Bakers' bottle, and all the while Alone felt his center leaking, threatening to explode. Finally he had no choice but to interrupt, asking his tormentor, "And which ship are you?"

The Voice hesitated.

"But you can't be the first ship," Alone said. "If you were carrying this nonexistence, you wouldn't know about the second ship chasing after you, trying to stop your work…"

In a mutter, the Voice said, "Yes."

"You must be the second Ship," he said.

"But a third choice exists," the Voice assured.

"No," said Alone.

Then in terror, he said, "Yes."

"I am," the Great Ship said.

"Both," Alone blurted. "You're that first ship bringing Nothingness, and you're the second ship after it has reached its target."

"Yes."

"But you can't stop the mission, can you?"

"Half of me has tried and cannot, and half of me will resist and nothing will change," said the Great Ship.

"You're both ships, both pilots."

"We are."

"Working for opposite ends."

"Yes."

"And these humans," Alone said. "They happily, foolishly ride you through their galaxy."

"Doom everywhere, and every moment ending us."

Alone felt weak enough to flicker out of existence, and an instant later, he was stronger than ever before. "Tell them," he said. "Why can't you explain it to them?"

"Why won't they hear me?"

"I hear you."

"At long last, yes."

"I could tell them for you."

"If you survived, you would explain. Yes."

"But…"

"It is too late."

Alone fell silent.

The Great Ship continued to talk, repeating that same tale of revenge and the chase, of nonexistence and the faint promise of redemption.

But Alone had stopped listening. He heard nothing more. With just the eye of his mind, he was gazing back across tens of thousands of years, remembering every step taken and each step avoided, and he could only marvel at how small his long life appeared when set against the light of far suns and the deep abyss of Time.

Bridge One

There is no reason to select that one girl. Yes, she is intelligent and watchful, but many creatures, thousands of creatures, have finer minds and quicker, more thorough senses. There have been moments and tiny incidents when she might have been influenced by another's influence, but then again, perhaps not. And yes, she seems nothing but capable, carrying herself with gentle confidence. But gifts such as capacity and self-assuredness often reach for hubris and arrogance and every flavor of disaster. Humans roam freely inside the Ship and beyond, which is why being human is a blessing, unless it is otherwise. Yet with an abundant species such as this, there must be better candidates. Where are the better candidates? What passes for eyes and a mind observes the newcomers, learning a little more about these sacks of lucid water and their elaborate implants, the species' brief history and their cherished beliefs, and even more critical, the gaps of belief that might play roles in what has barely begun.

No compelling reason demands to select the young Washen, and this is just another reason to let the search continue elsewhere.

A goal teases, always.

The universe has found the Great Ship, and they have found nothing. An object belongs to no one if it remains unknown, and humans have grabbed up a vast contraption that cannot be measured by any worthy scale. Ignorance rules. The captains are brilliant fools. Their uniforms are made of mirrored fabric, half-alive and regal, but their uniforms are also woven from arrogance and status and small experiences never tested properly and lessons never applied in suitable proportions. The fabric might fall away on occasion, but a naked captain squatting over a scented toilet is still a captain, bound by the office and buoyed by rank and to some degree or another endowed by senses of duty that can help feed what every animal would understand as raging, insatiable ambition.

The girl is no captain. She may never hold any rank onboard the Ship. After all, she is only ten years old, and though more mature than her peers, that means nothing. Maturity is a quality that humans will gather up eventually, in small doses. Physical strength and physical beauty are just as arbitrary. But these are her blessings for the moment, and Washen likes to use her strong muscles to swim the sea beside her home city.

Washen is no social creature, at least compared to her species' norms. She will swim and swim across open reaches of water, no one beside at the beginning or ever, and sometimes she will pause for no reason except to float—on the surface or deep below. The girl can hold her breath forever. Forever. Humans are rich with alternate metabolisms that ride secretly on their old mammalian organs, and better than most adults, the floating girl can close her eyes and blow the damp air from her chest, allowing her bones and hard muscle to carry her to depths where no light is welcome, where a soul can hover on the brink of hibernation while the frigid water holds tight.

She does not notice any mysterious voice or presence.

Yet she doesn't deny these ingredients either. And that is a small critical point, unnoticed at first and then well worth considering.

She hears nothing, but she appears willing to hear.

Perhaps this is why she floats in the dark, for a full hour of nothing; but eventually some urge comes and she touches a necklace that inflates into a vacuum collar that carries her to the surface where she remembers to breathe in deep long happy and very wet breaths.

The girl has many friends but doesn't require companionship. Being alone for a day or ten years wouldn't scare her. But walking the shore again, for the rest of that day and always, Washen is the person who is watched most closely. She is the golden child at the center of the classroom and the playground and at home. Adults and children alike tend to follow her motions, hang on her words, and if she is silent for a long while, they unconsciously and happily wait for whatever smart good or funny words will be worthy of breaking the silence.

Charisma is a rare talent, and sometimes it can be a fine talent.

But she remains more blind than not, more ignorant than not, more human than is probably best, and there is no compelling reason to single her out.

Yet the eyeless gaze continues to study her.

* * *

One day she sits on the basalt beach of her home sea, rump on rock while talking to the waves, to birds. She talks to no one. "I was born on the Great Ship," she says to no one. "I will never go anywhere else.

"I know this," she says.

"I don't know why I know this, but when the thought found me, I realized that I had always been aware of the truth," she says.

Then she rubs at the warm rock with both hands and both bare feet, saying, "I will live here as close to forever as I can, and do you know why?"

The wind gusts, carrying an affirmative urge.

But Washen doesn't feel or hear or even guess what passes through her, which is another fine reason to ignore her in favor of a thousand finer, more deserving candidates.

Except she offers an answer not expected.

"I love you," she says.

Who does she love?

"I love this big round puzzle of a spaceship," she says.

The wind gusts again, hard this time.

No ripe meanings come to her. Yet she holds her pretty face high, eyes tearing and the mouth open as if anticipating a first kiss, and there is no way to know exactly what will happen next.

Hoop-of-Benzene

1

A young captain was chosen because the task seemed quite minor and higher ranked souls had more vital and interesting duties to perform. What the officer knew was minimal: the apartment's location, a sketch of its history, plus the name and species of its current owner. But she brought clear orders and the sanctity of her office, and after centuries of training, she was accustomed to the mirrored uniform as well as its natural authority.

"Hello, sir," the captain began, offering the standard two-stomp greeting. A tall and naturally graceful woman, she was pretty in a human fashion, with an easy smile kept hidden for the moment. Employing a crisp, slightly angry voice, she announced, "My name is Washen."

The alien stared through the diamond door, saying nothing.

"Hoop-of-Benzene," she called out. Harum-scarums often appreciated a brash tone. "If that's your name, I wish to speak with you. And if you are someone else, bring Hoop-of-Benzene to me."

The breathing mouth opened. "I am Hoop," the alien replied.

She repeated the two-stomp greeting. "Three days from now, one of my superiors will visit your district, and the good captain has expressed interest in touring his former home. Which happens to be your apartment."

The mouth puckered. "Does this good captain carry a name?"

"For the moment, he does not. He prefers confidentiality. But I assure you that he's among the Master Captain's favorite officers."

"A Submaster, is he?"

"Perhaps," Washen allowed. "And perhaps not."

"In three days, you say." An enormous hand pressed against the door. "But why in three days? Can you surrender that much?"

Washen considered her audience. Harum-scarum society was built upon ceremony and rank, status and noisy bluster. "As I'm sure you are aware, sir…five thousand years ago, my people threw open the hatches of this great vessel, inviting all the species of the galaxy to share in our grand voyage. Fifty centuries of unrivaled success, and during this milestone year, to mark our countless accomplishments, the captains are holding a series of celebrations."

"I have heard about this business," Hoop allowed.

"The Master Captain is scheduled to visit your district. Her Submasters will be in attendance, plus a hundred lesser captains, and she will enjoy two feasts given in her honor, and a Janusian wedding, and the new Ill-lock habitat will be christened. As for the nameless captain, his stay here will last moments. Little longer. The man is not a sentimental creature, and I assure you, any disruption to your life will be minimal."

"No."

"Pardon?"

"The human creature may not visit my home."

Washen had imagined but never expected this turn. Concealing her surprise, she asked, "What is the difficulty, sir? Is it a matter of timing?"

"Why?" asked the breathing mouth. "Would the good captain accept a different day?"

"Possibly," she said.

"Yet I presume he wouldn't," Hoop decided. "Captains are exceptionally stubborn humans, and I believe you are trying to mislead me."

Washen allowed a grin to emerge. "Yes, sir. You've seen through my thin ape-skin, yes. The captain's schedule is quite busy, and he will probably not return to this district for a long, long while."

Even among his species, Hoop-of-Benzene was an enormous creature—a towering biped whose muscular body was covered with glistening armored plates and long golden spines. The broad black eyes stared at the young captain. Beneath the eyes were two mouths, one for speaking and breathing, the other intended for eating and delivering the worst insults imaginable.

"My schedule is equally rigid," announced the breathing mouth. "And since I do not wish to entertain visitors, not in three days or for the next three thousand years, I will not allow him inside my home."

The eating mouth made a soft, abusive noise.

"It is my right to turn away visitors," the alien continued. "I know the codes. I can quote the relevant statutes, if you wish. Even the Master Captain is forbidden from entering any premise where she is not welcome. The only exceptions demand sturdy legal causes, which do not apply in this situation. And even in the most urgent circumstances, mandatory warrants must be drawn up, sealed and registered, then delivered by the appropriate agents of the law."

Again, he made the rude sound.

Washen's eyes were nearly as dark as Hoop's. Her expression was curious and patient, with just a trace of nervous concern.

"You still haven't offered any name," the alien pointed out.

"I carry orders. My superior intends to remain anonymous." With a thin smile, she added, "I can tell you that he is a powerful figure onboard the

Great Ship. A force to be reckoned with, and once angered, he can be quite vindictive."

Harum-scarums had a genetic respect for tyrants.

Yet Hoop clucked a tongue as if amused. "I suspect, young captain, you must feel rather uncomfortable now."

Washen swallowed and said nothing.

"So tell me this…"

"Sir?"

"Why would a powerful, vindictive creature care who it is that strolls through these little rooms?"

"I cannot guess his mind, sir."

"I am not discussing the captain's mind," Hoop replied. "Perhaps I should remind you: Two powers are at play here."

"A worthy point," Washen said. Then with a wink and bright smile, "And you should consider the poor intermediary standing before you. She doesn't know the name of your game, much less its rules."

Again, the tongue clicked.

"This must be an important mission," Hoop observed. "To select such a quick-witted captain–"

"All missions are important," she interrupted.

The harum-scarum paused, perhaps considering his choices.

"If I fail to win your cooperation," Washen said, "a second, much higher-ranking captain will be sent. Or twenty subordinates wielding heavy legal weaponry will descend on your empire. As you say, captains are stubborn souls, and this one in particular is obstinate. He intends to step through your door at a specific hour, two days after tomorrow, and no one can halt the inevitable."

"Do I look helpless?" Hoop inquired.

"My name is Washen," the young captain repeated. "I just made my service files available to you. Absorb them at your convenience, and I will lie to my superior. I'll claim that you wish to meet with me tomorrow, and the two of us will come to terms with this nagging problem in our lives."

Then before Hoop-of-Benzene could respond, the young captain turned her back to him and strode off—in effect, making it difficult for a proper harum-scarum to refuse the little creature, when and if she found the courage to come to his door again.

2

A singular voyage through the wealthiest, most civilized regions of the galaxy: That was what the Great Ship offered. In principle, every individual and entire species could buy passage. Humans and aliens alike paid their way with simple capital, or they surrendered claims to starships and lucrative asteroids and sometimes entire worlds. But the Ship's owners had a weakness for deeper abstractions. Fresh science and raw, uncut data were popular trade items—subjects didn't matter as much as novelty. They also accepted revolutionary machinery and old-fashioned tools made better. And when some new species was powerful or peculiarly well-regarded, the Master Captain would make warm covenants between the newcomers and humanity, winning allies as the long thorough loop around the Milky Way began to take shape.

The Ship's builders, whoever they were, insured that every cubbyhole and grand ocean could be modified, matching the precise needs of alien physiologies. But what was not so easy—what was exceptionally difficult if not even possible—was to keep this menagerie happy enough and distracted enough to live under the same hull for hundreds of millennia.

The captains were the highest authority, steady hands on the tiller while their hard boots ruled every other facet of life onboard the Ship.

Harum-scarums were among the most important and abundant passengers. Older than humanity, they evolved on a watery, metal-starved world. Tiny continents and scarce resources shaped their long history; relentless, unapologetic competition was the hallmark of their mature civilization. Tens of millions of years were spent defending the same patches of dry ground, evolving elaborate codes of formal, trusted rituals. While proto-humans still brachiated their way through jungle canopies, harum-scarums were refining aluminum and building spaceships. Before *Homo habilis* jogged across Africa, the aliens had acquired hyperfiber and enhanced fusion star-drives, plus a collection of powerful tools that made both their bodies and minds functionally immortal.

Harum-scarum was the human name. The Clan of Many Clans was one inadequate translation of what the creatures called themselves. Like most high-technology species, once the Clan learned how to extend life spans, it stopped evolving. On thousands of worlds, the creatures still clung to their original natures—physically powerful entities filled with calculated rage as well as a startling capacity for acquiescence.

From the Clan's perspective, Washen's people were newcomers to the galaxy—untested and laughably optimistic, like children or pampered meat. For every air-cloaked rock that humans colonized, the Clan ruled a hundred mature worlds. Trillions of citizens were scattered across an entire arm of the galaxy, and they had more starships and better starships than anyone. If they had seen the Great Ship roaming the deep cold, they would have reached it first and claimed the artifact as their prize. But they didn't notice the giant wanderer soon enough. Humans did, and because of that blessing, humans achieved something that was deeply unlikely.

This was one reason why Hoop and his people found such pleasure insulting their hosts. "Monkey-men" was a popular barb. "Bare-fleshed fetuses." And perhaps the most caustic, damning name: "Luck-fattened souls."

The average human assumed that harum-scarums were embittered, jealous and probably vengeful monsters. But the responsible captain knew better than to read too much into a little hard noise. Once humans took legal possession of the ancient derelict—in accordance with the galaxy's ancient laws—the Clan had finished grieving. Ownership had been established. A contest won was a contest done. And if you were a good citizen of a worthy family, you turned away and carefully sharpened your spines, focusing on living your magnificent life.

Grudges and second acts were the province of weaker species.

Humans, for one.

* * *

"This makes no sense to me," the Submaster confessed. "You assured him that I was an important captain."

"Which you are," said Washen.

"Am I still anonymous?"

"Absolutely, sir."

"Yet the creature refuses to capitulate."

"For the time being, but I'll meet with him tomorrow and reach some understanding."

"Harum-scarums," the Submaster muttered. "I've dealt with them many times, and with much success. Once you push past their manners and moods, they're perfectly reasonable ogres."

Washen restrained a grimace.

The man was named Ishwish. By human measures, he was ancient and extraordinarily well traveled. Countless stories were told about the old Submaster, yet remarkably little was defined in his public biography. Ishwish had fought with distinction in several human wars, rising to a high rank in two militaries. More than once he had employed alien mercenaries, including the brigades of harum-scarums who helped make his career. Then after earning a strongbox full of medals, he retired to a quiet life, commanding colony starships during the first human expansion across the Milky Way. Those millennia made him a wealthy man with lucrative political connections. When the Great Ship was discovered, Ishwish expended his personal fortune, fitting a small asteroid with enormous engines and a minimal life support system and then hiring a crew to race out beyond the edges of the Milky Way. His starship was among the first to arrive at the Great Ship. And from that moment, Ishwish had worked tirelessly to maintain his rightful high rank among the first captains.

The Submaster remained silent for a few moments, most likely using a nexus to examine Hoop's files. The eyes flickered for a moment, meaning what? Then he sighed softly, and with a disappointed shake of the head, he said, "Frankly, I expected better things from an ambitious young captain."

Washen nodded as if agreeing, twisting the mirrored cap in her hands.

"There is no task that a captain cannot achieve," he reminded her.

"I know this, sir."

Ishwish's task of the moment was to sit alone before a large oak table, occupying the back corner of what was a very small eating establishment. This was the favorite haunt of the Master Captain, which made it popular to all of her Submasters. The man was exceptionally tall in his chair; Washen stood beside him, yet their eyes were nearly level. Handsome in an ageless, heavily polished fashion, Ishwish had bright gold eyes and a sharp joyless smile, and with every word and little motion, he betrayed enough arrogance to fuel two successful captains.

"What are little jobs?" he asked.

"'An impossibility of nature,'" she quoted from her training.

"And what are little honors?"

"'Blessings that fall on little souls,'" she said, quoting words he had used on more than one occasion.

Ishwish nodded, and the smile dimmed. "I am going to be awarded a declaration of merit, and it will come from the Master Herself."

"Congratulations, sir."

"For my long service to this fabulous ship, I will enjoy this stupendous honor."

"As is your right, sir."

"Our Master asked me, 'Where do you wish the ceremony to be held, my good friend? On the Ship's bridge? Or at the captains' dinner?' But after careful consideration, I decided on a small ceremony held inside the apartment where I first lived. I relish the image. And frankly, I am extremely fond of those little rooms and alcoves and such."

Even as she repeated her congratulations, Washen doubted the explanation. Creatures like Ishwish would want the largest possible audience to admire the treasured moment. And like the flickering of the eyes, the fact that he was lying now meant something. Though what this said about the circumstances, she couldn't yet say.

The Submaster glanced at her. "My memory tells me," he said quietly. "You were born in the Great Ship, weren't you?"

"Yes, sir."

"And your parents were not captains?"

"They were engineers," she admitted. But Ishwish surely knew that already, just as he seemed to remember every detail from her tiny life.

"You've never left the confines of the Ship," he said.

There was nothing confining about a machine with the mass of Uranus and enough caverns to explore for the next ten billion years. But she simply dipped her head, admitting, "I have not traveled far. No, sir."

"You haven't walked the harum-scarum worlds."

Washen shook her head, pretending to be disappointed in herself. "Never, sir."

"I have."

She waited for advice, or at least some tiny insight.

But Ishwish offered none. He lifted a utensil—a heavy crab-pincer—while glancing across the room. A colleague had just arrived, and in the smallest possible way, he waved the pincer and his elegant hand, offering his greetings to a fellow Submaster.

Washen bowed to the newcomer, then asked Ishwish, "Do you have any advice for a novice captain?"

"The Great Ship always needs new engineers."

His threat earned a small nod from Washen. But she was watching the newcomer stroll toward an empty table reserved for no one but her. Miocene was her name, and she was said to be the Master Captain's most loyal and dangerous officer. Since becoming a novice captain, Washen had spoken to the woman perhaps half a dozen times. None of those conversations held any substance. Yet the tall, imperious woman was looking at her now. Just for a moment. And for no obvious reason, Miocene tipped her head at the young officer, offering a dim but lingering smile…a smile that for no clear reason felt important…

3

"Where is your uniform?"

"It is doing its own business this morning." Washen confessed while giving a two-foot stomp. She was standing before the diamond door, wearing civilian clothes, including sandals and slacks and a pair of simple silk belts. If not for the small mirror-patch on the shoulder of her blouse, she would have been completely out of uniform, subject to a multitude of deserved punishments. "As I promised, I am here. And now I wish to step inside your apartment."

"No."

She nodded as if unconcerned. "Tell me why not."

"I don't crave visitors. Why is this so difficult to comprehend?"

Washen puckered her lips and blew air, making a doubtful sound. "As I understand these matters," she said, "your family clan is one of the largest. Your relatives stand tall on half a hundred worlds."

"Yes, we are great."

"Success hauls responsibility in its wake," she said.

"For more species than mine," Hoop said.

"According to your laws and honored conventions, you cannot turn away the weakest mouths. If a citizen with no status comes to your door begging for a small meal, it is your duty to feed her enough to live out the day."

Both of the harum-scarum's mouths snorted, amusement mixed with warm disgust. "You are far from weak," he said.

"Am I?"

"Perhaps you haven't noticed, my dear. But even a lowly captain commands respect from the multitudes."

"Not from you, sir."

"You do have my respect. I honor your office and rank. I'm just refusing to surrender my home to any captain."

With her best impression of a harum-scarum smile, Washen asked, "But what if I wasn't a captain anymore?"

The black eyes stared.

"If I surrendered my rank and authority, what would that mean to you…?"

"Nothing," he said.

Yet Washen acted as if she'd heard a different response, removing her blouse and the mirrored emblem attached to it, folding them into a small wad easily thrown over her naked shoulder. Then she kicked off the sandals and unfastened both belts, her slacks falling into a heap around her bare ankles. "As a traveler without rank or privilege, may I enter your home?"

"No," said Hoop.

She kneeled and bent low, slowly licking the granite floor of the avenue. Then employing a passable harum-scarum voice, she said, "Without food, I die."

"You are being silly," the alien said.

"I'm only following your example," she countered.

Hoop refused to answer. For a long while he remained motionless, spines and fingers held in relaxed positions. But there was pedestrian traffic in the avenue, and eventually half a dozen humans strolled past, pausing to watch this very peculiar scene. A Janusian couple joined them, and then a pack of Fume-dogs. Eventually half a hundred passengers stood in a patient half-circle, enjoying the spectacle of a former captain going mad, naked and splayed out on the hard chilled ground, muttering again and again in that harsh alien language, "Without food, I die."

Nothing in his demeanor changed until a pair of harum-scarums appeared down the avenue, leaving Hoop with no choice. This human creature had done nothing but follow orders, and the only worthy response was to invite her inside.

Just the same, he hesitated.

He didn't surrender until Hoop's brethren started kicking Fume-dogs out of the way, trying to see what was so interesting. Letting out a low wet sound, he backed out of sight, and an instant later, the thick diamond door split along every invisible seam.

4

Like many shipboard residences, the apartment began as a tiny portion of an enormous cavern. Walls were erected at convenient points, tunnels closed off, and a cozy ten hectares of floor space and high ceilings was created. No public record linked Ishwish to the place. The man lived there for his early centuries onboard the Ship, but wanting privacy, it was owned by an AI mask. Then the local district misplaced its cache. The Submaster and his mask acquired a more spacious and impressive address while the old apartment was sold to a human marriage—early passengers from a rich colony world. Over the next thousand years, two women and two men raised eight children from embryo to adulthood. Then came a difficult divorce and a quick sale to a gathering of Higgers—machine souls that promptly flooded the chambers and long passageways with the hot, pressurized silicone that they needed for survival. But Higgers have accelerated minds and painfully low thresholds for boredom, and fourteen years was too much time in one location. They sold to an investment conglomerate specializing in boondock properties. The new owners paid rather more than market value, but the Ship's population was growing rapidly, and better yet, shifting fashions and a parade of new species eventually lifted the district back to its former importance.

Hoop-of-Benzene acquired the property twenty-five centuries ago, draining the silicone and then renovating the interior with his own hands and curses, creating a volume that perfectly suited his needs.

He had lived nowhere else since boarding the Ship.

On bare feet, Washen walked upon the greeting-mat laid out in the hallway—the complex patterns of fuzzy rings displaying the name and important history of Hoop's family clan. The first of a hundred towering statues stood with their backs against the walls, each defending a block of ceremonial soil. Treasured ancestors had been carved from a ruddy wood alien to both of their species. A thick oily scent hung in the air, dark and disgusting to the human nose. But Washen took a deep sniff before turning to her host. "Tidecold-6," she said quietly.

Hoop gave no reply.

Then in his language—in the proper dialect—she named the tree. "Blood-twice," she said.

Considering the inadequate mouth, her diction was good.

The harum-scarum watched his guest absently scratch her bare ear, her bare breast. Then he studied her ribs and that patch of soft tissue where a beating heart could be seen. Perhaps he had never shared air with a naked human. Devoid of armor, Washen appeared exposed and ridiculously frail—a reaction tied to his oldest instincts—and as a consequence, the big hands pulled themselves into fists.

Washen returned to the standard human language. "Blood-twice trees are native to Tidecold-6."

"Botany is an interest?" he asked.

"It is, but I would have learned about them anyway." Throwing her own fist through the air was a gesture of respect. "I've done a respectable amount of research about you," she said.

He said nothing.

Washen started down the hallway, examining each of the life-sized statues. The first ancestors were the most ancient, the pink wood gone pale and dusty dry. But at some point the statues darkened, every slice of the old awls still deep, each figure decorated with scraps of clothing and jewelry, spines and plates of armor that belonged to each of the men and women being portrayed. They stood where the hallway curled sharply to the right. More statues waited out of sight, but Washen stopped and kneeled down, pretending to exam the meeting-mat beneath her feet. With a quiet, thoughtful voice, she said, "You came onboard my ship 2507 earth years ago."

Hoop watched her eyes, struggling to read the alien face.

"You came alone, a young, relatively wealthy man off on an adventure. Payment for your passage came through a universal account established on what you called your home world. Which was not Tidecold-6."

Hoop opened a huge hand. "This planet you keep naming…I have never seen the Tidecolds…"

She nodded agreeably, touching one of the mat's elegant rings. The fabric was young and clean. Pushing against the weave, she felt the living fibers moving in unison, debating if she was a threat and if she should be contested.

"Twelve light-years," she mentioned.

He was silent.

"Tidecold-6 was abandoned, and a portion of the survivors migrated to a hard little world twelve light-years removed. And to the best of their ability, they rebuilt. It was your clan that made new homes there, your people who had to weave the shame into their mats and then walk on."

The alien's spines straightened and the plates of armor pulled closer to his body, reflexively making ready to fend off any blow.

"That wicked ugly war of yours," she said.

Hoop's eating mouth made one wet sound.

"A harum-scarum apocalypse," she said.

"That is not possible." Staring at the tiny creature kneeling before him, he said, "My species aren't crazy apes. We do not fight to oblivion."

"Which makes your family history all the more tragic." Then Washen intentionally passed gas, her rectum offering the crudest possible curse—neatly underscoring the war's unbearable, unforgivable waste.

Their walk through the apartment continued in silence.

After the turn were the final few dozen statues. Washen paused beside a conspicuously empty slab of soil, and her host pushed ahead, polite in a harum-scarum fashion, entering the greeting room before his feeble guest.

Heavily pruned blood-twice forests grew in tall sapphire urns. Elegant furnishings meant for giants were scattered about the vast round space. The ceiling was a beautiful dome of polished green olivine. Light poured from everywhere, and nowhere. Some unseen functionary had just delivered a fresh meal to a greeting table set in the room's center. It was a dead meal, meat peeled from an immortal animal, seasoned and then cooked to a human's taste. In some other portion of the apartment, the meat's source was now recovering inside its spacious stable, feeling modest discomfort while eating its fill from the trough, damaged flesh rapidly patching the gaping wound.

The novice captain thanked Hoop-of-Benzene for going to so much trouble, and then she ignored the cooling feast.

"I have looked over your life," she mentioned again.

Hoop regarded her for a moment. "And what did you learn about me?"

"That I understand practically nothing."

Another silent stare began.

"I know something about the war," she said. "At least, I know one version of its history. Every few years, some young captain…someone even newer to his post than me…will pull me aside to ask, 'Do you know the story…?'"

"Which story?"

"My superior, the Submaster who refuses to be named, served as the captain to a small colony ship," she said. "His mission was to deliver ten thousand eager humans to a little world perched at the edge of the galaxy. A harsh young world, as it happens, and a huge challenge for ignorant monkeys like us, since we had almost no experience terraforming such marginal places."

Hoop's breathing mouth opened and then closed, forgetting to inhale.

"It was an unfortunate voyage," Washen said. "There were the usual problems with the engines and with life-support. But worst of all were the troubles between colonists. Personal qualms turned into political difficulties. Old feuds reignited in the quiet between the stars. The captain of any colony ship is responsible for his machinery and his human cargo, and this particular captain managed to keep the angry factions under control. But he lost his grip during the final decades, and a low-grade war broke out in the hallways and habitats. Plainly, his ship needed help, which was why he changed course, braking early and dropping into a low orbit around Tidecold-6."

With a slow voice, her host said, "Ishwish."

"I haven't mentioned names," Washen said, sitting on the edge of the greeting table, two fingertips riding up her bare stomach and sternum and neck. "The story that I have heard, and heard, and heard again, centers on the same few facts: Tidecold-6 was a large, mature world with oxygen and oceans and a vigorous biosphere. Two harum-scarum clans had lived there for eons. They were evenly matched, both in terms of population and resources. And that wasn't a coincidence. There had been half a thousand little confrontations already. But what would look like quick wars to humans were very formal, brutal on the edges but predictable in the meat. Your species is innately conditioned to spit and pummel one another, but the usual result is to reinforce some worthy status quo."

Hoop stared at her face, watching the weak little bones beneath her thin, practically useless skin.

"This is a consequence of your heritage." An appreciative smile broke out. "Your home world is eight billion years old, with worn-down islands and quiet seas and no reliable volcanism. Animals that evolve in similar circumstances, where resources are scarce and growth must be slow, often adapt along certain predictable lines."

"Am I an animal?"

She nodded. "You are a spectacular animal. And your ancestors were exceptionally expensive collections of bone and armor, muscle and energy. Without volcanic activity, key minerals are locked away in deep sediments. Soils are poor and the ocean is half-sterile, and it once took decades of slow, patient growth to wring enough calories and protein from some little patch of landscape, producing an adult as splendid as you. But evolution is a weave of complex calculations written in gore. You are a fabulous investment, and at the end of the day, you were a grand success."

Hoop gave an agreeable click of a tongue.

"What most humans should realize, but don't...if they are to work beside the Clan of Many Clans, they see furious, quick-tempered aliens. But most of what you do is for show. Not that what you do and say isn't real. The noise and fuming is not empty or unimportant. But when your powerful minds see nothing but disaster looming, you will give up. You will give in. Recognizing defeat, a sane and responsible citizen on any of your happy worlds will bow down and surrender to whatever clan or species has the battle won."

"How else should we behave?" asked Hoop.

"I agree. Every species in the universe should act this way," she said. "I know my sad people need a dose of your humility and wise nature. Particularly when you consider those human colonists: There was a new world to build, yet they felt it was more important to murder their own kind. If the unnamed captain had been shepherding two clans of harum-scarums across the galaxy, I guarantee you that there wouldn't have been any threat to the ship. Or to the mission. Or to the man sitting on the bridge, weighing his options."

"Ishwish came to Tidecold-6," Hoop said.

"He wanted to ask your species for help. Yes." Washen waited a moment. "I've heard this story too many times and always the same way. The human begged for aid, and it was given. But there were other players and another request for help was made, and after a few strokes of bad luck, what was simple became terribly complicated. What should have been finished in a few hours ended up filling most of eight days, and that poor world was butchered in the process."

Hoop squeezed tight both of his mouths.

"You must know a different version of the story, or at least a fuller telling. Am I right?"

"I know very little," Hoop said. "When this happened, my shadow hadn't been cast."

The naked captain said nothing, letting her silence work.

"But my mother," Hoop finally said, his voice faltering for a moment. "When I was old enough, she told me another history. Which is exactly the same as your story, except for the differences."

Hoop described the aliens' arrival: A crude, ungainly starship suddenly plunging from deep space, fusion engines struggling to kill its terrific momentum. Ishwish was the first human voice they ever heard, and the first human face they had ever seen for themselves; and in a pose of perfect submission, he begged the ruling clans for help. They gave permission for him to move into orbit, but the machine struggled with even that simple task. Once a sun-blasted comet, the ship was a fancy set of engines rooted in black tar and porous stone, the entire contraption bolstered with hyperfiber girders and incalculable amounts of luck. Ten thousand humans, plus supplies and an army of sleeping machines, had set out to make a new world habitable. But the colonists were plainly inexperienced at terraforming. Dressing a newborn world in a breathable atmosphere and a drinkable ocean would require more bodies than they had, as well as a heroic patience. Yet most alarming to the Clans was that their crude starship had been damaged, and not by natural means.

"Internal explosions," Washen said.

"Some flavor of fighting. Yes." The creature stared at a distant point, watching events he could only imagine. "We made scans, and the scans were followed by probes. Probes gave way to diplomats. A civil struggle had broken out among the colonists, we learned. Two governments had coalesced around opposing ideals, each occupying a different portion of the damaged vessel."

Washen nodded, saying nothing.

"Our world was relatively isolated," Hoop continued. "None of us had any direct experience with humans. To us, your species were abstractions. Well-drawn abstractions, since we had collected substantial files about your history and nature. But until your arrival, no one imagined that we would become neighbors, much less that you would slink up to our front door, pleading for aid."

She nodded. "To whom did the captain speak?"

"It was my father." Hoop extended a giant hand, palm up—a sign of charity for both species. "He was an Elder in my clan's council. Others urged distrust. But my mother told me, more than once, that my father felt it would be wise to make friends with humans. You were a bold young and foolish species, investing too much energy to place a few bodies on an ugly little planet that didn't look at all promising to us. But he believed that he liked you. In Ishwish, he found qualities that struck him as…the concept does not translate well…but in his eyes, the human captain was sympathetic and pathetic, honorable and powerfully intriguing…"

Washen quoted a Clan truism, declaring, "'Kindness is power; charity proves strength.'"

"Strength." Hoop repeated the word several times, in both languages, while the hand closed, a mailed fist turning slowly in the air between them. "My father led the delegation that met directly with Ishwish. Captain and crew as well as the loyal colonists were gathered around the engines, while rebel colonists controlled the bow and most major habitats. The fighting was constant, but sloppy. So the ship was still intact. Half of the humans were dead, but only temporarily. Their burnt, eviscerated corpses were mummified and kept locked away, mostly held as prisoners, waiting for one winner to be declared and for the ship's hospital to be reactivated."

Washen imagined herself sitting on a captain's chair. "The situation was treacherous."

"Chaotic and frightful, and to us, difficult to comprehend. How can two sides fight for decades with no winner standing over the loser?" The black eyes focused on her face. "Yet when he breathed the same air, my father was deeply impressed with the Ishwish creature. Returning home, he told my mother that he had felt as if the human had been his friend for ten thousand years. The creature offered perfect words, often in our language. How he spoke was flawless and soothing. And the stance of his little body…well, his performance was superior to yours today, my monkey dear…that great man clinging to the filthy black floor, licking at tar dusts and human blood, confessing to his guest that he was helpless to save his wicked, doomed ship."

"The captain had experience with your species," she said.

"Ishwish told us about those old human wars, yes. He named battles and offered dates that we found waiting in our files, and in all the respectable ways, he proved that he trusted us and that we could trust him. With our sweet help, he would regain control over the starship. And as final proof, Ishwish surrendered his name and wealth to my father, begging for our mighty clan to give him a few hands…just enough hands so that he could gain the momentum, defeating his enemies and winning this disgusting shambles of a war."

Washen struggled to picture the man she knew—the arrogant Submaster—reduced to such a state. "It would seem like a small request."

"Miniscule, yes," Hoop agreed. "A hundred hands with fifty fighters attached. But unknown to my father, a delegation of the rebellious colonists had made contact with our neighbor clan. A different tribe of monkeys begged in the same perfect fashion, requesting a few hands of their own."

Nothing was new. Washen had always understood the essential history of the disaster. But now she saw possibilities that she hadn't noticed before…subtle undercurrents that even a novice captain should have spotted, if only while listening to the gossipy chatter of her peers…

The towering figure continued speaking. "One day, long after those days, my mother grabbed hold of me and crushed me against her body, whispering that this was the moment when we should have realized what was true. Your Ishwish had experience with us, yes. But he seemed to be the only human with that distinction. We should have asked ourselves how the rebel leaders were able to speak and act with the same perfection, winning cooperation as well as a pledge of loyalty from our neighbors."

Washen took a breath, holding it deep in her chest.

Hoop made fists, saying, "Even in our ignorance, the situation was ours to control. We should have been able to stop our fighting after those first moments. You see, both clans sent the requested volunteers, and through what seemed like miserable luck, each attacked the other in the same awful instant. Plasma weapons were used, which meant that every soldier was annihilated. Which is where we should have stepped back then, waiting for the blood to dry." The mailed fists opened and dropped, fingers limp. "But the clans had made pledges, and both sides wished to earn respect from these newcomers. That's why larger blows were inflicted, in quick succession. Suddenly the space above our world was bright with fighting." The eating mouth pushed itself into a single hard point. "And then we came close to stopping again. After five days of mounting casualties, a pause erupted. A necessary rest began. And with an official truce in place, bids of peace were offered, and in another moment or another day, those bids would have been accepted."

Washen stared his slack, empty hands.

"Three tritium bombs," Hoop said. Then he paused, gathering himself before completing his story. "In the quiet of a truce, three sophisticated weapons in the five-hundred megaton range were delivered to three cities. In a single cowardly stroke, our clan lost one tenth of its population and much of its wealth. But even worse, the truce had been cheated, which was never done. One grand abomination demanded a suitable revenge, which is why my ancestors used three equally powerful weapons. And that should have been the end, if our enemies had been sensible. But they insisted on spreading lies. Against all evidence, they claimed that those first three weapons had not come from any stockpile or bad dream of theirs."

Washen said, "I see," even when nothing quite made sense.

"The tritium bombs simply had to belong to the enemy clan," Hoop reported. "My father digested every report, every shred of intelligence, and doubt was impossible. According to security eyes, the weapons were ceremonial Death-bringers, authentic to their isotope yields and the markings on their diamond jackets. They were launched from an enemy base in high orbit, and they were shielded by our usual methods, and lying about their culpability just made the horror worse. That was why another enemy city had to be destroyed; it was a punishment for the lie. Then the other clan annihilated three more of our cities, plus the honored site where our species first landed on our sweet world."

The giant face dipped, eyes losing all focus. "For three days, we ceased to be the Clan of Many Clans. We became what you call us: The harum-scarum. We were madmen filled with blind rage, wild actions devoid of thought and reason. Only when most of us were dead did we dare make peace, and then only on the condition that both of our miserable clans abandon our home, poisoned as it was by radiations, and worse, sickened by our grand stupidity."

Washen was crying. With a soft, slow voice, she asked, "Did your father die in the war?"

"No." Hoop's spines straightened, in reflex. "He survived and returned to his good friend, Ishwish, and did what he believed was best. He begged for help from the human animal. He bowed before the captain and colonists from both tribes, and licked the comet's tar until the help was given. In a gesture of extraordinary compassion, we were offered the same little world to which they had been traveling. 'It isn't much,' Ishwish admitted, 'but as a place for fresh beginnings, it might serve you well.'"

Washen blinked. "Your father met with every colonist?"

The alien showed a forest of little teeth inside his eating mouth. "Yes. While we were slaughtering one another, the humans had suddenly made their own peace."

Washen breathed quickly, the air stale and hot.

"Just enough ships for our journey were available," he continued. "My parents left for the new world, while the other clan retreated deeper into the galaxy, if only to place distance between the two of us. Twelve light-years had to be covered, but the voyage was productive. Even decimated by the war, there were more of us than there had been humans, and we had enough experience to make any new world habitable, if not comfortable. So my clan made its plans and refined them until we felt ready. And throughout the journey, messages arrived from our good allies. The human colonists were quickly cleaning up poisons and repairing the ecosystems. In the proper ways, they thanked us again for our charity, they promised to make our old home prosper, honoring our memories, and buried in their words was news that their mission's captain, dear Ishwish, had been awarded a tenth of the colony's future value—in thanks for his guidance and considerable bravery."

The Submaster was famously wealthy. But Tidecold-6 was an exceptionally rich world today—a favored destination for emigrants and every species of money—and ten percent of that single planet would make any man into a king.

Hoop had fallen silent.

Washen remembered the platform of ground waiting empty in the hallway, needing to be guarded. "Your father," she said. "What's the rest of his story?"

Quietly, the alien confessed, "He suffered terribly. A moment of clarity took him."

"What do you mean?"

"He woke one morning, as our new sun was growing bright…he woke and felt strong enough finally to ask questions that he hadn't dared pose until then. He turned to my mother and wondered aloud, 'But what if my very good friend, dear Ishwish…what if he was not what he seemed to be…?'"

Washen bit her bottom lip.

"Then as his strength drained, he asked, 'What if everything was other than it seemed to be…the civil war, the humans in despair, the three weapons appearing above our heads…?'"

Tasting blood, Washen said, "Maybe."

"Maybe," Hoop agreed.

"A captain could have played the colonists against each other. Fomented war, but kept it under control. And maybe he coached a few of the rebels, perhaps without even telling them his entire plan." She closed her eyes, envisioning what would have been both possible and necessary. "He could have bought those tritium bombs from somewhere else, using his military connections. He brought them all that way and prepositioned them in a higher orbit, ready to accelerate the hostilities." Her voice sputtered and then came back again. "But that would mean the beast had everything planned out, starting centuries before."

"This was what my father realized," said Hoop. "And that is why a great despair claimed his sorrowful mind. And about that good honorable man, I wish to say no more."

His father was dead, probably a suicide. No other conclusion to life was as dishonorable, not for a creature such as that, which was why there was no fatherly statue standing guard over his son's home.

Washen took them past that awful moment. "Help me now," she said. "When you purchased your home, this room and that hallway, did you know exactly who had lived here before?"

The black eyes brightened. "I knew about the Higgers," he said. "For years, I cleaned their silicone out of the cracks and pores."

"What about the past human owners?"

"I suspected nothing. I had no idea." He paused for a moment. "Until an acquaintance mentioned Ishwish to me, I was ignorant."

"An acquaintance?"

"A Clan woman. She mentioned the name and asked if I knew who he was. Had I ever seen him with my eyes? And after I explained what the man might be, she asked how it felt. What did it do to my soul to know that this awful human once shit in these rooms of mine?"

Washen nodded, considering. "And when was this conversation?"

"It was a year ago."

"Just one year ago?"

"Plus a few days," Hoop reported, which was the same as yesterday, when your life stretched for millennia.

"That is one spectacular coincidence," Washen mentioned. "Of all possible passengers, you end up living in the Submaster's old home."

Hoop rolled his face—the Clan equivalent of a nod. "I have asked these question many times. What are the probabilities? In a vessel of this size, with all these possible addresses to claim for myself…why must this be the home that I find for myself…?"

"The odds are long," she allowed.

"Which is why you and I are imagining along the same lines," he replied with quiet amazement. "What agent or force or malicious spirit is responsible for this conundrum…?"

6

A bowl of excessively sweet tea cooled on the oak tabletop. Washen stood close enough to smell alien spices. When the temperature dropped to a critical point, the Submaster took a pinch of maltose from a second bowl, sprinkling grains one at a time into the vaporous brew. There was no reaction, and then everything happened swiftly, with surprising drama. Like a sudden snow, supersaturated sugars fell out of solution, and what had been a fragrant brew turned into thick white syrup that could be spooned into dishes and served as a rare dessert.

The Submaster helped herself. Then glancing at Washen, she said, "You are early today. And Ishwish has been delayed. Some critical matter has ambushed his attentions, it seems."

"Yes, madam."

"If you would like, sit. Join me."

"I'd prefer to stand, madam." Washen was dressed again, in a full uniform. "But thank you for the invitation, madam."

"As you wish." Miocene was an elegant creature, tall and lovely, cold and effortlessly forbidding. But she had a rich dark voice, and when it was useful, a surprisingly engaging smile. After the first mouthful of dessert, she showed her smile. Then after a thoughtful silence, she said, "Something rolls in your mind, my dear."

"I'm thinking about Ishwish, madam."

"Yes?"

"And Tidecold-6."

The Submaster said nothing. But her face and manner appeared ready for the subject.

"Was my superior responsible for that tragedy?"

Miocene shrugged. "I'm not free to give details. But there were questions, and official inquiries, and unofficial meetings. Investigations were carried out by assorted agencies, among our people and the harum-scarums too." She pursed her lips for a moment, perhaps using a nexus to access old files. Or she was already familiar with the topic, and this was just a wonderful moment to savor her perfect dessert.

Washen waited at attention.

"The original colonists were interviewed, and each crewmember was interrogated. Ishwish himself underwent years of suspicion. But no credible account or chain of evidence has shown that there was any plan in place. Nobody wanted to cheat or in any way harm the harum-scarums, and the humans involved were left officially and forever clean."

With a nod, Washen said, "Good."

Miocene bit her lip. "He is a very careful man," she said.

"And he is shrewd," Washen said.

Miocene laughed softly. "You admire our colleague, as you should. The man has shown a small interest in your career, and it is important to appreciate the qualities of your superior."

"Yes, madam."

Miocene treated herself to a second bite of syrup and tea.

"Do you like Ishwish, madam?"

The Submaster tipped her head for a moment, swallowing. Then with a knife-like voice, she said, "I hope you can imagine what I think of the man."

Washen waited.

"Tell me my mind," Miocene prompted.

Washen took a quick deep breath. "Ambition is a wonderful trait. And the man is calculating and subtle, when he wishes. And those are excellent qualities to find in any captain."

"Go on."

"Ishwish carries authority and great responsibilities, but those blessings stem directly from decisions made thousands of years ago. Tidecold-6 made him exceptionally wealthy. That wealth brought him to the Great Ship, and being a captain was secondary. But once here, his ambition helped elevate him to the rank of Submaster." Washen paused. "Is that a fair accounting of his recent life, madam?"

"Don't dismiss his wealth," Miocene said. "Remember how difficult it was for us to reach the Ship first…how tenuous our hold was, and still is, on this ancient machine. With one command, Ishwish was able to mobilize an entire world, sending us more engineers and lines of credit to help us repair these old pumps and environmental systems. And with good words from him, he coaxed thousands of equally wealthy human passengers to come here—paying bodies who migrated from dozens of safe thriving worlds."

"He bought his rank," Washen said with distaste.

"I prefer to think in different terms."

"Do you accept his status, madam?"

"In the same spirit I accept each passing day."

"But do you think about Tidecold-6? Suspecting what you suspect, does it every leave your thoughts?"

"Will it escape your mind, Washen?"

"But I am not a Submaster."

"And you are modest in the worst ways."

"Perhaps." Washen offered a brief nod. "I've been given orders and intend to carry them out to the best of my ability."

"As is right."

"The investment group," said Washen.

Surprise showed in Miocene's narrow face. "To which group do you refer?"

"Inquiries," Washen said. "By several routes, I've made inquiries, and I think only one person stands behind the corporate mask. An unidentified human owns properties in an assortment of districts. And she once held title to a comfortable little apartment that now, purely by chance, belongs to an angry fellow named Hoop-of-Benzene."

The smile was respectful, perhaps even impressed. "Please, dear. Go on."

"When Hoop was searching for a home, he found help from an agent with ties to that investment group. The terms of the sale were very lucrative for the buyer. Someone made certain that this one passenger was placed inside that particular apartment, and more than two thousand years later, here we are."

"A captain did all this?"

"I know what seems to be, even if I can't prove anything."

The dessert was cooling, losing its delicate, precious flavors. Yet the Submaster seemed unconcerned, setting her spoon aside, focusing on the novice captain standing beside her.

"Hoop recently learned who once lived inside his home," said Washen. "You have no connections with the harum-scarum who delivered that news. As far as I can see, you are blameless. If there is any blame to be given, that is."

"That is so good to hear."

"Hoop doesn't want that man walking inside his house."

"I would imagine not."

"He intends to fight the invasion with every tool at his disposal."

"Which leads him where?" Miocene showed a big grim smile. "To his ruin, I would think. That's the only possible destination for the poor fellow."

Washen sighed. "But this decision to give Ishwish an award, to do it now and hold the ceremony in that location…I find it easy to believe you were the one who set this slippery business into motion…"

With a chilled glance, Miocene asked, "Is there anything else?"

"I don't understand."

"Define your ignorance."

Washen bent at the waist, explaining, "Until yesterday, Ishwish didn't realize who Hoop was or that he had roots in Tidecold-6. Until I delivered the refusal, Ishwish assumed that the harum-scarum would love the idea of a famous captain strutting about inside his rooms. But if the Submaster suspects trouble, then he will do whatever is possible to make this problem vanish."

"Whatever is possible," Miocene agreed with a tiny wink. "At this moment, my colleague is meeting with a team of advisors and confidantes. Yes, my dear, he has given up on you and your patient ways. New plans and brutal consequences are being considered. And by the end of this day, his problem will be solved."

"What plans?"

"I wouldn't know," Miocene replied. "But several minutes ago, our security soldiers have learned that we have a murderer among us—a brutal criminal who happens to be a tall, strong, and very dangerous harum-scarum."

"Not Hoop," Washen muttered.

"This is a matter for our courts, my dear. Not captains."

Washen fought with a scream.

For the moment, Miocene said nothing. Then with a soft pitying voice, she asked, "Why are you here? What did you believe would happen, if you and I happened to speak?"

"What am I supposed to do, madam?"

Miocene shrugged.

"Thousands of years ago, you put Hoop inside Ishwish's home. In some fashion or another, you are responsible for this situation. And now I've become your agent...although I don't see what it is you hope to gain..."

"Are you a captain, or aren't you?"

Washen threw back her shoulders. "Yes. I am."

"This ship of ours is still almost entirely empty," Miocene said. "But before the end of our voyage, we will be walking these hallways with a hundred thousand other species, and nothing will matter more than having a cadre of good captains...wise captains...human leaders who deserve respect from this multitude of odd entities..."

"Yes, madam."

"If you want to become one of the Great Ship's important officers," said Miocene, "you must be able to navigate your way to the best destination available. Without the help of anyone else, I might add. And even if this means, in one fashion or another, doing something that happens to be right."

7

Once more Washen returned to the diamond door. Hoop was surprised but gratified to see the human, and then she told him what she wanted. She told him what she wanted, offering no explanations why. Instinct took hold. Feet squared on the floor, shoulders tilting forward as the eating mouth pulled into a tight pucker. And once again, the young captain made her very simple demand, adding, "If you will not give me this, then I will fight you."

"No," Hoop replied. "I refuse your challenge."

There was little time remaining. With one nexus, Washen tracked an order-of-arrest as it moved past amiable judges, while another nexus watched a team of security officers gathered in a nearby bunker, preparing for the moment when every signature was in place.

She said, "You can't refuse.

"But I have," he protested.

Then the mirrored uniform fell away, and Washen took the proper stance for combat. "I demand this," she said, citing codes more ancient than her species.

Hoop nearly turned away from the door.

Suddenly harum-scarums appeared in the wide hallway. A few were neighbors, but most of the towering creatures were strangers from the far ends of the Ship. There were dozens of them, more arriving by the moment, and walking at the lead were a few wearing distinctive gold emblems on scales and spikes. The emblems marked them as belonging to the clan that had once fought Hoop's clan, both standing on a world that neither would keep.

Hoop looked at the bystanders and then glared down at tiny Washen. "You brought them," he said.

She said, "In their presence, I challenge you."

"And I will kill you."

"Break my bones and smash my heart," she said, "and I will heal again and stand here again. And I will launch a second challenge."

The diamond door opened up.

Out stepped the giant figure, peeling off his clothing while half-heartedly taking the defender's pose. "What is happening?" he asked.

"You have lost," she whispered.

"No."

She lifted a fist.

Again, he said, "No."

"But there are different ways to lose," she said.

Hoop said nothing.

On this public ground, Washen announced, "The challenge is accepted, and now I strike."

Her opponent smoothly deflected the first blow.

Then she drove left fist into his chest, and a human finger broke.

Twenty more blows were absorbed. Washen sliced her arms open against the spines, and every finger was shattered, and Hoop stood like a statue defending honored soil. But she kept hitting him, and beneath her increasingly miserable breath, she told the giant again that he was beaten and it didn't matter how and the only rational course at this point was to trust a friend to find the best route to make his retreat.

The forty-third blow astonished everyone.

The harum-scarum remained invulnerable. Covered with his opponent's blood, he had to do nothing and Washen would soon bleed dry and collapse. But there was frustration in Hoop's posture, and sorrow, and a measure of boredom too. Those were all fine reasons to end this chore. One fist tightened, and maybe he hesitated too long. But really, who would guess that the human had any strength to spend? Hoop hesitated and then swung at the naked captain, and Washen spun and wrapped one arm around her enemy's arm, clinging to him as she swung her entire body, throwing a bare foot into the armored neck.

The target was tiny. The harum-scarums decided that only an expert in alien physiology would recognize the weak point in an otherwise invulnerable throat, and of course there was luck involved. But humans did enjoy strong legs and a famous rage. Washen broke toes with the impact, but Hoop's head snapped back. He did not fall, not immediately. Anything looked ready to happen for a moment or two. Then the head dropped and pulled the rest of that great body to the floor, into the open doorway, and the bloodied victor took her rightful place on his chest, standing only on her good foot.

* * *

Security forces arrived to discover that a minor captain now owned the apartment and a wanted criminal had vanished. Neither the alien witnesses nor the captain knew where to find the harum-scarum, which was frustrating; and even worse, despite the severity of these charges, the arrest forms were suddenly turning into dream, evaporating despite the valiant efforts of their owners tried to hold tight to them.

8

"Brilliant," Ishwish said, walking in front of his new protégé. "That was a brave, bold, marvelous job. A little too noisy, I think. But still, you managed to find a solution to this difficult problem."

"There are no difficult problems," Washen said. "Not with a simple solution in hand."

The Submaster laughed amiably.

Washen's wounds had healed. But she still felt sick, and she wasn't sure what she believed, and then she decided that she was certain, yes, and that was why her entire body ached.

The procession had almost reached her new home. The Master Captain and Miocene were directly behind her, speaking about matters that seemed tiny to them and huge to a little captain like her. There were young captains like Washen, and others of higher rank, and every Submaster was there too. She glanced at the faces. She looked at her own face mirrored in Ishwish's back. Then she took the lead, hurrying to the diamond door, her presence causing it to open.

"Still the old furnishings, I see," said Ishwish.

The wooden harum-scarums guarding their original ground, with one new shape standing at the back of the hall, watching events.

"Oh, well. You've been too busy to see to every detail," he said with uncommon charity. Then he turned to face the other captains, golden eyes shining with a boyish joy. "Welcome," he said. "Welcome all. I'm so glad you could be here. And it is such a pleasure, coming back to this wonderful district that I remember so well."

"My home," Washen whispered.

"You are all welcome here," Ishwish declared. Then he turned to his protégé. The happiest creature in existence, he said, "This will be your first celebration in your lovely new home."

Washen nodded, and on quick legs, she stepped up to the door.

To the very important gathering, she said, "Come inside, my welcome guests." Then in the next moment, she turned back to Ishwish, whispering a few words that took the blood from his face and nearly knocked him to the ground.

"Except you, sir," she said. "In my home, you will never be."

Bridge Two

Starships are always exhausted on arrival, their fuel spent, every system crying out for repairs. And a good portion of the ships are damaged during the voyage, some mangled to the point where one more insult will collapse them to dust and bone. This is because the slowest vessel has to move fast enough to match velocities with the Great Ship, and the Great Ship plunges forward at one-third light speed. This is because the emptiest space is not empty. A hundred thousand kilometers of vacuum must be crossed every second. Place one cold stone on that path, or a lump of ice or someone's misplaced tooth, and the collision will transform that fleck of nothing into a fierce plasmatic bomb. Hyperfiber is formidable. Every starship wears at least a slathering of hyperfiber as armor. But quality varies and there are strict limits to its depth and mass, and even the premier grades will evaporate under a billion degree torch. Frailty is a fundamental truth of star travel. Passengers and crew can be ageless, but every sane traveler recognizes that one anonymous chunk of stone can strike without warning, erasing the Forever.

The typical starship is spun from high technologies that predate most of the species presently using them. But these vessels struggle to move significantly faster than the Great Ship, which is why the captains fire up the engines on occasion, tweaking their velocity just enough that decades later the Ship will fall under the spell of a muscular, compliant gravity well. Approached at the proper angle, at the perfect distance, a smoldering white dwarf star will throw the giant vessel into a fresh, profitable vector. Like a serpent happily wandering in tall grass, the Great Ship weaves and wobbles its way through the best portions of the galaxy, and if a sluggish transport is clever, following an exceptionally straight line, it will catch its goal before too many centuries pass.

But certain passengers demand a superior machine. Great wealth can buy long, arrow-shaped wonders called streakships. Streakships are tipped with the best hyperfiber and powered by supercharged engines, using fusion fire and antimatter spiking and strangelet tricks and hyperfiber endowments to shove against the possible, driving them across dangerous skies at better than two-thirds light speed.

Streakships and their slow cousins don't arrive at the Ship every day. But transports are always approaching, hundreds of them scattered across the light years and all begging for landing instructions—a steady rain of machines and old souls that is coming faster as the galaxy begins to appreciate the marvel that is snaking its way through the civilized realms.

The Great Ship is like nothing else.

Reliable and comfortable, luxurious and deliciously strange, it is a supremely safe mode of travel: Gravel and snowballs are nothing to its ocean-deep armor. Mountains and comets are trivial hazards. One fat asteroid could slam down on the Ship's bow, but the passengers would have no reason for fear. Maybe their luxurious homes would shake for a moment. Maybe they would awaken from some luscious dream. But afterwards the immortal travelers would journey to the hull—if permitted—standing on the lip of a broad crater that soon would be filled and patched, and gone.

Even little ships will be greeted with pageantry. Powerful aliens deserve spectacle and elaborate diplomatic receptions. Each new species is met by captains who have worked hard to understand them. This is critical. The average captain makes plans and more plans, making ready for the most unlikely guests. Parades and parties and elaborate banquets will stretch on for days and months, unless the newcomers prefer to be ignored, or they appreciate insults, or they cannot find any comfort unless one exceptional captain climbs inside a cavernous mouth, the ceremony demanding that she will be swallowed up whole and then ceremonially vomited back out again.

And sometimes, too many times, an approaching ship vanishes.

Disasters don't happen every day. A full year can pass between tragedies. But a big space liner might fail to report its progress and nothing more is heard, or an emergency beacon will flicker to life and then fall silent again, marking the death of a streakship.

There are ceremonies for every arriving ship and ceremonies to honor the dead as well.

Every approaching ship is logged on its first day, its passengers and crewmembers named and known. And there are a few captains who do little with their days but plan for every ship's death. Just in case. They compose speeches meant to honor lost souls, honoring all as friends, and they wrap their words around rituals designed to satisfy the species involved. Then all the surviving ships are warned about the loss and its location. Debris fields have formed, and they will keep charging ahead at some fraction of light-speed, spreading out and slashing at everything in their way. And the captains always share elaborate maps showing where the danger is greatest, and they always wish their future passengers safe travel, but even when odds are poor, they never tell anyone, "Change your course. Please, steer clear of us and save yourselves, please."

Mere

1

She should have been born with a fuller, richer name—a loving name bestowed by helplessly adoring parents—and she should have grown up happy and smug inside their loving grasp. Blessed with her native talents as well as the inherited wealth, all things good would have been inevitable. Life would have brought long years of trusted pleasure punctuated by tame adventures and the occasional romance, and as often happens in these cases, the daughter would have eventually fallen short of her family's lofty ambitions. But that wouldn't have prevented her from becoming a delightfully ordinary soul, raising her own little family or perhaps a series of families; and as the aeons mounted, that happy creature would have achieved the heavenly state that comes to the typical immortal: Entire centuries of existence would quietly escape her grasp, her mind reaching its natural limits, her snug and ordinary and generally untested existence shared with faces very much like hers and stories as eternal and as bland as her own little self.

But for a knob of black ice, that would have been the child's destiny. Her fate. She should have become someone else or she never would have been in the first place. But if you are one of the rare souls who both understand and believe as the Tila understand and believe, then you have no choice but accept the premise that your existence is a single thread, insubstantial to the brink of being unreal, and every thread is woven together by a universe of shadow and possibility, and buried among all those infinitely forgettable women is a strange and precious rope of pain and gold known as Mere.

* * *

Mere's parents were the wealthiest citizens on a distant colony world. Their piece of the universe wasn't as developed as some, and the available streakships were small and relatively short-ranged. But the Great Ship and its long voyage around the galaxy were too much of a temptation. How could they not take part in history? Husband and wife purchased the five best ships, then chopped them apart and cobbled together the finest pieces. In the end, there was no more powerful human-built vessel anywhere. The new streakship had efficient engines and redundant life-support systems, a talent for self-repair and just enough cabin space to house two people along with an entourage of twenty-three giddy friends. A slab of high-grade hyperfiber rode ahead of the bow and a few lasers clung to the armor, primed to attack every hazard. But the Great Ship was nearly out of range by then. Velocity was the critical need, and hard decisions had to be made. Studying projections of risk laid over time, the couple massaged the numbers until the numbers told a comforting story, and then they made themselves laugh, saying, "We'll just have to drag a little sweet luck along with us, and what is the mass of luck? Nothing, that's all."

Accelerating to a fat fraction of light-speed, they swung close to a quiescent black hole, and the AI pilot found the perfect course that would intercept the Great Ship in another nine hundred years, ship-time. Enough fuel was in reserve to kill half of their terrific momentum, allowing them to match velocities with their target and then dock. There was little margin for maneuvering, but for the next six hundred years, maneuvering didn't matter. The conscientious AI continually updated its charts, and then one morning, using a voice that was always sober and small, it announced they would soon pass through the outskirts of a diffuse and poorly charted Oort cloud.

By then, every woman and two of the men were pregnant. It was a colonist's tradition: Life begun as a promise to the future while every blastula was kept in arrested development, waiting more spacious quarters onboard the Great Ship. With everything at risk, their ship dove into the cloud. There was a series of little impacts and endurable damage. The armor was left pocked but structurally intact. Then they emerged from the cloud, slicing through a sharper vacuum, and the ship began repairing holes and refurbishing its exhausted lasers.

No warning was given. In the middle of spoken sentences, in the midst of pleasant little dreams, life ended with a flash of plasma and an abrupt, endless silence.

A knob of black cometary ice slipped through a temporary blind spot in the early-warning system, and at two-thirds the speed of light, it plowed through the armor and into the unprotected body of the ship.

Modern humans have tenacious, enduring bodies. But certain kinds of mayhem always prove fatal.

Every passenger was shattered and boiled and dead.

Only the ship survived, and only in the most limited sense. The AI was barely able to recover its identity and a few hints about its ultimate purpose. With insufficient resources, it managed to identify a single piece of still-viable tissue. A crude cabin was hurriedly fashioned out of hyperfiber shards and diamond panes, sealing the tiny volume and filling it with an atmosphere that could be breathed. Then the battered remains of the last autodoc realized that what was saved was the scorched chest and belly and upper left leg of a once wealthy woman. Everything else was stripped away, including her head and proud mind. The only complete nervous system was inside the corpse's uterus: A glistening bag of totipotent cells and salty water little bigger than a tear.

Unburdened by clear instructions, the AI did its imperfect best. It retrofitted the tiny cabin before coaxing the blastula to grow. What remained of the mother was nursed back into a state of mindless good health—in part to give the unborn child a functioning womb, but also because if the child survived, the living corpse would provide a storehouse of edible organics. As for the rest of the ship: Every communication system was shattered or stripped away, leaving the ship without any voice that could beg for help and no ears to hear its pleas left unanswered. Engines and fuel tanks had survived, but every control system was trash. There was no way to change course much less steer towards any safe port. Repairs could be made, but slowly, and since protecting the blastula was the central, the laser array and battered armor had to be rebuilt before any over system. And what would happen next? Using its tattered, very narrow intellect, the AI imagined an arrow-straight trajectory, leaving the local arm of stars and civilizations, passing closer to the galaxy's core before climbing into the next great arm—a bright wilderness where many thousands of years from now, according to a very tentative flight plan, the Great Ship was scheduled to pass.

Mere was born inside a warm, nourishing night. Her body came blessed with a multitude of genetic materials—old-style DNA, plus data reservoirs considerably more enduring and adaptable. Faint blue-shifted starlight was the only illumination. Her only companions were the heart-sized autodoc, her cold diamond walls, and the filthy food and several tiny waste ports. Growth was achingly slow, the ship recycling just enough matter to keep her uncomfortably alive. On occasion, it tried to speak to the child, moving the autodoc in a suggestive fashion or venting stale air to mimic a human voice. But the girl gave no sign of noticing, and other jobs were more important. Critical systems had been destroyed, and to keep both the ship and its holy cargo alive, the remaining systems were reconfigured every few moments. Relentless work and constant inspiration maintained an extraordinarily marginal existence. In one sense, the passenger was wrapped inside a vastness of pure nonexistence. She should never have been born. If a single fleck of shrapnel had followed a modestly different trajectory, she would have died. That she survived any given day was a minor miracle. The battered ship was far more vulnerable to impacts than ever, and when the little blows didn't kill the passenger, they were causing new damage, steadily eroding a deep poverty of bad, pathetic choices.

Happiness was quite impossible.

The girl's life lay cloaked in ethical ugliness. Trapped inside a suffocating blackness, she saw nothing but the slowly changing stars, and there was nothing to hear but the whine of air and her own miserable wailing. Only a monster or some pathological optimist would allow any organism to endure such relentless suffering. Perhaps both qualities played into the AI's nature. But it was motivated mostly by helpless—an injured machine controlled by a knot of simple, compelling instructions, no choice left but to do everything, by whatever means, to carry out its sole purpose.

Mere was born alone, and she lived that way for a very long while.

Ten thousand and eleven years can feel like forever—even if you are a tough, enduring little immortal.

2

Twin suns kissed as they danced around their mutual center of gravity.

Theirs was an unusual astronomical relationship, but not entirely rare. Many stars were born close together, and as their orbits decayed, their atmospheres began to touch—a precursor to another, more intimate embrace.

Four planets removed from the suns was a living world—yellow-green land and brown land and an ocean of soft blue partly shrouded in clouds. After centuries of relentless preparation, the AI could imagine no better option. Slide past the twins suns, and it would survive. But its lone passenger—a tiny unresponsive and mostly silent wisp of tissue and bone—would soon perish. The ad hoc recycling system was bleeding organics and air. Any moment, some crumb of ice might shatter a critical diamond pane or an irreplaceable wisp of machinery would fail. The best choice was to finish the voyage here, by whatever means, and perhaps enough luck was being dragged along to finally save the final passenger.

Blasted by ice and dust, the ship had eroded away quite a lot, and as a consequence, it was significantly less massive. With ad hoc controls, the AI managed to turn and fire the old engines, exhausting its fuel and draining away most of its velocity. But to kill the rest of the nagging momentum required a second brake. The pilot had wrestled with that problem for the last thousand years. What it had achieved unwrapped itself now: A portion of the hyperfiber armor laboriously rewoven, creating a low-mass and almost perfect mirror that was larger than most worlds, pulled taut by the light of two stars.

One day later, the light-sail was set loose and the attached cabin was jettisoned.

Luck as much as calculation provided the near-perfect trajectory. The passenger and her little home dove through the upper atmosphere—a glancing aerobraking blow that slowed her further—and then she swung out and swung back again, dropping onto the world's largest continent.

Moments before plunging past the twin suns, the AI assured itself that it had done its duty to the best of its ability. Looking back along a life well-lived, it nourished a cool, measured pride. And then for just a moment, it wondered what would happen to the tiny woman now: A tiny soul ten thousand years old, yet helplessly newborn. A human creature without name or history, lacking tools or the simplest training, trapped many thousands of light-years from every good human home.

* * *

The big male gypsum wing circled the burning forest, hunting for wounded meat. The still-warm wreck of the cabin lay where the wildfire began. Diamond panes glittered, drawing the eyes. The gypsum wing dropped and landed, one clawed foot clinging to the shattered hull until the residual heat was too much to bear, and then the other foot would take over the duty. That was why the great creature rocked slowly as he perched above the body. With deep black eyes, he studied burnt flesh and the oddly shaped limbs, some curious element inside him wondering what kind of creature this might be. Surely not like any he had ever seen, or imagined. It took courage to move closer, and as soon as he found the courage—as he set himself in a position to eat—the corpse jerked and made an abrupt sound, wet and sloppy.

His legs gave a start.

And the corpse jerked again, harder this time, the blackened skin splitting lengthwise, the fresh gash exposing what looked like a shockingly bright and smooth strip of newborn skin.

The gypsum wing returned to his perch and waited.

By nightfall, the corpse had been replaced with a thin and decidedly fragile body. The strange narrow face was drawn around big and sad and exceptionally empty eyes. There were no claws evident, no long teeth, and the gypsum wing was pleased. As soon as the creature was well enough to sit up, he flapped his wings once and leaped, landing on the bare head, grabbing hold and flapping again to spin his body, deftly shattering the slender neck. Then he dropped to the ground and jabbed at the big eyes, expecting a delicacy as a reward for his patience, but instead tasting something rancid—wet tissue laced with odd proteins and pseudoproteins, creating a toxic mouthful.

He spit up the poison and flew off.

Emergency genes continued working with the injured body, making inventories of the available tissues while organizing a hundred separate repairs. When she had eyes again, it was night. When she opened her eyes, she was on her back, gazing up at a wilderness of stars—a familiar sight, yet not. The lingering haze of smoke softened the starlight. Ten millennia of slow, placid change left her unsuited for this sort of novelty. She breathed, smelling smoke. She screamed, a low ugly wail bubbling out of her. Lifting her arms, tiny half-finished hands reached for the eternal walls of her cabin. But there were no walls. And just as strange, some crushing force pulled at her hands and the stick-thin arms, forcing them to collapse on top of her.

She screamed until she was exhausted.

Then for a brief while, she slept.

When she opened her new eyes, an enormous face was staring down at her. She had never seen a face before or even imagined the existence of another, but she had touched her own features countless times, which made her a little less fearful. Bright black eyes and a wide mouth lay in the midst of a huge oval. The mouth opened, revealing a furry gray tongue and a wealth of orange teeth. Once more, she lifted her arms, fighting their titanic weight while trying to touch the staring eyes. Fingers stretched until they were agonizingly close. And then a polished stone club was driven down into her face and her frail neck, and for the third time in less than a day, she was dead.

* * *

She was alive.

Death was sweeter, she sensed. Death existed free of time and pain and every fear. Alive again, her little limbs were too heavy to move, and she was surrounded by a treacherous wealth of sensations. She saw oval faces and the muscled bodies attached to the faces and simple woven furniture, and there were walls of bleached wood fixed against a wall of vertical rock, and through a long open window she saw a patch of sky wrapped around a pair of brilliant suns, each clinging desperately to the other. Winged worms were singing, and the nut groves were singing, and the wind soughed through branches and the open window. With every breath, she nearly choked on the smell of fires burning inside stone stoves and meals cooking and the lingering stink of happy farts. With every twitch, she felt the prickly brush piled beneath her, and the air was constantly moving across her bare flesh, and without pause, the gravity of an entire world pushed down on her laboring chest, trying to crush her sketch-like bones.

The Tila studied her, and more importantly, they studied the glimmering gray aura that surrounded her. The grayness told them as much as the creature herself could. She was small in the universe, and unlikely, but where she existed, she carried the mark of something that was plainly exceptional.

After a while, they began to discuss what they could see, voices soft and quick, whistles mixed with guttural syllables, their speculations making no sense to the tiny and exceptionally ill god.

No matter how weak it appeared, the creature had to be a god. Everyone had seen the mirrored sail filling the night sky, and that sign was followed by her plunge into the forest, igniting a blaze that burned two villages and killed hundreds of Tila. Yet she had survived both the fire and a determined blow from a blessed club, and how could she be anything but divine?

The local truth-seeker was curious and pragmatic. Using a sharp obsidian knife, she sliced off one of the god's big toes, and with the other village leaders watching over her shoulder, she studied the new toe erupting from the fresh stub. Then wielding a hard flint axe and most of her strength, she removed the left leg beneath the knee, and again, with an intoxicating astonishment, she watched the very peculiar blood clot, turning from red into black before the thick scab began to sprout new tissues, and over the next half-day, the crippled god managed to grow a new shin and ankle and foot nearly equal to what lay dead on the ground beside it.

Stealing flesh made the tiny god grow smaller. The truth-seeker made careful measurements. She dissected the severed leg, and then with strong people holding onto the god, she cut into the living right hand and reborn leg, studying the intricate bones and the soggy, quick-healing tissues wrapped around them. Both eyes and simple mathematics described what was happening: The god was reconstituting herself from whatever remained of her body. If they kept carving away at the creature, she would eventually perish, or more likely, shrivel to a state where she was too small to be seen.

Some answers were obvious.

At one time, this entity must have been enormous. Thinking of the vast light-sail, the truth-seeker described a creature as vast as their world and powerful beyond measure. But judging by her horrible fate, she must have angered the other gods. What lay here with the Tila was just a shard of the original deity. Yet perhaps they could make her large again. The truth-seeker saw the possibility, and despite the worries of others ordered the god's severed leg to be fed to her. A raw wet meal was pushed into the minuscule mouth, one bite at a time. And as predicted, every swallow led to a matching enlargement of her entire body—minus the demands of energy and the little inefficiencies of metabolism.

"Now let us feed her our own good food," the truth-seeker demanded. "Let's see if we can stack muscle on this soul."

But there were unsuspected difficulties. The native amino acids were unique to their world. The Tila succeeded only in making the nameless god violently sick. But after a few days, they learned what treats wouldn't cause her to vomit. They used the juices of certain fruits and clean water and small doses of nuts that had been crushed and partly chewed by their own mouths. Then they learned to season the meals with ash from old fires and let her suck on orange bones and a powerful lodestone.

A few weeks later, with much fanfare, the god had her first normal bowel movement. Then the Tila did what was natural for them: They fed the little god her own wastes. A second passage through the intestines could be a good thing for vegetarians. But not for a god, it seemed. The results weren't at all encouraging, and after long meetings and several important dreams, it was decided to set each day's feces in the temple for the public to observe and admire.

As promised, the god began to grow, if rather slowly. Plans were made. One village would never provide enough food to make her the size of a world, but perhaps she could gain the bulk of a respectable hill. Yet that meant food had to be brought from all lands. With this in mind, emissaries were dispatched to neighboring villages and far flung tribes, inviting diplomats and traders to visit. Every important visitor was shown the god. Some were impressed, others simply puzzled. There were questions about how fast the god was growing. With a quiet voice, the truth-seeker admitted that changes were rare. For whatever reason, no matter how much she was fed, this particular god stubbornly refused to become any larger.

Hearing that sad assessment, one foreign dignitary gave the Tilan equivalent of a shrug. And with a voice that couldn't have sounded more condescending, he announced, "This is the merest sort of god."

He said, "Really, she is scarcely worth anyone's trouble."

3

She was named Mere, but it took years for her to recognize that simple word or appreciate any portion of its significance.

Mere was unfathomably old, and she was nothing but a child. Her growth had been impoverished for millennia. Barely half a meter long when dropped from the void, she was twice as tall and able to stand. Yet even this slender, stunted human was bigger than all but the most gigantic Tila, and she enjoyed an alien sturdiness, those formerly twig-like arms thickened considerably, enhanced muscles fixed to hard white bone that almost never broke.

But the mind was in worse weaknesses than the body. Without adequate nutrition, the complicated landscape of wet neurons and dry neurons and neuroglia and bioceramic armor was only half-finished, and even more debilitating were the effects of relentless boredom—a hundred centuries drifting in space, the brain suffocating inside an infinite, solitary blackness.

Just to walk took years of hard practice.

Decades and infinite patience were needed to teach Mere a few words and their basic meanings.

If she weren't immortal, no one would have bothered. She would have been a novelty buried in a holy place, her and the ground soon forgotten. But because of the occasional success, and because the truth-seekers were naturally stubborn, each of them willingly invested their lives in this very slow undertaking.

One day, Mere asked, "What happened to the other one?"

Startled to hear a complete sentence, the truth-seeker's voice sputtered. "Who do you mean, madam?"

Mere squinted, trying to find a name to match with the missing face. But there was no name. Instead, she described the Tilan woman who had purposefully chopped off her big toe and her left leg, and then with others holding Mere still, had cut into her hand and newborn leg. "Where is this woman now?"

"Dead," the little male replied.

Dead things were food. True death meant that the food could never return as life again. Why should that happen to a truth-seeker?

"She grew old," he explained.

"I don't grow old," Mere said.

"And you never shall," was the quick, untroubled reply.

And then on another day, some years later, she asked the truth-seeker, "What is wrong with you?"

"I am dying."

"Good. May I watch?"

"Of course, madam."

What Mere saw was interesting, but then troubling. This dying business seemed too easy and far too simple. Afterwards she insisted on watching the corpse, studying its decay, and on occasion poking the bloated flesh with sharp tools or a curious finger. The newest truth-seeker agreed to these experiments: To the Tila, death was a tiny business involving just one of the infinite shadow realms. But once the remains were liquid and putrid, the truth-seeker suggested that the god please allow the mess to be taken away.

"Dead," Mere kept saying.

"Yes," the new truth-seeker allowed. "This is death."

"And I am a god?"

"The only god I know," he said.

She dwelled on this for another year. Then one morning, as light flooded into the temple, Mere strode forwards, bright human eyes examining the contents of a vast room that was decorated with polished copper mirrors and jeweled gypsum wings, little feet walking on a carpet woven from blessed shadow threads that multiplied as they spread outwards from the Creation. The diamond and hyperfiber ruins of her long-ago home stood in the room's center. Set on a golden pedestal beside them, illuminated by a beam of reflected sunlight, rested the pale and mummified toe that centuries ago had been sliced from her writhing foot.

"Why build this place?" she asked, for the last time.

"To honor you," her truth-seeker replied.

"Why honor me? I don't understand."

"Because you are holy."

Mere had heard that said many times.

"And because we love you very much, madam."

"Oh," said Mere, surprised.

From some deep place came the memory of warm nothingness, unvarying and awful. Then she remembered dying in the crash and dying under the gypsum wing, and after that she felt the wrenching sensation of a flint axe falling on her naked leg. With a grimace, she said, "I was wrong. I didn't understand."

"What didn't you understand, madam?"

"I always thought it was a bad thing, being a miserable god."

* * *

The Tilan brain was laced with delicate structures—crystalline proteins wrapped around tiny quantum wellsprings. Neurons like that, whether natural or synthetic, helped spawn quick thoughts and relentless intuition. But those benefits brought inescapable difficulties. For instance, the Tila possessed a keen sense of vision, but when they looked at any surface, particularly along the edge, they saw a thin gray aura that glimmered and endlessly changed shape. The aura might be meaningless noise precipitated by quantum imprecisions, but the Tila considered it to be quite a lot more—a true glimpse into the deepest, strangest workings of the universe. Their existence was just one narrow example of what was buried inside countless other possibilities. Whenever they looked at a lifelong friend, or a foolish god, or even a random stranger, they saw hints of the shadow realms filled with friends very much like theirs, and gods similar to theirs, and too many strangers to measure in a trillion lifetimes.

Mere had fine human eyes. But compared to her hosts, she felt blind. Truth-seekers constantly studied her aura, employing lessons from many generations, and their calm expert voices reported everything they saw and what it wanted to mean. The closest realms were full of creatures much like her. Some were happier, some taller and others smaller, and there were gods among the shadows who were considerably sadder than her. In that, Mere was part of a multitude, unspectacular by every measure. Of course each soul existed in a multitude of forms. But what made Mere unusual, even precious, was the narrowness of her existence. Every truth-seeker admitted that most of the realms don't know her. "To them, you don't exist at all. Or if you are real, you and the world live apart."

Mere didn't know how to interpret such news. But because it seemed easiest, she believed them, and with no tools but her imagination, she practiced seeing the world and its shadows in the infinite way that the Tila beheld every small thing.

4

What began as a substantial village gradually had grown into a full-bodied city. Just through her presence, Mere helped the community prosper and expand. Visiting diplomats signed trading pacts and traders brought goods from every end of the continent. The curious and the wealthy came to see this living god, and they left behind precious metals, or smelling opportunity, they would settle here. The trees that supplied food were cut down for lumber and homes, and new lands were put under cultivation—great golden forests heavy with nuts and sweet fruits covering the delta beside the warm blue sea. But there were little famines because there were too many mouths, and the City's leaders made the necessary decisions. Upriver were other villages, fiercely independent and powerful in their own right. An army was raised and sent marching, and after a long season the soldiers returned with their spoils. Mere watched the parade of victors. Sitting on a jeweled platform built specifically for her odd frame, she was as enthralled as anyone. The army looked spectacular, its armor polished and blood-blue paint on the victors' faces, and following behind were the prisoners—thousands of vanquished Tila lashed together, ropes secured around their thick necks, each of them bending under the food and cloth and other practical treasures.

The current truth-seeker sat on the adjacent platform—as beautifully jeweled and exactly as high as Mere's. Laughing, she told the god, "In every realm, these slaves are defeated and very sad."

Mere wondered if that were true. Surely there were enemies marching through different shadows, advancing as conquerors instead of lurching forward as helpless property.

"I own twelve to the third of these creatures," the truth-seeker said. "Tomorrow, before dawn, I will set them to building a new temple for our resident god."

Mere said, "Thank you," and tried to smile as a Tila should.

Then one of the leading slaves collapsed, bringing the procession to an ungainly halt. The others stood motionless, untroubled by their companion's dilemma. A pair of guards had to beat the weakling, and when that didn't inspire him, they cut him free and dragged him aside, killing him with their dullest, most painful spears.

Where the Tila saw millions of slaves dying across the endless shadow realms, Mere saw just the one soul perish. Watching the event brought neither pain nor genuine disquiet. What struck her was the odd, unexpected idea that even though she was immune to death, Mere seemed to appreciate what the creature was feeling, and what it feared, and what terrible thoughts passed through his dying mind and the silent blackness waiting on the other side.

* * *

Slaves built the new temple. Yet there was never enough room for all of the worshippers, which was why a fresh army of slaves was soon marshaled, erecting a grander perfection from carved stone and golden sunlight. Several more generations passed, a string of wars were won, and then the final temple was constructed by slaves and volunteers helping stonemasons and other artisans, a long spine of stone covered with a sumptuous, durable edifice made of polished marble inlaid with gems and heroic bones.

In her honor, Mere was given custody over the largest structure in the world—as a home and as a site where she could be celebrated. Because of Mere, all that was good found the City. Millions of citizens believed as much, and it was equally apparent to their resident god. She was a blessing. Her existence meant that her parents, the heavenly gods, approved of the City. From the highest room of her long home, she gazed across a chaotic river bottom jammed with artificial ridges, each ridge adorned with endless apartments and shops and important little offices. Downstream lay an ocean increasingly crossed by little ships, and upstream was a genuine empire woven together by good roads and army posts and beautiful little temples decorated with mirrors and shadow-thread rugs— spaces of devotion where stone Meres stood beside enameled bowls, alien hands beckoning for offerings in exchange for little blessings.

The god traveled, but only for the most special occasions. Most of her days were spent at home. Yet she read every word she could find about the empire, including the dry reports of distant officials. And with the painfully complex language of the City, she recorded the events of every day, making observations about the strange and the little that others would discount out of hand as being unimportant.

"The river is growing smaller," she said one day.

The current truth-seeker was a young man, intelligent along narrow lines. He accepted her observation and in the next breath added, "But it still is a magnificent river."

"And the weather is drier now," she said. "Drier, and hotter."

The truth-seekers had begun to paint their orange teeth white, and with intricate wigs woven from silky fabrics, they sported an approximation of a god's long brown hair. To the limits of their body, they walked like the deity. With wraps, they bound the extra joints in their arms, and by cutting themselves in the throat, they gave themselves deeper, more god-like voices. All those tricks were thought to help them speak to Mere. But hearing this unexpected observation, the truth-seeker seemed entirely baffled. What had this god just said to him?

"I have studied my journals," Mere continued. "Our winters are always warm now, and I can't find any mention of snow in the mountains for at least the last two hundred years."

"Our river is still strong," her truth-seeker replied. But his tone was mildly disapproving, shaping some form of warning. Then with a faint glimmer of curiosity, he asked, "Where do you think the problem lies?"

"Our suns are changing," she said.

"How do you know this?"

What she had found in her old journals, entirely forgotten until now, was a drawing made by her own hand. The twin suns were setting against the distant mountains, cloaked in enough haze to allow weak human eyes to discern the joined disks. The suns were the "stare" position, meaning they were perpendicular to her line of sight, and their outer edges had kissed two of the once-white peaks. Yet when the suns were last in that position, just last evening, she noted gaps between the peaks and the "stare"—as if their suns had fallen towards each other by a little ways.

Yet the truth-seeker had a ready response. "When the suns move around our world, they journey away from us a little distance and then back again. We have known this for ages. Our moon tries the same trick, but everything in the sky always falls back under our spell again."

Was that the explanation? Mere had doubts, but then again, she didn't understand the mathematics. So with a god's resolve, she said nothing more, deciding that she would have to wait out this rather stupid truth-seeker.

* * *

Regardless of reasons, their drought was real, and once mentioned, the heat grew noticeably worse. The river shrank over the next years. Its flow remained substantial, nobody suffering too badly in the City, but the upper reaches of the empire were turning to dust. Subjects starved while the surviving citizens struggled to keep hold of their own scant harvests. And with an equal inevitability, the army was dispatched to inflict appropriate punishments, winning a string of ugly battles before entire units lost their loyalties to the distant City and its inflexible, unfeeling leaders.

A new army emerged, rebels and the disaffected marching downstream. The solitary god studied the endless dispatches, but there was nothing in the reports but accounts of rebels being killed, in this little realm and presumably butchered in millions of other shadow realms too. Yet each victory was followed by an inexplicable retreat. Tales of victory were fictions, plainly. Mere began to question the worshippers who came to the great temple. She wanted to know every rumor, stories told by soldiers on leave, and what people had seen with their own sharp eyes, and her relentless skepticism left everyone embarrassed, perplexed.

Then the worshippers stopped coming. No footfalls sang on marble and no one chanted about their devotion and awe. Staring at the angry god, the now-elderly truth-seeker admitted, "Visitors are not welcome here any longer."

"Who decides that?"

The answer was a cold silence and a dismissive gesture.

"This is my temple," Mere said, "and they are and will always be my guests."

"But every road belongs to us," the old man replied. "And if we happen to block these roads, then they are nobody's worshippers. Isn't that so?"

Clean, sobering rage took hold of Mere. But there would always be time, she reminded herself. The best course was to keep silent and wait for the truth-seeker to die, which happened soon enough, and before the body was cold she met with his replacement. A young woman with brilliant white teeth and a shiny new wig, the new truth-seeker had been chosen by a council of leaders and lesser seekers, each of whom had carefully interpreted the shadow souls that clung tight to her. Better than every candidate—better than millions of her own shadow-selves—this soul was deemed wise and strong. Or maybe the judges saw nothing in the little woman's character that would worry them. Either way, the young woman was thrilled to occupy this great post, and Mere understood that for a little while, she might actually listen to a bothersome god.

With a well-practiced voice, Mere explained what she had learned about the seasons, and what she believed was the cause, and what she believed should be done now.

Together, they visited the City's leaders. Their audience was elderly souls, mostly. A little fat and harmlessly corrupt, of course. But they were intelligent citizens, each with children and grandchildren who needed their protection. Confident in her wisdom, the truth-seeker explained what was obvious: The suns were changing, bringing the heat and drought that had led to this crippling war, and if the arrow of change continued following its present course, the City was sure to be destroyed.

"How can we bend the arrow?" the old ones asked.

The truth-seeker offered a simple, pragmatic plan.

Mere's plan.

Then later, recalling her performance, the truth-seeker said, "We will seek peace with the rebels. I am quite sure of that."

The two allies were sitting in the temple again, in one of its smaller rooms. Maintaining a posture showing perfect respect, the truth-seeker said, "The City cannot win. So of course we will cut open our treasury and buy off the worst of our enemies."

It would be a temporary peace, Mere understood. But in this world, what wasn't temporary?

Then a soft voice asked, "Will you accept a worshipper, madam? I should like very much to see you."

Mere rose and said, "Yes. Always."

Her guest was dressed in a truth-seeker's gown, but his teeth were orange and there was no wig on his wide head. In his hands was a sheet of green copper, ancient and decorated with old words. Mere recognized the dialect with a glance. It was from the time when she first fell from the sky, and along the top margin of that single sheet was the official mark of the original truth-seeker. Beneath the mark, someone had written, "Should it become necessary, tomorrow or at the end of time, this is how you may kill the god."

Following the newcomer were twenty soldiers armed with keen swords and buckets full of fire. They stood together in a tight, nervous mass. There was a moment when Mere felt that she could convince them to surrender their weapons. But then the new truth-seeker threw a platinum coin to the floor, and he said, "In this one shadow of everything, you will become rich men. I promise."

The soldiers forgot their fears. They charged Mere, hacking both her and the defrocked truth-seeker to bloody pieces. Then they cooked the pieces in the burning buckets, and for good measure, they abused the severed heads until the new truth-seeker ordered them to stop. Yet when they turned, ready to collect their fortunes, they discovered that still more soldiers had appeared. For nothing but their basic wages, these newcomers gladly slaughtered those who had butchered their helpless god, and as he watched the carnage, the surviving truth-seeker stood on top of the platinum coin, enjoying the chill of metal against his little foot.

<h1 style="text-align:center">5</h1>

Mere fell into a protective coma.

She lived, but only barely. If she concentrated, summoning up an anaerobic metabolism, she could slowly open one of her eyes—usually her left eye—and a patchwork of light and shadow would fall into her sluggish mind.

She felt a hand carrying her by her long hair, and then there were long stretches when she was stashed inside dark, cramped places. Sometimes she smelled soil, sometimes rotting wood. Then came the searing white pain of a fire, and she woke in agony, her voiceless mouth opening, the tongue and her exposed lips burning to nothing.

The mind inside the slick white skull was still alive, but blind now, and deeply, perfectly asleep.

Mere dreamed in a fashion, and with practice, she learned how to control her dreams, carefully reliving her life. She saw mistakes made by others and by her own hand. She saw the stars. Sometimes she was floating in a different place—a tiny place far from the world—and then she was suddenly lying on her back, the gypsum wing reaching with his jaws spread wide, reaching for her lost eyes.

Later, another fierce blaze found her, consuming bone and teeth while her soul fell into perfect blackness, free of time and every dream.

And then she discovered eyes.

The eyes couldn't close, and they showed nothing but dull gray light. But her vision improved, and after an age or maybe just a day, she saw a Tilan face watching her, and surrounding the face, milky and thin but undeniably real, was the ghostly glimmer of countless others staring down at her from their shadowy high places.

Someone said, "Mere."

I have ears again, she thought.

She did, but the voice she heard was her own. "Mere. Mere. Mere," she kept saying.

A warm hand was laid across the new lips and tongue.

"We know who you are," said a stranger's voice. "Now quiet, please. And please, old woman, lay still."

★ ★ ★

One after another, her hosts described the last thirteen hundred years. To speak to her, each of the Tila had to master a language long extinct, and each became expert in the history of one eighty-year span. With a reverence for things ancient plus the natural pride of a talented student, each of the Tila wove a little portion of the endless thread, and at the center of everything rested the head of the reborn god.

The City had survived the siege. It seemed that its fat leaders were wiser than Mere, or at least they were shrewder. They outlasted their enemies, and when the drought finally broke, they reestablished the empire. But the new climate remained warmer and wetter than anything before. Snow never again fell on the mountains, and there were years full of rain and much darkness. Every old shoreline was inundated, and in winter the entire valley was submerged, people finding safety in the room where a god had been murdered.

Meanwhile, beyond the mountains were wild tribes riding half-tame gypsum wings. The floods and long plagues weakened the City, but it was the tribes that killed it. Mere's head was the great prize of war. From there, at least three major religions were spawned because of her. She was a messenger from the gods, and she was instilled with magical blessings, and if an army marched with Mere strung up beside their banner, then that army could never lose.

But armies always lost.

Unaware of any great event, Mere was carried away to a distant continent, and then due to the vagaries of politics and time, and the fragility of memory, her importance was forgotten and her eventual grave was mismarked.

"We were excavating inside a minor temple," the last teacher explained. "No one had seen you for so long that you had become a legend. For most of us, you were just another rusted old story, interesting to children and simple minds, but to sophisticated minds always a little silly and plainly, pathetically false."

The teacher was speaking the latest language. Over the last year, he and his colleagues had taught Mere its basics.

"When we found you, we brought you here."

"Which is where?"

"Near your old city, as it happens. But in the foothills, where you find cooler, drier breezes." The orange teeth shone brightly. The wide face was smooth and drab, showing its age. "We have built an institute of learning. The finest in the world, we would like to believe."

The Tilan glimmer was gone. Mere's eyes were complete, her focus good and sharp. And the rest of her body was almost finished, too. She could sit up. On a less taxing day, she might attempt to walk. Even her voice sounded more and more like her own. "Thank you for saving me," she said.

"No. Thank you, madam." The teacher made a circle with his two long arms, encompassing his happy face. Ages had passed, yet the Tila still employed the same artful gestures to prove their respect. "My entire life has revolved around your remains as well as my blundering attempts to make you live again."

Mere made her best circle, matching his respect.

"Because of you, we have learned much that matters about life and living flesh. We know your flesh as well as our own. Which are two quite different flavors of life, I should warn you."

She closed her hands around her face, saying nothing.

"The last few spans have been a golden age," the teacher continued. "My species is abundant and mostly at peace. There are no droughts and no winters anymore. The world is a paradise, and with so much easy wealth, we have learned what the world is."

"What is the world?" she asked.

Then in the next moment, with reflexive confidence, Mere answered her own question. "The world is the center of everything, and everything but the world revolves around us."

Those foolish words had to dissipate. Then with a sober little voice, almost an embarrassed voice, he said, "Madam, no."

She dropped her weary arms.

And a smile emerged, and the eyes became wide while the mouth formed a thin and toothless, perfectly flat line. With this long-anticipated moment suddenly before him, he had to breathe. He had to find strength. Then with what was little better than a whisper, he said, "Our world is a very little place, as it happens. And we believe, madam…some of us, at least…we believe we know where it is you came from, and what you very possibly are…!"

* * *

Gods were immortal, and gods could be tremendously powerful, and some of them were liable to act in mysterious ways. But a god's emotions and desires were always knowable. Where was the good in the indecipherable deity? A god served as a mirror held up to the self-aware soul. The image might be distorted and rather strange, but there was always something familiar—a quiet humor, a vengeful rage, or the simplest, most normal incompetence that the average citizen would recognize with a glance.

But an alien was infinitely stranger than any god.

The best minds of the age explained their verdict. Mere was the child of another world. In every detail, her body was unique—the shape of her bones and the stacking of her organs and the composition of her enduring mind. There was no place to insert her into the Tilan thread-of-life. Even the tiny workings of her flesh were unique. With delicate lenses, they showed Mere her blood and skin, and then they proudly displayed their own bubble-shaped cells, expert eyes identifying hundreds of obscure features that proved her complete Otherness. Then with giant mirrors and lenses, they forced her to gaze skyward: At the eleven worlds moving around the double suns, the thousands of asteroids and moons, plus millions of faraway suns that certainly were dancing with their own wet planets.

Ancient stories described silver wings filling the night sky, and then Mere fell to the world wrapped in fire. Those wings were likely some kind of ship. Pieces of odd material had been collected on all three continents—finer than any fabric, and fantastically strong. Recent discoveries about gravity and orbits pointed to her coming from outside their world's orbit. Perhaps she flew from one of the three giant gaseous worlds or their world-sized moons. Although it seemed to be very cold out there, and Mere was such a warm creature—an observation that turned a few imaginative minds to thoughts about distant, unknowable stars.

Whatever her origin, Mere was no god. She was utterly strange and crushingly alone, freed of every natural tie to this species and little world. The Tila respected her and in a lesser fashion still worshipped her, trying however they could to fill her needs; but instead of being a deity with some slippery noble purpose, Mere felt like the sole inhabitant of a privileged zoo, her days and nights spent in a soothing, suffocating isolation.

Her response was swift and determined. With a razor, she shaved her scalp and underarms and her legs and between her legs. Where she once walked with a comfortable stride, she now took care to mimic the walk of her hosts, forcing her hips and legs to dance in an unnatural fashion. She wore Tilan clothes that had been cut to enhance the illusion of the Tilan body. A leather noose tightened around her neck made her voice squeak nicely, and with lenses ground to order, Mere wore eyeglasses that gave every edge and every surface a slight aural shimmer.

In the past, whenever she was sad, Mere wept. It was a natural, godly way of proving her suffering. But determined practice allowed her to give up tears and sobs, invoking instead Tilan misery postures and woeful silences.

Never in the past, not once, had she taken a lover. But because it seemed essential now, she seduced not one lover, but many. Lessons learned with her hands and soft sticks were now applied to compliant alien bodies. Most were male, but gender didn't matter. The goal was in taking this next important step on the course to becoming Tilan. Mere even bonded with one young male in an official public ceremony—a little creature who was both a brilliant researcher, and according to even his most permissive colleagues, singularly odd.

For the rest of his life, they lived inside a little cabin on a remote mountaintop. Beside their home stood an old brick observatory refitted with the latest telescopes. Mere studied the double suns in the day and at night watched the nearby worlds, and to the best of her limited ability, she proved what she had sensed more than a thousand years ago: The twins were gradually and inexorably drifting closer to each other. Yet her success was dwarfed by her husband's triumphs. A genius and a theorist, he was armed with solitude and stacks of parchment, writing out a series of elaborate equations that played against each other, building revelations out of deep thoughts and abstract marks.

In a sequence of landmark publications, he explained how matter was just another form of energy. Compressed and heated hydrogen burned in a new fashion, releasing vast stores of energy as heat and light, and gravity could be described as twisted space and light and time. And finally, he gave a mathematical clarity to what all of the Tila knew by instinct: The universe existed as an infinite number of intricate shadows, each slightly different from all others, and with every tiny bite of time, these individual shadows effortlessly divided into countless shadows streaming away in every possible direction.

Upon his death, her husband was hailed as the finest mind that had ever lived inside this one particular shadow realm.

Mere walked behind the rotting corpse, fighting to maintain the ritual pose of the celebratory mate and feeling lonely again. A warm rain was falling. Heavy clouds obscured the twin suns. Looking through her thick glasses, she saw an unbroken crowd with long arms thrown up in worshipful circles, and surrounding them, on the brink of vision, she could almost see the nearest shadow realms where her husband was equally loved. Yet her grieving mind was filled with so much more: She imagined the infinite tangle of worlds where she had never been, where she never could be, and where for the entirety of their history none of these endless souls would bother to imagine a creature such as Mere.

6

The ageless widow selected her second mate from among a thousand talented suitors. Then using rudimentary AIs, she and her new husband worked together, trying to decipher the chaotic harmonics of the twin suns. The man began as a tireless and infinitely cheery soul, but his character changed over the years. More and more often, his work brought deep silences and an unshakable sadness. When they finally had what they felt were definitive results, he made an announcement to colleagues and the general public. With a cold grieving voice—a remarkable voice for a normally fatalistic species—he declared that the stellar cores were accelerating their merger. In another thirty spans—a little more than two thousand years—the suns would collapse into a single superheated body, and the resulting surge of light and heat would boil the seas and sterilize the land, launching a runaway summer leaving their tiny world dead, probably for all time.

Her third mate was her stepson. Almost as brilliant as her first husband, he was versed in every odd form of high thought. With superior AIs and the latest data, he continued his father's work, producing a new, even more damning timetable for the world's end.

Civilization had eighteen spans at most, with a cruel minimum of less than fifteen.

Mere's fourth mate was an elderly male—not an intellectual, but instead a shrewd and candidly lucky citizen who had built a fat fortune in biomechanics. As a gift, he had special eyes crafted for his bride. Mere's own eyes had to be cut free, the empty sockets treated with caustic agents to prevent any bothersome regrowth. Then the twin machines were implanted and integrated with her optic nerves, and when turned on, Mere found herself looking into the surgeon's face, seeing not only the woman's tight-mouthed smile and her bottomless black gaze, but also a multitude of whispery presences hovering close, smiling at her with that same professional pride.

The multitude was no simple illusion. With delicate, quantum-sensitive structures, her new eyes mimicked both Tilan sight and Tilan perceptions. What Mere saw was the vagueness of things small and ethereal. What the eyes gave her was the sensation—the deep and profound and unrelenting intuition—that she was one tiny creature walking along a narrow thread of reality.

In less than a year, Mere was widowed again. After another determined search, she settled on a young female with an infectious interest in space travel. Using Mere's inherited wealth, her new mate designed and tested a series of muscular rockets, and over the course of the next eighty-year span, Mere was able to build an observatory on the tiny Tilan moon—optical and radio telescopes of unprecedented power gazing out into the boundless wilderness of sky.

Her sixth mate died with a million others, drowned in a monster cyclone.

Armed with the latest data from Mere's observatory, her seventh mate revisited and refined the old projections of doom. The Tila still had twelve spans until their world died, but he foresaw the difficult and sometimes gruesome years between. Rising temperatures were already playing fits with crops, while the endless rains washed away key portions of the industrial infrastructure. Time was limited, but resources were even more precious. Mere demanded a divorce from him and then mated with a young scientist—a genuine savant who saw three routes to save the Tila: They could build enormous orbiting mirrors that would deflect the sunlight. Or massive asteroids could be pushed into new orbits, passing close enough to nudge the world into a more distant orbit. Or with ships not even imagined today, the Tila could carry part or all of their species to an elaborate refuge built somewhere in the outer solar system.

"Each path has the same essential problem," he confessed to his alien wife. Lying beside her, comfortably exhausted by a bout of lovemaking, he calmly said, "Each of these options is nearly impossible. Even with fifty spans, I doubt we could make any one of them succeed."

"Then our world is dead," she muttered, without hope.

"Perhaps we are entitled to our sad-silence, yes." He had to laugh at his mate's bleak tone. "But in other shadows, with different harmonics, our suns won't coalesce for another thousand spans. Or they were joined in some remote, pointless past, and nobody is here to complain."

Mere rose from the narrow mating pad. In the appropriate corner of the room, she relieved herself, and with an ease that had come gradually over these last centuries, she took a ceremonial nibble of her own feces. Little surgeries and large ones had radically changed her body and limbs. Extra joints in the arms allowed her to make convincing Tilan gesture. Her skull had been crushed in artful lines and then healed inside special containers, forcing it into a wide oval shape. She no longer grew hair of any kind, and her feet were longer and much narrower, and her vagina had an entirely different architecture. When the time seemed ripe, she intended to have her internal organs reshuffled, and her skin was going to be peeled away, the bloody tissues beneath treated to produce the same glossy pale skin that seemed so perfect and lovely in Tilan eyes.

"You said, 'Perhaps,'" she noted. Then with a wary interest, she guessed, "You aren't sure this world has to die. Is that what you mean?"

"If we attempt not one, but all three impossibilities, with the full focus of our entire world and species—"

"As interlocking projects, you mean?"

"If you notice, each hopeless task can help the other two. If we build a refuge near one of the gas giants, presumably on an icy moon, we can use it as a staging platform. If we are going to push a suitable comet or asteroid into some useful orbit, then it will slide close to our world and the gas giant, too. Why not make it carry passengers? And if we can manage that kind of presence in space, then perhaps we can also invent a simple way to manufacture truly impressive mirrors that could be brought here by the same asteroid that carries our people and gives our world the occasional little nudge." His black eyes became distant, and with an equally distant voice, he said, "Of course, darling…darling…there's one little nut of knowledge that would help us enormously…"

"What nut?"

Hung on the nearby wall, stretched tight like a treasured skin, was one of the surviving shreds of Mere's enormous light-sail. A mining dredge had found it on the deepest reaches of the sea. Despite being woven from badly degraded armor, under the most difficult conditions, and despite being further eroded by radiation and micrometeorites and its fiery descent through the atmosphere, the hyperfiber was in spectacular condition. It weighed almost nothing, and it was still the perfect mirror, and except along the failed edges, this tiny whiff of brilliant nothing possessed an impossible strength.

"If we could just make this wonder substance," her husband said. And then he carefully and conspicuously stopped talking.

"I wish I knew how to build it," she said.

Then the man looked at his mate—stared at her with a hard, cutting expression that betrayed secret distrusts—and with a suspicious voice, he said, "It has been suggested. More than once, suggested. That perhaps our resident alien knows more than she wishes to share with her little Tilans…"

That was Mere's eighth mate, and as it happened, he was the last.

The world grew hotter and wetter, its death pangs worsening each year. Cities were swept away by endless storms. Famine and opportunistic plagues killed millions, while filthy new industries and uranium reactors poisoned the hearts of the continents. Yet every catastrophe was endured and accepted and then left behind, and meanwhile the Tila accomplished miracles. Rockets and rail-guns lifted vast cargoes to space. Crude aluminum mirrors were built on the ground and deployed in useful orbits. A massive nickel-iron asteroid was selected as a planetary nudge, mass-drivers and chemical rockets, fuel tanks and mountains of perchlorate waiting for deployment. Driven past the nearest gas giant, the asteroid would borrow momentum that it would share when it raced past the Tilan world, easing it a little farther away from the colliding suns.

Even with a flock of asteroids, the process would remain unbearably slow. And even if the sky were filled with mirrors, the climate would never stabilize in a livable state. But one small, self-sufficient colony could be established on some far moon, and if the colony survived for ten thousand spans—if those few Tila walked one lucky thread—then their descendants would be able to return to a sterile but otherwise habitable world.

Mere would never become a colonist. That was a decision made in the early days of the work, and only on rare occasions did regret nip at her. Most of her wealth and possessions were given away to the powers in charge, and she missed none of it. What she retained was the old home perched on the rain-drenched mountaintop and its now useless observatory, and with her final resources, she built a little city around her where a few of the endless refugees could find the raw essentials of life.

As a rule, the Tila didn't waste resources on the doomed. But of course none of the homeless, starving souls were truly doomed. Creation was a magnificent home where everyone found extraordinary good fortune. Every little misery simply proved that somewhere else, on a cooler, drier world, these same Tila lived as sweetly and perfectly as any mind could envision.

Occasionally, Mere adopted one or two orphans. For the Tila, this was rarer than caring for the condemned, but it served to fill some ill-defined need in her alien heart. She took strength from newborns that had no bone-ties to her. Like any mother, she found delight in their successes and lost count of the disappointments; and after three hundred years of selfless work, she stood as the ageless matriarch of an enormous family—children and grandchildren and their descendants living in her little city, and elsewhere.

Mothers should never have favorite children, and they always do.

Mere's favorite was her last son, and he was special for the simplest reason: He looked as if he could be her own. He wore elements of her face and features, and he mastered her odd way of walking, and in his voice was a quality, a gait, that others heard in her voice. Like Mere, he was more persistent than authentically brilliant. He had a patience that could have come from her and an alien's sense of humor, and somewhere in his youth, he learned to sob as she still did on occasion, when one or the other of them was exceptionally sad.

The boy's name was Always.

While still a young man, Always left the world, taking a coveted student's posting on the moon's observatory. He was to be gone for three years, but before the first anniversary, without forewarning, he rode out of the clouds, his metal gypsum wing dropping him into the town's center.

Mere assumed trouble and imagined the worst.

But Always claimed that he was healthy and loved his studies, and better yet, his superiors thought that he wasn't too much of a dullard.

"Then why are you here?" Mere asked.

He smiled as she smiled, a weak little sob leaking free. A fresh rain had started, but he didn't notice. One hand reached into a satchel, retrieving a tiny light-pad that recognized his touch and came awake. Then with a smiling voice, Always said, "We just finished upgrading your old radio dishes. Made them bigger, more sensitive—"

"I know that," she interrupted.

He hesitated, suddenly nervous. Then as the rain worsened, drumming on their heads and the bare water-soaked stone on all sides, he said, "We heard something, finally. From the sky, we have an alien signal."

Mere flinched, saying nothing.

"Are you a little curious, Mother?"

"Never just a little," she said.

Satisfaction framed his voice. "I have been granted special permission," he said. "The official announcement comes as soon as I tell you the news."

"The news," she said.

"Look."

She was staring at the lighted pad, but her fancy mechanical eyes seemed to have failed. Why couldn't she see anything? She rubbed at them, and rubbed, and then she bent low to look at what seemed to be a child's toy. It was a ball of shiny gray glass, and erupting from one side of the ball were tubes or nozzles…or rocket engines of some peculiar design…

"Mother," he said. "Do you recognize the object?

"No," she said. "And why would I?"

"Some of us, a stubborn few of us…we believe this could be your starship."

With both hands, she cast that nonsense aside.

"Our hypothesis has weaknesses," he said. "The ship's current location and velocity show that it never actually passed through our solar system. And today it is several hundred light-years beyond its closest approach."

"How large is this machine?" she asked.

He told her.

Again, she believed nothing. "Why are you sure? How can you accept such insanity?"

"This is just one image," Always said. "The starship noticed our signals and sent us millions of images. And we have also received whole libraries of text and years of speeches and odd-sounding songs. A few pieces have been deciphered, and we've studied a portion of these very beautiful pictures, and what we can surmise is that this incredible vessel is indeed far larger than our own little world. And its crew…its god-like pilots…"

Her son paused and tilted his head back, rain flowing over the oddly shaped face.

To the clouds, he said, "The captains are your species, Mother. About that, everyone is certain. Your brothers and your sisters are guiding that marvel on a journey around the Wheel of Suns."

★ ★ ★

The harmonics of a single sun are wickedly complex, but two suns merging is an incalculable problem for even the most arrogant astronomer. The suns will mix their plasmas at changeable rates, and the fraternal magnetic fields can alternate between wrestling and dancing, while roaring pulses of sound will ignore one another or cancel each other out, right up until the moment when every busy force decides to join together—an event without warnings or mercies.

Brighter than both suns, the flare scorched the inner solar system with hard radiations and fantastic heat. Every grand mirror dissolved into an aluminum rain. All of the orbiting Tila were killed, as were the moon's inhabitants who weren't sheltered in deep bunkers. Mere's favorite son died in his sleep while the great telescopes were mangled by pulses of wild energy. The world's daylight hemisphere absorbed the blast, radiations blunted by the atmosphere but the heat punching down to the cloud-draped sea, cooking up storms that carried hot clouds higher than ever, piercing the increasingly sultry stratosphere.

One of the great-grandchildren woke the alien woman. Describing the ongoing disaster, the young woman used her most careful voice. Mere was a sensitive soul, always taking death news harder than the Tila could. Mere was sensitive because she was alien and because her immortality was woven inside a deep nest of good fortune. Some flaw in Mere's soul kept her from grasping what every Tila held with instinct: One soul might die in this narrow reality, but a billion trillion others just like her had to survive, walking along the neighboring threads, a few of them destined for perfect happiness.

The great-grandchild made these salient points. Then with a voice that sounded almost stern, she added, "Most of us have survived, madam. And most of the survivors will live out the year. If the climate worsens, so be it. We have options. Without so many bodies, we can migrate to the poles. Then, when necessary, we will ride airborne cities. And within another span, perhaps sooner, we will rebuild the orbiting factories and resume the colonization of the distant ice moon."

No expression showed on the ancient face. Nothing Tilan, and nothing alien. Mere stared blankly at the table between them, at one of the old pictures of the Great Ship. More and more, she spent her days alone, studying the alien texts and the wondrous images. "Hunting for useful gifts," was her excuse. Though the truth was that Tilan scholars had done all of the critical work.

"The new mirrors will be huge improvements," said the young woman. "Did you know? We will make them out of hyperfiber, just as your people, the great captains, taught us to do. And our next ships will be fusion-powered, swift and strong. And very soon, perhaps in just three spans, we'll begin lifting everyone to their new homes on the ice."

"And if another flare strikes?"

"Flares live on chance," said the great-grandchild, impatience tightening her voice. "If our thread happens to end here—"

"Another million threads carry us forward."

"Yes madam, exactly."

At last, the alien woman looked at her guest. Then with slow words and a strange tone, she asked, "Do you ever feel scared?"

"Scared?"

"Terrified," said Mere. "Your head fills with rational despair. Your entire existence is threatened, and everyone you care about is equally endangered. Does that kind of thinking ever find you?"

With an honesty suited to the Tila and the moment, the young woman said, "No. I never feel that way, madam."

"Since the universe is endless."

"Plainly, it is."

"And you are immortal, after a fashion."

"All that can be is eternal, madam."

"Perhaps so," the alien woman muttered. Then from a pocket on her hip she removed a knife, unfolding a mirrored blade that had been given to her as a gift just last year—a prototypical wisp of hyperfiber produced as an experiment, using a recipe supplied by the Great Ship.

"Perhaps so," she said again.

Then with that impossibly sharp blade, using her steadiest hand, she carefully hacked free both of her mechanical Tilan eyes.

* * *

Only Mere lived in the mountains.

Her human eyes had regrown, and she had allowed her human body to reemerge. The heat was awful, but her constitution never faded. Rains brought endless steam, but she could endure a hundred days of storm just to reach those rare moments when the rain stopped, allowing her to walk a certain ridge out to where she could look down on the river valley.

There was no forest anymore. Even the most determined weeds had retreated to the poles and the highest peaks. What lived in and beside the water were species of bacteria that tolerated the near-boiling temperatures. Colonies of purple and pale yellow and sickly orange microbes created a vivid carpet, and from her vantage point Mere would use one of her surviving telescopes to watch how the bacterial mats grew in elaborate patterns—threads of life branching out, twisting in the current, sometimes ending abruptly, sometimes breaking loose and riding the river towards the dying sea.

A voice said, "Mere?"

She turned, perhaps a little startled. The Tila seemed to be a stranger, although it was hard to feel sure. He was wearing a refrigerated suit and a bulky helmet that partly obscured his face, and when he spoke, the helmet muted his quiet, slightly nervous voice.

"Yes? What do you want?"

"I have a rock," he said with a distinct importance. "The rock is behind my back, in one of my hands. Guess which hand."

"Why?"

"Guess," he insisted.

She did as asked, and he brought the hand forwards and opened it, showing her a small wedge of eroded black slate.

"Under one of my feet," he continued, "I have a coin."

"Do I care?"

"Pick a foot," he insisted.

This game could not be more foolish. But something was intriguing about this business, which was why she selected one foot instead of the other.

The stranger lifted that foot, and an oval piece of platinum glowed in the cloud-soaked light.

"I have two pockets–" he began.

Before he could finish, Mere pointed at one pocket. And what he removed was a small holo showing a very peculiar object. Nozzles and fuel tanks were wrapped around each other. There may have been more to the structure, but turning the image in her hand, she saw ragged edges—places where pieces had been torn loose by irresistible forces.

"What is this thing?" she asked.

The stranger said nothing.

She threw his silence back.

Then he said, "Telescopes saw a faint spit of light following a highly eccentric orbit, and we assumed that it was a comet. But obviously it isn't, and what we imagine now is that the vessel passed close to the suns, and it was moving slowly enough to be captured, to begin a very long orbit…an orbit that is still a few years away from completing its first circuit."

"This is a starship?" she blurted.

"The wreck of a starship, yes."

Her hand squeezed the holo block until her skin bled. Then she quietly asked, "Is this my ship?"

"Presumably."

Despite the heat, Mere shivered, and she breathed deeply, calming herself before asking, "What will you do with this wreck?"

The Tila said nothing.

"How old is this image?" she pressed. "A first-generation holo means that it is twenty years old, at least."

Again, he said nothing. But he seemed to wring pleasure from Mere's unfolding astonishment.

"Can this ship function?" she asked.

"It can now," he said.

For a wild moment, Mere was imagining what was suddenly possible. Giant engines of this kind, given fuel and strapped to useful asteroids could accomplish wonders. And then a rational terror took hold, and she asked, "What was this game we just played?"

"You made the right choice three times, madam."

"I don't understand you."

"In thanks," he said. "And because you guessed correctly, madam, we can give you this gift of thanks."

8

Against Mere's wishes, they set her onboard the refurbished starship. Ignoring every argument, they showed her how to use the simple controls they had grafted into the remaining steering mechanisms. A minimal shield of battered hyperfiber was bolstered with aerogel and low-grade lasers. The engines had worked well enough on separate trials, and with the tanks filled to bursting with liquid hydrogen, there was just enough fuel to catch the Great Ship—finally—and with help from the captains, perhaps she would survive.

"You don't want to do this," Mere said.

Yet the Tila knew their minds exactly. Without the barest doubt, they said, "All paths are inevitable. This path is yours, madam."

"But you can save yourselves," she said. "These engines could carry thousands, maybe hundreds of thousands of citizens out to the new colonies, and then they could push and pull the asteroids wherever they need to be."

The rebuilt cabin was tiny, and with her company, quite crowded. Mere's supplies and a simple recycling system would keep her alive for the next few centuries, ship-time. Her luggage consisted of a few heirlooms and important trinkets, plus endless files containing the history and complete works of the Tila. In another few minutes, she would be underway, and by every conceivable means, they had assured Mere that she had no choice in this matter.

The original AI had been recovered, its shredded remains given a voice. In Tilan, the ship said to its single passenger, "It is time, Mere. This is the moment to resume our inevitable voyage."

She said, "No."

Enraged, she slapped and kicked at the Tila.

With just enough force, they restrained her. But she struggled again, and they worked together to break her arms and legs, shattering each bone badly enough that they wouldn't heal until after the long burn had begun.

"You cannot!" she said.

"Without this ship, you'll die!" she wailed.

One of the Tila—a large woman blessed with poise; a creature destined to be a truth-seeker in another age—made a careful final study of the alien. Then she laid her hand on the strange-boned face and with her own patience exhausted, she asked, "Has it occurred to you, madam? Have you ever considered this improbability? If somehow all of your threads die here, and if you never complete this journey of yours…that there is some destiny greater than ours that you will miss…a future will be cheated, madam…stolen away by little fears and tiny, tiny selfishness…?"

Bridge Three

The animals were perched on the narrowest circumstances. Friable, weak and short-lived, they drank water and breathed oxygen and feasted on almost any digestible object. One sex was relatively tall and strong, while the other was taller and more powerful. They spoke and hollered and sometimes sang and occasionally sang well. They made wealth using hands and slave-animals and slave-machines. They wandered widely and upon their return spun lies about what they had seen and done. They fashioned tiny charms full of power, and they painted magical figures on sacred walls, and whenever those animal eyes looked skyward, they saw nothing but spectacular versions of themselves striding free across the unreachable stars.

They acted like social beasts, gathering into blood clans and tribes and nation-states, and sometimes an empire would rise, conquering some little portion of the dry land. But their world was mostly ocean, and the sturdiest, wisest empires proved as fragile as the citizens. The animals were social, but bonds were tenuous, conflicted. They told stories and every story was about them, and the oldest tales involved the Creation and fertile, milk-heavy mothers giving birth to wild sons who disowned good fathers and brothers who happily murdered brothers.

Families always fell apart in a few generations. Every society was young enough to recall its humble birth and could see Death looming. No glorious mountain or sweet green river held the same name for long, and while everything in the world was in an uproar, the animal produced new tools and the first farms, and it invented cities and steel and radios and then slivers of magic electrified rock that began to think for themselves.

Turmoil was everywhere, but the beast clung to its nature.

Then a civilized voice found them

Speaking from a sky that wasn't filled with heroic humans, the voice sang out with laser light; and for the first time in their history, human beings fell silent, listening to the stark, elegant truths about the universe and their minuscule place inside the All.

* * *

The modern human still carries wet flesh on wet bone, and her voice is barely improved from the old voice, and she often talks in the same tireless gossipy fashion common to every marginally social, status-compulsive hierarchal beast. But living inside her old-fashioned flesh are machines: Ancient designs already proven in a multitude of unrelated species. The machines come in fleets, in multitudes. They provide her with strength and biochemical adaptability, quick healing and emergency healing and invulnerability to disease, plus a fabulous capacity to survive heat and pressure and violent, unexpected insults. Her soul is a vast sane mind that can memorize thousands of years and find the pleasure in most every moment. Little features and personal touches are attuned to the human species, but she still depends on the same trickery used by harum-scarums and Janusians and other species, common and rare. The woman will never age and never misplace an important thought, and if she is just a little bit careful, she will survive this elegant voyage around the Milky Way.

For a human—for any species—she is a beautiful creature.

Comfortably wealthy, she is free to sit where she wants and talk to friends all day and make new acquaintances when it suits her. Her company is usually human. Why wouldn't it be? The woman is beautifully ordinary. She is gorgeous and tirelessly pleasant, and perhaps this voyage and the Great Ship are not quite what she had imagined when she left the earth, but this immortal woman won't waste two moments of existence complaining to anyone about her tiny, trivial disappointments.

Sometimes she will be sitting at a large table, surrounded by her oldest finest loudest friends, and she will abruptly look away.

A lost expression comes to her, and someone notices.

Touching her hand, the man-friend says, "Quee Lee."

She does not hear him.

"Quee Lee," says a woman friend.

The pretty face tilts, and black eyes catch the fake sunlight while a deep clear voice asks, "Did you hear that?"

"Hear what?"

But she realizes that the sound, the sensation, vanished some time ago. And looking at these faces that she knows as well as her own, she discovers a larger, more dangerous question waiting.

"Why am I wasting my time here?"

But the lady has all the time in Creation, and she is far too polite to give that thought breath enough to live by.

The Remoras

1

Quee Lee's apartment covered several hectares within one of the human districts, some thousand kilometers beneath the Ship's hull. By no measure was it the most luxurious unit. Some of her friends owned as much as a cubic kilometer for themselves and their entourages. But it had been her home since she came onboard, quite a few centuries ago, and its hallways and cavernous rooms were as comfortable to her as her own body.

The garden room was a favorite. She was enjoying its charms one afternoon, lying nude beneath the false sky and sun, eyes closed and nothing to hear but the splash of fountains and the prattle of little birds. Suddenly her apartment interrupted the peace, announcing a visitor. "He has come for Perri, miss. He claims this is urgent."

"Perri isn't here," she said, soft black eyes opening. "Unless he's hiding from both of us, I suppose."

The apartment was momentarily silent, searching every crevice inside her property. Then it returned to say, "Perri is absent, and I have explained this to the man. But he refuses to leave. His name is Orleans, and he claims that he is owed a considerable sum of money."

What had her husband done now? Quee Lee made a guess and put on a bittersweet smile, and she sat up. *Oh, darling…won't you learn…?* She would have to dismiss this Orleans fellow herself, spooking him with a hard little stare. She rose and let an emerald sarong clothe her, and she walked the length of her apartment, never hurrying, commanding the front door to open at the last moment but leaving the security screen intact. And she was expecting someone odd. Even someone sordid, knowing Perri. Yet she didn't anticipate a bright lifesuit more than two meters tall and nearly half as wide, and she could never have imagined such a face gazing down at her with mismatched eyes. It took a moment to realize this was a Remora. An authentic Remora was standing in the public walkway, his fantastic round face watching her. The flesh was orange with diffuse black blotches that might or might not be cancers, and a lipless, toothless mouth seemed to flow into a grin. What would bring a Remora down here? They never, ever came below the hull.

"I'm Orleans." The voice was sudden and deep, slightly muted by the security screen. A speaker hidden somewhere on the thick neck told her, "Dear lady, I need help. I'm sorry to disturb you, but I'm desperate. I don't know where else to turn."

Quee Lee had seen Remoras and even spoken to a few, although those conversations were aeons ago and their substance was buried deep, beyond her immediate reach. They were such strange creatures, stranger than most aliens, even if they possessed human souls.

"Dear lady?"

A good person would be welcoming. Yet Quee Lee couldn't help but feel repelled, the floor rolling under her and her breath stopping short. Orleans was a human being, one of her own distant brothers. True, his genetics had been transformed by hard radiations. And yes, he normally lived apart from ordinary people. But inside the orange flesh and cancers was a tough, potentially immortal mind. Quee Lee wanted to have compassion for everyone, even aliens, and she managed to find her wits before saying, "Come inside." She said, "If you wish, please do," and with her invitation her apartment deactivated the invisible screen.

"Thank you, dear lady." The Remora walked slowly, almost clumsily, his lifesuit producing harsh grinding noises that rose up from the knees and hips. That was not normal; Orleans should be graceful, his suit dancing with power, serving him as an elaborate exoskeleton.

"Would you like a drink?" she asked out of habit.

"No, thank you," he replied, his voice perfectly pleasant.

The question was foolish. Remoras ate and drank only suit-made concoctions. They were permanently encased in their shell, functioning as perfectly self-contained organisms. Food was synthesized, water recycled, and they were possessed by dreams of purity and independence.

"I don't wish to bother you, dear lady. I'll be brief."

The politeness was another surprise. Remoras were famously distant, even arrogant. But Orleans continued to smile, watching her. One eye was a muscular it filled with thick black hairs, and she assumed the hairs were light sensitive. Like an insect's compound eye, each one might build a piece of an image. But contrast, its mate was ordinary, white and fishy with a foggy blue center. Mutations could do astonishing tricks. An accelerated, halfway planned evolution was occurring inside that suit, even while Orleans stood before her, boots stomping on the stone floor, a single spark arcing toward her.

"I know this is embarrassing for you," said Orleans.

"No, no," she lied.

"And it makes me uncomfortable too. I wouldn't have made this trip for any small reason."

"Perri is gone," she said again, "and I don't know when he'll be back."

"But that is what I was hoping for."

"You were?"

"Though I would have come either way."

The apartment, loyal and vigilant, wouldn't let anything nasty happen to Quee Lee. She took one step forward, then another. "This is about some money being owed. Is that correct?"

"Yes."

"Owed for what exactly?"

"Think of it as an old gambling debt." Orleans didn't want to offer clear descriptions; it was better to imply much and then press on. "This is a very old debt, I'm afraid. And Perri has refused me a thousand times."

She could imagine that. Her husband had his share of failings, incompetence and a self-serving attitude among them. But she loved the man in a disciplined fashion, and she accepted the flaws that he wore so easily and openly—unlike other men that she preferred not to think about now.

"I am sorry, sir," she said. "But I am not responsible for his debts."

The odd eyes continued to stare at her.

Making her voice sound hard was best. "I hope you didn't come all this way because you heard that he married well."

"No, no, no!" The grotesque face seemed injured. Both eyes became larger, and a thin tongue, white as dry ice, licked at the lipless edge of the mouth. "Honestly, we don't follow the news about passengers. I assumed Perri was living with someone. He usually does. My hope was to come and make my case to whomever I found, winning a comrade. An ally. Someone who might become my advocate." There was a hopeful pause, and then he said, "When Perri appears, will you explain to him what's right and what is not? Would you, please?" Another pause, and then he added, "Even a lowly Remora knows the difference between right and wrong, miss."

That was an ugly trick, calling himself lowly, and he was painting her to be some flavor of bigot, which she wasn't. Besides, she felt that their souls were linked in a profound fashion—joined together by a charming and handsome, manipulative user...by her darling husband...and Quee Lee discovered a sudden anger directed at the man who should be standing between them.

"Dear lady?"

"How much does he owe you, and how soon will you need it?"

Orleans answered the second question first, lifting an arm with a sickly whine coming from his shoulder. "The sound is my seals begging to be replaced, or at least refurbished. Yesterday, if possible." The arm bent and the elbow whined. "I had savings, but they vanished when I rebuilt my reactor."

Quee Lee appreciated his circumstances. Remoras lived on the open hull, standing on the most dangerous places for hours and days at a time. One split seal was a disaster. Any opening would kill most of his body, and even when his mind was safe inside a protective coma, Orleans would be at the mercy of radiation storms and comet showers. A balky suit was an unacceptable hazard on top of the normal dangers, and what could she say?

She felt deep empathy for the man.

Orleans appeared to take a breath. "Perri owes me fifty-two thousand hectos, dear lady."

"I see." She swallowed. "My name is Quee Lee."

"Quee Lee," he said. "Yes, dear lady."

"He and I will have a painful conversation, as soon as he comes home."

"I would be grateful if you did."

"I promise."

The ugly mouth opened, revealing blotches of green and gray-blue against a milky throat. Those could be cancers or pigments or perhaps strange new organs. The strangest sort of human was standing before her, and despite every myth, despite tales of courage and reckless sacrifice, Orleans appeared fragile. He even looked scared, that wet orange face shaking in despair as he turned away. His suit made an awful grinding noise, and his voice said, "Thank you, Quee Lee. For your time and patience, and for everything."

Fifty-two thousand hectos! More than that and she would have screamed. She promised herself to scream as soon as she was alone. Perri had done this man a great disservice, and he would hear about it. Fifty thousand wasn't a grand fortune, even for a woman raised by a family of misers, but it would allow Orleans to refurbish his lifesuit, which was as much a part of his body as that furry eye or the five hearts beating inside his belly.

Orleans was through her front door, turning around to say good-bye. False sunshine made his suit shine, and his faceplate darkened until she couldn't see his features anymore. He might have any face, and what did a face mean? Waving at the visitor, sick to her stomach, Quee Lee considered giving him the sum now, erasing the old debt.

But no, that wouldn't happen. She was suspicious and a little angry, and worst of all, she lacked the required compassion. And having made up her mind, she ordered the security screen to reengage, helping mute the horrid grinding of joints as the Remora shuffled off for home.

2

Perri began as a story shared by immortal ladies.

One day, Quee Lee was in the Make-ling district, enjoying an ordinary luncheon with a dozen acquaintances. The gollings were breeding in the canyon below. Perhaps that's why the subject of the moment was sex, although frankly there didn't have to be any excuses to let that topic reign. One acquaintance was a Martian woman with a flair for sexual intrigues, and she took the lead, boasting about a certain local boy who had done this and allowed that, and my, she hadn't had so much fun in decades. Sordid details were her specialty. She gave the ladies and a couple husbands quite a lot to think about while the gollings continued to screech and wail. But then the superlatives began to flag, and needing something else to talk about, the woman mentioned, "Oh, yes. And Perri also tells these long wonderful and interesting stories."

"What kinds of stories?" Quee Lee asked.

With a smirk and gently mocking tone, she said, "The young man likes to travel around the Great Ship. His dream, his life-plan, is to swim in every puddle and walk every tunnel, poking his business into every willing crevice and hole."

The bawdy people laughed hard.

Quee Lee sat quietly, watching a golling rising into view. The Martian had a history of embellishments and outright lies, and who knew if there was any Perri behind the name? The moment passed without significance. The golling was a female glowing deep in the UV range, and her male suitors attacked her from below, slashing at the weakest parts of her body. Hydrogen gas bled into the open air and then detonated—blue flames felt by the audiences gathered on the balcony. Countless eggs started their blazing fall to the ground below. The mother would have died in the ancient past, bones and ashes feeding her children. But gollings were just as immortal as humans, and the giant lady would eventually heal. Of course every egg was infertile; there were limits to reproduction among the Ship's passengers, particularly among aliens. Yet the females endured the incendiary misery because it was their nature, and because it defined them as a unique, eternal species.

The subject of young lovers was forgotten.

For years, Quee Lee didn't think about the name Perri.

Then a woman friend vanished without warning, missing for a long while and then suddenly back again. Explaining her whereabouts, she told Quee lee about an empty river running down the middle of an uninhabited cavern system and a handsome fellow named Perri who acted as her guide and sole companion. Nothing much had happened, except for the usual things that a bored woman does with a healthy male body. Perri proved himself to be a talker although she didn't believe half of what he said, and he was a funny and very pretty man, and they enjoyed quite an adventure that day when they came across a secret camp of Hall'al'amans being sought by the captains for some important crime.

Quee Lee concluded that Perri did exist, but he was tiny in her thoughts, and as the decades mounted, he once again vanished.

Millions of humans lived onboard the Great Ship, and Quee Lee had never met anyone as old as her. But one of her dearest friends was eight days her junior. Both were from Earth, specifically from Old China. They often sought each out to share meals or wander through some touristy adventure, and they were often invited to the same parties—day-long affairs where thousands of bodies, mostly human, would trade gossip and observations, long stories and ancient jokes with tiny new twists.

The friend came to one grand party with a young-faced human on her arm. Quee Lee was unimpressed with the boyfriend. He looked vain and silly and far too proud of himself. And when they were introduced, Perri acted utterly indifferent to this ancient creature from the home world. The three of them stood together, women making all of the polite noise. Then the friend spotted an ex-husband who needed to be abused public, and as she left, she jokingly warned Quee Lee not to steal anything of hers.

Two strangers were left beside a tidal pool. Quee Lee watched the helt-trilobites dancing over beds of glass mussels. The man calmly studied her, and he said nothing. Then Quee Lee began looking for the perfect excuse to extract her from this misery. But that was the moment when her future husband threw a radiant smile at her, quietly saying, "I know quite a lot about you."

"Your girlfriend talks about me," she guessed.

"Sometimes, but I have a far more reliable source than that," he said.

Quee Lee named the other two women who spent time with this unexceptional man. But Perri shook his head, saying, "No, neither of them ever mentioned you."

"So who has told you about me?"

"My intuition," he said.

A moment passed, and then she laughed at him and at the entire situation.

Perri was neither surprised nor offended. Nothing dimmed the smile, and he reached out with one hand, fingers closing on her elbow. It was the first time he touched her, and then he said, "Madam, I think you are the most important person here."

She continued laughing at him.

He shrugged and let go of her.

"All right," said Quee Lee. "So you think that I'm the most important person in this room."

"In this room and everywhere," Perri said, winking once before turning and walking away.

3

Perri failed to come home the next day, and the next. Then ten days had passed, and Quee Lee had left messages with nexuses and his usual haunts. She was careful not to explain why she wanted him. Nothing about the silence was unusual. Perri was probably wandering somewhere new, and he liked to isolate himself as much as possible. For her part, Quee Lee was skilled at waiting, her days defined by visiting friends and little parties thrown for any small excuse. It was her normal life, never anything but dreamily pleasing; yet she kept thinking about Orleans, imagining him walking on the open hull with his seals bursting, his strange body starting to boil away…that poor man…!

Taking the money to Orleans was an easy decision. The hectos weren't an impressive sum, particularly when wrapped inside AI guardians. But wasn't it better to have Perri owing her instead of owing a Remora? She had the better chance to recoup the debt, and besides, she doubted that her husband could raise the money without borrowing from others—aliens as well as humans. For the nth time, she wondered how she had ever let Perri charm her. What was she thinking, agreeing to this crazy union?

But her husband was a blessing, and not just a little blessing. Ridiculously young and wearing his youth with verve, he gladly shared what he had in abundance, including enthusiasms and boundless energy. He was an excellent lover, but rarer than that, Perri knew when to stop and what to do next. He could listen when it was important, and nothing she told him was misunderstood or conveniently forgotten. Not once had he tried to rob Quee Lee from her money, and his personal tastes could never be confused for expensive. Besides, the man was a challenge. No doubt about that. Maybe her friends didn't approve of the man. Flings and long affairs were not the same as legal bonds, as more than a few wise voices had pointed out. But to a woman of her vintage, in the beginning millennia of a five hundred thousand year voyage, Perri was something fresh and remarkable. And Quee Lee's old friends, quite suddenly, seemed like fossils doing nothing but sitting inside museum exhibits.

"I was born on the Ship, did you know?" he explained at the beginning. "Just weeks after my parents came onboard. They were riding as far as a colony world, but I stayed behind. My choice." His laughs came in countless flavors. Laughing and gazing into the false sky of her bedroom ceiling, he asked, "Do you know what I want to do with my life?"

"Explore every corner of the Great Ship," she said, repeating what she was told years before.

"Except the Ship isn't the point," he said. "The aliens are what matter. Where else in the galaxy can you find thousands of species and their assorted civilizations woven together? Each species is fascinating, and most have never seen one another up close. For instance, there's a giant spidery creature with a scent-name which roughly translates as Webmaster, and tiny machine aliens called G/gloons live with them. Two species from a thousand light-years apart, but the G/gloons build cities on the sprawling webs, and each Webmaster collects rent in the form of addictive pheromones."

Quee Lee had to be impressed. Who else in her small life could tolerate aliens, what with their overbearing odors and impenetrable minds? Perri was remarkable. Even her most critical friends admitted that much. And even the old friend who lost a lover to Quee Lee made a habit of forgetting her jealousies, begging to hear the latest Perri adventure as told by his foolish, indulgent wife.

"Can you afford to stay on the Ship?" she asked him.

"I'm paid up for the next ninety thousand years," he claimed. "Minus my day-to-day expenses, but that's all right. Believe me, when you've got armies of wealthy souls in one place, there are always opportunities to make a living."

"By legal means?"

"Glancingly so." He had a rogue's humor, all right. Yet later, in a more sober mood, he said, "I have grown a few enemies. I'm warning you, my love. Like anyone, I've made more mistakes than seems fair—my youthful blunders—but at least I'm honest about them."

Blunders, indiscretions. Crimes, perhaps. Yet Perri had nothing to earn her distrust.

"We should marry," he proposed one evening. "We like each other's company, yet we seem to weather our time apart too. And from what I see, you don't need a partner who shadows you day and night. Do you, Quee Lee?"

She didn't. True enough.

"A small tidy marriage, complete with rules and barricades," he assured her. "I get a home base, and you enjoy your privacy, plus my considerable entertainment value." Those words demanded a big long laugh, from both of them. Then he said, "I do promise. You'll be first to hear my latest tales. And I'll never be any kind of leech, darling. The mayhem will be out of sight, and with you, I will be the consummate gentleman."

* * *

Quee Lee carried the money and AIs in a camouflaged pouch, traveling to the hull by cap-car. There was one Orleans in the crew listings, no mention made if he was a Remora or not, and the only address was Port Beta. The facility was enormous—a towering cylinder lined with shops and capped with a kilometer-thick hatch—and there were days when Beta was filled with workers and robots and elegant streakships freshly arrived from new worlds. But this was a different day: The floor was an empty sweep of gray hyperfiber. An engineer stood nearby, but she didn't notice the visitor; wrapped in shifting lights that formed numbers and intricate technical plans, she calmly some unseen person that they were prone to profound little errors. Besides Quee Lee, the only tourists were aliens, some kind of fishy species encased in bubbles of ammonium hydroxide. The fish wiggled their fins and their bubbles rolled forward in response. It was like standing inside a school of wise tuna, the sharp chatter audible and Quee Lee unable to decipher any of it. Were they mocking her? She had no clue, and it made her all the more frustrated, leaving her feeling lost and more than a little homesick because of it.

By contrast, the first Remora seemed quite normal. Walking without any grinding sounds, it covered ground at an amazing pace. Quee Lee had to run to catch it. To catch her. Somehow the lifesuit seemed feminine, and a woman's voice responded to the urgent shouts.

"What, what, what?" asked the Remora. "I'm busy."

Gasping, Quee Lee asked, "Do you know Orleans?"

"Orleans?"

"I need to find him. It's quite important." Then she wondered if something had happened, something terrible, and she had arrived too late.

"I do know someone named Orleans, yes." The face had comma-shaped eyes, huge and black and bulging, and the mouth blended into a slit-like nose. Her skin looked like silver, odd bunched fibers running beneath the surface. Black hair showed along the top of the faceplate, except at second glance it wasn't hair. It looked like ropes soaked in oil, the strands wagging with a slow stately pace.

The mouth smiled. Then the utterly normal voice said, "Actually, Orleans is one of my closest friends."

True? Or was she making a joke?

"I really have to find him," Quee Lee said. "Can you help me?"

"Can I help you?" The strange mouth smiled, gray pseudoteeth as big as thumbnails, the gums the same silver as her skin. "I'll take you to him. Does that constitute help?" And Quee Lee found herself following, walking onto a lifting disk without railing, the Remora standing in the center and waving to the old woman. "Come closer. Orleans is up there." Skyward gestures were delivered with both gloved hands. "A good long way, and I don't think you'd want to try this alone. Would you?"

★ ★ ★

"Relax," Orleans advised.

She thought she was relaxed, except she found herself nodding, breathing deeply as a secret tension began to evaporate. The ascent seemed to take ages. Save for the rush of air slipping past her ears, it had been soundless. The disk had no sides at all—a clear violation of safety regulations—and Quee Lee needed to grasp hold of the Remora's shiny arm, surprised to feel rough spots in the hyperfiber. Minuscule impacts had left craters too tiny to see. Remoras were very much like the ship itself—enclosed biospheres taking abuse as they pushed through raw space.

"Are you feeling wonderful?" Orleans asked.

"I feel better." First she endured a thirty kilometer ride through the cavernous port, clinging tight a Remora, and now this. She and Orleans were inside some tiny room not five hundred meters from the vacuum. Did Orleans live here? Studying the bare walls and stubby furniture, she was tempted to ask. But no, this was too spare, too ascetic to be anyone's home, even Orlean's. Evading that subject, she asked, "How are you feeling?"

"Tired. Fresh off my shift, and devastated."

Ten days had changed the face. The orange pigments were softer, and both eyes were the same sickening hair-filled pits. How clear was his vision? How did he transplant cells from one eye to the other? There had to be mechanisms, reliable tricks…and she found herself feeling ignorant and glad of it, thank you.

"What do you want, Quee Lee?"

She swallowed. "Perri came home, and I brought what he owes you."

Surprise emerged from the face. Then a cool voice said, "That is the best news."

Out from the pouch she pulled one newly minted coin, fifty-two thousand hectos tied into its circuits, and working not to sound mistrustful, she mentioned that its AI would shepherd the money, making certain that the funds were used where it was needed.

His shiny palm accepted the gift, and when the elbow gave a harsh growl, she said, "I hope this helps."

"My mood already is improved," he said.

What else? She wasn't sure what to say next.

"I should thank you somehow," Orleans said. "May I give you something for your troubles?" One eye actually winked at her, hairs contracting into their pit and nothing left visible but a tiny red pore. "How would you like a very quick tour?"

Looking at the bleak room, she asked, "What sort of tour?"

"Outside, on the hull," he said. "We'll find you a lifesuit. We always have them waiting, in case some captain wants to embarrass himself." A big deep laugh filled the chamber. "Once every thousand years, they come, whether we need their help or not?"

What was he saying? She had heard him, yet she hadn't.

A smile and another wink prepared the next moment. "I am serious, Quee Lee. Would you like to take a little stroll?"

"I don't know," she said. "I never considered—"

"Safe as safe will be," he said, whatever that meant. "Listen, this is the best place for a jaunt. We're behind the bow, which means that impacts are nearly impossible. But we're not close to the engines and their radiations either." The next laugh included a waving hand. "Oh, you'll get a snack of gamma rays, but nothing important. You're nothing but tough, Quee Lee. Does your fancy apartment have an autodoc?"

"Of course."

"Well, there is no problem at all."

She wasn't scared, at least in any direct way. What Quee Lee felt was excitement and fear born of excitement. She had no experience to compare with what was happening. A creature of habits, rigorous and ancient, she couldn't guess how she would respond _out there_. No habits had prepared her for this moment.

"Here," said her gracious host. "Come in here."

No excuse offered itself. They walked inside a closet full of lifesuits. She let Orleans select her suit and then dismantle it with his growling joints. "Yours opens and closes, unlike mine. And it lacks two layers of redundancies. Otherwise, ours are identical."

On went the legs, the torso and arms and helmet; she banged the helmet against the low ceiling and put a shoulder into the wall with her first step.

"Follow me," said Orleans, "and stay slow."

Wise words. The locker room led to a tunnel that zigzagged toward space, ancient stairs fashioned for a nearly human gait. Each bend had a demon door that held back the Ship's thinning atmosphere. They began speaking by radio, voices close, and she could feel through the suit's skin, pseudoneurons interfacing with her own. Here gravity was stronger than earth-standard, yet despite her added bulk she moved with ease, the helmet striking the ceiling as she climbed. Thump, and thump. She couldn't help herself.

Orleans laughed pleasantly, the sound intimate, comfortable. "You're doing fine, Quee Lee. Relax."

Hearing her own name made her feel courageous.

"Remember," he said. "Your servomotors are potent. Lifesuits make motions large. Don't overcontrol and never act cocky."

She wanted to succeed. More than anything in recent memory, she wanting to pass as close to perfect as possible.

"Concentrate," he told her.

Then her gait changed, and he said, "That's better, yes."

They arrived at a final turn and a hatch, and Orleans paused and looked back at her, his syrupy mouth making a preposterous smile. "Here we are. We'll dance outside for a little while, all right?" A pause, then he added, "When you go home, tell your husband what you've done. Amaze him."

"I will," she whispered.

And he opened the hatch with one arm—the abrasive noises just audible across the radio—and a bright glow washed over them. "Beautiful," the Remora observed. "Isn't it beautiful, Quee Lee?"

4

Perri didn't return for several more weeks.

"I was rafting Cloud Canyon and didn't get your five thousand messages," he said. "What's so very important, my love?"

Just then Quee Lee realized that she wasn't going to tell him about her adventure, nor the money. And having decided on secrecy, she crafted a worthy reason: She would wait for the better time, that weak moment, when Perri's guard was down for repairs.

The messages were nothing. She said that she had missed him and been worried about him, and how was the rafting, and who went with him?

"Lovely and Tweewits," said Perri, chuckling softly. "The rafting was lovely, but Tweewits are big hulking baboons and not particularly pretty." He smiled until she smiled. He looked thin and tired; but that night, without prompting, he made love to her twice. And the second time was special enough that she was left wondering how she could so willingly live without sex for long spells. It could be the most amazing pleasure.

Perri slept, dreaming of artificial rivers roaring through artificial canyons, and Quee Lee sat up in bed, in the dark, whispering for her apartment to show her the view from Port Beta. The images were projected on her ceiling, twenty meters overhead, the shimmering aurora changing from crimson to purple, then gold and green—force fields wrestling with every kind of spaceborn hazard.

"What are you thinking, Quee Lee?"

Standing on the hull, Orleans had asked the question, and she answered it once again, in a soft awed voice. "Lovely." Then she shut her eyes, remembering the hull itself had stretched into the distance, flat and gray, bland yet somehow serene. "It is lovely."

"And the view is more impressive on the bow," her companion had said. "The fields are thicker, stronger. The big lasers pound the comets that are ten million kilometers in front of us, softening them up." His voice was slow and soft when he told her, "You can feel the Ship moving when you look up from the bow. You honestly can."

She had shivered inside her lifesuit, out of pleasure more than fear. The passengers who walked on the hull had permission. She did not. No doubt rules were being broken, which was another unexpected pleasure. On the hull she had felt exposed, profoundly naked. And maybe Orleans had measured her mood, watching her unremarkable face lit up by the flickering pulses. "Do you know the story of the first Remora?" he asked.

Did she? She wasn't certain.

"Wune," he said with his voice smooth and quiet. "She came to the Ship as a registered criminal, a habitual repeat offender who could escape prison by signing on as a crew member."

"What crimes?"

"Do the details matter?" The round orange head shook off the question. "Bad deeds were responsible. But the point is that Wune arrived without rank, glad for the opportunity, and like any good mate, she took her turns working on the exposed hull."

Quee Lee had nodded, staring at the far horizon.

"She was pretty, like you. Maybe prettier. Between shifts, she did typical typicals, exploring the Ship and having affairs of the heart and then grieving those affairs when they went badly. Like you, Quee Lee, she was smart. And after just a few centuries, Wune saw the trends: Captains were avoiding their shifts on the hull. Meanwhile certain people, guilty of small offenses, were pushed into double-shifts in their stead."

Status. Rank. Privilege. She could understand these things too well.

"Wune led the rebellion," Orleans said with pride. "But instead of overthrowing the system, she conquered it with an embrace. She built a lifesuit with its semi-forever seals and the hyperefficient recycke systems. She created a machine that she would never have to leave, and then she began to live on the hull, in the open, sometimes alone for years and for decades."

"Alone?"

"The prophet's contemplative life." He glanced fondly at the smooth gray terrain. "Wune stopped purging her body of cancers and other damage. She let her face—her beautiful face—become speckled and scabbed with dead tissues. Then she taught herself to manage the mutations, with discipline and strength. And once she was the master of her body, she selected friends equally without status, teaching them tricks while explaining the peace and purpose she found while living in the open, contemplating the universe without clutter, without obstructions."

Without instructions indeed!

"A few hundred became the First Generation. Attrition convinced our great captains to allow children, and the Second Generation numbered in the thousands. By the Third, we were officially responsible for the Ship's exterior and the deadliest parts of its engines. A quiet conquest had claimed a world-size realm, and today we number in the millions."

She had sighed and said, "I would like to meet Wune."

"Except there was a heroic death," Orleans had said. "A comet swarm was approaching. A repair team was caught on the bow, their shuttle dead and useless."

"Why were they there if a swarm was coming?"

"Patching a previous crater, of course. Remember. The bow can withstand most any blow, but if comets struck one on top of the other, unlikely as that sounds—"

"Disaster," she had said.

"For the passengers below, yes." A strange smile tried to cut the orange face in two. "Wune died bringing out a fresh shuttle. She was vaporized when ice and rock turned to plasmas."

"I'm sorry," Quee Lee had whispered.

"Wune was my great-great-grandmother, which makes me Fifth Generation," said Orleans. "And no, she didn't name us Remoras. That began as an insult, some captain happily responsible. You're from the earth, perhaps you know this already. Remoras are ugly fish that cling to sharks and eat their scraps. Not a pleasing image, yet Wune embraced the word. To us being Remora means spiritual fulfillment, independence and a powerful sense of self."

She had nodded, listening to each word.

"Do you know what I am, Quee Lee? I am a god ruling the universe that fills this suit. In ways you cannot appreciate, I am the ultimate authority over my body, over my own self."

Staring at him, she could not move.

A glove and hand lifted, placing thick fingers against his faceplate. "My eyes. You're fascinated by my eyes, aren't you?"

A tiny nod. "Yes."

"Do you know I sculpted them?"

"No."

"Tell me, Quee Lee. How do you close your hand?"

She had made a fist, as if to show him.

"Neurons fire and muscles contract, and how can you manage something that complex without being able to describe it in full?"

"Habit," she had said, suddenly proud of the word.

Orleans had used a large, engaging laugh. "And I have thousands of years of stubborn habit helping me sort through my mutations, spreading my favorite metastasized cells to where they can do the most good—as naturally as you make fists and walk across new ground."

Opening her hand, she had said nothing.

"Transformation is my every day, and this is why my life is so much richer than yours," Orleans had said. Then with a final wink, he had told her, "I cannot count the times that I have reinvented vision."

Again Quee Lee looked at her bedroom ceiling, at a curtain of indigo dissolving into salmon and blush.

"You think Remoras are vile, ugly monsters," Orleans had said. "Don't deny it. I won't let you deny it."

She hadn't made a sound.

"I know: When you saw me standing at your front door, all of that ordinary blood of yours drained out of your face. You were so pale, so terribly weak, Quee Lee. By any measure, horrified."

She couldn't deny it. Not then or now.

"Which of us carries the richest life, Quee Lee? And be objective. Is it you or is it me?"

She pulled the bed sheets over herself, shaking.

"You or me?"

"Me," she whispered, but with doubt in that word. Just the flavor of uncertainty. Then Perri stirred and rolled toward her with his face trying to waken. Quee Lee enjoyed a last glance at the projected sky and then had it quelched. Then Perri was grinning, blinking and reaching for her.

"Can't you sleep, love?"

"No," she said.

Then she said, "Come here, darling."

"Well, well. Aren't you in a mood?"

Absolutely. A feverish mood, her mind leaping from subject to sensation to wild ideas, every thought intense and abrupt, Perri on top and her old-fashioned eyes gazing up at the darkened ceiling, still seeing the powerful surges of changing color that obscured the bright dusting of stars.

* * *

They took a honeymoon-of-renewal, Quee Lee's treat. Halfway around the Ship was a famous resort beside a small tropical sea, and for several months they enjoyed scenery and beaches, floury sands dropping into azure waters where fancy corals and fancier fish lived. Every night brought a different sky, the Ship supplying images of nebulas and strange suns; and they made love in the oddest locations, in odd manners, strangers coming upon them on occasion, humans and various aliens sometimes pausing to watch.

Yet she felt detached throughout the vacation, as if hovering over the scene as an observer. In the afternoon, Perri would dress in fins and gills and leave her alone on the powdery sand, allowing her to use her nexuses to do research, learning whatever she could about Remoras. But their faith and history existed only as sketches, full of holes and often self-contradictory. Sex proved to be a richer, odder subject. Coitus involved electrical stimulation through the suits, and reproduction meant pulling totipotent cells from each partner, children conceived in vitro and grown inside a hyperfiber envelope. The envelope was expanded as needed. Birth came with the first independent fusion reactor. Remoras thrived in the oddest circumstances, but then again, many human societies seemed bizarre. Some refused immortality. Some married AIs or lived in a narcotic haze. Spiritual groups and splinter factions were normal, and why was it so difficult to learn anything certain about Wune's children?

And the better question: Why had Quee Lee been allowed a glimpse of Orlean's private world?

The resort had to be a suffocating trap for an adventurer like Perri. Everything about the place was clean and predictable. Yet he remained pleasant and attentive, and if he ever said a negative word about the burdens, he saved them for when he was drifting under the sea.

"I know this is work for you," Quee Lee said one evening, greeting her husband as he climbed out of the surf. "But old women appreciate winks and smiles."

"Winks and smiles to the young lady," Perri said, kneeling at her feet.

They returned home soon afterward, and Quee Lee was disappointed with her apartment. It was the same as she remembered, and the sameness was depressing. Even the large garden room failed to brighten her spirits, and she found herself wondering if she had ever lived anywhere but here, the stone walls cold and closing in on her.

"What's the matter, love?"

She didn't answer her husband's question.

"Because something is wrong," he said.

"I forgot to tell you something," she began. "A friend of yours visited…oh, it was nearly a year ago."

The roguish charm surfaced, reliable and nonplussed. "I have ten million friends. Which one?"

"Orleans."

Perri didn't respond at first, hearing the name but not allowing his expression to change. Was that what he was doing? He stood motionless, not quite looking at her; and Quee Lee noticed a weakness in the mouth and something glassy about the smiling eyes. Uneasy, she almost asked Perri what was wrong. Then Perri asked, "What did Orleans want?" His voice was too soft, almost a whisper. A sideways glance seemed to steal away his balance, and then he muttered, "Orleans came here?" None of these words were making sense.

"You owed him some money," she said.

Perri didn't speak, didn't seem to hear anything.

She said, "Darling, I paid him."

"But…but what happened…?"

She told him and she didn't. She mentioned the old seals and some other salient details, and then in the middle of her account, all at once, what was obvious and awful finally occurred to her. What if there hadn't been any debt? She gasped, asking, "You did owe him the money, didn't you?"

"How much did you say it was?"

She repeated the figure.

He nodded. He swallowed and straightened his back, and with the most solemn voice that she had ever heard from him, he said, "I'll pay you back…as soon as possible…"

"Is there any hurry?" She took his hand, telling him, "I haven't made noise until now, have I? Stop worrying." Pause. "I just wonder how you could owe the man so much."

Perri shook his head. "I'll give you five thousand now, or six…and I'll raise the rest. Soon as I can, I promise."

She said, "Fine."

"I'm sorry," he said.

"Orleans is one of your ten million friends," she said, trying for a joking tone.

"I'd nearly forgotten, it was so long ago." He summoned a smile which engaged his old charm. "You should know, love. The Remoras aren't anything like you or even like me. Be very careful with them, please."

She made appreciative sounds yet never mentioned her jaunt to the hull. The incident was past anyway, and why had she brought it up at all? Perri announced he was leaving immediately, needing to find some nameless creatures that owed him quite a lot. The best he could manage today was fifteen hundred hectos, admitting, "That is a very weak down payment, I know.

Quee Lee felt a decision take hold, and the decision put her in such a fierce mood that she could tell him, "Have a good trip, and come home whenever you want. I will always be waiting."

Perri was the most darling man when vulnerable. "Soon," he promised, kissing her hard before walking out the front door.

Quee Lee was leaving an hour later, convinced she was going to the hull to confront her husband's old friend. What was this mysterious debt? Why did it bother him so much? But the long cap-car ride diluted her resolve, and by the time she reached Port Beta, she had realized that a confrontation would accomplish nothing but further embarrass Perri, and that wasn't what she wanted.

"What do I want?" she whispered to herself.

And there stood the answer, in plain view: Another walk on the hull, of course.

5

His flesh had turned blue, and the eyes were much larger, each filled with black hairs that shone in the light, something about the face distinctly amused. Two little tusks showed in the corners of the mouth. The cool voice said, "I suppose we could go for a stroll." They were standing inside the same small room or one just like it; Quee Lee wasn't sure about directions. "We could," Orleans repeated, "but if you want to bend the rules, why stop with the little ones? Why not pick the hefty canons?"

"What canons?" she asked.

"Of course this will take months or maybe a few years," he said. "But that shouldn't scare someone with centuries to fill."

She waited.

"But I think I know you. You've gotten curious about me, about us." Orleans moved an arm, not so much as a hum coming from the refurbished elbow and shoulder. "We'll make you an honorary Remora, if you're willing. We'll borrow a lifesuit, set you inside it, and then transform you in a hurry-up fashion."

"You can do that," she said.

"We'll use aimed doses of radiation for a foundation, and then we'll wrap proven mutations inside smart cancers, and they'll migrate to the proper spots and grow."

She was frightened and intrigued, her heart kicking harder.

"This won't happen overnight, of course. And it depends on how much you want done." The black hairs pulled together, studying her. "Of course nothing about this conversation is strictly legal. The captains have disdain for putting passengers even a little bit at risk."

"How much risk is there?"

Orleans said, "The transformation is easy enough, in principle. I'll dredge our records, making sure of the finer points." He paused, eyes relaxing into two unkempt tangles. "We will need you to be in a shallow coma. Intravenous feedings, no nexus activity, and you'll be perfectly safe. Lie down with one body and waken with another. The new Quee Lee will be much improved, I would like to think. How much risk? None at all, believe me."

She felt numb. Small and weak and numb.

"You won't be a true Remora. Your basic genetics won't be touched, I promise. But an outsider looking at you will believe you to be genuine."

For an instant, with utter clarity, Quee Lee saw herself along on the great gray hull, walking the path of the first Remora.

"Are you interested?"

"Maybe. I am."

"You'll need a lot more interest before we can start," he said. "We have expenses to consider, and I'll be putting my crew at risk. If the captains find out, it's suspensions for everyone."

She said nothing.

"Are you listening, Quee Lee?"

"You want money."

Orleans gave a figure.

But she was braced for a much larger sum. Two hundred thousand hectos was large but quite bearable. One year at any lazy, prosaic resort would cost at least that much.

"You've done this before," she said.

"Not for a long time, no."

She didn't ask what seemed obvious, that Perri and his debts had come from a similar transaction.

"Take a year," Orleans counseled. "Research the matter, measure your thoughts, and feel sure."

But she had already decided.

Looking at the Remora, she asked, "Can I pick my own face? Can you wrap it inside a smart cancer and give it to me?"

"Certainly." A great fluid smile emerged, framed with tusks. "Pick and choose whatever you want."

"Your eyes," she said.

"They are yours," he declared, offering a little wink.

* * *

Arrangements had to be made, and what surprised her most—what she enjoyed more than the anticipation—was the subterfuge, converting the money into the proper flavor, and then telling friends and her apartment nothing except that she would be gone for an indeterminate period, at least a year and perhaps much longer. Orleans hadn't put a cap on her stay, and what if she enjoyed the Remoran life? Why not keep her possibilities open?

"And what if Perri returns?" the apartment asked.

He was to be greeted as a treasured member of the family, naturally. She thought she'd made herself clear.

"No, miss," the voice said. "What do I tell him about you?"

"Explain...explain that I have gone exploring."

"Exploring?"

"Tell him it's my turn for a change," she said, leaving without so much as a backward glance.

* * *

Orleans found help from the female Remora, the same one who had taken Quee Lee to him twice now. Her comma-shaped eyes hadn't changed, but the mouth was smaller and the gray teeth had turned black as obsidian. Quee Lee lay between them as they worked, their faces smiling but the voices tight and shrill. Not for the first time, she realized that she never heard their true voices. Wet mutterings had to be translated by the lifesuits, which was why throats and mouths could change so much without having any audible effect.

"Are you comfortable?" asked the woman. But before Quee Lee replied, she asked, "Any last questions?"

Encased in the lifesuit, a sudden panic took hold. "When I go home, when I am done…how fast can I return to my normal self…?"

"Cure the damage, you mean." The woman laughed gently, her expression changing from one unreadable state to another. "There is no firm answer, dear. Do you have an autodoc in your apartment? Good. Let it excise the bad and help you grow your own organs again. Consider this a very bad accident." She looked up. "It should take what, Orleans? Ten days to be purged and cleaned up."

The man said nothing, busy with the controls inside the suit's helmet. Quee Lee could barely see his face above and behind her.

"Ten days and you can walk in public again," said the woman.

"I didn't mean it that way." Quee Lee swallowed, pressure building against her chest—dread becoming panic, and terror waiting to strike. She wanted nothing now but to be home again.

"Listen," Orleans said, and then he said nothing.

Finally Quee Lee said, "Tell me."

He knelt beside her. "You'll be fine. I promise."

The confidence was missing from the voice. Perhaps he hadn't believed she would go through with this adventure. Perhaps the offer had been a bluff, something that no sane person would find appealing, and now he was inventing an excuse to stop everything.

But then he stood up and said, "Seals tight and ready."

"Tight and ready," said the woman.

Smiles appeared on both faces, though neither inspired confidence. Then Orleans said, "There is a very tiny chance that you'll die on the hull, like a Remora. And there's a somewhat greater risk of getting blistered by too much radiation, precipitating too many novel mutations, and the strangeness will get buried too deep. A thousand autodocs won't be able to root out the damage."

"Vestigial organs," the woman said. "And maybe an odd blemish or two."

"But nothing bad will happen," said Orleans.

"It won't," Quee Lee said.

A feeding nipple appeared before her mouth.

"Suck and sleep," Orleans told her.

She swallowed the chemical broth.

The woman said a few muddled words, and Orleans responded with a hard, sharp curse.

Then the woman said, "Oh, she's asleep."

But Quee Lee was beyond sleep. She found herself in a dreamless, timeless void, her body being pricked with needles—little white pains marking every smart cancer—and it was as if nothing else existed but Quee Lee, floating in that perfect blackness while the universe was remade.

* * *

"How long?"

"Not so long. Seven months, almost."

Seven months. Quee Lee tried to blink and couldn't, couldn't shut the lids of her eyes. Then she tried touching her face, lifting a heavy hand and setting the palm on her faceplate before she finally remembered the suit. "Is it done?" she said with a sloppy, slow voice. A stranger's voice. "Am I finished now?"

"You're never done," Orleans said. "Haven't you been paying attention?"

She saw a figure, blurred but familiar.

"How do you feel, Quee Lee?"

Strange. Through and through, she felt very strange.

"That's normal enough," he said. "Another two months, and you'll be perfect. Have patience."

She was a patient person, she remembered, eyes closing of their own volition. Then her mind was sleeping again. But this time she dreamed. She was with Perri and Orleans at a beach. Her husband was naked, sunning himself on the bright white sands, and the Remora seemed to be doing the same, odd as that looked. She even felt the heat of the false sun, felt it baking her bones, and then she touched herself, not even a little surprised to feel the invulnerable skin of hyperfiber under her fingertips.

She woke and said, "Orleans."

"Here I am."

Her vision was improved now. The wrong-shaped mouth could breathe normally, but each word was a slurring, frustrating struggle that her suit turned into coherent noise.

"How do I look?" she asked.

Orleans was the only other person in the room. He smiled down at her and said, "You are gorgeous."

His face was blue-black, or it was something else. Sitting up, looking at the plain gray room, she realized how the colors had shifted. Her new eyes perceived the world differently, sensitive to the same spectrum but in novel ways.

Climbing slowly to her feet, she asked, "How long?"

"Nine months, fourteen days."

No, she wasn't finished. But the transformation had reached a stable plateau, and it was wonderful to be mobile again. A few tentative steps didn't end in disaster. She found the date on her nexuses but little else; her presence here was heavily shielded, keeping her out of view from friends and captains alike. Making clumsy fists with her too-thick hands, she lifted the hands and gazed at the hyperfiber gloves and imagined the strange new fingers inside.

"You should see yourself," Orleans said.

Now? Was she ready?

Her friend's tusks glinted in the room's weak light. He offered a large mirror, and she bent closer until her face came into focus. She saw a sloppy mouth full of mirror-colored teeth and a pair of hairy pits for eyes. She took one deep breath and shivered. Her skin was lovely, golden with the texture of fine leather. Hard white lumps of tissue formed patterns on her cheeks, and her nose was a slender beak. She wished she could touch herself, hands stroking her faceplate. But Remoras could only touch themselves by stripping away the suits that made them Remoras in the first place.

"If you feel strong enough, you can go with me," Orleans said. "My crew and I are going on a patching mission, out to the bow."

"When do you leave?"

"Right away." He lowered the mirror. "The others are waiting in the shuttle. Stay here for a couple more days, or follow me."

"I'll follow."

"Good." He nodded. "They're eager to meet you. They want to see what sort of person becomes a Remora."

A person who doesn't want to be locked away inside a bland gray room, she thought, all those bright mirrored teeth smiling now.

6

They had all kinds of faces, unique myriad eyes and twisting mouths and oddly drawn noses and openings that had no clear function, all wrapped inside flesh of every color. Quee Lee counted fifteen Remoras, plus Orleans, and she worked to learn names and acquire some feel for her new friends. The shuttle ride was like a party, an informal party of strangers that she had wandered into by chance, and she had never met happier people, listening to Remoran jokes and how they teased one another, and how they gently teased her. They were also curious, asking about her apartment—how big; how fancy; worth how much—and they wanted stories about her long life. Was it as boring as it sounded? Quee Lee laughed at herself, nodding and saying, "No, nothing changes often or goes far. The centuries bleed into one another, sure."

One Remora with an operatic masculine voice and a contorted blue face shouted at the others, "People pay fortunes to ride the Ship, and then they do everything in their power to hide deep inside it. But the joy of the ride is out here, out where the eyes and mind can see where we are going."

The cabin erupted in laughter, the complaint an obvious favorite.

"Immortals are cowards," said the woman beside Quee Lee.

"Foolish cowards," said the woman with the comma-shaped eyes. And then glancing at their guest, she said, "With a few exceptions, of course."

Quee Lee felt uneasy, but not for long. Looking through a filthy window, she watched the smooth landscape and glowing sky, one constant while the other never stopped changing. That view soothed her. Eventually she closed her new eyes and slept, waking when the pilot announced their arrival.

The shuttle was dropping and slowing. Looking at her friends, Quee Lee saw smiles meant for her. The Remoras beside her took her hands, and everyone prayed, "No comets today but plenty tomorrow, because we want the overtime."

They hovered and fell and then settled.

Orleans joined Quee Lee, touching his faceplate to hers. "Stay close," he said, "yet don't get in our way, either."

The hyperfiber was older than the earth and deeper than most oceans, and at least in this one place the hull was covered with a soft faint dust that was kicked up easily, clinging to the machinery and lifesuits. High above, the aurora and flashes of laser light dwarfed the brilliance of three nearby stars. Quee Lee followed the others, listening to their radio chatter. She ate

Remoran soup—her first conscious meal in months—and she tried to map her new architecture, feeling the meal slipping down her throat. Her stomach seemed unchanged, but did she have two hearts? The beats were wrong, unless two hearts were nestled side by side, working in rhythm. Orleans was three bodies ahead. She approached him and said, "I wish I could look at myself, just once. Slip of the suit to take in all of me."

He glanced her way and then looked ahead. "No."

"I realize—"

"Remoras never remove their suits."

His anger was followed by a deep chilling silence from everywhere. Quee Lee looked about and swallowed before saying, "But I'm not a Remora."

Silence persisted, quick looks exchanged.

"I will climb out of this contraption eventually," she said.

Orleans stopped walking. Then a softer, more tempered voice said, "Maybe we seem too rough and wild, but we do have taboos."

"I'm sure."

"These lifesuits are as much a part of our bodies as our guts and eyes, and being a Remora, a true Remora, is the one sacred pledge that you take for your entire life."

Every face was stern, stolid.

The comma-eyed woman stepped up. "The one sacrilege is removing your suit, no matter the reason."

"Unthinkable," said the opera voice.

Yet everyone was thinking about nothing else.

Then Orleans made a show of touching her, his hands warm and comforting through the suit. The next smile felt summoned, and the look in the eyes was guarded for some reason. Yet he said, "You are nothing but our guest, and we like you. I wouldn't have invited you if I didn't enjoy your company. But you won't ever know us, or much less know how to return the pleasure, unless you can appreciate our beliefs."

"Ideals," said the woman. "Our truths."

"And accept our contempt for those that we don't like," Orleans said. "Do you understand, Quee Lee?"

* * *

The crater was vast and rough along its lip and only partway patched. Giant tanks already had been towed to the site along with the largest machines. Pouring fresh liquid hyperfiber was more art than craft. There was a proper speed to make the pour, and the curing process never happened the same way twice. Each shift added another twenty meters to the smooth crater floor.

Orleans explained little pieces of the job to Quee Lee. This was going to be a double shift, and she was free to watch and learn. "But stay back and stay safe," he said again, the tone vaguely parental.

She promised. And for the first half-day, she was happy to sit just beneath the crater's lip, on the ridge of tortured, refrozen hyperfiber, watching labors and listening to the radio chatter while imagining the comet that must have made this mess. Not a large comet, she knew. Major impact blasted wide holes that would reach into the distance, and an army of Remoras would be scattered before her. But this wasn't a small collision either. A room-sized bolide must have slipped past the lasers—probably a fragment of a fragment that descended as part of a swarm of comets. With that in mind, she watched the intense beams cutting through the aurora. Her new eyes captured amazing details: Every beam was invisible until it kissed dust. Then the shock waves turned to violet phosphorescence, swirls of orange and cobalt and snowy white flowing outwards. The sky was beautiful and only beautiful, but then the lasers fired faster, a spider web of beams focused on far flung targets. The radio crackled ominously. Another swarm of comets lay directly in front of the Ship, pinpointed by navigators and paranoid AIs rooted somewhere below—millions of kilometers of emptiness hiding ice and mud and rock that was closing fast.

The lasers fired still quicker, and the aurora surged, bathing the hull in warm yellowish light.

For no rational reason, Quee Lee bowed her head.

One sharp impact arrived with a flash and the faint rumble dampened by the hull. The new crater wasn't particularly close and it probably wasn't particularly big, but it made Quee Lee's next breaths feel special. She watched plasmas rising in a plume, gases pushed high enough to be snagged by the aurora, and each charged particle was grabbed and then concentrated and pumped inside, helping replace the volatiles that were lost every time a streakship embarked or one of the giant rockets was ignited.

The Great Ship was an organism feeding on the galaxy. That was the familiar image, the trusted cliché, yet suddenly it seemed quite fresh, even profound. Quee Lee laughed quietly, looking out over the crater floor while turning her attentions inward. Aware of her breathing, aware of the bump-bumping of the wrong hearts, she sensed changes happening with every little motion. Her body had an odd indecipherable quality. She felt every muscle fiber, every twitch and stillness. No one could live for thousands of years and not experience this kind of excitement, yet she couldn't recall ever feeling so alert, so self-absorbed and wondrous, and for a long while she did nothing but relish this giddy, infectious amazement.

If she was a true Remora, then she would be a world onto herself. A world like the Ship, only tiny, its organic parts enclosed in armor and forever in flux. The passengers below were changing, and the cells in her body were changing. She was feeling her body evolving, and how did Orleans control this relentless process? How could a human re-evolve sight, gaining unique eyes and a kind of vision that had never existed before and would never become real again?

What if she stayed with these people?

The possibility took her by surprise.

What if she took whatever pledge was necessary, embracing their taboos and proving that she belonged among them? Did such things happen? Could adventurous, virtuous passengers actually convert?

The sky turned red again, lasers punching through the aurora, each beam aimed at a point directly overhead. The silent barrage was focused on a substantial mountain or lost little moon, vaporizing its surface before cracking its heart. Then the beams separated, assaulting the big pieces first and then the shrapnel. She felt helpless and glad of it. There was nothing to do but sit, exhilaration married to terror, watching the aurora turned yellow and then white. Force fields killed the momentum of the surviving grit and atomic dust. Sudden tiny impacts kicked up the dusts around her. Something struck her leg, the heat of a sun blossoming, following by dull pain. She wondered if she was dead, and then she was certain that she was badly injured. But the only mark was a tiny crater etched above her left knee, barely a blemish and the meteor shower already finished.

Quee Lee rose to her feet, shaking and happy.

Orleans' commands were forgotten. She began picking her way down the crater wall, full of insights and compliments that she had to share. Twice she nearly tripped, finally reaching the work site while gasping, her air stale from her exertions. Her new body had its own taste, unfamiliar and thick and a little bit sweet.

"Orleans," she said.

"You're not supposed to be here," one man said.

The comma-eyed woman said, "Stay there. Stay. Orleans is coming, and you do not move."

A lake of fresh hyperfiber was cooling and curing as stood beside it, a thin skin already forming, flat and silvery. Mirror-like. Quee Lee saw the sky reflected, and she leaned forward even when she knew that was wrong. She risked falling, endangering herself and ruining the day's work. But she wanted to see her face again.

The nearby Remoras watched her, saying nothing.

She knelt and grabbed a lump of old hyperfiber, using it as a fulcrum as she leaned forward, and then the lasers flashed again, making everything obvious.

She didn't see her face.

Or rather, she did. But it wasn't the face she expected, the face from Orleans' obedient mirror. Here was the old Quee Lee, mouth ajar, those pretty but ordinary eyes wide in amazement.

She gasped, knowing everything. A considerable sum had been paid, nothing given in return. Nothing here had been real. An enormous and cruel joke was the goal, and now the Remoras were laughing, hands to their untouchable bellies and their awful faces twisting in new ways, ready to rip apart from the sheer brutal joy of the moment.

7

She talked quickly, not waiting for any response. "Your mirror wasn't any mirror, just a synthesized image. And you drugged me, probably with an elaborate cocktail that keeps adapting to my body, fending off its attempts to make me see and feel normally again. My nexuses weren't just compromised. I think months have passed, but I suspect it's been a matter of days, even hours. And despite your promises, you probably didn't even shoot me with hard radiation, did you? Did you?"

"Would you have wanted that?"

"One honest incident would feel refreshing, yes." Quee Lee remained inside the lifesuit, just the two of them flying back to Port Beta. Everyone had agreed there was no point in keeping her on the bow. Orleans would see her on her way home. The rest of the crew was still working, and he would have time to return and finish his shift.

"You owe me money," she said.

Orleans' face was bluer than before. His tusks framed a calm icy smile. "Money? Whose money?"

"I paid for a service, and you never met the terms."

"I don't know about any of this," he said, laughing.

"I will report you," she said, using all of her venom. "I know captains, and they know me."

"Then you'll embarrass yourself even more." He was confident, cocky. "Our transaction would be labeled illegal, not to mention disgusting. No captain will look at you as being anything but a silly rich woman, believe me." A long laugh ended with a growl. "Besides, you can't prove any of this. Your nexuses weren't just befuddled, but we erased everything that we said in each other's presence. Maybe you gave your funds to someone, but that attached AI will testify that the gift was used properly, and I promise, you don't want people to know what that money was supposed to deliver."

The shame was brilliant and horrible, and Quee Lee crossed her arms while saying nothing, trying to wish herself home again.

"The drugs will wear off soon," he said. "You'll feel like you deserve to feel, a gentle complacent creature all over again."

Softly, with a breathless little voice, she asked, "How long have I been gone?"

"Three days."

She felt ill to her stomach, and it still wasn't her real stomach.

The Remora watched her for a long while, remorse mixed into the expression. Or was she misreading those features?

She used the best insult she could find, speaking with certainty. "You aren't spiritual people. Your ancestors were monsters, and you couldn't live below if you were handed the chance, and this is the best place for you, and you have to die here. Probably soon."

Orleans said nothing, watching her. Then he looked out the window beside Quee Lee, absorbing the endless gray landscape. "We try to follow Wune's path. We try to be many things and maybe a little spiritual too." The armored shoulders shrugged. "Some of us do better than others. We're human, after all."

"Why?" she asked.

"Why do this to you?"

She nodded.

"Oh, Quee Lee. You haven't been paying attention at all." He grasped her helmet, pulling her face next to his face. She saw nothing but the eyes, each black hair moving and nameless fluids circulating through them, and the voice rolled over her like hard surf, saying, "This has never, ever been about you, Quee lee. Not for one instant."

* * *

Perri was already home.

"I was worried," he said, sitting in the garden room, honest relief on his lovely face. "The apartment says you are going to be missing for a year or more. So I was scared for you."

"Well," she said, "I'm back."

Her husband tried not to appear suspicious, and he worked not to ask certain questions. Quee Lee could see him holding the questions inside. She watched him decide to try charm, smiling when he said, "So you went exploring."

"Not really."

"Where did you go?"

"Cloud Canyon." She had practiced the story all the way from Port Beta, yet it sounded false. A three year-old girl could tell a better lie.

Yet her husband didn't hesitate. "Did you go into the canyon?"

"I rented a boat, but I didn't have the courage. I couldn't even make myself step onboard."

Perri grinned, relieved enough to enjoy one deep breath. Then he said, "By the way, I raised almost eight thousand hectos and struck a coin for you."

"Fine."

"I'll find the rest too."

"I can wait, Perri."

Relief faltered. Confused, he said, "You don't look right."

"No?"

"You don't sound like yourself."

"I am tired, and maybe a little embarrassed."

He brightened. "Then let's go to bed."

Perri was compliant, making love to her before falling into a deep sleep, apparently as exhausted as Quee Lee. Yet she insisted on staying awake, sliding into her private bath and giving her autodoc a drop of Perri's seed. "I want to know what's right and what is odd," she said.

"Yes, miss."

"And scan him, without waking him."

The machine set to work. Almost instantly, Quee Lee was being shown lists of abnormal genes and shriveled, long useless organs. She didn't bother to read about them. Staring at her own hands, she remembered what Orleans had told her after he had admitted that she was nothing but an incidental bystander. "Perri was born Remora, and he left us. A long time ago, by our count, and leaving the fold is the worst kind of insult." His voice was slow, measured, and poisonous. "Every so often, one of us visits his current home, choosing a moment when he has gone wandering. Slip a little dust into our joints makes them grind, and we do a pity-game to whomever we find."

Her husband had lied to her from the beginning, about everything.

"We'll trick the lady into making good on old debts. And sometimes, when the situation is ripe, we find clever ways to make more money, just as we've done with you."

"You want vengeance," she said.

"Our eventual goal is, yes." Orleans didn't laugh and he didn't seem proud. His attitude was cool and complacent, like a worker doing his job. "Eventually every rich woman is going to know Perri's story. He will run out of hiding places, and money, and he won't have any choice but to come back to us. We just don't want to rush the process. You see, this is like curing the hyperfiber—it takes patience and a flair for perfection."

Quee Lee looked up from her hands. The abnormalities were tiny and rigorously cataloged. Perri wasn't someone who had lived on the hull for a few years. He probably had to work to appear so completely human, coping with the mutated genetics. She was living with a full-blooded Remora who had committed the worst crime, removing his suit and living below, safe from the mortal dangers of the universe. Quee Lee was just the latest ignorant lover, and she knew precisely why he had selected her. More than money, she offered a useful naiveté and sheltered ignorance, and she was absolutely within her rights to confront him, confront his lies and demand that he leave at once.

"Erase the lists," she said.

"Yes, miss."

Then she told her apartment, "Project the view from the bow. Put it on my bedroom ceiling, please."

"Of course, miss."

She stepped out of the bath, lasers and exploding comets overhead. She fully expected to do what Orleans anticipated, putting her mistakes behind her. Sitting on the edge of her bed, on Perri's side, she waited for him to wake on his own. He would feel her gaze and open his eyes, seeing her framed by a Remoran sky.

She hesitated.

Taking a breath and holding it, she glanced upwards, remembering that moment on the crater's lip when she had felt a union with her body; an intoxicating sense of self. Induced by drugs and ignorance, yet it still seemed true. Here was a perception worth any cost, and she set that against Perri's imagined future, hounded by the Remoras, every human friend stripped away, the man left with no choice but the hull and his left-behind life.

She looked at him, the peaceful face stirring.

Compassion. Pity. Not love, but there was something not far from love drawing her to the fallen Remora.

"What if?" she whispered, beginning to smile.

And Perri smiled in turn, eyes closed and busy, watching some lazy dream that in an instant he would surely forget.

Bridge Four

Fourteen rocket nozzles stand high over the stern, imposing yet sleek, each nozzle the size of a small world. Eleven identical engines are fed by billions of kilometers of pipe and conduit, most of which have never been used and never will be used—back-ups to back-ups, all presumably as clean and ready as the day they were built. Every engine has nineteen gargantuan impellers ready to force compressed liquid hydrogen into the reaction chambers, though only three impellers are necessary to feed a nuclear firestorm. Again, no system exists without profound redundancies. In addition, there are tens of thousands of lesser impellers and pumps and compression valves and spindle injections serving to feed fuel and enhancements into a maelstrom which can generate energy and thrust unmatched by other ships or even by the heart of the hottest star.

Attached to the centermost engine and nozzle, one giant impeller has never been awakened yet has been used constantly since the human arrival. Bigger than most cities, the machine is filled with vacuum and motors and grand arching blades of hyperfiber, valves measured by the kilometer and control systems built to withstand radiation and time and the natural creep of unwatched atoms. Humans have studied every aspect of the impeller. The brightest, most creative engineers have measured and probed, and on the basis of numbers built models that run for aeons of simulated time. The impeller is not eternal; no device can be. But these simulations have reached out for five hundred billion years of constant work, and the machine never pauses. A thousand thousand little systems can fail, but what hasn't been used even once is nonetheless eager to run flawlessly for as long as a trillion years, shoving hydrogen into an engine that is just as durable, just as perfect, and just as puzzling as any other portion of the Great Ship.

* * *

Engineers are not spiritual or transcendent or pious or divine. Truth is composed of numbers and the relationships between those numbers and how the equations stack on top of one another and how they manage to stand apart when need be.

Engineers are the same, their flesh and mechanics and chemical fires being factors in the maintenance of the soul's essential equations.

The true engineer recognizes beauty as a dance between elegance and the worthy task.

Genius is rare, and it is laudable until it proves too clever or too proud for the task in hand, and then genius has to be set aside, or if it proves stubborn, choked to death by the strongest available means.

Engineers appreciate other engineers, regardless of species, while humans and aliens outside their ranks are regarded with skepticism, bafflement, and interlocking layers of indifference.

Without exception, engineers onboard the Great Ship train inside that one impeller. Nothing about the object is sacred and especially honored. When every ancient machine is perfect, chance determines which one is special. The premier engineering school is set beneath the impeller, which is a fine reason to make it the laboratory for high technologies utilized to their very best. Every student walks the same access tunnels. Control systems that have never throbbed with power have been mapped and modeled and redesigned ten thousand times, no ever making improvements. At the impeller's core is one periwinkle-shape blade famous for the unerring precision of its angle and the gradations within its hyperfiber. Of course every surface is resilient, but the stress-bearing spots are reinforced just enough, no farther. This is an important, even revelatory observation. The finest human engineers always overcorrect. Incans building stone walls and Incans building space elevators will brace what doesn't strictly need more bracing, if only to let themselves sleep well. But ancient temples and hundred thousand kilometer towers would stand just as well with a little less help, and materials have been wasted, and time has been wasted, and no genuinely competent engineer should ever worry about sleep.

The impeller is not a cathedral, and it isn't holy or blessed or capable of the smallest miracle.

Saying otherwise, even implying otherwise, merits scolding from teachers and demerits to the worst offenders.

The mechanism was built according to a plan, and while nobody doubts that fact, there is no useful data about the vanished builders. Without data, opinions are gusts of wind best used for other purposes.

And yet.

Every engineer student and hoary old instructor secretly feels the Builder's presence. They scale blades that have never moved, tug on nanoweave wires that haven't carried any current, and walk down throats that where not two drops of cold fuel have dribbled through, and they cannot help themselves. Say what they want, but here stands a temple to what is possible, a temple that mocks every little thing that they will accomplish, and no engineer escapes those moments and those years when she wants to drop to her knees and kiss the gray face of this wondrous perfect example of why they became engineers in the first goddamn place.

Rococo

$$1$$

Drifting in the middle of the tiny cabin, Aasleen was sleeping and then she was otherwise. The tickling tug of her nexus wished to be noticed, telling her that a message had just arrived, swaddled inside human encryptions. But opening her eyes and then her bed, she realized this wasn't the only reason she was awake. The perfect silence of space was lost, replaced by watery sounds and rhythmic vibrations. She couldn't see through the milky white cabin walls, but it was obvious that the ship beyond was reconfiguring its body, reinventing its hull and engines for the next leg of this extraordinarily painful voyage.

Warily, she unpacked the message.

Hazz appeared to her mind's eye. He was a tall, handsome captain dressed in the crisp mirrored uniform of his station. Personable and capable of great charm, he smiled at his chief engineer, saying, "About Rococo, we have news…"

A cold spike pierced Aasleen's belly.

"The Scypha have picked up his trail again." The voice was deep and slow, possessing the practiced clarity found in actors and great captains. "Six days ago, he was still hiding inside the Stone Ring but anchored to an asteroid nearly fifty million kilometers from his last known position. Nowhere close to where anyone was looking, naturally." Hazz paused. "By the way, the asteroid rides the Ring's inner edge."

The implications were obvious.

"Our hosts are certain about their verdict," said Hazz. "This isn't another false lead, or so they claim."

Hazz's face and clear voice was just the tiniest portion of a dense data rain. Most of the rain was an elaborate map that Aasleen fed to her ship's library.

"Show me," she ordered.

Her cabin was woven from dense bioglass. The glass instantly turned black, and the new map blossomed inside the walls. Stretching before her was the Stone Ring—hundreds of thousands of rough gray worlds, each tumbling along some private path, circling the cool orange sun. Two spaceships were delineated with vector lines: The human starship lay outside the Ring, while Aasleen's tiny vessel traveled above it, nine degrees over the plane of the ecliptic. Only one asteroid deserved to be circled in blue. Touching that speck of dust, a tiny portion of the map expanded, filling an entire wall. Ten kilometers across, the battered world was dotted with bubbles of green water and green air, plus one tiny fueling station tucked inside the deep polar crater. The obvious explanation was that her brother had stopped at the station, probably in a bid to steal fuel. But no, every marker drew her attention to a blunt mountain standing on the world's equator. The location was without charm or obvious significance. Why would Rococo, or anybody in his desperate state, waste two moments in that empty, exposed place?

The image shifted to a recently recorded feed. Scypha hunters were scattered across the rounded summit. The aliens didn't exist as species in any traditional sense; each individual was a unique collection of totipotent cells. But every hunter was assembled in the same basic pattern—a spherical green body cloaked in a clear nacre lifesuit, countless busy spines gripping the rocky landscape while dozens of hemispherical eyes searched for clues that the first twenty searches had missed.

The critical discovery lay at the base of the mountain. Six earth-days ago, an exhausted ship buried itself in the dusty regolith—a violent maneuver, but no more spectacular than a million other impacts among the asteroids. Then yesterday, a lone Scypha hunter noticed the fresh crater buried by a convenient landslide. On a hunch, it recruited some of the locals—lobster-like workers brandishing claws wrapped in steel and diamond teeth. Under the hunters' guidance, those workers uncovered the tangled remains of a human shuttle. But there was no trace of the hated pilot.

Examining the wreckage, Aasleen triggered a recorded response woven into her captain's transmission.

"See if you can puzzle this out," said Hazz. "Why did your brother visit this non-place?"

As an older sibling, Aasleen couldn't find any worthy answers. But as a trained engineer, the solution was obvious.

"What else has been recovered?" she asked the data rain.

There was only one item of substance. In the shadow of a room-sized boulder, somebody had hurriedly buried a hyperfiber satchel. It had ruby-rope straps that allowed it to be carried, and the main pocket was locked by several methods, including a diplomat's seal. She recognized the article immediately. For as long as she had known him, her brother had carried the satchel everywhere, his personal journal locked inside.

"I want that," she said loudly.

Then with a more careful tone, she explained why. It would take a human agent to break the seal, and its contents were possibly valuable but most likely booby-trapped. An expert in human ingenuity was essential if the security systems were to be subverted. Aasleen deserved the discovery because nobody else could hope to find and interpret whatever clues were hiding inside.

Her plea was sent to Hazz and to the Scypha hunters and to a hundred important little worlds—by agreement, every word Aasleen said to her captain was shared with their alien hosts.

There was more to see inside the data rain, but she responded first to Hazz's question. "I know why my brother was there," she said. "If he fled the Stone Ring inside that stolen shuttle, we would have spotted him. And judging by his position in the system, he probably didn't have any fuel left, much less the velocity necessary to avoid us any longer.

"So Rococo crashed at a prearranged location, then unburied himself and climbed to the summit. Alone and wearing nothing but a minimal lifesuit." The tiny world had a quick spin, its gravity falling to almost nothing along the equator. "This is a problem in mass and force," she said. "I'm sure what he wanted was to hide his shuttle before jumping into space. Any kind of rocket assist, and he might have been noticed. But his leg strength should have been adequate. I'm guessing, but leaving the satchel behind was probably a last-moment decision. For whatever reason, he wasn't convinced that he was strong enough to make it into orbit with an extra kilo or two."

She imagined her brother kneeling on summit, his face grim but determined. A little worried, perhaps, but definitely sure about his cause, whatever the crazy cause was.

"He jumped into a low orbit, but you won't find him there either." Aasleen hesitated, her belly twisting into a hard lump. "It's exactly what everybody is scared of, that the man is not working alone. What's likely is that another ship has come to play—a quick vessel we haven't been looking for. It passed by recently, and it was there for no purpose but to snatch him up."

The recorded image of the captain put on a broad smile, and the last of the data rain opened up. Suddenly the asteroid pulled back and back, revealing a great arcing swath of the Stone Ring. Then a blue line—the color of alarm among the Scypha—was laid across the grand map. The line marked the course of a single vessel. A Scypha seeder, judging by its designations and lazy motions. The seeder had been traveling slowly along the Ring's inner edge, cutting close to various asteroids, making a series of intricate maneuvers that eventually took it past Rococo's last known position. That was several days ago and nothing changed immediately. But a few thousand kilometers later, the seeder's course straightened unexpectedly, powerful engines bursting to life to shove it toward the system's largest world. Any fleshy passengers would have been crushed by the gees, but flesh heals and Rococo would have made a full recovery long before he reached his ultimate goal.

Once again, Aasleen grew aware of the vibrations extending beyond her tiny cabin. Obviously her situation changed while she slept. She asked the ship to make the walls transparent, which it did; and then she studied the machinery as it gracefully shifted positions around her—engines and fuel tanks realigning themselves, while the extra mass was being cobbled into a crude but useful heat shield. What was built to be a swift pursuit vessel able to dance among the asteroids was now being transformed into something even faster but decidedly less graceful, getting ready for the voyage's last leg.

According to the dangerous blue vector, two days ago Rococo's new ship had crashed into the system's largest world: Chaos.

For a sad, sorry moment, Aasleen imagined her brother watching the cold gray planet grow huge before him—a world built upon endless violence and relentless, unpredictable rebirth. But his smart, always confident voice interrupted her daydream, asking, "Do you really think you could have stopped me, Sister? How would you believe, knowing me as you do, that preventing any of this was remotely possible?"

2

Despite sharing parents and the same home world, Aasleen and her brother were profoundly different people. In part, it was their ages: Rococo was a thousand years younger than his big sister. In part, it was the long and very separate lives they had led. But they were poles apart mostly because they were siblings, which meant that what was the same between them wasn't half as important as the attitudes and oddities making them feel unique.

Aasleen grew up on a young, UV-blistered world on the edge of the galaxy—a harsh body that demanded nothing from its citizens but strength and pragmatic, selfless genius. Her first centuries were spent mastering the rough, reliable machinery preferred by colony worlds. Then as the colony's conditions improved—as wealth and free time gained toeholds—she earned degrees in five species of engineering. The colonists had brought every possible tool from Earth, but most of those tools existed only as impossible plans locked inside data vaults. On an alien world with its own peculiarities, people had limited resources with almost no industrial base to spare. Yet Aasleen opened the vaults and picked what she needed, adapting plans to fit local conditions. Against the responsible advice of her parents and few friends, she set to work on a continent far removed from where humans had always lived. Alone, she built a generation of high-functioning AIs, equipping them with tough bodies and relentless work ethics. Her machine army set to work, manufacturing a giant tent of nanotubes and microlasers. The fabric was transparent to most flavors of light but selectively permeable to gases. Her plan was to drape the tent over a corner of the empty continent, terraforming one broad piece of terrain. There were setbacks, naturally, and then a string of disasters that destroyed the first tent and rendered the next three useless. What succeeded was the fifth tent—a structure designed entirely by her, borrowing the shape of an earthly conk shell. Within a hundred years, the tent's internal atmosphere was free oxygen and nitrogen, carbon dioxide and water vapor. No other place on the world allowed people to walk naked beneath the blue-white sun, and nowhere else where they could enjoy deep, unfiltered breaths. Inside twenty years, most of the original colony domes had been abandoned for the new lands, and Aasleen's grand dream made every life easier and wealthier, particularly for herself.

When she was eight hundred and three years old, staggering news arrived: A human probe had discovered the Great Ship, and every local human colony was assembling scarce resources, trying to mount expeditions to reach the

Ship before any other species. With an engineer's gaze, Aasleen examined the technical problems any mission would face, including the mortal dangers, both known and probable. Then after two minutes of hard consideration, she made her decision. She would surrender her new fortune and the lands that she still owned. Then she would purchase the colony's original tug, and she and her AIs would refurbish it and then travel to a distant rendezvous point where Belters were carving up an asteroid, building one of the swiftest starships ever attempted. The plan was to offer herself and her loyal machines as trained engineers and as hundreds of willing hands; and if these captains were rational souls—a great leap of faith, that was—then Aasleen would be immediately welcomed into their grand adventure.

But her parents didn't want her to leave. They believed this mission was an idiotic business, dangerous and without gain, and they didn't wish to lose the daughter that had brought them delicious local fame. And because they were parents with a single child, they used guilt and every awful trick, shamelessly trying to make her crumble under their will.

But ninety days later and despite the heroic efforts, Aasleen proved her traitorous nature, abandoning that teary, anguished home, never to return.

Two centuries later, she and her loyal machines were serving onboard a historic starship. The retrofitted asteroid had been named for a bird of legend—Olympus Peregrine. Rough quarters were set between cavities jammed full of metallic hydrogen, the hydrogen feeding five enormous engines, each boosted by antimatter and stranglet accentors. The ship was only beginning its long, dangerous journey out of the galaxy, and in that moment of glory and great danger, a brief message arrived from home.

"Hello, darling," Aasleen's mother said with a tight, bitter voice.

Beside her sat her father, happier than he had ever looked, and with a fond hand, he was patting the back of a small, very handsome boy of perhaps ten years, or eleven.

"His name is Rococo," her mother said.

Then with a menacing smile—the kind of look that only the most determined parent achieves—she added, "We've told him about his sister, and now he knows all there is to know about you, darling."

3

By the time they slipped back inside the galaxy, Aasleen and her colleagues felt they had mastered the Great Ship's timeless machinery. Most of the cavernous chambers remained dark and empty, but configuring each volume to suit the needs of alien biology was usually a simple matter. Far, far harder was deciding which creatures to accept, and even more difficult, determining how many and for what exceptional but fair price.

This was no task for engineers.

Captains claimed the right to refuse any creature that might prove violent, toward humans or the other, more responsible passengers, but even the most arrogant officer clung to any opinion or advice that lent them some measure of confidence.

The Scypha were early conundrums.

One captain explained the situation to his chosen crew. "Scypha live in a three-sun system. Their home star is K-class, with millions of asteroids and only one substantial world. There's also an M-class sun traveling in a long elliptical orbit, plus a G-class sun that's practically next-door. It's the final sun and its jovian-class world that interest us. The world and several massive moons orbit inside its biosphere. None of those moons have significant life today, but with minimal expense, human colonists could terraform three of them."

Hazz was a pleasant, gracious and genuinely liked captain rumored to be enjoying a hard boost up to the Submaster ranks.

"Our mission," said Hazz, grinning to a small room jammed with carefully selected souls. "We will take one of our original starships to visit to the Scypha. One of the new streakships might seem more reasonable, but there are cultural/species-specific factors at work. The onboard teams will include scientists and diplomats. Scientists will have three intense years to study our gracious, perplexing hosts, and our diplomats will have the same three years to cobble together a worthwhile agreement. What we want is legal title to the jovian world and all of its moons. What we'll settle for is something less, but that's for the diplomats and Master Captain to determine. And what the Scypha want—what they have told us in our initial contacts—is to be granted their own modest habitat onboard the Great Ship."

The "original starship" was the Olympus Peregrine. No wonder Hazz was plucking Aasleen away from her routine duties, or so she assumed. Nobody knew the ship's engines better—their capacities and histories and genuine limits. In the intuitive ways of engineers and lovers, she had a natural feeling for the ship's difficult, rewarding personality.

A hand rose from the front row, and with a nod from Hazz, the first question was asked.

"What sort of species is the Scypha?"

"I could give a partial answer," Hazz said. "But instead of underscoring my limits, I'll let a better voice have this chance."

The captain glanced to his right.

A tall figure strode into the room. With a first glance, Aasleen felt an instant and deep, almost painful connection. The man shared her build and mannerisms, long in the body, with sturdy limbs and a precise, determined way of marching forward. And like Aasleen, the visitor's skin was as black as human tissue could be. But immigrants were coming from every colony world now, and plenty of them demanded protection from UV light. The coincidence was tiny. And what if their faces shared same oval form, elegant and smooth, and what if their teeth were a buttery yellow and their eyes set far apart? Maybe this fellow came from her gene pond, but even that wouldn't be much of a coincidence. By now, hundreds of the crew, if not thousands, shared that left-behind world with her.

Hazz whispered his welcome, then turning to his future crew, explained that their distinguished guest was an exobiologist as well as a member of the diplomatic corps, and his name was "Rococo", and these were his various ranks.

When Aasleen heard the name, she became deaf.

Their guest was carrying a small hyperfiber satchel. He set it down and graciously thanked the captain, and then with a bright, inescapable charm, he turned to his audience and delivered a well-rehearsed lecture about the curious origins of the Scypha, and their nature and incredible numbers and obvious potential. But Aasleen was still struggling to listen, studying records yanked through an array of nexuses, reconstructing the man's life from this moment backwards to that distant point in space and in time when their shared mother gave birth to him.

"To the Scypha," said her brother, "there is no concept called a 'species'."

What was that?

Rococo showed his audience a thousand distinct body types, each one adapted to low-gee conditions or pure free fall. Each was different from the others in highly unpredictable ways. Yet to Scypha eyes, every one of those organisms was the same. No matter its size or its architecture, they were recognized as belonging to a union, a shared and decidedly holy lineage.

"The Scypha are not one species or fifty million species," he said. "They are a distinct line of totipotent cells. Each cell is capable of living alone, subsisting on minimal food and water. But in times of wealth, those same cells will grow and divide, and thousands or trillions of them can join together, forming elaborate bodies."

He paused, staring at the wall behind his audience.

"But why take this path for life?" he asked. "Because the Scypha evolved in an extraordinary environment—a world with a special, perhaps even unique history. But when the Scypha achieved space flight, they immediately abandoned their home and colonized their system's extensive asteroid belts. This is the environment where they have prospered. Make a rough count of the sentient cellular conglomerates, and their total population stands in excess of one and a half trillion bodies."

Selected images were fed into Aasleen's nexuses. Comets in the far flung Ice Ring were wrapped in monomolecular bags and lit up with hot fusion torches. Silica-rich asteroids in the Stone Ring were turned to slag and pulled into elaborate shells, transparent and filled with warm, bright air. Orbiting beside the orange-white K-class sun was a dense belt of iron-rich bolides, unpopulated but actively mined for their precious ores. And between the Iron Ring and Stone Ring was an empty zone where a single moonless world moved in a circular orbit. With half the mass of the Earth, the rocky gray sphere sat inside a deep dirty atmosphere, under which lay shallow seas and silted lakes and great ringed basins, as well as hundreds of sharp, relatively small craters formed over the last million years.

"This is the Scyphas' birthplace," said Rococo. Then with a broad, intense smile, he added, "Calculate the odds and marvel: Multicellular life should never evolve on such a body, in a solar system as dangerous as this. And not only did life emerge in this unlikely womb, but it is still alive. It can even thrive on occasion. And that despite the certainty that every few thousand years, on average, some fat bolide kicked out from the Rings ends up impacting here—blistering, apocalyptic events on par with those that killed the dinosaurs, and before that, obliterated all of the multicellular creatures on ancient Mars."

The declaration earned prolonged silence.

Then one hand rose. It was a broad black hand, strong and wearing on its fingertips the hard callus presently fashionable among engineers—as if the hand had been toughened up by genuine physical labor.

Rococo nodded. "Yes, Aasleen."

She stood. Her intention was to greet her brother. She had planned every word, ready to say, "Welcome, and I didn't know you were onboard, and by the way, how are our dear distant parents?" In a very public way, she wanted to define their relationship: The siblings were far from close. Everyone needed to know that her brother had joined the crew in secret, never mentioning his presence to his respectable sister. Of course this was an enormous vessel, and they had very different duties, but it seemed important for her to paint the young brother as being less than polite.

Yet when Aasleen spoke, unexpected words ran from her mouth.

"Do the Scypha today live on their home world?"

"No," Rococo said, the grin turning wary but his eyes smiling.

"Yet they definitely came from there."

He nodded. "About half a million years ago was a period—a unique period—of fifty or sixty thousand years. There were no major impacts, just a few showers of two and three kilometer asteroids. In other words, their home world was given a window of peace. And the Scypha lineage prospered well enough to develop basic spaceship technologies."

Aasleen studied images of that left-behind world. It appeared cold now, which was only reasonable. The world orbited its sun at an earthly distance, but its sun was notably weaker than Sol. Her terraforming skills allowed her to build a simple mental model of climate, and she realized that without constant impacts—the steady and reliable battering of two and ten and forty kilometer bolides—that little world would soon fall into a deep, impoverishing ice age.

"That world's name," she began.

"Yes," he said expectantly.

"Wait," she said, interrupting herself. "First of all, are there other lineages? And if so, do they still live on the home world?"

Rococo couldn't have looked happier. "There is evidence of at least six hundred distinct lines of totipotent cells," he said. "From that menagerie, only the Scypha climbed into space."

"And did all of the Scypha emigrate?"

The smile tightened, just a little. It was an expression Aasleen knew well, since it came across her face whenever she found herself in uncomfortable corners, unable to say everything that was in her mind.

What Rococo did say was, "Our alien hosts are presently extinct on their home world."

She started to nod.

"Chaos," he said.

"Pardon me?"

"You were going to ask for the name of their birthplace. When translated, using our best tools, their language boils down to the word 'Chaos.'"

She squinted, considering the news.

"Chaos means danger to the Scypha. It refers to disasters that arrive from the unexpected avenues."

Humans nodded, pretending they understood the alien minds.

"The home world is being held in quarantine," Rococo said. "The Scypha want nothing to do with it, nothing at all. And that has been the situation for the last several hundred thousand years."

Aasleen was honestly confused. "Why?"

Her brother offered no simple answer. He made a show of shrugging his shoulders, reminding the entire audience, "We'll have three years to decipher meanings and reach our best judgments. Will the Scypha make good passengers? And will they pay a reasonable fee for the privilege?" Again, he shrugged. "Speaking as an exobiologist, I want everyone too scared to make premature guesses or biasing notions."

"That sounds very diplomatic," Aasleen said softly.

Rococo chuckled with a diplomat's grace. Then he threw a knowing wink in her direction, saying, "The politics of a family can be very difficult."

Aasleen laughed loudly and said, "No."

"You don't think so?"

"Families are simple," she said. "Just so long as they aren't your own family, that is."

4

The Scypha built spaceships much as they built themselves: Mechanical embryos were generated, each containing the guiding principles used by every ship in their enormous fleet. But the growth of each vessel was a nonlinear, wildly unpredictable business. A hundred identical embryos could be instructed to form slow freighters of a specific size, yet no two vessels ended up with identical schematics. To the human engineer, that system was no system, and the results were both astonishing and terrifying. Aasleen would be the first to admit that Scypha machinery was adaptive, tough and reasonably efficient. If necessary, their vessels could heal most damage with the resources on hand, and should one of their freighters need to update its shape and job, the transformation took remarkably little time. But no pair of freighters could reliably exchange components. Hull shapes and engine designs were full of quirks and one-of-a-kind features. And mistakes were inevitable—catastrophic failures in design waiting for that ripe wrong moment to arrive—and that was a grim possibility that Aasleen could never, ever accept.

On the other hand, human ships were standardized and tenaciously, even dangerously reliable.

Rococo had no expertise as an engineer or pilot. Yet he had been able to learn enough about human-built shuttles to steal one of them, and without much trouble, he crippled the three sister shuttles remaining behind in the Peregrine's dock.

"How long for repairs," Hazz had asked.

"Twenty-three hours," was Aasleen's best guess. "That's for bringing all three ships back on line and refueling them, and that's assuming our colleague didn't sabotage their AI managers, too. Because if that's the case, it's going to take time to discover where and how, and then it could be three days, or four, until we can launch even one shuttle."

A captain's poise obscured what had to be a terrible rage. Hazz nodded and said nothing, considering the situation.

It was the chief diplomat who couldn't contain her emotions. "Your brother," she said, the two words sounding like the most terrible curse. "Where is he going? What in hell is he planning?" A young-faced woman named Krill, she appeared to be little more than a child, yet she was older than anyone else present. Thousands of careful years had been invested in a career that looked ready to shatter. "If we can't catch your brother soon, then we'll have to tell the Scypha and let them corral him for us."

"If they can manage that," Aasleen said.

Krill grimaced and looked at their captain.

Hazz understood the situation clearly. But he thought it best to let Aasleen explain.

"Your subordinate," she began, staring at the diplomat's smoke-colored eyes. "You're your diplomat just took our best shuttle. It is exactly the same as these other three, except it has a secondary hull that can be reconfigured. I designed that hull, under direct orders from you, madam. We were planning for contingencies, and you suggested that we have at least one shuttle that could look rather like a Scypha ship. 'Just in case,' you said. Madam. 'In case our hosts aren't as friendly or forthcoming as they should be. It would help if we could move among them, unseen.'"

The blood drained from the young face. Then a sorry old voice dribbled out. "Now I really don't want to tell the Scypha."

"Are there choices?" Aasleen asked.

"None," Hazz said. Then with a crisp voice, he instructed the ranking diplomat, "Confess everything we know, and everything we can reasonably guess. No secrets here. Do you understand me? But make certain our man wears the majority of the blame."

* * *

For twenty-three hours, Aasleen went about her business, overseeing repairs and managing one delicious fifteen-minute nap. She also listened to every rumor and examined the official updates for anything that might prove enlightening, and several times, she caught glimpses of the resident Scyphas. For nearly a year now, an alien delegation had been living onboard the Olympus Peregrine. They were high-ranking members of a government council that seemed to wield considerable power. For reasons of civility or simple functionality, they had grown bodies not unlike the human form—bipeds with single heads and single mouths, a pair of hemispherical eyes made from calcite crystals. They usually kept to their own little portion of the ship, which made it unnerving to see them drifting through the dock, one by one, glassy eyes staring at the broken shuttles and the AIs that were repairing them, and in particular, studying the chief engineer who was trying to do her job while ignoring all the damned rumors and briefings and official declarations that kept finding their way to her.

In the end, it was determined that Rococo hadn't damaged the AI managers. But that didn't particularly matter. With a full day's jump on ships that were no faster than his, he had already won every likely race.

Other answers were needed. Aasleen was working on contingencies when Hazz called her to his quarters. By then the rumors were running in the same direction, but she ignored them. Aasleen entered the captain's meeting room with three different plans ready to offer. Even when she saw the entire Scypha delegation drifting around the central table, she refused to accept the obvious explanation. Through a nexus, she fed her captain the latest update of the repairs. Then she told him and Krill, "I think we can see through his camouflage. And if we find him, we'll use our own com-laser to cripple his shuttle, neat and easy."

Hazz thanked her on a private nexus. But the latest stories proved generally correct. Speaking for humanity and the aliens, Krill said, "Everyone is outraged by what your brother has done," she told Aasleen. "We are outraged and appalled. Stealing the shuttle is a minor evil. The Scypha believe, and now we concur, that Rococo has been in secret contact with one or more of the nonScypha lineages. For what purpose, we do not yet know. But he has acted against every order that I have given and every code that our captain has set down as law. And since he is ours—a body that belongs to our great lineage—we must send one of our own into the hunt. Because, as our hosts make plain, that is what justice demands."

Aasleen glanced at the bright-eyed aliens, then at Hazz.

Her captain spoke. "I've considered every crew member for this assignment. We've had a few volunteers drift forward, which has been gratifying, but there isn't much doubt about who is the best qualified. Is there, Aasleen?"

Shaking her head, she admitted, "No, there probably isn't."

Then she mentioned the most obvious difficulty. "But that leaves the problem of finding a suitable ship for me, since we don't seem to have any craft that can actually catch him."

A new voice emerged, a little too loud, utterly precise. "A fully-loaded deuterium freighter is soon to pass. Within a thousand kilometers of this place, it will pass." The speaker was a smallish biped with a yellowish-green skin. Regardless of their body form, the Scypha retained a photosynthetic surface. It was a tradition and a consequence of their complex genetics: Under the proper circumstances, any one of these creatures could collapse into a trillion cells, and from those anonymous pieces, an entire jungle of plant-like organisms would spring forth.

"The freighter is changing its nature now," the Scypha promised. "The ion-drive is being replaced by three fusion engines, and its body is creating a small but comfortable cabin for its guest. For you."

"Am I the pilot?" she asked.

"No," Hazz replied, fully expecting that question.

Then the human diplomat pointed a stiff finger at Aasleen. "You'll go where you need to go, particularly if your brother manages to reach places where our good hosts cannot intrude."

Chaos was the implication.

"But about my brother," Aasleen began. Then she hesitated, wondering if she should risk offering her thoughts.

"A creature of your blood," said the ranking Scypha.

"Except I don't know my blood particularly well," Aasleen said. And just to be certain that everyone understood, she quickly explained the histories of their unshared lives.

"But he is of your immediate line," the creature insisted. Then the alien mouth attempted a smile, and it said to her and to every human, "You know him exceptionally well, or you know nothing at all."

* * *

Aasleen made herself ready for the mission, packing a few belongings in a field kit while studying grim orders in detail. As soon as she was ready, she would ride one of the newly repaired shuttles out to an empty point in space where it would rendezvous with the promised freighter/hunter ship. The last word was that Rococo had vanished completely. But now the Scypha were actively searching for him, using tricks that Aasleen had surrendered willingly, and there was no way that he could remain hidden much longer.

Only an idiot would believe he could escape this sort of attention.

But Rococo was not an idiot, which led her mind to travel in new, equally painful courses.

Obviously, the charmer had more tricks waiting.

"And I'll have to be ready for them," she muttered to herself, leaving her quarters with her kit in tow.

A single Scypha was drifting in the wide hallway outside her door. It was wearing a loose-fitting gown and gecko shoes and the same yellow-green flesh that all of them cherished. But it was definitely not the delegate that had spoken at the meeting. Its voice was identical, but the body had more height and many more ribs, and the arms had extra joints for no sensible reason.

That familiar voice said, "Listen to me."

Aasleen touched the floor with her own shoes, killing her momentum.

"About us, what you know is not enough."

She couldn't agree more. "I'm a tool-bearing tool. Most my friends are machines. Even human beings are usually too complicated for me."

But that wasn't apparently the creature's point. Its face was twisted around a squarish skull and the lidless calcite eyes absorbed every photon, giving it the nearly perfect vision that the Earth surrendered when the trilobites went extinct. After a long, thoughtful silence, it asked Aasleen, "Which is more problematic, the shape of the body or the shape of the mind?"

She hesitated.

"If I look like no one else, how can one trillion minds think the same ways as any single mind does?"

And then that very peculiar creature turned its back on her, and on gecko toes, practically ran away.

5

The engines were firing again, this time killing some portion of their terrific momentum. Aasleen was strapped into her crash chair, a thousand invisible hands pressing down. On her orders, the bioglass walls had been left as transparent as gin, and when she wasn't studying the Scypha and their long history, she gazed out at the graceless, doomed ship. Its fuel tanks were black cylinders mostly drained of their precious deuterium, and strung between them was a maze of pipes and pumps constructed from diamond and other soft materials. Three reaction chambers were woven from a low-grade hyperfiber, each chamber barely restraining the tiny sun burning inside. The newly constructed heat shield was vast and insubstantial—a stubborn cloud of carbon soot braced with nanowhiskers. Staring beyond the engines, Aasleen searched for Chaos, but the world was still hiding beyond the plasma plumes. Only between the black fuel tanks could she make out the blackness of empty space. Periodically the Scypha sun would peek in at her, filling the cabin with a blinding light, and sometimes she would see its sister star and the lone silver speck beside it—the giant jovian world maintaining a loyal distance. And the Ice Ring was always visible somewhere, appearing as smoky bands of glowing greenish haze. Millions of tiny worlds were moving, rich with life, linked to each other by com-lasers and trade lanes, by leaked air and lost water, by culture and eternal genetics. For tens of thousands of years, the Scypha had ruled a gigantic realm. Yet they never built any kind of starship or sent even one asteroid drifting off into the interstellar wilderness. And there was absolutely no evidence that they ever, even on the tiniest scale, attempted to colonize the jovian's empty moons.

At least two ships were on a rendezvous course with Aasleen. One of the human shuttles had been given permission to slowly approach Chaos, while a swift Scypha drone was charging straight toward her, nothing onboard but Rococo's left-behind satchel.

If she had the satchel in her hands now, she could crack its seals and study its contents, and more important, that conundrum would give her the excuse to do something other than other people's nonsense and conjecture.

But there were no excuses. With one nexus, Aasleen reached deep into her data vault, picking random studies and learned papers, teaching herself a little more about the Scyphas and their home world. Yet experts were far from perfect. Even the exobiologists agreed on little but their own ignorance.

And despite weeks of reading and contemplation, Aasleen was still barely a novice who could follow maybe half of any text, asking little questions when they occurred to her—clumsy questions answered easily by the vault's AI, or countered with a simple, "That is not known," response.

She was misreading an account about Scypha politics when Hazz appeared to her mind's eye.

"It's almost certain now," the message began. "The ship that grabbed up Rococo has been traced back to the Iron Ring. That's where it first appeared. It was pretending to be a drone bringing up a load of refined metals. It didn't change its shape or programming until he had crash-landed on the asteroid. A few hours ago that new ship touched down on Chaos. On the eastern shore of the central ocean, we're sure. Our telescopes saw it smack into the atmosphere, and our hosts are reporting the same observation." He paused for a moment. "But I don't need to remind you that our esteemed colleague might not have been onboard."

Inside a hyperfiber lifesuit, the human body could drop almost anywhere and recover. Its descent would look like a meteorite, and since thousands of little impacts occurred every minute, there was no way to be certain about Rococo's destination.

"But at least you can pick up a trail there," Hazz continued. "Follow him as best you can. Our hosts have assured us that all of the local lineages will be helpful. Or at least, they will not get in your way."

She sighed, barely relieved.

"And maybe there's some more luck coming," Hazz said. "As it happens, the dominant local lineage is an ally to the Scypha. At least as much of an ally as you're going to find…"

The man's face said more than any words. Hazz looked worried, suspicious and only grudgingly hopeful. It was an expression that an alien probably couldn't read—even if the encryptions and other seals were broken.

"The Dun," he said.

A thousand entries in her data vault began to glow with a soft pink light.

"They're closely related to the Scypha lineage. At least that's what our biologists claim."

Hazz paused once again, pretending to gather his thoughts. But he knew exactly what he wanted to say. Quietly, with genuine warmth, he told Aasleen, "I am sorry. If I could have found a better candidate, you would have stayed here with me. This isn't your profession, and these are awful circumstances, and I won't remind you again about the time factors involved."

Successful or otherwise, their mission had to end in just a few weeks. Otherwise it would be difficult for their starship, even with healthy engines and full tanks of metallic hydrogen, to catch up to the Great Ship.

Hazz shook his head angrily. "It does seem obvious. For whatever reason, Rococo is trying to ruin everything."

Aasleen nodded.

Hazz pushed a hand through his kinky hair. "This isn't your normal work, but this isn't a job for diplomats. Or biologists. Or anyone else who happens to be under my command."

In reflex, Aasleen reached along her nexus, taking another quick inventory of the traveling kit lying beneath her crash chair.

"None of this is fair," said Hazz. "But Rococo has entered a place where he isn't allowed, and you're the best hope we have to solve this ugly conundrum."

The kit was filled with exactly the types of devices that a talented engineer would want in reach, including a powerful plasma torch that could chisel through hyperfiber, or if necessary, boil the brains of one lucky man.

"Good hunting," the captain said to his assassin.

Then he vanished, and Aasleen purged the message while leaving the Dun files highlighted. And again, she began skimming random texts, reading those parts that seemed most important, asking questions when they occurred to her, and swallowing every urge to scream or sob, or worse of all, just give up the fight and fall back to sleep.

6

The experts that hatched this mission had been of one mind: Olympus Peregrine—the retrofitted asteroid that helped carry the first humans to the Great Ship—would astonish their primitive hosts. The Scypha often rebuilt bolides, some even larger than the Peregrine. But their work was primitive by every standard, including mass-drivers and crude fusion engines that could barely nudge the little worlds into new orbits. The aliens didn't possess high-grade hyperfiber, nor did they know any of the big cheats necessary to build a functional star-drive. Even as an elderly machine, the Peregrine possessed its burnished beauty, and it didn't hurt that the enduring symbol of everything good and noble about human achievement was built inside a common piece of stone.

But Aasleen didn't share the optimism. With a rather different estimate of her aging starship, she knew that good fortune was at least as important as good engineering when the Peregrine made its famous journey out to the Great Ship. Yes, the tiny voyage to the Scypha consumed only sixty years, but for the chief engineer, this mission felt like one intense, unbroken day jammed with work and major crises, plus three genuine disasters involving the ship's increasingly problematic engines.

To reach the goal, the Peregrine needed to race ahead of the Great Ship while dropping through the plane of the Milky Way. Making this possible meant pushing hard enough so they could afford to slow down again, lingering in one location for three lazy years. And assuming that humans and the Scypha achieved some workable understanding, then the Peregrine wouldn't just have to make the return voyage, but it would also have to bring home a few thousand adults—enough bodies and grown minds to build a functional colony somewhere onboard the Great Ship.

But return voyages weren't guaranteed. While still inbound, Aasleen met with Hazz and his immediate staff, showing them projections and models, hard numbers and soft gloomy numbers. Then as a final touch, she set a worn valve-fiber in front of her captain. It had been poured from what was once the finest hyperfiber made by humans, but that was thousands of years ago. The telltale darkening was obvious, revealing fractures deep inside the normally invincible material. Pointblank, she explained that only two of their main engines were reliable. What's more, the trustworthy two were divided among the five present engines. "In other words, I'm going to cannibalize all five just

225

to make a good pair, which leaves me needing to build three new engines just to give us a ninety percent chance of returning home."

Hazz's face grew soft and sorry. "What exactly are you proposing?"

She explained. The challenge wasn't a surprise, and her solutions shouldn't have been either. But it took Hazz half an hour to study the concepts, and several more hours to embrace what she wanted to do with their museum-worthy machine. A complete renovation of the starship was called for. Hyperfiber factories and fresh reactors would have to be built wherever there was room, and work had to be accomplished on the proverbial fly, using the inadequate tools on hand. Boast all they wanted about human genius, but the grim, inglorious truth was that their species was close to drowning.

Aasleen rarely saw her brother during those next months and years. But it seemed as if every twenty-four hours, she would talk to a person or two who mentioned Rococo. The diplomat/exobiologist often gave briefings to the crew, and he ate frequently with Hazz; and most likely, the affable fellow would pass someone in a hallway, and just to be pleasant, he would strike up a brief but undeniably memorable conversation.

Unlike his sister, Rococo was an intensely social organism, and better than most, he had the gift. Bring up his name, and faces would smile. Ask why, and the most retiring engineer or simplest AI-worker would replay a conversation word for word, catching some joy that nobody else could see. Of course nothing important was ever said. Aasleen noted that Rococo could speak buoyantly about the shallowest subjects. He was amusing at times but never more than that. And he told a good story, but not a great one. Yet her brother had some kind of chokehold on the hundreds of people they were traveling with—people she knew by name and face, some counted among her friends. But none of those people were so thrilled by her attentions that they would run to her brother, stopping him in the middle of his important work, distracting him by saying, "Oh, I saw your sister today. What a fun, good person Aasleen is!"

Rococo was fun, and he was good. He was also exceptionally skilled at managing his sister's emotions—knowing how often to meet with her, and for how long, and somehow finding the sweetest way to orchestrate the event so that both of them felt as close to comfortable as possible.

Wisely, Rococo never brought up their parents or the distant home world. That duty was left in Aasleen's lap.

And when she asked about his childhood—how could she not?—the man sitting before her always put on a careful face, measuring his words and muting their tone before offering the narrowest response.

The world Aasleen remembered was gone; Rococo described a planet transformed by human hands. Her gossamer smart-tent proved to be just a brief step on the way to larger adventures. By the time he emigrated, the entire atmosphere was fully oxygenated, the continents covered with soil made from comet crusts and ocean muck, and the latest crop of engineers were busily draping a tough monomolecular curtain over the entire world—a much larger version of Aasleen's tent, its central purpose filtering out the blistering UV light.

Aasleen was disappointed, and she didn't mind saying so.

"We weren't born on the Earth," she said. "And we always had the means on hand to adapt to these hazards. UV is something we can easily tolerate."

"That's absolutely true," he said without hesitation.

"And our engineered flora and fauna were going to depend on the hard radiation, that rich free abundant energy bolstering the biosphere's productivity." She looked at her hands, ancient feelings emerging. "We agreed. Before I left, votes were taken, and the colonists decided to let the planet stay as alien as possible…to force us to meet it at some good and worthy middle point."

Her brother nodded amiably, his face sharing her disgust. But later, replaying the conversation, she noticed that Rococo avoided the opportunity to come out and say, "Yes, you are right, sister. I'm on your side here."

Because he didn't agree with her, she realized. Nor did he agree with the vote, either.

"What about my tent?" she asked.

His eyes widened while his mouth pulled into a small knot.

"Is anything left of it?"

Rococo shook his head. Then with another expression of diplomatic disgust, he admitted, "The entire structure was dismantled for scrap."

Aasleen wasn't vain by nature. But this was a pivotal event in her life, which was why she asked, "Yes, but is there some little statue, maybe? Is there a monument or plaque, just to let people know?"

"People know," he said. "It's part of our history."

"History," she echoed. Then with a scorn that took both of them by surprise, she said, "I was hoping for a little more than some cryptic notes in a dusty historical file…as forgotten as everything else…"

Rococo was charming and soothing, and in ways few souls could match, he could deftly step into difficult circumstances, creating a false but welcome peace. But he had an even more unusual gift: With his sister and perhaps other difficult souls, he knew that it was best sometimes not to attempt peace. These were very old feelings for Aasleen's, making them exceptionally stubborn. And even at their worst, the feelings were harmless, and by their nature silly, and if he let her spout on, they quickly lost their teeth and fury.

The siblings' last social engagement was a late night meal for the entire crew. The Peregrine was halfway rebuilt, the most difficult jobs already completed. By chance or by someone else's planning, Aasleen was sitting next to her brother, sharing the back corner of the ship's largest galley. His journal was beside him—a portable slab of plastic encased in a diamond sleeve. He never touched it, but he didn't put it inside the satchel, either. Much later, replaying the moment, Aasleen could appreciate how her little brother had played her. Very softly, he mentioned receiving a note from their mother. The woman was constantly sending digitals and little messages to her much-loved son, and that unfailingly bothered Aasleen. She bristled at the news. As he knew she would, she began to offer disparaging words about being dead to her home world. But this time, for the first time, Rococo interrupted the pity-play. "But you are doing enormous work now," he said with feeling. "These things you're involved in…these are adventures far more important than terraforming an obscure colony world. For instance, the future history of an entire species is being determined here. And you, Aasleen…you are playing a pivotal role in the drama…"

She saw the mistake. But instead of correcting him, she shrugged and stabbed her grilled eland.

"You know," Rococo said. Then he fell silent.

"What do I know?"

Throwing a wink at her, he warned, "I won't be here much longer. The diplomatic corps will come and go as necessary. But until our last couple months, I plan to live among the Scypha. Full-time, on various worlds."

The wall beside them wore images harvested from the approaching solar system. The Rings were highlighted, the largest and most important asteroids glowing green. She glanced at them and the simple gray speck that was Chaos. Nodding, she asked, "Are you giving tonight's briefing?"

That was the reason for this gathering. All but a skeleton staff was sitting in the galley, waiting to hear the latest news about their mission.

"I'll generate a few words," Rococo said.

"Because I can't stay," she admitted. "I've got a rocket nozzle to inspect. And there's a diagnostic that's turning up new problems."

"Are we in trouble?"

"No worse than usual." She set down her knives and dabbed her lips with a piece of sticky ice. "It's just that we're going to being asking a lot out of engines that are either well past their prime or too new to trust…"

Her voice trailed away.

Rococo nodded with compassion, as if her burdens were riding his shoulders too. Then he touched the wall—touched it low and brought up the menu—and without a word of explanation, he asked for an image of Chaos.

Aasleen was thinking about slipping away. Had she shown her face long enough? Would Hazz or his staff put a black mark on her record? Then a flash struck the corner of her eye—a soundless, brilliant, and enduring light—and she turned in time to watch a blister of plasma rising from the shore of an alien sea.

The image was ancient, or it was invented. Either way, she was witnessing an event that had happened perhaps a billion times in the past. An asteroid or lost comet had plunged onto that battered world, vaporizing the entire sea and melting a portion of the crust, producing shockwaves that burned up every organic body that happened to be trapped on the surface.

Four billion years ago, this was the Earth.

She and her brother had spoken about this many times. Or rather, Rococo had made the noise, and she had listened, interested in what he was saying even when she already knew the details.

Nobody knew for sure how many times life evolved on the Earth.

But in the early eons, when hundred-kilometer bolides were falling like rain, the ancient ocean was repeatedly boiled off and the crust turned to magma, and even the toughest little bugs were killed. Only later, when nothing bigger than fifty kilometers was crashing down, life survived, if barely. Microbes found places to survive—usually in porous rock deep underground. The best guess was that by the bombardment's end, a single line of *Archaea*—the thermophilic bacteria—had endured the worst abuse, and that plucky survivor was grandmother to every crawling, talking organic beast that managed to spring up on their cradle world.

But the bombardment had never ceased on Chaos.

Grind up an earthly sponge into mush, and the individual cells would gradually migrate back together again, slowly forming another adult organism.

On a much grander scale, Chaos took that course. Many lines of life developed during its early history, and most of them evolved multicellular forms. But there were critical differences in their genetics and physiology as well as the makeup of individual cells. Far tougher than Precambrian worms, each of those early lineages left behind spores that would wait for the heat and fire to fade away. Then they would come alive again, growing in the wreckage and the warm springs. Eventually those tiny children would come together, killing and eating those that didn't belong to their lineage, while joining with the cells that did. Inside each viable nucleus was enough genetic information to put together a wide array of body plans. Usually the creatures were photosynthetic, and occasionally they looked like clumsy animals. Successful lineages left the most spores. And since there was no way to know when the next asteroid would fall, or where, natural selection continued to move in a most jerky, gloriously unpredictable fashion.

Watching Chaos endure the gigantic blast, Aasleen asked, "Is this what I'm going to miss? Are you briefing us about old history?"

Rococo shook his head. "No, not at all."

"Then why show this to me?"

"Because I think it is interesting," he allowed. "Of all the places I'm going to visit, all the wondrous sights I'll witness…there's no way for me to embrace the most interesting and important world of all."

Of course he couldn't visit Chaos. That cradle world was under a strict quarantine, and Aasleen could appreciate their hosts' reasons: Each lineage was embroiled in a constant against every other lineage. This was not war. This was older and much vaster than any battle of armies, and there was no chance of lasting forgiveness. The Scypha had been lucky to escape their home world, and it was only natural for them to keep their enemies out of reach.

But the muddy alien politics didn't interest her. Rococo mentioned his fascination with Chaos, and Aasleen nodded agreeably, thinking nothing more about it. Then after making her own assessment of human politics, she saw the opportunity to float away.

But Rococo put his hand on top of hers, the gesture not quite gentle. "You were right, you know."

"What was I right about?"

"Families," he said. "When you belong to a family, everything can seem like a spectacular mess."

She couldn't agree more.

"But when you stand apart, immune to personal histories and private passions…well, what matters most is perfectly easy to see…"

She hesitated.

Then quietly, she said, "Species."

"What's that?"

"When you were talking before, you mentioned that I was helping with something big, something that would determine a species' future." Shaking a callused finger, she reminded him, "Scypha do not exist as species. Not so we would recognize them, at least."

Rococo nodded, smiled.

Then he bent close and kissed his sister lightly on the cheek—he had never kissed her before, in any fashion—and into her ear, he whispered, "But Aasleen, I wasn't thinking about the Scypha."

7

For three years, the gray face of the world was simple and unlovely—a bland fleck of light not worth a bare-eyed glance. But as Aasleen plunged toward that face, the world became huge, revealing a multitude of complications as well as a dirty, unpolished brand of beauty. Two seas rode the visible hemisphere—shallow round bodies of muddy water straddling the dawn line, the southern sea wearing a stubborn patch of early summer pack ice. The cold flat desert between was home to a dust storm, ruddy and fragile, working its way to the east. Elsewhere volcanoes stood alone, dormant and possibly dead, young glaciers flowing from their summits, grinding rock into fresh eager dust. Peel away the world's dust and a landscape of overlapping pocks and blisters would be revealed—the cumulative damage wrought by six billion years of tireless abuse. Like a plow turning soil, the impacts had shattered the crust down to the mantle. Without enough internal heat to generate tectonics, Chaos depended on those good hard blows. Ten million years ago, a massive carbonaceous asteroid had blasted out a basin stretching most of a thousand kilometers across. The molten plain spouted fire and red-hot projectiles big as mountains. Portions of the atmosphere and crust were thrown into space, and every sea boiled away and then fell again as a scalding rain. But after the rain cleared and the rock froze, warm water collected inside the newborn crater, and life prospered in what was a sudden tropical climate, there and everywhere on Chaos. Dry ice and water ice and fossil methane had been kicked loose from the regolith, producing a sultry wet heat that was maintained by a gracious string of lesser impacts—the beginnings of a persistent, much-treasured golden age that lasted, without serious pause, until a just few geologic moments ago.

The heat shield was positioned for impact; Aasleen couldn't see the world with her own eyes. A live, unmagnified feed revealed patches and twists of color emerging slowly from the endless gray. From a thousand kilometers overhead, she could make out slivers of gold and violet, watery blue splotches and green dots in several distinct shades. Each color stood alone. Sun-facing slopes were popular, as were the rare river valleys. One giant shield volcano wore perhaps three-dozen oases—tiny, wholly unique communities huddled around hot springs or their tepid, fondly recalled remnants. And along the sunny shore of the largest sea, at the end of the line she was following, ran a ribbon of pale yellow-green larger any other living zone, yet encompassing barely fifty thousand square kilometers.

The Dun.

Strewn among Aasleen's scholarly references was every lecture delivered by her brother. Over the last several hours, she had studied any portion pertaining even slightly to that one patch of shoreline. No other lineage on Chaos was as closely related to the Scypha. The fission came after the massive impact that brought on the golden age: Two isolated populations emerging on opposite sides of the world, each quickly dominating its own hemisphere. Even today, the Dun remained the dominant force on the home world. They had a functioning, marginally vigorous biosphere. They wielded nuclear power and irrigation and other high technologies. And no other lineage could even pretend to build spaceships, which was perhaps why Rococo had invested the breath and time on the ill-understood entities.

Aasleen didn't attend her brother's longest, best lecture, but she watched one moment at least ten times. A crewmember lifted a hand and then stood before making his point. "I don't understand," he said. "One lineage succeeds masterfully while its sibling accomplishes what? Very little, from what I can tell. I mean, I'm sure that the Dun are comfortable on that beach. But what makes them so different from the Scypha?"

Rococo nodded patiently, throwing his warmest smile out at everyone. Then with the nicest possible voice, he told the fellow, "No, you don't understand the situation at all."

The slight had been delivered with a diplomat's soothing voice.

The man slouched and agreed. "I guess I don't understand. I'm sorry if I missed something obvious."

"Try and think of it this way." Rococo winked slyly. "You're assuming there was some pre-Scypha, pre-Dun lineage. You imagine a shared ancestor dividing into two equal parts. But this isn't at all like evolution on the Earth, sir. These lineages haven't split into two streams. No, one of them has remained true to its ancestral beginnings, while the other is the upstart—more the bastard child than an equal sibling."

The galley was full of thoughtful, mystified faces.

"Which lineage is which?" the lecturer asked. Then with a bright grin, he answered his question with more questions. "Which one lives exactly as it always lived? And which one has completely and forever walked away from home?"

* * *

Two hundred kilometers above Chaos—at long last—a slight impact jostled Aasleen. The swift little drone that chased her across the solar system had just arrived, making a rough docking with her ship.

The cabin's hatch opened with a tiny wind pushing an envelope of pure, high-grade hyperfiber toward her. Grabbing one of the ruby-rope straps, she pulled the satchel close. Its various locks remained intact. The diplomatic seal was undisturbed. If anyone had tinkered with the mechanisms, she would see it now. But nobody had. Like a birthday girl, she shook the satchel side to side, one object rattling. She couldn't imagine anything but Rococo's journal, abandoned because of its mass. Or if her brother had anticipated this moment, maybe he left it behind for his sister to keep safe.

There was no time to break the seal. Aasleen stowed the satchel, focusing again on the world below. Only a sprinkling of young impact craters stared back at her. Dust and cold water ruled, and Rococo had repeatedly lectured about that detail: Aeons ago, once the Scypha had populated the various asteroid belts, they learned how to predict the endless motions of every substantial bolide. Little nudges and the occasional hard shove were what kept those little worlds from in place. Collisions between the asteroids had fallen to nothing, and nothing substantial wandered free of the Rings, and with that triumph, the home world was suffering quietly, growing colder and drier, every failed lineage collapsing back into oases that might live for another thousand years, or even another twenty million. But the inevitable was approaching. The gray world would become gray at every distance, and a traveler would see nothing alive, even as her ship began to slam into the first high whiffs of atmosphere.

8

Machines rose up to meet the falling machine.

Tiny, erosive devices, they struck the charred heat shield, burrowing into seams and points of weakness. Hard pops were felt more than heard, shaped explosions creating surgical gashes that swiftly peeled off the shield. Then a second wave of machines peppered the hull itself. Aasleen had just enough time to unfasten her straps and kick free of the crash chair, holding Rococo's satchel close to her stomach, her kit on her back. The Scypha ship was being dismantled around her, and now a third wave of machines—larger, more sophisticated models—grabbed each sliver and disabled component, measuring its composition before using acids and blistering heat to tear into everything. This was the antithesis of engineering, taking a sophisticated device and creating in its stead something utterly simple, fundamental and pure.

The bioglass cabin was the final target. It shattered along a hundred lines, and Aasleen found herself surrounded by cold thin air, spinning heels over head through a rain of elemental particles.

After a few wild turns, she managed to clear the debris field.

Holding her tuck, she let her body settle on a point of balance. Her head was leading the way. With deep painful gasps, she clung to consciousness, and after another minute the air thickened at least to where it wasn't a miserable struggle to keep her mind clear.

The yellowish-green land was forest, low and dense, every tree sporting one or two or three trunks and a tangle of branches. Wide blackish blocks of glass were scattered about the terrain—windowless structures that might or might not have been buildings, arranged without any obvious pattern. Curved spines of transparent glass rose up into the bright dusty sky, and the spines were moving, she realized. Like fingers possessing an infinite number of joints, they curled and reached, their tips diving into the canopy, grabbing up whatever was worth claiming from the treetops: Sweet foods grown to feed the animal bodies, perhaps. Perhaps.

Every living cell was a Dun. The individual tree was just one of the lineage's manifestations, the same as the animal-like masses which ate the tree fruits and tree leaves. If the Earth had evolved in similar directions, if totipotent lineages had dominated land and sea, there wouldn't be such a thing as an ancestor. No close cousins or living parents, either. Humans and elands, walnuts and trilobites would be equal citizens embraced by a single identity.

And more to the point, there would be no such creature as a human, every bipedal omnivore constructed in its own unique, never quite human way.

The engineering of the Dun and Scypha and the other lineages was fascinating and gorgeously complex. Every cell had a compressed, efficient genetic language. Once built, no gene was discarded, and no avenue of development could be forgotten, which was the only way that such a plastic, thoroughly inspired system could work.

Aasleen continued falling toward the pale green forest. Even with the lower gravity, her velocity would shatter bones and possible dislodge limbs. But humans didn't rely on sloppy old DNA anymore. Repairs would begin instantly, disaster genes awakened from repositories scattered throughout her fractured body. There would be pain, sure. Pain was just as instructive today as when people were mortals. But with a lucky bounce or two, she might be alive again in a few minutes and walking normally within the hour, and then the next phase of this ugliness could begin.

But as the air continued to thicken, a sturdy wind began to push, carrying Aasleen out over the thick whitish water of the sea.

Turning onto her back, her face pointed at the gray sky, she clenched her eyes shut as the agony took hold, fierce but brief.

The body died. The shallow muddy water was pushed aside, and her momentum shoved the muck out of her way, and then the muck flowed back over her. Aasleen's mind retreated into a brief coma, and she survived by consuming fat through anaerobic pathways—metabolisms more ancient than oxygen, enlivened by new enzymes and a biochemistry full of modern efficiencies.

When her body found the strength, she attempted to sit up. But the mud was deep and stubborn, and above it laid enough seawater to smother her again. Reaching with her right arm, she clung to Rococo's satchel with her left. But the satchel felt different now. Lighter? No, heavier. The sealed flap had somehow come open, and mud and cold water had filled it up. But how could hyperfiber give up that easily? Then, just as she guessed the only likely answer, something pushed down into the water and grabbed her right hand. Another hand had taken hold of hers, a hand as cold as the sea, but possessing fingers and a helpful mood.

She was yanked up into a sitting position.

The air was still thin and unpleasantly chilled. Her first breaths found alien stinks and a profoundly rancid taste. But her companion looked utterly human, down to the black face and bright eyes and an expression not too unlike a warm, familiar smile.

The creature could be Rococo.

But it wasn't. An elaborate machine was encased inside the native mud. A facsimile of a human had built from the cheapest material available, and she didn't expect it to sound at all like Rococo.

Yet it did.

"Hello, Sister."

She tried to speak, and coughed instead.

"Do you know why they hated you so much?" the apparition asked, its wet face drawn around a mechanical mouth and diamond eyes.

She asked, "Who hated me?"

With a mouth full of mud, she had a stranger's voice.

"Our parents," the apparition said. "They were so angry with you. For centuries, they were livid. And I suppose they still are and won't ever stop. Yet when I emigrated to the Great Ship, they viewed it as a good and honorable adventure that was worth embracing, and they wished me all the sweet fortune I could find."

Hate made her feel warm, alert.

"Do you know the difference between us, Sister?"

"No," she said.

"It is the distance between intense fury and furious pride." The machine lifted a sticky hand, two fingertips clamped tightly together. "It is this much. It is this little. Those emotions are spectacularly close to being the same awful thing."

9

"Where's my brother?"

With bright eyes, the machine regarded her for a speculative moment. Then her companion said, "Follow me," and turned away, long legs pulling through the muck and shallow water.

Aasleen poured the slop out of Rococo's satchel, making sure nothing else was waiting inside. Then she collapsed its sides and stuffed it inside her own kit—a dirty sack woven from sapphire and spider silk—and with a touch, she told the kit to levitate and let her pull it by its handle.

The sea had no distinct shoreline, no defined edge. The water simply grew shallower and more turbid, and at some ill-defined point, there was more land than liquid beneath her. The tracks left by the machine looked like human footprints, bare feet with high arches and long toes, and the sculpted mud retained its human shape, picking up excess mud. The machine paused where the land was dry, using fingers to clean between the toes. Aasleen was wearing field boots that cleaned themselves. She caught up and bent low, studying the entity's motions. The illusion of muscle clung to a human-shaped skeleton. Except for a mud-cloth hanging about its middle, the machine appeared naked. Watching it was like watching Rococo, down to the smallest flourish of the fingers.

"Harum-scarum," she said.

The machine lifted its gaze, yellow teeth and a bright pink tongue showing inside the smile. "Yes?"

"You're a harum-scarum facsimile." A widespread species, ancient compared to humans, they possessed quite a few technological tricks. "Harum-scarums love to model their brains and use facsimiles for rituals and the most difficult jobs."

"Yes."

"And for fun," she added.

"Isn't that what this is? Fun?" The machine straightened and walked toward the forest.

"That's not my point." Aasleen kept on its left, using a similar stride. "Believe me, I know every last tool we brought with us. I've got the Peregrine's full inventory in my head. And I don't remember anything about stockpiling this particular trick."

The machine offered nothing.

241

"Rococo brought you with him. Didn't he?"

The toothy smile seemed appreciative. "Is this important?"

"Yes," she said. "Because if he left the Great Ship carrying you—a secret machine stowed inside his personal gear—then he had a pretty clear idea that he'd need you. And that tells me quite a lot."

"I didn't know that I would employ this," he said. "But it seemed like a prudent item to keep close."

"Why prudent?"

Silence.

She walked in front of Rococo—that's how she thought of the machine now; it was the same as her brother—and with an accusing tone, she said, "When I first saw you, at that initial briefing on the Great Ship…you already had a very clear idea of what you were going to do here…"

"What was possible was obvious," her brother replied.

"Before we boarded the Peregrine, you visited one of the harum-scarum districts and purchased this device, and then you had to pay somebody an additional fortune to have it reconfigured for our species and your mind. Since you couldn't have done either job yourself, my guess is."

The first traces of vegetation were decidedly ordinary—what might have been an earthly grass starved of nutrients, left yellow and a little thin on the crusted surface of sun baked mud. Aasleen looked at the plants and the bright forest beyond, and then she glanced over her shoulder. The sun lay close to the horizon, the empty mud flat and smooth, marred only by two sets of determined tracks. "The water level dropped recently," she said.

Rococo squinted, lips pursing.

"The Dun are heating the water," she said.

"Are they? How?"

"They drained off the top meter of this sea. No, wait. The bottom meter would be better. Easier. They'll drop the coldest, oxygen-poor water into subterranean chambers and let the world's heat percolate into it, and then they bring the warmer water up to irrigate desert and moderate the local climate."

The yellow smile was encouraging, the voice thrilled. "You know, this is exactly what I promised them."

"What is?"

"That you're an exceptional talent. A gifted thinker carried by a rare set of instincts." Rococo's voice practically sang when he said, "I promised them the very best mind for a difficult job. And the fact that you are practically in my personal lineage was an added benefit, naturally."

But Aasleen couldn't stop thinking about seawater and heat. "But it's just a temporary measure," she said. "Every liter of warmed water is going to bleed more heat away from the deep crust."

"Naturally."

They were past the grassy shoreline. A volume of shaded air took hold of them—cool damp air still barely thick enough to be breathed normally. The jungles on a million worlds were not too different from this one. Trees of different heights and different ages stood around them, each one a variation on some common theme built along the same photosynthetic system and unwavering metabolisms. There were things that weren't quite animals wrapped around traditional architectures, including insects and worms, limbless and many-legged, and there were big-eyed climbers that were busily staring at the alien and alien machine that were strolling past their nesting sites. But even the same kinds of creatures had differences. One six-limbed monkey sported thick green fur while its companion had a feathery covering. The eyes held different positions, as did the mouths and large nostrils. Only one lineage ruled here, a grand and plastic and multitudinous species that was too inventive to produce the same body-plan twice in succession. Endless inspiration was wrapped around the same unchanging set of instructions, and despite genetic similarities, this was not the Scypha. The Dun was something else, smaller in numbers and power but equally as remarkable, and what Aasleen had known intellectually for years was suddenly gnawing at her. Stopping in the chilled sunshine of an open glade, she felt a deep disquiet, unable to ignore the emotion any longer.

Rococo's voice called off into the shadows, telling watchful souls to step forward and have their own look.

Intelligent Dun emerged on all sides.

They were bipeds, more than not. Perhaps they looked halfway human in order to honor their guest. More likely, this was a convenient form taken from what organic life had to offer. Some had many eyes, others just one. A few bodies sported two heads, while many more had their faces buried in their chests. Hands and hand-like feet were grown to serve very precise jobs. But every hand was lifted up now, extended and flattened, an endless array of fingers held erect, the gesture looking utterly human.

An open-hand sign of peace, Aasleen assumed.

The Dun were inventive and persistent, yes. But their world was cooling off, a little more every year. Yet wasn't this state of affairs perfectly natural? When the Great Freeze came, each of these bodies would leave behind viable spores, trillions of them hiding in the deep dusts and glacial ice. And just one hypercompetent spore knew enough to resurrect the Dun forests and faces, just as soon as conditions changed for the better.

Which would be when?

Aasleen was thinking about all of it. Problems and solutions. What was easy, and what was nearly impossible. "If the Scypha never let the asteroids fall," she asked quietly, "what happens?"

"But you know that answer already," said the Rococo facsimile.

Then something else obvious showed itself. Aasleen straightened her back and swallowed, and she had no choice but laugh at herself and everyone else too.

The Dun faces regarded her with their bright, unreadable eyes.

It was the machine beside her that seemed intrigued, smiling for a long moment before asking, "What is it, Sister?"

"Nothing."

"Are you certain?"

Aasleen nodded, telling her companion, "Let's keep walking. Keep talking. And by the way, are you taking me to my brother?"

"Perhaps," said the diplomat's voice. "Perhaps."

10

Sometimes the subject wormed its way to the surface.

During those periodic lectures, a crewmember might pose an innocent query that brushed against Chaos. Then everyone found himself thinking about that untouchable place, and perhaps a second hand would lift, and a second voice would ask about that mysterious, increasingly hostile realm. With concern, perhaps even a measure of sadness, they would refer to their hosts, wondering aloud if maybe the Scypha were intentionally strangling their cradle world to death.

But Chaos was not dying. The ranking diplomat had made that salient point enough times to convince ten million people of its veracity. Borrowing from the exobiologists' manual, Krill reminded audiences how the spores represented every lineage, and how they would remain for eons to come, waiting patiently inside the planet-wide dust. In some locations, more spores than dust were lying on and inside the ground. And while there was no way to know the future, it was easy to envision a different day when the Scypha would loosen their grip on the Rings, allowing a fire-shower of rock and ice to trigger another rebirth.

"It's not as if our hosts are fighting the other lineages," she pointed out, her tone reasonable and responsible, her young-girl face glowing with infectious confidence. "We aren't visiting a war zone here. We haven't seen extinctions, and we won't. I promise. If struggles are happening, they're between the little lineages, all which is rigorously natural, since the inhabitants of Chaos have always fought for resources, for water and warmth. If you look at these circumstances as I do, you see a thousand failed lineages unable to make peace with one another, much less find any lasting prosperity.

"The Scypha are something else entirely.

"I won't concede them to be innately superior to their sister lineages. Frankly, I don't have the expertise to make judgment. But it's not a small point to remind ourselves that the Scypha have accomplished wonders. On their own, they have escaped their limited beginnings. And in exchange for allowing a tiny population of their infinitely plastic bodies to come onboard the Great Ship, humanity will be given three empty worlds, which is a spectacular gesture on their part, the gift delivering new homes to millions of humans, complete with happiness and prosperity and the promise of long, luminous futures."

Krill could afford to be effusive; she was a very different beast than any exobiologist. But Chaos was descending into a long hard sleep, and the ultimate results depended on the viability of the spores, which was hard to determine from a range of a hundred million kilometers. Who knew what ten million years of unbroken drought and ice would do to the tiny dormant bodies? In their darkest moods, the experts liked to point out that these weren't simple bacteria buried beneath Martian permafrost. Spores produced by the Scypha were substantial bodies, visible to the eye and covered in a hard, jewel-like cuticle. In principle, it was a magnificent and enduring system. But on the other hand—a grim, obstinate second hand—Chaos had never known dormancies as long as this one promised to be. Asteroid impacts had been uneven but inevitable events, and at most, the coldest driest deadest times had probably lasted not much longer the present drought.

One day an old friend asked Aasleen, "Does it concern you?"

"Does what concern me?"

"Our part in what is happening to that world. And what isn't happening to it. Do these events make you uneasy?"

The AI technician was drifting beside her. "Help me," she said. "Define your subject a little more clearly."

The machine said, "Chaos."

"I know," Aasleen said. "But since when does that world concern you?"

"In the last few moments, the idea struck me." The rubber face put on a tight, worried expression. "I suddenly found myself dwelling on my critical role in this horrible business."

Aasleen had built this machine thousands of years ago. It had helped her erect the short-lived terraforming tent, and later, it had gladly accompanied her to the Olympus Peregrine and eventually to the Great Ship. And now they were together again, finishing the retrofitting of the last nuclear engine. It wasn't unfair to claim that this thoughtful, talented machine was Aasleen's oldest and possibly dearest friend, and there were even lonely moments when it was much more than that. But the machine was not sentient, not in any legal or compelling way, it wasn't.

"Someone been talking to you," Aasleen guessed. "Somebody brought up the subject in your presence."

The machine said, "No."

Then it said, "Perhaps."

"Who?"

"I don't know."

"Rococo?"

With confidence, the AI said, "I haven't shared time with your brother, not since several days before he and the other diplomats disembarked from the Peregrine."

Aasleen nodded, considering possibilities. "What bothers you most?"

"I am doing nothing," it said.

"About that world, you mean."

The machine nodded. "If I was a moral entity, and if the galaxy was watching my inactions, then a million worlds would be entitled to ask, 'Should we entrust our bodies and minds to the care of this lucky but exceptionally young species? That AI might be able to maintain the Great Ship, but can it maintain a proper ethical climate for its diverse passengers?'"

These were fair questions, regardless of the source.

"If I was a free citizen," the AI continued, "I would argue that the Scypha are morally reprehensible, and the only just, reasonable action on our part is to break off negotiations and refuse them entry to the Great Ship."

How would somebody tinker with the machine's mind? Aasleen considered that question more as a friend than an engineer. "But you aren't a free citizen," she said.

"For which I am thankful."

With one hand, Aasleen began to pull off the warm rubber face. "Why are you thankful?"

"The galaxy cannot despise me," the entity responded. Then one of its many hands touched her hand fondly, asking, "What are you doing, darling?"

"I want to examine your mind," Aasleen said.

"But we have our engine to finish."

The chief engineer hesitated.

"And now I'm thinking about tertiary pumps and accentor chambers," the machine reported. "Nothing else is in my mind. That spell, whatever it was, seems to be finished."

11

The Dun territory ended with a slow climb onto an old crater wall. The Rococo facsimile led the way, offering little doses of information about the terrain and its long history. At least twenty different lineages were mentioned, most too obscure to be given a human name like Scypha or Dun. But each had ruled some portion of the crater, its sea or the once-young walls. Her brother's voice described violet forests and oily black forests and towering gray spires with roots reaching deep into the still-hot interior, living off chemical energies that were spent long ago. "Each lineage creates its own biosphere," said the machine, its face and the music of the voice the same as Rococo's. A wry smile was flashed back at her, the mud features giving an impressed shake of the head. "Each lineage has its own physiology and its culture and a personal history and a tenacious, gorgeous will to survive."

They were being followed, at a distance, by perhaps a hundred of the bipedal Dun. But when the facsimile entered a deep gully high on the crater slope, the Dun hesitated, gathering together in a green mass, their stance and silence implying caution falling short of genuine concern.

Aasleen followed her guide.

The air was as thin as it would taste on the highest earthly mountains. An impoverished frost had formed in the shadows and survived through the long day. The gully turned north, ending with a flat slab of wind-polished rock that felt the full brunt of the sun's weak light; and from the rock's base came a weak flow of water—a spring barely strong enough to be considered a trickle, and judging by the vivid orange stains, severely contaminated with metals and salts.

Around that spring grew a forest, each tree no taller than a thumb. The oily black color was a giveaway. Aasleen attempted to name the lineage, amusing her companion in the process.

He laughed, and then he wasn't laughing.

Kneeling beside the tiny woods, he said, "There are thousands of places like this. Lineages huddled around oases too insignificant for names. The most successful lineages might have a hundred homes. But not this one, no." Despite the machine's heat, its mud face was beginning to freeze, a bright white frost appearing along the chin and cheeks and across the tall forehead. "According to the Dun, this lineage has no other sanctuary. Except for some spores left behind on the wind, it exists this close to total annihilation."

Aasleen nodded, asking, "Have you spoken to the Dun?"

"They have spoken to me, yes."

"I'm talking about Rococo. Did he make forbidden contacts?"

The icebound face gave a cracking sound as the smile grew. "He did not associate with them, no."

"Then where did he find the help to come here?"

Her companion waited a moment. "You know where. And I don't have to be your brother to see that you know."

She breathed the thin air, nodding. "How many Scypha don't agree with the present policy?"

"There are one million and nine dissenters, or fifty billion and six." The facsimile shrugged its shoulders. "Numbers are guesses…except that one or two members of the official delegation are maintaining opinions far outside what is considered normal."

"Families," said Aasleen.

"Pardon?"

"When you mentioned our parents and showed me the difference between fury and pride, you weren't talking only about our family."

Yellow teeth shone at her.

"It's a muddled familial mess, and the Scypha are pretty much helpless when it comes to finding an easy way out. That's what you've been telling me. Probably from the beginning, I suppose."

The facsimile rose to its feet.

"Do you want to put an end to our mission?" She shook her head. "It must sicken you, sensing what's being lost—the lineages, the unmet potentials. We have an opportunity to accomplish good works, yet the rest of the galaxy will see…the story that will be told…is that you and I and every other human took possession of three worlds, and in return we promised one lineage a long ride while ignoring their neighbors' quiet murder."

Rococo's white-rimmed face seemed pleased. But the voice was measured, even grim. "All that I want is for our mission to be an enormous success, for all of the lineages, including humans."

"Good," she whispered.

"Which is exactly what Krill and my other associates want. The trouble is, they have a rather different assessment of events and consequences."

"And why am I here?" Aasleen asked.

"You're smarter than I am," Rococo assured her. "I think you can piece together my fondest hopes."

She had never hated her brother more. But this collection of mud and machine wasn't Rococo, and her rage would only waste time.

"I'm going to climb on top," she said.

"To contact Hazz?"

"Piece that together for yourself." She pulled her kit along as she climbed the less steep face of the gully. Finally in the open, standing in the raw dry wind, she pulled out a portable com-link, letting it acquire a signal and aim itself, pulling in a constant transmission that was updated according to changes and looped when there was no change.

"Our shuttle reaches Chaos in eight days," Hazz reported, his expression stern and vaguely disgusted. "The Scypha have agreed to let us drop as close to you as low orbit, and they claim that the Dun will lift you to the shuttle once your mission is finished. This is in exchange for several hundred kilos of enriched uranium, which is a relatively cheap price for a good engineer." Her captain sucked on his teeth, gathering himself. "Will you finish soon? Our gracious good and very persistent hosts very much wish to see justice done."

That was when Aasleen understood all of it.

She began to laugh in relief, and she wept for a few moments. Then a new sound bounced up along the gully walls, and looking into the shadows and the bitterest cold, she saw the Rococo facsimile smashing tiny black trees under its frozen feet. The entity was walking back and forth, calmly and efficiently destroying the ancient forest, finishing what the Scypha had begun.

Aasleen reached into her kit dragging out the plasma torch.

But she hesitated. The torch had to build a charge, and she needed to set up a transmission, showing her audience what they wanted to see. Then to the sky, she said, "In eight days, I'll be back with the Dun. Or I'll be coming back. I might get lost on this desert once or twice."

She aimed her weapon at a shape that was identical to her missing brother.

It was easy, letting loose that blue bolt of energy. Mud and machine never looked at her, exploding with a crack of thunder. Then she let torch charge again, and again, and she etched a crater into the forest floor, and she dug into soggy rock of the spring, water slowly, slowly pouring into the clean raw hole, warm enough to steam, turning what had been a tragedy for an ancient lineage into a blessing born from above.

12

With fifteen hours to spare, the shuttle slid into the berth where it would sleep for the next three decades. Aasleen disembarked to find Hazz was waiting, accompanied by Krill and the Scypha delegation as well as the few AI technicians that weren't making final preparations for the Peregrine's return voyage. Long meetings had been held to orchestrate these next few minutes. The delegates had insisted on personally thanking the human for undertaking this critical mission, and with a quick dry voice, their leader referred to Aasleen as being a courageous warrior, duty-blooded and honorable enough to be a Scypha, and most astonishing, she had survived her journey to a world as cruel as any.

"Your entire lineage has been strengthened by your strength," it said. "And as a consequence, one grave failure has been diminished." Then it extended a bony olive-colored hand, and Aasleen accepted it in the required fashion—her hands sandwiched above and below, squeezing as hard as she could for a ridiculously long time.

Drifting nearby was the Scypha with extra joints in its arms—the same delegate that once spoke to her about the variability of minds. Like its peers, it remained silent, watching the ceremony with bright calcite eyes. Did it know what actually happened on Chaos? And did it agree with what Aasleen had done? Staring at the alien face, she wondered if perhaps every Scypha understood what had happened: This great adventure was nothing more, or less, than an elaborate means by which more than a trillion entities could find what they wanted to find in the human lineage, whatever that happened to be.

Once the Scypha reclaimed its hand, humans and machines were free to greet one of their own. Smiling in a sad, almost pained fashion, Hazz said, "Good to have you back." Then dropping the captainly façade, he added, "I know, I know. This was an awful to ask of you."

"It was," she agreed.

Shamed, Hazz retreated.

Krill kicked in close. That youthful face was sorry and thrilled, in equal measures. She might be crying for both reasons, and with a voice not unlike the alien's, she repeated most of what the Scypha had just said, pale pink hands claiming Aasleen's hand, proving that this woman had invested too much time with her alien friends.

Aasleen's kit and Rococo's satchel drifted beside them.

253

Krill reached for the satchel, but Aasleen grabbed one ruby-rope strap and pulled it to her belly. Locks and seal were in place again. Nobody but her could easily open the pouch.

"These are my brother's ashes," she said.

But the diplomat reached again for the prize, at which point Aasleen added, "I'm carrying him back to the Great Ship. My rights and duties include giving Rococo a proper burial."

Every human fell silent.

Most of the Scypha acted uninterested in their enemy's corpse. Already turning away, they were making for the vessel that would soon lift them free of the Peregrine. None of them would travel to the Great Ship. Their colonists were onboard elsewhere, safely sealed away inside specially prepared cabins. Only the many-jointed Scypha bothered to look at the satchel, and then an AI pushed in front of it, unable to wait any longer.

"Welcome home, madam!"

"Thank you," she said.

"And will you help me, please? One of our new accentor chambers has confessed a minor flaw, and we don't think it's worry-worthy but we require the ranking officer to sign off."

"And she will," Aasleen said. The abrupt intrusion of normal life was a joy, a blessing. "Except first let me look at the analysis, my friend…"

* * *

The first ten seconds of the burn were critical. Problems might betray themselves as sputtering plumes or one catastrophic blast, and if anything substantial went wrong in any one of ten thousand critical systems, it would take centuries to return home to the Great Ship. Unless of course the blast cracked the Peregrine open, hopefully killing its chief engineer quickly enough that she wouldn't feel embarrassed by her mistakes.

But the three new engines ignited without incident, matching the output and harmonics of their rebuilt sisters. The next thousand seconds would lift their acceleration well past a full gee, and the circumstances were tense enough to make the most confident human forget to breathe. But every system was operating within the narrow blue zone dubbed "Perfect". Save for two minor failures on the outskirts of the Scypha system, the same perfection held sway past every other critical juncture.

The familiar life fell across Aasleen's shoulders.

But there was more here than the old life she had inspired her for thousands of years. Human engineers regarded her with new fondness: A dangerous duty had been foisted upon her, and she'd done what was asked of her. In the process, she visited a world like none other, walking its surface for almost nine unbroken days. And because there was no other choice, she had executed her only brother—a dangerous criminal who had broken rules and ignored smart laws, acting out of pure selfishness while putting their mission at risk.

Other humans—crewmembers who didn't know Aasleen—were far less understanding about the dead brother. Nobody said it to her face, at least not with words. But there were looks offered in the galley and averted eyes in the hallway, and sometimes a faraway person would point in her general direction, giving a hard opinion or two to whichever allies were standing close.

Everyone onboard the Peregrine had enjoyed Rococo's company, and very few could understand just how dicey the situation had been.

Aasleen kept her brother's satchel inside her cabin, locked away in a hyperfiber bubble. If a superior officer asked to see the ashes, she was prepared to tell the truth. She had incinerated nothing but a facsimile of the criminal, and she had lied convincingly about everything that happened. And no, she would admit that she never came across Rococo while wandering on the barren, nearly dead surface of Chaos.

About his whereabouts, she could shrug her shoulders, honestly admitting, "I don't know where he is. But abandoned on an alien world seems a lot like death, if you want my opinion."

Yet nobody asked about the satchel's contents or her point-of-view.

Not even Hazz.

After three years and few days of constant acceleration, they began throttling back to where every engine was comfortable, where the chance of meltdowns and magnetic hiccups became deliciously small.

Aasleen gathered up diagrams of the Peregrine's interior, every recent plan laid over everything ancient and nearly forgotten. For good reasons, she assumed she would be searching walled-off hallways and locked closets for the next twenty years. But the sweetest, most logical answer occurred to her after less than a minute's consideration.

Not far from the central fuel tank was a tiny cabin cut off by a series of violent renovations. To reach that unnamed place, she had to walk through an inoperative pump and down an empty fuel line, and then chisel through a diamond wall that had to be patched before continuing—in the remote chance that the main fuel line would fail and somebody would push the hydrogen through here. Afterward that were a series of little hallways, each more familiar than the last, and she ended up standing before a locked doorway that still recalled the touch of her hand. Ages ago, when this starship was new and outbound to the Great Ship, Aasleen had slept in these quarters nearly four hours every night.

She touched the door, and a voice beyond said, "Wait. I'm not dressed."

"I'm tired of waiting," she said. "Hurry up."

"All right. Enter."

Rococo was sitting on a hard cot. He looked rested and a little soft, his body unaccustomed to exercise of any kind. His face seemed thinner, eyes brighter. His personal journal was opened on the desk beside him, waiting for whatever thoughts he wanted to transcribe next. Stolen monitors and narrowband connections allowed him to secretly watch happenings and nonhappenings around the ship. His most recent meal lay half-finished on a grimy plate—rations synthesized in a portable field kitchen—and the tiny volume of air smelled of sweat and subtle decay and too little oxygen.

"Your recycke system is in trouble," Aasleen said.

Then a wide, joyous grin broke out, and with her voice cracking, she said, "You miserable dog."

Laughing, Rococo said, "You were worried about me."

She wouldn't admit it. Instead she tossed his satchel to the floor between them, admitting, "This is yours."

"When did you figure me out?"

"I don't think I'm done picking apart your mind," she said. "But when I first stood up on Chaos—when I saw your face drawn with mud—I realized just how long you'd been planning this adventure. For decades, probably. And of course if a person brings one fancy stand-in for himself, then it's not much of a jump to imagine two facsimiles. Each meant to do a different job, of course."

"Of course."

"You never stole that shuttle," she said. "At least, you weren't the creature piloting it. That was the first facsimile's job, and it flew into the asteroid and then walked up onto the mountaintop and leaped to the sky."

"After leaving this behind," Rococo said, referring to the satchel.

"You assumed I'd be chosen to follow, which was an obvious guess. And you'd hoped I would get your left-behind possession. Working out the vectors and timetable had to press you, I'm guessing."

"But I had help," he said, smiling with that eternal charm.

"Among the Scypha." She nodded. "I once had a chat with one of your coconspirators."

"I know. I was watching."

Of course.

"You never left this room. Did you, Rococo?"

He shook his head.

"Which means that you never broke the Scypha quarantine. Not according to them, and not according to our Krill's orders either."

"The facsimile is a gray area," he conceded.

"But as you say, you enjoyed official help. You didn't deal with the Dun or any other out-of-bounds lineage. One of the Scypha delegates was your contact, which gives this scheme its scent of legality. In the end only one human walked the surface of Chaos, and she had full permission granted by all of the Scypha."

"And what was my scheme?"

She hesitated, smiled. Then she kicked the hyperfiber satchel to him, saying, "It's jammed full of dust."

"Just dust?"

"Dust mixed with a peculiar grit that looks like tiny, tiny jewels." She could say from experience, "On Chaos, there are hollows and dry valleys where the prevailing winds brings dust from every corner of the world. Where a woman can use her bare hands and scoop up a remarkably full sampling of the lineages, alive and dead."

"I knew you'd see my madness," he said.

"But why does this matter? You can hide here until we make it home, but you have to emerge. There has to be a board of inquiry. Maybe you're cleared of any wrongdoing. But after that, what are we supposed to do with the spores inside this silly sack?"

"I see at least two worthy answers," Rococo said. "First, we need to recognize that a multitude of species—richer, older species than ours—are watching us. Our actions and inactions are establishing our reputation throughout the Milky Way. We own the Great Ship, but that isn't enough to make us great. Others will wonder: Are humans wise enough to be trusted? Are they gracious enough to endear?" He set a foot on top of the satchel, pointing out, "Whatever we do with this pregnant grit, it must be a noble and worthy gesture, respectful by almost every measure."

"Granted," she said.

"And second, what I'll tell the Master Captain—what I will argue using rational reason as well as every gram of charm—is that there is one simple, even obvious solution waits for us. And when you think about the consequences, the cost won't be all that steep."

Aasleen offered her guess.

And with a wink, Rococo told her that she was right.

Then he stood and stepped close enough to gently place his arms about her shoulders—he smelled sour and warm and very brotherly—and with a genuine scorn, he said, "Families."

Shaking his head, he asked, "Can you imagine, Aasleen…how wonderful the universe would be if we could simply jump from one family to the next until we found happiness…?"

13

Two centuries later, the Olympus Peregrine returned.

Its minimal crew was made up of facsimiles—machines wearing uniforms and sacks of water draped over a network of false bones. Only one of the Peregrine's big engines was still operational, but that was no problem. The necessary momentum had already been won; nothing more was required but tweaks of the final course. At half-light speed, the much-traveled asteroid plunged out of the darkness, streaking above the green Rings of Ice and Stone and then over the Iron Ring and past the orange sun. Then the engine let loose one last long burst of plasma. Chaos was a tiny gray dot, undistinguished and soon left behind. The final hour of the voyage began with the swift passage over the Rings again, then a quick plunge into the yellowish light of the sister sun—a realm now partly owned and controlled by the human species.

"Here's a question worth asking," said the Rococo facsimile. "Why didn't the Scypha ever colonize this neighboring solar system?"

Standing beside him was a machine strongly resembling his sister. With a nod, she admitted, "That always puzzled me too. Those three moons shouldn't be too difficult to adapt to or rebuild. Even if they had still room to grow in the Rings, I think they'd want to hedge their bets with fresh colonies elsewhere."

"And they could have easily built a fleet of slow starships," said Rococo's voice. "How difficult would that have been, traveling out to all the worlds within five or ten light-years?"

"It is a big old conundrum," Aasleen's voice replied.

The facsimiles were simple in design—little more than likenesses with embedded personalities and cherry-picked memories. It would have been immoral to send sentient organisms, machine or otherwise, on a mission like this. That's why the two of them had enjoyed this conversation at least a thousand times: This was based on a recording made by Rococo's journal, back when the Peregrine was still chasing after the Great Ship.

"Aliens are peculiar people," the Aasleen facsimile mentioned. "Who knows what makes sense to them?"

"But I know why," her brother promised.

Racing toward them was the jovian world and its family of tightly bound moons. Staring at the crescents, Aasleen said, "So explain it all to me."

"Simple ordinary fear," he offered. "That's what held them back from attempting colonies."

"And what were they scared of?"

"If they had populated some new world—a large environment radically different from their home Rings—there's a good chance, a certainty, that little variations would have taken hold. In genetics, in culture. A fissure of their great lineage was possible, not unlike how they split away from the Dun ten million years ago."

The inner two moons were strongly volcanic and washed by the jovian's radiation belts. But magma was a resource, and there wasn't so much radiation that shields and artificial magnetic fields couldn't protect a human population. By contrast, the outer moon was relatively unscathed by toxins, and it was smaller and less volcanic—a quieter realm not too unlike the unterraformed Mars.

"Ten million years have passed," said Rococo, "and that wound still aches."

"I can appreciate that," she replied, laughing gravely.

"Which is the same reason why they never sent asteroids to the stars," he continued. "Colonists would surely form new lineages, and perhaps someday they would return here and raise hell."

"What about the Scypha onboard the Great Ship? Isn't their goal to spread their lineage across the galaxy?"

"They'll be a thousand light-years from here, or twenty thousand."

Out of reach, lost forever.

"My impression," Rococo said. Then he hesitated for a moment, staring at the worlds before them. "My impression is that the Scypha were utterly thrilled to give these worlds to us. They wanted that temptation gone. More than anything, they see humans as a chance to cut old bonds with their past, to slowly find new directions and a fresh sense of purpose."

Aasleen's facsimile nodded. Fixed to the wall beside her was a small hyperfiber bubble, and she touched it gently now, some tiny portion of her recorded thoughts dwelling on its contents.

"So you understand the aliens," she said.

"What I understand is fear and family," Rococo said.

The belted, beautiful jovian world was the largest object in their sky, but the smaller moon was growing swiftly. It looked cold and dirty, ruddy dust gathered around extinct volcanoes, little caps of frozen water clinging to both poles.

"What I appreciate most is how the past shapes what we are," he said, "and how weak the future is whenever it tries to change us."

In a few moments, Olympus Peregrine would dive out of the sky, colliding with that sleepy outer moon. A substantial bolide moving at half the speed of light, its enormous mass would be converted into light and heat, pumping energy into a mantle that had been close to dead for the past billion years.

In another century, a second, much smaller vessel would streak into a close orbit, waiting for the molten crust to stiffen. Then the atmosphere would be doctored and the spores that Aasleen had stolen from Chaos would be strewn across the surface, and whatever lineages survived would have a new world to fight for—a world owned and maintained by a benefactor called Man.

Again, the Aasleen facsimile touched the bubble. The hyperfiber was the very finest grade available, and it was thick enough to survive the coming impact. Inside its tiny center was a small plaque with her name and her bother's name and several important dates. Nothing more, but that seemed like a wonderful gesture, even if you were nothing more than a simple machine acting along narrow parameters.

After today, the Scypha would continue to slowly strangle their cradle world. Though who could say what would happen in another ten million years?

Meanwhile human colonists on the other two moons would watch over New Chaos, perhaps flinging down the occasional spent starship or thousand-megaton bomb…just be the good neighbor…

The Aasleen facsimile laughed quietly.

"What is it?" asked her brother's facsimile.

"Something just occurred to me." A thousand times before, she had said those words, and as always, she looked at him now, smiling for a long happy moment. Just before the Peregrine plunged to its death, she asked, "How do we know the Scypha left their world willingly? That's what they claim, I know, but maybe…maybe the other lineages simply got tired of them and booted them off into space…?"

Rococo laughed. "Certainly that would explain things, wouldn't it?" he always replied.

But he didn't offer those words, not this time.

Both of the machines hesitated, big eyes brilliant and wonderstruck, gazing down at a blank, utterly drab landscape that in another instant would be entirely and forever remade.

Bridge Five

Life is the living fire.

Inventive and relentless, life feeds by burning sugar and fat, or it burns acetylene, or it eats electrical sparks, or it squeezes a whiff of hydrogen until the atoms fuse, creating helium ash and scorching heat as well as a swift mist of neutrinos.

Life is the cautious, thoughtful fire that can plan and can move. When conditions are ripe, fire creates little sparks and embers that fly away with their own faces and identities and stories. The most complicated of these blazes are self-aware: They never stop measuring the fuel in hand and the fuel in easy reach, and every moment is spent guessing the next moment, and a portion of these individual flames have the capacity—the capacity and the urge—to burn without interruption for millions of happy years.

Immortality shapes the galaxy.

Only so much fuel exists, and there are only so many hearths, and flickering beside an eternity, each flame quickly appreciates the stark, infinite limitations before them.

Offspring can be produced and loved and sometimes loved dearly, but the children must be nourished, and if they live forever, then they become competitors of the worst sort—rough mirrors of their parents and grandparents and every other generation that sips sunlight and fusion light, dreaming of how they will fill the next ten billion years.

Every sentient fire understands: If each of them runs wild, the galaxy would be consumed in a million-year moment—a grand doomed inferno that would leave nothing but ravaged suns and cold sorry worlds.

This is why the galaxy is laced with powerful, ancient regulations. Ownership of worlds and every fleck of dust are subject to strict, unimpeachable property rights. Fertility and willingness barely matter. There are few opportunities to spread across the sky, even if the fires are tiny and mortal. And when immortals spawn, the capital demands are enormous, and even the brightest, wealthiest blazes are slow to make children, and many of them use every means to avoid even that possibility.

But there are incidents and odd circumstances where rapid growth is possible. The cool wet human fire claims an empty starship as salvage, legally taking full and eternal ownership, and enriched by the luck, a conflagration is set loose on the galaxy.

But when they think hard, humans are not fools. They would be within their legal rights to kick every other species off the Great Ship and breed like plankton inside their home, filling every cavern and obscure crevice with their kin. But they can understand what Forever means, and what Forever demands, and this is why most of the Ship remains empty—countless volumes set aside for future needs—while they cede most of the inhabited corners to obedient alien flames.

River of the Queen

1

Every voice spoke of the Queen. "Where is She? Ascending! Do you see Her? In my dreams, yes! Do you smell Her? Absolutely, yes! The All ends, the new All walking in its tracks! Praise the Queen! Bring us the Queen! Where is She now? Ascending!" Stirred among the voices were animal grunts and hollers; better than any words, they captured the wild anticipation—a chorus of piercing, wordless roars that almost obscured the tumbling thunder of the great river. And behind the voices and roars were the percussive clack of nervous limbs and the extruded symphonies of pheromones, a giddy sense of celebration laid so thick across the setting that even a pair of human beings—mere tourists—could appreciate the unfolding of great, glorious things.

Quee Lee shivered beneath her robe, purring, "This is wonderful. Remarkable. And really, it hasn't even begun yet."

Perri nodded and smiled, peering over the edge.

"Can you see Her?" she joked.

"But I see the entourage," he said. "Down in the mists. Can you make them out?"

The railing was created from thick old vines grown into elaborate knots, golden leaves withered, dried spore-pods ready to burst. Quee Lee leaned against the top vine. A beautiful woman in a thousand ways, she gazed into the mayhem of plunging water and endless snowstorms, her smile widening when a few wisps of black appeared for the briefest instant. Long albatross-style wings were resting inside bubbles of calm air; a few of the Queen's devoted attendants had to gather themselves before resuming their long climb.

"Will the wind-masters reach us?" she asked.

"Most won't." Perri still wore a young, almost pretty face, fine features amplifying a pair of clear bright eyes that could only be described as sweet. He had turned to the right, watching the main lane, watching thousands of Dawsheen wrestling for position. "The last time I was here, barely a handful of those big flyers survived the climb."

"Is it too far?"

The cliff was more than eleven kilometers tall.

"It's more the cold and snow, I think. And not just the wind-masters suffer. Most of Her entourage dies along the way." Then in the next breath, with an easy conviction, he said, "But still, this is the best place to be. This is Her final gathering point. Being here is an enormous honor."

"I know," Quee Lee sang. "I know."

Perri didn't mention costs. His wife had donated a substantial sum to the Dawsheen, and nothing would come from it but this brief opportunity to endure the glacial cold, standing among the alien throngs, every kind of eye trying to catch a glimpse of the fabled Queen. Their private vantage point was an ice-polished knob of black basalt. The river was to their left—a shrunken but still impressive body of water hugging the cavern wall, flowing hard and flat until it reached the neatly curled lip of the towering cliff. The city lay to their right, perched on the higher ground. Beneath the city, where the cliff was a dry black wall, a single zigzagging staircase had been etched into the stone. By custom and for every good reason, the Queen never took a step upwards. Her assistants carried her beautiful bulk, using the honored old ways. On foot and with the fading strength of their limbs, they were bringing her up the final eleven kilometers of a grand parade that began centuries ago, in the warm blue surf of the Dawsheen Sea.

"She won't arrive for a little while," Perri cautioned. Then touching Quee Lee with a fond hand, he added, "This is our ground. Nobody can take it from us. So why don't we go somewhere warm, and sit?"

"I don't want to miss—"

"'Any little thing.'" One of his sweet eyes winked. "But remember. This is a wonderful city in its own right, and in another week or two, there won't be anything left to see."

"We should walk around," she agreed.

Stepping back from the dying vines, he said, "And maybe we can treat ourselves..."

"'To a little drink or two,'" she said, doing a seamless imitation of her husband's voice.

"'To be social,'" he said, imitating his wife's voice and mannerly sense. "'To be polite.'"

Then together, inside the same moment, they thought of the city's fate. In another two weeks, it was dead and buried under the relentless blizzards; and with that thought, a sudden respectful silence waked with them as they moved hand in hand down their own little set of carved stone stairs.

2

In ancient times, Perri would have looked like a man in his early twenties—adulthood just achieved, childhood still lurking in the face and manners. But time and age were different creatures today. The youngster was thousands of years old, and during that busy long life, he had explored just a tiny fraction of the avenues and caverns, chambers and odd seas that lay inside the Great Ship.

By contrast, Quee Lee preferred an older, more mature appearance. She moved like a woman who had forever to accomplish the smallest deed—a suitable façade, since she was considerably older than her husband. She was a young girl when the first alien words and images were captured by telescopes. From the time of the pharaohs, wealthy old women had been embarking on great voyages. She was the wife walking up the wide lane with her boyish husband, hands clasped and heads tipping towards one another whenever one of them spoke. Sometimes a finger would point, some little question asked and answered, or the question was repeated to a buried nexus, dislodging a nugget of information from some data ocean, another tiny piece of the Dawsheen existence explained to the curious tourists.

The lane was covered with hard sheets of living wood, turquoise and photosynthetic when the weather was warm, but now turning black and soggy in the cold. No one shared the way with them. Heaps and ridges of hard dirty snow stood to the sides, and behind the snow were vegetable masses, dome-shaped and crenulated where they pushed through, their sides punctured with doorways leading into chambers of every size. What passed for leaves had died with the first hard freeze. The masses themselves were dying, choking under the snow while their roots froze with the soil. But the hollow chambers in their wooden hearts remained inhabited. Sheets were draped across the doorways, the heated air inside making them ripple, and the sloppy, half-melted ice on the thresholds was littered with the long, faintly human prints of busy feet.

In one sense, Dawsheen biology was perfectly simple. Diversity was low, ecosystems few and trimmed to a minimum of trophic levels. One species always held prominence based on intelligence and tools. For convenience's sake, the rest of the Ship referred to those creatures as the Dawsheen. Tripeds with a single burly arm in front and two flanking arms tipped with delicate hands, in the high country they tended to be round-bodied and short. Their skin was the color of sun-bleached straw, and their hair turned from black to gold as they aged. They were normally vegetarian. The Dawsheen home world had small continents, and feeding a large population meant eating low on the food chain. But whenever the All collapsed into winter, meat became a cheap, holy indulgence. As the lovers strolled away from the cliff, the air filled with the smell of burning fats and spiced vitals. With a hungry sigh, Perri said, "There was a restaurant last time, on that hilltop, overlooking the river."

"Last time," she said.

That was nearly a hundred centuries ago. But with a tug on the arm, he reminded Quee Lee, "The Dawsheen are compulsive traditionalists."

Sure enough, another eating establishment was perched on the summit. But the hill was smaller than Perri remembered, the rock scrapped down by the last glaciation. And the view wasn't quite the spectacle that he had promised Quee Lee. For that, he apologized. Snow was falling again, fed by the drenched air and gathering cold. They sat together in one of the communal booths, on the steeply tilted bench, gazing at a gray expanse of water and the swirling white of the snow, and except for the occasional slab of ice being carried towards the falls and its death, nothing seemed to change outside.

But that was fine. There was the building itself to enjoy—a great home-tree hollowed out by worms, the flat floor and immovable furniture carved with a million relentless mouths. They could happily study the creatures sitting and walking about. There were several species of tourists, plus Dawsheens too old and feeble to stand in the cold, waiting for their Queen. The indoor air was warm and smoky. Most of the patrons stared at an interior wall sprinkled with live images from downstream. The Queen Herself was never quite shown; She was too important to be reduced to a mere digital stream. Instead, audiences were treated to the celebrations held in distant cities. Beneath the illusion of a warm blue sky, millions of Dawsheen stood in the open and sang, wishing their Queen luck and bravery on the trails awaiting Her, and in the trials awaiting their species.

What passed for a waiter approached the two humans. Speaking through a translator, he called out, "Adore the Queen!"

"Adore the Queen!" they replied, amiable words transformed into an amiable singsong.

The alien face was narrow and stiff. The crest of hair had turned a dull whitish gold. His breath smelled of broiled fish and exotic oils. Three pearl-colored eyes regarded them with no obvious emotion, but the translator made the voice sound angry. "She is a slow Queen," their waiter exclaimed. "A late Queen, at this rate."

Quee Lee glanced at her husband, waiting for advice.

With a shrug of shoulders, he told her to say nothing.

"If this weather worsens," the alien continued, "we will all be dead and frozen before she can Gather us."

A few elderly patrons growled in agreement.

The humans shifted their weight against the polished wood. They had no menus, and no fees were expected. Where was the value of money when the world was dying? An enormous fire pit was dug into the middle of the room and lined with rock. Perri was ready to point at one of the platters of blackened food. But Quee Lee was a problem. As a rule, she didn't appreciate heads attached to her dinner.

"You've still got time," another voice called out. "The glacier isn't going to out race your little Queen!"

Perri didn't immediately notice what was different about the voice. Then he heard the singsong translation following in its wake, and curious now, he turned. Four humans were sitting in a distant booth. The largest man was glowering at their waiter. Two other men were cutting at the seared flesh, eating with famished urgency. The final man stared out at the falling snow, saying nothing and apparently paying no attention to his companion's complaints.

The waiter turned towards them, lifting one leg while standing on the other two—the standard Dawsheen insult.

The talking man didn't notice the gesture. "I want a fresh plate, and I want you to stop badmouthing your Queen."

The Dawsheen dropped his leg and faced Quee Lee, a slow tight voice asking, "What would you like to eat, madam?"

"Nothing," she said.

"Ask me," the loud man called out. "I want something. Come here!"

"And you, sir?" the Dawsheen said to Perri. "There is a large pudding char that died of old age. I have been saving it for an adventurous set of stomachs."

Perri said, "Yes."

"Hey!" the loud man shouted. "Before you're dead, old man. Why don't you pay a little attention to—"

<u>Crack.</u>

The sound was abrupt and astonishingly loud. No one was watching the loud man, and then everybody was. His face was beginning to bleed. His shattered nose hung limp on his face, too damaged to heal itself quickly. Two of his companions laughed quietly while they ate, enjoying his discomfort and embarrassment. The other man continued to stare out the window, studying the relentless snow, his face and posture unchanged, while his left hand slowly and carefully set an empty iron platter back on the worm-carved table where it belonged.

3

The Dawsheen home world was a cyclic snowball.

Many worlds were. Even the young Earth passed through its own snowball phase. Watery bodies with a few small continents were most susceptible, particularly when their continents lay scattered along the equator. If the sun's energy flagged, or if the world's orbit shifted by the tiniest margin, the dark open waters at the poles would abruptly freeze over. Sea ice was a brilliant smooth white. Light and heat were hurled back into space, allowing the climate to cool further. The newborn icecaps expanded rapidly, reaching into normally temperate regions. And as the world brightening further, it cooled again, and again, the ice spreading, and over the poles, beginning to thicken.

Seven hundred million years ago, the Earth's climate collapsed. A murderous cold reached to the equator. Glaciers born on the high peaks rumbled into once-tropical valleys. The ocean froze to a depth of nearly a full kilometer, and the water beneath was black and choked of oxygen. The cold was enormous, and enduring. But without evaporation, there were no clouds or fresh snows, and the desiccated glaciers began a slow retreat. Deserts of glacial till covered the barren land, frigid winds piling up towering dunes. But even in the most miserable chill, volcanoes kept rumbling and churning, spitting carbon dioxide into the sky. Without rainwater or plant life, the greenhouse gas built up to staggering levels. A tripping point was achieved, and the seas began to melt, and snows fell again, the glaciers growing even while the heat continued to soar.

In a matter of decades—in a geologic blink—the glaciers burned away, and the world moved from snowball to furnace.

On the earth, the snowball cycles eventually moderated. The continents gathered together and drifted away from the equator, while the aging sun grew warmer. But with each glaciation, earthly life was battered. Entire lines of multicellular species were pushed into extinction. The biosphere that eventually arose—the world of grass and men and jeweled beetles—owed its existence to the tiny few survivors clinging to the deep-sea vents or swimming in the hot springs on the shoulders of the great volcanoes.

But the Dawsheen world never moderated.

The largest moon of a massive gas giant, it was a blue body with tiny continents and tidal-churned tectonics. With the precision of a pendulum clock, the climate continued swinging in and out of the snowball state. Predictability was a blessing. Predictability allowed the ancient Dawsheen to adapt to their suffering. Obeying the season, terrestrial plants threw spores on the wind, trusting that one in ten trillion would survive the cold drought. Animals climbed into the high mountains, building nests inside deep caves and stuffing them with thick-shelled eggs. The ocean's creatures changed their metabolisms, borrowing the slow, tiny ways of anaerobic organisms, living sluggishly in the deep darkness while the ice creaked and roared above them.

Every winter was a savage winnowing.

And every thaw left the world stripped and lifeless, defenseless and full of promise.

Surviving the winter wasn't enough. Success meant spreading quickly, furious breeding, children adapting rapidly to a landscape transformed by glaciers and eruptions. Success meant being first to swim into the first dark thread of open seawater, and spawning before anyone, and fending off every rival to a rapidly growing empire.

Cooperation brought the greatest successes.

The early queens were ensembles: Species hiding together in the largest, most secure redoubts, existing as totipotent spores and fertilized eggs along with a dowry of mummified bodies and dried shit—organic wealth brought to feed and fertilize what was, in simple terms, an ark that was waiting for the next All.

That was a billion years ago.

Life on the Earth was little more than a film, a gray tapestry woven of single-celled bacteria; while on Dawsheen, the Queen was becoming more interesting and more elaborate, gradually but inexorably evolving into what the world would see as a spectacular, utterly beautiful woman.

4

"Bride of the world, Bride of the All!"

They could scarcely hear their own translators. At this penultimate moment, the city's entire population was standing along the main lane, every Dawsheen chanting in a wonderfully smooth chorus, the melded voices loud enough to shake stone and passionate enough to make humans shiver and smile at one another. Quee Lee turned to her husband, winking in a certain way. "It's as if we've wandered into an orgy."

"What?" Perri shouted.

"We've stumbled across an orgy!" But that wasn't quite true, and reconsidering, she added, "No, no! It's a salmon run. Coho spawning! That's what this reminds me of!"

"Accept our selves," their translators screamed. "Accept our offerings, accept our souls!"

The crowd was a blur, a vivid living mass of the Dawsheen lining the parade route, plus another twenty or thirty, or perhaps forty animal species visible from that little knob of basalt. The bulky species stood alone, clambering little bodies dancing on their shoulders and backs. Limbs rose high. Every creature was full-grown, and many were elderly. Why make children when this world was about to perish? Trembling bodies shoved against neighbors, forming two astonishingly straight lines.

Nothing mattered but the Queen. Nothing else existed. Her exhausted vanguard moved onto the wide lane. Leading the procession were the intelligent Dawsheen, each wearing elaborate ceremonial robes and carrying relics from great, long-past Alls. Behind them, big work-grazers pulled wagons filled with a tiny sampling of Her wealth—sacks of blessed soil, armored plates made from titanium and cultured diamond, slabs of pasteurized fat sealed in plastic, and one long banner lit from within by electrified gases, showing the redoubt that had been prepared for Her at the top of the cavern, at the birthplace of the Long River.

"There…I see Her…!" Quee Lee cried out.

The Queen was being lifted up the last long flight of stairs, rising over the cliff's lip at a slow pace that might have been majestic, but more likely signaled great fatigue. She was huge. Resembling an enormous caterpillar, she was adorned with turquoise plates and gold emblems that shone in the snowy light. What might be legs were wrapped securely around the trunk of a sky-holder tree. Handles and saddles had been fastened to the tree, and every possible species helped carry Her. Work-grazers and Dawsheen and bounce-maidens and three-cautions and whisper-winds; and in the middle of the tree trunk, a pair of massive hill-shakers strode along, each with six pillar-like legs, each leg stepping with practiced care, setting the pace for the others.

A centuries-long climb was nearly finished.

But the achievement wasn't quite as astonishing as it seemed. The sky-holder tree was mostly hollow, saving weight. And the Queen's body was nearly as empty. The carapace was a tough, enduring contrivance—diamond fibers woven into a structure able to endure the angry weight of entire glaciers. The Queen's true self was astonishingly small. But as Perri liked to explain, "Small makes sense. A little body is easier to move and protect. The little queen can fall into hibernation faster, and then awaken first." Over the recent centuries, on various occasions, he had reminded his wife, "Really, you don't need much space to hold a world's genetics. A sampling of every species…a few million examples, each no larger than a single cell…you could hold that treasure inside one trustworthy hand…"

Thundering chants reached a higher, brighter pitch. The cliff seemed to be shaking, ready to collapse. And then the enormous Queen was in view, and the mood changed, the crowd falling into sudden silence.

Quee Lee sighed, and shivered.

Perri looked back across the city. Thousands of spore-pods began to leap high, home-trees and vines and the living lanes throwing their genetics into the damp, snowy wind. And in the next moment, the pods detonated, filling the air with talc-like dust. Perri coughed, and Quee Lee sneezed. But the natives remained silent, focused on this ultimate moment. As the Queen passed, each Dawsheen approached. The two lines pushed inwards, bodies clambering on top of bodies. With the aliens came the rough equivalent of rats and scorpions, dogs and sparrows, and underfoot, furry worms and tiny bugs. With quiet solemnity, every creature opened its clothes or parted its fur—in some way exposing itself–needle-like penises and distended vaginas delivering their cargo with a minimum of fuss, and just enough bliss.

Quee Lee nudged Perri with her elbow. He followed her gaze. Half a dozen giant wind-masters were still trying to finish their long climb. Exhausted, ancient and nearly starved, their movements were weak but precise, using a last little updraft somewhere in the cold, dense air. Perri began to say, "Too bad." They were majestic creatures. He had hoped at least one of them would glide above the parade; that would make the spectacle complete.

But not today, he thought.

Then a new motion grabbed his gaze. Skimming along the edge of the cliff, just above the falls, was a black and elegantly slender wind-master, large even at a distance, flapping the long wings once and then twice again, twisting its body as the body rose up level to Perri and Quee Lee.

He nudged her with an elbow, and nodded.

Quee Lee whispered a few words.

"What?"

"Stronger," she said.

The enormous flyer was powerful enough to flap hard and quick, gaining velocity as it continued its ascent. In another moment it was above them, vanishing into the snow and spores. Perri thought he heard air racing, which was ridiculous. The deep rumbling of the waterfall wouldn't let him hear anything as subtle as wings or breezes. Then inside that same instant, he heard a new chant from the Gathering, unexpected and sloppy, and not half as loud as before.

"No, no, no!" their translators cried out.

Then with bluntly descriptive voices, the machines said, "PANIC. THIS IS THE SOUND OF PANIC."

Again, air was rushing overhead.

Almost too late, Perri looked back at the Queen. A strange little fire had erupted along Her back, a haze of blue plasmas brightening and lifting like a flap of iridescent flesh. Then there was a clean sharp explosion, and the Queen's carapace shattered and fell off its perch on the sky-holder tree, and out of the clouds dove something narrow, black, and wingless. It swooped low and stopped instantly, absorbing that terrific momentum. Mechanical hands delicately reached inside the Queen's jeweled carapace, retrieving a squirming gray body not much larger than a human being.

"What is it?" Quee Lee asked.

The machine had lifted again, vanishing into the endless snow storm.

"What just happened?" she wanted to know, more puzzled than worried, more disappointed than angry.

Perri said nothing.

He was studying the ongoing panic—arms swaying in agony; voices cursing wildly; waves of tiny sparrow-like flyers struggling to chase after their stolen Queen—and then with an expression that looked a little amused, and thrilled, and focused, he turned to his wife and shook his head, telling her, "Stay with me. Stay close!"

5

The building only resembled its neighbors—a home-tree façade encompassing a set of rounded rooms that pretended to have been shaped by determined worms. But every surface was cultured diamond braced with threads of hyperfiber. The furnishings had a slick, impervious feel promising durability as well as ease of cleaning. One of the back rooms, visible at the end of a remarkably straight hallway, was enclosed with hyperfiber bars—horizontal, not vertical—and inside that large cage stood half a dozen Dawsheen, a single harum-scarum sitting behind them, threatening to crush anyone who came near her.

Many things in the universe were not universal, Perri reflected. But police stations very nearly were.

"I have no authority," said the officer on duty.

Quee Lee halfway laughed, saying, "And I'm not precisely sure why we have come here."

The Dawsheen looked at Perri. "I have no authority," he repeated. "Do you claim special knowledge about a criminal incident?"

"Maybe," Perri said.

The alien spoke, and with a flat, incurious tone, three separate translators asked, "Which criminal incident?"

"The kidnapping."

The translators struggled to deliver that simple concept. A blur of barks and tweets ended with the station's translator taking charge of the interview. Its AI asked Perri directly, "Do you mean the Queen?"

"Yes."

"Do you know Her whereabouts?"

"No." Then he shook his head, deciding that wasn't quite true. "Or maybe I do. Maybe."

"But you have some useful knowledge?"

"I think so. Yes."

The officer sat listening to the conversation between machine and man. One leg was thrown behind his tilted bench, the others locked in front. Every hand lay in a pile on the little desk set before him. He wore a greenish-black uniform of densely woven yarns. His face with covered with bristly golden hairs. Every eye was open, but there was no way to determine if he was even a little interested in what was being said.

Finally, he muttered a few syllables.

"My superiors are searching for Her," he offered. "I have no authority, but I will listen to whatever you say."

"I saw some men," Perri said. "Human men. My wife and I noticed them before the Gathering."

Quee Lee glanced at him, sensing some little portion of his reasoning.

"I recognized one of those men," Perri said.

"What do you know about the man?"

"He's a smuggler, on occasion."

Quee Lee was neither surprised nor disappointed. Her husband knew all kinds of people, and a tangle of questions could wait until later. For now, it was enough to make a dismissive cluck with her tongue, smiling and staring back at the jail cell.

"You recognized this smuggler?"

"I think so," said Perri.

"His appearance was familiar to you?"

"No."

"No?"

"His face had been modified. Disguised. Smugglers have to have tricks."

"But his voice was familiar," the officer pressed.

"No. It's a new voice, and that also means nothing. Every time that I've seen him, he sounds different." Perri cut the air with one hand—a Dawsheen gesture promising that he was telling the truth. "I've known this man for centuries. I know his manners, his methods, how he moves his hands and his tongue. Lately, he's been working with a pair of brothers. There were brothers with him today. And the fourth man in their party was a stranger, but he seemed to be in charge."

Like any cop, the Dawsheen had to ask, "How is it, sir, that you are familiar with a notorious smuggler?"

Never hesitating, Perri said, "Because I know just about everybody."

Quee Lee's willpower came close to breaking, but she managed to say nothing.

"I have no authority," said the Dawsheen one final time. "My superiors are searching upriver. The Queen will be recovered soon." An unreadable expression passed across the narrow, bristly face. "Or she is already ours again," he promised someone, perhaps himself. "But you can be sure that I have already relayed your words to every one of my superiors."

"Every escape route is closed," Perri said. "Am I right?"

The officer said, "Yes."

"But how can you be sure?" Quee Lee asked.

Perri spoke. "Up and down the Long River, every tunnel and little doorway has been closed. They are closed and sealed and not one Biggolow flea can get inside this cavern, much less escape." Then he looked at the officer again. "Is that why you're confident?"

The Dawsheen replied and the translator snapped, "Yes."

"Loon Fairbanks," Perri offered. "That's the smuggler's name. And believe me, he anticipated every measure that you have employed already and whatever you might do ten moments from now. He knows your security systems, your psychology, your weather and every other factor. Loon will have a good, solid plan. If those men and your Queen are still inside the cavern, they won't be for long. And if he can get Her out here, what chance do you have to find Her inside the Great Ship?"

The officer fell silent, white eyes dulling slightly.

"I can help you," Perri said. "I want to help you. I don't particularly like that man, and I wish to be of service to your Queen."

The alien stood abruptly.

"I have the authority," he shouted with astonishing energy. A cabinet jumped open, a hyperfiber vest and two weapons flying across the room. He put on the vest and pocketed the weapons, and then one of his little hands touched a control, causing the cage in back to open. The horizontal bars fell into a neat triangular pile at the feet of the prisoners. In a scream, he told the Dawsheen, "You have been freed. Go home and wait for the glacier."

The harum-scarum rose to her feet, towering above the rest. From her speaking mouth, she snarled, "What about me?"

"I do not like you. You have earned my scorn and my distrust, and if you can live with that burden, you also are welcome to leave."

6

Slowly, slowly, the Dawsheen biosphere grew more sophisticated, intricate, and robust. The brutal winters both delayed and inspired the wheel of evolution. There were never many species, but each was highly adaptable. Native genetics were intricate and miserly. No gene, useful or otherwise, was thrown away. Who could guess when or how one of these developmental oddities might become precious again?

In little steps, intelligence arose. Simple civilizations flickered into existence—in the scattered valleys, typically–and each was summarily crushed under the next river of ice. Yet there are advantages to the occasional Death. What society wouldn't relish the chance to wipe your world clean and begin again? The young Dawsheen began to educate their Queens, leaving them with elaborate instructions. Each All began with hints and advice, and clear warnings left behind by the wise departed. Each All blossomed with the help of thousands of past Alls. Every new city was superior to its forbearers. Every new society was quicker to grow and more likely to remain at peace. Gradually, the Dawsheen acquired industry and high technology. Like humanity, they cobbled together enormous telescopes—radio ears listening to alien gossip. With that burst of knowledge, they built starships and found empty worlds. But where most spacefarers embraced some flavor of immortality, the Dawsheen resisted. Their winters and the purging glaciers were too important, too deeply embedded in their bones. They bolstered their lifespans, but only to a few thousand years. And learning to control their climate, they made their winters as brief as possible. But they wouldn't surrender their most powerful myth: The Dawsheen as creatures of endless change, born from relentless reinvention. The occasional Death was a blessing, and each new All was fresh and full of potentials. In their lustrous white eyes, most alien species seemed humdrum, and stodgy, as well as pleasantly, even deliciously, contemptible too.

7

Perri sat in the back of the little ship studying his own holo-map.

"You may examine our map," the Dawsheen remarked, sitting at the ship's controls, carefully touching nothing. The AI pilot was keeping them close to the river's face, ice piled on ice, tiny leads betraying the cold black water beneath. "My map is accurate to the millimeter, and updated by the instant."

"Thank you," said Perri, his voice distracted. "But no, thank you."

Quee Lee was sitting beside the Dawsheen, her high-collared robe pulled snug across her squared shoulders. Suspicious and a little amused, she looked back at her husband as he stared into that maze of colored lines and pale spaces. "My husband is very proud of his map," she said. "He loves it more than he loves me, I think. There are entire months when I can't pry his nose away from it."

Perri seemed enthralled with his own narrow business. The tiny projector in one hand threw up a comprehensive view of the Long River, and he poked and prodded with his free hand. For no obvious reason, certain points needed to be enlarged and studied in detail. He let his instincts steer him. Quietly, he said, "You have an enormous area to search. The river starts under the hull—here—and twists and turns its way back and forth, down down down, into your little sea. The drop is nearly three thousand kilometers. Except near its source, it's a lazy river. A couple meters down for every kilometer crossed. The river is one and a half million kilometers long, making it the longest river in the galaxy, no doubt. And since the cavern has an average width of twelve kilometers, your living area is roughly equal to the lands on your home world."

"It is a satisfying relationship," the officer interjected.

Leasing an enormous habitat required frightful sums. The Dawsheen had surrendered titles to half a hundred worlds—difficult planets with climates too stable or seas too tiny to feed deep ice ages; perfect for an inventive ape that could terraform and colonize, making homes for billions of prosperous souls.

"This is a maze," Perri cautioned. "This is a huge and intricate and beautiful maze. And I don't think you can search it in the time left, no."

"We have sealed every exit." The officer had no better response, and he repeated what he believed. "There is no way to escape."

"You're searching mostly upriver," Perri continued. "But they could have taken the Queen downstream."

"No," the Dawsheen replied. "We tracked them coming this way."

"I bet so." Perri touched an approaching sector, asking for an enlargement. A thousand square miles of ice and raw stone appeared before him. And again, he fingered portions of the map, gazing into the wasteland's corners.

Quee Lee smiled gently.

"It just realized that I don't know your name."

The Dawsheen uttered something quick and soft. His translator said, "Lastborn Teek."

With genuine sadness, she repeated, "Lastborn."

"A common name," the Dawsheen explained. "As Firstborn is common at the beginning of an All."

The river was frozen over, and the weather continued to worsen, snow falling in thick white waves, hurricane winds trying to push them out of the sky. The worst gusts made the ship tremble, but shape-shifting wings and powerful engines kept them on course. Lastborn studied his controls and listened to reports from distant search parties, empty hands closing and opening again with a palpable nervousness.

Quee Lee looked over her shoulder.

"Darling?"

Perri didn't react.

She said, "Darling" again, with a certain weight.

He noticed. A soft sigh proved it, and he blinked, his poking hand held steady for a moment.

"What are you thinking, darling?"

He wasn't sure. Until the question had been asked, his thoughts were utterly invisible to him.

"Our friend deserves to know." She reached back. Her hand was small and warm, soft in every way, little fingers wrapped around the man's elegant young hand as she pulled gently, insistently, saying again, "Lastborn deserves to know."

"The flyer is up in the glacier," Perri guessed. "It's going to be buried, but not that deep. Camouflaged, but not that well."

Lastborn said nothing.

"And there's going to be at least three trails worth following. Heat trails, boot prints, and there will be signs of a second flyer, probably."

Alien fingers tightened into knots.

"Have there been any ransom demands?"

With a touch, the Dawsheen took the controls away from the AI pilot. In a near-whisper, he spoke for a long moment. Then his translator admitted,

"The flyer was discovered a little while ago. It was left empty, hiding in a rock crevice. Not in the ice."

Quee Lee smiled with nervous pride.

"The flyer was empty almost from the beginning," Perri explained. "If I was stealing the Queen, I would have slipped her into a second ship. A better, far less visible ship. Then I'd double back, probably somewhere below the city."

"Every passageway out of our world is closed and secured—"

Lastborn paused, as if hearing his own voice for the first time.

Then with a new tone, he asked, "Where?"

"Here."

Perri pulled his view back a hundred kilometers, passing over the city and dropping with the enormous falls. Beside and beneath the Dawsheen habitat were more caverns and tunnels, plus innumerable fissures too tiny to wear names. "A lot of things in this universe are difficult, but cutting a new door isn't difficult," he said. "In fact, with the right tools, it's about the easiest job that there is."

8

Ten thousand years ago, Perri came home from a long wandering.

His wife greeted him in every usual way. She made love to him, and he returned the pleasure. She fed him and let him sleep, and then woke him with fond hands, using his body until both of them were spent, breathless, and dehydrated. Then they staggered into Quee Lee's garden—a many-hectare room filled with jungle and damp hot air—and naked, they kneeled and drank their fill from a quick clear stream. Where the stream pooled, they swam and bathed, tired legs barely able to carry them back onto shore. With a voice frank and earthy, Quee Lee spoke to her husband. She explained how much she had missed him. She had craved his voice and stories and his pretty mouth against her mouth, and in her dreams, she had played cruel, sordid games with his delicate parts. She never spoke to anyone else with those words. No other lover, not even to pretend. Perri had been gone longer than usual—several years, and without a word. "Where were you?" she finally asked. "Where did you take that lovely little friend of ours?"

Perri laughed, gently and happily. Then with a matching voice, he described his adventures. With like-minded idiots, he had explored one of the Great Ship's engines—a moon-sized conglomeration of machines with pumps as big as cities. Strictly speaking, he didn't have permission and sentries were stationed at every turn, and it consumed most of his time, remaining undetected. Then he went gambling, playing twenty-deck poker with a platoon of humans and harum-scarums and Blue Passions and AI souls. In less than sixteen days and nights, Perri managed to surrender most of the allowance given him by his very generous wife. He had let himself look embarrassed and a little desperate, smiling painfully at the better gamblers, asking for one more chance. "One more hand? With a fresh twenty-decks, maybe?" He charmed and begged, and of course when the cards were dealt, every suspicious eye was fixed on Perri. But his awful luck held. He had nothing. The Blue Passion at the far end of the table gathered up the enormous pot with suckered fingers; and three days later, in an entirely different corner of the Ship, the same alien surrendered Perri's share of the profits, along with her weepy thanks.

"She was in awful trouble," Perri explained. "She absolutely needed that money."

"You're so noble," Quee Lee teased. "Anything for a lady in need."

With his earnings, Perri bought a used slash-car, and in the depths of the Ship, in a looping tunnel used only for racing, he had raced. And won. And won again. He described the car and how it was to drive, hands wrapped around an imaginary wheel, the stone and hyperfiber walls blurring around him. Then just as Quee Lee was about to ask to see his new toy, Perri said, "I crashed it. Mangled it, and myself. I was clinically dead for a full week. It took most of my winnings to reclaim my body. The autodocs asked if I wanted improvements, but I honestly couldn't think of one. Being perfect, as I am."

Both laughed.

And then, with a very slight change of tone, Perri said, "The Long River." He rolled onto his back, asking, "Do you know much about it?"

"I've heard it mentioned. Yes."

"And the Dawsheen?"

She knew about them, but not much.

Perri explained the snowball world and its enduring biosphere. Quietly, slowly, he described the city perched beside the eleven-kilometer falls, and its inhabitants, and the amazing parade. A Queen had been carried past. An entire world gave Her its seed. And after the Queen was gone, safely entombed in a redoubt high above the blue ice, Perri had waited, watching the river freeze solid while the enormous snows fell, thousands of Dawsheen buried in their homes, happily falling into the eternal sleep—their bones and souls crushed beneath the newborn glacier.

It was a sad, spectacular event to witness.

The voice that began soft and happy turned softer and awed. Perri was lying naked on the bank of the stream, on his back, staring at the illusion of stars floating inside the room's high ceiling. With her frank, practiced hands, his wife measured his mood, and when nothing happened, she admitted defeat. Curling up beside him, she tenderly asked, "What happens to the Queen?"

"She waits," he said. "Safe and high, she waits. Everything below her is frozen now, glaciers stretching to the sea. But in another century, maybe two, spring comes. The heat soars, and the ice melts, and safe inside that tough shell, she rides the flood down to the sea."

"And then?" she whispered.

"The Queen is a repository, a living, sentient ark. But she only holds the land-dwelling species. Fishes and sea creatures…they rely on a second ark…a different sort of body waiting under the sea ice…"

"Is that a second Queen?"

"Yes," he said. Then in his next breath, he said, "No. It's not a Queen. It's something else entirely."

"Her King?"

He said, "No." And then with a second thought, he allowed, "Maybe. In a certain fashion, I suppose so."

Quee Lee slid her hand across his young chest and belly. In countless ways, she was grateful that Perri had survived. There were moments when she wanted to beg him to remain home, giving her the same devotion that he willingly gave to his adventures. But that would never happen. Outside of a daydream, there was no way for that to happen. Rubbing the perfect skin, she took a deep breath, and finally, with a quiet firm and determined voice, she surprised both of them.

"Take me," she said.

She said, "The next time winter comes. Show me."

Here was a fresh twist on a very old conversation. Perri tried to smile, reminding her, "You don't normally enjoy my adventures."

"I want to meet the Dawsheen," she said. "I want to see their Queen."

"Maybe someone should take you."

"Maybe I should go myself."

"It's going to be cold and uncomfortable," he said. "Watching a world die…it can't be anyway but grueling. Do you think you're strong enough to endure that sort of fun?"

"And you think you're strong?" she asked.

Then with her smallest finger, she touched the corner of a newborn eye, gathering up the glistening remains of a tear.

9

The world was white, and damned. The snow fell in waves, burying the dead lanes and high roofs, wiping away every last trace of the city. Huddled inside their homes—inside their graves—the citizens could do nothing but wait for any good news, nursing little hopes amid wild despair. Only the river held the thinnest promise of life. Flat slabs of ice moved in a great parade, immune to fear or caution, holding their pace until their prows pushed out into the air, and dipped, each slab falling with smooth inevitability, dropping over the brink of the falls, still floating on the face of the water as it plunged into a cold, fierce maelstrom.

Lastborn took them over the brink, and down.

Eleven kilometers of air and spray and thunder lay below them, and behind the water stood the basalt cliff. Sensors began working, hunting for things that were surely trying to hide—a few bodies and probably some machinery, plus every trick of camouflage that a smuggler could drag along.

The sensors found plenty, none of it remarkable. Each vertical kilometer was examined in detail, and then the Dawsheen took them back towards the sky, flying along the waterfall's lip, peppering the current with tiny probes better suited for other, easier jobs.

Perri ignored the search, or pretended to ignore it.

"No one is here," Lastborn declared.

Perri was squinting into his elaborate map, studying an empty maze of tunnels situated on the far side of the cliff.

Again, the Dawsheen said, "There is no one." Then with an improving sense of things, he turned to Quee Lee, confessing, "My tools and patience are exhausted. I will leave you inside the jail, where you will be safe."

"No."

Both of them said that word. Quee Lee spoke with a begging tone, while Perri nearly shouted.

The map dissolved and Perri pocketed his tiny projector. "Leave us at the base of the falls," he told Lastborn. "I've got one good place to look."

"There is, I promise, no one." But the alien relented, dashing over the little knoll where the couple had watched the Gathering, then dropping fast. Where the cliff was exposed, it formed a massive black wall decorated with that single zigzagging white line. That line was the staircase covered with snow. Now and again, little shapes came into view, crawling their way up through the

295

snow. Half a dozen secondary parades were attempting the long, hard climb. These were the Queen's little sisters. Evolution and pragmatism demanded their existence. What if disaster struck? But no Queen had been lost during the last ten thousand Alls. They were symbols only—emergency repositories of genetic matter accompanied by smaller entourages, each encasing only a fraction of the genetic wealth held by their big sister.

The base of the cliff was bare rock, the freezing mist reducing visibilities to a soggy arm's length.

"Where?" asked Quee Lee.

Perri looked at her for an instant. "Maybe you should stay here."

She leaped first, and again, loudly, she asked, "Where?"

"We'll work our way along the base," he said. "Stagger closer to the falls."

The rocks were treacherous, slick and jumbled. Sensing the terrain, their boots sprouted crampons, and their robes shed the freezing water, channeling it off to their downstream side. Too late, Quee Lee turned to say, "Thank you," to Lastborn. But he had already lifted off. Then to her husband, with a modest concern, she asked, "Won't the water crush us? Or the falling ice?"

"Probably," he said, stepping into the lead. "But the ice is slush before it reaches bottom, and the river is choked to a trickle. Compared to what it was."

"You pray," she said.

He laughed, saying, "Yes, help me pray. That just about doubles its effectiveness."

They marched. Rock litter and massive boulders quickly vanished beneath a frosting of new ice. In a sense, it was an easy walk. The cliff was always to their left, always close. A foot might plant wrong, but the boot invented some way to faultlessly hold the balance. Sometimes Perri moved ahead too quickly, and vanished. But later, as Quee Lee grew accustomed to the pace, she would catch him, a gloved hand set firmly against his back, reminding him of her presence and urging her to hurry.

There was some ill-defined moment when they moved behind the great falls.

Half a kilometer later, they were blind. The robes were pushing against their functional limits, and the sleet sounded like an avalanche of gravel. Quee Lee refused to quit, but she was regretting her stubbornness. Never again, never, would she let herself ignore her rational instincts, following after Perri in one of his little miseries.

Perri stopped in the wet blackness. Crouching, he activated his holo-map. But instead of checking their position, he ordered up one of the Ship's main reactors. Then he magnified that portion of the map, peering inside the reactor chamber. The light was sudden, brilliant and pure. This was a traveler's trick: Dial to a bright place, and let the map illuminate your surroundings.

The image of fusion threw a white glow against the base of the cliff. They saw a cavern or maybe an overhanging spur of rock. A glimmer came back at them, and Perri stood and walked straight for the glimmer and it brightened gradually, and lifted, and Quee Lee looked up to see motion overhead. She was watching two figures apparently walking on their heads.

The ceiling was hyperfiber.

The Great Ship's bones lay exposed. Tumbling waters must have chiseled away the basalt, revealing the supporting strata. She looked at herself—a sloppy, pale version of herself—and then she looked ahead again, hurrying after Perri, the air drying while the roar of the sleet fell into an angry rumble.

She didn't see the kidnappers.

Perri slowed and dimmed his map, and he kneeled, saying nothing. With a hand in the air, he asked her to drop beside him. Then he extinguished the map, letting a second light burst into view.

The cave ended with a wall of high-grade hyperfiber. Three men stood before the wall, manipulating a plasma drill, using slow measured bursts to peel away the barrier in millimeter bites. Work fast, and someone might notice the energy discharges. Work too slow and someone might stumble into their hiding place. The men seemed perfectly attuned to their task, urgency married to patience. Burn, clean the new surface, and wait. Burn, clean, wait. Burn, clean, wait. The rhythm was steady and relentless, and very nearly silent. The only voice belonged to the man who had yelled at the Dawsheen waiter. "Now," he would say every minute. And the other two men would step behind opaque shields, letting the drill spit out another carefully crafted pulse.

"How did they get here?" Quee Lee asked.

Expecting the question, Perri was already pointing into the shadows. "We just walked past their ship. It looks like a boulder, because it is a hollow rock, reequipped and very sneaky."

She nodded, and squinted.

The drill pulsed, washing the scene with light, but she couldn't see what she wanted to see.

"The Queen," she said.

"I don't know," he said.

A minute later, the man called out, "Now."

And again, the drill pulsed. This time, Quee Lee glanced to her right, spotting two figures. The human was sitting on a flat slab of gray-black stone. The Queen was sitting, too. Was that really Her? They weren't too far away. In the gloom, the creature resembled any Dawsheen. But there her features were smooth, almost plainness, like a hurried sketch of something infinitely more complicated. She was wearing a plain cloak, nothing about her distinctive. There was no hair or plumage, no flourishes. She was sitting across from her kidnapper. Again, the drill pulsed, and the injured hyperfiber continued to glow. With a voice that wasn't right for a Dawsheen, the Queen said a few words. The man was wearing an odd wide smile, and he said a few words of his own, his voice sounding like the bleating of a child's toy.

Quee Lee tried to make sense of the scene.

And then she felt something, or heard something. For no conscious reason, she looked back over her shoulder, turning in time to see a boot perched on an adjacent rock, and the trousers tucked into the boot, the trousers lifting into a rounded body that was wearing the dark, thoroughly drenched uniform of a Dawsheen police office.

She put her elbow into Perri's side.

He started to turn.

Lastborn aimed his weapon with a practiced touch, but his nervousness fought against an easy shot. It took another moment for him to feel sure enough to fire. The gun drained itself in one full blast, and the world turned white, the screaming ball of plasmas rolling towards its target. But a set of transparent diamond shields absorbed the blast, keeping the Queen from being incinerated.

Perri said, "Shit," and stood.

Lastborn unholstered his second weapon, and with the same nervous earnestness aimed at the Queen.

Her shields had evaporated. She tried to run, and the human threw himself between Her and the attacker—a fearless, useless gesture—and Perri managed to throw a loose rock overhand, catching Lastborn on the back of his head.

The second blast hit the ceiling and faded.

In reflex, Quee Lee sprinted at Lastborn.

The alien was working with his first gun, trying to find enough residual power for a second shot.

"Why?" she screamed. "Why?"

She grabbed the lead foot, and yanked, accomplishing nothing.

"Why—?"

And then what felt like a great hand descended on them, and there was nothing else to see.

10

Every morning, She would walk with her instructors, and listen. The beach was sand made by the glaciers and living wind-reefs built from the same sand. The Sea was blue and warm and just a little salty. When her instructors spoke, the tropical blue air filled with words about duty and history and honor and the great noble future. The duty was Her own, demanding and essential; while the honor was entirely theirs. Who wouldn't wish to nourish and educate the newborn Queen? Together, the instructors shared a history reaching back into a mist of conjecture and dream; while the future lay before Her, as real as anything can be that has not yet been born.

She was an empty vessel walking beside the warm blue water—a large vessel filled with empty spaces, every space begging to be jammed full of important treasure.

Her powers were obvious. Animals fell silent and still as she passed, staring at her simple body with the purest longing. Every bush and fruited blade threw out its spores, hoping to find Her blessing. Even the tiniest microbe struggled to reach her, crawling wildly across a dampened grain of quartz while one of Her vast and noble feet rested in the lazy surf.

The Queen's little sisters didn't elicit such dramatic responses. One day, She looked back at them and at their own little entourages, and with simple curiosity asked, "What is their future?"

Her first instructor was an elderly Dawsheen woman. She answered with a dismissive tone, as if to say, "What happens to them does not matter." But then, sensing the Queen wasn't satisfied, she explained, "They will follow you, always. And hibernate in their safe havens. And your children will eat their sleeping bodies, except for the one or two of them will be sent away—"

"Sent where?"

"Another world, perhaps." The face was full of indifference. Little sisters couldn't be more insignificant to this old woman. "We roam the galaxy for a purpose," she reminded her student, gesturing to the illusion of a sky. "At this moment, my people are hunting for suitably empty worlds."

That was when the Queen realized that she did not like this woman.

Then there was a different walk, on an entirely different day. She sensed eyes staring and a silence. But the stare didn't come from the trees or soil this time. Looking out at the little waves, she spied what resembled a mossy stone bobbed in the surf, a pair of enormous black eyes watching nothing but Her.

She had never seen one of the Others.

For the briefest instant, with a mixture of curiosity and desire, She returned the gaze. And then her instructor covered Her eyes with every hand, and a sudden voice, tight and angry, warned her, "It should watch your sisters, not you. That one is not yours."

But the eyes kept staring, and She returned their gaze.

"Your Magnificence," the old woman said. "Your Other has already been chosen, infinitely suited for You and Your glorious duty. Please, please, turn your eyes away. Everyone knows that that Other is sick, and peculiar, and you do not want to know anything more about it...!"

Perri woke slowly.

"There's a general alert," someone said. Then after a pause, the same voice said, "Shit."

Perri pried his eyes open and breathed. His pain told him that he still had hands and feet, and an intact body. His skin was warm and bare, arms and legs were lashed down. Someone sat beside him, similarly restrained. Quee Lee. Was she awake? Maybe. He wasn't certain. Then he looked at two figures sitting on the floor opposite him—a human hand lay hidden inside the Queen's Dawsheen hands—and what was meant to look like a human face betrayed bliss and simple, corrosive horror.

Finally, Perri understood.

Again, Loon said, "Shit."

The male creature sitting before Perri spoke in a whisper, and a translator buried in the false throat asked, "What is wrong now?"

The smugglers sat at the front of the little cap-car, each eavesdropping on a different sliver of the security net. A third time, Loon said, "Shit." Then he turned and grimaced, saying, "We'll slip past fine. I've got emergency routes waiting. I've beaten these general alarms plenty of times."

Quee Lee stirred and quietly called to her husband.

Perri nestled against her. "You're all right now."

"And you?"

He didn't answer. With a rapt intensity, he stared at the Queen, and when she seemed to look back at him, he asked, "Why?"

The man-figure looked at him now.

"Why?" Perri repeated.

Neither entity answered that deceptively simple question.

Then Loon threw up his arms, saying, "This shouldn't have happened. If you'd let me kill that Dawsheen–"

The Queen bleated, and her translator said, "No."

"No killing," said her companion. "I explained."

"One old, doomed Dawsheen. Good as dead already." Loon shook his head, frustrated and enraged, and helpless. "But of course we had to leave him. We had to give him the chance to get off a warning."

Again, Perri asked, "Why?"

Quee Lee was naked. Her robe, like Perri's, had been taken away, along with every link to their buried nexuses. But they were unhurt. Loon was a smuggler. In the right circumstance, he might kill an alien, but murdering human beings was an entirely different crime.

"I don't understand," Perri said. "Explain this to me. Why?"

Dipping her head, Quee Lee said, "Because the two of them, in some uncommon sense, are in love with each other."

Perri shook his head, a thin laugh breaking out. "Except that's not what I'm asking them."

Both aliens stared at him, wary but curious.

"I know what you want," Perri said. "You want each other. You're hoping to escape, to get onboard one of the little starships bound for somewhere else…another world, and some kind of freedom…and that's why you've gone to all this work and risk."

"Yes," the Queen rumbled.

"And that's why they want you to die," said Perri. "You're a traitor, in their eyes. A danger. An abomination!"

"Shut up," Loon told him.

"But you're not dangerous," Perri said, "and you're not any kind of abomination. Believe me, I understand. All you want is to join together. You want only what Queens and Others have desired from the beginning of time. An empty world, a fresh beginning, and the chance to realize your own future…"

Again, Loon started to say, "Shut up."

But the Other lifted one human hand, in warning. And with a smooth male voice, it said, "We have a beautiful, beautiful world to build."

"I can believe that," Perri said.

Then the Queen spoke, her musical voice diluted into the inadequate words, "A new world unlike any. A lovely, elegant All that will never be born if we do not make the proper journey!"

An alarm sounded, loud and urgent.

Loon cursed and abruptly changed course.

Quee Lee leaned forward, smiling at their shared hands. "It must be extraordinarily important to you, to make you sacrifice so much."

The Queen spoke for several moments, which the translator distilled to the single word, "Yes." But Her voice held the meaning, longing and sad desperation fixed to the faint, dying hope that something worthy would come out of all this crazy wanting.

Then one last time, Perri said, "I still want to understand why."

Queen and Other stared at him, baffled.

Then he asked, "Why did you hire Loon Fairbanks? Why did you think he was going to be your salvation?"

No answer came.

Loon rose to his feet. To nobody in particular, he shouted, "Will you just shut the hell up now!"

"That man," Perri said. "He smuggles objects, and he's not even the best at that. You need the finest. You deserve nothing less!"

The Other asked, "Who is the finest?"

"Me. I am."

Silence.

"What you should do is fire Loon," said Perri. "Dismiss him, and do it now. Do it this moment. Then I will hire him and his crew as my subcontractors, and I'll try to get you what you desire, and deserve."

The Queen spoke, no translation offered.

With the tone of a sorry confession, her mate and collaborator admitted, "But we have no more money to give."

"Goodness, that's no obstacle," Quee Lee blurted. And with an effusive grin, she said, "Believe me. This darling man works for surprisingly little!"

Her neighbors let her live alone for the next few years, enduring her shame. Her embarrassment. The shocking notoriety. Then a gradual, relentless process began. They began to invent ways to cross paths with Quee Lee. She might be shopping in a market or walking in one of the local parks, and one of her human acquaintances from a nearby apartment would appear without warning, wearing a benign smile, muttering, "Hello," before mentioning in the same breath, "We haven't seen nearly enough of you lately."

Even alone, they always spoke for the "We." The tiny word implied that each person stood among many, many like-minded souls. "We've worried about you," they might say. Or, "We miss you, Quee Lee. Come visit us, when you have the strength."

Strength wasn't a limiting issue. She couldn't remember when she last felt this strong. And their worry was genuine, but only to a point. No, there were other fine reasons to be alone. Quee Lee let her old friends speak among themselves, and gossip, and out-and-out spy. Only when it felt right did she begin walking the neighborhood again, visiting one or two of the wealthy souls who lived along her particular avenue. About her troubles, no one said a word. About her adventures…well, nobody could stop thinking about what had happened. She saw it in their staring faces. There was wondering and outrage and the almost comical fear that blossomed whenever they remembered that their dear friend had been involved in things illegal, violent, and strange.

About Quee Lee's husband, nobody asked. Fifty years had to pass before a woman-friend felt bold enough to look at the ancient woman with a mixture of concern and simple nosiness, and then risk saying the name.

"Perri."

"What about my husband?" Quee Lee asked.

"How is he?" the woman inquired. Then fearing that she had overstepped her bounds, she foolishly said, "Is he comfortable, where he is?"

What could she say? The truth?

Never that, no.

Instead, Quee Lee shrugged and remarked, "He's comfortable enough. And he looks reasonably contented."

"How often do you see him?"

"Every three weeks, for twenty-one minutes per visit," Quee Lee said. "Those are the terms of his sentence. One visitor every twenty-one days, and the rest of his time is spent among the general population."

"You poor soul," the friend moaned. "We're all so sorry for you."

"Don't be," was Quee Lee's advice. "Really, it's not that awful. It's not even that unpleasant, considering."

The wicked truth was that Perri adored prison. Surrounded by strange aliens and dangerous people, he was in his element. The Ship's enormous brig was an entirely new wilderness open for his explorations. He spoke in whispers and code while Quee Lee was visiting, offering hints of great new stories that would have to wait for another century to be told.

In principle, they were supposed to be alone in the visitation chamber, but you could never feel secure about your solitude. The chamber was a hyperfiber balloon. A molecule-thick screen stood between them. Permeable to light and sound, but not touch, the screen allowed them to undress and perform for each other, and sometimes that's what they did. Sometimes Quee Lee didn't care who might be watching them. And with an honest longing, she always told her husband, "I miss you. I want you. Make the years hurry up, would you?"

"I will," he always said, the perpetual laugh quiet and sweet.

Perri's sentence was one hundred and one years. An excellent attorney and a surprisingly law-abiding record had helped reduce his punishment. What hadn't helped was his stubborn refusal to implicate any other player or players in that very peculiar crime.

Sixty years before any neighbor dared mention the crime.

It was another good friend who finally bit into the topic. He was sitting with Quee Lee, sitting in her little jungle and helping her drink some of her more exotic liquors, and when the drugs and silence got too much, he blurted out the words, "What in hell were you thinking?"

She knew what he meant. But to be stubborn, she asked, "When?"

"Because you had to know all about it," he said. "You went off with Perri on that little vacation of yours, and ship security claims that you were with him and those two Dawsheen—"

"They weren't Dawsheen," she interrupted. "They were sentient genetic repositories."

"According to the Dawsheen, they were criminals." Sixty years of waiting was erased. The man was too drunk and self-consumed to let this issue pass for another moment. "I saw those security digitals, Quee Lee. Everybody has watched them."

"Well, that isn't legal," she said. "Those are confidential recordings."

"Well, then I am a criminal too," he said. "Call the Master Captain, if you want."

She fell silent.

"I saw the digitals," he said again. "From twenty angles, I watched your husband and that Dawsheen criminal. Sorry, I mean that sentient genetic repository criminal. Dressed up to look human, and walking with Perri and that storage trunk with the Queen stuffed inside."

"Is that what happened?" she said. "I never knew."

The sarcasm made him angrier. "Your husband was trying to slip them onboard that star-taxi. He got them past security…I don't know how…and then he waved good-bye and turned just as someone noticed a detail that was wrong…"

Quee Lee said nothing.

"That alien with the plasma gun. He was a real Dawsheen."

"One of their police officers, named Lastborn. Yes."

"The trunk was floating beside that human-looking repository, the Other, and then the trunk was gone. Destroyed. The Queen was dead."

"I know."

"It was public place, for goodness sake. Some innocent could have been killed."

She held her tongue.

"Such a scream, that Other gave. It roared and exposed that weapon and dropped to its knees, and…" His voice failed him. Immortal memories can seem new for aeons, and the will danger of that scene still bothered him after all these years. "He shot himself. I mean, it shot itself."

"I know what happened."

"A thousand innocent travelers running everywhere, screaming in well-deserved terror."

"I saw it happening," Quee Lee confessed. "I know."

Eyes widened. "So you really were there?"

She didn't answer him.

"Were you the woman walking the pet leopard? Or maybe you were disguised as one of the Blue Passions."

With a little finger, she wiped at one eye and then the other.

"We understand that your husband refused to implicate anyone else. He was protecting your good name, I suppose."

"Maybe."

"Protecting his sweet money tit," the man said.

A cold moment passed. Then with a black, hard voice, Quee Lee said to her long-time friend, "Really, it would be best if you left. Now, this moment. And if you can, I think you should run. Because in another moment, or two, I'm going to find a very long knife, and I'm going to cut out your ugly heart."

13

A century and a year had passed.

Perri strolled out of the Ship's main brig, and before anything else, hugged his wife. Then they left together on a very long journey. Like honeymooners, they enjoyed resorts and beaches and odd, out-of-the-way hotels that specialized in supplying fun to people who were accustomed to nothing else. In the middle of their travels, in full view of any watchful eyes, they rented a private suite in one of the deepest districts. For a full week, as far as any eavesdroppers could assume, they didn't leave those luxurious confines.

A hidden passageway and an unlicensed cap-car allowed two people to travel a thousand kilometers, reaching an empty corner of the Great Ship.

A second, equally anonymous cap-car carried them a little farther.

Pressed together, Perri and Quee Lee crawled up the narrow confines of a nameless fissure. He didn't know their precise destination. He relied on his wife to say, "Stop," and then, "There. That wall."

A hidden doorway let them pass.

The cold was abrupt, and brutal, and wonderful. The tilted floor of the cavern wore a river of blue ice. Above them, hidden in the rocks and snow, was a tiny redoubt; and fifty kilometers downstream was a brief, deep lake with just enough room for a single creature to swim in the dark, waiting for the inevitable spring.

"Another few years," Perri mentioned.

The Queen would awaken and ride the spring floods, following her own little river to its mouth.

Inside this tiny volume, the two Dawsheen repositories would merge into one, reshuffling and reformulating their genetics, creating an entirely new lineage of species and phyla. The basis for a new world would blossom inside several dozen square kilometers; and later, when the time was ripe, another new Queen and her Other would be born.

That was when Perri would finally slip them off the Ship, bound for an empty young world.

"It is going to be lovely," said Quee Lee. "Whatever they make here, I'm sure it will be wonderful."

Perri looked across the rugged ice and snows, and then he turned, smiling happily at his wife.

"Let's walk around," he suggested.

She shivered under her robe, asking, "Now? What could we possibly find here now?"

"I don't know," he said with a boyish giggle. "And that's why it's worth walking around."

Bridge Six

As sound, as scent, as florid bursts of EM or the crudest, roughest marks riven in the most ordinary stone, voices are everywhere. They are everywhere and growing larger by the year, the day, the breath. The loudest of them are never truly loud, despite what their important owners might believe, and none are constant and certainly none are eternal. But the accumulation of pheromones and vocalizations and holo images and flat images and shared dreams and private, secret dreams—that grand wild mounting of thought and expression—long ago erased every silence onboard this machine. The Ship shivers with the wild, undisciplined racket. Two and five and twenty voices together can use the same formulas, the same shared intents, but there are thousands of species and each individual can employ tongues, and between the rivers of words and every attached concept lay a multitude of understandings. A second species or even an creature from the same ranks will fail to hear what is said. True intents will be lost. No matter how simple or profane the fact, it can escape in an instant, escape without notice, and the orators play into the ignorance, which is another reason why voices will only grow louder with the passage of time.

Ignorance is a wound, and its victims fight to dispel what is misunderstood and what has never been known.

From birth to her ultimate end, every entity shouts, sings, wails, and whispers, and some of the finest thoughts are shared with soft touches and hard blows from fists and claws. Yet no one understands the other. This is a fundamental quality embedded in the universe, this monstrous incompetence welcoming every moment of existence.

If each beast knew the meaning behind every roar, then the Ship would press on through a much quieter Creation.

But the roars are dipped in mystery, in confusion, and this is perhaps the universe's finest, oldest hope: In the midst of foolishness and misdirection, in unexpected places and times, lost entities will understand one another perfectly, and the grandeur of those shared voices will cause the rest of the nonsense fall away, like the cold white sound that one hears when listening to the edges of the sky.

Night of Time

1

Ash drank a bitter tea while sitting in the shade outside his shop, comfortable on a little seat that he had carved for himself in the trunk of a massive, immortal bristlecone pine. The wind was tireless, dense and dry and pleasantly warm. The sun was a convincing illusion—a small K-class star perpetually locked at an early-morning angle, the false sky narrow and pink, an artful haze of dust pretending to have been blown from some faraway hell. At his feet lay a narrow, phenomenally deep canyon, glass roads anchored to the granite walls, with hundreds of narrow glass bridges stretched from one side to the other, making the air below glisten and glitter. Busier shops and markets are set beside the important roads, and scattered between were the hivelike mansions and mating halls, and elaborate fractal statues, and the vertical groves of cling-trees that lifted water from the distant river: The basics of life for the local species, the 31-3s.

The Ash, business was presently slow and it had been for some years. But he was a patient man and a pragmatist, and when you had a narrow skill tied to a well-earned reputation, it was only a matter of time before the desperate or those with too much money came searching for you.

"This will be the year," he said with a practiced, confident tone. "And maybe, this will be the day."

Any coincidence was minimal. It was his habit to say those words and then lean forward in his seat, watching the only road that happened to lead past his shop. If someone were coming, Ash would see him now. And as it happened, two figures were ascending the long glass ribbon, one leading the other, both fighting the steep grade as well as the thick endless wind.

The leader was large and simply shaped—a cylindrical body, black and smooth, held off the ground by six jointed limbs. Ash instantly recognized the species. And he decided that the other entity was human—a creature like himself, and at this distance, entirely familiar.

They weren't going to be clients. Most likely, they were sightseers. Perhaps they didn't even know one another. The two entities happened to be marching in the same direction. But as always, Ash summoned a seductive premonition. Then he finished his tea and ate the drowned ii-link beetle on the cup's bottom, relishing the acrid taste as he listened to the world, and after a little while, despite the heavy wind, he heard the quick dense voice of the alien—an endless blur of words and old stories and lofty abstract concepts born from one of the galaxy's great natural intellects.

When the speaker was close, Ash called out, "Wisdom passes."

A Vozzen couldn't resist such a compliment.

The road had finally flattened out. Jointed legs turned the long body, every eye focusing on the tall, rust-colored human sitting inside the craggy tree. The Vozzen continued walking sideways, but slowly, fatigued by the long march. His only garment was a fabric tube, black like his carapace and with the same slick texture. "Wisdom shall not pass," said a thin, shrill voice. Then the alien's translator made adjustments, and the voice softened. "If you are a man named Ash, this Wisdom intends to linger."

"I am Ash." He immediately dropped to his knees. The ground was rocky but acting like a supplicant would impress the species. "May I serve your Wisdom in some time way, sir?"

"Ash," the creature said. "The name is Old English. Is that correct?"

Genuine surprise brought laughter. Ash said, "Honestly, I am not quite sure."

"English," the creature repeated. The translator was extremely adept, creating an unnervingly human voice—mature and male, and pleasantly arrogant. "There was a tiny nation-state, and an island, and as I recall from my studies, England and its confederate tribes acquired a rather considerable empire that briefly covered the face of your cradle world."

"Fascinating," said Ash. The second figure was climbing the last long grade, pulling an enormous float-pack, and despite his initial verdict, Ash realized that the creature wasn't human at all.

"But you were not born on the Earth," the Vozzen continued. "Your flesh and your narrow build are revealing some very old augmentations."

"Mars," Ash said. "I was born there."

"Mars," the voice repeated. That simple word triggered a cascade of memories, facts and telling stories. Dipping into the flood, the Vozzen selected his next offering. "Old Mars was home to some fascinating political experiments. From your earliest terraforming societies to the Night of the Dust—"

"I remember," Ash interrupted, trying to gain control over the conversation. "Are you a historian, sir?"

"I am conversant in the past, yes."

"Then perhaps I shouldn't be too impressed. You seem to have been looking for me, and for all I know you've already researched whatever little history is wrapped around my life."

"It would be impolite not to study your existence," said the Vozzen.

"Granted." With another deep bow, Ash asked, "What can this old Martian do for a wise Vozzen?"

The alien fell silent.

Ash glanced at the second creature. Its skeleton and muscle were much like a man's, and the head wore a cap of what could have been dense brown hair. There was one mouth and two eyes but no visible nose, and the mouth was full of heavy pink teeth. Many humans had novel genetics, but this creature was not human. Ash sensed it, and using a private nexus, he asked his shop for a list of likely candidates.

"Ash," the Vozzen said. "Yes, I have made a rather full study of your considerable life."

Dipping his head, Ash drove his knees into the rough ground. "I am honored, sir. Thank you."

"I understand that you possess some exotic machinery."

"Quite novel. Yes, sir."

"And talents. You wield talents even rarer than your machinery."

"Unique talents," Ash said with effortless confidence. Lifting his gaze, he smiled, and wanting the advantage in his court, he rose to his feet, brushing the grit from his bloodied knees as he told his potential client, "I help those whom I can help."

"You help them for a fee," the alien remarked, disdain in the voice.

Ash approached the Vozzen. "My fee is a fair wage," he said. "A wage determined by the amoral marketplace."

"But I am an impoverished historian."

Ash gazed at the many bright black eyes, and with a voice tinged with careful menace, he said, "It must seem awful, I would think. Being a historian, and being Vozzen, and feeling your precious memories slowly and inexorably leaking away."

2

It was Ash's good fortune to be one of the first passengers onboard the Great Ship, and for several centuries he remained a simple tourist. But he had odd skills leftover from his former life, and as different aliens arrived, he made acquaintances bearing new ideas and fresh technologies. His shop was the natural outgrowth of that learning. "Sir," he said to the Vozzen. "Would you like to see what your money would buy?"

"Of course."

"And your companion–?"

"My aide will remain outside. Thank you."

The human-shaped creature seemed to expect that response. Walking under the bristlecone, he tethered his pack to a whitened branch, and with an unreadable expression stood at the canyon's edge, staring into the glittering depths, watching for the invisible river, perhaps, or perhaps watching his own private thoughts.

"By what name do I call you?"

"Master is adequate."

Every Vozzen was named Master, in one fashion or another. With a nod, Ash approached the shop's doorway. "And your aide–"

"Shadow."

"Shadow is his name?"

"Shadow is an adequate translation." Several jointed arms emerged from beneath the long body, complex hands tickling the edges of the door, one tiny sensor slipped from a pocket and pointed at the dark tunnel inside. "You are feeling curious, Ash."

"An occasional affliction of mine, yes."

"My companion's identity is a little mystery to you, I think."

"It is."

"Have you heard of the Aabacks?"

"But I have never seen one." Then after a brief silence, he said, "They are a rare species with a narrow intelligence and fierce loyalties, as I understand these matters."

"They are rather simple souls," Master said. "But whatever their limits, or because of them, they make wonderful servants."

The tunnel grew darker, and then the walls fell away. With a silent command, Ash triggered the lights to awaken, a great chamber suddenly revealed. The floor was simply tiled and the pine-faced ceiling arched high overhead while the distant walls lay behind banks and banks of machines that were barely awake, spelling themselves for those rare times when they were needed.

"Are you curious, Master?"

"Intensely and about many subjects," said the Vozzen. "What particular subject are you asking about?"

"How this magic works." Ash gestured with an ancient, comfortable pride. "Not even the captains can wield this technology. Within the confines of our galaxy, I doubt if there are three other facilities equally well-equipped."

"For memory retrieval," Master said. "I know the theory at play here. You manipulate the electrons inside your client's mind, enlarging their tiny effects. And you also manipulate the quantum nature of the local universe, reaching into a trillion alternate but equally valid realities. Then you combine these two subtle tricks, temporarily enlarging one mind's capacity to reminisce."

Ash stepped up to the main control panel.

"I deplore that particular theory," his client said.

"I'm not surprised."

"That endless-world image of the universe is obscene. It is grotesque and relentlessly ridiculous, and I have never approved of it."

"Many feel that way," Ash allowed.

Genuine anger surged. "This concept of an individual electron existing in countless realities, swimming wild in an endless ocean of potential, with every potential outcome creating what can only be described as an infinite number of outcomes—"

"We belong to one twig of reality," Ash interrupted. "One slip of wood riding on one giant tree, lost in the endless canopy of the multiverse forest."

"We are not," Master said.

The controls awoke. Every glow-button and thousand-layer display had its theatrical purpose. Ash could just as easily manipulate the machinery through nexuses buried in his own body, but his clients normally appreciated this visible, traditional show of structured light and important sound.

In Vozzen fashion, the hind legs slapped each other in disgust. "We are not a lonely reality lost among endless possibility," he said. "I am a historian and a scholar of some well-earned notoriety. My considerable life has been spent in the acquisition of the past, and its interpretation, and I refuse to believe that what I have studied—this great pageant of time and story—is nothing more than an obscure leaf shaking within an impossible-to-measure shrub."

"I'm tempted to agree with you," said Ash.

"Tempted?"

"There are moments when I believe..." Ash paused, as if to select his next words. "I can see us as the one true reality. The universe is exactly as it seems to be. As it should be. And what I employ here is a trick, one shifty means of interacting with ghost realities, magnetic whispers and unborn potentials. In other words, we are the trunk of the only tree, and the dreamlike branches have no purpose but to feed our magnificent souls."

The alien regarded Ash with new respect. The respect showed in the silence, and then with hands opening, delicate fingers wearing spiderweb patterns that were presented to the historian's equal.

"Is that what you believe now?" Master asked.

"For this particular moment, I do." Ash laughed quietly. Two nexuses and one display showed the same information: The historian had enough capital to hire him and his machinery. "And I will hold this faith for the rest of the day, if necessary."

Master said, "Good. Wonderful."

Ash turned toward him, bowing just enough. "What is it that you wish to remember, Master?"

The alien eyes lost their brightness.

"I am not entirely sure," the voice confessed with simple horror. "I have forgotten something important...something essential, I fear...but I can't even recall what that something might be..."

3

Hours had passed, and the projected sun hadn't moved. The wind was unchanged but the heat only seemed worse as Ash stepped from the cool depths of his shop, his body momentarily forgetting to perspire. He had left his client alone, standing inside a cylindrical reader with a thousand flavors of sensors fixed to his carapace and floating wild inside the ancient body and mind. Ash kept close watch over the Vozzen. Nexuses showed him telemetry, and if necessary, he could offer words of encouragement or warning. But for the moment his client was obeying the strict instructions, standing as motionless as possible while machines made intricate maps of his brain—a body-long array of superconducting proteins and light-baths and quantum artesians. The alien's one rebellion was his voice, kept soft as possible, but always busy, delivering an endless lecture about an arcane, mostly forgotten epoch.

The mapping phase was essential and relentlessly boring.

From a tiny slit in the pink granite wall, Ash plucked free a new cup of freshly brewed, deliciously bitter tea.

"The view is pleasant," a nearby voice declared.

"I like it." Ash sipped his drink. As a rule, Aabacks appreciated liquid gifts, but he made no offer, strolling under the bristlecone, out of the wind and sun. "What do you know about the 31-3s?"

"I know very little," Shadow said. The voice was his own, his larynx able to produce clear if somewhat slow human words.

"Their home is tidally locked and rather distant from its sun. Their atmosphere is rich in carbon dioxide, which my Martian lungs prefer." Ash tapped his own chest. "Water vapor and carbon dioxide warm the dayside hemisphere, and the prevailing winds carry excess heat and moisture to the nightside glaciers, which grow and flow into the dawn, melting to complete the cycle." With an appreciative nod, he said, "The Ship's engineers have done a magnificent job replicating the 31-3 environment."

Shadow's eyes were large and bright, bluish gray irises surrounding the black pupils. The pink teeth were heavy and flat-crowned, suitable for a diet of rough vegetation. Powerful jaw muscles ballooned outward when the mouth closed. A simple robe and rope belt were his only clothes. Four fingers and a thumb created each hand, but nothing like a fingernail showed. Ash watched the hands, and the bare, almost human feet. Reading the dirt, he was certain that Shadow hadn't moved since he had arrived. He was standing in the sun, in the wind, and like any scrupulously obedient servant, he would remain on that patch of ground until exhaustion claimed him.

"The 31-3s don't believe in time," Ash continued.

A meaningful expression passed across the face. Curiosity? Disdain? Shadow glanced at his companion and then looked down into the canyon again. "Is it the absence of days and nights?"

"Partly. But only partly."

Shadow leaned forward slightly. On the bright road below, a pack of 31-3s was dancing along, voices like brass chimes rising through the wind. Ash recognized his neighbors. He threw a little stone at them, to be polite. "The endless day is one factor, sure," he said. "But they've always been a long-lived species. On their world, with its changeless climate and durable genetics, every species enjoys a nearly immortal constitution. Where humans and Vozzens and Aabacks had to use modern bioengineering to conquer aging, the 31-3s evolved in a world where every lucky organism can live almost forever. That's why time was never an important concept to them. And that's why their native physics is so odd, and lovely: They formulated a vision of the universe that is almost, almost free of time."

The alien listened carefully, and then quietly admitted, "Master has explained some of the same concepts to me, I think."

"You're a good loyal audience," said Ash.

"It is my hope to be."

"What else do you do for Master?"

"I help with all that is routine," Shadow said. "In every capacity, I give him aid and free his mind for great undertakings."

"But mostly, you listen to him."

"Yes."

"Vozzens are compulsive explainers."

"Aabacks are natural listeners," said Shadow, with pride.

"Do you remember what he tells you?"

"Very little." For an instant, the face seemed human. An embarrassed smile and a shy blinking of the blue-gray eyes preceded the quiet admission, "I do not have a Vozzen's mind. And Master is an exceptional example of his species."

"You're right," said Ash. "On both accounts."

The alien shifted his feet and stared down at the 31-3s.

"Come with me."

"He wants me here," Shadow said. Nothing about the voice was defiant or even a little stubborn. He intended to obey the last order given to him, and with his gentle indifference, he warned that he couldn't be swayed.

Sternly, Ash asked, "What does Master want from this day?"

The question brought a contemplative silence.

"More than anything," said Ash, "he wants to recover what's most precious to him. And that is—"

"His memory."

Again, Ash said, "Come with me."

"For what good?"

"He talks to you, and yes, you've likely forgotten what he can't recall." With one long sip, Ash finished his tea and rolled the beetle into his mouth. "But likely and surely are two distinct words. So if you surely wish to help your friend, come with me. Come now."

4

"I do not deserve solitude," the Vozzen said. "If you intend to abandon me, warn me. You must."

"I will."

"Thank you."

"Do you feel that, Master?"

"Do I…what…?"

"Can you sense anything unusual?"

The alien was tethered to a fresh array of sensors, plus devices infinitely more intrusive. Here and in a hundred trillion alternate realities, Master stood in the same position, legs locked and arms folded against his belly. With his voice slightly puzzled, he said, "I am remembering my cradle nest."

"Is that unusual?"

"It is unlikely," the Vozzen said.

"And now?"

"My first mate," he said. "We are in the nest, overlooking a fungal garden. The garden needs tending."

"And now?"

He paused and then said, "Your ship. I am seeing the Great Ship from space, as my shuttle makes its final approach."

Ash said nothing.

"It's a historian's dream, riding inside a vessel such as this."

"And now?" said Ash.

Silence.

"Where are you?"

"Inside a small lecture hall," Master said.

"When?"

"Eleven months in the past. I am giving a public lecture." He paused for a moment. "I make a modest living, speaking to parties about whichever topics interest them."

"What do you remember about that day's lecture?"

"Everything," Master said. But the voice had no confidence, and with a doubting tone he said, "A woman?"

"What woman?"

"A human woman."

"What about her?" Ash pressed.

"She was attending…sitting in a seat to my right…? No, my left. How odd. I usually know where to place every face."

"What was the topic?"

"Topic?"

"Of the lecture. What did your audience want to hear?"

"I was giving a general history of the Great Wheel of Smoke."

"The Milky Way," Ash said.

"Your name for everyone's galaxy, yes." With a web-like hand, the alien reached in front of his own face. "I was sharing a very shallow overview of our shared history, naming the most important species of the last three billion years." The hand closed on nothing and retreated. "For many reasons, there have been few genuinely significant species. Some might be modestly abundant, and others relatively wealthy. But I was making the point…the critical line of reasoning…that since the metal-rich world began spawning intelligence, no one species or clusters of related sentient organisms have been able to dominate more than a small puff of the Smoke."

"Why is that?"

The simple question unleashed a flood of thoughts, recollections, and abstract ideas, filling the displays with wild flashes of color and elaborate, highly organized shapes."

"There are many reasons," Master said.

"Name three."

"Why? Do you wish to learn?"

"I want to pass the time pleasantly," said Ash, studying the data with a blank, almost impassive face. "Three reasons why no species can dominate the Milky Way. In brief, please."

"Distance. Divergence. And divine wisdom."

"The distance between stars…is that what you mean…?"

"Naturally," the historian said. "Star-flight remains slow and expensive and potentially dangerous. Many species are compelled to remain at home, safe and comfortable, reengineering the spacious confines of their own solar system."

"Divergence?"

"A single species can evolve in many fashions. New organic forms. Joining with machines. Becoming machines. Sweeping cultural experiments. Even the obliteration of physical bodies. No species can dominate any portion of space if what it becomes are many, many new and often competing species."

Ash blinked slowly. "What about divine wisdom?"

"This is the single most important factor," said Master. "Ruling the heavens is a child's desire."

"True enough."

"The galaxy is not a world, or even a hundred thousand worlds. It is too vast and chaotic to embrace, and with maturity comes the inevitable wisdom to accept that some dreams are impossible."

"And what about the woman?"

"Which woman?" Master was startled by the question, as if another voice had asked it. "The human female. Yes. Frankly, I don't think she's important in the smallest way. I don't even know why I am thinking about her."

"Because I'm forcing you to think about her."

"Why? Does she interest you?"

"Not particularly." Ash looked up abruptly, staring at the black eyes. "She asked you a question, didn't she?"

"I remember. Yes."

"What question?"

"She asked about human beings, of course." With gentle disdain, the historian said, "You are a young species. And yes, you have been fortunate. Your brief story is fat with luck as well as fortuitous decisions. The Great Ship is a prime example. Large and ancient, and empty, and you happened to be the species that found it and took possession. And now you are interacting with a wealth of older, more knowledgeable species, gaining their gifts at a rate rarely if every experienced in the last three billion years."

"What did she ask?"

"Pardon me. Did you just ask a question?"

"I want to know what the woman said."

"I think…I know…she asked, 'Will humanity be the first species to dominate the Milky Way?'"

"What was the woman's name?"

Master said nothing.

Ash feathered a hundred separate controls.

"She did not offer any name," the historian said.

"What did she look like?"

Again, with a puzzled air, the great mind had to admit, "I didn't notice her appearance, or I am losing my mind."

Ash waited for a moment. "What was your reply?"

"I told her and the entire audience, 'Milk is your child's food. If humans had named the galaxy after smoke, they wouldn't bother with this nonsense of trying to consume trillions upon trillions of worlds.'"

For a long while, Ash said nothing.

Then, quietly, the historian asked, "Where is my assistant? Where is Shadow?"

"Waiting where you told him to wait," Ash lied. And in the next breath, "Let's talk about Shadow for a moment. Shall we?"

* * *

"What do you remember...now...?"

"A crunch cake, and sweet water." Shadow and Ash were standing in a separate, smaller chamber. Opening his mouth, the subject tasted the cake again. "Then a pudding of succulents and bark from the Gi-Ti tree."

"And now?"

"Another crunch cake. In a small restaurant beside the Alpha Sea."

With mild amusement, Ash reported, "This is what you remember best. Meals. I can see your dinners stacked up for fifty thousand years."

"I enjoy eating," the alien said.

"A good Aaback attitude."

Silence.

And then the alien turned, soft cords dragged along the floor. Perhaps he had felt something—a touch, a sudden chill—or maybe the expression on his face was born from his own thoughts. Either way, he suddenly asked, "How did you learn this work, Ash?"

"I was taught," he said. "And when I was better than my teachers, I learned on my own, through experiment and hard practice."

"Master claims you are very good, if not the best.

"I'll thank him for that assessment. But he is right: No one is better at this game than me."

The alien seemed to consider his next words. Then, "He mentioned that you are from a little world. Mars, was it? I remember something that he said, something that happened in your youth. The Night of the Dust, was it?"

"A lot of history happened back then."

"Was it a war?" Shadow pressed. "Master often lectures about human history, and your worlds seem to have a fondness for fighting."

"I'm glad he finds us interesting."

"Your species fascinates him." Shadow tried to move and discovered that he couldn't. Save for his twin heart/lungs and the mouth, every muscle in his body was fused in place. "I don't quite understand why he feels this interest."

"You attend his lectures, don't you?"

"Always."

"He makes most of his income from public talks."

"Many souls are interested in his words."

"Do you recall a lecture from last year?" Ash gave details, and he appeared disappointed when Shadow said:

"No, I don't remember. There must not have been any food in that lecture hall."

The Aaback and human laughed together.

Then Ash said, "Let's try something new. For the sake of calibrations, I want you to think back as far as possible. Describe the very first meal that you can remember."

A long pause ended with, "A little crunch cake. I was a child, and it was my first adult meal."

"I used to be an interrogator," Ash said abruptly.

The other's eyes were gray and watchful.

"During that old war, I interrogated people, and on certain days, I tortured them." He nodded calmly, adding, "Memory is a real thing. Maybe it is the most real thing, Shadow. Memory is a dense little nest made, like everything, from electrons—where the electrons are and where they are not—and you would be appalled, just appalled, by the ways that something real can be hacked out of the surrounding bullshit."

* * *

"Quee Lee."

"Pardon?"

"She is the mysterious human woman." Ash began disconnecting his devices, leaving only the minimal few to keep shepherding the Vozzen's mind. "It was easy enough to learn her name. A lecture attended by humans, on such-and-such day. When I found one lady, she told me about another. Who mentioned a good friend who might have gone to listen to you. But while that woman hadn't heard of you, she mentioned an acquaintance who had a fondness for the past, and her name is Quee Lee. She happened to be there, and she asked the question."

Relief filled Master, and with a thrilled voice, he said, "I remember her now, yes. Yes. She was interested in human dominance over the galaxy."

"Not quite, no."

Suspicion flowered, and curiosity followed. "She didn't ask the question?"

"She did, but it was her second question, and strictly speaking, it didn't belong to her." Ash smiled and nodded. "The woman sitting beside her wanted it asked, and as a favor, Quee Lee repeated the question, since she had your attention in hand."

A brief pause ended with a wary question. "What then did the woman ask first?"

Ash stared at the remaining displays, and with a quiet, firm voice said, "I've spoken with Quee Lee. At length. She remembers asking you, 'What was the earliest sentient life to arise in the galaxy?'"

The words generated a sophisticated response. An ocean of learning was tapped, and from that enormity a single turquoise thread was pulled free, and offered. Five candidates were named in a rush. Then the historian rapidly described each species, their home worlds, and eventual fates.

"None survived into the modern age," he said sadly. "Except as rumor and unsubstantiated sightings, the earliest generation of intelligence has died away."

Ash nodded and waited.

"How could I forget such a very small thing?"

"Because it is so small," Ash said. "The honest, sad truth is that your age is showing. I'm an old man for my species, but that's nothing compared to you. The Vozzen journeyed out among the stars during my Permian. Your mind is enormous and dense and extraordinarily quick. But it is a mind. No matter how vast and how adept, it suffers from what is called bounded rationality. You don't know everything, no matter how much you wish otherwise. And your surroundings today are enriched, full of opportunities to learn. So long as you wish to understand new wonders, you're going to have to allow, on occasion, little pieces of your past to fade away."

"But why would such a trivial matter bother me so?" asked Master.

And then in the next instant, he answered his own question. "Because it was trivial, and lost. I'm not accustomed to forgetting. The sensation is quite novel. I suppose it must have preyed on my equilibrium, and wore a wound in my mind.

"Exactly," lied Ash. "Exactly, and exactly."

5

After giving him fair warning, Ash began to leave the historian. "The final probes still need to disengage themselves," he said. Then with a careful tone, he asked, "Should I bring your assistant to you? Would you like to see him now?"

"Please."

"Very well." Ash pretended to step outside, turning in the darkened hallway, centuries of practice telling him where to step. Entering the secondary chamber, he used a casual voice, mentioning to Shadow, "By the way, I think I know what you are."

"What I am?"

With sudden fierceness, Ash asked, "Did you really believe that you could fool me?"

The alien said nothing, and by every physical means, he acted puzzled but unworried.

Ash knew better.

"Your body is mostly Aaback, but there's something else. If I hadn't suspected it, I wouldn't have found it. But what seems to be your brain serves as an elaborate camouflage for a quiet, nearly invisible neural network."

The alien reached with both hands, yanking one of the cables free from his forehead. Then a long tongue reached high, wiping the gray blood from the wound. A halfway choked voice asked, "What do you see inside me?"

"Dinners," Ash reported. "Dinners reaching back for billions of years."

Silence.

"Do you belong to one of the first five species?"

The alien continued tearing out the cables, but he was powerless to void the drifters inside his double-mind.

"No," said Ash. With a sly smile, he said, "I don't think you're one of the five. I can tell. You're even older than that, aren't you?"

The tongue retreated into the mouth. A clear, sorry voice said, "I am not sure, no."

"And that's why," said Ash.

"Why?"

"The woman asked the question about the oldest species, and you picked that moment because of her." He laughed, nodded. "What did you use? How did you slice a few minutes out of a Vozzen's perfect memory?"

"With a small disruptive device–"

"I want to see it."

"No."

Ash kept laughing. "Oh, yes. You are going to show me the tool."

Silence.

"Master doesn't even suspect," Ash said. "You were the one who wanted to visit me. You simply gave the Vozzen a good excuse. You heard about me somehow, and you wanted me to peer inside his soul, and yours. You were hoping that I would piece together the clues and tell you what I was seeing inside your peculiar mind."

"What do you see?" Shadow asked.

"Two basic elements." A thought severed every link with Shadow, and with professional poise, Ash said, "Your soul might be ten or twelve billion years old. I don't know how that could be, but I can imagine: In the earliest days of the universe, when stars were young and metal-poor, life found some other way to evolve. A completely separate path. Structured plasmas, maybe. Maybe. Whatever the route, your ancestors evolved and spread and then died away as the universe turned cold and empty. Except on occasion, when they managed to adapt. Using organic bodies as hosts, from what I can see."

"I am the only survivor," Shadow said. "Whatever the reason, I cannot remember anyone else like me."

"You are genuinely ancient, and I think you are smarter than you pretend to be. But this ghost mind is limited, unsophisticated. Vozzens are far smarter, and most humans too. But when I was watching your thoughts, when you were contemplating crunch cakes, I saw other dinners, secret dinners, reaching back for a billion years, at least. And that kind of vista begs for an explanation."

Ash took a deep breath. "Your mind is limited, but your memory has help. Quantum help. And this isn't on any scale that I've ever come across, or even imagined possible. I can gather the collective conscience from a trillion Masters, but with you, I can't pick a number than looks sane."

The alien showed his pink teeth, saying nothing.

"Are you pleased?" Ash asked.

"Pleased by what?"

"You are probably the most common entity in Creation," said Ash. "I have never seen such a signal. This clear. This deep and dramatic. In one form or another, you exist in a fat, astonishing portion of all the possible realities."

Shadow said, "Yes."

"Yes what?"

With a tiny nod, a human nod, he said, "Yes, I am pleased."

6

The sun always held its position in the fictional sky. And always, the same wind blew with relentless calm. In such a world, it was easy to believe there was no such monster as time, and the day would never end, and a man with old and exceptionally sad memories could convince himself, on occasion, that there would never be another night.

Ash was last to leave the shop.

"Again, thank you for your considerable help," said the historian.

"Thank you for your generous gift." Ash found another cup of tea waiting for him, and he sipped down a full mouthful, watching Shadow untether the floating pack. "Where next?"

"I have more lectures to give," Master said.

"Good."

"And I will interview the newest passengers onboard the Ship."

"As research, I presume."

"And as a pleasure, yes."

Shadow was placing a tiny object beside one of the bristlecone's roots. "If you don't lend me the disruptor," Ash had threatened, "I'll explain a few deep secrets to the Vozzen."

Shadow had relented, of course.

Sipping tea, Ash quietly said, "Master. What can you tell me about the future?"

"About what is to come–?"

"I never met a historian who didn't have opinions on that subject," Ash said. "Consider my species, for instance. What will happen to us in the next twenty million years?"

Master launched into an abbreviated but dense lecture, explaining to his tiny audience what was possible about forecasting the future and what was unknowable, and how every bridge between the two was an illusion.

His audience wasn't listening.

With a whisper, Ash asked Shadow, "But why do you live this way? With him, in this kind of role?"

In an Aaback fashion, the creature grinned. Then Shadow peered over the edge of the canyon, speaking to no one in particular when he explained, "He needs me so much. This is why."

"As a servant?"

"And as a friend, and a confidant." With a very human shrug, he asked Ash, "How could anyone survive even a single day, if he didn't feel as if he was, in some little great way, needed?"

Bridge Seven

Ruling the skin of one living world are the bacteria and the bugs, giant megaplegs marching through forests of gaul-trees and scurrying heart roaches, and gilled wanderers and quirks and the atolls of rhom-clams that speckle the face of the Twin Seas. That skin, that fierce light-washed biosphere, has a mass. Every physical attribute can be measured precisely, to the nearest microgram and milliliter, and that is for a single planet of no great significance but for its perfect lack of all significance.

Now repeat the study with a thousand other worlds.

Gas giants can be sterilized by exploding stars and their own internal furnaces, and cosmic accidents along with grand oversights will strip away the self-replicating and self-improving from uncounted terrestrial worlds. But where life exists, bacteria and viruses dominate. Buried oceans are ubiquitous, common inside large comets and the sunless planets cast into the interstellar silence. Each ocean has its thin population of mindless tenacious slow life. Wet stony crust and cold slurries of methane and rock-hard ice hold their own multitudes. Apply any kind of lasting energy to one of those bodies—sunlight or tides or radionuclides, and everything else arises: Communal cells and elaborate organisms and organs that produce nothing but thought. Intelligence arises. Societies and grand histories emerge. Machines will be built from carved plastics and titanium and quilts of silicon that think for others and then for themselves, and then machines become another mass of viable, measurable life.

This is all to say that the galaxy is rich with life.

Measured as mass and as volume, a staggering quantity of material can live happily somewhere and survive in many other places. The galaxy is thick with naturally made starships, and even the poorest inhabited world is a wondrous vessel, loyally following its sun or wandering free in the dark, carrying far too much possibility to be measured, to be calculated, to be known.

The Great Ship is so very small by comparison.

A fleck of simple, sterile rock and pure hyperfiber, reactors and rockets, it carries assorted chambers filled with haphazard examples of life—slivers of great biospheres bound for other places, or nowhere.

Each planet is a ship that never stops moving.

The Ship is merely swifter than the rest, and odder. But no grand authority seems able to give the true compelling reason why the Great Ship should be considered valuable, or even notable.

Ignore me, the voice pleads.

Get off me and forget me and I promise, I will vanish, into the smothering gloom, with the barest fuss.

Aeon's Child

1

Pamir was a captain of consequence. His ageless frame was tall and strong, partly because passengers seemed to expect both from the ship's officers, and a large, pleasantly homely face conveyed confidence and a burdensome wisdom. In uniform, he drew long looks, whether from humans or sighted aliens. And unlike most captains, he had risen in the Ship's hierarchy without depending on friendships or flattery. It was said in his presence, with all the best intentions, that Pamir could have become a Submaster by now, earning a seat at the Master Captain's table, if only he would attempt to play the game.

"Give gifts," Washen advised. "Memorable gifts, and durable. Gifts that will say, 'Pamir,' for ten thousand years."

He knew the game but feigned ignorance. "What would I give that could impress a Submaster?"

"There's that alien weed you like to grow. The one that sings."

"The llano-vibra."

"Is that its name?"

He nodded, removing his mirrored captain's cap and setting it on one of the obsidian busts fixed to the table's corners. "You think I should be giving away weeds."

"Pretty ones," she said. "Why not? Offer a reason."

Disgusted, he said, "People would see the unmistakable calculations."

"Then again, maybe you don't deserve any promotion." Washen was tall and strong—a captain of roughly equal rank—and she was pretty in a smooth, unconscious way. They were lovers once, but that was so long ago that the details had evaporated. Friend to friend, she argued, "A captain must believe in calculations. How else can he do his job? Formulas for acceleration, for stress loads. For managing passengers, for ass-kissing. If you don't respect your equations, maybe you don't belong at the Master Captain's table."

"I agree with you." Their drinks rose from the table's center. Claiming his rain-of-tears, Pamir said, "I don't deserve anything, and we can move to other business."

"Such as?"

"I don't know. You wanted to see me, as I recall."

"And I can't linger," she complained. "I'm greeting a shuttle full of Y'uy'uy. Have you heard of them?" No, he hadn't. "A social species, and tiny.

A couple million of them are arriving, and if I don't wiggle my fingers at each one, in the proper way, the entire nest is my enemy."

As if practicing, Washen curled and uncurled a ring finger.

Pamir looked across the lounge, through the long transparent wall. The shallow black surf sloshed against the rocks below. Poisonous to earth life, alien plankton were rapidly consuming the false sunlight and water, and a host of little fish were growing swiftly. In another few months the lake would become a stiff coal-colored gelatin—the only food for the ten thousand Bloom onboard. Arriving in force, the Bloom would throw a celebration, and the lounge would be jammed with onlookers, watching their fellow passengers chop out feasts and snacks and the trapped succulent fish.

"But hey," said Washen. "Speaking of newcomers…"

Pamir turned. Puzzled, alert.

"I found one for you. And he fits most of your parameters." With a sweeping, overly dramatic gesture, she handed him a memo chip. "The odd bioscan. A very peculiar ship. And a port of origin that doesn't quite seem real."

The chip was a giant snowflake worn simple by countless hands, its whiteness magnified by the tired black stone of the tabletop.

"A peculiar ship," she repeated. "Wooden, but not like any wood I know. He sold it for scrap. I've got the recyke reports. How many times have you seen a starship built from lumber?"

Pamir reached across the table, making a fist. "Who is he?"

"Don't you know? You asked me to watch for him."

Loudly, he asked, "How long has he been here?"

"You should see yourself," said Washen. Then she laughed, shaking her drink and inhaling the gases that rose out of solution. "I don't think I've ever seen quite that face on you."

"When did this passenger come onboard?"

She tapped the snowflake, as if answers would spring forth. "More than a week ago. But I was too busy to handle the case, and you were off-duty somewhere, and besides, you never offered any reason to sound alarms."

Pamir wrestled with adrenaline, feigning self-control.

"Wood," she repeated. "Tough, weird wood. Cellulose laced with non-terran proteins configured for strength and durability. Except it doesn't give much protection from radiation, or from impacts, and I'm surprised how fit the passenger seemed to be."

"An organic ship," he said.

"In places, yes." She sniffed her drink again, enjoying the temporary corrosion of her nervous system. "The engines had metals where you need them, and ceramics, and the guts were good-enough diamond. But there wasn't anything like hyperfiber, and the scrap value was nil."

"A starfaring tree." Pamir consumed the rest of his drink, barely tasting the salt, wishing all the while that this was some enormous, curious coincidence.

"I did some research for you." Again she tapped the chip. "There's a report of another ship like this one. Organic and sloppy. But it didn't stay with us, as it happens."

"Thank you," he said.

"A sketchy, misfiled report." Washen was staring at a point behind his eyes. "I don't even know who wrote it."

Pamir lifted his cap with both hands, placing it on his head, at an angle calculated to give the passengers confidence in him. At least the human passengers. Again, he said, "Thank you."

"The man calls himself Samara."

He barely heard the voice.

"Human, but not completely. From a colony world that exists, only we didn't pass within five hundred light-years of it."

What should happen next? It was centuries since Pamir had considered this scenario, and he felt lost, cold and ill, fears building between those gaping weaknesses.

"Samara qualified as primarily-human." Another tap at the snowflake. "If you need his address, it's waiting for you."

Washen was a close friend, and she was doing him a great favor. Yet he was so consumed by his troubles that when he looked at the captain he felt anger—a blistering, sloppy, unfair rage. He wanted to ask how such a creature could get onboard. But instead of speaking, he tugged on the violet-black epaulets, thick fingers struggling to remain gentle.

"Some advice," said Washen. "Come to the Master Captain's dinner this year. Bring your singing weeds, call them calculations, and smile until your face hurts." She showed him a gracious smile and two flirtatious winks, all framed by her mirrored uniform and cap. "Sit beside me, if you'd like."

Pamir could think of nothing to say except, "I don't raise llano-vibra anymore."

"No?"

"Not in ages," he said, claiming the memo chip and again looking through the transparent wall, gazing at the strange black lake while struggling not to think about death.

2

The Great Ship was safer than any other starship, but it was also far larger and substantially more complicated. There were fine districts and wondrous, important neighborhoods, and there were poverty wards famous for crime and novel forms of madness. Samara had taken an apartment in the most notorious ward. Pamir learned that from the chip and from his own research. Yet the newcomer was a relatively wealthy passenger, offering more than just a wooden starship to the local markets. He had brought vials of giant molecules, intricate and irreproducible, considered high art by various species. He also brought the mummified feet of another alien, collected on the home world and sold to grieving, grateful relatives. Plus Samara was the reputed author of a billion-word novel meant for the AI readers, already purchased by an onboard publisher and released to lukewarm reviews.

Whatever Samara was, he was distinctive.

A minor captain had interviewed him. His humanness was a central question. There were oddities in the bioscans, and shown the details, Samara nodded and smiled, tiny teeth flashing in a small, thin-lipped mouth. Then a voice more suitable for a bird said, "Yes, yes. A consequence of my home world. But those bodies are inert. Take all you want and watch them. Feed them. Torture them, if you wish. Nothing will happen because they aren't alive." The bodies were organic, convoluted and holding a passing resemblance to mitochondria. "They're produced by the natives. They get inside us, and there's no ridding of them. Unless you want to endure a cell-by-cell scrubbing, which I'm willing to do if you believe this grit might pose some kind of threat…"

Samara was small and almost pretty, attempting charm but not quite succeeding. If Pamir had been the interviewer, knowing nothing, he would have pressed the man for more information. Why leave the home world? What was his ultimate destination? There was ample reason to delay, pulling new tests from the bottomless bag that every captain possessed. But that little captain had avoided any ugliness, moving toward short-term issues. "How will you live here?" he had asked.

"How will I pay my way?" A songful laugh. A human hand swept through hair that seemed blond until it was touched, then for an instant, at certain angles, became a bright golden-green. "I've done my research, and believe me, I plan to live cheaply. Without complaints."

Captains like to hear promises of compliance.

"You've seen my ship," said Samara, using another grin. "To have come this far, and in such a vessel…doesn't that prove sincerity?"

It proved desperation, but the interviewer had seemed impressed with the logic, nodding and smiling in turn.

Pamir made a note to reprimand the officer, if he could do so without being noticed by anyone higher up. Then he hunted through every shipboard record in his grasp. A thousand-year passage was paid off. The cramped apartment was rented and then left empty. After a long search of security digitals—and several turf wars with security troops—Pamir pieced together portions of the man's last few days, including a talkative lunch with a familiar face.

"Perri," said the captain. "Out of everyone, and he finds you."

Several hours later, he was inside a wealthy human district, at the front door of what passed for a modest local apartment. Long ago, Perri had been a member of the crew, but he quit for the high life of a gigolo, eventually fooling an ancient lady into marriage.

The wife met him at the door.

Pamir had several excuses at the ready, but Quee Lee just smiled at the unexpected captain. "You probably need to see my husband. Am I right?"

"Yes, ma'am."

In the same moment, she and the apartment called for Perri. But there were hectares of rooms behind her, and she had enough time to invite him into the stone hallway, and reading his public nexus, she said his name. She said, "The Pamir Mountains are one of the earth's backbones. Unless they were torn down since I left, I suppose."

"I wouldn't know, ma'am."

"I climbed several of the peaks, but that was ages ago."

The captain didn't know what to say.

"I am such a humdrum creature anymore," she said, amusement working within the words.

Pamir was thankful when the husband finally appeared, and the wife kissed him and whispered a few words before retreating out of sight.

With the natural smile of a charmer, Perri asked, "What do you want, friend?"

Friend was an insult. Showing a digital, he said, "Samara."

"I remember his name."

Pamir said, "You ate with him."

"I guess I remember that too." Something here was quite funny. "And you want to know what we talked about."

"I know what you said."

The gigolo was weighing Pamir's mood.

"Samara learned that you are a traveler, that you know the Ship better than anyone else."

"Not better than the captains, of course."

Pamir ignored that noise. A lip-reading AI had prepared the transcript, and while parts of conversation were invisible, the gist of the luncheon was easy to see. "Samara asked about secret places, private wildernesses, and any quiet location that never quite makes the public maps."

"The intriguing rooms in our house, yes."

"What does he want?" asked the captain.

"He seems to be a traveler in his own right. But he didn't name any specific goal."

"Can you guess?"

"Conjectures are light. It doesn't take much to throw one."

"Where does our sewage go?"

"Down," said Perri, laughing quietly and shrugging his shoulders. "Yes, he asked about sewage, and you already know that."

"There are treatment plants, and they are off-limits. Just a jumble of machines, you told him." Pamir was breathing in ragged, wet gulps. "Big facilities as old as the Ship, doing nothing but scrubbing the water clean. And there's nothing interesting to see in any of them."

Perri leaned against the polished stone wall, waiting.

"You told him there's no point in visiting the treatment plants, then you claimed that you've never been there."

"Because I haven't been."

Pamir took him by the throat, squeezing for emphasis. It was an ancient gesture, useless today and yet woven into every human's innate fear. A choking hand remained an effective crudeness, and so did a low angry voice. "Lie and I'll hurt you," said the captain. "If I don't believe you, I will ruin you."

"I didn't tell him." Perri's face was red and wet. With both hands, he tried to punish Pamir's forearm. "I told him…nothing…!"

"Because you knew I was watching."

Perri gave him a hard kick to the groin.

The pain was savage, and it was nothing. "You met with him later, in secret," said Pamir. "That's when you told Samara what you saw."

"I saw nothing," the smaller man said. "And we didn't meet later. I saw that man just once." Then Perri wrapped both of his hands around Pamir's choking hand, and a sly odd and almost mischievous look came into his bulging eyes. He started to squeeze, adding to the pressure, and a major bone inside his neck shattered with a quiet snap.

Pamir let go.

Leaning against the wall, Perri felt his neck healing, and he coughed in pain and then in less pain. Blood came up with the spit. Both men looked at the mess on the back of the small hand, and then a thick, slow voice said, "I promised not to tell, and I didn't tell, and I wouldn't know what to say if I had the urge, since I barely saw the place."

"Samara offered to pay you handsomely."

The gigolo charms had been set aside. Lucid fury filled the eyes. "Maybe you didn't notice, but I don't need money. And I paid for my own damn lunch." Massaging the broken neck, he said, "Besides, I like Samara even less than I like you."

Pamir was surprised. "Oh, what don't you like?"

No easy answer was waiting. "There's something wrong with Samara, and there's not enough that's right." The coughed-up blood was retreating into his skin. He swallowed twice, the pain lessening, and then he said, "The entity is deep water. Whatever he is, he's mostly hidden."

Pamir's surprise had doubled. He believed the man, despite all odds, and he felt utter pleasure in the fact that two people didn't approve of this new immigrant.

"Darling?"

The hapless wife was emerging from the shadows, walking with a deliberative gait, looking at Pamir while she asked her husband:

"Are you all right, sweetness?"

Another cough, and Perri said, "Absolutely fine."

Quee Lee stopped just short of them. She was small and pretty, and the pretty face was set. "Sir, I think you should leave now." With a chilled voice, she said, "Captain or not, I want you out of my home."

As if Pamir was the villain here.

3

Captain had their preferred districts, usually just beneath the hull, and in this one slender case, Pamir had obeyed the tradition. His apartment was relatively small, set away from the traffic areas, in a portion of a catacomb that nobody entered by mistake. The private realm had several hundred meters of tunnels, rooms of a hectare or two, and a whirlpool pond with bronze-colored orfes swimming endlessly in the spinning water, beds of blackpot mussels fixed to the bottom, preventing erosion for the last ten thousand years.

Before the mussels, Pamir had used hypersaline corals and wise-squids from Karta's World.

Before corals, he just let the water gnaw at its basin, sculpting the greenish olivine however it wished.

Staring at the unkempt surroundings, the rare visitor might mention that cleaning your home wasn't a crime. After all, nobody knew who the Ship's builders had been, and what if one of them returned suddenly: Wouldn't you want to keep their property presentable?

But Pamir relished the slumping, oxidized walls. He loved the palpable sense of titanic age, the possibilities of history. In the early centuries, he had spent every off-duty moment inside his largest room, staring a wall covered with crosshatched scratches, trying to decipher meanings that might not exist. It was another delicious, unanswerable mystery inside a machine with more mysteries than inhabitants. In the same room, Pamir began culturing the delicate llano-vibra plants, mastering their byzantine genetics to create songs of fragile, surreal beauty. But then the hobby drifted away from him, and the plants went wild, crossbreeding at will while losing all sense of pitch and rhythm.

A harsh, incoherent wail rose when Pamir entered the room. Barely noticing, he halfway ran through the tangled growth, bending to touch a certain knob of damp green stone.

The floor beside him neatly dropped out of sight.

The cap-car waiting below didn't exist, and it used nothing but energy stolen from nonessential machinery. The hatch sealed with a hiss. As Pamir sat, the car accelerated, taking him through a network of empty tubes and passageways, never repeating any previous course.

Sensors watched for any fool trying to follow him.

Nobody ever did.

But he imagined Samara hunched over an identical panel, watching him with a cool, amoral malevolence. The image made him anxious when he was awake, and then its way into his dreams while he slept; and only in the last thousand kilometer fall could Pamir genuinely rest, shaken awake with the berthing.

Pamir undressed, his uniform left hanging in the car. Stepping through a second camouflaged doorway, he was attacked by a screaming mist, gray and toxic. Hands to the mouth, he pushed ahead slowly, eyes tearing and sinuses catching fire, his naked feet splashing through caustic puddles and over a slope of badly eroded, diamond-sharp hyperfibers—a last line of defense to dissuade the curious and the feeble.

A thousand sewers fed into the district's purification center. Spent water, industrial wastes and the byproducts of alien biologies came roaring from orifices on all sides. The nearest sewer flowed from human places, and it was a genuine river, swift and familiarly rancid, beaten white by the ceaseless turbulence.

Years ago, Perri had ridden with that filth, his body encased in a hyperfiber suit, both hidden inside a whale's rotting carcass. The self-styled adventurer evaded every security system and survived the maelstrom, expecting to find great machines at work—filters and distillers and atom-cracking wonders older than vertebrates, and more durable.

But to his amazement, he found the Child instead, and with it one naked and enraged captain.

Breathing between his fingers, Pamir felt his throat swell and bleed. There was a thin and wobbly trail beneath him that he could feel more than see, and he avoided it, preferring the thin carpet of mock-fungi, gray and bristly, thriving on a diet of toxins. The sewer's roar was vast, uncomplicated. Other fluids were moving underground, the air reverberating with thunderous swallowing sounds. Eventually the mists thinned and then vanished, leaving him on the shelf where he always stopped. He lowered his burned hands. The flesh was already healing. Eyes blinked and dripped for a few moments, reclaiming their superior vision, and he lifted his gaze, turning in a slow circle, absorbing his surroundings.

The ceiling was an inverted bowl, a peach-colored sun strung from the apex, both sun and ceiling obscured by banks of water-fat clouds. The floor was like a shattered plate—a ten thousand square kilometer plate—its shards loosely reassembled, every gap a canyon where a different sewer flowed. In the center was an ocean of sand—countless grains of scrap hyperfiber and catalytic metals—and on top of the sand lay a shallow lake being perpetually drained, its overflow bound for reservoirs that would slake millions of thirsts.

The old machines and every surface were built of hyperfiber, yet little of the wonderstuff was visible.

Life covered every surface.

Dense and vibrant.

Noisy.

Tireless.

Kilometer-long mock-vines. Mock-trees taller than starships. Mock-fungi wearing elegant shapes and vivid fluorescent colors. And all were linked, roots and fleshy tendrils locked together, a perfect biological embrace extending into the sewers, absorbing and lifting the tainted water, xylem pulling it through filtering gills and kidneys and more gills. Everything of value was harvested. Everything else—the filth of modern technology—was destroyed, if not on the first try then on the next, or the thousandth. However long the work took, it took; the Child was nothing if not tenacious, doing its job without failure or complaint.

As was the custom, Pamir whispered, "Hello."

The reply was diffuse and immediate. Millions of mouths and other orifices exhaled as one, mangling the words, "Hello," and "Captain," and "Friend Pamir."

The ground shook under the Child's voice.

Pamir moved, head down, stepping wherever the vegetation looked soft and sturdy. His footprints didn't linger. Every trace of him was erased. Bacterium and viral bodies, skin flakes and dislodged hairs were caught and digested. Everything but the captain became the Child, incorporated and annihilated, then refashioned to serve some critical task.

Several times each year, during off-duty time, Pamir visited the Child.

Their relationship was centuries old.

Yet even now he had to remind himself that here was one inhabitant, one organism—a multitude of forms but all linked, like the cells inside his own durable body.

Only better.

Mock-animals appeared, and mock-insects and mock-rodents and sharp little bodies that looked more like tools than organisms. A herd of mock-okapi grazed on poisoned foliage, shitting sweet treasures as they moved closer. Then a mock-angel arrived, shaped like a winged human female, gliding into a meadow of mock-grass, its umbilical linking with the grass and the Child, the gesture as automatic as breathing.

Neural bodies spoke through the angel. A feminine voice observed, "You are early, friend, and by a long measure."

Pamir tried to speak and then stopped himself, unsure how to proceed.

Cloud-colored wings lashed at the air, causing the dew to leap from the gold-green blades—a clean chill rain in reverse—and with concern on its human face, the angel asked:

"What is wrong, friend Pamir?"

Pure, raw fear made him shiver and hold himself.

The Child tasted fear compounds boiling from him, and each body sobbed the same question from whatever passed for a mouth:

"What is wrong?"

Then again, in a thunderblast:

"WHAT IS WRONG?"

Pamir cupped his hands to his dampened face, legs buckling, knees diving into a mat of sweet-scented mushrooms. Beneath them was a solvent, gray and alien. Suddenly exposed to the air, its rank odor made him cough, tasting blood again. He wished he could fall unconscious but he didn't. He had no choice but to say, "The Monster." His voice was quick, almost soundless. "The Monster's here, and I'm sorry. Sorry."

But the Child had already guessed as much; what else could be so awful?

The mock-okapi came forward, placid herbivorous faces dropping, big cobalt tongues lapping at the solvent as the eyes gazed through him; and the angel spoke, a small pitiful voice asking, "Will you help me?"

Spores exploded into the air, tasting of cinnamon and things unnamed.

"Please, friend Pamir, will you help me?"

Even before he answered, Pamir wondered why the Child would have to ask. After everything he had risked, staking so much on the survival of this one organism…why did he still have to prove his devotion, and with something as thin as words…?

4

A minor captain had handled the initial interview, tabulating each discrepancy against the subject's sketchy background. Then with an absence of spirit, he left the would-be immigrant waiting in the quarantine cell while he went to his superior. The second captain chastised him for doing nothing, and then she approached a still higher-ranked officer with a reputation for not giving a shit. But bureaucrats trained by millennia of ritual and small decisions needed the occasional blood-letting. Even a thousand years later, Pamir recalled the prolonged, deeply inspired dressing-down giving to both of his whimpering colleagues. Why, why, why should he get dragged into something as minuscule as one inappropriate passenger? Throw the idiot back into his ship, or kick him overboard. Then as the captains turned to run, he amended himself, saying, "No, I'll do the throwing and kicking. Watch your nexuses, and learn."

The immigrant had a fictional name and a dubious biography. Smaller than any human adult, he bore a glancing resemblance to a child, his fine features emphasizing the huge green eyes and a young boy's oversized head. Yet he claimed to be an adult, both in words and under bioscans. His starship was a wooden-hulled, crude and profoundly unsafe vessel, and he had built it himself. His home was a tiny, little-known colony world. From a region without humans, Pamir knew, and he pressed the man-child on that subject, making him admit that the home was a lie, that his identity was fabricated, and his bioscan was exactly what it seemed to be: A collection of odd, even bizarre features scattered inside a glancingly human shell.

The body was camouflage, and it wasn't especially good camouflage.

"You're alien," said Pamir. "Admit it. There's no harm. We like aliens here. We don't even know how many kinds are riding with us." A lie. Each species was registered, regardless of intelligence or numbers. "Maybe you're a criminal on your home world. These things happen. There's no shame or embarrassment, or whatever you call your suffering. We are a human venture, and the grand crimes of your planet might not make us blink. How do you know? Until the truth shakes free, nobody knows."

"I am not a criminal," said the creature, tears running and the bottom lip pushing out in a shamelessly human gesture.

The eye-rich face was a calculation, Pamir knew, and these emotions arose from the same calculation.

357

And none of this would matter.

"I have done nothing wrong," said a soft, resolute voice.

"Not a criminal, but a saint. Huh." A pitiless gaze and hard laugh seemed useful. "We can use saints. All we can find. But you see, the rules require me to ask: Saint or not, how do you intend to pay for your passage?"

The mouth closed tight and then opened slightly, words dribbling from it. "You can have my ship."

"Your ship is trash," the captain said. "How it's held together this long, I don't know."

Now the green eyes were dry but infinitely fragile.

Pamir shook his head. Laugher was a weapon, and he attacked with it, battering the victim before asking another good question. "How did you learn so much about us?"

"I monitored your broadcasts."

"And you're alien. Just say, 'Yes.'"

"Yes."

"See? And here you sit, still safe and whole."

The alien dipped its head, soft golden hairs breaking the light into tiny rainbows.

"What sort of beast are you?" Pamir pointed a thick finger at his victim, and he lied. "Give details and you won't be punished. Honest details might even earn you rewards."

"I like humans."

"Which are words that mean so little," said Pamir. "You've gone to the trouble of manufacturing a human carriage. Like me or not, the intent is to mislead my species, and sad to say, that in itself is a significant and punishable offense."

"I will do no harm," it said, trying tears again.

"What are you?"

"A refugee."

Watching the tears, Pamir wondered if they were just a little genuine. "Son," he said, "let me show you real honesty in action. Yes, we see quite a few refugees, but we are a commercial vessel on a pleasure cruise, every last passenger obliged to pay his way: In goods, or services, in any of several abstract monetary systems, or with rich gifts of knowledge."

The alien nodded and began to stand.

"What are you doing?" Pamir asked.

"I don't know," it whispered.

"You saw our broadcasts. Weren't you suitably warned?"

No response.

Through a nexus, Pamir started the eviction procedure. Then almost as an afterthought, he asked, "Are you certain that you don't have some useful skill?"

"I have many skills."

"Fine. Name one."

The alien took several steps before finding the right direction. Then it asked Pamir, "May I retrieve something from my ship?"

"But I'll be watching you," he said. "Remember."

That was another lie. Pamir concentrated on the legal essentials. He had no reason to watch a small tragedy unfold, which was why he mandated that an engineer would examine the wooden starship first, and if found unworthy, the alien would remain in captivity until a berth could be found on a willing transport.

He didn't notice the Child's return.

A weak breath was heard, and Pamir lifted his eyes. Nestled in the boyish hands was an open vial full of some thick black liquid. "Can you scan this, please?" asked the Child. Easily, in an instant, and the results showed a stew of aggressive toxins and carnivorous oxides. One drop on the skin would destroy a healthy man's body. Pamir's first thought was that the foolish organism was going to play the Let-me-stay-or-I-will-kill-you gambit.

A trio of defensive systems was awakened, added to the usual tools.

But there was no threat, verbal or implied. The Child simply lifted the vial to its mouth and drank it dry, and then with ungulate teeth grown in the last minutes, it chewed the crystal glass to slivers and swallowed them too.

Pamir's laugh felt forced. "Okay, you are a tough little bug. You're put together differently than me, and so what? It doesn't matter. On my authority, I am expelling you from the Ship. Good luck to you, and good-bye."

"I'll clean this water," the Child promised. Begged. "If you will wait a moment—"

"Toward what end?" Pamir interrupted. "What you're doing is not special, much less spectacular. Not if your aim is shipboard entertainment. Not with hundreds of millennia waiting ahead of us, no."

The Child approached him, its breath scalding.

"Before this, I drank your water," it said.

"My water."

"After I spoke to the first captain, I tasted what you drink." A pinching of features; a visible pain. "Sour water."

Pamir said nothing, waiting.

"Your recycling systems are ill, I think."

That was a class-one secret. This district's purification system was struggling with the pollutants of so many species. But the contamination was at such a low level that no organism, or even a bioscan, would be able to tease out the part-per-trillion impurities.

"I can help you."

Pamir built a weak smile, swallowed and said, "Maybe you can clean up the occasional mouthful and liter, my friend. But multiply that by rivers of sewage, night and day, and what possible good are you?"

The Child had hoped to be accepted as human, and if that failed, as an ordinary alien. But with both prospects finished, it had no choice but honesty. Pamir couldn't be trusted—how could it have faith in an organism so unlike itself—but it was out of choices, save death.

In a quiet, stolid fashion, it said, "I have more than this mouth."

"Is that so?"

"I can be large," it promised.

Pamir didn't respond, gathering his belongings, ready to leave.

"Once," said the Child, "I was vast."

"As big as me?"

Realizing it was being mocked, and either out of anger or rage, the Child grabbed Pamir at the waist and lifted him from the ground. Then with its stinking, blistering breath, it told him, "I was once as large as a world."

"A world?"

"If you had known me, you would describe me as..." A pause. "As being..." The face was changing, gaining color and a rock's stillness, eyes shrinking to hot white points. "As being Gaian. I am, that."

The captain kicked at the air, not believing the words but unable to discount them either.

Moments passed with that strange little organism holding the giant man far from the floor.

Then Pamir asked, "What are you?"

If he heard that impossible word again—"Gaian"—he could laugh out loud and then dismiss the creature and its nonsense out of hand. That's what he believed before the Child suddenly dropped him.

"I am small," it said.

Black tears streaking its changing face.

"I have become small, and weak, and I beg you, wondrous sir, will you allow me to stay here with you?"

5

The Monster had arrived, and after delivering the news, Pamir remained with the Child for several more days and nights. Old contingencies were resurrected. Various actions and defensive schemes were examined in detail. The Child was already altering its nature, still cleaning the incoming waters but pulling more and more flesh into fighting bodies unlike anything the captain had ever seen. Mock-okapi collapsed and died. Mock-rodents grew poisoned fangs and spurs. And the mock-angels ate corpses while transforming themselves into griffin-like creatures, hot-blooded and enormous, gills sucking in oxygen like ramjets as they learned to fly, great roaring flocks of them patrolling just beneath the clouds.

The furious activity comforted Pamir. The Monster was close, but it hadn't yet found the Child. And even if it did, he couldn't believe that a tiny organism without allies or resources could prevail. He said as much to his companion, and the Child responded with silence. The entire cavern paused, save for the rushing waters. Then a griffin landed nearby and said, "Perhaps you are right, friend Pamir." But there was no confidence behind the words, and he wondered in which ways he had disappointed the creature.

Boarding the cap-car, Pamir started for home.

The long-ago interview felt new again, and he began doubting himself. A more ambitious captain would have worked the opportunity, dragging the Child before a Submaster or perhaps the Master Captain herself. The Gaian would have been granted official asylum, responsibilities passing along the links of command; and today, the Monster would be facing the official resolve and pooled resources of the united Ship.

But doubts soon collapsed. Pamir's superiors might not have understood the situation, evicting the Child out of fear and ignorance. Or more likely, the Submasters would have seen blessings wrapped inside the creature's singular genetics, and they would have done any ugly thing to render a profit. And even if through some lack of judgment they acted honorably, granting asylum to the Child, security measures would have grown weak over time. Captains talked. Most of them were babblers who told passengers any astonished thing, just to impress. And with passengers coming and going, in short order this entire arm of the galaxy would have known about the Child, and the Monster would have arrived even sooner, wearing even better camouflage.

No, Pamir had picked the least-awful solution. There were regulations, and there were places never imagined by regulations; he used a vague directive allowing a captain to take a single entity into temporary protective care. That's why he had faked the Child's eviction. With the two other captains watching, he had said, "There are no Gaians, and you think that I'm an idiot." He faked data that would explain the magic trick, and then to sell the lie, he had launched the wooden starship toward the nearest inhabitable world. Its engine was sabotaged but without reason, the reactor failing on its own. A few decades later, there was a flash of light against the stars, and the ship was gone, and Pamir comforted his subordinates by reminding them that rules had reasons and the blame was his to wear, not theirs, and just to keep this between the three of them, he would put the proper files where they couldn't be found.

By then, Pamir had wrested control of a faltering sewage plant from another captain. The colleague went away thinking that she was the crafty one, getting out from under that onerous station. Nobody asked questions or thought to complain. Gradually, as the Child grew larger and more competent, Pamir put the ancient machines to sleep. Insoluble problems were gone. Effluents were absorbed and simplified, and water pure to the billion-trillion levels ran from every tap. And for nearly a thousand years, lies and the occasional bribe were able to deflect every official who showed the least little curiosity in trash.

The Child became his friend, and more.

Intelligent. Awesome. Beautiful beyond measure: And that from an ancient human who had grown tired of stars and nebulae, human lovers and his chosen profession.

The Child was a miracle, and the captain was its savior. Pamir's visits began with a thunderous voice of welcome and a thousand charities. Fruits and meaty pods were invented, no two tasting alike. Mock-lovers took every lubricious form. Visual spectacles, in light and in fire, made Pamir forget to breathe. Singing in unison, a trillion mouths made his scraggly llano-vibra seem pathetic. Astonishing creations rose from the malleable body—sauropods bigger than hills; dragons spitting narcotic clouds of perfume; butterflies with hectare-sized wings; and once, a living giant with Pamir's face and body, the mirrored uniform and the perfectly tipped cap. And between the marvels were multitudes of flying flowers and burning fungi and impossible species evolved in a night and extinct before the next day's end.

The other captains would say, "How do you use your free time? We don't see you anymore."

It didn't occur to Pamir that they missed his company. They were just nosy people, and he forgave them, shrugging his shoulders while saying, "I do a little traveling, alone. Or I stay home. Whichever suits my grumpy mood."

"That's funny," a few captains told him. "From the symptoms, we thought you'd found a new lover."

And Washen went farther, saying, "She must be incredible, and I'm guessing that you're ashamed of her."

Ashamed? Never. And he wouldn't use the word "lover", except perhaps in the most abstract, ethereal sense.

But leaving the Child so soon felt like abandoning a lover. Pamir missed its company after he was underway, and for every conscious instant after that. And because the Child hadn't liked his hopeful attitude, he stopped feeling it. He purged his moods, feeding a nugget of gloom until there was nothing else, a useful piece of him terrified that the Monster—this Samara creature—would attack now, in his absence, robbing Pamir of his chance to die with his perfect friend.

Home again, slipping through the invisible entrance, Pamir's first thought was to contact the Child through one of several secure means. He just wanted to know that it was safe. But that was a risk in itself, and instead he activated his sleeping nexuses, reengaging with captains and messages and little duties and fond notes from people that he hadn't seen in ages.

A familiar face was waiting for him, the sexless voice saying, "Hello, Pamir."

Pamir triggered the digital by saying, "Hello."

"Once you have extricated yourself from the Child, you must meet with me,' said Samara. "We need to share the same air."

Why was he surprised? He had no right to feel startled, and the glacial cold building inside him was another useless distraction.

"We can meet on neutral ground. You select the place." Samara paused and smiled, and the background slid into focus. The creature was sitting in a captain's lounge, and behind it, perched beside a second table, was the captain who had first interviewed the Child.

Samara laughed, anticipating Pamir's reaction.

"I will assure you of your safety," it said. "Honestly, sir, I hold no malice towards you."

Inside his enormous life, Pamir had never felt this alone, small and vulnerable.

A child-sized hand appeared, lifting a glass to thin, smiling lips. "Dear captain, how could you hope to hide anything so large?" Samara asked, taking a sip of chilled water.

Hope was a game, a makeshift shelter for ego and pride, and how could Pamir ever hope to keep the Child a perfect secret, belonging to no one but himself?

$$6$$

Full, unedited maps were only available to captains—in principle—but Samara claimed to know how to find their meeting place. The Ship had been mapped by robots, tiny and self-replicating; set free inside tunnels, they doubled their numbers with each branching, employing sound and radiation to peer into the chilled metal and stone surrounding them. One robot had walked into Pamir's selected chamber, but finding no other exits, it turned and retreated. No human hand had ever touched that space, which was its chief attraction. Anything organic, down to the smallest, most desiccated spore had to be linked to the captain, or more likely, to Samara.

As clean as medicine and persistence could make him, Pamir arrived early for the encounter. Robot tracks showed the way, nothing else marring a thin coating of gray-white dust. No contamination, claimed his scanner. He brightened his torch's beam. And of all things, he clearly remembered the first time that he had stepped inside his apartment, billions of years of peaceful darkness shattered and a weak, self-important part of the man grieving because of it.

There was a sound.

From out there?

"Welcome," said a voice. It was familiar and not, neither warm nor cold. Then a diffuse orange glow silhouetted a human figure, both of them tiny to begin with and apparently distant.

Pamir took another bioscan, unable to find the slightest hint of anything that didn't belong to him.

The chamber was a cube, precisely fashioned and intended for no known purpose. A little more than a kilometer on a side, it seemed both vast and relentlessly claustrophobic; Pamir had to concentrate to make his legs walk, the sound of his boots crisp and steady, each footfall swallowed by the darkness.

"Welcome," said the voice once more. Louder, nearer.

Pamir hesitated, took a ragged breath, and asking, "What do you want?"

Said the Monster, "I want what you expect me to want. I intend to kill your friend."

There. At least it was said.

Again he was walking, halfway across the square floor, and then farther, still nothing organic but his own throng of tailored microbes and wayward cells. Yet there was a vivid glowing mass of something, presumably alive, and

Pamir could only guess where his opponent had stolen the materials and energy to construct it.

No, "construct" was the wrong word.

He straightened his cap, extinguished the torch, and stepped at a faster clip. Everything was Samara—the luring orange light and human shape were extensions of the hidden genetics, the mammoth potentials. And still, the damned machine refused to show any trace of it.

"You're kind to see me," said Samara. Its body was the same as when it stepped onboard, except nude and blatantly sexless, empty hands offered and the face seemingly amused when Pamir stopped short, refusing to touch it. "I promised not to hurt you. I meant my words."

"Leave us alone," said Pamir, his voice not quiet, not at all, but still far softer than the other voice.

"You call it the Child."

"What I call it is my business."

"But I have certain knowledge, and I understand the creature's preferences, its tendencies." The body took a small step forward. Dangling between it and the radiant orange mass was a tendril, neural impulses flowing in both directions. The Samara body was no more than a finger to the whole. "Answer this, if you can: Whose child is it?"

"Aeon," said Pamir.

Samara repeated that name several times, wrapping the word inside a questioning tone. "And what else do you know?"

"Everything."

"Indeed." A jovial smile lingered for a long moment. "You are a captain and a rather good captain, as I understand these matters. Unlike most of your peers, you nourish skepticisms about every part of your job, your duties, and perhaps the entire human mission. But sorry as it is to admit, you are small. You have a small, streamlined mind that cannot hold more than a sliver of 'everything', and despite the well-practiced stubbornness, your precious cynicism is marred with weaknesses and looming gaps."

"You murdered Aeon." Pamir was panting and weak, a piece of him wishing Samara would murder him here, drawing the wrath of the captains. "The Child told me where it came from and what you are and that you murdered its parent."

"Well," the body said, "in those stark terms, I am guilty."

Pamir took a half-step forward. If he died, nexuses would release files to certain trusted captains, including Washen. Maybe they wouldn't defend the Child, but a captain's killer would never escape the Ship.

"For my edification, and for my entertainment too," Samara said. "Slice off a piece of this 'everything'. Simplify. Clarify. And perhaps we can reach an accommodation." What might or might not be teeth shone inside the narrow mouth. "And if you can, hurry. This has been a long chase. I'm eager to get to the end, please."

* * *

The history had been told dozens of times, in a wondrous array of voices. Hunched low, the original Child related it in careful words, and then later, a variety of bodies found new possibilities. Flowing script grew on living wood, and the curled leaves read the epic poem aloud. Tailored drugs brought on lucid dreams. The Child's nightmares were injected straight into Pamir's nervous system. Trillions of torchflies formed a dense cloud overhead, weaving a cold living picture, majestic and tragic, and then the story was finished and their desiccated bodies fell as snow over Pamir. But his preferred form was the single voice, usually an angel's voice, her wings and arms embracing him while the whispered words moved him to astonishment and awe, and rage, and something indistinguishable from love.

Aeon had been a Gaian in the truest, rarest form: A vast, interlocking organism carpeting one rich world, the simplest algae and most sophisticated mock-animals linked in a glorious Whole.

Evolutionary accidents built the Gaian. There was a steady climate, a devoted sun, and few if any asteroid impacts battering the status quo. Runaway symbioses were the beginning. Neural networks arose from a gently parasitic worm; it was the worm's spores that the bioscans had found, each spore filled with the makings of an intellect. Only one world in ten thousand ever showed Gaian properties. Fewer than one in ten million generated worldwide consciousness. And according to Pamir's research, none were self-aware, and experts and sophisticated models doubted that any world in the galaxy wore an authentic soul.

But the Gaian wasn't born alone. Aeon had a sister complete with an atmosphere and two small, salty oceans. The two worlds were in a tidal lock, the same faces staring at each other as they turned around their center of gravity, sixteen hours to the day. With countless eyes, night and day, Aeon watched its companion, marking the changing of seasons, the advance and retreat of glaciers, and the eras of relative abundance when the land and swollen water became a golden sweet green.

The moon was alive, and knowing nothing else, Aeon assumed a Gaian entity.

From its first conscious day and for a very long while, Aeon tried speaking to its sister. It groomed forests and bright grasslands, and it painted the clouds with flights of mock-birds and torchflies, and the ocean's plankton fluoresced on command, the night washed away by the extravagant radiance. Every display built symbols. There were pictures of their two worlds, and crisp patterns linked to numbers and counting and time, images of favorite bodies, favorite shores, jungles and mountains and deep cold waters. But there was no response—nothing clear and unambiguous—and Aeon was forced into more desperate means.

Wings could fly only so high, and living balloons might reach the ends of the atmosphere, but then their gases escaped and their bodies froze, descending like spent leaves to the forest floor.

New ideas were needed, plainly.

Specialized, oversized neural centers were grown and spoiled. Silly ideas with a smidgen of genius were cataloged, and that's where the simple idea of rockets was created. Within days, the first wood-and-flesh bodies were born and launched, and found wanting. Yet that direction became the focus of hope: New materials; new fuels; radical fresh methods of growth. Specialized bodies mined the crust, purifying and reshaping elements scarcely needed in the past. The next rockets had metal guts, and a few of them achieved orbit; and then even better rockets landed on the moon's surface, their mock-animal crews examining and deciphering, and then returning to disgorge memories of immeasurable worth, immeasurable gloom.

The sister world had a thin dry impoverished atmosphere and a climate subject to rapid, chaotic change. The poles were brutally cold while the equator broiled until the land was baked dead, every wind carrying the dust away in choking clouds. Life was scarce and divided. It was split into units—bitter, independent species—and even within one species there was competition, each body fighting for water, for food, for homelands and mates and the poor opportunity of making offspring that were never the same as the parents.

There was nothing Gaian to find, nothing to relish.

In the most fundamental ways, Aeon was alone.

Looking at its neighbor now, it saw pain and waste and daily tragedies, and after careful consideration it saw no choice but to act.

Rockets were sent by the thousands.

The alien flesh was not too different from its own—the result of shared origins in the mysterious past, no doubt. Aeon taught that flesh how to cooperate, sharing without hesitation or agendas. Neural masses were grown from local tissues, scattered but linked, and they shared thoughts yet never quite joined together. There was competition and tiny alliances that would last a day, if that long, and the little world remained splintered. So every mass was killed, and Aeon repeated the pattern, the weave inside its own responsible minds, and that was when the collective intelligence was born.

Ages passed, productive beyond measure.

The Gaians spoke, faces to faces. Aeon discovered radio waves and lasers, and working together, they fashioned a single network of mirrors and antennae, orbiting and landlocked, all watching the great emptiness engulfing tiny them.

Eventually they heard creatures speaking, star to star to star. The universe was rich with thought, yes. But the minds were strange, minuscule and swift, often cooperative but never in the Gaian sense, and abundant beyond all calculation.

The sister was first to suggest building a genuine link—a physical connection to make them One.

Aeon invented the means. Why not a great bridge? No wood or metal would be strong enough. But ultrapure carbon, if properly cultivated and aligned, could be laid down like coral, a great strong perfect bridge accreting with the ages.

Aeon's deepest water was directly beneath the other's waist. To support its end of the bridge, it grew a small continent—a mammoth hunk of living wood and hollow aluminum—and the bridge was one endless tree, then many trees growing in a ring, and finally one magnificent tube bigger around than most mountains.

The other world lacked the water and bodies, but a matching tube rose into space, and the two structures met, merged.

There was a ceremony.

A celebration.

A grand embrace.

Aeon allowed its fellow Gaian to build huge muscular pumps, and the pumps took in a modest quantity of ocean water, spilling it over the bitter plains. But the gift was a symbol. "No more than this," Aeon warned. Long-range rockets were returning with news of water. A thin belt of comets waited in the dark, and they were made of water ice and rich organics. Wasn't it reasonable to work together, with patience, bringing the wealth home to both of them?

Yet the neighbor had no intention of waiting. Without warning—without any declaration of intent—it stole the floating continent. Neural pipelines and mock-animals arrived, the latter built to be warriors. Bladders full of careful poisons burst open, killing Aeon's helpless flesh. It was that moment, recoiling in retreat, when it named its opponent the Monster, every other name stricken from its mind.

A slow, enormous war was waged.

The pumps roared, joined by still larger pumps. Cubic kilometers of seawater flowed across the bridge, flooding deserts and filling new seas, the Monster's face turning blue as a gemstone.

Aeon tried to fight back, and failed.

What did it know about competition? How could it learn treachery and cruelty, and master them fast enough? Obviously peaceful, selfless Gaians were scarce for a reason; and centuries and too much thought were wasted dwelling on the unfairness of the universe, the grossness of life.

The ocean dropped as the disaster's pace accelerated. The continental shelves lay exposed, and the once-verdant continents grew cold and dry. The floating continent—an ancient, badly abused slave—was anchored several kilometers beneath its starting point. Sunken volcanoes stood as tall mountains. Aeon's shores fell straight into deceptively tranquil seas. The new poverty brought dust storms and rumbling glaciers and cold droughts without end, and no river lived for long, while outside sheltered valleys, life was more likely to die than live.

Meanwhile, the Monster prospered. The smaller world was submerged beneath the stolen waters. Floating continents of mock-kelp and sponges fed on sunlight and fusion power. Aeon watched the transformation, wishing for some stopping point, some moment and mood where the first Gaian would be maimed yet alive. Surrendering to hope, it called out for a meeting, sending diplomats across the front lines, a thousand mock-dragons escorting them to the cursed bridge.

A newer, even larger pumping facility was starting to work; the Monster happily showed off its machinery. Now the atmosphere was being absorbed, pressurized and liquefied, then carried away. A great chill wind was blowing up the new shaft. One of the diplomats was thrown in for emphasis. The survivors asked how much air would be enough air? And the Monster responded with a great laugh, every mouth saying, "I will leave nothing here but bare stone and pure vacuum."

"But why?" asked a single diplomat.

"What else should I do?" it said, utterly amused. "There are no negotiations, since I have won, and you will soon die and be lost, and why did you waste flesh on this ridiculous mission?"

The diplomats were killed in painful manners, their neural centers returned for Aeon's edification.

A few centuries later, a single working starship lifted from the highest peak on Aeon's far side. The pilot was the self-sufficient Child, and the Child was carrying a portion of its parent's memories and the wrenching lessons as well as Aeon's character and desires.

The strongest of the nearby signals led to the Great Ship.

What choice did it have but to believe the transmissions, expecting to find a tolerant and charitable crew of unlinked animals, and in such a gigantic vessel, any tiny berth for its little self?

Mercy, in whatever truncated form, had to exist in the universe.

Without mercy, why should one ever bother with life, or even bother with the smallest single breath?

* * *

Samara listened to the tale, never interrupting.

Afterwards it remained silent, and Pamir realized that this was the first time that he had ever told the story to another, in any form.

A wan smile appeared on the alien, and he said, "That was delicious. A delicious, satisfying lie."

Pamir mopped at the sweat on his homely face. "What do you mean? That this never happened?"

The body shrugged like a human, and the orange glow behind it flared, dilating orifices belching gases that instantly caught fire. Then it said, "In these last days, at last, I have come to understand your species. Tiny minds, and old. Your thoughts are so hardened by habit and wish that none of you seem capable of asking the obvious."

"I'm expelling you," Pamir said. "I intend to contact the Master Captain and see you thrown off our ship."

"You can't expel what you can't catch, old man."

Again, Pamir hoped to be murdered. A heroic, short-sighted part of him saw no other solution, and only after another moment of life did he bother to wonder why he was thinking this way. This was not the man that he had been just ten centuries ago.

The orange mass moved, retreating like a vast amoeba. There was a vivid sloshing as it watery self crept into hairline fissures, unmapped and uncountable. That's how it got here, the captain realized. It slipped through the Ship's cracked, aged body; and how could anyone corner such a creature?

Then Samara asked, "Who is the Child?"

Pamir stared at the basalt, saying nothing.

"Maybe the Child is that one fragment of Aeon, the creature that happens to be your friend. Or maybe it's Aeon's world-sized creation." The body stepped backward, pausing against the ancient wall. "Perhaps both are its children. But since I arose from the first and truest child, perhaps I should be given that cherished name. Yes?"

"Stay away from me," Pamir said.

Samara responded with a prolonged gaze, eyes pained and disappointed. Then it asked another question:

"If sisters tell two stories…which sister will you believe?"

The body was merging with the wall, and the orange glow was the weakest, coolest light imaginable.

"Which of us?" asked the vanishing mouth.

Pamir gave no answer.

"A fair warning to you," Samara said. "I intend to relish my work, and good-bye. Forever, I hope."

The many-billion-year night had returned, undiminished by that one weak sliver of day.

"Weapons," said Pamir, speaking as much to himself as the Child. "I know sources. There are markets. You can't make these kinds of weapons for yourself–"

"Thank you."

"And they're designed for humans. Another pair of hands? Does that sound worthwhile?"

"Friend Pamir," the Child replied, speaking through the nearest griffin. "When it's time, I hope you leave me. I can't ask you to fight, and for the sake of truth, I should mention that you are tiny and weak and more a burden than an effective soldier." The voice was certain, logic and empathy smeared together. "What I've asked you to do, you have done. What more can I want?"

"Let me take my chances," said Pamir. Then, for emphasis, he added, "You'll have to use more than words to keep me away."

The Child didn't react to the banality, except to beat the griffin's wings. Huge eyes watched the human, golden pupils pulled wide, threatening to swallow Pamir whole.

The captain turned, walking just to be walking.

An alien sewer flowed beside him, rushing between high canyon walls. Here the water should be clean and sweet, but as more of the Child was readied to fight, less of the wastes were being absorbed and purified. Soon no work would be done, and raw sewage would percolate through the central sands, into a reservoir that Pamir had left empty for this day. The AI overseers were long ago recalibrated; months could pass, and no one needed to know what was happening. Yet that act—the sabotage of one warning system—reminded Pamir that he wasn't acting as a captain, his first duty no longer directed at the Ship and its smooth, dignified operation.

Fumes rose from the river, tickling his nose, scorching flesh. Pamir coughed but refused to back away from the shoreline. Nestled inside the torrent was a mock-fish, camouflaged to match the brown poisons, suction cups holding it to the hyperfiber streambed while its armored back was visible in the deeper troughs. This species was first built during the long war. Its eggs were shaped like dead shells and fat plankton—harmless detritus swept up with the stolen ocean—and they would hatch inside the giant pumps and along the length of the interplanetary bridge. With palpable pride, the Child had explained how the fish stole energy from the moving water while building flesh laced with unstable compounds. Each body was a bomb, and Aeon was trying to ignite a single apocalyptic blast. But the Monster anticipated the attack, no significant damage done, and afterward it mocked its enemy for the transparent, foolhardy nontrick.

Pamir wondered what good a few fish would do now, and he coughed harder, tasting blood as he turned to look at the canyon walls and sky.

It was easy to forget where he was: The Child had transformed itself. Every vegetable mass was covered with spines and piercing threads, a thousand proven, reborn poisons waiting to be injected, another ten thousand fresh poisons crafted from the alien sewage, ready to be thrown into the breach. No mock-animal, no matter how small or scarce, lacked a killing function. Fruiting bodies were engorged with napalms. Bacteria generated tons of necrotic enzymes. The griffins were growing larger and swifter, and more ominous, they were resting more than training, shepherding their energies in case of a sudden attack. Even the Child's color hinted at deadly work, a blackness of flesh and bark swallowing the soft orange sunlight, hiding details under a velvety sameness that would make an attacker's job ever so slightly more difficult.

Pamir couldn't wander at will. Toxins and spring-loaded blades would make a nightmare out of the shortest stroll.

The Child was right; his body was a small weak burden.

But he was a captain too, and that helped immeasurably. Samara would have to enter through one of the orifices; the hyperfiber floor and ceiling were too dense and perfect to allow passage. That known, Pamir had an army of sensors above and below the facility, and booby-traps hid inside the sewage lines, inorganic bombs and electrified screens set to maim anything that might be alive. And Pamir himself had crawled inside the ancient machinery, behind the canyon walls, inventing at least one good trick to help the Child, if it ever came to that...

The griffin gently draped one huge talon over Pamir's shoulder. Its beak and talons were sheathed in hyperfiber, mirror-colored and sharp. Pamir had ordered them from a friendly supplier, paying through an official account—another lapse as a captain, and he didn't care.

With the gentlest possible voice, the griffin asked, "What kinds of weapons can you offer, and where will you find them, friend Pamir?"

He answered the first question with vagaries but no specifics. As for the second question, he said, "I can't be certain, since I've never actually tried to assemble this kind of gear."

The Child waited.

"But captains know all the illegal markets," he said.

Myriad eyes watched him. Then the griffin said, "There is something else here."

"What is here?"

"I know your expressions," it said. "You have words that you want to tell me, perhaps."

"I told you what's important," he said.

The Child knew about his meeting with Samara, but Pamir neglected to mention the parting words. He wanted to forget them, and sometimes it felt as if he could. But the face showed too much, and the Child had reasons to ask, "Is this a trivial matter? Is it silly? Why not just say it and get it done with, friend Pamir?"

He felt like a lover admitting to an indiscretion. "The Monster tried to tell a different history."

"Yes?"

"Different," he repeated.

The bright talon lifted. A small voice said, "I can imagine."

"I don't know any details. All it did was throw out noise about a two-sided story."

"The creature is clever," said the Child.

"I realize that." There was no place to hide his eyes, cold sweat making his skin shine. "It gave me some vague shit about sisters, and I don't know where it would have led."

"Because you can imagine anything. You have that power, which it knows full well."

Pamir had worked hard for days, avoiding daydreams, keeping his liquid thoughts in safe places. Captains—even a sordid, failed captain—knew that doubt was a killer. The decision made and then aborted was often worse than a simple, clean mistake.

"It is cunning," said the griffin, with confidence.

Pamir nodded, and after a long uncomfortable pause, he said, "I'll keep one weapon in reserve, for my own use."

"If you wish."

"And I will be here when Samara comes."

"As you wish, friend Pamir."

The griffin sprang into the air, wings beating once, then again, carrying it toward a high perch where the hyperfiber lay exposed, griffins by the hundreds set shoulder to shoulder, doing nothing.

Then something soft stroked Pamir's back. He wheeled, startled to find a reborn angel. The body was taller than him, perfect breasts in his face, while its face—a lean strong lovely favorite—sang to him, "For you."

New hands stroked his chest, no human hand so soothing.

But Pamir said, "Not now, no." He managed a blind backward step, his heel jabbed with an electrified thorn. "Take it away. Build something useful." In other words, cobble together something strong, and brutal, and fatal.

The angel's eyes were deep, hiding worlds.

Stepping into the churning waters, its flesh painlessly dissolved as it moved, the beautiful body embraced and annihilated in moments; and Pamir left behind in what passed for solitude.

* * *

He took an official leave of absence.

The Submaster was not known for her charm or warmth. Taking tight hold of Pamir's hand, Miocene said, "Enjoy your rest. But remember, endless rest is Heaven, and Heaven does not exist."

A Remora sold Pamir five dozen plasma guns, homemade from stolen parts and capable of incinerating everything short of medium-grade hyperfiber. As was customary, the officer told the seller that he was taking friends on a hunt, their quarry large and mechanical and decidedly nonsentient. That would be the excuse in case of trouble. Then Pamir set to work, adapting all the guns but one for griffins' paws. He was working at home, nearly finished, when Washen arrived at his front door.

"We should meet for drinks," she said. "Meet and talk."

"That would be great," Pamir lied, standing in the hallway, a munitions depot hiding around the first corner. "The week after next week might be best."

Washen smiled for a moment. Then she said, "Your friend has vanished."

The Child was what he thought about first. Instinct crafted a story where the Gaian had decided not to fight, following instead the escape route that Pamir designed, or maybe another avenue…but that was stupid, and he realized what she meant with the word "friend".

"Samara," she said. "Remember him?"

"Barely." Pamir blew through his teeth.

"Either way, he's gone." Washen offered a rich little smile, as if some special knowledge was being shared. "And I thought you'd want to know, since you seemed fascinated about him."

"Not him, no. I was wrong."

She knew better but didn't press. "I heard a rumor that you are taking some time off."

"A little while, yes."

"Who's doing your jobs?"

He named captains, leaving one responsibility unaccounted for.

Washen didn't mention what was obvious, and a tacit conspiracy had begun. What did she suspect? But nothing could be as strange as the truth, which lent the moment its thin satisfaction.

Then his friend, peer, and ex-lover said, "She must be astonishing."

"Who?"

"The woman, whatever she is." A slicing look brought jealousy cloaked in a vapid, unwelcome pity. "But you don't even realize it, do you? How much you're in love. How deep the holds reach."

"That's not me," he said.

And against long odds, he believed those words.

Washen's gaze wandered down the hallway and back to him again, and she said, "The week after next then. All right?"

"Yes."

She left, and in a mad rush, Pamir loaded the big cap-car and set out for the Child, following the most direct route. The last gun was ready with minutes to spare, and that wealth of idle time allowed him to admit a few hard truths to himself. He even promised himself to admit his affections when he arrived. But stepping through the final hatch, Pamir couldn't say the planned words. He found a griffin waiting on the other side, its eagle-eyes staring through him, and in a hushed voice, the Child told him:

"Samara. Is here."

8

Holding to form, their enemy arrived as Drought.

Every sewer was blocked. Plugs of rubbery flesh were lodged upstream, beyond the reach of booby-traps. The river below Pamir—the one from human districts—had fallen to a greasy blue-green rivulet, its fish dead and dying, the Child absorbing and reallocating their bodies in the grandest kind of panic he had ever witnessed.

Griffins took every plasma gun but his.

The first griffin remained behind, asking for quick training.

Pamir showed how to link the gun's umbilical to the Ship's power supply, and then he gave a demonstration, melting and sealing the hatch behind him with a thunderous blast. An instant later, an alarm sounded. Something was moving in the nearest tunnels; sensors disgorged phenomenal volumes of vague, conflicting data. Pointing the barrel at the dry river's source, the captain said, "It's massive, and it's flowing, and every bomb is detonating."

Yet the orifice remained empty and silent, no motions betrayed.

The gun's barrel began to twist, correcting for Pamir's little failures.

"Hide," begged a hundred small voices. "Will you please?"

He pointed at a small intake port exposed by the drought. The griffin carried him and his gun to the makeshift redoubt, and a second griffin brought a hyperfiber suit, trim and lightweight, with a double-thick helmet and a sealed environment. Examining his reflection in the hyperfiber wall, Pamir decided that he felt as expected: Strong. Scared, but determined. And tired, yet existing outside the need for normal rest.

"How soon?" he asked the reflection.

The Child gave no answer.

Pamir relinked and calibrated the gun. Every high cloud had evaporated, the moisture stored and the bare ceiling reflecting the rich blackness below. Nothing happened in the next minute, and the next hour was the same. It became possible to imagine that Samara would wait as long as possible, studying their strengths while letting their weaknesses grow.

What was that?

A million faces tilted. Something was felt, heard. Pamir glanced at the readouts from the sensors, countless signs of motion making his heart race.

"Now!" screamed the Child's nearest face.

It was a leathery, fanged face, droplets of alien plague arcing through the dry, dry air.

Pamir squared his shoulders, telling his reflection, "I guess I am. Ready."

* * *

Through the closest orifice, in one titanic push, came life, unformed and full of energies that bled out of it as light and screaming white noise. The electrified screens had shattered. Winged beasts sprang from the plastic goo, born in flight, driving for the Child's center. And in reflex, fruits exploded, and living nets launched themselves, engulfing and slicing the enemy's bodies. Then the armed griffins worked as a well-trained unit, bolts of plasma evaporating bodies and breaking molecules, leaving incandescent vapors that hung in the air, for a moment, before they were absorbed by a second wave of screaming winged enemies.

Pamir aimed and fired, nanosecond pulses cutting. Boiling. Doing remarkably little good.

Samara was vast. It wasn't as large as the Child, but its first assault killed as much as it lost, and it absorbed casualties from both of the sides, reshaping and reanimating the spoils, then launching those newborn troops.

The second assault dwarfed the first.

The third nearly reached Pamir's hiding place, and he fired until a haze of boiled blood hung as a curtain before him.

"Retreat," the Child said.

Then another sound arrived. More distant, and louder, it was a piercing wail rising through the crimson fog. Pamir retreated deeper into the port, and he lifted his gun, and a vast winged creature plowed into the riverbed before him. It was one of Samara's bodies. Fresh cacti impaled it, needles pumping lethal stews into the bleeding flesh. A smaller beast sprang from lifeless back, and it too was grabbed by the spines, dying in turn. But then its corpse instantly gave birth to a pair of wings—dragonfly-style; more delicate than smoke—and the wings flapped hard, Pamir watching with a mixture of astonishment and fatalism. They were wings with a thread-like body between, and what could such a little thing accomplish?

Behind him stood a griffin, unnoticed until now.

Springing forward, it swatted at the dragonfly with both paws, encasing it inside the hyperfiber claws.

The blast threw the griffin and Pamir deep inside the machinery. They ended up in a shared heap. The paws were shattered, the hyperfiber lost, possibly stolen. And the battle grew louder, wilder. Two worlds were battling, and the emotion was blatant and rank—combatants wasting air and energy to scream what felt like ancient, eternal curses.

Pamir ripped the umbilical free and retreated through a maze of mirrored tunnels. There were no straight-line courses. He wasted too much time before reaching the next downstream port, where he replugged and aimed firing steadily for thirty seconds. Then Samara was looming, and he retreated again. "Go, go, go!" he screamed to himself. Strong, scared legs carried him past the third port. He stopped at the fourth, for just a moment. A gaseous mass was drifting overhead. It was a bubble, a balloon. Detached from Samara's body, the menace was riddled with wounds, leaking gas and blood, yet it held together as jets of air carried it past him, descending slowly, with stateliness and inevitability.

Pamir didn't see the impact. Retreating underground, he heard the roar of an explosion while wind pushed into his face, oxygen racing to feed a mammoth blaze. Then a sudden deep quiet began, marking endless death, and he ran a curling path through the sleeping purification system—twenty kilometers crossed before he dared stop inside a deep hole, attempting to rest.

Twelve more roundabout kilometers brought him to a buried port. He had to carve a passage through damp black earth, reaching the surface to find the false sun extinguished. Too much ground had been lost; the Child didn't want to share free photons. But Pamir could see by the light of fires, the blue electric discharges. Some brutalized little creature dragged itself close, plugging its rectal umbilical into the Child, and it said, "Friend Pamir." Then it stood tall on its three best legs, adding, "What a fucking mess."

Nothing had gone well. Worst-case plans hadn't look this bleak, and Pamir wondered why he had ever felt any optimism.

A glowing wall of unformed flesh was closing, moving like syrup down the riverbed, and the human fired until fumes condensed on his pitted faceplate, half-blinding him. A griffin arrived, shouting, "Hold on here!" And beating its wings, fighting gravity and its own exhaustion, the griffin lifted him and his armored suit and the precious plasma gun out of danger.

How long had they been fighting?

A full day had passed. But it felt like ten minutes, and it felt like a very long year. Pamir was bouncing between exhilaration and a drugged hunger for sleep. The griffin carried him over the flat dry sands—a newborn desert—landing at a prearranged, marginally secure point from where he could measure the disaster's dimensions. This was one of the original control stations, a kilometer-tall ridge of hyperfiber covered with leathery skin and spines. The griffin looked back at Pamir, ready to leave, and he handed over his gun, saying what was obvious:

"You can do more with this than I can."

Not that it would make a difference one way or the other.

Pamir took drugs to sleep and then woke when a distant blast lit the cavern from end to end. The battle formed a U-shaped line, the Child struggling to hold the interior. Samara was attacking the stems in irregular, unpredictable bursts, plainly striving to collapse the U into a tiny circle set in the middle of the defenseless sands.

Samara's size and its effortless success were spellbinding. How could captains hope to control such an organism? In a whisper, he said, "If the Monster wants, it could steal the whole Ship for itself."

"I told you so," said the Child.

A small hand touched the human's elbow, setting off an alarm in his armored suit.

He jumped and spun, finding a child-like figure staring up at him. Another resurrected figure; it was identical to the body he had interrogated some thousand years ago.

"I told you," the Child repeated, the grim expression lit by distant napalm and the fluorescence underfoot. "The Monster is black-hearted and treacherous. Didn't you believe me?"

"Not well enough," he said.

That body could be the last hope. If the Child was beaten here, Pamir and this tiny totipotent construction would retreat, using the Ship's volume to hide. That is, unless Pamir died, and then the captains would be alerted. Except Washen and the troops might be defeated too, and Samara would grab hold of the Ship, shaking it hard until its enemy was found.

"Keep fighting," Pamir said weakly.

The Child never quit its struggle. But another two days reduced its ground to the central sands and Pamir's little ridge.

The final encircling attack had begun.

Bloodied, half-dead griffins landed at the bunker, desperate for nourishment. They fed through umbilicals and their mouths, and they fired the last few guns. Then another great balloon rose out of Samara, pushing overhead, and it dove and spread like an octopus, engulfing whatever lay in its reach. The nearest tendril flowed up the slope, within a hundred meters of Pamir. He could smell the flesh, a sweet, delicate fragrance that turned sour an instant before it exploded.

Eleven griffins were killed instantly.

The Child's lifeboat body, dressed in its own armored suit, turned to Pamir, giving him a nod and then a despairing smile.

Beside them stood a wall of controls.

Ancient.

Asleep.

With a captain's authority, Pamir initiated a series of commands, coaxing the machinery into wakefulness, and then he told the systems that an awful mess had come here, defining Samara as a grievous toxic spill.

With a sequence of dull grinding rumbles, creations older than worlds set to work, instantly busy doing some much needed housekeeping.

* * *

Samara was vast and undeniably cunning. But the attack seemed to take the creature by surprise. Great twisting chunks of it were sucking into the ports, chopped into smaller chunks with the water dragged free and purified while the organics were torn down to their atoms, stripped of identity and purpose, then fed back to the Child's residues. With orchestrated, professional brutality, Pamir stood at the controls fighting the Gaian. After several days, Samara was forced to retreat, and it shrank, and the Child grew to where it had a thin hold on nearly half of the cavern's floor.

Then the machinery faltered.

Slipping inside the workings, Samara discovered ways to overwhelm some systems, confound others. Another long day was spent in stalemate. Finally Pamir brought secondary systems on line, and the tertiary systems, and as their opponent once more started to retreat, the Child launched one final counterattack. But every purification system failed, and the attack failed, bodies retreating over bodies, struggling to destroy everything of use between them and the ridge.

The griffins were extinct. Weaker, smaller bodies fired the final three plasma guns. Like a ring of warm pudding, Samara came across the bare sands, flowing and glowing softly and sometimes spawning little bodies that would run toward the ridge, but not quickly, the fight and fire of the originals spent long ago.

"Look," said the lifeboat body. "The Monster is nearly dead."

But the Child was just a few hundred hectares of scales and spines, without depth or bodies and sick with poisons. Only one gun was operating. The orange pudding reached the base and started crawling upwards, endless mouths scraping the hyperfiber clean. To take stock of the situation, Pamir stepped from the control room. He was struck hard, knocked flat and senseless. The lifeboat body dragged him back into cover. His helmet was cracked, and a captainly shard of him calculated the force required to break this gauge of cultured diamond.

The Child pushed the last gun into Pamir's hands, and he said, "It is time now! Time!"

They began the final, beaten retreat. A secure escape route was waiting. Pamir and the Child still had time to slip away. Of course Pamir would lead the way. Aiming the weapon at nothing, using the lowest setting to illuminate the darkness, he came around each turn of the hallway to find nothing, working his way toward the hidden, stealthy cap-car. But a feeling started to chew after the third turn, and he paused, knowing what was wrong before he looked at the hallway behind him, as dark and empty as the one ahead.

Where was the Child?

Outside, Samara was working its way up the faces of ridge.

A great wet roar preceded an explosion. The last of the Child's spare flesh had changed its nature, combusting with a yellowish light that filtered down to him and rapidly faded, accomplishing nothing. But Pamir had seen the light through a side hallway, implying an alternate passageway to the surface. Turning, he ran up a set of steep stairs, stopping only when he saw a human-shaped figure silhouetted against the black sky. The figure wore armor and stood inside a thick bubble of diamond, and the bubble was perched high on scaffolding that helped support a huge apparatus that shouldn't be there. The gemstone and metal machine was perched on top of a makeshift fuel tank, and it was discolored and battered and crude. Yet the device was familiar, and Pamir took another step and another, and then said, "Oh, shit."

Here stood the worn out engine of a starship—a ship that according to every record was recently sold as scrap. Pamir expected to feel astonished, and to some degree he was. And he waited for the horror and grief to grab hold, except those reflexes didn't have the anticipated grip. He had always understood what was obvious. Nothing here was a surprise. Truth was a plastic, fickle substance, and why wouldn't every Gaian be good at shaping it to fill a need?

Samara's stardrive had been reassembled inside a vertical room hacked out of many smaller rooms. Every ceiling had been removed. Above them was darkness ending with an inverted, almost indestructible bowl of high-grade hyperfiber.

Oblivious to the approaching human, the Child grabbed the controls with both hands. Then it paused, watching monitors, examining images of the cavern and its nemesis and the willingness of the fusion engine.

Pamir dropped the gun and began to climb the scaffolding.

Then the Child smiled, razor-cold serenity defining the eyes while the little mouth pursed, lips saying the words, "Now, you die."

A sun was born just meters away, the flash and plasmas blinding Pamir as he leaped for the floor. His head was tucked and his back was exposed, and that single burst of light hammered the hyperfiber ceiling, energies absorbed but the residue bouncing down on their heads, washing the realm clean.

And Pamir lay beneath the engine, guessing everything else, including the scope of his own magnificent ignorance.

9

Samara—the bulk of Samara—had been turned to gas and ash. But one surviving splinter was alive, huddling beneath a half-melted desiccator. The body wore the same human shape and face that had first stepped onboard the Ship, but radiation had seared the flesh, and the legs were too weak to lift it from the ground. Yet the Gaian acted amused regardless. Cocky and sharp-tongued, it said, "What did you accomplish? Nothing. More of us are coming, and they know what I know, and what does it matter if it takes millennia to kill that thing?"

Pamir was holding the plasma gun.

The Child was unarmed, its armor cracked by the stardrive and discarded.

"Burn the Monster," said the Child.

Samara's green-gold eyes found the captain. "The Monster is prepared for a million-year hunt," it said with glee. "What could be more patient than a vengeful Gaian?"

The Child moved to strike it, or worse.

Pamir lifted the barrel, saying, "No. I want to hear this. Stand back." There was no plug for the weapon's umbilical, but its batteries were halfway charged. Turning to Samara, he said, "Tell me a new story."

"No," the Child said.

Pamir threw a burst of plasma into the desiccator, earning silence.

Samara looked into the distance, seeing the past and left-behind places. "My home wasn't a Gaian world, no. It didn't have a self, a soul. But Aeon gave it both. And it gave the world its first name: The Child.

"Before becoming the Monster, I was Aeon's little offspring, weak and well aware of its weakness. But stronger by the century, and more experienced. And like any Child, I imagined the future and how I would act differently than my parent, and maybe I could improve on Aeon's way."

Pamir stood where he could see both of them, and he nodded.

Samara looked at the other Gaian, with an expression more complex than disgust. "We fought each other, yes. As you heard, we fought over water. Aeon wouldn't share the abundance. But other resources were rationed, and it tried to forbid certain knowledge. Aeon demanded oaths of fealty. And when words didn't convince, it invented physical acts to prove the same. But no proof was adequate. The Child gave and gave of itself, begging for acceptance and winning none. With each word, every gesture, Aeon found flaws, minuscule and often invented. And when the Child tried to claim freedom, its parent battered with curses and far, far worse."

The creature was panting, slowly rocking back and forth.

"That bridge between the worlds was built by Aeon, for Aeon. It was to help maintain control—an avenue where griffins, armies of griffins, could descend on the bothersome Child."

"Lies," spat the other Gaian.

Pamir drew a circle with the gun's barrel, and he nodded.

"Aeon also put mirrors and curtains in space. Changing the sunlight, it could bring drought and endless dust storms. 'I am hurting in order to teach,' it would say. 'I am doing these little things to help you, Child.'"

Pamir felt weak, cold.

"But I didn't surrender or even pretend to relent, and Aeon decided to murder me, sterilizing land and both seas before taking the little world for itself." Samara paused, a hearty smile building. "But you can guess the rest. All that effort to teach the Child, and what was learned? The importance of misery and treachery and of course I put every good lesson to work, and that's why the rest of the story is mostly the story you know…"

The other Gaian began to jump.

But Pamir was ready, firing between them, the sand rising in a fountain as the air between the grains burned.

The gun's batteries were past half-drained now.

"Lies," said the current Child, again and again.

"No no no," Samara said.

In some form or another, real truth existed. There was a history and a string of ugly events leading to this moment. But these creatures were built by entities that shaped flesh at will, and couldn't memories be molded too, and every chance of doubt chiseled out of their helpless souls?

Pamir looked at the current Child. "How did you acquire that stardrive?"

A vulnerable look turned to resolve.

"I can see the records. It was purchased by a harum-scarum." He named the individual before asking, "Do you know him?"

Resolve became haughtiness. "I have met him, yes."

"How did that happen?"

With a stiff voice, it said, "Friend Pamir."

"But I'm rarely here, and you are a huge talented creature," Pamir said. "For all I know, you have spent centuries manipulating aliens and humans, building a little empire of helping hands and eyes."

"How can that possibly matter to you?" it asked.

"I learned about Samara's arrival, and I came here immediately to tell you…but you already knew, didn't you…?"

"I don't love the others," the Child said. "I love you. You were the one that I wanted with me today. But what if some disaster took you? An accident could have happened, and I needed safeguards."

Pamir used silence.

"Safeguards," the Child repeated, in a mutter.

He turned toward Samara. "More like you are coming. Is that your promise?"

"There are many more of us, each more clever than the last."

"But you have to kill this one," said the Child.

Pamir watched Samara, studying the eyes. "But what if this creature is dead? Will these others keep threatening the Ship?"

"Never. They are built for vengeance, nothing more."

Then he glanced at the Child. Its face was changing shape and color as claws sprouted on the hands that were just beginning to reach out.

"All right," the captain said. "I have decided what to do."

His arms held the weapon steady, and two bursts were fired, the air filled with the vivid stink of evaporated flesh, and steam, and the brief beginnings of twin screams cut short by the boiling of their respective tongues.

<h1 style="text-align:center">10</h1>

"You look different."

"I'm out of uniform."

"We're chasing you. I saw the arrest warrant and the charges."

"I know. I've seen them too."

"You destroyed an entire facility. If we didn't have the water reserves, we'd already be drinking our own urine."

"I built the reserves," Pamir said. "And everything will be fixed years before anyone suffers."

"Mention those facts at the trial," Washen said, taking a tentative step toward the fugitive. "Whatever has happened, you need to turn yourself in and let the Submasters examine the evidence."

"Why? I'm guilty."

"What do you know? You're not a Submaster."

Pamir laughed. Washen's home was rather like his, but cleaner and brighter. Against one wall, in a tiny, root bound pot, a tired clump of llano-vibra sang in hushed voices about everlasting love.

"Are you curious about what happened down there?" he asked.

"Tell me," she said.

He shook his head. "Sorry. I can't."

She took another step. "Will you turn yourself in to me?"

"No."

"Will you surrender to anyone?"

"Not intentionally, no."

She paused, probably wondering if she could physically restrain him. Not now, not in these circumstances. With a quiet, calculating voice, she said, "I don't see why you sneaked in here, frankly."

"I have a gift for you."

She exhaled, entirely surprised.

"You advised me to give gifts, didn't you?"

"What is it?" Washen asked.

He laid a biovial on the nearest tabletop and passed a small kinetic gun to his other hand, yanking a memo chip from his trousers' pocket. "These are the instructions." It was the same chip that she had given him, resembling a worn snowflake. "It's all pretty straightforward, once you get past the strangeness. That is, if you are willing to help."

"Help you?"

The homely face smiled. "No. I don't want that."

She looked at the vial and gun and snowflake. "What happened down there? Give me that much."

"Do whatever you believe is right, but promise me, you need to study everything in the chip."

She nodded but her expression drifted into pity and gloom. "Where will you go, Pamir?"

He said nothing.

"We won't stop hunting you."

The grin brightened. He stepped to one side and past her, making for the apartment's emergency hatch. "Good-bye, darling. And thank you."

Washen grabbed the vial, and hoping to delay him, she lifted it overhead, aiming at the olivine floor.

Pamir didn't give even a backward glance. "It's flesh," he said. "Barely living, perfectly stupid flesh."

"Yours?"

"Yes. And theirs too."

"Whose?" she asked.

He stepped through the open hatch.

"Who else is this, Pamir?"

The hatch closed and a shaped charge melted its mechanisms. Then after a moment's contemplation, Washen set down the biovial and picked up the old snowflake, tapping it as if to coax the answers to spring forth, explaining every mystery without fuss, without delay.

11

She called him the Child, and she called herself his mother, even when both knew that no part of her was incorporated into him. The Child lived in his mother's home, growing faster than human children but requiring far longer to mature. His talents were baffling and incomplete. His mistakes were painful for both him and his botched creations. But he persisted with his education, imagining the future, some ambitious part of him eager to become vast, and powerful, and wise.

His mother-who-wasn't-his-mother told him what little she knew.

When the Child dreamed of the past—worlds he didn't know; violence beyond measure—she would comfort him, wetting his forehead with damp rags while saying, "That isn't you. You are not them."

Yet *they* were part of him.

Tiny, tiny bodies floated inside each of his myriad cells, giving him magical powers over bone and meat.

"The others were enemies," she taught him. "They came here and fought—a terrible, brutal war—and then they killed each other."

"But why, Mother?"

She didn't know, but she made guesses. She talked about greed and jealousy, and fear—human emotions, which made them suspect. Then she said, "Tiny parts of them survived. But not enough to remake either, which is why your father bound those pieces with his own flesh."

A human was his father. The Child couldn't stop asking about him.

"I don't know where he is," she said, her face grave, sorrowful. "I don't even know if he's alive anymore."

"I will find him," the Child said.

But one day, instead of acting happy when he repeated that promise, Mother shook her head and told him, "You won't do that, no. Never. You're getting too strong, too skilled. I think it's time that you leave."

He had never left the apartment. "You want to walk out the door?"

"No, I need you to leave the Ship." She showed images of a young, barely living world. Its sun was ruddy and fixed in the sky. Its ocean was thick with organics and simple bugs. "Your father left instructions. Once you were ready, he wanted you to go to a place like this and live. Do you like it?"

Not at all. In the Child's mind, the world seemed ugly.

Yet then again, the prospect of embracing an entire planet seemed wondrous, even inevitable.

They went to one of the Ship's ports, to a tiny vessel that would carry him to the new world. Kneeling before him, Mother straightened his useless clothes, and she cried, saying, "Remember. Two of your parents hated each other so thoroughly that they couldn't see anything else. They lived badly, and they hurt one another, and how do you erase their terrible crimes...?"

"I will live properly," he said, with feeling.

"What does 'properly' mean?"

"With kindness to all of my parts, and to whatever life forms that I meet along the way."

She sobbed and said, "Be good."

The eternal motherly advice.

Suddenly the Child looked over her shoulder, focusing on something distant.

"A man," he said.

She turned.

"He was watching me. But he's gone now."

"Did he look like you?"

"Maybe." He thought harder, and then said, "No, he didn't. He was much more handsome than me."

She straightened his clothes again, smiling bravely.

"I think you're lovely," she told him. "Just beautiful, if you ask me."

Bridge Eight

The finest minds are cold or believe they are cold.

A small dense superconductive brain enjoys the swiftest thoughts. Whiskers of silicon can travel anywhere while demanding very little, and if those were the only criteria, then the galaxy would be awash in thoughtful dust. But physical law limits what the small mind can embrace, and being quick is rarely best. This is why one liter of bioceramic sentience is a more popular size. Thinking fast enough for most occasions and then survive its mistakes, that kind of mind can walk about on two legs, or fly with four wings, or happily sit inside a cool box on a high safe shelf. And that is the mind that can hold thousands of years of memory, each moment and every year patiently waiting for the chance to speak.

Inspiration flourishes in the big mind.

Memories like to talk to one another, and Genius is the beast that sits to the side, eavesdropping on the roaring conversation.

A million years can be bottled inside a liter-sized maelstrom, and the chaos spits out dreams and little ordinary thoughts and sometimes great mad wonderful ideas, and sometimes Genius will take away what seems new or wise or nothing but fun.

It is a nature of the universe to make minds.

But even a feeble, barely self-aware soul realizes that minds are never the priority. What matters in the universe is dark energy and then cold dark matter and then come the little stars and the worlds circling those stars and the worlds lost between.

Thought is a contaminate woven through the dark cold.

Consciousness can look like a flaw, a mistake.

Yet even scarce, minds continue to bear down on each vivid moment, and Genius contemplates what it can, and the universe expands while it cools as the stars begin to wink out, and minds die, and certain questions are asked and answered in the same reliable ways, and sometimes the survivors can find the peace to sleep awhile and let the dreams roll on.

The Caldera of Good Fortune

1

The hamlet was forbidden to wear any name, and by decree, its population and borders were never allowed to grow. Tucked inside a high valley, the tiny community was flanked on three sides by dense, ancient rock—walls of black rock flecked with white and dubbed "granite" because of a passing resemblance to the bones of Old Earth. Stunted forests of cold-adapted, light-starved trees grew wild on the slopes, while the caldera's rim was reserved for native life forms. Visiting the rim required special permission from the Luckies, and without exception, one of the hamlet's permanent citizens had to act as an Honored Guide.

Twenty-five hundred humans, aliens, and AIs lived permanently in the nameless hamlet. On the strength of an address, even the laziest among them made excellent livings. Passengers came from the far reaches of the Great Ship to walk the high rim and gaze into the caldera's magnificent lake. But when the prolonged winter was finished—when the signs pointed at catastrophic change—the fattest of the fat times began. When the lake began to simmer and bubble, news quickly spread among the wealthy. Tens of thousands of strangers would ride the tram into the high valley, dressed for the brutal cold, happily paying insane fees for the chance to sleep in somebody's cellar or attic, or be stacked like logs in the back of a little closet. The hamlet was transformed by bright cheery souls who sang drinking songs and spent fortunes on the overpriced food, all while watching vapor rising from behind the towering rim. Guests were constantly searching out the natives, asking them when the caldera would finally erupt. "Soon," was a safe reply, but these decisions were made entirely by the Luckies. Ten Ship-days was the average length of an eruption—time enough for the entire lake to boil skyward and freeze solid. And how big and beautiful would the new mountain be? "It will be enormous and gorgeous," the residents promised. And that wasn't just because they wanted to peel more money from these prosperous souls; even the most jaded, sun-starved citizen looked forward to the spectacle of fragile, moon-washed ice hanging over their drab little home.

Narrow trails crisscrossed the valley walls, eventually leading to the rim. But hiking was thankless work and a considerable investment of time. Antique cable cars offered quicker, easier journeys. For thousands of years, tourists had gathered inside the spacious, overheated station, and locals who wanted work sat with their backs to the caldera, gossiping with one another, patiently waiting for the first worthwhile offer.

Crockett had planned to do nothing that day but sleep. The lake had been steaming for weeks, and he'd made plenty already. But a friend mentioned that today and today only, a certain pair of security officers was patrolling in and around the station grounds.

As it happened, those officers were very beautiful and wonderfully human.

When the hamlet was jammed with strangers, outsiders were hired to fill critical jobs. Included in their ranks was a platoon of security officers, human and otherwise. Judging the age of immortals was difficult; but those two women carried a palpable, delicious sense of youth. They smiled constantly—weightless, untroubled grins common to barely grown people. In their walks and the secure tilt of their heads, they looked unaffected by responsibility. Another clue was their skin, as smooth and clear as any Crockett had ever seen: After centuries of life, most humans cultivated artful wrinkles near the eyes, hinting at wisdoms that might or might not exist. If appearances could be believed, the duo was thrilled to be living in the hamlet, however briefly. They patrolled together and whispered to each other constantly, sharing giggles and various knowing looks; and several times, Crockett had spied them standing in the middle of a crowded street, ignoring the shoving bodies and lustful glances while they held gloved hands, gazing up at the distant rim of the caldera and the curtain of fresh steam that rose into the gloom and then froze, falling where the winds let it fall as this spring's first snow.

Those girls were the reason Crockett walked to the cable car station and sat with his neighbors, making small talk while deflecting the tourists: He was waiting for to see the objects of his affection.

"Is my offer not enough?" asked a lumbering Tamias.

"Your offer is most generous," Crockett replied, examining the alien's rodent-like face with an appropriately indirect gaze. "But my ass is comfortable, and I will leave it where it is for now."

Soon a Hippocamus shuffled forwards—a pregnant male, by the looks of its belly. The creature took a deep breath and held the rich air inside his long neck, assessing the captured odors. Then he bowed to Crockett, but before he could speak, the human warned, "I am claimed by others, my friend. At present, I am helpless to help you."

Without complaint, the alien stepped down the line and took another defining breath, and after a few moments of conversation, hired a little Janusian couple to be his Guide.

Human tourists noticed the rebuff. They looked like a married couple, and married for a very long time. The wife was less pretty than her husband, carrying quite a few millennia on her bones. Both of them had stepped off a cable car that just returned from the rim, wearing smiles and heavy, self-heating coats and tall boots that had recently walked in the snow. The pretty man approached Crockett. "We wish we could have stayed longer," he confessed. "But our guide was tired, and we had to ride back with her."

Crockett shrugged. "The Luckies won't let you stay up there alone."

The old woman mentioned a respectable fee. "For a second peek. Would that be all right?"

Crockett was tempted, but only to a point.

"Not enough, is it?" asked her husband.

"I'm a little nervous." Crockett threw a dramatic glance over his shoulder. "This eruption is late. It could come any time now."

"Are you being honest?" the woman asked, plainly suspicious.

"There's honesty in my noise," Crockett conceded with an amiable laugh. "Our lake's been simmering longer than usual, and eventually, all that warm water has to leap into the sky."

He had no predictive skills. Only the Luckies knew when a full eruption was imminent, and they never gave clues.

"Warning away the fools," said the pretty man. "That seems like a good career."

"It would be noble work," Crockett said.

Then the wife tugged on her husband's elbow. "Maybe we should go back to our room, dear."

Crockett liked to believe that he understood women. One of the attractions of living in this nameless place was the parade of wealthy, carefree ladies. This particular old woman gave every sign of wanting attention, and Crockett imagined that he was her husband. She seemed like an elegant creature, accustomed to wealth but not spoiled by the stuff. He appreciated that old-fashioned face and build, and maybe there was an old-fashioned address in her past. Could she have come from the Old Earth? That was a fascinating prospect, and watching the amorous couple stroll off into the darkness, he promised himself that he would find them tomorrow. For a modest fee, he would offer his valuable services as an Honored Guide, testing his guesses against whatever they revealed about their cultivated lives.

Besides Crockett, the only Guides were a pair of rubber-faced AIs and a fiery little vesper. But the little sun had just set, and as often happened when night began, tourists grew more interested in dinner than a walk through the cold. The vesper soon rose and danced his way home. The AIs plugged into each other, vanishing in their own unimaginable ways. Crockett was alone, and the two objects of interest—those delightful security officers—had yet to pass through the station. Were they delayed? Did some criminal business ruin their timetable? Crockett turned in his chair, watching the banks of steam illuminated by moonlight; and then he heard a sound and looked forward again, exactly at the moment when the two lovelies strode into the almost empty room.

He offered a smile and soft sigh.

Effervescent as always, the officers responded with as much of a glance as he could have hoped for. They were delightful young ladies, each lovely in her way. The shorter one was muscular, with meaty breasts and a buoyant ass. By contrast, her companion was tall and elegant, blessed with a lip-rich mouth and eyes that couldn't have been brighter.

"Hello," Crockett managed.

Giggling, their hands met for a moment.

That they were lovers seemed self-evident. But Crockett's favorite rumor was that while they were passionate toward one another, they left the room and grace to invite a third party into their passion.

"Everybody else is home or on the rim," he said.

Really, couldn't he find anything more memorable to offer?

"We should visit the rim sometime," said the taller girl. With a flip of that pretty head, she declared, "You know, we could make it up there and back again before our dinner break is done."

They must have a very long break, Crockett thought.

Since the officers weren't permanent residents, the Luckies—the aliens who owned this realm—wouldn't allow them close without a Guide. Seeing his opportunity, Crockett came up with an amount that would make him the perfect companion: Not too much, but then again, not so cheap that they'd think he was begging for the honor.

For a long, delightful moment, two lovely faces stared at him.

Then together, without one word being said, they approached the twin AIs, using pointed fingers and sparks of static electricity to alert their Guides.

Moments later, a cable car pulled out of the station, four passengers rising silently into the darkness.

Well, this hadn't worked out at all. Dignity demanded that Crockett wait for a few moments, as if the next action wasn't connected to the past; and then he stood, putting on his hood, preparing for the sad walk home.

A lone figure stepped into the vacant station.

Countless aliens were passengers on the Great Ship. According to official counts, thousands of species were among the wealthy, exceptionally important souls onboard, and some aliens took a multitude of physical forms. Of course not every entity visited the Caldera of Good Fortune, but Crockett had never met the species standing before him. Even a rapid search of reliable databases came up with nothing but a few similar creatures. The entity was humanoid and small, with a tiny sucking mouth and smoky white eyes large enough to nearly fill its elliptical face. Those odd eyes regarded Crockett for a contemplative moment, and then through its translator, the creature asked, "What would be a fair price to ride with me to the top…?"

Crockett sliced what was fair in half.

He would have done it for free, happily. But then again, he was still a little upset that his girlfriends had so brazenly ignored him.

<h1 style="text-align:center">2</h1>

During those years and decades while the caldera slept, tourists arriving at the hamlet were as likely to gaze at the sky as to stare down at the Luckies. Habitats onboard the Great Ship wore elaborate disguises—scented atmospheres and precise climates, false horizons painted on cavern walls and a simplified cosmos projected on what was only rock and timeless hyperfiber. But most illusions demanded pragmatism over accuracy. Modest telescopes focusing on any of those stars would reveal the fiction: This artificial universe was composed of simple, bland specks of light. Only the brightest few mock-suns pretended to spit out flares and gas, and only the nearest were accompanied by the faint glows of pretend worlds. Point the same telescope at the blackness between any two stars, and a thousand dimmer suns might be waiting to be found. But if you built even larger mirrors out of polished glass and photon traps and then peered out toward some galaxy floating on the edge of Creation, there always came a point—that well-defined and inevitable line of exhaustion—where the dimmest stars and oldest galaxies were missing, were not.

The Luckies had their own limits. But their ceiling was managed by an army of dedicated AIs working with the best available squidskin—an intricate medium that produced light and darkness on an atomic scale. The illusions eventually broke down, but that kind of telescope was far beyond what most tourists could carry or drag up to the hamlet, much less all the way to the high ridge.

"I love this view," Crockett allowed, hoping to generate conversation. Or even just a neutral comment.

But the alien seemed to cherish its silence.

Luckies loved their sky, and with reason. Their home world was tucked inside a thick bright arm of the Milky Way, not far from an active star nursery. Gaze north, away from the ridge, and the false sky had beauty and majesty that even the shallowest soul would notice. But the local space was even richer: Five massive moons orbited a substantial brown dwarf, and the brown dwarf was dancing with a quiet little K-class sun. The Luckies' lived on the third moon, tidally locked and constantly massaged by its hefty neighbors. The inner neighbors were volcanic superstars, baked in radiation and their own fierce internal heat, while the outer moons were originally ice-clad and exceptionally cold, but with deep seas waiting beneath their surface.

Crockett preferred the illusionary sky to the illusionary landscape. Distant cavern walls were decorated with images of a frigid, bleak and deceptively bland terrain—a slow-moving chimera showcasing volcanoes and stubborn glaciers and wide expanses of lifeless, inert stone.

The Honored Guide turned, and not quite looking at those enormous white eyes, he introduced himself by name.

His companion offered no sound or visible motion.

"Luckies have rules," Crockett said. "I'm allowed to live here because ages ago, I won a lottery. I'm exceptionally lucky, for a human. And with my address comes the understanding that I can bring only my friends to the ridge."

The alien offered a soft, metallic chirp.

"Let's go through the motions," Crockett suggested. "For the sake of law and custom, tell me your name."

A moment passed, and another. Then the alien chirped again, and its translator said, "Doom."

"Doom?"

The translator spoke for itself. "That is my best approximation. But it is imperfect, and I apologize."

"What language does the creature use?"

"I cannot say."

"You aren't free to name it?"

"Perhaps I am. But my expertise feels incomplete."

The cable car had been accelerating since leaving the station, riding on a nanowhisker too small to be seen. Once and then twice again, descending cars sped past them, brightly lit, filled with visitors and their newfound friends. Crockett waved at his neighbors. Then he shut down his car's lights, allowing the full effect of the sky to work on odd, silent Doom.

The brown dwarf was a flattened disk barely visible through the vaporous clouds. But an inner moon lay far enough to one side to be visible—a rough orange and black blister of a world, chunks of its crust melting and exploding outwards with a violence that only looked impressive.

"You know," Crockett said. "The amount of computing power goes into these stars, the brown dwarf, and every major and minor moon…"

Then he intentionally stopped talking.

After a long pause, his companion said, "I am listening."

"The Luckies have peculiar personalities," said Crockett. "And a rather unique biology, as I understand it. They're an old species, yet it took them forever—a billion years, nearly—to build starships. Not that they weren't interested in the stars. The sky means more to them than almost anything.

You see, their preferred habitat are these hot caldera lakes. Each caldera had its vantage point, its unique view of the heavens. And whenever different populations spoke, they spent most of their time explaining what they could see—star for star; moon for moon."

Doom did not speak. But the big eyes were gazing upward, at least accidently showing interest.

"You probably know all of this," Crockett continued, "but during their entire history, the Luckies have built only a handful of starships. These were elaborate ships and very reliable, but exceptionally difficult to piece together." He held up his hand, squeezing two fingers close together. "A single Lucky is only this big."

The size of a dust mite, in essence.

"Autochemotrophic metabolisms. Low energy, minimal complexity. Not only aren't they particularly bright creatures, when taken alone, but they're pretty much helpless too."

Was he interesting his client, or boring it? Either way, Crockett was enjoying his impromptu lecture.

"A few million Luckies are about as sharp as one average human brain," he said. "But they don't feel at home until they number in the hundreds of trillions. That's what lives on the other side of this mountain. A nation of tiny entities all tied together. Together, they build giant eyes that float on their lake home, catching every wandering photon. And when enough of the Luckies think hard on one subject, they can dream up the greatest thoughts imaginable."

Crockett shrugged. "So what if it took millions of years to accrete a workable starship out of hot ores and salty, acidic water? They had time, and the patience. Really, if you want my opinion, they're incredible, wonderful organisms."

Several more cable cars passed by, looking like gaudy balloons being dragged down to a lower altitude. Without exception, the faces inside the balloons were happy, either glad for their adventure or glad to be returning home again.

"Wonderful creatures," he said.

Doom was certainly alien, but Crockett sensed emotion. The eyes were jumping inside their sockets, and the mouth was cocked in a way that didn't look comfortable. It was nervous. <u>He</u> was nervous. Plenty of species lacked a sense of gender, but Crockett had spent most of his life riding inside these cars with aliens, and that gave him a healthy respect for his own intuitions.

"Luckies have a weird, interesting model of reality," Crockett continued. "I'm sure you know this too. But the idea enjoys repetition."

A tight little breath was audible over the cold hum of the wind.

"Our universe is nothing more, or less, than a very pretty and intensely busy picture. The Creation is an illustration that hangs on the wall of someone else's living room. If only we had some eye that could reach out far enough—out into those realms hidden by the Grand Inflation—then the stars would cease to be. The galaxies and quasars and dark-matter masses…all those magnificent illusions would vanish…"

"Nothing is real," Crockett said.

Then he sad, "To the Luckies, everything and everyone is a fiction. And existence is simply the oldest, finest illusion."

Crockett's new friend whimpered. That was the best description for the mournful little sound. Then the big eyes closed, the lids rising from below, and he chirped and his translator said, "Well, perhaps we should hope these little creatures are correct."

3

Regardless of origins and no matter the vagaries of physiologies, trees adapted to severe cold and darkness often shared physical traits. Large, almost weightless leaves, mirrored and spread wide in the daylight, gathered the glow of the weak illusionary sun, bouncing it into a central bud or vein that was always black or purplish—a spherical receptor encased within an organic crystal, transparent but heavily insulated, clinging to every trace of useable heat. What was living inside any tree was tiny. Think of a man's dead body with a busy heart still beating in the chest; those were the normal proportions. Trees growing in the hamlet had the richest, easiest environment. Warmth leaked from the homes, and the streetlamps were blessings. But it took a hundred years for even the most vigorous Ganymede pine to expand as much as a good heart filling with hot, living blood.

Perhaps there were other ways to build cold trees. But Crockett had no experience with them. He came to the hamlet as a young boy and never left. He couldn't afford to go anywhere, since that meant losing his cherished residence status. But he was free to travel by virtual routes, which he did on occasion—witnessing habitats inside the Great Ship and across the galaxy. In general, Crockett favored hot bright places where trees grew tall as hills, leaving behind beautiful wood that he would buy with a tiny portion of his savings, using it to add accents and warmth to the walls of his own tiny house.

Beneath the cable car, the meager local forest was vanishing, and a moment later, it was gone.

Half a dozen cable cars were sliding past, and with a rough calculation, Crockett decided that only one or two more remained above. The security officers hadn't given up. Smiling, he let himself imagine the girls waiting for him. He pictured them standing side-by-side, pretty faces obscured by the layers of heated clothing, but their breath coming quickly with anticipation, emerging into the gloom before mixing with the rising steam and the falling snows.

The eruption would come today, or next week. Or after several more months of patient bubbling, the heat would dissipate, the artificial magma allowed to cool until this carefully regulated hazard was past.

Eruptions were much the same on the Luckies' home world. Quakes followed chaotic logic. Rising plumes were relentlessly fickle. But a new volcano would always build somewhere and then explode, leaving a gaping wound. Heated groundwater would percolate through the fractured crust, filling every hole with a fresh young lake. The first colonists to arrive inside a new caldera were the fortunate ones. They and their descendants ruled until the next eruption. Hence the name: Luckies.

Most cold worlds were marginal for life, or at best had stunted forests incapable of feeding the slowest bug. But the Luckies' home world enjoyed its own good fortune. The soggy, constantly shifting crust was filled with microbes using every metabolic trick, dancing with energetic irons and sodiums, carbon monoxides and nitrates. But the real producers were root-like giants—underground forests that choked every crevice, every pore, feasting on piezoelectric reactions and the physical flexing of the ground. Some of them even pumped water into the magma pools, creating steam that powered elaborate, turbine-like organs.

Every eruption was preceded by a season of rapid, joyous growth.

The Luckies riding the Great Ship had just this one caldera. Cataclysmic eruptions weren't possible, much less desirable, but the general rhythms of their old life held sway. The lake simmered and then boiled. The tiny crystalline bodies separated from one another, growing tough spore-like shells. Then the volcano erupted, flinging the water skyward as a scalding cloud, and trillions of tiny bodies were flung high by that carefully calibrated blast. Most of the tiny aliens fell outside the caldera, and they were dead. But those that found their way home again were blessed and knew it, and within a few months, they would be well on their way to rebuilding the society from Before.

Even the hamlet's residents referred to the rim community as a forest. But except for a passing resemblance to dead, leafless trees, the landscape had more in common with leaf litter, or better, with compost. The pale gray remains of dead roots had been pushed out of every hole, expelled by what was still living underground. Unlike the mirror-forests below, this realm had animal life—small crawlies and bigger crawlies, everything cloaked in fur and fat and tough genetics and variable metabolisms. But instead of the usual chirps and drummings, Crockett heard only silence. This was new and probably important. Yesterday the forest was still jabbering away; but now, for the first time, he found himself wondering if the eruption was imminent.

The cable car slid into its empty berth.

Only one other berth was filled, its passengers presumably on the far side of the ridge, gazing down at the bubbling, seemingly bottomless lake.

Their car stopped, a polite voice warning everyone about the cold to come, and then the main door slid open.

But the chill wasn't awful. Crockett guessed the air wasn't worse than seventy below—much warmer than the hamlet on any sun-scorched day. He stepped out onto the wide porch where tourists normally paused to acclimatize themselves, investing a few moments thinking of the witty things that he might say.

His client remained in the car.

Puzzled, Crockett stepped back inside. Doom was standing where he had always stood, but now his eyes were closed.

"Have you changed your mind?" asked Crockett.

The alien didn't speak.

"You're worried about the eruption," Crockett said. "Well, you shouldn't. It's a surprisingly peaceful event. I've known plenty who stayed up here while it happened. Keep inside the shelters, or find a likely hole, and your body won't die for more than a few hours."

There was a brief silence. Then with a quiet rattle, his friend said, "I will not be returning."

Crockett blinked. "What was that?"

"You are welcome to go, if you wish."

"I can't. Not and leave you here."

"But I need to be here," Doom said. "And besides, I do not require your presence. Since I have their permission."

"Whose permission? The Luckies?"

"Yes."

"Then why bring me at all?" Crockett asked.

Doom had six fingers on each hand, arranged three-and-three. One of his hands had just reached inside his heavy coat, digging deep while white eyes scanned the Luckies' false-forest.

"Maybe I should go home," Crockett allowed.

"But you will have to walk," Doom warned. "Neither cable car is operational. I am certain they will have seen to that detail."

"Who saw to what?"

The creature's gaze fixed on a distant point.

Crockett asked the car door to close, but nothing happened.

Then Doom began to retrieve his hand, and with a firm, half-loud voice, he said, "My good friend, I am sorry for your involvement in this."

"Sorry–?" Crockett began.

And then the world turned to fire and a searing golden light.

4

Drifting back into consciousness—in that instant when misery and clarity were roughly balanced—Crockett decided that the caldera had erupted. Where else would the flash of light come from? How else could his body have been flung hard against the floor? But then he gently set his gloved hand against his worst ache—the top of his head—and discovered that the insulated hood was missing, and his long golden hair was missing, and a palm-sized patch of the scalp had been burnt down to the hard bone.

A thousand emergency systems were awake, throwing their talents into protecting the brain and knitting new flesh. Adrenalin and fancier stimulants enlarged his senses, slowing time to a contemplative crawl. Crockett wasn't scared, much less panicked. He felt alert and focused and incapable of fear, absorbing his surroundings with curiosity and a powerful, intoxicating detachment. One focused blast had punctured the cable car, destroying the door and then the far end. The wind blowing up the valley was drifting through the gutted vehicle and then out again, carrying away the final traces of smoke and burnt flesh. Doom lay in a corner, limp and headless. Whatever had knocked Crockett to the floor had struck the alien with its full force, evaporating tough tissues and the skull, and whatever lay beneath.

Was the brain lost?

Was his client dead?

A pragmatic voice asked how this was possible. The slow wet eruption of the caldera couldn't produce the energies necessary to kill. Maybe the rising steam and falling snow had produced some exotic species of ball lightning. But even the most murderous example of meteorology couldn't produce this kind of disaster, which left him with a much-worse explanation.

A military-grade weapon was at work here.

Someone higher on the ridge could have taken the shot, and a plasma gun would have gutted the car. Except who would own such a device, and why would they, and for what conceivable reason would make anyone shoot at Crockett?

But of course he wasn't the target.

If he were, he would be dead. Plainly.

At long last, useful terror emerged. Crockett managed one deep breath and dropped down, throwing both arms over his wounded head. Except a second blast wouldn't be impressed with a few obscuring limbs. He needed to move, to hide. But his terror had swollen out of control suddenly. He couldn't move, even to save himself. He lay there like a scared, whimpering boy, waiting for another flash and the sudden removal of his existence.

Then the corpse sat up.

The six-fingered hand continued the motion begun before death, revealing some kind of ballistic weapon with a wide stubby barrel that lifted now, the blind hand aiming by memory or by unsuspected senses. A soft, almost musical report could be heard. An object flew out of the shattered car, followed by a muscular blast that rolled across the slope above them.

The corpse stood and began to walk, its free hand digging into a new pocket while the first gun fell on the floor beside Crockett. Brandishing a second weapon, the blind corpse fired twice again and ran through the open door. The next blasts shook the ridge and knocked it off its feet, but it was a determined apparition, rising once more and breaking into a run.

Crockett sat up for no other reason than to keep watch on what seemed to be the most unexpected, incredible sight of his sheltered little life.

Then from behind, a small sorry voice said, "Help me, my friend. My Crockett."

He turned, and the fighting corpse was forgotten.

A spider as wide as a dinner plate rose high as it could, on six jointed black legs. The body was thick and solid, fashioned from some tough species of bioceramic alloy. A mouth built only for speech was in front, and with a familiar voice, it said, "I will pay you…all I have left…"

"Doom?" the human muttered.

"All that remains of my wealth, it is yours."

Crockett had heard about such tricks: Organisms in the most dangerous circumstances would peel off their bodies, and sometimes even the bone or gelatin surrounding their living minds. Then their minds were secured inside a lifeboat, tough and temporary, able to weather all but the worst abuses.

"What do you want?" Crockett asked.

More blasts peppered the slope, followed by the sizzle of a second plasmatic bolt.

"I must reach the lake."

"You want to get to the Luckies," he assumed.

"I have no help but yours," said the spider.

"And if I don't?"

"I apologize, but these ladies are professional murderers," Doom warned. "And since you are a witness to their attempted crime–"

Another blast was unleashed, higher up the slope this time.

Crockett snatched the alien gun and stood.

"My friend–?"

"We aren't friends," Crockett said.

"But you will help me?"

"Yeah, that too," he promised. "I'll help both of us, if I can."

5

Some visitors to the hamlet didn't require local guides. Diplomats representing various distant worlds had received permission, or they were scientists intrigued in the robust biosphere. But a few souls had no obvious qualifications. They were peaceful, profoundly focused individuals who preferred not to ride the cable car to the ridge, but instead would walk the steep trails, investing time and some effort into the last moments of normal life.

The hamlet residents might discuss their fate, but not often and rarely with much feeling. Free sentient entities could do any fool thing they wished, so long as no one else was hurt. And besides, there was always the chance that somebody would come looking for those who were lost, and there was money to be made from that very peculiar work.

One day, a human woman arrived on the tram. She was handsome and queenly and reserved and alluring. Rumors swirled about her desires, and Crockett gladly put himself where he could impress an old lady with his professionalism and strong back.

She hired him, promising ten days of constant labor.

The first six days were spent loading the cable car with equipment that was lifted to the end of the line and then carried over foot-worn trails, up to a rocky shelf on the far side of the caldera's ridge. The lake lay below them. In the middle of winter the deep water was barely warm enough for a bath, and it was spectacularly clear—a vertical realm filled with swimming shapes and flexing tendrils and the delicate, rib-like reefs where the communal Luckies enjoyed their easy times. Alien eyes covered nearly a quarter of the lake surface—thin, profoundly black disks made of light-sensitive neurons. They were lidless and unsleeping eyes, missing nothing that happened in the sky. By comparison, the woman's telescope was tiny, feeble, and perhaps even laughable.

Crockett laughed, but only when he reached home again.

Six full days were needed just to bring the pieces of the machine up to the high shelf, and another three days were spent standing in the brutal cold. The two worked in clumsy partnership, assembling and calibrating all the components and photon traps and the generator and its backup, struggling to meet the deadline that came on that last, tenth day. By then, the Luckies' weak sun had dropped beneath the illusionary horizon. A sky that had been suffused with soft purple tones fell into total darkness. Bright stars became brilliant, and thousands of unseen stars leapt out of the night. Glancing through the viewfinder, Crockett saw more detail than he had ever imagined possible. Each one of those miniscule stars was nothing more, or less, than a colorful mark painted on an otherwise invisible ceiling. And not painted once, but endlessly—a succession of tiny, intense images that if examined closely would reveal flares and sunspots and perhaps the occasional, consistent transit of worlds. And by the same inherent logic, each tiny round patch of shadow, smaller than a virus, was itself imbued with a thorough, finely rendered map, mountains giving birth to twisting rivers that ran unseen down to the invisible seas.

The Luckies had to feel utterly comfortable with their sky.

Crockett understood that logic, the alien mind…or at least he accepted the creatures' strangeness well enough to make them familiar, and in the fashion of a tapestry hung for too long on the wall, forgettable.

But his client didn't care about stars, bright or otherwise.

The vagaries of orbits had brought both of the outer moons into view. In reality, the outermost moon was sold to humans as payment for passage onboard the Great Ship. Colonists had rapidly terraformed the prize, transforming the ice crust into a blue ocean where millions of humans lived in floating cities and submerged cities and walked along beaches designed to be idyllic. Sometimes, in a mocking mood, Crockett would tell neighbors, "I wouldn't mind visiting that place." And everybody laughed, enjoying his weak humor even as they secretly wondered how walking that sand would really feel.

The nearer moon was half-full, and following the orbit of its namesake, on that day it reached opposition with the Luckies' home moon. The two celestial bodies couldn't have been closer. That icy neighbor was as large as possible, big as a big palm riding on the end of the short arm; and while it wasn't near enough to touch, at least it managed to look genuine and immediate, even when the eyes knew it was a smear of light.

A picture.

Nothing.

Except for his presence as an Honorable Guide, Crockett wasn't needed anymore. His client told him to step away, which he did willingly. For the next few hours, he staved off boredom by watching the caldera's lake. He studied the banded face of the old brown dwarf. Then with eyes closed, he imagined sleeping with this woman with whom he had shared effort and time and very little else.

The telescope was a broad, blunt machine focused hard on one of the cities of that nearby moon. With limited success, Luckies had colonized their neighbor's natural hot springs. Starships had brought other species, and later, the Great Ship brought even more. With the available resolution, the woman found a certain building, and when the light was good, she could make out a solitary figure standing on its roof. Then with a laser barely strong enough to throw its beam across a very large room, she sent a message, and after the appropriate delay, she received an answer that made her laugh quietly and then sob to herself.

Hours passed while she conversed with that dead person.

Crockett never learned who it was. Human? Alien? Was it a former lover, or just some lost friend? In a roundabout fashion, he made inquires. But his client pretended not to hear him, and later, she mentioned that perhaps this was none of his business, thank you.

"I was just curious," he muttered. "Sorry, never mind."

In the Luckies' sky, no object was so thoroughly rendered as that neighboring moon. Knowledgeable voices claimed that not even the Ship's captains had the computing power that was being focused on that one illusionary body. Every city on the visible hemisphere was real, as were the cities on the far side: How else could the entire organic world be maintained? Each city had its population, and every citizen had a name and address and life and loves, including the fierce hates and passionate disinterests and all the other untidy, inelegant, and wonderful hallmarks of existence. Some self-declared experts claimed the vast imagery was so thorough that every mote of dust had its own label. Every snowflake knew its place; every gust of wind had its story. And that was why the Luckies could demand fortunes from those souls who were desperate enough or odd enough to have themselves killed: Killed so those strange mite-sized creatures could tear their minds apart, revealing every memory, every cherished secret, and then slather whatever they learned to the plaster on their busy ceiling.

Finished at last, the woman turned away from the telescope and wept again.

When her grieving was finished, she called Crockett over, and together, they dragged the telescope to the edge of shelf and gave it one shared push. An apparatus worth plenty tumbled into the warm water. And alien bodies instantly tore it apart—the rare metals and hyperfibers most likely part of her payment.

Together, the two strangers returned to the cable cars.

In silence, they rode back down to the hamlet—a tiny place full of warm homes and real people and organisms that were as good as any person.

Only in the station, at the end, did Crockett suggest to his client that she might enjoy an evening spent with him. He meant sex, but he didn't say it. He meant to sound friendly and fun, and that was exactly how he came across. But she reacted instantly, decisively. A knife in the belly wouldn't have made her straighten up any faster, and with a tight, small voice, she asked, "Why would you ever think such a thing would be half-possible?"

He blinked, too startled to react.

"You're the one living a dream," she informed him.

This was not the first time, nor was it the last, that Crockett wondered if perhaps he didn't know women quite as well as he believed.

6

The two AIs were sitting together in the false-forest, in the middle of the main path, a thin coat of new snow obscuring their faces and their high functions removed and burnt to ash.

Six mechanical legs had wrapped themselves around Crockett's waist, the tip of each leg fused with its mate. Doom was riding him, the spidery body snug against the small of his back. The lifeboat weighed almost nothing, and sometimes it was almost possible to forget about the alien. Crockett could run naturally, long legs slicing through the deep fresh snow. He carried the bomb-throwing gun in one hand, then the other. There were moments when he almost forgot why he was running. Then the plasma weapon discharged somewhere in the Luckies' forest, and he heard fire and saw a flash of light, followed by the stink of burning wood.

"Who are they?" Crockett whispered.

"Hired killers."

"I know. I mean…" What did he mean? "They were security officers. Ours. Children, nearly—"

"They aren't young," the alien warned.

"Okay." Crockett was following the narrow, unpopular trail that he once used to carry the telescope to the high shelf. "The women aren't what I guessed. But I want to know—"

An explosion shook snow off the gray roots.

"My body has expired," Doom reported. Then with a curiously buoyant joy, he added, "But it did earn us time and distance."

Crockett stumbled.

"Careful," said his companion.

"I want to know," Crockett managed as he stood. "Who hired your killers?"

"My enemies."

"Well, yes…"

"If you learned their identities, perhaps you would know too much."

"So what are you?" Crockett asked. "And why did you deserve this—?"

"I am nobody, and I did nothing." The alien adjusted his grip as the trail began to climb. "Nobody and nothing," Doom repeated.

Crockett glanced at the weapon. Could his hands use this thing?

"I boarded the Great Ship to escape my enemies."

"That happens a lot," Crockett agreed.

"But they came with me, my enemies did. They hate me that much."

From behind and far below, a woman's voice shouted out a single word: "Tracks."

Crockett muttered, "Shit," and ran harder.

"Eight centuries, I have been onboard this wonderful starship. I have made a habit of regularly changing identities and habits. But my enemies always find me, and three times before, they have sent agents to put an end to me."

"Go to the captains," Crockett suggested. "Can't they help?"

Silence.

"They won't, will they? Why now? Are you some kind of criminal?"

"If I was," the alien pointed out, "then my enemies would invite the captains' aid in finding me."

Probably so.

"This is a private, difficult concern."

The trail angled to the right, flattened and then lifted steeply again. A single plasmatic round passed overhead, near enough that the air warmed, and with the brilliant yellowish glare, the surface of the snow turned to fresh vapor.

"I am sorry to involve you, my friend."

"We aren't friends," Crockett gasped.

"Of course not."

"Will this be the end?" he asked. "If you reach the Luckies…will it put an end to everything…?"

"I believe so."

"Because you'll be dead."

Silence.

How much farther? Crockett had walked this path thousands of times, but never in these awful circumstances. Never this fast, and never this slow. He felt as if he was in a nightmare, the snow growing deeper for no reason other than to fight every stride. He was aching and sick with fear, and sometimes he caught himself wondering what would happen if he just dropped the damned bug. It would probably crawl after him, he guessed. So then he'd turn and give the creature a good finishing kick.

Crockett tried to sprint, stumbled and slid backward a few meters.

As he tried to rise, the legs around his belly tightened. "No," said Doom. "Remain where you are."

Crockett could taste the steam rising off the boiling lake—a rich, acrid scent created by shredded organics and heavy metals. "Why?" he muttered.

"Here you are invisible to them."

"But they're coming," he pointed out. "They're going to find us—"

"Please wait."

The runaway terror had returned.

A very tiny eye lifted high above the spider's body. "Below us stands a substantial rooting body," Doom explained. "He is parabolic in shape, and much taller than any of his neighbors."

"What do you want?"

"With both hands, grasp the weapon's trigger mechanism. Yes, that is the technique. In a few moments, I would like you to sit up and aim at that large root…and please, twist the trigger until the magazine is empty…"

"Will that stop them?"

"With luck, you will earn us more time," Doom replied.

Crockett took a deep breath, fighting to clear his head. "Letting the Luckies kill you…" he began. "Is that a reasonable solution…?"

"I am living in death now," the creature pointed out. "By doing this, I will simply be exchanging one afterlife for another."

Crockett breathed again.

"Now, my friend. Turn. Shoot. And then, please run…!"

7

Explosions tore apart the dead wood, and secondary charges ignited the airborne chunks and splinters, creating a rolling blaze that pushed its way down the slope, melting and searing all that lay in its brilliant orange path.

Crockett threw down the empty weapon and sprinted uphill, his frantic shadow leading the way. For an instant, from out of the firestorm, he heard what might have been a single voice screaming in misery. Or it was random noise. Then the voice vanished within the boiling crackle of sap, and he reached the crest of the ridge and gratefully started down the other side.

In a few steps, there was no snow underfoot.

The air turned blacker and denser, choked with moisture and a miserable heat. A quick succession of hard shocks sprang from some deep, angry place. Crockett stumbled. He stood and then stumbled again. From his left came the ominous rumblings of a thick, newborn geyser. Finding his feet and balance, he warned, "The eruption's starting."

"Run," the alien kept advising.

"Where?"

"To the lake."

"But the eruption—"

"It has not arrived," Doom replied. "My saviors shared with me the moment of the Birth Catastrophe, and we have several minutes remaining…"

Crockett discovered that the air was less awful when he bent low, and that was how he ran—a clumsy pitched-forward stride—and when he could see nothing useful, which was most of the time, he would close his burning, tearing eyes, navigating by a mixture of feel and panicked memory.

The trail suddenly flattened out.

Here was the high rock shelf where he and that odd woman had assembled the telescope. But the sky was stolen away. Stars and the elaborate moons were hidden behind a growing flume, superheated vapors rising from the lake's center, lifting countless spores with them. Crockett took a step and coughed and managed two more steps before his windpipe began to scald. Then he paused, kneeling forward for what was supposed to be a brief, brief rest. But without oxygen, his body was descending into emergency metabolisms. Energies were dipping, and his eyes refused to stop weeping, and when he tried to rise it was too soon, and he tripped and fell again, losing all sense of direction.

The spidery machine deployed more eyes.

"Let go of me and run," Crockett advised.

"Quiet," said Doom.

"I'm slowing you down," Crockett argued.

Then his companion yanked the jointed legs, threatening to cut his body in two. And very softly, Doom said, "One is with us. The tall one is here."

With both fists, Crockett wiped at his eyes. Then he forced the lids to open, but he saw nothing except for the perfect blackness. The universe was him and this apparition that refused to release him, plus nothingness without end or purpose, comfort or hope. But at least his anaerobic metabolisms were awake now. He had enough strength to stand, and from that new perspective, he realized that he could hear the boiling lake lying straight ahead.

He took three increasingly small steps, feeling for the edge.

Each motion caused Doom to pull his legs in close again, but the creature didn't offer so much as a whisper of advice.

With the third step, a new shape appeared before Crockett—a geometrical simple shape composed of dark lines joined together, each line moving slowly according to its own desires. Too late, he understood what he was seeing. The beautiful tall killer was standing directly in his path, probably fully aware of his presence and his hopelessness. Yet Doom chose that moment to speak again—in an abrupt, rather loud voice—telling his companion, "Run. Past her, and jump over the edge—"

"I'll die," he interrupted.

"My saviors will not let that happen. I promise."

Even if the alien was telling the truth—if the Luckies would willingly digest his brain and volunteer their computing power to let an extra illusion to walk their nonexistent moon—this wasn't what Crockett wanted. Never. With both hands, he grabbed the encircling legs, hard tugs accomplishing nothing while he cried out, "Get off me. Drop!"

The alien refused.

Crockett sucked in the hot black air and screamed. "Here I am! I've got him here. Here!"

Doom pulled his legs close, crushing the human guts.

The tall girl stepped closer, and then she set off a floating flare that lifted several meters overhead, throwing a hard bluish glare across the black rock of the shelf. A transparent mask lay over her pretty face, allowing her to breathe slowly and naturally. As always, she looked like a supremely happy soul. With a warm joyful smile, she watched Crockett fighting with his companion. She seemed utterly amused by the situation. Without question, she had won, but why didn't she use the plasma gun riding in her long left hand? Then another figure emerged from the fumes—a short strong human, badly burnt but already beginning to heal.

The second killer said, "Hello," to her partner.

She wasn't wearing a breathing mask. It was lost or destroyed, or maybe she didn't feel it was necessary anymore.

"I was waiting for you," the tall girl allowed.

"Thank you." That beautiful face had been destroyed, eaten to the bone by the firestorm. A sloppy mouth remained, withered lips and the stump of a tongue barely able to speak. "You almost made it," she managed, studying Crockett with a pair of freshly grown eyes. But she was speaking to the alien. She said, "Mr. Doom," and broke into a mocking laugh.

Too late, Crockett stepped toward the lake.

The tall girl had a second weapon—a tiny kinetic gun that neatly shattered both of his shins, leaving him sprawled out on his right side.

"You want your friend pulled off?" the tall girl asked.

The short girl fell to her knees. For a moment, she teased Crockett with that brutalized mouth, threatening to give him a dry, sooty kiss. Then she reached around back and used a special tool, and the machine-spider released its grip and fell helplessly onto its back.

"Make sure," the short girl advised.

The tall girl deftly opened the armored carapace, and what she saw made her pause. Crockett couldn't see the lovely face against the glare directly overhead, and perhaps she couldn't see anything well enough because of her own shadow. Then she rocked backward, letting the full light of the flare fall into the cavity—a cavity designed to carry a mind that was most definitely missing.

"The crafty shit," the tall girl muttered.

"A second lifeboat," her partner muttered. "There must have been, and I didn't notice—"

"You didn't," the tall girl agreed testily.

From the beginning, Crockett realized, he had been carrying an empty vessel—a package of programs and contingencies that was masquerading as a poor miserable soul facing death.

"He lied to me," Crockett complained.

The short girl laughed at him, or herself.

"The shit," said the tall girl once again.

Then the two of them traded glances, and the short girl climbed to her feet and moved out of the way. And her partner said, "Nothing personal," and pointed her plasma gun at Crockett's cowering face—

The empty spider flinched and leaped high.

When it detonated, the six long legs were driven hard into both women, cutting through spines and bones, leaving them in mangled wet piles...and allowing Crockett just enough time to crawl into a crevice where he wedged his own battered body, the next moment or two spent thanking his own considerable luck.

And with that, the caldera exploded.

8

Watching the eruption from below, various neighbors recalled having seen three friends accompanying clients to the ridge. Did they return in time? No? Well, incidents like this always seemed to happen, and usually more bodies were involved. But neither the hottest water or deepest snow could kill, and from experience, they understood that it was best to wait several days, letting the new mountain build itself to where its foundation was stable and as predictable as could be hoped for.

The deep lake continued to explode upwards, and the thick white steam cooled, falling again as waves of snow and delicate formations of ice. Gas bubbles and volcanic soot complicated the complex, ever-changing layering. No two mountains were ever the same, and this particular eruption built the tallest peak in memory—a lofty, single-vent ice volcano that looked as if it was willfully reaching for the ceiling, and with that, trying to touch the painted stars.

Steam was still pouring upwards when the rescue party found the burnt out cable car, and shortly after that, the two dead AIs.

What had seemed routine was not.

More volunteers joined in the desperate efforts. Portable heaters cut half a dozen tunnels up the ridge and down the other side. Two more days passed before the next body was discovered: One of the temporary security officers, horrifically maimed but conscious enough to point at her colleague. "It was the alien," she managed to say with her frozen, half-healed face. "Watch for him, and be careful," she warned. Then someone asked about Crockett's whereabouts, and she paused for a moment, in thought, before directing them toward the shelf's edge, into the scorching depths of the caldera itself.

"The poor bastard," was the general consensus.

The other officer's body was dug out of the ice, and both victims were carried back down to the hamlet; and after a full day of intense medical care, the two ageless women got out of bed and grabbed each by the hand, and a few moments later, they walked to the tram and rode away, leaving the habitat for places unmentioned.

A few hours later, one of the local vespers was hired to bring a married couple into the temporary ice tunnels. It was the woman, Quee Lee, who discovered Crockett's mangled body. With her husband's help, she dragged the lucky man into a convenient chamber. The vesper wanted to leave Crockett there and chase after help. But the humans decided to feed the man their modest dinners, and by keeping their patient warm and comfortable, it took only a few hours for him to recover to where he could stand on his own and walk slowly.

Crockett told what had happened. He claimed that he wanted to go home, but at the last moment, standing inside an empty car, he had a sudden change of mind.

"But I wish to leave now," the vesper snapped.

"I'm staying here," said Crockett. Covering his head with a makeshift cap, he turned to his saviors, adding, "You're welcome to walk with me."

"What's the fee?" asked the husband, with a suspicious tone.

"Perri," his wife snapped. "Does it matter–?"

"For nothing," said Crockett. Then he smiled weakly, adding, "For the fun of it. How would that be?"

Tourists were exploring the new landscape—a giant gray-white dome of ice and air pockets and vantage points that would never exist in quite this way again. In another few weeks, the residual heat of the eruption would begin melting the mountain's bones. Small quakes and a few large ones would cause spectacular avalanches. Eventually the caldera would fill with slush and dirt and the sleeping Luckies too, and the lake would be reborn, and a civilization that was already ancient when Earth was ruled by single-celled life would gracefully begin all over again.

But for this particular moment, three humans could walk safely on the face of the mountain.

Again, Crockett told his story.

Slowly, carefully, Perri and Quee Lee asked little questions, forcing him to explain those points that were hardest to explain. The sun was down, as it happened. And the nearest moon had risen just an hour ago—a almost full circle of ice and warm villages and unreal cities and teeming millions. Assuming that he had reached the lake, Doom was living there now. Or at least some elaborate bottle of intelligence, with his name and identity, believed that it was living on that spot of light cast up on that finite sky.

"He isn't safe," Crockett muttered.

His companions listened patiently.

"His enemies...they won't stop just because of this...inconvenience..." A keen sorrow ran through the voice. Quietly, he said, "One year from now, or in a thousand and one years...somebody will pass through the hamlet, pretending to be like all the others who want the Luckies' tricks. The stranger will want to make his family rich, or maybe he won't have anything else to lose. The reasons don't matter. All that counts is that he'll walk up a trail and surrender his body to the aliens, and the Luckies will put him up on that moon there, and in another year, or fifty thousand years, he'll finally accomplish what he was hired to do." Crockett sighed, gesturing at that patch of cold light. "One way or another, Death is going to find its way there."

"It's the same for all of us," Perri whispered.

Crockett glanced at him. For a moment, his face twisted with genuine horror; but then the horror slowly faded, replaced by a strange, bright expression that looked like pure wild joy.

During the cable car descent, Crockett asked his new friends if they often traveled around the Great Ship.

"Sometimes we stop wandering," Quee Lee replied with a self-deprecating laugh.

"Name your hundred favorite destinations," said Crockett. Then he added, "The warm, bright places, I mean. Alien and human both."

Perri quickly supplied a list of more than a hundred habitats.

The car slid into its berth, and Crockett thanked both of them for everything, and then he walked out of the station, past his home and the little party of friends and neighbors who were waiting inside to surprise him…past them and out of the hamlet entirely, stepping onto the first tram available, and without one backward glance, leaving behind the unreal for those things that truly had to matter.

Bridge Nine

Little shards of far flung worlds never stop rising.

The purest strongest most elaborate materials have been cobbled into elegant streakships that climb to the Great Ship, dropping into prepared berths inside Port Beta, each welcomed by celebrations and suitable music, or if preferred, long silences designed to honor the onboard species. Slower ships are more common but just as reveled: Ungainly taxis and battered freighters, hyperfiber balloons and waspish yachts. Ships come from every important place in this arm of the galaxy, enduring risks and damage and sometimes severe damage. Many will never fly again. Chopped into salvage, they can be woven into new machines wearing ten million improvements. Fueled and crewed, they will then embark for worlds out in the dusty deep where new species and fresh experiences will be waiting, paying premiums for space onboard the Great Ship.

Mechanical shards carry living shards. Drips and sacks of alien fluid walk on bony legs, or they have jointed exoskeletons, or they make due with mobile roots or perfumed trails of slime. Many supremely wet creatures live inside larger drips and sacks. Liquid water is a necessity, or liquid methane, or molten sulfur, or ammonium hydroxide, or perchlorate, or silicone, or a different flavor of silicone, or gases compressed to high densities. Yet there are biologies that have no use for fluids. They can be machines or entities indistinguishable from machines, and there are species that don't pretend to belong to one camp or the other—cyborgs born from old traditions or difficult environments, or perhaps recent marriages between unlikely, loving mates.

In some way shape or form, every species has been designed.

Evolution is the first master. Chance and cold practicality push the simple species into their basic, boilerplate structures. But natural selection often bows to experience and genetic manipulations. Disease is banished. Immortality is routine. Fashion has its influences, as do political certainties and political uncertainties. But tradition counts for quite a lot: Humans still look like apes, and they sing like apes, but the flesh and their young minds have been transformed by tricks older than the Krebs' cycle.

Humans used to be the most common shards to step onboard, but those times are done. Human space was a thin belt of metal-poor worlds and sterilized worlds and odd planets that would probably never be entirely stable or safe for life, and the Great Ship passed out of that realm long ago, entering more civilized and wealthier and considerably more intriguing neighborhoods. Harum-scarums and Ginas and blue-passions and Janunsians are older, far more abundant species, and they are just a tip of the proverbial tentacle.

Life wears its culture and history and names, and humans have favorite names for the new passengers that never stop arriving.

*In one average century, Undersheens and Jakks and cocoHarols and Lol*Tings step into the yellow, Sol-inspired lights of Port Beta. Quaker Maids ride on columns of compressed air. Channelmen and Ravvens are flyers—beautiful, unrelated creatures sporting wings and crimson plumage—while X(66)s are ugly beasts with voices so lovely, perfect and lovely and fluid, that the echoes of their arrival can be heard for years.*

And this menagerie is nothing compared to the drips and circuits that arrive with the intelligent life forms. Each new passenger has its entourage. Microbes and fleas and important intestinal worms come onboard with the pets and domesticated livestock. Habitats and little apartments have critical plants and pretty plants and the special rare species that are supposed to be carried to the far end of the galaxy. Every alien body is precious, unique, and rich with tiny environments where little beasts and quick swift minds can hide from easy view, or in some cases, use their hosts as platforms to show the universe their own magnificence.

The humans own the Great Ship, and they rule it, and one key activity is to count the species that step and fly and swim their way inside.

Numbers always look precise, even when they fall short of the truth.

The Ship is eighty thousand years into a voyage scheduled to last half a million years, and it already can be said that no body in the galaxy, or perhaps even the universe, contains so much diversity.

There is no way to calculate the potential that lives beneath the deep hard hull.

But that doesn't stop humans from building models, charting the promise and dangers. They use biology and sociology, history and other oracles. Weighty equations will say whatever they want to say, and perhaps a few captains believe one result over countless others. But even the fools among them would never risk their endless lives for any of these fantastical, deeply subjective guesses, while the wisest few realize that each result is important only because it shows another future that will never come to pass.

Camouflage

1

The human male had lived on the avenue for thirty-two years. Neighbors generally regarded him as a solitary creature, short-tempered on occasion, but never rude without cause. His dark wit was locally famous, and a withering intelligence was rumored to hide behind the brown-black eyes. Those with an appreciation of human beauty claimed that he was far from handsome, his face asymmetrical, the skin rough and fleshy, while his thick mahogany-brown hair looked as if it was cut with a knife and his own strong hands. Yet that homeliness made him intriguing to some human females, judging by the idle chatter. He wasn't large for a human, but most considered him substantially built. Perhaps it was the way he walked, his back erect and shoulders squared while the face tilted slightly forwards, as if looking down from a great height. Some guessed he had been born on a high-gravity world, since the oldest habits never died. Or maybe this wasn't his true body, and his soul still hungered for the days when he was a giant. Endless speculations were woven about the man's past. He had a name, and everybody knew it. He had a biography, thorough and easily observed in the public records. But there were at least a dozen alternate versions of his past and left-behind troubles. He was a failed poet, or a dangerously successful poet, or a refugee who had escaped some political mess—unless he was some species of criminal, of course. One certainty was his financial security, but where his money came from was a subject of considerable debate. Inherited, some claimed. Others imagined gambling winnings or lucrative investments on now-distant colony worlds. Whatever the story, the man had the luxury of filling his days doing very little, and during his years on this obscure avenue, he had helped neighbors with unsolicited gifts of money and sometimes more impressive flavors of aid.

Thirty-two years was not a long time. Three decades was little different than an afternoon, and that's why for another century or twenty, locals might still refer to a neighbor as the newcomer.

Such was life onboard the Great Ship.

There were millions of avenues like this one. Some were short enough to walk in a day, while others stretched for thousands of uninterrupted kilometers. Many avenues remained empty, dark and cold as when humans first discovered the Great Ship. But some had been awakened, made habitable to human owners or the oddest alien passengers.

This particular avenue was almost a hundred kilometers long and barely two hundred meters across. And it was tilted. Wastewater made a shallow river that sang its way across a floor of sugar-and-pepper granite. For fifty thousand years, the river had flowed without interruption, etching out a shallow channel. Locals had built bridges at the likely places, and along the banks erected tubs and pots filled with soils that mimicked countless worlds, giving roots and sessile feet happy places to stand. A large pot rested outside the man's front door—the vessel made of ceramic foam trimmed with polished brass and covering nearly a tenth of a hectare. When he first arrived, the man poisoned the old jungle and planted another. But he wasn't much of a gardener, apparently. The new foliage hadn't prospered, weed species and odd volunteers emerging from the ruins.

Along the pot's edge stood a ragged patch of llano vibra—an alien flower famous for its wild haunting songs. "I should cut that weed out of there," he would tell neighbors. "I pretty much hate the racket it's making." Yet he didn't kill them or tear out the little voice boxes. And after a decade or two of hearing his complaints, his neighbors began to understand that he secretly enjoyed their complicated, utterly alien melodies.

Most of his neighbors were sentient, fully mobile machines. Early in the voyage, a charitable foundation dedicated to finding homes and livelihoods for freed mechanical slaves leased the avenue. But recently organic species had begun cutting their own apartments into the walls, including a janusian couple downstream, and upstream, an extended family of harum-scarums.

The human was a loner but by no means a hermit.

True solitude was the easiest trick. There were billions of passengers onboard, yet the great bulk of the Ship was full of hollow places and great caves, seas of water and ammonia and methane, as well as moon-sized tanks filled with liquid hydrogen. Most locations were empty. Wilderness was everywhere, cheap and inviting. Indeed, a brief journey by cap-car could take the man to any of six wild places—alien environments and hidden sewage conduits as well as a maze-like cavern that was rumored to never have been mapped. That was one advantage: He had more than one escape route. Another advantage was his neighbors. Machines were always bright in easy ways, fountains of information if you knew how to employ them, but indifferent to the subtleties of organic life.

Pamir lived as a hermit for a time. That was only sensible. Ship captains rarely abandoned their posts, and captains of his rank and great promise never made ruins out of an important facility—regardless whether they had good reasons or not.

But thousands of years had brought changes to his status. By most accounts, the Master Captain had stopped searching for him. Two or three or four possible escapes from the Ship had been recorded, each placing him on one the new colony worlds that humans were building as they traveled through the galaxy. Or maybe he had died in some ugly fashion. The best story put him inside a frigid little cavern. Smugglers had killed his body and sealed it inside a tomb of glass, and after centuries without food or air, the body had stopped trying to heal itself. Pamir was a blind brain trapped inside a frozen carcass, and the smugglers were eventually captured and interrogated by the best in that narrow field. According to coerced testimonies, they confessed to killing the infamous captain, though the precise location of their crime wasn't known and would never be found.

Pamir spent another few thousand years wandering, changing homes while remaking his face and name. He had worn nearly seventy identities, each elaborate enough to be believed, yet dull enough to escape notice. For good reasons, he found it helpful to wear an air of mystery, letting neighbors invent any odd story to explain the gaps in his biography. Whatever they dreamed up, it fell far from the truth. Machines and men couldn't imagine the turns and odd blessings of his life. Yet despite all of that, Pamir remained the good captain. A sense of obligation forced him to watch after the passengers and Ship. He might live on the run for the next four hundred millennia, but he would always be committed to this great machine and its precious, nearly countless inhabitants.

Now and again, he did large favors.

Like with the harum-scarums next door. Giants by every measure, adorned with armored plates and spine-encrusted elbows, they were possessed by an arrogance caused by millions of years of wandering among the stars. But this particular family was politically weak, and that was a bad way to be among harum-scarums. They had troubles with an old Mother-of-fathers, and when Pamir saw what was happening, he interceded. Over the course of six months, by means both subtle and decisive, he put an end to the feud. The Mother-of-fathers came to her enemies' home, walking backwards as a sign of total submission, and with a plaintive voice begged for death, or at the very least, a forgetting of her sordid, graceless crimes.

No one saw Pamir's hand in this business. If they had, he would have laughed it off, and moments later, he would have vanished, throwing himself into another identity inside a distant avenue.

Large deeds always demanded a complete change of life.

A fresh face.

A slightly rebuilt body.

And another forgettable name.

That was how Pamir lived. And he had come to believe that it wasn't a particularly bad way to live. Fate or some other woman-deity had given him this wondrous excuse to be alert at all times, to accept nothing as it first appears, helping those who deserved to be helped, and when the time came, remaking himself all over again.

And that time always came…

2

"Hello, my friend."

"Hello to you."

"And how are you this evening, my very good friend?"

Pamir was sitting beside the huge ceramic pot, listening to his llano-vibra. With a dry smirk, he mentioned, "I need to void my bowels."

The machine laughed a little too enthusiastically. Its home was half a kilometer up the avenue, sharing an apartment with twenty other legally sentient AIs who had escaped together from the same long-ago world. The rubber face and bright glass eyes worked themselves into a beaming smile, while a happy voice declared, "I am learning. You cannot shock me so easily with this organic dirty talk." Then once again, he said, "My friend," before using the fictitious name.

Pamir nodded, shrugged.

"It is a fine evening, is it not?"

"The best ever," he deadpanned.

Evening along this avenue was a question of the clock. The machines used the twenty-four hour ship-cycle, but with six hours of total darkness sandwiched between eighteen hours of brilliant, undiluted light. That same minimal aesthetics had kept remodeling to a minimum. The avenue walls were raw granite, save for the little places where organic tenants had applied wood or tile facades. The ceiling was a slick arch made of medium-grade hyperfiber wearing a thin coat of grime and lubricating oils and other residues. The lights were original, as old as the Ship and set in the thin dazzling bands running lengthwise along the ceiling. Evening brought no softening of brilliance or reddening of color. Evening was a precise moment, and when night came…in another few minutes, Pamir realized…there would be three warning flashes, and then a perfect smothering blackness.

The machine continued to smile at him, meaning something by it. Cobalt-blue eyes were glowing, watching the human sit with the singing weeds.

"You want something," Pamir guessed.

"Much or little. How can one objectively measure one's wishes?"

"What do you want with me? Much, or little?"

"Very little."

"Define your terms," Pamir growled.

"There is a woman."

Pamir said nothing, waiting now.

"A human woman, as it happens." The face grinned, an honest delight leaking out of a mind no bigger than a fleck of sand. "She has hired me for a service. And the service is to arrange an introduction with you."

With a flat, unaffected voice, Pamir said, "An introduction." And through a string of secret nexuses, he brought his security systems up to full alert.

"She wishes to meet you."

"Why?"

"Because she finds you fascinating, of course."

"Am I?"

"Oh, yes. Everyone here believes you are most intriguing." The flexible face spread wide as the mouth grinned, never-used white teeth shining in the last light. "But then again, we are an easily fascinated lot. What is the meaning of existence? What is the purpose of death? Where does slavery end and helplessness begin? And what kind of man lives down the path from my front door? I know his name, and I know nothing."

"Who's this woman?" Pamir asked.

The machine refused to answer him directly. "I explained to her what I knew about you. What I positively knew and what I could surmise. And while I was speaking, it occurred to me that after all of these nanoseconds of close proximity, you and I remain strangers."

The surrounding landscape was unremarkable. Scans told Pamir that every face was known, and the nexus traffic was utterly ordinary, and when he extended his search, nothing was worth the smallest concern. Which made him uneasy. Every long look should find something suspicious.

"The woman admires you."

"Does she?"

"Without question." The false body was narrow and quite tall, dressed in a simple cream-colored robe. Four spidery arms emerged from under the folds of fabric, extending and then collapsing across the illusionary chest. "Human emotions are not my strength. But from what she says and what she does not say, I believe she has desired you for a very long time."

The llano-vibra were falling silent now.

Night was moments away.

"All right," Pamir said. He stood, boots planting themselves on the hard pale granite. "No offense meant here. But why the hell would she hire you?"

"She is a shy lady," the machine offered. And then he laughed, deeply amused by his own joke. "No, no. She is not at all shy. In fact, she is a very important soul. Perhaps this is why she demands an intermediary."

"Important how?"

"In all ways," his neighbor professed. Then with a genuine envy, he added, "You should feel honored by her attentions."

A second array of security sensors was waiting. Pamir had never used them, and they were so deeply hidden no one could have noticed their presence. But they needed critical seconds to emerge from their slumber, and another half-second to calibrate and link together. And then, just as the first of three warning flashes rippled along the mirrored ceiling, what should have been obvious finally showed itself to him.

"You're not just my neighbor," he told the rubber face.

A second flash passed overhead. Then he saw the shielded cap-car hovering nearby, a platoon of soldiers nestled in its belly.

"Who else stands in that body?" Pamir demanded.

"I shall show you," the machine replied. Then two of the arms fell away, and the other two reached up, one violent jerk peeling back the rubber mask and the grit-sized brain, plus the elaborate shielding. A face lay behind the face. It was narrow, and in a fashion lovely, and it was austere, and it was allowing itself a knife-like smile as a new voice said to this mysterious man:

"Invite me inside your home."

"Why should I?" he countered, expecting some kind of murderous threat.

But instead of threatening, Miocene said simply, "Because I would like your help. In a small matter that must remain—I will warn you—our little secret."

3

Leading an army of captains was the Master Captain, and next in command was her loyal and infamous First Chair. Miocene was second most powerful creature in this spectacular realm. She was tough and brutal, conniving and cold. And of all the impossible crap to happen, this was the worst. Pamir watched his guest peel away the last of her elaborate disguise. The AI was propped outside, set into a diagnostic mode. The soldiers remained hidden by the new darkness and their old tricks. It was just the two of them inside the apartment, which made no sense. If Miocene knew who he was, she would have simply told her soldiers to catch him and abuse him and then drag him to the Ship's brig.

So she didn't know who he was.

Maybe.

The First Chair had a sharp face and black hair allowed to go a little white, and her body was tall and lanky and ageless and absolutely poised. She wore a simple uniform, mirrored in the fashion of all captains and decorated with a minimum of epaulets. For a long moment, she stared into the depths of Pamir's home. Watching for something? No, just having a conversation through a nexus. Then she closed off every link with the outer world, and turning toward her host, she used his present name.

Pamir nodded.

She used his last name.

Again, he nodded.

And then with a question mark riding the end of it, she offered a third name.

He said, "Maybe."

"It was or wasn't you?"

"Maybe," he said again.

She seemed amused. And then, there was nothing funny about any of this. The smile tightened, the mouth nearly vanishing. "I could look farther back in time," she allowed. "Perhaps I could dig up the moment when you left your original identity behind."

"Be my guest."

"I am your guest, so you are safe." She was taller than Pamir by a long measure—an artifact of his disguise. She moved closer to the wayward captain, saying, "Your origins don't interest me."

"Well then," he said.

And with a wink, he added, "So is it true, madam? Are you really in love with me?"

She laughed abruptly, harshly. Stepping away from him, Miocene studied the apartment again, this time focusing on its furnishings and little decorations. He had a modest home—a single room barely a hundred meters deep and twenty wide, the walls paneled with living wood and the ceiling showing the ruddy evening sky of a random world. With a calm voice, she announced, "I adore your talents, whoever you are."

"My talents?"

"With the aliens."

He said nothing.

"That mess with the harum-scarums…you found an elegant solution to a difficult problem. You couldn't know it at the time, but you helped the Ship and my Master, and by consequence, you've earned my thanks."

"What do you wish from me tonight, madam?"

"Tonight? Nothing. But tomorrow—early in the morning, I would hope—you will please apply your talents to a small matter. A relatively simple business, we can hope. Are you familiar with the J'Jal?"

Pamir held tight to his expression, his stance. Yet he couldn't help but feel a hard kick to his heart, a well-trained paranoia screaming, "Run! Now!"

"I have some experience with that species," he allowed. "Yes, madam."

"I am glad to hear it," said Miocene.

As a fugitive, Pamir lived among the J'Jal on two separate occasions. Obviously, the First Chair knew much more about his past. The pressing question was if she knew only about his life five faces ago, or if she had seen back sixty-three faces—perilously close to the day when he permanently removed his captain's uniform.

She knew his real identity, or she didn't.

Pamir strangled his paranoia and put on a wide grin, shoulders managing a shrug while a calm voice said, "And why should I do this errand for you?"

Miocene had a cold way of smirking. "My request isn't reason enough?"

He held his mouth closed.

"Your neighbors didn't ask for your aid. Yet you gave it willingly, if rather secretly." She acted angry though not entirely surprised. Behind those black eyes, calculations were being made, and with a pragmatic tone, she said, "I promise not to investigate your past."

"Because you already have," he said.

"To a point, and maybe a little farther than I first implied. But I won't use my considerable resources any more, if you help me."

"No," he said.

She seemed to flinch.

"I don't know you," he lied. "But madam, according to your reputation, you are a bitch's bitch."

In any given century, how many times did the First Chair hear an insult delivered to her face? Yet the tall woman absorbed the blow with poise, and then she mentioned a figure of money. "In an open account, and at your disposal," she said. "Use the funds as you wish, and when you've finished, use some or all of the remaining wealth to vanish again. And you should hope to do a better job of it this time."

She was offering a tidy fortune.

But why would the second most powerful entity on the Ship dangle such a prize before him? Pamir considered triggering hidden machines. He went as far as activating a tiny nexus, using it to bring a battery of weapons into play. With a thought, he could temporarily kill Miocene. Then he would slip out of the apartment through one of three hidden routes, and with luck, escape the pursuing soldiers. And within a day, or two at most, he would be living a new existence in some other avenue…or better, he would stand alone in one of the very solitary places where he had stockpiled supplies.

Once again, Miocene confessed, "This is a confidential matter."

In other words, this was not official business for the First Chair.

"More to the point," she said, "you won't help me as much as you will come to the aid of another soul."

Pamir deactivated the weapons, for the moment.

"Who deserves my help?"

"There is a young male you should meet," Miocene replied. "A J'Jal man, of course."

"I'm helping him."

"I would think not," she replied with a snort.

Then through a private nexus, she fed an address to Pamir. It was in the Fall Away district—a popular home for many species, including the J'Jal.

"The alien is waiting for you at his home," she continued.

Then with her cold smirk, she added, "At this moment, he is lying on the floor of his backmost room, and he happens to be very much dead."

4

Every portion of the Great Ship wore at least one bloodless designation left behind by the initial surveys, while the inhabited places enjoyed one or twenty more names, poetic or blunt, simple or fabulously contrived. In most cases, the typical passenger remembered none of those labels. Every avenue and cavern and little sea was remarkable in its own right, but under that crush of novelty, few were unique enough to be famous.

Fall Away was an exception.

For reasons known only to them, the Ship's builders had fashioned a tube from mirrored hyperfiber and cold basalt—the great shaft beginning not far beneath the heavy armor of the ship's bow and dropping for thousands of perfectly vertical kilometers. Myriad avenues funneled down to Fall Away. Ages ago, the Ship's human engineers etched roads and paths in the cylinder's surface, affording views to the curious. The crew built homes perched on the endless brink, and they were followed by a wide array of passengers. Millions now lived along its spectacular length. Millions more pretended to live there. There were more famous places onboard the Great Ship, and several were arguably more beautiful. But no other address afforded residents an easier snobbery. "My home is on Fall Away," they boasted. "Come enjoy my view, if you have a free month or an empty year."

* * *

Pamir ignored the view, and when he was sure nobody was watching, he slipped inside the J'Jal's apartment.

The Milky Way wasn't the largest galaxy, but it was most definitely fertile. Experts routinely guessed that three million worlds had evolved their own intelligent, technologically adept life. Within that great burst of natural invention, certain patterns were obvious. Half a dozen metabolic systems were favored. The mass and composition of a home world often shoved evolution down the same inevitable pathways. Humanoids were common; human beings happened to be a young example of an ancient pattern. Harum-scarums were another, as were the Glory and Aabacks, the Mnotis and Striders.

But even the most inexpert inorganic eye could tell those species apart. Each humanoid arose on different life-trees. Fur and plumage and armor and neatly folded fat enclosed the dissimilar bodies. Some were giants built for massive worlds, others frail little wisps that could barely survive the Ship's gravity. Even among naked mock-primates, there was an enormous range when it came to hands and faces. "I am nothing like a human," shouted the elegant bones, while the flesh itself was full of golden blood and DNA that proved its alienness.

And then, there were the J'Jal.

They had a human walk and a very human face, particularly in the typically green eyes. Diurnal creatures, they were hunter-gatherers from a world much like the Earth, having roamed an open savanna for millions of years, using stone implements carved with hands that at first glance, and sometimes with a second glance, looked entirely human.

But the similarities reached even deeper. The J'Jal heart beat inside a spongy double-lung, and every breath pressed against a cage of rubbery white ribs, while the ancestral blood was a ruddy mix of salts with iron wrapped inside a protein similar to hemoglobin. In fact, most of their proteins had a telltale resemblance to human types, as did great portions of their original DNA.

Convergence could happen when species evolved in similar environments, but mutation-by-mutation convergence was preposterous. A common origin, however unlikely, was ten million times more practical. The Earth and J'Jal must have been relatively close neighbors in the past. One world evolved simple, durable microbial life. Then a comet splashed into the ocean, and a piece of living crust rose into space. With a trillion sleeping passengers safely entombed, the wreckage drifted free of the solar system, and after a few light-years of cold oblivion, the crude ark slammed into a new world's atmosphere where at least one microbe survived, happily eating every native pre-life ensemble of hydrocarbons as it and its children conquered the new realm.

Such things often happened in the galaxy's early times. At least half a dozen other worlds shared biochemistries with the Earth. But only the J'Jal world took such a similar evolutionary pathway.

In effect, the J'Jal were distant cousins, and for many reasons, they were poor cousins, too.

* * *

Pamir stood over the body, examining its position and condition. Spider-legged machines did the same. Reaching inside the corpse with sound and soft bursts of x-rays, the machinery arrived at a rigorous conclusion they kept to themselves. With his own eyes and instincts, Pamir wished to do his best, thank you.

It could have been a human male lying dead on the floor.

The corpse was naked, on his back, legs together and his arms thrown up over his head with hands open and every finger extended. His flesh was a soft brown. His hair was short and bluish-black. The J'Jal didn't have natural beards. But the hair on the body could have been human—a thin carpet on the nippled chest that thickened around the groin.

In death, his genitals had shriveled back into the body.

No mark was visible, and Pamir guessed that if he rolled the body, there wouldn't be a wound on the backside either. But the man was utterly dead. Sure of it, he knelt down low, gazing at the decidedly human face, flinching just a little when the narrow mouth opened and a shallow breath was drawn into the dead man's lungs.

Quietly, Pamir laughed at himself.

The machines stood motionless, waiting for encouragement.

"The brain's gone," he offered, touching the forehead with his left hand, feeling the faint warmth of a hibernating metabolism. "A shaped plasma bolt, something like that. Ate through the skull and cooked his soul."

The machines rocked back and forth on long legs.

"It's slag, the brain is. And some of the body got torched too. Sure." He rose now, looking about the bedroom with a careful gaze.

A set of clothes stood nearby, waiting to dress their owner.

Pamir disabled the clothes and laid them on the ground beside the corpse. "He lost ten or twelve kilos of flesh and bone, and he's about ten centimeters shorter than he used to be."

Death was a difficult trick to achieve with immortals. And even in this circumstance, with the brain reduced to ruined bioceramics and mindless glass, the body had persisted with life. The surviving flesh had healed itself, within limits. Emergency genetics had been unleashed, reweaving the original face and scalp and a full torso that couldn't have seemed more lifelike. But when the genes had finished, no mind was found to interface with the rejuvenated body. So the J'Jal corpse fell into a stasis, and if no one had entered this apartment, it would remain where it was, sipping at the increasingly stale air, its lazy metabolism eating its own flesh until it was a skeleton and shriveled organs and a gaunt, deeply mummified face.

He had been a handsome man, Pamir could see.

Regardless of the species, it was an elegant, tidy face.

"What do you see?" he finally asked.

The machines spoke, in words and raw data. Pamir listened, and then he stopped listening. Again, he thought about Miocene, asking why the First Chair would give one little shit about this very obscure man.

"Who is he?" asked Pamir, not for the first time.

A nexus was triggered. The latest, most thorough biography was delivered. The J'Jal had been born onboard the Ship, his parents wealthy enough to afford the luxury of propagation. His family's money was made on a harum-scarum world, which explained his name: Sele'ium—a play on the harum-scarum convention of naming yourself after the elements. And just a youngster, barely five hundred years old, Sele'ium carried a life story that couldn't seem more ordinary.

Pamir stared at the corpse, unsure what good that did.

Then he forced himself to walk around the apartment. It wasn't much larger than his home, but with a pricey view making it twenty times more expensive. The furnishings could have belonged to either species. The color schemes were equally ordinary. There were a few hundred books on display—a distinctly J'Jal touch—and Pamir set loose a little flat-scribe to read each volume from cover to cover. Then he lead his helpers to every corner and closet, to new rooms and back to the old rooms again, and he inventoried every surface and each object, including a sampling of dust. But there was little dust, which meant that the dead man was exceptionally neat, or somebody had carefully swept away every trace of his own presence, including bits of dried skin and careless hairs.

"Now what?"

He was asking himself that question, but the machines replied, "We do not know what is next, sir."

Again, Pamir stood over the breathing corpse.

"I'm not seeing something," he complained.

A look came over him, and he quietly laughed at himself. Then he requested a small medical probe, and the probe was inserted, and through it he delivered a teasing charge.

The dead penis pulled itself out of the body.

"Huh," Pamir exclaimed.

"All right," he said, shaking his head. "We're going to search again, this place and the poor shit's life. Mote by mote and day by day, if we have to."

<h1 style="text-align:center">5</h1>

Built in the upper reaches of Fall Away, overlooking the permanent clouds of the Little-Lot, the facility was an expansive collection of natural caverns and minimal tunnels. Strictly speaking, the Faith of the Many Joinings wasn't a church or holy site, though it was wrapped securely around an ancient faith. Nor was it a commercial house, though money and barter items were often given to its resident staff. And it wasn't a brothel, as far as the Ship's codes were concerned. Nothing sexual happened within its walls, and no one involved in its mysteries gave his or her body for anything as crass as income. Most passengers didn't even realize that a place such as this existed. Among those who did, most regarded it as an elaborate and very strange meetinghouse—like-minded souls would pass through its massive wooden door to make friends, and when possible, fall in love. But for the purposes of taxes and law, the captains had decided on a much less romantic designation. Borrowing an ancient human word, the space was labeled to be an accredited library.

On the Great Ship, routine knowledge was preserved inside laser files and superconducting baths. Access might be restricted, but every word and captured image was within reach of buried nexuses. Libraries were an exception. What the books held was often unavailable anywhere else, making them precious, and that's why they offered a kind of privacy difficult to match, as well as an almost religious holiness to the followers of the Faith.

"May I help you, sir?"

Pamir was standing before a set of tall shelves. His arms were crossed and his face wore a tight, furious expression. "Who are you?" he asked, not bothering to look at the speaker.

"My name is Leon'rd."

"I've talked to others already," Pamir allowed.

"I know, sir."

"They came at me, one by one. But they weren't important enough." He turned, staring at the newcomer. "Are you important enough to help me, Leon'rd?"

"I hope so, sir. I do."

The J'Jal man was a little taller than Pamir, wearing a purplish-black robe and long blue hair secured in back as a simple horsetail. His eyes were indistinguishable from a human's green eyes. His skin was a pinkish brown. As the J'Jal preferred, his feet were bare. They could be human feet, plantigrade and narrow, with five toes and a similar architecture of bones, the long arches growing taller when nervous toes curled up. With a slight bow, the alien remarked, "I am the ranking librarian, sir. I have been at this post for ten millennia and eighty-eight years. Sir."

Pamir had adapted his face and clothing. What the J'Jal saw was a security officer dressed in casual garb. A badge clung to his sleeve, and every roster search identified him as a man with honors and a certain clout. But his disguise reached deeper. The crossed arms flexed for a moment, hinting at lingering tensions. His new face tightened until the eyes were squinting, affecting a cop's challenging stare. The pinched mouth looked ready to curse, but all he said was, "I'm looking for somebody."

To his credit, the librarian barely flinched.

"My wife," Pamir said. "I want to know where she is."

"No."

"Pardon me?"

"I understand what you desire, but I cannot comply."

At that moment, a giant figure stepped into the room. The harum-scarum noticed two males facing off, and with an embarrassment rare for the species, she carefully backed out of sight.

The librarian spoke to his colleagues, using a nexus.

Every door to this chamber was quietly closed and securely locked.

"Listen," Pamir said.

Then he said nothing else.

After a few moments, the J'Jal said, "Our charter is clear. The law is defined. We offer our patrons privacy and opportunity, in that order. Without official clearance, sir, you may not enter this facility to obtain facts or insights of any type."

"I'm looking for my wife," he repeated.

"And I can appreciate your—"

"Quiet," Pamir said, arms unfolding, the right hand holding a small, illegal plasma torch. With a flourish, he aimed at his helpless target, and he said one last time, "I am looking for my wife."

"Don't," the librarian begged.

The weapon was pointed at bound volumes. The smallest burst would vaporize untold pages.

"No," Leon'rd moaned, desperately trying to alert the room's weapon suppression systems. But none were responding.

Again, he said, "No."

"I love her," Pamir said.

"I understand."

"Do you understand love?"

Leon'rd seemed offended. "Of course I understand—"

"Or does it have to be something ugly and sick before you can appreciate, even a little bit, what it means to be in love."

The J'Jal refused to speak.

"She's vanished," Pamir said.

"And you think she has been here?"

"At least once, yes."

The librarian was swiftly searching for a useful strategy. A general alarm was sounding, but the doors he had locked for good reasons suddenly refused to unlock. His staff and every other helping hand might as well have been on the far side of the Ship. And if the gun discharged, it would take critical seconds to fill the room with enough nitrogen to stop the fire and enough narcotics to shove a furious human to the floor.

Leon'rd had no choice. "Perhaps I can help you, yes."

Pamir showed a thin, unpleasant grin. "That's the attitude."

"If you told me your wife's name—"

"She wouldn't use it," he warned.

"Or show me a holo of her, perhaps."

The angry husband shook his head. "She's changed her appearance. At least once, maybe more times."

"Of course."

"And her gender, maybe."

The librarian absorbed that complication. He had no intention of giving this stranger what he wanted, but if they could just draw this ugly business out for long enough, allowing a platoon of security troops to swoop in and take back their colleague…

"Here," said Pamir, feeding him a minimal file.

"What is this?"

"Her boyfriend, from what I understand."

Leon'rd stared at the image and the attached biography. The soft green eyes had barely read the name when they grew huge—a meaningful J'Jal expression—and with a sigh that sounded human, he admitted, "I know this man."

"Did you?"

Slowly, the implication of those words was absorbed.

"What do you mean? Is something wrong?"

"Yeah, like I said, my wife is missing. And this murdered piece of shit is the only one who can help me find her. Besides you, that is."

Leon'rd asked for proof of the man's death.

"Proof?" Pamir laughed. "Maybe I should call my boss and tell her that I found a deceased J'Jal, and you and I can ask the law do its important and loud and very public work."

A moment later, with a silent command, the librarian put an end to the general alert. There was no problem here, he lied; and with the slightest bow, he asked, "May I trust you to keep this matter confidential, sir?"

"Do I look trustworthy?"

The J'Jal bristled but said nothing. Then he stared at shelves at the far end of the room, walking a straight line that took him to a slender volume that he withdrew and opened, elegant fingers beginning to flip through the thin plastic pages.

With a bully's abruptness, Pamir grabbed the prize. The cover was a soft wood stained blue to identify its subject as being a relative novice. The pages were plastic, thin but dense, with a running account of the dead man's progress. Over the course of the last century, librarians had met with Sele'ium on numerous occasions, and they had recorded his uneven progress with this very difficult faith. Audio transcripts drawn from a private journal let him explain his mind to himself and every interested party. "My species is corrupt and tiny," Sele'ium had confessed with a remarkably human voice. "Every species is tiny and foul, and only together, joined in perfect union, can we create a worthy society—a universe genuinely united."

Several pages held holos—stark, honest images of religious devotion that most of galaxy would look upon as abominations. Pamir barely lingered on any picture. He had a clear guess about what he was looking for, and it helped that only one of the J'Jal's wives was human.

The final page was the key. Pamir stared at the last image, and with a low snort and a disgusted shake of the head, he announced, "This must be her."

"But it isn't," said the librarian.

"No, it's got to be," he persisted. "A man should be able to recognize his own wife. Shouldn't he?"

Leon'rd showed the barest of grins. "But I know this woman rather well, and she is not—"

"Where's her book?" Pamir snapped.

"No," the librarian said. "Believe me, this is not somebody you know."

"Prove it."

Silence.

"What's her name?"

Leon'rd straightened, working hard to appear brave.

Then Pamir placed the plasma torch against a random shelf, allowing the tip of the barrel to heat up to where smoke rose as the red wood binding of a true believer began to smolder.

The woman's journal was stored in a different room, far deeper inside the library. Leon'rd called for it to be brought to them, and then he stood close while Pamir went through the pages, committing most of it to a memory nexus. At one point, he said, "If you'd let me just borrow these things."

The J'Jal face flushed, and a tight hateful voice replied, "If you tried to take them, you would have to kill me."

Pamir showed him a wink.

"A word for the not-so-wise?" he said. "If I were you, I wouldn't give my enemies easy ideas."

6

How could one species prosper, growing in reach and wealth as well as its numbers, while a second species, blessed with the same strengths, exists for a hundred times longer and still doesn't matter to the galaxy?

Scholars and bigots had deliberated that question for ages.

The J'Jal evolved on a lush warm world, blue seas wrapped around green continents, the ground fat with metal ores and hydrocarbons, and a massive moon riding across the sky, helping keep the axis tilted just enough to invite mild seasons. Perhaps that wealth had been a bad thing. Born on a somewhat poorer world, humans had evolved to live in tiny, adaptable bands of twenty or so—everyone related to everyone, by blood or by marriage. But the early J'Jals moved in troops of a hundred or more, which meant a society wrapped around a more tolerant politics. Harmony was a given. Conflicts were resolved quietly, since nothing was more precious to the troop than its own venerable peace. And with natural life spans reaching three centuries, change was a slow, fitful business brought on by consensus, or when absolutely necessary, by surrendering your will to the desires of the elders.

But quirks of nature are only one explanation for the future. Many great species had developed patiently. Some of the most famous, like the Ritkers and harum-scarums, were still tradition-bound creatures. Even humans had that sorry capacity: The wisdom of dead Greeks and lost Hebrews was followed long after their words had value. But the J'Jal were far more passionate than humans when it came to ancestors and their left-behind thoughts. The past was a treasure to them, and their early civilizations were hide-bound and enduring machines that would remember every wrong turn and every quiet success.

Humans stepped into space after a couple hundred thousand years of flint and iron, but it took the J'Jal millions of years to contrive reasons for that kind of adventure.

And that was a murderous bit of bad fortune.

The J'Jal solar system had metal-rich worlds and watery moons, and its neighboring suns were mature G-class stars where intelligence arose many times. While the J'Jal sat at home, happily memorizing the speeches of old queens, three different alien species colonized their outer worlds—ignoring galactic law and ancient conventions in the process.

Unknown to the J'Jal, great wars were being waged in their sky.

The eventual winner was a tiny creature accustomed to light gravity and the exotic technologies. The K'Mal were cybernetic and quick-lived, subject to fads and whims and sudden convulsive changes of government. By the time the J'Jal launched their first rocket, the K'Mal outnumbered them sixty-to-one inside their own solar system. For millions of years, that moment in history still brought shame. The J'Jal rocket rose into a low orbit, triggering a K'Mal fleet to lift from bases on the moon's hidden face. The rocket was destroyed, and suddenly the J'Jal went from being the masters of Paradise to an obscure creature locked on the surface of one little world.

Wars were fought, and won.

Peace treaties held, and collapsed, and the new wars ended badly.

True slavery didn't exist for the losers, even in the worst stretches of the long Blackness. And the K'Mal weren't wicked tyrants or unthinking administrators. But gradual decay stole away the wealth of the J'Jal world. Birthrates plunged. Citizens emigrated, forced to work in bad circumstances for a variety of alien species. Those left at home lived on an increasingly poisonous landscape, operating the deep mantle mines and the enormous railguns that spat the bones of their world into someone else's space.

While humans were happily hamstringing mammoths on the plains of Asia, the J'Jal were a beaten species scattered thinly across a hundred worlds. Other species would have lost their culture, and where they survived, others might have split into dozens of distinct, utterly obscure species. But the J'Jal proved capable in one extraordinary endeavor: Against every abuse, they managed to hold tight to their shared past, beautiful and otherwise; and in small ways, and then in slow large ways, they adapted to their far flung existence.

7

"You'll be helping another soul."

Miocene had promised that much and said little else. She knew the dead J'Jal would point him to the library, and she had to know that he was bright enough to realize it was the human woman who mattered. Why the First Chair cared about the life of an apparently unremarkable passenger, Pamir couldn't guess. Or rather, he could guess too easily, drawing up long lists of motivations, each entry reasonable, and most if not all of them ridiculously wrong.

The human was named Sorrel, and it had been Sorrel since she was born two centuries ago. Unless she was older than that, and her biography was a masterful collection of inspired lies.

Like most of the library's patrons, she made her home on Fall Away. Yet even among that wealthy company, she was blessed. Not one but two trust funds kept her economy well fed. Her rich father had immigrated to a colony world before she was born, leaving his local assets in her name. While the mother—a decorated member of the diplomatic corps—had died on the ill-fated Hakkaleen mission. In essence, Sorrel was an orphan. But by most signs, she didn't suffer too badly, appearing happy and unremarkable through her early years of wealth.

What was the old harum-scarum saying?

"Nothing is as massive as the universe, but nothing is half as large as a sentient, imaginative mind."

Then the young woman began to change.

Like many young adults, Sorrel took an early vow of celibacy. With a million years of life stretching before her, why hurry into sex and love, disappointment and heartbreak? She had human friends, but because of her mother's diplomatic roots, she knew quite a few aliens too. Her closest companions were a Janusian couple—double organisms where the male was a parasite rooted in his spouse's back. Then her circle of alien friends widened, which again seemed perfectly normal. Pamir searched the archives of forgotten security eyes and amateur documentaries, finding glimpses of luncheons and shopping adventures in the company of oxygen breathers—the traditional human allies. Then came the luxury cruise across a string of little oceans spread through the Ship's interior—a relatively brief voyage accomplished in the midst of the circumnavigation of the Milky Way—and near the end of that tame adventure, while drifting on a dim cold smooth-as-skin methane sea, she took her first lover.

He was a J'Jal, as it happened.

Pamir saw enough on the security eyes to fill in the blanks.

Cre'llan was a spectacularly wealthy individual, and ancient, and in a Faith that cherished its privacy, he flaunted his membership and his beliefs. Elaborate surgeries had reshaped his penis to its proper form. Everyone involved in the Many Joinings endured similar cosmetic work; a uniform code applied to both genders, and where no gender existed, one was invented for them. During his long life, Cre'llan had married hundreds if not thousands of aliens, and on that chill night he managed to seduce a young virginal human.

After the cruise, Sorrel tried to return to her old life. But three days later she visited the library, and within the week, she underwent her own physical reconfigurations.

Pamir had caught glimpses of the surgery in her journal—autodocs and J'Jal overseers hovering around a lanky pale body. And when he closed his eyes now, concentrating on the buried data reserve, he could slowly and carefully flip his way through the other pages of that elaborate yet still incomplete record.

After a year as a novice, Sorrel purchased a bare rectangle of stone and hyperfiber some fifty kilometers directly beneath the library. The apartment she built was deep and elaborate, full of luxurious rooms as well as expansive chambers that could be configured to meet the needs of almost any biology. But while every environmental system was the best available, sometimes those fancy machines didn't interact well with one another, and with the right touch, they were very easy to sabotage.

* * *

"Is it a serious problem, sir?"

"Not for me," Pamir allowed. "Not for you, I'd guess. But if you depend on peroxides, like the Ooloops do, then the air is going to taste sour. And after a few breaths, you'll probably lose consciousness."

"I understand," the apartment offered.

Pamir was standing in the service hallway, wearing his normal rough face as well as the durable jersey and stiff back of a life-long technician. "I'll need to wander, if I'm going to find your trouble. Which is probably an eager filter, or a failed link of code, or a leak, or who knows what."

"Do whatever is necessary," the soft male voice replied.

"And thanks for this opportunity," Pamir added. "I appreciate new business."

"Of course, sir. Thank you for your diligence."

The apartment's usual repair firm was temporarily closed due to a bureaucratic war with the Office of Environments. A search of available candidates had steered the AI towards the best candidate. Pamir was releasing a swarm of busy drones that vanished inside the walls, and he continued walking down the hallway, pausing at a tiny locked door. "What's past here?"

"A living chamber."

"For a human?"

"Yes, sir."

Pamir stepped back. "I don't need to bother anyone."

"No one will be." The lock and seal broke. "My lady demands that her home is ready for any and all visitors. Your work is a priority."

Pamir nodded, stepping through the narrow slot.

His first thought was that captains didn't live half as well as this. The room was enormous yet somehow intimate, carpeted with living furs, art treasures standing about waiting to be admired, chairs available for any kind of body, and as added feature, at least fifty elaborate games laid out on long boards, the pieces playing against each other until there was a winner, after which they would play again. Even the air tasted of wealth, scrubbed and filtered, perfumed and pheromoned. In that perfect atmosphere, the only sound was the quiet precise and distant singing of a certain alien flower.

Llano-vibra.

Pamir looked at monitors and spoke through nexuses, and he did absolutely nothing of substance. What he wanted to accomplish was already done. The apartment was now infested with hidden ears and eyes, and everything else was show that would lend him more credibility.

A tall diamond wall stood on the far side of the enormous bedroom, and beyond, five hectares of patio hung over the open air. A grove of highly bred llano-vibra was rooted in a patio pot, its music passing through a single open door. The young woman was sitting nearby, doing nothing. Pamir looked at Sorrel for a moment, and then she lifted her head to glance in his general direction. He tried to decide what he was seeing. She was clothed but barefoot. She was strikingly lovely, but in an odd fashion that he couldn't quite name. Her pale skin had a genuine glow, a capacity to swallow up the ambient light and cast it back into the world in a softer form. Her hair was silver-white and thick, with the tips suddenly turning to black. She had a smooth girlish face and a tiny nose and blue-white eyes pulled close together, and her mouth was broad and elegant and exceptionally sad.

It was the sadness that made her striking, Pamir decided.

Then he found himself near the door, staring at her, realizing that nothing was simple about her sadness or his reactions.

Sorrel glanced at him a second time.

A moment later, the apartment inquired, "Is the lady a point of technical interest, sir?"

"Sure." Pamir laughed and stepped back from the diamond wall.

"Have you found the problem? She wishes to know."

"Two problems, and yes. They're being fixed now."

"Very well. Thank you."

Pamir meant to mention his fee. Tradesmen always talked money. But there came a sound—the soft musical whine of a rope deploying—that quickly fell away into silence.

The apartment stopped speaking to him.

Pamir asked, "What?" while turning to look outside again. The woman wasn't alone anymore. A second figure had appeared, dressed like a rock climber and running across the patio towards Sorrel. He was a human or J'Jal, and apparently male. From where Pamir stood, he couldn't tell much more. But he saw the urgency in the intruder's step and a right hand that was holding what could be a weapon, and an instant later, Pamir was running too, leaping through the open door as the stranger closed on the woman.

Sorrel stared at the newcomer.

"I don't recognize his face," the apartment warned her, shouting now. "My lady—!"

The inertia vanished from her body. Sorrel leapt up and took two steps backwards before deciding to stand and fight. It was her best hope, Pamir agreed. She lifted her arms and lowered them again. She was poised if a little blank in the face, as if she was surrendering her survival to a set of deeply buried instincts.

The stranger reached for her neck with his left hand.

With a swift clean motion, she grabbed the open hand and twisted the wrist back. But the running body picked her off her feet, and both of them fell to the polished opal floor of the patio.

The man's right hand held a knife.

With a single plunge, the stranger pushed the blade into her chest, aiming for the heart. He was working with precision, perhaps by feel. He was trying to accomplish something very specific, and when she struggled, he would strike her face with the back of his free hand.

The blade dove deeper.

A small, satisfied moan leaked out of him, as if success was near, and then Pamir drove his boot into the smiling mouth.

The stranger was human, and furious.

He climbed to his feet, fending off the next three blows, and then he pulled out a small railgun that he halfway aimed, letting loose a dozen flecks of supersonic iron.

Pamir dropped, hit in the shoulder and arm.

The injured woman lay between them, bleeding and pained. The hilt of the knife stood up out of her chest, a portion of the hyperfiber blade reflecting the brilliant red of the blood.

With his good arm, Pamir grabbed the hilt and tugged.

There was a soft clatter as a Darmion crystal spilled out of her body along with the blade. This was what the thief wanted. Seeing the glittering shape, the man couldn't resist the urge to grab at the prize. A small fortune was within reach, but suddenly his own knife was driven through his meaty forearm, and he screamed in pain and rage.

Pamir cut him twice again.

The little railgun rose up and fired once, twice, and then twice more.

Pamir's body was dying, but he still had the focus and strength to lift the man—a bullish fellow with short limbs and seemingly an infinite supply of blood. Pamir kept slashing and pushing, and the railgun was dropped and left behind, and now the man struck him with a fist and his elbows and then tried to use his knee. Pamir grabbed the knee as it rose, borrowing its momentum as well as the last of his own strength to shove the thief against a railing of simple oak, and with a last grunt, flinging him over the edge.

Only Pamir was standing there now.

Really, it was a beautiful view. With his chest ripped open and a thousand emergency genes telling his body to rest, he gazed out into the open expanse of Fall Away. Thirty kilometers across and lit by a multitude of solar-bright lights, this was a glory of engineering, and perhaps a masterpiece of art. The countless avenues that fed into Fall Away often brought water and other liquids, and the captains' engineers had devised a system of airborne rivers—diamond tubes that carried the fluids down in a tangle of spirals and rings, little lakes gathering in pools held aloft by invisible means. And there were flyers moving in the air—organic and not, alive and not—and there was the deep musical buzz of a million joyous voices, and there were forests of epiphytes clinging to the wall, and there was a wet wind that hadn't ceased in eighty thousand years, and Pamir forgot why he was standing here. What was this place? Turning around, he discovered a beautiful woman with a gruesome wound in her chest telling him to sit, please. Sit. Sir, she said, please, please, you need to rest.

8

The Faith of the Many Joinings.

Where it arose first was a subject of some contention. Several widely scattered solar systems were viable candidates, but no expert held the definitive evidence. Nor could one prophet or pervert take credit for this quasi-religious belief. But what some J'Jal believed was that every sentient soul had the same value. Bodies were facades, and metabolisms were mere details, and social systems varied in the same way that individual lives varied, according to choice and whim and a deniable sense of right. What mattered were the souls within all of these odd packages. What a wise soul wished to do was to befriend entities from different histories, and when possible, fall in love with them, linking their spirits together through the ancient pleasures of the flesh.

There was no single prophet and the Faith had no birthplace, which were problems for the true believers. How could such an intricate, odd faith arise simultaneously in such widely scattered places? But what was a flaw might be a blessing, too. Plainly, divine gears were turning the universe, and this unity was just further evidence of how right and perfect their beliefs had to be. Unless of course the Faith was the natural outgrowth of the J'Jal's own nature: A social species is thrown across the sky, and every home belongs to more powerful species, and the entire game of becoming lovers to the greater ones is as inevitable and unremarkable as standing on their own two bare feet.

Pamir held to that ordinary opinion.

Glancing at his own bare feet, he sighed and then examined his arm and shoulder and chest. The wounds had healed to where nothing was visible. Unscarred flesh had spread over the holes, while the organs inside him were quickly pulling themselves back into perfect condition. He was fit enough to sit up, but he didn't. Instead, he lay on the soft chaise set on the open-air patio, listening to the llano-vibra. At the moment he was alone, the diamond wall to the bedroom turned black. He spent his time thinking about what was obvious, and then he played with the subtle possibilities that sprang up from what was possible.

The thief—a registered felon with a long history of this exact work—had fallen for several kilometers before a routine security patrol noticed him, plucking him out of the sky before he could spoil anybody else's day.

The unlucky man was under arrest and would probably serve a century or two for his latest crime.

"This stinks," Pamir muttered.

"Sir?" said the apartment. "Is there a problem? Might I help?"

Pamir considered, and said, "No."

He sat up and said, "Clothes," and his technician's uniform pulled itself around him. Its fabric had healed, if not quite so thoroughly as his body. He examined what could be a fleck of dried blood, and after a moment, he said, "Boots."

"Under your seat, sir."

Pamir was giving his feet to his boots when she walked out through the bedroom door.

"I have to thank you." Sorrel was tall and elegant in a shopworn way, wearing a long gray robe and no shoes. In the face, she looked pretty but sorrowful, and up close, that sadness was a deep thing reaching well past today. "For everything you did for me, thank you."

A marathon of tears had left her eyes red and puffy.

He stared, and she stared back. For a moment, it was as if she saw nothing. Then Sorrel seemed to grow aware of his interest, and with a shiver, she told him, "Stay as long as you wish. My home will feed you, and if you want, you can take anything that interests you. As a memento..."

"Where's the crystal?" he interrupted.

She touched herself between the breasts. The Darmion was back home, resting beside her enduring heart. According to half a dozen species, the crystal gave its possessor a keen love of life and endless joy—a bit of mystic noise refuted by the depressed woman who was wearing it.

"I don't want your little rock," he muttered.

She didn't seem relieved or amused. "Thank you," she said one last time, planning to end this here.

"You need a better security net," Pamir remarked.

"Perhaps so," she said, without interest.

"What's your name?"

She said, "Sorrel," and then the rest of it. Human names were long and complex to the point of unwielding. But she said it all, and then she looked at him in a new fashion. "What do I call you?"

He used his most recent identity.

"Are you any good with security systems?" Sorrel inquired.

"Better than most."

She nodded.

"You want me to upgrade yours?"

That amused her somehow. A little smile broke across the milky face, and for a moment, the bright pink tip of her tongue pointed at him. Then she shook her head, saying, "No, not for me," as if he should have realized as much. "I have a good friend…a dear old friend…who has some rather heavy fears…"

"Can he pay?"

"I will pay. Tell him it's my gift."

"So who's this worried fellow?"

In an alien language, she said, "Gallium."

Genuinely surprised, Pamir asked, "What the hell is a harum-scarum doing, admitting he's scared?"

Sorrel nodded appreciatively.

"He admits nothing," she said. Then she smiled again…a warmer expression, this time. She looked fetching and sweet, even wonderful, and for Pamir, that expression seemed to last long after he walked out of the apartment and on to his next job.

9

The harum-scarum was nearly three meters tall, massive and thickly armored, loud and yet oddly serene at the same time, passionate about his endless bravery and completely transparent when he told lies. His home was close to Fall Away, tucked high inside one of the minor avenues. He was standing behind his final door—a slab of hyperfiber-braced diamond—and with a distinctly human gesture, he waved off the uninvited visitor. "I do not need any favors," he claimed, speaking through his breathing mouth. "I am as secure as anyone and twelve times more competent than you when it comes to my defense." Then with a blatant rudeness, he allowed his eating mouth to deliver a long wet belch.

"Funny," said Pamir. "A woman wishes to buy my services, and you are Gallium, her dear old friend. Is that correct?"

"What is the woman's name?"

"Why? Didn't you hear me the first time?"

"Sorrel, you claimed." He pretended to concentrate, and with a little too much certainty said, "I do not know this ape-woman."

"Is that so? She knows you."

"She is mistaken."

"So then how did you know she was human? I hadn't quite mentioned that detail yet."

The question won a blustery look from the big black eyes. "What are you implying to me, little ape-man?"

Pamir laughed at him. "Why? Can't you figure it out for yourself?"

"Are you insulting me?"

"Sure."

That earned deep silence.

With a fist only a little larger than one of the alien's knuckles, Pamir wrapped on the diamond door. "I'm insulting you and your ancestors. There. By the ship's codes and your own painful customs, you are now free to step out here, in the open, and beat me until I am dead for a full week."

The giant shook with fury, and nothing happened. One mouth expanded, gulping down deep long breaths, while the other mouth puckered into a tiny dimple—a harum-scarum on the brink of a pure vengeful rage. But Gallium forced himself to do nothing, and when the anger finally began to diminish, he gave an inaudible signal, causing the outer two doors to drop and seal tight.

475

Pamir looked left and then right. The narrow avenue was well-lit and empty, and by every appearance, it was safe.

Yet the creature had been terrified.

One more time, he paged his way through Sorrel's journal. Among those husbands were two harum-scarums. No useful name had been mentioned in the journal, but it was obvious who Gallium was. Lying about his fear was in character for the species. But how could a confirmed practitioner of this singular faith deny that he had even met the woman?

Pamir needed to find other husbands.

A hundred different routes lay before him. But as harum-scarums liked to say, "The shortest line stretches between points that touch."

* * *

Gallium's security system was ordinary, and it was porous, and with thousands of years of experience in these matters, it took Pamir less than a day to subvert codes and walk through the front doors.

"Who is with me?" a voice cried out from the farthest room.

In J'Jal, curiously.

Then in the human tongue, he asked, "Who's there?"

Pamir said nothing.

And finally, as an afterthought, the alien shouted, "You are in my realm, and unwelcome." In his own tongue, he promised, "I will forgive you, if you run away at this moment."

"Sorrel won't let me run," Pamir replied.

The last room was a minor fortress buttressed with slabs of high-grade hyperfiber and bristling with weapons, legal and otherwise. A pair of rail-guns were tracking Pamir's head, ready to batter his mind if not quite kill it. Tightness built in his throat, but he managed to keep the fear out of his voice. "Is this where you live now, in a little room at the bottom of an ugly home?"

"You like to insult," the harum-scarum observed.

"It passes my time," he said.

From behind the hyperfiber, Gallium said, "I see an illegal weapon."

"Good. Since I'm carrying one."

"If you try to harm me, I will kill you. And I will destroy your mind, and you will be no more."

"Understood," Pamir said.

Then the human sat—a gesture of submission on almost every world. He sat on the quasi-crystal tiling on the floor of the bright hallway, glancing at the portraits on the nearby walls. Harum-scarums from past ages stood in defiant poses. Ancestors, presumably. Honorable men and woman who could look at their cowering descendant with nothing but fierce contempt.

After a few moments, Pamir said, "I'm pulling my weapon into plain view."

"Throw it beside my door."

The plasma gun earned a respectful silence. It slid across the floor and clattered to a stop, and then a mechanical arm unfolded, slapping a hyperfiber bowl over it and then covering the bowl with an explosive charge set to obliterate the first hand that tried to free the gun within.

The hyperfiber door lifted.

Gallium halfway filled the room beyond. He was standing in the middle of a closet jammed with supplies, the armored plates of his body flexing, exposing their sharp edges.

"You must need this work," he observed.

"Except I'm not doing my job," Pamir replied. "Frankly, I've sort of lost interest in the project."

Confused, the harum-scarum stood taller. "Then why have you gone to such enormous trouble?"

"What you need is a small, well-charged plasma gun. That makes a superior weapon."

"They are illegal and hard to come by," argued Gallium.

"Your rail-guns are criminal, too." Just like with the front doors, there was a final door made of diamond reinforced with a visible meshwork of hyperfiber. "But I bet you appreciate what shaped plasma can do to a living mind."

Silence.

"Funny," Pamir continued. "Not that long ago, I found a corpse that ran into that exact kind of tool."

The alien's back couldn't straighten anymore, and the armor plates were flexing to their limits. With a quiet voice—an almost begging voice—Gallium asked the human, "Who was the corpse?"

"Sele'ium."

Again, silence.

"Who else has died that way?" Pamir asked. It was a guess, but not much of one. And when no answer was offered, he said, "You have never been this frightened. In your long, ample life, you have never imagined that fear could eat at you this way. Am I right?"

Now the back began to collapse.

A miserable little voice said, "It just worsens."

"Why?"

The harum-scarum dipped his head.

"Why does the fear get worse and worse?"

"Seven of us now."

"Seven?"

"Lost." A human despair rode with that single word. "Eight, if you are telling the truth about the J'Jal."

"What eight?"

Gallium refused to say.

"I know who you are," Pamir said. "Eight of Sorrel's husbands, and you. Is that right?"

"Her past husbands," the alien corrected.

"What about current lovers–?"

"There are none."

"No?"

"She is celibate," the giant said with deep longing. Then he dropped his gaze, adding, "When we started to die, she gave us up, physically as well as legally."

Gallium missed his human wife. It showed in his stance and voice and how the great hand trembled, reaching up to touch the cool pane of diamond while he added, "She is trying to save us. But she doesn't know how."

He paused, and a ball of coherent plasma struck the pane. No larger than a human heart, the ball dissolved the diamond and the hand, and the grieving face, and everything that lay beyond those dark lonely eyes.

<h1 style="text-align:center">10</h1>

Pamir saw nothing but the flash, and then came a concussive blast that threw him off his feet. For an instant, he lay motionless. A cloud of atomized carbon and flesh filled the cramped hallway. He listened and heard nothing. He was completely deaf. Keeping low, he rolled until a wall blocked his way. Then he started to breathe, scalding his lungs, and he held his breath, remaining absolutely still, waiting for a second blast to shove past.

Nothing happened.

With his mouth to the floor, Pamir managed a hot but breathable sip of air. The cloud was thinning. His hearing was returning, accompanied by a tireless high-pitched hum. A figure swam into view, tall and menacing—a harum-scarum, presumably one of the Gallium's honored ancestors. The hallway was littered with portraits of the dead. Pamir saw a second figure, a third. He was trying to recall how many images there had been…because he could see a fourth outline now, and that seemed like one too many…

The plasma gun fired again. But it hadn't had time enough to build a killing charge, and the fantastic energies were wasted in a light show and a gust of blistering wind.

Again the air filled with dirt and gore.

On elbows and feet, Pamir crawled away.

Gallium was a nearly headless corpse, enormous even when mangled and stretched out on his back. The little room was made tinier with him on the floor. With their owner dead, the rail guns had dropped into their diagnostic mode, and waking them would take minutes, or days. The diamond door was shredded and useless. When the cloud fell away again, in another few moments, Pamir would be exposed and probably killed.

Like Gallium, he first used the J'Jal language.

"Hello," he called out.

The outer door was open and still intact, but the simple trigger would react only to pressure from a familiar hand. Staring out into the hallway, he once again shouted, "Hello."

In the distance, a shape began to resolve itself.

"I am dead," he continued. "You have me trapped here, my friend."

Nothing.

"Do what you wish, but before you cook me, I'd love to know what this is about."

The shape drifted one way, then back again.

Pamir lifted one of the dead arms, trying to lay the broad palm against the wall, close to the door's trigger. But that was the easy part of this, of course.

"You're a clever soul," he said. "Allow the human to open the way for you. I outsmart the harum-scarum's defenses, and then you claim both of us."

How much time before another recharge?

A few seconds, he guessed.

Suddenly the corpse flinched and the arm dropped with a massive thunk.

"Shit," Pamir muttered.

On a low shelf was an ornate little dinner plate, pressed from nickel and covered with cooked blood. He took hold of it, made a few practice flings with his wrist, and once again called out, "I wish you would tell me what this is about, because I haven't got a guess."

Nothing.

In human, Pamir asked, "Who the hell are you?"

The cloud was clearing, revealing the outlines of a biped standing in the hallway, maybe ten meters from him.

Kneeling, Pamir again grabbed the dead arm. Emergency genes and muscle memory began to fight against him, the strength of a giant forcing him to grunt as he pushed the hand beside the trigger. Then he threw all of his weight on the hand, forcing it to stay in place. He panted. He grabbed the heavy plate with his left hand. With a gasping voice, he said, "One last chance to explain."

The biped was lifting both arms, aiming.

"Bye-bye, then."

Pamir let the dead hand drop as he flipped the plate, aiming at a target three meters away. A slab of hyperfiber slid from the ceiling, and the final door was shut. It could withstand two or three blasts from a determined plasma gun, but eventually it would be gnawed away. Which was why he threw the plate onto the floor where it skipped and rolled, clipping the edge of the shaped charge of explosives that capped his own gun.

A sudden sharp thunder struck.

The door was jammed shut by the blast, and Pamir spent the next twenty minutes using a dead hand and every override to lift the door far enough to crawl underneath. But a perfectly symmetrical blast had left his own weapon where it lay, untouched beneath a bowl of mirror-bright hyperfiber.

His enemy would have been blown back up the hallway.

Killed briefly, or at least scared away.

Pamir lingered for a few minutes, searching the dead man's home for clues that refused to be found, and then he slipped back out into the public avenue—still vacant and safe to the eye, but possessing a palpable menace that he could feel for himself.

11

A ninety-second tube ride placed him beside Sorrel's front door. The apartment addressed him by the only name it knew, and with alarm creeping into the officious voice, it asked, "Do you know how badly you are injured, sir?"

"I've got a fair guess," said Pamir, an assortment of shrapnel still buried inside his leg and belly. "Where's the lady?"

"On the patio, where you left her, sir."

Everybody was terrified, except for Sorrel. But why would she worry? She had only been knifed by a quick-and-dirty thief, which on the scale of recent crimes was practically nothing.

"I'll meet her in her bedroom."

"Sir?"

"I'm not talking in the open anymore. Tell her."

"What about her friend?"

"Another husband is dead."

Silence.

"Will you tell her?" Pamir asked.

"She is already on her way, as you have requested." Then after a pause, the apartment suggested, "About Gallium, please…I think you should deliver that sorry news…"

★ ★ ★

He told it.

She was dressed in slacks and a silk blouse made by the communal spiders of the Kolochon district, and her bare feet wore black rings on every toe, and while she sat on one of the dozens of self-shaping chairs, listening to his recounting of the last brutal hour, her expression managed to grow even more sad as well as increasingly detached. Sorrel made no sound, but there was always the sense that she was about to speak. The sorry and pained and very pretty face would betray a new thought, or the pale eyes would recognize something meaningful. But the mouth never quite made noise. When she finally uttered a few words, Pamir nearly forgot to listen.

"Who are you?"

Did he hear the question correctly?

Again, she asked, "Who are you?" Then she leaned forward, the blouse dipping in front. "You aren't like any environmental technician I've known, and I don't think you're a security specialist either."

"No?"

"You wouldn't have survived the fight, if you were just a fix-it man." She tried to laugh, a little dimple showing high on the left cheek. "And even if you had survived, you'd still be running now."

"I just want you to point me in the safest direction," he said.

She didn't respond, watching him for what seemed like an age. Then sitting back in the deep wide chair, she asked, "Who pays you?"

"You do."

"That's not what I mean."

"But I'm not pushing too hard for my wages," he said.

"You won't tell me who?"

"Confess a few things to me first," he said.

She had long hands, graceful and quick. The hands danced in her lap for a little while, and when they finally settled, she asked, "What can I tell you?"

"Everything you know about your dead husbands, and about those who just happen to be alive still." Pamir leaned forward. "In particular, I want to hear about your first husband. And if you can, explain why the Faith of the Many Joinings seemed like such a reasonable idea."

12

She had seen him earlier on the voyage and spoken with him on occasion—a tall and slender and distinguished J'Jal man with a fondness for human clothes, particularly red woolen suits and elaborately knotted white silk ties. Cre'llan seemed handsome, although not exceptionally so. He was obviously bright and engaging. Once, when their boat was exploring the luddite islands in the middle of the Gone-A-Long Sea, he asked if he might sit on the long chaise lounge beside hers. For the next little while—an hour, or perhaps the entire day—they chatted amiably about the most ordinary of things. There was gossip to share, mostly about their fellow passengers and the boat's tiny crew. They made several attempts to list the oceans that they had crossed to date, ranking them according to beauty and then history and finally by their inhabitants. Which was the most intriguing port? Which was the most ordinary? What aliens had each met for the first time? What were their first impressions, and second impressions, and what did they think today? And if they had to live the next thousand years in one of these little places, which would they choose?

Sorrel would have eventually forgotten the day. But a week later, she agreed to a side trip to Greenland.

"Do you know the island?"

"Not at all," Pamir lied.

"I never understood that name," Sorrel admitted, eyes narrowing as if to reexamine the entire question. "Except for some fringes of Martian moss, the climate is pure glacial. The island has to be cold, I was told. The upwellings in the ocean and the sea's general health are at stake. Anyway, there is a warm current upwind, which brings the moisture, and the atmosphere is a hundred kilometers tall and braced with demon-doors. The snows are endless and fabulous, and you can't sail across the Gone-A-Long Sea without visiting Greenland. At least that's what my friends told me."

"Was Cre'llan in your group?"

Somehow that amused her, a little laugh leaking free. "No, everybody was human, except for the guide, who was an AI with a human-facsimile body."

Pamir nodded.

"We power skied up onto the ice. An incredibly hard snowfall was falling, but when we on the glacier, our guide turned to us, mentioning that it was a clear day, as they went. And we should be thankful we could see so much."

At most, they could see twenty meters in any direction. Sorrel was skiing with a good friend—a child of the Great Ship like her, but a thousand years older. She had known the woman her entire life, sharing endless conversations and attending the same fine parties, and their shopping adventures had stretched on for weeks at a time. They always traveled together. And in their combined lives, nothing with real substance had ever found them.

The glacier was thick and swiftly built up by the waves of falling snow. Sorrel and her friend skied away from the rest of the group, scaling a tall ridge that placed them nearly a kilometer above the invisible sea. Then the snow began to fall harder—fat wet flakes joining into snowballs that plunged from the white sky. They were skiing close together, linked by a smart-rope. Sorrel happened to be in the lead. What happened next, she couldn't say. Her first guess, and still her best guess, was that her friend thought of a little joke to play. She disabled the rope and untied herself, and where the ridge widened, she attempted to slip ahead of Sorrel, probably to scare her when she was most vulnerable.

Where the friend fell was a bit of a mystery.

Later, coming to the end of the ridge, Sorrel discovered that she was alone. The natural assumption was that her friend had grown tired and gone back to rejoin the others. There wasn't cause for worry, and she didn't like worry, and so Sorrel didn't give it another thought.

But the other tourists hadn't seen the young woman, either.

A search was launched. But the heavy snowfall turned into what can only be described as an endless avalanche from the sky. In the next hour, the glacier rose twenty meters. By the time rescue crews could set to work, it was obvious that the missing passenger had stumbled into one of the vast crevices, and her body was dead, and without knowing her location, the only reasonable course would be to wait for the ice to push to the sea and watch for her battered remains.

In theory, a human brain could withstand that kind of abuse.

But the AI guide didn't believe in theory. "What nobody tells you is that this fucking island was once an industrial site. Why do you think the engineers covered it up? To hide their wreckage, of course. Experimental hyperfibers, mostly. Very sharp and sloppy, and the island was built with their trash, and if you put enough pressure on even the best bioceramic head, it will crack. Shatter. Pop, and die, and come out into the sea as a few handfuls of fancy sand."

Her friend was dead.

Sorrel and the woman hadn't been lovers, and she didn't feel any bond unique just to the two of them. But the loss was heavy and persistent, and for the next several weeks, the young woman thought about little else.

Meanwhile, their voyage through the Great Ship reached a new sea.

One night, surrounded by a flat gray expanse of methane, Sorrel happened upon the J'Jal man wearing his red jacket and red slacks, and the fancy white tie beneath his nearly-human face. He smiled at her, his expression genuine with either species. Quietly, he asked, "What is wrong?"

Nobody in her own group had noticed her pain. Unlike her, they were convinced that their friend would soon return from oblivion.

Sorrel sat with the J'Jal. For a long while, they didn't speak. She found herself staring at his bare feet, thinking about the fragility of life. Then with a dry low voice, she admitted, "I'm scared."

"Is that so?" Cre'llan said.

"You know, at any moment, without warning, the Great Ship could collide with something enormous. At a third the speed of light, we might strike a sunless world or a small black hole, and billions would die inside this next instant."

"That may be true," her companion said. "But I have invested my considerable faith in the talents of our captains."

"I haven't," she said.

"No?"

"My point here..." She hesitated, shivering for reasons other than the cold. "I have lived for a few years, and I can't remember ever grabbing life by the heart. Do you know what I mean?"

"Very well," he claimed.

His long toes curled and then relaxed again.

"Why don't you wear shoes?" she finally asked.

And with the softest possible touch, Cre'llan laid his hand on hers. "I am an alien, Sorrel." He spoke while smiling, quietly telling her, "And it would mean so much to me if you could somehow, in your soul, forget what I am."

★ ★ ★

"We were lovers before the night was finished," she admitted. A fond look passed into a self-deprecating chuckle. "I thought all J'Jal men were shaped like he was. But he explained that they aren't and why he wasn't, and that's when I learned about the Faith of the Many Joinings."

Pamir nodded, waited.

"You know, they did eventually find my lost friend." A wise sorry laugh came out of her. "A few years later, a patrol working along the edge of the glacier kicked up some dead bones and then the skull with her mind inside. Intact." Sorrel sat back in her chair, breasts moving under the blouse. "She was reconstituted and back inside her old life within the month, and do you know what? In the decades since, I haven't spoken to my old friend more than three times.

"Funny, isn't it?"

"The Faith," Pamir prompted.

She seemed to expect the subject. With a slow shrug of the shoulders, Sorrel observed, "Whoever you are, you weren't born into comfort and wealth. That shows, I think. You've had to fight during your life...probably through much of your life...for things that any fool knows are important. While someone like me—not a fool, I hope—walks through paradise without once asking herself, 'What matters?'"

"The Faith," he repeated.

"Think of the challenge." Staring through him, she asked, "Can you imagine how very difficult it is to be involved—romantically and emotionally linked—with another species?"

"It disgusts me," he lied.

"It disgusts a lot of us," she replied. For an instant, she wore a doubting gaze, perhaps wondering if he was telling the truth about his feelings. Then she let the mistrust fall aside. "I wasn't exceptionally horrified by the idea of sex outside my species, which was why I wasn't all that interested either. Somewhere in the indifferent middle, I was. But when I learned about this obscure J'Jal belief...how an assortment of like-minded souls had gathered, taking the first critical steps in what might well be the logical evolution of life in our universe..."

Her voice drifted away.

"How many husbands did you take?"

She acted surprised. "Why? Don't you know?"

Pamir let her stare at him.

Finally, she said, "Eleven."

"You are Joined to all of them."

"Until a few years ago, yes." The eyes shrank, and with the tears, they grew brighter. "The first death looked like a random murder, horrible but imaginable. But the second killing was followed a few weeks later by a third. The same weapon was used in each tragedy, with the same manner of execution..." Her voice trailed away, the mouth left open and empty. One long hand wiped at the tears, accomplishing little but pushing moisture across the sharp cheeks. "Since the dead belonged to different species, and since the members of the Faith…my husbands and myself…are sworn to secrecy—"

"Nobody noticed the pattern," Pamir said.

"Oh, I think they saw what was happening," she said. "After the fifth or sixth death, security people made inquiries at the library. But no one there could admit anything. And then the killings slowed, and the investigation went away. No one was offered protection, and my name was never mentioned. At least that's what I assume, since nobody was sent to interview me." Then with a quiet, angry voice, Sorrel added, "After linking the murders to the library, nobody saw any reason to care what happened next."

"How do you know that?"

She stared at Pamir as if he were a perfect idiot.

"The authorities assume this was some ugly internal business among the Joined. Is that what you think?"

"Maybe," she said. "Or maybe they received orders telling them to stop caring."

"Who gave those orders?"

She looked at a point above his head and carefully said, "No."

"Who wouldn't want these killings stopped?"

"I can't," she said, shaking her head. "Ask all you want, but I won't tell you anything more."

"Do you consider yourself in danger?"

She sighed. "Hardly."

"Why not?"

She said nothing.

"Two husbands are alive," Pamir reminded her.

She worked him over with a suspicious expression. "I'm guessing you know which two," she said.

"There's the Glory." Glories were bird-like creatures, roughly human-shaped but covered with a bright, lovely plumage. "One of your more recent husbands, isn't he?"

Sorrel nodded. "Except he died last year, on the opposite side of the Great Ship. The body was discovered only yesterday."

Pamir flinched. "My condolences."

"Yes. Thank you."

"And your first lover?"

"Yes."

"The J'Jal in the red suit."

"Cre'llan, yes. I know who you mean."

"The last man standing," he said.

That earned a withering stare from the pained cold face. "I don't marry lightly, and I don't care what you're thinking."

Pamir stood and walked up beside her, and using his best stare, he said, "You don't know what I'm thinking. Because I sure as hell don't know what I've got in my own soggy head."

She dipped her eyes.

"The J'Jal," he said. "I can track him down for myself, or you can make the introductions."

"It isn't Cre'llan," she whispered.

"Then come with me," Pamir replied. "Come and look him in the eye and ask the old man for yourself."

13

As a species, the J'Jal were neither wealthy or powerful, but there were a few individuals of enormous age who had prospered in a gradual, relentless fashion. On far flung worlds, they served as cautious traders and inconspicuous landowners and sometimes as the bearers of superior, profitable technologies; and while they would always be alien, they had adapted well enough to feel as if they were home.

Then the Great Ship arrived, and their young, arrogant human cousins promised to carry them across the galaxy—for a fee. The boldest of these wealthy J'Jal left a hundred worlds behind, spending fortunes for the honor of gathering together. They had no home of their own, yet it was easy to hope that a new planet was waiting, reminiscent of their cradle world, yet for some reason empty, waiting to be claimed as their own. Some of the J'Jal believed that given time and small measures of luck, they would perhaps even match the human accomplishments, blending into the ranks of their highly successful relatives.

"But neither solution gives me pleasure," said the gentleman wearing red. "The boundaries between the species are a lie and impermanent, and I hope for a radically different future."

According to his official biography, Cre'llan was approximately the same age as <u>Homo sapiens</u>.

"What's your chosen future?" Pamir inquired.

The smile was bright and a little cold. "My new friend," the J'Jal said, his voice nearly human. "I think you already have a fair assessment of what I wish for. And more to the point, I think you couldn't care less about any dreams or utopias that I happen to entertain."

"I do have guesses," Pamir agreed. "And you're right, I don't give a shit about your paradise."

Sorrel sat beside her ancient husband, fondly holding his hand. Divorced or not, she missed his company. They looked like lovers waiting for the holo portrait to be taken. With a whisper, she warned Cre'llan, "He suspects you, darling."

"Of course he does."

"But I told him…I explained…you can't be responsible for any of this…"

"Which is the truth," the J'Jal replied, his smile turning into a grim little sneer. "Why would I murder anyone? How could it possibly serve my needs?"

The J'Jal's home was near the bottom of Fall Away, and it was enormous. This single room covered nearly a square kilometer that was carpeted with green timber and quick little streams, and the ceiling was so high that a dozen tame star-rocs could circle above and never brush wings. But all of that grandeur and wealth was dwarfed by the outside view: The braided rivers that ran down the middle of Fall Away had been set free some fifty kilometers above their heads, every diamond tube ending at the same point, their contents exploding forth under extraordinary pressure. A flow equal to ten Amazons roared past Cre'llan's home, water and ammonia mixing with a spectacular array of chemical wastes and dying phytoplankton. Aggressive compounds battered each other and reacted, bleeding colors in the process. Shapes appeared inside the wild foam, and vanished again. A creative eye could see every face that he had ever met, and he could spend days watching for the faces that he had worn during his own long, strange life.

The window only seemed to be a window. In reality, Pamir was staring at a sheet of high-grade hyperfiber, thick and impervious to most any force nature could muster. The view was a projection, a convincing trick. Nodding, he said, "You must feel remarkably safe, I would think."

"I sleep quite well," Cre'llan replied.

"Most of the time, I can help people with their security matters. But not you." Pamir was being entirely honest. "I don't think the Master Captain has this much security. That hyperfiber. The AI watchdogs. Those blood-and-meat hounds that sniffed our butts on the way in." He showed a wide smile, and then mentioned, "If I'm not mistaken, you would never have to leave this one room. For the next ten thousand years, you could sit where you're sitting today and eat what falls off these trees, and no one would be able to touch you."

"If that was what I wished, yes."

"But he is not the killer," Sorrel muttered.

Then she stood and stepped away from the ancient creature, her hand grudgingly releasing his grip. Pamir watched her approach, how she looked at him without looking, settling on the ground before him. Suddenly the woman looked exceptionally young, serious and determined. "I know this man," she said. "You have no idea what you're suggesting, if you think that he could hurt anyone, for any reason."

"I know the species," Pamir said. "In fact, I once lived as a J'Jal."

Sorrel leaned away from him, taken by surprise.

"I dyed my hair blue and tinkered with these bones, and I even doctored my genetics far enough to pass half-assed scans." Pamir was telling too much. Nonetheless, he didn't feel as if he had any choice. "I even kept a J'Jal lover.

For a while, I made her happy. But she saw through my disguise, and I had to steal away in the middle of the night."

The other two stared at him, bewildered and deeply curious.

"Anyway," he continued. "During my stay with the J'Jal, a certain young woman came of age. She was very desirable. Extraordinarily beautiful, and her family was one of the wealthiest onboard the Ship. Before that year was finished, the woman had acquired three devoted husbands. But someone else fell in love with her, and he didn't want to share. One of the new husbands was killed. After that, the remaining two husbands went to the public hall and divorced her. They never spoke to the girl again. She was left unattached, and alone. What rational soul would risk her love under those circumstances?" Pamir shook his head, studying Cre'llan. "As I mentioned, I ran away. But I kept track of the community, and several decades later, an elder J'Jal proposed to the widow. She was lonely, and he was not a bad man. Not wealthy, but powerful and ancient, and in some measure, wise. So she accepted his offer, and when nothing tragic happened to her new husband, everyone understood who ordered the killing. And not only that, but they accepted it too, in pure J'Jal fashion."

With a flat, untroubled voice, Cre'llan said, "My soul has never been thought of as jealous."

"Yet I am accusing you of jealousy," Pamir countered.

Silence.

"Conflicts over females are ordinary business for some species," he continued. "Monopolizing a valuable mate can be a good evolutionary strategy, for the J'Jal as well as others. And ten million years of civilization hasn't changed what you are, or what you can be."

Cre'llan snorted. "I would never embrace that old barbarism."

"Agreed."

The green gaze narrowed. "Excuse me, sir. I don't think I understand. What are you accusing me of?"

"This is a beautiful, enormous fortress," Pamir continued. "And as you claim, you're not a jealous creature. But did you invite these other husbands to live with you? Did you offer even one of them your shelter and all of this expensive security?"

Sorrel glanced at the J'Jal, her breath catching.

Pamir said, "You didn't offer because of a very reasonable fear: What if one of your houseguests wanted Sorrel for himself?"

The tension was physical, ugly.

"In your mind, every other husband was a suspect, with the two harum-scarums being the most obvious candidates." He looked at Sorrel again. "Gallium would be his favorite—a relatively poor entity born into a biology of posturing and violence. His species is famous for stealing mates. Both sexes do it, every day. But now Gallium is dead, which leaves your husband with no one to worry about, it seems."

"Except I am not the killer," Cre'llan repeated.

"Oh, I agree," Pamir said. "You're innocent of that crime, yes."

The statement angered both of them. Sorrel spoke first, asking, "When did you come to that conclusion?"

"Pretty much the moment I learned who your husbands were," Pamir said, sitting forward in his chair, staring out at the churning waters. "No, Cre'llan isn't the murderer."

"You understand my nature?" the J'Jal asked.

"Maybe, but that doesn't particularly matter." Pamir laughed. "No, you're too smart and far too old to attempt this sort of bullshit with a human woman. Talk all you want about every species being one and the same. But the hard sharp damning fact is that human beings are not J'Jal. Very few of us, even under the most difficult circumstances, will be able to ignore the fact that their spouse appears to be a brutal killer."

Cre'llan gave a little nod, the barest smile showing.

Sorrel stood, nervous hands clenching into fists. She looked vulnerable and sweet and very sorry. The beginnings of recognition showed in the blue-white eyes, and she started to stare at the J'Jal, catching herself now and forcing her eyes to drop.

"And something else was obvious," Pamir said.

With a dry little voice, Cre'llan asked, "What was obvious?"

Pamir said nothing.

"What do you mean?" Sorrel asked.

"Okay," Pamir said, watching her face and the nervous fists. "Let us suppose that I'm killing your husbands. I want my rivals dead, and I want a reasonable chance of surviving to the end. Since Cre'llan enjoys the most security...better than everyone else combined, probably...I would hit him before he smelled the danger..."

That earned a cold silence.

Pamir waved one hand, then the other, as if brushing away some little irritant. "The killer wants the husbands out of your life. From the start, I think he knew exactly what was required. The other ten husbands had to be murdered, since they loved you deeply and you seemed to love them. But this gentleman J'Jal…well, he's a different conundrum entirely, I'm guessing…"

Cre'llan appeared interested but distant. When he breathed, it was after a long breathless pause, and he sounded a little weak when he said, "I don't know what you are talking about."

"You told me," Pamir said to Sorrel.

"What did I tell you?"

"How you met him during the cruise. And what happened to you and your good friend just before you went to bed with this alien man."

"I don't understand," she said.

Cre'llan said, "Be quiet."

Pamir felt a pleasant nervousness in his belly. "Cre'llan wanted you, I'm guessing. He wanted you very badly. You were a wealthy, unattached human woman. The Joining can talk all they want about the equality of the species, but the J'Jal adore their cousins. And you would bring him a generous amount of status. But seducing you was going to be a challenge, which is why Cre'llan paid your friend to vanish on the ice in Greenland, faking her own death."

She said, "No."

"He wanted to expose you emotionally, with a dose of mortality."

"Stop that," she told him.

Cre'llan said, "Idiot," and little more.

"The AI guide was right," Pamir told her. "The chances of a mind surviving the weight of that ice and the grinding against the hyperfiber shards…well, I found it remarkable to learn that your good friend was found alive.

"So I made a few inquiries.

"I can show you, if you wish. A trail of camouflaged funds leads from that woman back to a company formed just hours before her death. The mysterious company made one transfer of funds, declared bankruptcy and dissolved. Your skiing partner was the recipient. She was reborn as a very wealthy soul, and the principal stockholder in that short-lived company happened to have been someone with whom your first lover and husband does quite a lot of business."

Sorrel's mouth closed and opened, in slow motion, and then it began to close again. Her legs tried to find the strength to carry her away, but she looked about for another moment or two, finding no door or hatchway to slip through in the next little while. She was caught, trapped by the awful and true. And then, just as Pamir thought that she would crack into pieces, the young woman surprised him.

Calmly, she told Cre'llan, "I divorce you."

"Darling–?" he began.

"Forever," she said. Then she pulled from a pocket an ordinary knife. A sapphire blade no longer than her hand was unfolded, and it took her ten seconds to cut the Darmion crystal out of her chest—ripped free for the second time in as many days—and before she collapsed, she flung the gory gift at the stunned, sorry face.

14

Pamir explained what had happened as he carried her into the apartment. Then he set her on a great round bed, pillows offering themselves to her head while a small autodoc spider-walked its way across the pale blue sheets, studying her half-healed wound before opening more penetrating eyes, carefully examining the rest of her miserable body.

Quietly, the apartment said, "I have never known her to be this way."

In his long life, Pamir had rarely seen any person as depressed, as forlorn. Sorrel was pale and motionless, lying on her back, and even with her eyes open, something in her gaze was profoundly blind. She saw nothing, heard nothing. She was like a person flung off the topmost portion of Fall Away, tumbling out of control, gusts of wind occasionally slamming her against the hard walls, battering what couldn't feel the abuse anymore.

"I am worried," the apartment said.

"Utterly reasonable," Pamir said.

"It must be a horrid thing, losing everyone who loves you."

"But someone still loves her," he countered. Then he paused, thinking hard about everything again.

"Tell me," he said. "What is your species-strain?"

"Is that important?"

"Probably not," said Pamir.

The AI described its pedigree, in brief.

"What's your lot number?"

"I do not see how that matters."

"Never mind," he said, walking away from their patient. "I know enough as it is."

Pamir ate a small meal and drank some sweet alien nectar that left him feeling a little sloppy. When the head cleared, he slept for a minute or an hour, and then he returned to the bedroom and the giant bed. Sorrel was where he had left her. Her eyes were closed now, empty hands across her belly, rising and falling and rising with a slow steady rhythm that he couldn't stop watching.

"Thank you."

The voice didn't seem to belong to anyone. The young woman's mouth happened to be open, but it didn't sound like the voice he expected. It was sturdy and calm, the old sadness wiped away. It was a quiet polite and rather sweet voice that told him, "Thank you," and then added, "For everything, sir."

The eyes hadn't opened.

She had heard Pamir approach, or felt his presence.

He sat on the bed beside her, and after a long moment he said, "You know. You'd be entitled to consider me—whoever I am—as being your main suspect. I could have killed the husbands, and I certainly put an end to you and Cre'llan."

"It isn't you."

"Because you have another suspect in mind. Isn't that right?"

She said nothing.

"Who do you believe is responsible?" he pressed.

Finally, the eyes pulled open, slowly, and they blinked twice, tears pooling but never quite reaching the depth where they would flow.

"My father," she said.

"He killed your husbands?"

"Obviously."

"He's light-years behind us now."

Silence.

Pamir nodded, and he waited until the moment felt right, and then he asked, "What do you know about your father?"

"Quite a lot," she said.

"But you've never seen him," he reminded her

"But I've studied him." She shook her head and closed her eyes again. "I've know his biography as well as I can, and I think I know him pretty well."

"He isn't here, Sorrel."

"No?"

"He emigrated before you were born."

"That's what my mother told me."

Pamir leaned closer, adding, "What did she tell you about the man?"

"That he is strong and self-assured. That he knows what is right and best. And he loves me very much, but he couldn't stay with me." Sorrel chewed on her lip. "He couldn't stay here, but my father has agents and ways, and I would never be without him. Mother promised me."

Pamir just nodded.

"My father doesn't approve of the Faith."

"I can believe that," he said.

"My mother admitted, once or twice…that she loved him very much, but he didn't have a diplomat's ease with aliens. His heart can be hard, and he has a capacity to do awful things, if he sees the need…"

"No," Pamir whispered.

The pale blue eyes opened. "What do you mean?"

"Your father didn't do any of this," he said. Then he thought again, saying, "Well, maybe a piece of it."

"What do you mean?"

Pamir set his hand on top of her mouth, lightly. Then as he began to pull his hand back, she took hold of his wrist and forearm, easing the palm back down against lips that pulled apart, teeth giving him a tiny swift bite.

A J'Jal gesture, that was.

He bent down and kissed the open eyes.

Sorrel told him, "You shouldn't."

"Probably not."

"If the murderer knows you are with me…"

He placed two fingers deep into her mouth, J'Jal fashion. And she sucked on them, not trying to speak now, eyes almost smiling as Pamir calmly and smoothly slid into bed beside her.

15

One of the plunging rivers pulled close to the wall, revealing what it carried. Inside the diamond tube was a school of finned creatures, not pseudofish nor pseudowhales, but instead a collection of teardrop-shaped machines that probably fused hydrogen in their hearts, producing the necessary power to hold their bodies steady inside a current that looked relentless, rapid and chaotic, turbulent and exceptionally unappealing.

Watching the swimming machines, Pamir decided that this was how he had lived for ages now. Then he showed a shrug and soft laugh, continuing the long walk up the path, moving past a collection of modest apartments. The library was just a few meters farther along—a tiny portal carved into the smooth black basaltic wall. Its significance was so well hidden that a thousand sightseers passed this point every day, perhaps pausing at the edge of the precipice to look down, but more likely continuing on their walk, searching richer views. Pamir turned his eyes toward the closed doorway, pretending mild curiosity, hands on the simple basalt wall that bordered the outer edge of the trail, eyes gazing down at the dreamy shape of the Little-Lot.

The massive cloud was the color of butter and nearly as dense. A trillion trillion microbes thrived inside its aerogel matrix, supporting an ecosystem that would never touch a solid surface.

The library door swung open—J'Jal wood riding on creaky iron hinges.

Pamir opened a nexus and triggered an old, nearly forgotten captain's channel. Then he turned towards the creaking sound and smiled. Sorrel was emerging from the library, dressed in a novice's blue robe and blinking against the sudden glare. The massive door fell shut again, and she quietly said, "All right."

Pamir held a finger to his closed mouth.

She stepped closer, speaking through a nexus. "I did what you told me."

"Show it."

She produced the slender blue book.

"Put it on the ground here."

This was her personal journal—the only volume she was allowed to remove from the library. She set it in front of her sandaled feet and asked, "Was I noticed?"

"I promise. You were seen."

"And do we wait now?"

He shook his head. "No, I'm too impatient for that game."

The plasma gun was barely awake when he fired it, turning plastic pages and the wood binding into a thin cloud of superheated ash.

Sorrel put her arms around herself, squeezing hard.

"Now we wait," he advised.

Not for the first time, she admitted, "I don't understand. Still. Who do you think is responsible?"

Again, the heavy door swung open.

Without looking, Pamir called out, "Hello, Leon'ard."

The J'Jal librarian wore the same purplish-black robe and blue ponytail, and his expression hadn't changed in the last few days—a bilious outrage focused on those who would injure his helpless dependents. He stared at the ruins of the book, and then he glared at the two humans, focusing on the male face until a vague recognition tickled.

"Do I know you?" he began.

Pamir was wearing the same face he had worn for the last thirty-two years. A trace of a smile was showing, except around the dark eyes. Quietly, fiercely, he said, "I found my wife, and thanks for the help."

Leon'ard stared at Sorrel, his face working its way through a tangle of wild emotions. "Your wife," he said.

Then he tipped his head, saying, "No, she is not."

"You know that?" Pamir asked.

The J'Jal didn't respond.

"What do you know, Leon'ard?"

Leon'ard glanced back across a shoulder—not at the library door but at the nearby apartments. The man was at his limits. He seemed frail and tentative, hands pressing at the front of his robe while the long toes curled under his naked feet. Everything was apparent. Transparent. Obvious. And into this near-panic, Pamir said, "I know what you did."

"No," the J'Jal replied, without confidence.

"You learned something," Pamir said. "You are a determined scholar and a talented student of other species, and some years ago, by design or idiot luck, you unraveled something. At the knot's center was a secret that was supposed to remain a deep, impenetrable."

"No."

"A mystery about my wife," he said.

"What is it?" Sorrel asked.

Pamir laughed and said, "Tell her."

The blood had drained out of Leon'ard's face.

"No, I agree," Pamir continued. "Let's keep this between you and me, shall we? Because the poor kid doesn't have any idea what this means."

"What means what?" she asked.

"She is not your wife," the librarian said.

"The hell she isn't." He laughed. "Check the public records. Two hours ago, in a civil ceremony overseen by two Hyree monks, we were made woman and male-implement in a legally-binding manner."

Sorrel stepped in front of him. "What do you know about me?"

Pamir stared only at the J'Jal. "But somebody else knows what we do. Doesn't he? Because you told him. You said a few words in passing, maybe. Unless of course you were the one who devised a simple, brutal plan, and he is your simple accomplice."

"No!" Leon'ard screamed. "I did not dream anything."

"I might believe you." Pamir looked at Sorrel, and he winked. "When I showed this man an image of one of your dead husbands, his reaction didn't feel quite right. I saw the surprise, but the J'Jal eyes betrayed a little bit of pleasure, too. Or relief, was it? Leon'ard? Were you genuinely thrilled to believe that Sele'ium was dead and out of your proverbial hair?"

The librarian looked pale and cold, arms clasped tight against his shivering body. Again, he glanced at the nearby apartments. His mouth opened and then pulled itself closed, and then Pamir said, "Death."

"What did you say?" Leon'ard asked.

"There are countless wonderful and inventive ways to fake your own death," Pamir allowed. "But one of my favorites is to clone your body and cook an empty, soulless brain, and then stuff that brain inside that living body, mimicking a very specific kind of demise."

"Sele'ium?" said Sorrel.

"What I think." Pamir was guessing, but none of the leaps were long or unlikely. "I think your previous husband was a shrewd young man. He grew up in a family that had lived among the harum-scarums. That's where his lineage came from, wasn't it, Leon'ard? So it was perfectly natural, even inevitable, that he could entertain thoughts about killing the competition, including his own identity."

"You know nothing," Sorrel said.

"Almost nothing," Pamir agreed. "Leon'ard is the one who is carrying all the dark secrets on his back. Ask him."

The J'Jal covered his face with his hands. "Go away."

"Was Sele'ium a good friend and you were trying to help? Or did he bribe you for this useful information?" Pamir nodded. "Whatever happened, you pointed him toward Sorrel, and you must have explained, 'She is perhaps the most desirable mate on the Great Ship—'"

A sizzling blue bolt of plasma struck Pamir's face, melting it and obliterating everything beyond.

The headless body wobbled for a moment and then slumped and dropped slowly, settling against the short black wall. Leon'ard leaped backwards, flattened hands waving in the bright air, while Sorrel stood over the remains of her newest husband, her expression tight but calm—like the face of a sailor who has already ridden through too many storms.

16

A pedestrian wandered past, his gaze distracted and his manner a little nervous. He seemed embarrassed by the drama that he had happened upon. He looked human. The cold blond hair and purplish-black skin were common on high-UV worlds, while the brown eyes were as ordinary as could be. He wore sandals and trousers and a loose-fitting shirt, and he stared at the destroyed body, seeing precisely what he expected to see. Then he glanced at Sorrel, and with nothing but warmth, he said, "You do not know…you cannot appreciate…how much I love you…"

"Sele'ium," she said doubtfully.

He started to speak again, to explain himself.

"Stay away," she said. "Leave me alone!"

His reaction was to shake his head with his mouth open—a J'Jal refusal—and then calmly and with considerable malice, he informed her, "I am an exceptionally patient individual."

A bitter thin laugh came out of her.

"Not today, no, and possibly not for a thousand years," he said. "But I will approach you with a new face and name—every so often, I will come into your life—and there will be an hour and a certain heartbeat when you come to understand that we belong to one another."

Suddenly the corpse kicked at the empty air.

Sele'ium glanced at the distraction. Then slowly, he realized that Pamir's body was shrinking, as if it were a balloon slowly losing its breath. How odd. He stared at the mysterious phenomena, not quite able to piece together what should have been obvious. The headless ruin twitched hard and then harder, one shrinking leg flinging high. And then from blackened wound rose a puff of blue smoke, and with it, the stink of burnt rubber and cooked hydraulics.

With his left hand, Sele'ium yanked the plasma gun from inside his shirt—a commercial model meant to be used as a tool, but with its safeties cut away—and turning in a quick circle, he searched for a valid target.

"What is it?" Leon'ard called out.

"Do you see him?"

"Who?"

More puzzled than worried, the young J'Jal refused to panic, his mind ticking off the possible answers, settling on what would be easiest and best.

In the open air, of course.

"Just leave us," Leon'ard begged. "I will not stand aside any longer!"

Sele'ium threw five little bolts into the basalt wall, punching out holes, making a rain of white-hot magma.

Somewhere below, a voice howled.

Sorrel ran to the wall and looked down, and Sele'ium crept up beside her, the gun in both hands, its reactor pumping energies into a tiny chamber, readying a blast that would obliterate everything in its path.

He started to peer over and then thought better of it.

One hand released the weapon and the free arm wrapped around Sorrel's waist, and when she flung her elbow into his midsection, he bent low. He grunted and cursed softly and then told her, "No."

With his full weight, he drove the woman against the smooth black wall, and with his chin on her left shoulder, they bent together and peered over the edge.

Pamir reached up and grabbed the plasma gun, yanking hard.

And Sorrel tried to jump away.

The two motions combined to lift her and Sele'ium off the path, over the edge and plummeting down. Pamir's gecko-grip was ripped loose from the basalt, and he was falling with them, one hand on the gun, clinging desperately, while the other arm began to swing, throwing the fist into the killer's belly and ribs. Within moments, they were falling as fast as possible. A damp singing wind blew past them, and the wall was a black smear to one side, while the rest of Fall Away was enormous and distant and almost changeless. Airborne rivers and a thousand flying machines were out of reach and useless. The three bodies fell and fell, and sometimes a voice would pass through the roaring wind—a spectator standing on the path, remarking in alarm, "Who were they?"

Three bodies were clinging and kicking. Sele'ium punished Pamir with his own free hand, and then he let himself get pulled close, and with a human mouth only a few days old, he bit down, chewing hard on a wrist, trying to force the stranger to release his hold on the gun.

Pamir cried out and let go.

But as Sele'ium aimed at his face, for his soul, Pamir slammed at the man's forearm and pushed it backwards again, and he put a hard knee into the elbow, and a weapon that didn't have safeties released its stored energies a thin blinding beam that coalesced inside the dying man's head, his brain turning to light and ash, a supersonic <u>crack</u> leaving the others temporarily deafened.

Pamir kicked the corpse away and clung to Sorrel, and she held tight to him, and after another few minutes, as they plunged toward the yellow depths of a living, thriving cloud, he shouted into her better ear, explaining a thing or two.

17

Again, it was nearly nightfall.

Once again, Pamir sat outside his apartment, listening to the wild songs of the llano-vibra. Nothing looked out of the ordinary. Neighbors strolled past or ran past or flew by on gossamer wings. The Janusian couple paused long enough to ask where he had been these last days, and Pamir said a few murky words about taking care of family troubles. The harum-scarum family was outside their apartment, gathered around a cooking pit, eating a living passion ox in celebration of another day successfully crossed. A collection of machines stopped to ask about the facsimile that they had built for Pamir, as a favor. Did it serve its intended role? "Oh, sure," he said with a nod. "Everybody was pretty much fooled, at least until the joke was finished."

"Was there laughter?" asked one machine.

"Constant, breathless laughter," Pamir said. And then he mentioned nothing else about it.

A single figure was approaching. He had been watching her for the last kilometer, and as the machines wandered away, he used three different means to study her gait and face and manner. Then he considered his options, and he decided to remain sitting where he was, his back against the huge ceramic pot and his legs stretched out before him, one bare foot crossed over the other.

She stopped a few steps short, watching him but saying nothing.

"You're thinking," Pamir told her. "Throw me into the brig, or throw me off the Ship entirely. That's what you're thinking now."

"But we had an agreement," Miocene countered. "You were supposed to help somebody, and you have, and you most definitely have earned your payment as well as my thanks."

"Yeah," he said. "But I know you. And you're asking yourself, 'Why not get rid of him and be done with it?'"

The First Chair was wearing a passenger's clothes and a face slightly disguised, eyes blue and the matching hair curled into countless tight knots, her cheeks and mouth widened but nothing about the present smile any warmer than any other smile that had ever come from this hard, hard creature.

"You know me," she said.

A moment later, she asked, "Will you tell me who you are?"

"Don't you know yet?"

She shook her head, and with a hint of genuine honesty admitted, "Nor do I particularly care, one way or the other."

Pamir grinned and leaned back a little more.

"I suppose I could place you under custody," Miocene continued. "But a man with your skills and obvious luck…well, you probably have twelve different ways to escape from our detention centers. And if I sent you falling onto a colony world or an alien world…I suppose in another thousand years or so, you would find your way back again, like a dog or an ugly habit."

"Fair points," he said.

Then with a serious, warm voice, he asked, "How is Sorrel?"

"The young woman? As I understand it, she has put her apartment up for sale, and she has already moved away. I'm not sure where."

He said, "Bullshit."

Miocene grinned, just for a moment. "Perhaps I do have an idea or two. About who you might be, I mean."

"She knows now."

The woman's face seemed to narrow, and the eyes grew larger and less secure. "Knows what?"

"Who her father is," said Pamir. "Her true father, I mean."

"One man's conjecture," the First Chair reminded him. Then with a dismissive shake of the head, she added, "A young woman in a gullible moment might believe you. But she won't find any corroboration, not for the next eternity, and eventually she will have to believe what she has always believed."

"Maybe."

Miocene shrugged. "It's hardly your concern now."

"And it never was," he allowed. Then as the overhead lights flickered for the first time, he sat up straighter. "The robbery was your idea, wasn't he? The thief who came to steal away the Darmion crystal?"

"And why would I arrange such a thing?"

"What happened afterwards was exactly what you were hoping for," he said. "An apparently random crime leaves Sorrel trusting me, the two of us emotionally linked."

With a narrow grin, Miocene said, "I must be a very clever person."

"And you assumed that the killer, whoever he was, would likely put an end to me. Exposing himself in the process, of course."

"Wicked as well as clever," she said.

A second ripple of darkness passed along the avenue. Pamir showed her a stern face, and quietly, he said, "Madam First Chair. You have always been a remarkable and wondrously awful bitch."

"I didn't know it was Sele'ium," she confessed.

"And you didn't know why he was killing the husbands, either." Pamir stood up slowly. "Because the old librarian, Leon'ard, pieced together who Sorrel was. He told Sele'ium what he had learned, and he mentioned that the Sorrel's father was a woman, and as it happens, that woman is the second most important person onboard the Great Ship."

"There were some flaws in the public records, yes." She nodded, adding, "These are problems that I have resolved already."

"Good," he said.

Miocene narrowed her gaze. "And yes, I am a difficult soul. The bitch queen, and so on. But my life is enormous and very complicated, and for a multitude of reasons, selfless as well as selfish, it is best if my daughter remains apart from my life and from me."

"Maybe so," he said.

"Look at these last few days. Do you need more reasons than this?" Then she took a step closer, adding, "But you are wrong, in one critical matter. Whoever you are."

"Where is the error?"

"You assume I wanted you to be killed, and that's wrong. It was a possibility and a risk. But as a good captain, I had to consider the possibility and make contingency plans, just in case." She took another little step, saying, "No, what all of this has been…in addition to everything else that it seems to have been…is what I have to call an audition."

"An audition," said Pamir, genuinely puzzled.

"You seem to be a master at disappearing," Miocene admitted. Then she took one last step, and in a whisper, she said, "There may come a day when I cannot protect my daughter anymore, and she'll need to vanish in some profound, eternal fashion."

The third ripple of darkness came, followed by the full seamless black of night.

"That's your task, if you wish to take it," she said, speaking into the darkness. "Whoever you happen to be…are you there, can you hear me…?"

18

Sorrel had been walking for weeks, crossing the Indigo Desert one step at a time. She traveled alone with her supplies in a floating pack tied to her waist. It was ten years later, or ten thousand. She had some trouble remembering how much time had passed, which was a good thing. She felt better in most ways, and the old pains had become familiar enough to be ignored. She was even happy, after a fashion, and while she strolled upon the fierce landscape of fire-blasted stone and purple succulents, she would sing, sometimes human songs and occasionally tunes that were much harder to manage and infinitely more beautiful.

One afternoon, she heard notes answering her notes.

Coming over the crest of a sharp ridge, she saw something utterly unexpected—a thick luxurious stand of irrigated llano-vibra.

Louder now, the vegetation sang to her.

She approached with care.

In the midst of the foliage, a shape was sitting. It was a human shape, perhaps. A male, by the looks of it. He was sitting with his back to her, his face obscured by the shaggy black hair. Yet he seemed rather familiar, for some peculiar reason. Familiar in the best ways, and Sorrel stepped faster now, and smiled, and with a parched voice, she tried to sing in time with the alien weed.

Bridge Ten

Space is structure and relentless logic.

Hydrogen atoms are identical to one another, and the galaxies are nearly the same as one another, and certain grand patterns reach back to the Beginning even while stretching past starlight and gravity and cold time.

Space is as good as infinite.

Infinity always loves some telltale shape.

Everything great and important is built upon a few clean principles. Galaxies and atoms build life. Life swarms and spreads and dies away but never completely. One totipotent spore can survive ten holocausts before dropping onto the perfect face of a warm sterile pool, and there it grows into a greasy purple slime that is carried away when a storm breaks, and in another moment, a sterile ocean is conquered.

Life is mindless until it isn't.

But intelligence only reaches so far. Mistakes are made. The smartest, most subtle minds can murder their own world and themselves. But what survives the carnage will learn and adapt. Wisdom is a stubborn power—a nearly infinite power—and the wisest minds will soon fall deeply in love with a few reliable principles that can be repeated without end.

The galaxy is thick with living worlds, and the worlds speak to each other in a wild chorus that shakes the cosmos.

But something is wrong here.

Voices are unaccounted for, lost and missing.

The galaxy's interior is too quiet and too dark, and what makes the most sense is that that silence has meaning.

Listen deeply, and what is not heard?

And now listen to closer places—as close as can be:

Standing in a bright avenue, on the most ordinary day, one mouth says nothing while the mind behind it seems drained of thought. The entity appears ordinary, yet it is impenetrable, and worse still, the shape of its silence resembles the mystery at work in the galaxy's heart.

The Man With the Golden Balloon

1

Quee Lee learned about the Vermiculate from an unlikely source—a painfully respectable gentleman who never took pleasure from adventuring or the unexpected. But their paths happened to cross during a feast given by mutual friends, and after the customary pleasantries, he gently pulled the ancient woman aside, remarking, "I have some news that might be of interest to you."

"Well, I have interest to spare," she said.

Then with a precise, mildly perturbed voice, he explained how one tiny portion of the Great Ship had never been adequately mapped.

"How can that be?" Quee Lee asked skeptically. "The captains' first priority was to locate every shipboard cavern and dead-end tunnel. Even the tiniest crevice wears some unique name."

"Oh, the captains were thorough," the man admitted, never one to openly doubt authority. "But the Ship has the mass and volume of Uranus, with engines bigger than moons and fuel tanks that can swallow oceans whole."

Yes, mapping the enigmatic body was a challenge. But the early captains were clever, stubborn souls. Their survey began with several million robots—small, elegantly designed machines bristling with sensors and curious limbs. Scrambling through the Ship's interior, the robots memorized every empty volume, and whenever a passageway split in two, the robots paused, feasting on the local rock and metal while building copies of their obsessive selves. As prolific as carpenter ants or harum-scarum fleas, those early scouts soon numbered in the trillions, and ruled by simple unyielding instructions, they moved ever deeper inside the Ship, eventually scurrying down every hole, fashioning a precise three-dimensional model of the Ship's vacant interior.

But the method had limitations. Doorless bubbles and pockets and finger-wide seams lay out of reach; more than a few long caverns were sealed beneath kilometers of iron and hyperfiber. Yet with sonic probes and neutrino knives, the Ship's engineers made even those buried places visible. The only unmapped region was the Ship's distant core. The Master Captain was being honest when she stood on the bridge, proclaiming that her fabulous machine had been mapped in full; and its crew and countless passengers had little reason but believe every promise that this voyage would remain routine—a blissful journey that would eventually circumnavigate the bright heart of the Milky Way.

Quee Lee explained all of this, and her companion bristled.

"I understand how the Ship was mapped," he said. "What I'm telling you is that despite everyone's best efforts, a few empty spaces are lurking out there."

"And how do we know this?"

"Because the Master Captain owns a team of AI savants—brilliant machines designed to do nothing but ponder the Ship and its mysteries. One of those AIs recently made a fresh analysis of old data, and one glaring gap was discovered. One blank spot on the captains' map and nobody understands how this could have happened."

"And when did we learn this?"

"But we haven't learned anything," he countered, his voice breaking at the edges. "This is a very grave, very important business. Only the highest ranking captains know about the flaw."

"And you," she pointed out.

"Well, yes, I know portions of the story. But I can't tell how or why, and please don't ask me."

"And why are you telling me?"

"Because it occurred to me," he said, producing a hopeful smile. "You of all people would appreciate hearing this news."

Give a rich secret to the blandest soul, and he will turn into a fountain of knowledge. And Quee Lee was a charming presence as well as a very desirable audience: A wealthy woman from the Old Earth and one of a handful of humans onboard the Ship who could remember that precious moment when their species turned a sensitive ear to the sky, hearing intelligent sounds raining down from the stars. In that sense, she was a remarkable and very rare creature—a lady of genuine fame inside the human community. She was also beautiful and poised, socially gifted and universally liked. Given this kind of opportunity, any healthy, insecure heterosexual male would work hard to impress Quee Lee.

"Our captains are worried," her confidant said. "The Master Captain took the trouble of waking one of the old surveying robots and putting it down a promising hole. And do you know what happened?"

"You're going to tell me, I hope."

"The robot lost its way." The man shivered, bothered by this turn of events. "The machine fumbled around in the darkness, and then with nothing to say for itself, it climbed back out of the hole again."

"Fascinating," she said.

"I knew you would enjoy this," he whispered, offering a smile and quick wink. After millennia of traveling together, he had finally managed to engage the interest of this beautiful creature.

"Perri will want to hear this story," she mentioned.

"But I wish you wouldn't mention it," the man said. Then a worse possibility occurred to him. "I understood your husband is traveling now. He isn't here with us, is he?"

"Oh, but he is." For the last several weeks, Perri had been riding a saddle strapped to the back of a squid-like alien called the Gi-Gee, enjoying wild swims in a frigid river of ammonium hydrate. But by chance, he had just now slipped into the party. Of course her husband would want to learn of this news. A thousand souls were scattered across the room, human and otherwise. Most of the celebrants were dressed in gaudy, look-at-me costumes—which was only proper, since these were among the wealthiest, most powerful individuals to be found in the galaxy. But looking past the towering egos, Quee Lee waved at the only human male dressed in plain, practical clothes.

"I don't want this to be known," the man said. "Not outside our little circle, please."

The tone was the message: Perri was neither wealthy nor important, which made him unacceptable.

But Quee Lee laughed off the insult as well as the earnest pleas for silence. "Oh, I'm sure my husband's already heard about the Vermiculate," she said. "Perri knows the Ship as well as any captain does, and he knows everyone onboard who matters too." Then she winked, adding sweetly, "And he knows you, of course."

"Of course."

Yet for some reason Perri wasn't familiar with this rumor. He listened intently as Quee Lee related the mystery, and yes, he was familiar with the region called the Vermiculate. It was an intricate nest of dry caves, very few entrances leading to a million dead ends. But he never knew that some portion of those caverns had escaped mapping.

The other man rocked nervously side to side.

"Tell it again," Perri demanded, tugging at the fellow's elbow. "From the beginning, everything you know."

But there weren't many new details to share.

"I think I see what's happening," Perri said. "This is just an old rumor reborn. The first two passengers to come onboard the Great Ship started this story. Over drinks or in somebody's bed, they convinced themselves there had to be secret places and unmapped corners. It helped heighten the sense of adventure, don't you see? And every century or two, without fail, that same old legend puts on a new costume and takes its walk in public."

"But this is no rumor," the man said. "And I don't approve of legends. What I told you is the truth, I swear it."

"Yet you won't name your source," Perri pointed out.

"I cannot," the man said. "Frankly, I wish I hadn't said this much."

Unlike all of the well-moneyed souls in the room, Perri wore a boyish face and a pretty, almost juvenile smile. When it served his needs, he played the role of a smart child surrounded by very foolish adults. "It scares the hell out of you, doesn't it, sir? You hear about this puzzle, and you're the kind of creature who won't fall asleep unless every puzzle is solved, every question mark erased."

"And what is wrong with that?" asked the rumor's source.

"What's right about it?" Perri asked.

Quee Lee had expected that response, and when it came, she laughed softly.

The gentleman bristled, looking at her. "My dear, I thought you would be interested in this matter. But if you're going to tease me—"
"I didn't mean that," she began.

But the man had his excuse to turn and march away. No doubt he would avoid Quee Lee for the rest the day, and if genuinely angry, she wouldn't see him for the next fifty years.

"I shouldn't have laughed," Quee Lee admitted.

"And he shouldn't forgive you," said Perri. "But he will."

True enough. Fifty years of chilled silence was nothing among immortals. All but the most malicious slights were eventually pardoned, or at least discarded as memories not worth carrying any farther. "It's too bad that the story isn't true," she said. "I wish there was an unmapped cave hiding out there."

"Oh, but there is," said Perri.

Quee Lee worked through the possibilities. "You lied to me," she complained. "You'd already heard about the Vermiculate."

"I didn't, and I haven't."

"Then how can you say—?"

"Easily," he interrupted. "Your friend might be a wonderful soul. He might be charitable and sweet—"

"Hardly."

"But the man has never once shown me the barest trace of imagination. I seriously doubt that he could dream up such a tale, and I know he wouldn't repeat some wild fable, unless it came from a reasonable, responsible source."

"Such as?"

"One of the captains," said Perri.

"But why would an officer take any passenger into his or her confidence?" She hesitated, and laughed. "I suppose our friend is rather wealthy."

"Wealthier even than you," Perri agreed.

"And if he happened to be sleeping with a captain…"

"That's my cynical guess."

Nothing about her husband's mind was unknown. "You already know which captain it is. Don't you?"

"I have a robust notion," he said.

"Tell"

"Not here." Stroking her arm with a fond hand, he said, "My candidate has rank and connections, and she's desperately fond of money. And if you mix those qualifications with the fact that she, like that prickly man sulking over there, doesn't appreciate mysteries…"

"Is the Vermiculate unmapped?" she asked.

"If any place is." With long fingers, he drew elaborate shapes in the air between them. "Join all of those empty caves together and straightened them out, and you'll have a single tunnel long enough to reach from your Earth to Neptune and partway home again. So yes, it's easy to imagine that some AI expert could massage the old data, and one corner here and one little room there might have escaped notice and naming. And maybe after eighty thousand years of sleep, one of the original survey robots gets awakened and shoved down a hole, but because of its age, it malfunctions, which makes these events far more mysterious than they actually are."

On her own, Quee Lee had narrowed the list of suspect captains to three, perhaps four. With a quiet, conspiratorial voice, she asked, "Who's going to make our discreet inquires? You or me?"

"Neither of us," Perri said.

"Then you're not my husband," she teased. "The man I married would want to finish the mapping himself."

Perri shrugged and grinned. "We can make our own good guesses. Besides, if we get ourselves noticed, what began as a tiny anomaly mentioned on a pillow becomes much more: An area of potential embarrassment to the godly rulers of the Great Ship. Then our nameless captain will personally march into that empty corner, and keep me from having my little bit of fun."

"And me too," said Quee Lee.

"Or quite a lot of fun," Perri added, wrapping an arm around his wife's waist. "If you're in the mood for a little darkness, that is."

2

Yet nothing was simple about this simple-sounding quest. Finding holes inside the existing maps required months of detailed analysis by several experts paid well for their secrecy as well as their rare skills. Meanwhile, half a dozen of Perri's best friends heard about his newest interest, and by turning in past favors earned slots on the expedition roster. Then Quee Lee decided to invite two lady-friends who had been pressing for centuries to join her on a "safe adventure", which was what this would be. The Vermiculate might be imperfectly known, but there was no reason to expect danger. The dry caves were filled with the standard minimal atmosphere—nitrogen and oxygen and nothing else. There were no artificial suns or lights, and the only heat was thermal leakage from the nearby habitats and reactors. Even if the worst happened—if everyone lost their way and their supplies were exhausted—the result would be a bothersome thirst and gradual starvation. Bioceramic minds would sever all connections with their failing bodies, and when no choice was left, ten humans would sit down in the darkness and quietly turn into mummies, waiting for their absence to be noted and a rescue mission to track them down, waking them up and then teasing them endlessly.

But Perri didn't approve of losing his way. Meticulously recording their position on the new, modestly improved map, he earned gentle ribbing and then not-so-gentle ribbing from the others. Of course the Vermiculate was far too enormous to explore, even a thousand years. But their flex-skin car took them to areas of interest, and before stepping away from each base camp, he made his team memorize the local tunnels and chambers. Everyone had to stay with at least one companion, he insisted. He begged for the others to carry several kinds of torches as well as locator tools, noisemakers and laser flares. But eighteen days of that kind of mothering caused one of Quee Lee's friends to break every rule. She picked a random passageway and ran for parts unknown, at least to her. Carrying nothing but one small torch and a half-filled water bottle, she invested ten hours into solitary adventuring, and then discovered that she had no worthwhile ideas where she was in the universe.

Perri and Quee Lee found the explorer sitting in a dead-end chamber, shivering inside her heated clothes—shivering out of anxiety and the first hunger experienced in ages. But it was a lesson that took, and from that moment on, everyone's wandering was done with at least the minimal precautions.

Boredom was what began defeating the explorers.

The Vermiculate's walls were stone buttressed with low-grade hyperfiber. No human eye had ever seen these tunnels, but the novelty was minimal. Some places were beautiful in their shape and proportions, but it was an accidental beauty. The Ship's builders might have had a purpose for each twist and turn, every sudden room and the little tubes that gave access to the next portion of the maze. But living eyes found nothing strange or interesting, and after two months of wandering, the novice adventurers were losing their interest.

One by one, the expedition shrank.

First to leave was the woman who hadn't gotten lost. Then Perri's friends complained about these dreary circumstances, each demanding a ride to the nearest exit point. The only ones left were identical twin brothers and that dear old friend of Quee Lee who had gotten lost and scared, and who since then, to the surprise of everyone, had discovered a genuine fondness for spelunking.

Or maybe it was the brothers who held her interest. One night, when the camp lights were dropping down to a nightly glow, Quee Lee spotted the twins slipping into her friend's little shelter—entering her home from opposite ends, and neither appearing again until morning.

Another month of roving brought few highlights. Half a dozen tunnels showed evidence of foot-traffic over the last few thousand years. The desiccated slime trail of a Snail-As-God was a modest surprise. Inside one cave was the broken scale from a harum-scarum shin, and a few meters farther along, a liter of petrified blood left behind by a human male. And then came that momentous afternoon when they discovered a graveyard of surveying robots—ten thousand machines that had pulled themselves into neat, officious piles before dropping into an eternal diagnostic sleep.

Two days later, Perri brought his team to the bottom of a deep, deep chimney. Mathematical wizards had labeled that location as "mildly interesting". The Vermiculate displayed patterns, sometimes predictable and occasionally repeatable, and according to sophisticated calculations, that very narrow hole should lead to a large "somewhere else". But the unknown refused to expose itself with a glance. Two little tunnels waited at the bottom of the chimney, yet every sonic pulse and cursory examination showed that they were long and exceptionally ordinary repositories of the same-old-shit.

The five humans broke into two groups.

Perri and Quee Lee slipped into the shorter tunnel. As always, they brought tracking equipment as well as the sniffers constantly searching for organic traces left by past visitors, and they carried heated clothes and survival rations and a variety of lights to offer feeble glows or sun-blazing fires. But the most effective sensor came in pairs, and it was the bluish-yellow eyes that noticed the sudden hole in the floor.

"Stop," said Perri.

Quee Lee paused, one gloved hand dropping, fingertips reaching to within a hair's width of the emptiness.

"Look," he advised.

"I see it," she said. But she didn't know what she saw. After days and weeks of staring at structural hyperfiber, she recognized that here was something different. The area surrounding the hole was peculiar. Holding a variable beam to the floor, she slipped through a series of settings. Hyperfiber was the strongest baryonic substance known—the bones of the Ship and the basis of every starfaring civilization—yet she had never seen light flickering against hyperfiber quite like this. It was as if the floor could feel their weight, and the photons were betraying the floor's tiny vibrations.

"Do you know what this is?" Perri asked.

"Do you?"

"The source," he said. "The source of our rumor."

She shone a second light up and down the tunnel. There was no sign of disabled robots or the detritus left by mapping crews. But the captains could have cleaned up their trash, since captains liked to keep their secrets secret, particularly when it came to curious passengers.

"This hole is fresh," Perri said. And when Quee Lee reached toward the edge, he said, "Don't. Unless you want to cut off a finger or two."

The floor was pure hyperfiber—a skin only a few atoms thick at its thickest. Because the stuff was so very thin, the light flickered. What they were trusting with their combined weight was close to nothing, like worn paint stretched across empty air, and the edge of the hole was keener than the most deadly sword.

"But a robot should have noticed," she guessed. "If we can see that the floor here is different…"

"Yeah, I've given that some thought too," said Perri. "We're about as deep into the Vermiculate as you can go, or so we thought. A few surveyors probably started working above us, and when they were overwhelmed, they stopped and ate the rock and replicated themselves."

"Imperfect copies," she said.

"Flawed but not badly, and nobody noticed." He shrugged, enjoying the game without taking anything too seriously. "Whatever the reason, the machine that first crawled into this tunnel wasn't paying close attention. It didn't notice what should have been obvious, and that's why the Ship's map was incomplete."

"Just like the rumor says," Quee Lee agreed. "Except there isn't much mystery, because if the captains found something remarkable—"

"We wouldn't get within ten kilometers," Perri agreed.

With every tool, including her warm brown eyes, Quee Lee examined the floor and the hole and the blackness below.

Perri did the same.

And then for the first time in perhaps a hundred years, one of them managed to surprise the other.

It wasn't the adventurous spouse who spoke first.

Pointing down, Quee Lee said, "That hole's just wide enough for me."

"If we string tethers to the ceiling," Perri mentioned. "And if there's another floor worth standing on below us."

"What about our friends?"

"I'll go gather them up," he began.

"No." Then for the second time, she surprised her husband. "We'll leave a note behind. We can tell them to follow, if they want."

Perri smiled at the ancient creature.

"This is our adventure," she concluded. "Yours, and mine."

3

What lay below was the same as everything above. The sole difference was that no public map showed these particular cavities and chimneys, and the long tunnels and little side vents always led to a wealth of new places devoid of names. Perri's navigational kit claimed that they had wandered twelve kilometers before beginning their hunt for a campsite. A series of electronic breadcrumbs led back to the original hole and their left-behind note, and speaking through the crumbs, Quee Lee discovered that her lady-friend and the twins hadn't bothered to look for them. She mentioned why that might be, and the two enjoyed a lewd laugh. Then following one promising passageway around its final bend, they entered the largest room they had seen in weeks.

The floor of the room was an undulating surface, like water stirred by deep currents. They selected a spacious bowl of cool gray hyperfiber, and with the camp light blazing beside them, they made love. Then they ate and drank their fill, and at a point with no obvious significance, Perri strolled over to his pack and bent down, intending to snatch some tiny item from one of the countless pockets.

That was the moment when every light went out.

Quee Lee was sitting on her memory-chair, immersed in sudden darkness. Her first instinct was to believe that she was to blame. Their camp light was in front of her. Had she given it some misleading command? But their other torches were extinguished, the night total, or perhaps for some peculiar reason her eyes had suddenly decided to go completely blind.

Then from a distance, with a moderately concerned voice, her husband asked, "Darling? Are you there?"

"I am." Perri was blind too, or every one of their lights had failed. Either way, something unlikely had just occurred. "What do you think?" she asked.

"That it's ridiculously dark in here," said Perri.

Perfectly, relentlessly black.

"Do you feel all right?" he asked.

"I feel fine," she said.

"I do too." He was disappointed, as if some little ache might help answer their questions. "Except for being worried, I suppose."

Perri's foot kicked the pack.

"Darling?"

"I'm hunting for the echo-catchers."

"Good."

Then he said, "Found one."

She listened for the high squeak of sonar.

But he said, "Nope. Not working either."

She rubbed her eyes.

"Sing to me," he said. "I'll follow your voice."

Softly, Quee Lee sang one of the first tunes that she had ever learned—a nursery rhyme too old to have an author, its beguiling lyrics about rowing and time wrapped around a long dead language.

Moments later, she heard Perri's soft steps and one deep breath as he settled on the ground directly to her right.

She stopped singing.

Then Perri called from off to her left, from some distance, telling her, "Don't quit singing now. I'm still trying to find you, darling."

A long moment brought nothing. The darkness remained silent and unknowable. And then from her right, from a place quite close, a voice that she did not recognize softly insisted, "Yes, please. Sing, please. I rather enjoy that wonderful little tune of yours."

4

Quee Lee began to jump up.

"No, no," the voice implored. "Remain seated, my dear. There is absolutely no reason to surrender your comfort."

She settled slowly, warily.

Perri called her name.

Clearing her throat, Quee Lee managed to say, "I'm here. Here."

"Are you all right?"

"Yes."

"But I thought I heard–"

"Yes."

"Is somebody with you?"

Inside the same moment, two voices said, "Yes."

Then the new voice continued. "I was hoping that your wife would sing a little more," it remarked. "But I suppose I have spoiled the mood, which is my fault. Please, Perri, will you join us? Sit beside Quee Lee, and I promise: Neither of you will come to any harm. A little conversation, a little taste of companionship…that's all I wish for now…"

Again, with urgency, Perri asked, "Are you all right?"

How could Quee Lee answer that question? "I'm fine, yes." Except she was startled, and for many rational reasons, she was scared, and with the darkness pressing down, she was feeling a thrilling lack of control.

Her husband's footsteps seemed louder than before. In the perfect blackness, he stepped by memory, and then perhaps sensing her presence, he stopped beside her and reached out with one hand, dry warm fingertips knowing just where her face would be waiting.

She clung to his hand with both of hers.

"Sit, please," the stranger insisted. "Unless you absolutely must stand."

Perri settled on one edge of her soft chair. His hand didn't leave her grip, and he patted that knot of fingers with his free hand. As well as she knew her own bones, Quee Lee knew his. And she leaned into that strong body, glad for his presence and confident that he was glad for hers.

"Who are you?" asked Perri.

Silence answered him.

"Did you disable our lights?" he asked.

Nothing.

533

"You must have," Perri decided. "And my infrared corneas and nexus-links too, I realized."

"All temporary measures," the stranger said.

"Why?"

Silence.

"Who are you?" asked Quee Lee asked. "And what's your name?"

Something here was funny. The laughter sounded genuine, weightless and smooth, gradually falling away into an amused silence. Then what might or might not have been a deep breath preceded the odd statement, "As I rule, I don't believe in names."

"No?" Quee asked.

"As a rule," the voice repeated.

Perri asked, "What species are you?"

"And I will warn you," the voice added. "I don't gladly embrace the concept of species either."

The lovers sat as close as possible, speaking to each other with the pressure of their hands.

Finally, Quee Lee took it upon herself to say, "We're human, if that matters to you."

There was no response.

"Do you know our species?" she asked.

And then Perri guessed, "You're a Vapor-track. Nocturnal to the point where they can't endure even the weakest light—"

"Yes, I know humans," the stranger responded. "And I know Vapor-tracks too. But I am neither. And I am not nocturnal, nor diurnal. The time of day and the strength of the ambient light are absolutely no concern to me."

"But why are you down here?" Quee Lee asked.

Their companion gave no response.

"This is a remote corner of the Ship," Perri said. "Why would any sentient organism seek out this place?"

"Why do you?" was the response.

"Curiosity," Perri confessed. "Is that your motivation?"

"Not in the least."

The voice was more male than female, and it sounded nearly as human as they did. But those qualities could be artifacts of any good translator. It occurred to Quee Lee that layers of deception were at play, and what they heard had no bearing at all on what, if anything, was beside them.

"I could imagine that I am a substantial puzzle for the two of you," the voice allowed.

The humans responded with their own silence.

"Fair enough," their companion said. "Tell me: Where were each of you born?"

"On the Great Ship," Perri volunteered.

"I come from the Earth," Quee Lee offered.

"Names," the stranger responded. "I ask, and you instantly offer me names."

"What else could we say?" asked Quee Lee.

"Nothing. For you, there are no other polite options. But as a rule, I prefer places that don't wear names. Cubbyholes and solar systems that have remained outside the catalogs, indifferent to whichever label that a passerby might try to hang on its slick invisible flesh."

Quee Lee listened to her husband's quick, interested breathing.

After reflection, Perri said, "And that's why you're here. This is one place inside the Great Ship that has gone unnoticed, until now."

"Perhaps that is my reason," the voice allowed.

"Is there a better answer?" Perri asked.

Silence.

"You have no name," Quee Lee pressed.

The silence continued, and then suddenly, an explanation was offered. "I don't wear any name worth repeating. But I do have an identity. A self. With my own history and limitations as well as a wealth of possibilities, most of which will never come to pass."

They waited.

The voice continued. "What I happen to be is a government official, one of the harmless and noble followers of rules. But when necessary, I can become a brazen, fearless warrior. Except when my best choice is to be a coward, in which case I can flee any threat with determination and remarkable skill. Yet in most circumstances, I am just an official: The loyal servant to any exceptionally fine cause."

"Which cause?" both humans asked.

"In service to the galactic union," the entity replied. "That is my defining role…a role which I have played successfully for the last three hundred and seven million years, by your arbitrary and self-centered count."

Human hands squeezed, relaxed.

Quee Lee took it upon herself to confess, "I'm sorry. But we don't entirely believe you."

"You claim you were born on the Earth. Is that true, my dear?"

She hesitated.

"'Earth.' Your home planet carries a simple utterance. Am I right?"

She said, "Yes."

"I happen to know your small world. But when I made my visit, the stars were completely unaware of that self-given name."

"And what do you know about the Earth?" Perri asked.

"Actually, quite a lot," their companion promised. Then once again, it fell into a long, long silence.

5

Separately, Quee Lee and Perri had come to identical conclusions: The voice was rhythmic and deep, not just easy to listen to but impossible to ignore. Every word was delivered with clarity, like the voice of a highly trained actor. But woven through that perfection were hints of breathing and little clicks of tongues or lips, and once in a great while, a nebulous sound that would leak from the mouth or nostrils…or some other orifice hiding in the darkness. Whatever was speaking to them was slightly taller than their ears, and their best guess was that the creature was sitting on a lump of hyperfiber less than three meters from them. There was mass behind the voice. Sometimes a limb moved, or maybe the body itself. Perhaps they heard the creak of its carapace or the complaining of stiff leathery clothes, or maybe a tendril was twisting back against itself. Unless there was no sound except what the two humans imagined they could hear out in the unfathomable blackness.

As far as they could determine, their nameless companion was alone. There wasn't any other presence, or a whisper of a second voice. Somehow the creature had slipped into their camp, perhaps even before the lights died, and neither one of them had perceived anything out of the ordinary.

Or maybe there was nothing but the voice.

Sound. Or a set of elaborate sounds, contrived for effect and existing only as so much noise produced by nothing but the unlit air or the fierce motions of individual atoms.

Somebody could be playing an elaborate joke on the two of them. Perri had many clever friends. A few of them might have worked together, going to the trouble to bring him and Quee Lee into this empty hole, snatching them up in some game that would continue until the fun was exhausted and the lights returned. Quee Lee could envision just that kind of trick: One moment, a mysterious voice. And then just as suddenly, a thousand good friends would be standing around them, congratulating the married pair for some minor anniversary.

"Is this a special occasion?" Quee Lee asked herself.

That route seemed lucrative. She smiled, and the nervousness in her body began to drain away. How many months and years of work had gone into this silly joke? But she had seen through all of the cleverness, and she even considered a preemptive shout and laugh, perhaps throwing out the names of the likely conspirators.

Meanwhile the creature continued to explain what might not be real. "My preferred method of travel is to move alone, and always by the most invisible means. This is standard behavior for officials in my station. We will finish one task in some portion of the Union, and that success brings another task to bear. Since news travels slowly across the galaxy, entities like ourselves are granted considerable freedom of action. No other organization is confident enough to tolerate such power in their agents."

"What kind of tasks?" Perri asked.

"Would you like an example?"

"Please."

"I am thinking of a warehouse that I had built and stocked—a hidden warehouse in an undisclosed location. And in the very next moment, I was dispatched to my next critical mission."

"A warehouse," said Perri.

"Not a romantic word, I grant you. But it was, and is, a vast, invisible facility full of rare and valuable items. I haven never returned to the site, but it most likely remains locked and unseen today. Idle but always at the ready. Waiting for that critical, well-imagined age when its contents help with some great, good effort. But that is the Union's way: We have an elaborate structure, robust and overlapping, enduring and invincibly patient; which is only natural, since we are the oldest, most powerful political entity within this galaxy."

"The Union," Perri said dubiously.

"Yes."

"I thought you didn't approve of names."

"I offer it because you expect some kind of label. But like any contrivance, 'the Union' doesn't truly fit what is real." A smug, superior tone had taken hold, but it was difficult for the audience to take offense. After all, this was just a voice in the night, and who could say what was true and what was sane?

"Simply stated, my Union is a collection of entities and beliefs, memes and advanced tools, that have been joined together in a common cause. And what you call the Milky Way happens to be our most important possession—the central state inside a vast, ancient empire."

"No," Perri said. "No."

Silence.

Quee Lee felt her husband's tension. Leaning forward, she told their companion, "There are no empires."

A long black silence held sway, and then came a sound not unlike the creak of a joint needing oil.

"Many, many species have tried to build empires," she continued, naming a few candidates to prove her knowledge of the subject. "The galaxy's first five sentient races accomplished the most, but they didn't do much. The galaxy is enormous. Its planets are too diverse and far too numerous to be ruled by a thousand governments, and star travel has always been a slow, dangerous business. When one species rises, it gains control only a very limited region. Measure the history of empires against the life stories of suns and worlds, and even the most enduring régime is a temporary and tiny."

She concluded by saying, "No one authority has ever controlled any substantial portion of the galaxy."

"I applaud that generous sense of doubt," said the stranger. "May I ask, my dear? What are you?"

"What do you mean?"

"By blood, I think you must be Chinese. Am I right?"

"Mostly, yes," she said.

"And the city of your birth?"

"Hong Kong," she whispered.

"Hong Kong, yes. A place I know, yes. Of course you understand that your China was a great empire, and more than once. And as I recall from my studies of long-ago Earth, there was a period—a brief but not unimportant time—when the port of Hong Kong belonged to the greatest empire ever to exist on your little world. A minor green island sitting in a cold distant sea called itself Great Britain, and with its steam-driven fleets, it somehow managed to hang its flag above a fat fraction of the world's population."

"I know about Britain," she said.

"Now tell me this," their companion continued. "An old rickshaw driver plies his trade on the narrow Hong Kong streets. Does that lowly man care who happens to serve as governor of his home city? Does it matter to him if the fellow on top happens to have yellow hair, or is a Mongol born on the plains of Asia, or even a Han Chinese who is a third-cousin to him?"

"No," she said. "He probably doesn't think much about those matters."

"And what about the Hindu peasant who struggles to feed himself and his family from a patch of land downstream from Everest…the ruler of a farm that has never even once fallen under the indifferent gaze of the pale Northern man who works inside a distant government building? Does that farmer concern himself with the man who signs a long list of decrees and then dies quietly of malaria? And does he care at all about the gentleman who comes to replace that dead civil servant…another Northern man who bravely signs more unread decrees before he dies of cholera?"

Quee Lee said nothing.

"Consider the Mayan lady nursing her daughter in Belize, or the Maori cattle herder in Kenya who happens to be the tall strong lord to his herd. Do they learn the English language? Can they even recognize their rulers' alphabet? And then there squats the Aboriginal hunter sucking the precious juice out of an emu egg. Is he even aware that fleets of enormous coal-fired ships are landing and then leaving from his coast each and every day?

"Each of these souls is busy, embroiled in rich and complex, if painfully brief lives. Within the British Empire, hundreds of millions of citizens go about their daily adventures. The flavor of each existence is nearly changeless. Taxes and small blessings come from on-high, but these trappings accomplish little, regardless which power happens to be flying the flags. A peasant's story is usually the same as his forefathers' stories, and if the peasant's children survive, they will inherit that same stubborn, almost ageless narrative."

Neither human spoke.

"Do these little people ever think of that distant green island?"

"I wouldn't be surprised if they didn't," Quee Lee allowed.

"But if they do think of Britain," the stranger began.

"What then?" Perri prompted.

"Would they love the Empire for its justice, order, and the rare peace that it brings to the human world?"

Neither of them responded.

"Of course they do not. What you do not know, you cannot love or despise. This is true for every life that has walked two moments of time. So long as the lives of these peasants remain small and steady, hating the British is not an option."

The voice paused, and what might have been a deep breath could be heard. "Make no mistake—I am not claiming that these are unsophisticated souls. They are far from simple, in fact. But their lives are confined. By necessity, the obvious and immediate are what matter to them. And the colors and shape of today's flag could not have less meaning."

"Suppose we agree," said Perri. "We accept your premise: For humans, empires tended to be big, distant machines."

"As it is for most species," was the reply.

In the dark, Quee Lee and her husband nodded.

"But I don't agree with that word 'big'," the stranger continued. "I believe that even the greatest empire, at the height of its powers, remains vanishingly small. To the brink of invisible, even."

"I don't understand," said Quee Lee.

"Let me remind you of this: Several million whales swam in your world's little ocean. They were great beasts possessing language and old cultures. But did even one species of cetaceans bow to the British flag? And what about the tiger eating venison on the Punjab? Did he dream of the homely human queen? And what role did the ants and beetles, termites and butterflies play in the world? They did nothing for Britannia, I would argue…and Britannia had no place in their relentless little minds."

Perri tried to laugh.

Quee Lee could think of nothing useful to say.

"The trouble," the voice began. Then it paused, perhaps reconsidering its choice of words. "Your mistake," it continued, "is both inevitable and comforting, and it is very difficult to escape. What you assume is that the names in history are important. Because you are smart, educated minds, you have taught yourselves much about your own past. But even the most famous name is lost among the trillions of nameless souls. And every empire that you think of when the subject arises…every political entity, no matter how impermanent and trivial…was visible only because it wasted its limited energies making certain that its name would outlive both its accomplishments and its crimes."

"Maybe so," Quee Lee allowed.

"Names," the voice repeated. "The worlds you know wear that unifying trait. The name brings with it a sense of purpose and a handle for its recorded history. Attached to one or a thousand words waits some center of trade, a nucleus of science, and you mistakenly believe that the most famous names mark the hubs of your great cosmopolitan galaxy."

Perri squeezed his wife's hand, fighting the temptation to speak.

"But the bulk of the galaxy…its asteroids and dust motes, sunless bodies and dark corners without number…those are the features that truly matter."

"Matter to whom?" Quee Lee asked.

"To the weaver ants and lowly fish, of course. The beetles and singing whales, and our rickshaw driver who knows the twisting streets of Hong Kong better than any Chinese emperor or British civil servant. Nameless citizens are those with substance, my dear." Something creaked, as if their companion shifted its weight, and the voice drifted slightly to one side. "I will confess that my empire is like all the others, only more so. The Union that I love and that I have served selflessly for eons is vast and ancient. But where England made maps and gave every corner its own label, my Union has wisely built itself upon places unknown."

Husband and wife contemplated that peculiar boast.

Then Quee Lee recalled an earlier thread. "You have visited the Earth, you claimed."

"I did once, yes."

"Was this before or after your invisible warehouse?"

"Afterwards, as it happens. Not long after."

"You mentioned receiving a new mission," Perri coaxed.

"Which leads indirectly to an interesting story." The next sound was soft, contented. "My orders arrived by a usual route. Whispered and deeply coded, the instructions from my superiors that were designed to resemble nothing but a smeared flicker of light thrown out from a distant laser array." The words were strung together with what felt like a grin. "Alone, I left my previous post. Alone, I rode inside a tiny vehicle meant to resemble a shard of old comet, using a simple ion motor to boost my velocity to where my voyage took slightly less than forty centuries—"

"By our arbitrary and self-centered count," said Perri.

"Which is not such a very long time." Those words were ordinary and matter-of-fact. Yet somehow the sound of them—their clarity and decidedly slow pace—conveyed long reaches of time and unbounded patience. "I traveled until I came to a nameless world. There was one ocean and several continents. The forests were green, the skies blue with white watery clouds. To fulfill the demands of my new mission, I selected an island not far from the world's largest continent: A young volcanic island where the local inhabitants built boats driven by oars and square sails, and they put up houses of wood and stone and planted half-wild crops in the fertile black soil. And their moments of free time were filled with the heartfelt worship of their moon and sun—the two bodies that ruled a sky that they would never truly understand."

"Was this was the Earth?" asked Quee Lee.

There was a pause, and inside the darkness, motion.

And then the voice told them, "When these particular events occurred, my dear, there was no planet yet called 'the Earth'."

Quee Lee wrapped both hands around her husband's arm.

"Remember this," the voice continued. "The Union is the only power of consequence. And the Union holds its interest only in those dark realms that appear on no worthwhile map."

6

"A king happened to rule that warm, sun-washed island. He was simple and rather old, and I was tempted to kill him in some grand public fashion before taking his throne for myself. Yet my study of his species and its superstitions showed me a less bloody avenue. The king's youngest wife was pregnant, but the child would be stillborn. It was a simple matter to replace that failed infant and then bury what was Me inside healthy native flesh. Once born, I proved to the kingdom that their new prince was special. I was a lanky boy, physically beautiful, endowed with an unnatural strength and the gentle grace of wild birds. I didn't merely walk at an early age, I danced. And with a bold musical voice, I spoke endlessly on every possible subject, people fighting to kneel close to me, desperate to hear whatever marvel I offered next.

"The wise old women of my kingdom decided that I must be a god's child as much as a man's. Like a god's child, I predicted the weather and the little quakes that often rattled the island. I boasted that I could see far into the skies and over the horizon, and to prove my brave words, I promised that a boat full of strangers would soon drift past our island.

"My prediction was made in the morning, and by evening, I was proved right. The lost trireme was filled with traders or pirates. On a world such as that, what is the difference between those two professions? Whatever their intentions, my people were waiting for them, and after suitable introductions, I ordered the strangers murdered and their possessions divided equally among the general populace."

The voice paused.

In the dark, Quee Lee leaned hard against her husband.

And the story continued. "I was almost grown when that little old king stood before his people and named his heir. Two of my brothers were insulted, but I had anticipated their clumsy attempts at revenge. In a duel with bronze swords, I removed the head of the more popular son. Then I turned my back, allowing my second brother to run his spear through my chest—a moment used to prove that I was, as my people had always suspected, immortal.

"With my two hands, I yanked the spear from my heart.

"In anguish, my foe flung himself off one of our island's high cliffs.

"'Someday I will follow my brothers into the Afterlife,' I promised the citizens. 'But for the rest of your days, I will remain with you, and together we shall do the work of the gods.'

543

"And that was the moment, at long last, when the heart of my mission finally began."

Their companion paused.

"Are you going to explain your mission?" Perri asked.

"Hints and teases. I will share exactly what is necessary to explain myself, or at least I will give you the illusion of insights, placing you where your imaginations can fill in the unnamed reaches."

"About these natives," Quee Lee began. "Your people...what did they look like?"

Quietly and perhaps with a touch of affection, the voice explained, "They were bipedal, as you are. And they had your general height and mass, hands and glands. Like you, they presented hairless flesh to the world, except upon their faces and scalps and in their private corners. As a rule, most were dirty and drab, and on that particular island, their narrow culture reached back only a few generations. But their species had potential. Following ordinary pathways, natural selection had given them graceful fingers and an evolving language, busy minds and a compelling sense of tribe. In those following years, I showed my people how to increase the yields and quality of their crops. I taught them how to purify their water, how to carve and lift gigantic stones, and I helped them build superior ships that could chase the fat fish and slow leviathans that could never hide from my godly eyes. Then in the shadow of their smoldering volcano, I laid out a spacious palace surrounded by a solid homes and wide avenues, and for three generations, my devoted followers built the finest city their species had ever known."

Once again, the voice ceased. But the silence was neither empty nor unimportant, accenting a sense of time crossed with clear purpose. Then a smooth laugh came, and their companion remarked, "If the two of you were dropped into similar circumstances, you would accomplish most if not all of my tricks. You are borderline immortals. Spears through your hearts would be nuisances at day's end. Armed with the knowledge common to your happy lives, you could visit some nameless world and convince its residents that you were divine, and in the next breath, you could call for whatever riches and little pleasures that your worshippers might scratch together for you.

"But what pleasures me is serving the Union.

"What I wanted...what my orders demanded from this one place, inside this single moment...was the construction of a significant machine, a device that would demand the full focus of a half-born civilization..."

"What machine?" asked Perri.

"If it proves important to know that, then I will tell you."

But Perri couldn't accept that evasive answer. "How many people lived in your city? Five thousand? Fifty thousand? I don't know what you were building, granted. But you're implying advanced technologies, and I'd have to guess that you'd need a lot more hands and minds than you would ever find on a tiny island in the middle of the sea…"

The first answer was prolonged silence.

Then the sharp creak of a limb or cold leather could be heard, and with quiet fury, the entity said, "You have listened carefully enough, sir. Pay strict attention to everything that I tell you."

"Remind me what you said," Perri said.

Another silence ended with what might have been a sigh. "I sat on my throne for seventy summers and several months," said the voice. "Then one day, I abruptly announced that my city was failing me. With a wave of my fist, I told my followers that they were not truly devoted, and they were not sufficiently thankful for my wise counsel, and I was contemplating the complete obliteration of their island-nation.

"With the next sunrise, the great volcano erupted. The rich rocky earth split wide. Ash was coughed into the blackened sky, and lava flowed into the boiling sea, and boulders as big as homes were dropped onto the cowering, inadequate heads around me. Then I pretended a sudden change of mind. I showed pity, even empathy. On the following day, after the dead were buried and the damage assessed, I dressed in a feathered robe and walked to the summit where I told the mountain to sleep again—which it would have done on its own, since the eruption had run its course. But a single moment of theatre erased the last shreds of doubt. Again, I had convinced my followers that I was supreme. You could not hear one muttered complaint about me, or doubts about my powers, or the slightest question concerning each of my past decisions.

"That seamless devotion was necessary.

"You see, the eruption was not a random event. And I didn't make the mountain tremble and belch just to scare the local souls.

"Even as I sat on my throne, I had been working. My assignment demanded the kinds of energy generated by top-grade fusion reactor. But reactors produce signatures visible at a great distance. Neutrinos are difficult to shield, and I didn't want prying eyes to notice my industrial plant. So instead of a reactor, I employed the lake of magma directly beneath our feet, creating an inefficient but enormous geothermal plant. When that plant awoke—when the first seawater poured down the pipes and into the reaction vessels—my island was shoved upwards like a balloon inflating. Watchful eyes noticed that every tide pool was suddenly baking in the sun. Our island was significantly taller, and a thousand hot springs flowed out of the high crevices, and the black ground was itself warm to the touch.

"On that good day, I ordered every woman of breeding age to come to the palace, to arrive with the evening bell, and I welcomed each of them individually, giving them a feast and plenty to drink, as well as jewelry and robes finer than anything they had known. Then to this nervous, worshipful gathering, I announced that each of them was carrying a child now.

"I promised my wives untroubled pregnancies and healthy, superior babies.

"Both promises came true.

"And you are correct, Perri. Sir. Fifty thousand followers would never have been enough. No natural species can bring the mental capacity demanded by this kind of delicate, highly technical work. So I enlarged the natives' craniums and restructured their neural networks, flinging them across fifty thousand generations of natural selection. Then I served as the children's only teacher. I taught them what they needed to know about the high sciences, and I made them experts in engineering, all while carefully preparing my kingdom for the next change."

Perri said, "Wait."

In the dark, Quee Lee felt her husband's body shifting. She recognized his excitement and interest, his emotions mirroring her own.

Again, he said, "Wait."

"Yes?"

"I've been thinking about what you've told us."

"Good."

"Where your logic leads..."

Silence.

"If you were willing to rewrite the biology of one species," Perri said, "you could just as well reshape others too."

"Ants?" Quee Lee blurted. "Were you a god to the island's ants?"

"Ants have no need for gods," the voice corrected. "They demand nothing but a queen blessed with spectacular fertility. But you've seen my logic, yes. You are paying attention. But then again, I knew that the two of you would prove a worthy audience."

Some small object clattered against hyperfiber—a clear, almost bell-like sound expanding and diminishing inside the gigantic room.

The voice returned. "By the time my first grandchildren were born, the ocean around my island was lit from below. Which was only reasonable, since the city above was just one portion of a much greater community—a nation numbering in the billions. My people supplied the genius, but to serve them, I had built a multitude of obedient minds trained for narrow, exceptionally difficult tasks. A full century of careful preparation had made me ready to begin the construction of a single mechanical wonder.

"Which was the moment, I should add, when all of my many troubles began…"

7

In the smothering blackness, Quee Lee held her husband by an arm, by his waist, and then she twisted her body in a particular way, inviting a groping hand, not caring in the least that the nameless entity might be able to perceive their timeless, much-cherished intimacies.

Perri started to ask the obvious question: "What troubles?"

But the voice interrupted. Louder than before, it said, "Human beings are an extraordinarily fortunate species. Wouldn't you agree?"

"I feel lucky," Quee Lee said.

But Perri guessed, "You're talking about something specific. Aren't you?"

"Tell me your opinion," the voice said. "Is this vessel a true blessing for you and yours?"

"You mean the Great Ship," she said.

"I mean the machine that surrounds us," it said. "The name itself has zero significance."

Perri laughed. "Well, I know at least a thousand other species that could have found it first. They were more powerful, more numerous, and far older than we are. All of them should have grabbed it up before we ever knew it existed."

"It is a magical machine," Quee Lee offered.

The entity made a few soft, agreeable noises. "Our galaxy has stubbornly refused to be dominated by any single species. But humans stumbled across this prize, claimed it first, and have held on to it since. A single possession has lifted the human animal into an exceptionally rare position. Your best captains have no choice but thank the stars and Providence for this glorious honor. Today, your artisans and scientists are free to drink in the wisdom of the galaxy. Your wealthiest citizens can make this long journey in safety, sharing their air with the royalty of a hundred thousand worlds. But I think your greatest success rises from the hungriest, bravest souls among you.

"Each year, on average, seventeen-and-a-third colonial vessels push away from the your ports. How many of your willing cousins are dropped to the surface of wild worlds and lucrative asteroids? How many homes and shops are being erected, new societies sprouting up in your wake? Now multiply those impressive numbers by the hundreds of thousands of years that you plan to invest in this circumnavigation of the galaxy. The totals are staggering. No society or species or even any compilation of cooperative souls has enjoyed the human advantage, and there is no reason to believe it will happen again.

"And consider this: How many species buy your berths? Thousands arrive each year, and in trade for a safe journey, they surrender every local map, cultural experiences and open-ended promises of help. That's why each of your new colonies has a respectable, enviable chance of survival. And that's why your species is hugging a small but respectable probability of dominating the richest portions of the galaxy.

"So now I ask you: When will this galaxy of ours become known everywhere and to every species as 'the Milky Way'?

"In other words, when will this wilderness become your possession?"

Considering that possibility, the humans couldn't help but smile.

But then Quee Lee sighed and shook her head, saying, "Never. Is that the answer you want?"

The voice turned quiet again, nearly whispering as it explained, "That kind of success shall never happen. No, never. Even in your blessed circumstances, this little whirlpool of creation remains too vast and far too complex for any species to dominate. Your makeshift empire is doomed at its birth. The best result that you might achieve—and even this is an unlikely future—is for this machine to complete its full circuit of the galaxy without being stolen from you, and for you to leave scattered in your wake twenty million human worlds. But what are twenty million names against those trillions of rocks big enough to be called planets? I promise that no matter its blessings, each one of your colonies will struggle. It is inevitable. Your species is relatively late on the scene. Easy rich worlds are scarce and typically walked by someone else. By the minute, your galaxy grows older. And with every breath, the sky grows more crowded. New species are evolving, and thinking machines are designing their next generations, and almost everything that lives strives hard to live forever, or nearly so."

The smiles had vanished.

For a long moment, neither human spoke.

Then Quee Lee suggested, "Maybe our empire should stop naming our worlds. If we emulated your Union…if human beings decided to rule the dark and empty and the unmapped–"

"No," the voice interrupted.

Then with a palpable scorn, it added, "I will share with you one common principle known by every true empire. Whether you are British or Mongolian, Roman or American: You may never, ever allow a competing empire to sprout within your sacred borders.

"My Union stands alone.

"Never forget that.

"And when the inevitable future arrives…when the final star burns out and the universe pulls itself into a great empty cold…my Union will persist, and it will thrive, living happily on this galaxy's black bones: A force as near to Always as that word shall ever allow."

8

The humans felt chastened and a little angry, powerless to respond yet nonetheless intrigued by the stark implications. They held one another in ways that spoke—the touch of fingers, the pressure of a fat-clad knee, and the shared tastes of expelled air carrying odors that could only come from Perri, and only come from Quee Lee.

The voice returned, quietly mentioning, "My mission to the blue world had begun so easily, with much promise. Yet now its nature changed. In relatively quick succession, three problems emerged, each capable of threatening the project and my sterling reputation."

A thoughtful pause ended with a brief, disgusted sound.

"Remember the pirates mentioned before? The seafarers whom I let my people kill? They had floated out from the main continent, and with another hundred years of experience, their descendants were eager to return. That rocky green wilderness still lay over the horizon, but now it was speckled with dirty cities and fledging nations. Unlike my little island, those far places had always enjoyed culture and a deep history, every corner of their rich landscape adorned with some important little name.

"Bronze-and-brick technology was at work. Kings and educated minds were beginning to piece together the first, most obvious meanings of the universe. The largest triremes could wander far from land, and their captains knew how to navigate by the stars and moon. That those captains would try to visit my island was inevitable, which is why I took precautions. The leviathans patrolling my bright waters were instructed to scare off every explorer, and should fear not work, they were entitled to crush the wooden hulls and drown those stubborn crews.

"A few ships were sunk off our coast.

"The occasional corpse washed up on shore, swollen by rot and chewed upon by curious or vengeful mouths.

"One of the dead had been a scientist and scholar, and even as he drowned, he managed to grab hold of his life's work—a long roll of skin covered with dense writing and delicate sketches.

"The body was looted, and the book eventually found its way into the appreciative hands of one of my grandchildren.

"The island's original natives could never have understood the intense black scribbling, but my grandchild was more than intelligent and highly creative, he was also curious and unabashedly loyal to me. Using code-breaking algorithms, he taught himself the dead man's language. In his spare moments, he managed to translate the text in full. His purpose, it seems, was to make me proud of his genius. He was certainly thrilled of his own accomplishment, which was why he shared what he had learned with close friends and lovers. Then he walked to the palace and kneeled before my throne, presenting both the artifact and his translation for my honest appraisal.

"'They speak of us,' the young man reported. 'The rest of our world believes we are gods or the angels of gods or we have descended from the stars. They have convinced themselves that if they defeat the sea monsters and outsmart the currents, they can row themselves into our harbor and stand among us, and they will be heroes in the gods' eyes. And for their extraordinary bravery, we will award them with the secrets of All…'"

A brief pause.

"I'll ask this question again," said Perri. "This species…were they human…?"

A sound came, soft but perhaps disgusted.

"Atlantis," Quee Lee whispered. "Is that this story?"

"My guess exactly," said Perri, hugging her until her ribs ached. Then he said the ancient name for himself, in the appropriate dead language.

"Once again, you have forgotten: The galaxy had no name for that world, much less for that long-ago island. But I won't stop you from imagining your Earth and its legendary lands, and I won't fight the labels that help you follow what I happen to say."

In the darkness, Perri squeezed his wife again, and she pushed her mouth into his ear, saying with relish, "It must be."

They had decided, together.

It was Atlantis.

"My grandchildren," the voice continued. "Several generations had passed since the first of them were born, and I should confess to one inevitable event. I have always taken lovers from the locals. A lover supplies information and oftentimes can be a tool for good methodical management. Bedding those who are most beautiful and intriguing is a natural consequence of my station. But one of those grandchildren proved more irresistible than usual. She was a young woman, as it happened. Though it just as likely could have been a man…

"By the standards of her species, she was physical small and exceptionally lovely.

"Among her gifted peers, she was considered brilliant and singularly blessed. The finest of the fine…

"That I took her into my bed was natural. That she retained her virginity until that night only enhanced her reputation with her people, and to a degree, with me. The bloodied sheet was hung from the palace wall for a full day, and when she appeared again in public, cheers made her stand tall as a queen—the center of attention smiling at her appreciative world.

"I was very fond of that little creature.

"As a lover, she was fearless and caring, bold and yet compliant too. And when we were not making love, she would ask me smart little questions about all matters of science and engineering. Her particular expertise involved the heart of the device that we were building together. There were puzzles to work through, matters that I didn't understand fully myself. I had never built such an object, you see. That's why the brilliant grandchildren were critical. But even though she understood many of the ideas behind our work, she always wanted to know more, and if possible, hold what she knew more deeply.

"Charming and crafty, she was, and I let myself be fooled. I confessed that there were subjects that could never, ever to be discussed with her people. 'You will repeat none of this again,' I warned. 'Not even to the wind.'

"She promised to remain mute.

"Then I explained to her the true shape of the galaxy, and its great age, and I told the violent history of our glorious universe.

"And yes, there were moments when I mentioned the Union and my small, critical role within it.

"Then because she seemed so interested in the subject of Me, I confessed my age and gave a brief thorough accounting of past missions as well as some of the tricks that I was capable of."

The voice fell away.

In the blackness, a body stretched until the bones or carapace creaked, a sharp dry crack coming at the end.

"That lover was my second challenge," said the voice. "Although at that particular moment, I didn't appreciate the danger."

Quee Lee leaned away from Perri, begging her dark-adapted eyes to find any trace of wayward light. If she could just make out the creature that was sitting so close to them–

No. Nothing.

"One of our shared nights never seemed to end," said the voice. "Normal fatigues don't trouble me, but my lover, no matter how much improved genetically, needed sleep. She lived for dreams. Yet the girl somehow resisted every urge to close her lovely dark eyes. Twice in the dark, she managed to surprise me with tricks she had never shown before. I was appreciative. How could I not be? But then as the full moon set and the bright summer sun began to rise, she whispered, 'I was wondering my lord…about something else…'

"'What?' I asked.

"'But maybe I shouldn't,' she conceded.

"'Ask me anything,' I said, never voicing the obvious possibility that I wouldn't reply, or that I might simply lie.

"With a sleepy slow voice, my lover confessed, 'I am curious. When you speak of old missions, you usually seem to be out between the stars, or huddled beside some dying star, or cloaked inside a storm cloud of interstellar dust…'

"I nodded, and for a moment, she seemed to drop into sleep.

"But then she roused herself with a gasp, straightening her little body before asking, 'Why come here? Why visit our little world, my lord?'

"'It suits my present mission,' I conceded. 'Your volcano and the sea water are rich with rare elements and useful minerals—'

"'But you have told me this before…in other nights, you explained that in the baby days of any solar system, some if not most of the new worlds are flung out into the night. Their oceans freeze. Their atmospheres fall as snow. But radiation keeps their iron cores molten, and volcanoes still bubble up beneath the bitter ice, and a god like you could surely bring temporary life to those unnamed realms…'

"I listened to her, perhaps not quite believing just how bright she was.

"Then very quietly, I reminded her, 'Like those cold places, this world possesses no name. As far as the universe is concerned, your home is a random lump of dust and still-simple life forms.'

"For a long while, she stared at me.

"Those beautiful dark eyes…I cannot mention those eyes and not feel shame…a burning disgrace that keeps me from describing to you just how deep their hold was on me…

"But then the eyes closed, and my lover drifted into a rich, much deserved sleep. I thought the matter was finished. I didn't want to entertain any other possibility. And really, what reason did I have to believe that this worshipful little creature was a threat, or even if she was a threat that she could be ever present a genuine danger to the likes of me?

"I covered her with a fine linen sheet.

"Then for the following days and months, and years, nothing changed. No word or incident raised even the tiniest suspicion on my part. My lover was the same to me as she had always been, and I was as pleasant and giving to her and to all of my people.

"And then my third challenge arrived. This danger came from the sky, and even at a great distance, it brought the worst possible trouble. Out on the edge of the solar system was an automated probe. A harum-scarum probe was moving at a small fraction of light-speed. The harum-scarums have always been aggressive in their explorations and colonizations, and now one of their sharp-eyed robots was plunging out of the darkness, threatening to fly past my world while taking note of everything that might bear interest.

"I couldn't allow myself or my good work be seen.

"And sadly, the machines that I had left in orbit couldn't protect me. I needed to leave the island. Wisely, I didn't offer reasons or predict when I would return. As far as my people knew, I would be back among them before the next sunset or the coming full moon. But I begged them to continue our work—the delicate fabrication of a single machine that meant everything to me and to them."

In the dark, the voice dropped into a long airy sigh.

Then quietly, but with an unhealed pain, their companion said, "This was the moment when the rebellion began. And I think you can guess who stood on the silk cushions of my empty throne, whirling a titanium hammer above her head, shouting to the throng, 'It is time to save our world, my friends! To rescue our futures and gain control over our souls!'"

9

Emotions lay rich and fresh in the silence, born out of a sadness that could not be forgotten. Or maybe there was only silence, black and seamless, and the misery and burning sense of loss were supplied entirely by the human audience. It was impossible to tell which answer was correct, or if both were a little true. But then the humans heard a limb flex, the invisible body creaking as it shifted, not once but three times in quick succession. When the voice returned, it seemed slower. Each word was delivered alone, and between one word and the next laid a tiny silence, like a cold black mortar pushed between warm red bricks.

"I could have destroyed the automated probe at a distance. I could have used methods that would have made harum-scarum scientists believe that bad luck was responsible. Some random rock, a cosmic hazard that slipped past the machine's various armors. Nothing would seem too unusual about that. But erasing the danger was not the only problem. Harum-scarum probes are relatively common in our galaxy, and if I blithely obliterated them whenever our paths crossed, somebody would eventually see the pattern in my clumsiness.

"No, what I did was rise up into the sky to meet the danger directly.

"Like you, I am the loyal subject to a variety of laws concerning motion and energy. I had to race out into the solar system for a considerable distance, and then with methods that I cannot share, I invisibly changed my trajectory, racing back again, making certain that my momentum carried me close to the probe's vector.

"Together, that machine and I dove into the hot glare of the sun. I studied my opponent while it absorbed images of the two inner worlds. Then we climbed away from the sun, and at a moment when I would escape notice, I drifted closer and touched the machine with a thousand fingers, allowing its giant eyes to do their work even as I changed a small portion of what it could see.

"Together, we passed between the gray moon and my blue-green world.

"And then the danger was finished. The probe turned its attentions to the little red world coming next, and with my chore accomplished, I glanced backward, examining my home with my own considerable eyes.

"The rebellion was well underway.

"Twenty different security systems had been fooled, or by various means disabled. And now my clever little grandchildren had full control over their land and the ocean around them.

"Feigning loyalty, they had continued building the machine.

"Pretending subservience, most of them moved through their lives in the expected ways. But others openly prayed that I was dead, even while they planned my murder should I return. And still others pretended to die, their names removed from the city's rosters, freeing them to journey over to the mainland, taking with them tools and skills as well as a story that would inspire the primitive souls they would find waiting there.

"I was furious.

"In ways quite rare to me, I felt the powerful, consuming need for revenge.

"But motion and energy still held sway. I could not roar home in the next instant, and if I didn't wish to be noticed by the probe beside me, I would have to be patient enough to obey my original plan.

"Easing away from the probe consumed many days.

"I spent another month pushing against the universe, slowing myself to a near-halt before turning and plunging back into the brilliant sunshine.

"By then, the harum-scarum eyes were distant. But if the probe happened to glance back at my world, it might have noticed an island exploding before its time, a dark cloud spreading while a deep bubbling caldera defined the island's grave. But I resisted that instinctive violence. Destroying my own work would have been an unacceptable cost, and worse, it would have been graceless.

"And of course I could have remotely shut down the entire operation, protecting my investment from malicious hands. But that meant new risks as well as long, embarrassing delays.

"Instead, I decided to dance with complete disaster, but aiming for total success."

After those words, a long pause seemed necessary.

Finally, Perri said, "You won't tell us. I know. But we would appreciate to know what the stakes were."

"I would like to know," Quee Lee said.

"What exactly you were building?" her husband pressed.

"Britannia," the voice replied. "Like any empire worth its salt…" A weak laugh washed over them. "How can you separate a true empire from all of the little pretenders? What did the British possess that their vanquished opponents lacked? Why were those Northern men superior to the tropical peasants in the field and the dogs in the street?

"Any good empire holds at least one skill that is its own.

"The Greeks had their highly-trained hoplites and several unique if contradictory forms of government. The Chinese had the most enduring civil services ever seen on your world. Romans were possessed by their engineering and brutal legions. And so long as British boats owned the seas, their power was accepted by a world that saw no option but bow in their mighty presence.

"An empire is always smarter than its competition.

"And my Union is far, far smarter than the human species. Or any other species you can name, for that matter.

"The device I was building…? Well, I will tell you that it was a single component meant to be set inside a much larger machine. And that it was extremely rare and very valuable, embodying sciences that you have never mastered. Once assembled, the full apparatus can wield principles that your most brilliant minds might recognize as possible, but only that. The apparatus is magic. It is gorgeous. It was, and is, worth every cost."

A brief pause ended with Quee Lee's voice.

"So you returned to the Earth," she said. "To Thera, or Atlantis. Although it wore different names then, I suppose."

"Whatever the world, whatever the island," said the voice. "Yes, I returned, yes. To find my grandchildren engaged in an artful rebellion."

There was a long, contemplative pause.

Finally Perri asked, "And what happened then?"

"Worth every cost," the entity said once again. "I speak without doubts, telling you what I did that day. And for that matter, what I would do on this day, in an instant, if I saw any threat to my enduring Union.

"I would protect what I love."

10

Until that moment, the voice had been just so much noise. It was interesting and entertaining noise, the words intriguing if not completely believable. The narrative was compelling enough for the humans to feeling empathy for the creatures that could well have been their own ancestors. Every portion of the disjointed tale deserved their attention as they tried to predict what would happen next and next after that; but there was no moment when they stopped wondering what kind of body was connected to the voice. Until then, that was the central question that kept begging to be answered.

Then they heard the words, "My enduring Union," and that simple utterance changed everything.

Wrapped around a bald statement was stiff, unyielding emotion. Quee Lee and Perri heard the threat, the promise, the conviction and purpose—and they instantly believed what they heard. Now both of them were considering what it would mean if this story, unlikely as it seemed, was in some fashion or another true. And that was when the formless entity beside them—mysterious and unknowable, bristly and proud—became markedly less interesting than the grim bit of history it was sharing with them now.

Human hands grabbed one another.

Each lover felt the other's body bracing for whatever came next.

Another silence was what the voice decided to offer. And then from the perfect darkness came a sound not unlike a tongue or two licking against lips threatening to grow dry.

Quee Lee and Perri had been married for tens of thousands of years. But as long as that might seem, marriage was infinitely older than their single relationship. And there were species that took intimacy to higher levels than humans could manage. The Janusians, for instance: Their little husbands rooted into the body of female hosts, literally joining into One. Yet among the human animals, Quee Lee and Perri were famous. Their relationship had evolved gradually into a complex and robust, enduring and very nearly impossible to define melange. There were a few humans who spent more time together than the two of them. Unlikely as it seemed, some married souls enjoyed their physical lives even more than these two managed. But no one could believe that any other human pair, on the Ship and perhaps anywhere else in the universe, was emotionally closer than that ancient Earth-born lady and her boyish life-mate.

At some point, everybody tried to tease them.

The happy couple generally welcomed good-natured barbs and admiring glances. But when asked to explain their success—when some friend of a friend insisted on advice for less-perfect relationships—they grew testy and impatient, even a little defensive. The truth was that they were helpless to define their relationship. A marriage was always larger than its participants, and what they possessed here was as mysterious and unlikely to them as it seemed to distant eyes. They couldn't understand why they had drawn so closely together. They didn't see why life had not yet found the means to yank them apart. But they were undeniably intimate and deeply dependent, up to the point where Quee Lee and Perri could never imagine being separated from one another in any lasting, hellish way.

"Can you read each other's thoughts?" people wanted to know.

Not at all, no.

"But it seems you can," some maintained. "The way you know what each other wants, what you're about to say and do—"

Did they do that?

"There's a trick at work," a few declared. "Dedicated nexuses let your minds share thoughts and feelings. Is that what you're doing right now...?"

Not even a little. In fact, they made a point of avoiding mechanical shortcuts to authentic tongue-and-expression conversation.

Eventually somebody would ask, "When have you felt closest?"

What did that mean? Close how...?

"What was the day—the incident—when you felt as if you were a single brain shared by two independent bodies...?"

There were thousands of stories worthy of repetition, each able to satisfy the audience if not themselves. Several dozen favorites had become minor legends among the passengers. But the best answer was never offered, not even to the closest, dearest friends. It happened on that particular evening as they sat inside the perfect darkness, deep within the unmapped Vermiculate, immersed in the most isolated corner yet discovered within the Great Ship. That proud and stern and eternal voice promised them that it would do anything to protect what it loved, which was the Union; and for a singular moment, Quee Lee and Perri were one irreducible soul.

Now they finally believed the unlikely story.

Unseen tongues licked at dry lips, and the two lovers held each other with strong arms, sharing of flurry thoughts, speaking with nothing but the touch of fingers, the sound of breathing, the push of heavy breasts and the telltale flinch of a nervous penis.

"There is a Union," they decided together. "It is real."

And in the next moment, it occurred to them that the Union's loyal servant would never do anything that did not, in small ways or great, help its ageless cause.

Quee Lee pressed hard against her husband, and she shivered, and just before the voice spoke again, she whispered an obvious possibility into her husband's ear and skull:

"Our friend is on a mission! Now!"

And in the next instant, with thrilled horror, both of them thought, "It's telling us the story for a reason…and we are the mission!"

11

With a sense of deeply buried pain, or at least an old, much-practiced anger, the voice continued.

"At last, I returned to the island. At last, I touched down in the Sunset Plaza, on an ellipse of crimson glass brick reserved for my shuttle and my immortal body. The plaza was flanked by tall apartment buildings buried beneath masses of vines—engineered greenery that thrived in the volcanic warmth, producing enough fruit and sweet nuts to feed the residents within. A thousand of my grandchildren quickly gathered around me, while thousands more sneaked looks from behind the curtains of their comfortable little homes. Every face made an effort to smile. Every head dipped in a show of respect—a gesture that I had never demanded from my subjects, that arose long ago on its natural own. Only one important face was missing, but the brave traitors anticipated my first question. Several knelt before me, palms to the sky, and they explained that I had been gone longer than anticipated, and my arrival had proved quite sudden, but yes, my mistress was as happy as anyone could be. In fact, she was waiting for me at the palace, rapidly making herself ready for my pleasures.

"The avenue was lined with pruned trees thriving inside big copper pots and rows of intricate geometric sculptures cut from the black native stone. The smallest citizens barely noticed my passing. They were the ants and fat beetles that I had reinvented for the purpose of little jobs, and unburdened by the demands of awe, they continued cutting down the weeds and disposing of trash. But a crew of enhanced crabs was pulling superconductive cables under the pavement, and when I passed near, they paused long enough to salute me with their elegant pincers—a signal learned from the grandchildren.

"Everybody was working hard to appear worshiping. Everybody wanted to shine with joy. And a few even managed to convince themselves that they were being honest. 'You were gone too long,' several complained, at different moments but always with the same worried, slightly put-upon tone. And then one or two remarked, 'We feared you were lost, that some horrid disaster had claimed you.'

"If that is what they wanted, those voices kept their thoughts hidden.

"Then at the mouth of an alleyway, I noticed a very young grandchild standing in the shadows, waiting for something. Not for me, it seemed…but in his stance and attitude, I could see anticipation.

"I paused and asked his name, even though I had already found his face in the public files. He introduced himself, and with a charming little smile mentioned that he had no memory of me. I had left for my errand among the stars while he was still just a toddler.

"He was barely more than that now. I smiled, telling him that it was my pleasure to meet him.

"He mentioned that I looked exactly as he expected, except I wasn't tall enough of course, and then his gaze drifted off toward the island's slumbering volcano.

"'What are you waiting for?' I inquired.

"'For you,' he replied. But before there was any misunderstanding, he added, 'I'm waiting for you to pass, and then I can go about my business.'

"'What is your business?'

"'To walk down to the Sunset Plaza and watch the night come,' he explained.

"'You like the setting sun, do you?'

"The young eyes smiled, and the mouth too. Then a smart little voice said, 'Yes,' and nothing else.

"The bodies surrounding us began to relax.

"With a fond hand, I stroked the boy's thick black hair and kissed him on the nose, and then continued with my triumphant stroll to the palace.

"No one was invited to follow me inside, and no one asked to join me. My shadow passed first through the iron gates and beneath the brass arches and into the grand hall. The air was scented with spice and smoke. The floor and walls and high ceiling were tiled in a fractal pattern, cultured sapphires and diamonds lending accents to an example of mathematical beauty that I have always appreciated. My throne stood at the end of the hall—the oldest object in the palace, gold flourishes and silk laid over my adoptive father's original chair.

"My shadow hesitated, and so did I.

"My grandchildren stood in a crowd outside, waiting for me to vanish.

"Suddenly a great damp shape emerged from a back door, walking on long mechanical legs. The creature was a leviathan whose ancestors had swum the local sea. I had made him smaller while changing his lungs and flesh to where he could thrive in indoors, adeptly serving me with whatever little duty that I might require.

"With a high-pitched warble, he welcomed me home.

"Whatever plots were lurking about, I sensed he was not involved and almost certainly unaware.

"I asked if I had been missed.

"'Always,' he replied with a quick series of clicks.

"'Where is she now?' I inquired.

"'In your quarters, lord.'

"'And has she been faithful to me?'

"'No,' the creature replied, without hesitation. 'I have seen her use her hands and several plastic devices. And once, the edge of a large pillow.'

"'Thank you for your honesty,' I said. 'And good evening to you.'

"No shadow led the way now. Alone, I climbed a long flight of dimly-lit steps and entered a narrow hallway that only seemed endless…an illusion lined with tall doors meant to impress and confuse the rare visitor. I walked a short distance and opened what seemed to be a random door. There was only one bedroom inside the palace, and it never occupied the same position twice. I entered through a random wall, and my lover flinched in surprise, starting to pull the sheets over her naked body before realizing it was me, only me.

"Together, we celebrated my return.

"I had been absent even longer than I had anticipated. The young creature that I had left in this bed was noticeably older. A few white hairs and a hundred little erosions marked the natural decline of a creature not born immortal and never told to expect such blessings. But she was just as fierce a lover as always, maybe more so. She insisted on satisfying herself by various means, and whenever my attentions seemed to waver, she would offer encouragements or measured complaints.

"'What kind of god are you?' she teased me once, in the dark. 'Are you going to let this old lady beat you at your game?'

"'I am tempted to lose, yes,' I confessed.

"Perhaps she heard more than one message in those words, because she paused and pulled away from me. Then like a hundred times before, she settled on my chest, legs spread, the smell of her thick and close.

"In a whisper, she mentioned, 'Your journey must have been considerable.'

"'My task was difficult,' I said.

"'We have continued with our work.' She said, 'Our work,' to make certain that I would hear the loyalty in those words. Then after a pause, she added, 'But of course you kept track of our progress.'"

"'Always,' I said.

"'Have we missed any goals?'

"'Never.'

"'Are you proud of us?'

"'Along the narrowest tangents, yes. Yes, I am very proud.'

"She refused to be surprised by my measured answer. And what worry she let show was small and easily controlled. The creature was exceptionally bright, after all. And she was wise in rare, precious ways. Extraordinary dangers were lurking, and she must have realized there was no way to keep me from seeing pieces of her scheme.

"Silently, she dropped her face to my face and kissed me.

"Then I placed my hand against her little throat, feeling her breath and the flinching of soft muscles, and I eased her back up into a sitting position. With a flat, cool tone, I said, 'It was reasonable, holding to the work schedule. And I was most impressed by how you managed to fool my security systems.'

"Perhaps her plan was to claim innocence. 'I didn't try to fool anything,' she might have said. 'I don't know what you're accusing me of.' Denial might have given the plotters precious time. But it also might have angered me, which would have brought my wrath down on them even sooner than they had planned.

"So instead of lying, my lover decided on poise. She shrugged her shoulders, asking, 'What do you know?'

"'That the good machine being built inside our mountain is almost finished. But your lieutenants have surreptitiously slipped other devices into its workings. You devised some very clever, extremely powerful bombs that you hope won't be noticed, and you will soon obliterate the purpose of my coming to this world.'

"Most souls would have tensed, hearing those words. Many would have panicked. But for my lover, that moment brought relief. Her duplicity was laid bare, and the simple fact that she was alive meant that perhaps she still retained some little chance of success here.

"I felt her throat relax against my hand.

"Then with great seriousness, I added, 'I also know you hope to murder me. Tonight, if possible. You have an array of weapons hiding here, and you have modified any piece of machinery that might injure me. I can even see dangers inside you, darling. Your body fat has been laced with acids that can be set free with a thought, turning you into a burning puddle that falls over my writhing, helpless body…'

"She stared down at me.

"In her gaze, I could see her asking herself if this was the moment for suicide. But why would I lie beneath her if I felt at all at risk?

"With a reasonable tone, she asked, 'Can we kill you?'

"'If I was foolish and a little blind, perhaps. But I am not, and I am not.'

"She nodded, accepting that verdict.

"And then she tensed through the shoulders and along her back, and with a small furious voice, she asked, 'But why shouldn't we try to kill you? When your work is finished, you intend to murder all of us. Isn't that so?'

"I didn't respond immediately.

"'You told me as much,' she claimed. 'When you sang about your secret Union and your need for nameless places…you practically confessed that when you were finished with this place, you wouldn't leave witnesses behind.'

"I waited for a moment. Then I warned her, 'You don't quite understand.'

"Then I dropped my hand, the fingers and broad palm stroking her body down to the point where her legs joined together. 'You are a special, special soul,' I told her. 'My work would have been finished in another few years, and my plan was to take you with me. Out to the stars, out into the rich cold darkness.'

"The shock rolled across her features.

"Quietly, almost angrily, she said, 'No, you're lying.'

"But I was speaking the truth.

"With a fond, slightly paternal voice, I asked, 'How do you think I was brought into the Union? No one is born into this noble service. The rank and responsibilities are earned only on exceptionally rare occasions. In my case, another servant visited my home world and built several marvels before retreating back into the darkness with his treasures, and one of the treasures was the man lying beneath you now.'

"'No,' she whispered.

"And then, in pain, she said, 'Maybe. But this changes nothing. I wouldn't abandon my world, and I certainly won't let you to blow up this volcano and make it as though this place never was.'

"'Is that what you think will happen?' I asked. 'That I would slaughter you and yours for no reason but my convenience?'

"She hesitated. Then with a figurative acid on her tongue, she asked, 'What do you mean?'

"'Unless provoked, I will not murder.'

"By the light of the moon, my lover looked into my face, and the beginnings of an explanation occurred to her. 'You won't murder, but you might take back all of your gifts. Our minds. The genetic manipulations. Wipe clean the ideas and concepts you brought down here to serve your damned Union.'

"I threw my palm across her mouth.

"Then I yanked her close, saying, 'Yes. That was my kind, responsible plan. You would come with me, and my magical device would come with us, and the other grandchildren would wake the following morning to discover…nothing. There would be a shared dream of a magical civilization, a public memory that would turn to legend in another day, and in another ten generations that would vanish into a muddled, impossible story.'

"She lay against me, her heart beating against what passed for my ribs.

"'I am sorry,' she told me.

"Into my ear, she said, 'Really, we haven't done anything wrong. Not yet. I can give commands, and every weapon will be put away, and you won't have to worry about any of us lifting so much as a lard-knife against you.'

"'That is not enough,' I said.

"'And you can kill me,' she promised. Then she repeated her offer, sounding as if she was begging. 'Kill me, and maybe the other adults. But leave our children. They don't know anything.'

"'Like the boy I spoke to? That child waiting between the plaza and the palace?'

"She hesitated.

"'At this moment,' I said, 'that tiny fellow is sitting beside the water, bare toes in the surf. And do you know what he is watching with all of his interest, every shred of passion? He watches the sky.'

"She did not move.

"'The sky,' I repeated. 'And in particular, he stares at this night's brightest stars.'

"The woman could not breathe.

"'You are a crafty soul, my dear. My darling.' I told her, 'I am extremely impressed by the thoroughness and audacity of your plan. Threatening the machine as well as my own immortal self…those are the tactics that anyone would expect. But you also dispatched a team of technicians to the mainland. You convinced the worshipful souls living there that they should help you. Since then, our people and theirs have been living in a distant valley, secretly fabricating an amazing machine of their own.

"'A radio beacon, as it happens.

"'To the best of your ability, you have been marking my passage across the heavens. You guessed that I was subverting a set of prying eyes, and you were correct. Your hope was to broadcast a huge, important signal. You wanted to be noticed. You wanted the probe to see you, perhaps. Or if you missed that mark, then at least one loud intelligent scream would race its way through the heart of our galaxy…

"'Your secret hope was to accomplish what I would never allow…you wanted to name your world, and to name it in exactly the manner that would make the universe take note of your presence.

"'And you were right, my sweet darling. That would have been your only hope of salvation.

"'But I visited that far valley and your secret beacon. Just this morning, I destroyed the dishes and power plant, and I slaughtered everyone in my reach, but I left the local communication system intact. During these last hours, every time you spoke your fellow rebels, you were actually speaking to me.'"

Finally, the voice paused.

In the perfect darkness, a deep useless breath was taken.

Then the entity was talking again, quietly admitting, "I gave my lover one last freedom. She could be the last to die, or first. She chose to be first, and she did that herself, releasing the acids inside her body. But I was already standing at a safe distance from our bed, my back to the carnage. Hearing the screams and smelling the blistered flesh, I kept my eyes averted, reminding myself that the worst of this awful night was finally finished."

12

The two humans clung to one another.

In the same moment, in a rough chorus, they asked, "What happened? What did you do? What about the other people? What?"

A tight slow creak was audible, old leather or old bones moving.

From a point markedly closer than before, a mouth opened and breathed and then breathed again.

"I did precisely what I promised." The voice seemed to be within arm's reach. "However imperfectly, I have always strived to serve my cause, and that includes punishing those who dared rise up against me. I had no choice but gather the worst of the offenders on the Sunset Plaza, and with the rest of the grandchildren watching, I removed them from the living world. Then I ordered the low-animals to clean the bricks of blood and pink tissues, and the dead bones were ground up and piled high on the nearest beach. And within five years, those who had survived my justice had managed to make up for lost time. Within ten years, my work was finished, and I carved away the gray summit of the volcano and pulled from the hot workroom a single machine encased in the finest hyperfiber—a wonder of genius and competence that made my stay on that world worth any cost."

The voice drifted even closer, and feeling the intrusion, Quee Lee instinctively leaned away.

Perri held her and spoke past her, asking, "When did the mountain erupt?"

Nothing.

"After you abandoned the world, did the island explode?"

A sound of amusement, weary and cool, ended with the simple pronouncement, "Never, no."

They waited.

"Your assumption has been that this was the Earth. And that is a reasonable, wrong assumption. But I let you believe what you wanted. As a rule, every species, no matter how open to odd notions and alien fancies, will find its own stories to be the most compelling.

"No, this wasn't your cradle world. And its people were perhaps not quite as human as I might have let on."

"What happened to them?" Quee Lee pressed.

"As I promised my lover, I undid my fancy tinkering. I made her citizens simple again, just as I pulled back the engineering of the other species. The population scattered. The palace was abandoned. Without trained hands to make repairs, the city fell into ruins. Within a few years of my departure, the island was a mystery already famous across half of that world. But its mountain would never erupt. My work had stolen away too much heat, and the magma lake below had cooled and turned to stone."

The voice paused.

Then with a matter-of-fact tone, it explained, "The Earth is blessed in many ways. It has a mature, very stable sun. Comets are rare beauties in the sky, not constant hazards. And it possesses a relatively thin crust, easily pierced and quick to bleed. But this world that I speak of is notably different. Its skin is much thicker than the Earth's, and much more resilient. As its core generates heat, oceans of magma build up slowly, millions of years required to reach that critical point when a thousand eruptions come at once.

"That harum-scarum probe surely recognized the inevitable—a world perched on the margins of a grand, yet thoroughly natural disaster.

"I left that world and placed my magical machine in a secret place. A new mission called to me from the sky, and I was en route when that nameless world suddenly and violently attacked itself. The sulfurous gases and blistering lava flows achieved everything that I had counted upon. Every convincing trace of my visit was erased. The continents were wracked by quakes. Ten thousand volcanoes spat ash and fire, and they exploded, flinging their poisons into the stratosphere. Every forest burned. Every breath brought blisters and misery. The ocean floors were wrenched upwards, forcing saltwater over the coastlands. My little island was washed clean beneath a quick succession of tsunamis, erasing even the palace. The human-like creatures were reduced to a few scattered populations, ignorant and desperate. And after another thousand years of geologic horror—when the skies finally cleared and the lava cooled to glass—not a single example of that very promising species could be found in Creation."

Those deadly words were absorbed in silence.

Then Quee Lee said, "How awful."

Softly, the voice asked, "In what way is this awful?"

"You allowed that to happen," she began.

"But the people were doomed," it said. "Long before I knew of their existence, they had a fate to face, and despite my considerable powers, there was little I could have done, except delaying the story's end by one day, or at the very best, maybe two."

The humans said nothing.

"If you need righteous anger," it continued, "direct your emotions toward the harum-scarums. Their probe saw the same future that I saw. Three of their colonies were near enough and powerful enough to launch rescue missions. Better than me, they could have saved a worthy sampling of those people before they passed out of existence. But no missions were launched. Their costs and the benefits were too much and too little, respectively. The battered world remained nameless until a starship eased its way into orbit. That particular ship was bringing colonists, I should mention—people who didn't care about the bones under their feet, people who wanted nothing but to start new lives on this rich empty place."

Quietly, Perri asked, "Is it a harum-scarum world?"

"No," the voice replied, "it is not."

"Then who has it?"

"Who else would be a likely suspect, my friend? Remembering all that we have discussed by now…"

Humans had claimed the empty world. The colonists might even be humans that had come from the Great Ship…people whom Quee Lee and Perri had met and even known well at one time or another…

Quee Lee was desperate to talk about anything else.

And Perri was too. With a scornful, demanding tone, he said, "I still don't believe in your Union."

"No? In what ways do you doubt it?"

"When you describe this organization, it sounds like an exclusive club or somebody's secret society. Not the imperial underpinnings of a powerful political machine."

A long pause ended when the voice said, "Power." It said the word four times, each utterance employing a different emotion. Amusement was followed by disgust, and then came contempt, and finally, a different species of amusement—a joyful, almost giddy rendering of the word, "Power." After that, there was a laugh that lingered until the voice decided to speak again.

"As you must have guessed by now," it told them, "I am embroiled in a new task in the service of my Union. A mission full of facets and difficult challenges, yes, and it is not something to be accomplished in an easy few centuries, either."

The humans held their breath.

The voice pushed even closer, less than an arm's length away, and from a mouth that they could only imagine came the reminder, "I did once visit your cradle world. Your Earth. Yes, I did."

Quee Lee nodded.

"Before it was named," Perri recalled.

"Moments before," the voice added. And then the bulk of an invisible body drifted even closer, hovering within a tongue's length of Quee Lee's ear, and an intimate whisper offered her a single date. A specific time. Then a place inside a city that she would never see again.

Quee Lee shivered.

Perri reached out with one arm, aiming for the face that had to be lurking in the blackness…but his hand closed on nothing, and nothing else came from the voice, and after a few moments more of clinging comfort with one another, their camp lights returned—a scorching white glare of photons that left them blinking, blinded in a new way altogether.

13

They didn't sleep that night, and they didn't miss sleep until the middle of the following morning. By then, Perri and Quee Lee had thoroughly explored the enormous room and most of the little tunnels leading out from it. But they didn't find any trace of visitors other than themselves. Their sniffers tasted surgically clean surfaces and cold air uncluttered by even a single flake of lost skin, and just as puzzling, none of their machines could explain why they had failed last night. Whatever the voice was, it had been careful. With its absence, it proved its great power…at least when it came to fooling a couple peasants who were ignorant of the real powers of a galaxy that they had barely begun to know.

There was talk about returning to the flex-car, or at least contacting their missing friends.

But one last tunnel needed a quick examination. And with Perri at the lead, they marched up into an increasingly narrow space that turned sharply, revealing a pair of security robots waiting for anyone who might wander where they didn't belong.

The robots were in slumber-mode, facing in the opposite direction.

Perri retreated, pulling his wife behind him. "They're the last in a string of sentries," he decided. "I bet if we found our way to the other side, we'd come across barricades and official warnings from the captains not to take one step farther."

"The captains don't know about our route?"

"Not yet," he said. Then with a soft conspiring voice, he added, "Maybe we should hurry home. Now. Before we get noticed."

They discovered their friends waiting at the flex-car. An argument had just ended, and one of the twin brothers refused to say anything to anyone. Apparently he had lost on the competition for the rich woman's affections, and his anger helped Quee Lee and Perri avoid the expected questions.

The tiny expedition abandoned the Vermiculate before evening.

Home again, the old married couple made love and ate enough for ten hungry people, and throughout the sex and the dinner, they discussed what they should do next, if anything. And then Quee Lee slept hard for three dream-laced hours. When she woke, Perri was standing over her. He was smiling. But it was a grim, concentrated smile—the look of a man who knew something enormous but unsatisfying.

"Want to hear a rumor?" he asked.

She sat up in bed, answering him with a look.

"Like we heard before, the captains did discover the hole in their maps, and they sent an old robot down into the hole. But it got lost and climbed out again, and it couldn't explain where it had gone wrong."

"That's the story I remember," she said.

"Engineers tore open the robot. Just to identify the malfunction. And that's when they found a message."

Quee Lee blinked, and waited.

"Addressed to the Master Captain," he continued, his smile warming by the moment. "After a thousand security checks, the invitation was delivered. Except for the Master Captain, and maybe a few Submasters, nobody knows what the message said. But a few days later, alone, the Master Captain walked down that tunnel and vanished for nearly five hours. And when she emerged again, she looked sick. Shaken sick. The rumor claims that she actually cried in the presence of her security troops, which is why the whole story refuses to get wings and soar. It doesn't sound at all like the benign despot we know so well."

His wife agreed with a nod. "When did this happen?" she asked.

"Ten years ago, nearly."

"And since then?"

"Well," said Perri, "the Master Captain has quit weeping. If that's what you're curious about."

She lay back on her pillows.

"No," her husband said.

"What else?"

"I didn't wake you just to tell you something that might have happened. Or even to give you another mystery to chew on."

"Then why am I awake?"

"I know a man," Perri said. "And he's very good pulling old memories out of very old skulls."

* * *

The magician was named Ash.

He was human, but he lived inside an alien habitat where the false sun never set. Sitting in a room full of elaborate machinery, Ash told his newest clients, "I can make promises, but they don't mean much. This date is a very big problem, madam. You were alive then, yes. But barely. This is a few years before bioceramic brains came into existence. You could have been the brightest young thing, but my tricks work best with the galactic-standard minds…brains that employ quantum many-world models to interface with a trillion sister minds…"

"Can you do anything?" Perri asked.

"I can take your money," Ash replied. "And I can also dig into the old data archives. You claim you have a place in mind?"

"Yes," Quee Lee said. Then she repeated the location just as the voice had given it to her.

"I assume you think you were there then," Ash said.

"I don't know if I was."

"And this is important?"

"We'll see," she said.

Ash began to work. He explained that on the Earth, for this very brief period of history, security systems as well as ordinary individuals tried to keep thorough digital records of everything that happened and that didn't happen. The trouble was that the machinery was very simple and unreliable, and the frequent upgrades as well as a few nasty electromagnetic pulses wiped clean a lot of records. Not to mention the malicious effects of the early AIs—entities who took great delight in creating fictions that they would bury inside whatever data banks would accept their artistic works.

"The chances of success," Ash began to say.

Then in the ancient records, he saw something entirely unexpected, and lifting his gaze, he mentioned to Quee Lee, "You were a pretty young lady."

"Did you find me?" she asked expectantly.

"Too easily," he allowed. Then he showed her a portion of the image—a girl who was nine or maybe eight years old, dressed in the uniform mandated by a good private school.

With a shrug, Ash allowed, "No need for paranoia. This does happen, on occasion." He gave commands to a brigade of invisible assistants, and then said, "If I can dig up a few more records, I think I can piece together what you and the man talked about."

"What man?" she asked.

Perri asked.

"The man standing beside you," Ash remarked. "The man with the golden balloon." Then he showed an image captured by a nearby security camera, adding, "I'm assuming he's your father, judging by his looks."

"He's not," she whispered.

"And now we have a second digital record," Ash said happily. "Hey, and now a third. See the adolescent boy down the path from you? Wearing the medallion on his chest? Well, that was a camera and a very good microphone.

His video has been lost, but not the audio. I can't tell you how unlikely it is to have this kind of recording survive this long, in any usable form."

"What is the man saying to me?" Quee Lee asked nervously.

"Let me see if I can pull it up…"

And suddenly a voice that she hadn't thought about for aeons returned. The young girl and the stranger were standing in Hong Kong Park, on the cobblestone path beside the lotus pond. A short white picket fence separated them from the water. Standing in the background were towers and a bright blue sky. With the noise of the city and other passersby erased, the voice began by saying, "Hello, Quee Lee."

"Hello," the young girl replied, nervous in very much the same fashion that the old woman was now. "Do I know you?"

"Hardly at all," the man replied.

The girl looked about, as if expecting somebody to come save her. Which there would have been: Quee Lee was the only child to a very wealthy couple who didn't let her travel anywhere without bodyguards and a personal servant. "Where are my people now?" she seemed to ask herself.

The voice said, "I will not hurt you, my dear."

Hearing that promise didn't help the girl relax.

"Ask me where I came from. Will you please?"

The youngster decided on silence.

But the strange man laughed, and pretending the question had been asked, he remarked, "I came from the stars. I am here on a great, important mission, and it involves your particular species."

The girl looked up at a face that carried a distinct resemblance to her face. Then she looked back down the path, hoping for rescue.

"In a little while," said the stranger, "my work here will be complete."

"Why?" the girl muttered.

"Because that is when one of your mechanical eyes will look at the most lucrative portion of the sky, at the perfect moment, and almost everything that you will need to know about the universe will be delivered to your doorstep."

The pretty black-haired girl hugged her laptop bag, saying nothing.

"When that day comes," said the man, "you must try and remember everything. Do you understand me, Quee Lee? That one day will be the most important moment in your species' history."

"How do you know my name?" she asked again.

"And this is not all that I am doing on your world." The man was handsome but quite ordinary, nothing about him hinting at anything that wasn't human. He was wearing a simple suit, rumpled at the edges. His right hand held the string that led up to a small balloon made from helium and gold Mylar. He smiled with fierce joy, telling her, "It has been decided. Your species has a great destiny in service of the Union."

In the present, two people gasped quietly.

"What's the Union?" the girl asked.

"Everything," was the reply. "And it is nothing."

The girl was prettiest when she was puzzled, like now.

"You won't remember any portion of our conversation," the man promised. "Ten minutes from now, you won't remember me or my words."

One hand smoothed her skirt, and she anxiously stared at her neat black shoes.

"But before I leave you, I wanted to tell you something else. Are you listening to me, Quee Lee?"

"No," she claimed.

The man laughed heartily. Then he bent down, placing their faces on the same level, and when he had her gaze, he said, "You were adopted, only your parents don't know that. The baby inside your mother had died, and I devised you out of things that are human, but also elements inspired by a wonderful old friend of mine."

The girl tried to step back but couldn't. Discovering that her feet were fixed to the pavement, she looked down and then up at the other adults walking past the long brown pond, and when she tried to scream, no sound came from her open mouth.

"I am not gracelessly cruel," the stranger told her. "You may think that of me one day. But even though I live to aid the workings of an enormous power, I make certain that I find routes to kindness, and when it offers itself, to love."

The little girl couldn't even make herself cry.

"Part of you," he said. Then he paused, and from two different perspectives, the audience watched as his free hand touched the girl's bright black hair. "The shape of your mind was born on another world, a world too distant to be seen today. And I once lied to that mind, Quee Lee. I told it that I could stand aside and watch it die forever."

She had no tears, but the man was crying, his face wet and sorry.

"I wish I could offer more of an apology," he said. And then he rose up again, pulling the balloon's string close to his chest while wiping at his wet face with a wrinkled sleeve. "But much is at stake…more than you might ever understand, Quee Lee…and this is as close to insubordination as this good servant can manage…"

Then he glanced at the security camera hidden in the trees and handed the string and balloon to the girl beside him. "Would you like this, Quee Lee? As a little gift from your grandfather?"

The girl discovered that she could move again.

"Take it," he advised.

She accepted the string with one little hand.

For a brief instant, they were posing, staring across the millennia in a stance that was strained but nonetheless sweet—the image of a little girl enjoying the park with some undefined adult relative.

"I will see you later," he mentioned.

Quee Lee released the string, watching the gold ball rise faster than she would have expected—shooting into the sky as if it weighed nothing at all.

When her eyes dropped, the stranger had stepped out of view.

And a few moments later, her father ran up the path to join her, asking, "Where did you go? I couldn't find you anywhere."

"I didn't go anywhere," the girl replied.

"Tell me the truth," the scared little man demanded. "Did you talk to somebody you shouldn't have talked to?"

She said, "No."

"Why are you lying?" he asked.

"But I'm not lying," she protested. Then with a wide, smart grin, the young Quee Lee added, "The sky is going to talk, Father. Did you know that? And he promised me, he did, that I am going to see him again later...!"

Bridge Eleven

Every irreducible moment brings the New. Nothing will ever remain where it was and how it was. Matter is transformed. Energy and thought are transformed. With endless hands, the universe frantically shuffles its pieces, and every part of the universe must move and grow colder or move and grow temporarily warmer, and every possibility is manifested, and no mind finds any happiness to inhabit forever, and even what seems stable and true skids upon a razor balanced upon another razor perched upon the thinnest, keenest slice of luck.

Five hundred thousand years is the promise—one circuit through the finest portions of the galaxy. Increasingly competent entities are thoroughly in charge, and nothing goes wrong. Nothing is wrong. A thousand centuries of relative peace and occasional bliss can make the mind believe that the next centuries will be very much the same. But the Great Ship is not alone. Even when the Ship appeared empty, drifting beyond any reach, there was Marrow. Marrow is the world sitting snug at the Ship's center, and after not being noticed for so very long, it is suddenly discovered and explored, settled and named, and certain ideas get loose inside its children.

The inevitable moment arrives, and the Ship's old course is thrown aside.

The Polypond waits before the Ship—a black cloud full of rage and intelligence and the joy of oblivion.

The Polypond tries to kill the Great Ship, and Everything.

Inside a multitude of futures, it succeeds.

But one little possibility springs up like a root—a blind sickly colorless root that pushes out of the Milky Way, pushes into the deep familiar cold of true space, achieving very little beyond surviving through this moment, and the next moment, and perhaps the moment after that…

Hatch

1

Yes, the galaxy possessed an ethereal beauty, particularly when magnified inside the polished bowl of a perfect mirror. Every raider conceded as much. And yes, the rocket nozzle where they lived was a spectacular feature, vast and ancient, its bowl-like depths filled with darkness and several flavors of ice lain over a plain of impenetrable hyperfiber. Even the refugee city was lovely in its modest fashion, simple homes and little businesses clinging to the inside surface of the sleeping nozzle. But true raiders understood that the most intriguing, soul-soaring view was found when you stood where Peregrine was standing now: Perched some five thousand kilometers above the hull, staring down at the Polypond—a magnificent, ever-changing alien body that stretched past the neighboring nozzles, reaching the far horizon and beyond, submerging both faces of a magnificent starship that itself was larger than worlds.

The Polypond arrived thousands of years ago, descending as a violent rain of comet-sized bodies, scalding vapor and sentient, hate-filled mud. The alien wanted to destroy the Great Ship, and perhaps even today it dreamed of nothing less. But most of the city's inhabitants believed the war was over now. In one fashion or another, the Ship had won. Some were convinced that the alien had surrendered unconditionally. Others believed that the Polypond's single mind had collapsed, leaving a multitude of factions endlessly fighting with one another. Both tales explained quite a lot, including the monster's indifference to a few million refugees living just beyond its boundaries. But the most compelling idea—the notion that always captivated Peregrine—was that human beings had not only won the war but killed their foe too. Its central mind was destroyed, all self-control had been vanquished, and what the young man saw from his diamond blister was nothing more, or less, than a great corpse in the throes of ferocious, creative rot.

Whatever the truth, the Polypond was a spectacle, and no raider understood it better than Peregrine did.

Frigid wisps of atomic oxygen and nitrogen marked the alien's upper reaches, with dust and buckyballs and aerogel trash wandering free. That high atmosphere reached halfway to the hull, and it ended with a sequence of transparent skins—monomolecular sheets, mostly, plus a few energetic demon-doors laid out flat. Retaining gas and heat was their apparent purpose, and when those skins were pierced, what lay below could feel the prick, and on occasion, react instantly.

Beneath the skins was a thick wet atmosphere, not just warm but hot—a fierce blazing wealth of changeable gases and smart dusts, floating clouds and rooted clouds, plus features that refused description by any language. And drenching that realm was a wealth of light. The glare wasn't constant or evenly distributed. What passed for day came as splashes and bright winding rivers, and the color of the light as well as its intensity and duration always varied. After spending most of his brief life watching the purples and crimsons, emeralds and golds and the myriad blues that stretched from the brilliant to the soothing, it had suddenly occurred to Peregrine that each color and every intricate shape held some important meaning.

"A common belief," Hawking had told him. "But your translator AIs can't find any message, or even the flavor of genuine language."

"Except I wasn't thinking language," Peregrine countered. "Not at all."

His friend wanted more of an answer, signaling his desires with silence and circular gestures from his most delicate arms.

"I meant plain simple beauty," the young man continued. "I'm talking about art, about visual poetry. I'm thinking about a magnificent show performed for a very special audience."

"You might be the only soul holding that opinion," Hawking counseled.

"And I feel honored because of it," Peregrine had laughed.

The Polypond's atmosphere was full of motion and energy, and it was exceptionally loud. Camouflaged microphones set near the base of the rocket nozzle sent home the constant roar of wind sounds and mouth sounds, thunder from living clouds and the musical whine of great wings. But even richer than the air was the watery terrain beneath: Tens of kilometers deep, the Polypond's body was built from melted comets mixed with minerals and metals stolen from vanished worlds. This was an ocean in the same sense that a human body was mere saltwater. Yes, it was liquid, but jammed inside the wetness was structure and purpose. Alien tissues supplied muscles and spines and ribs, and there were regions serving roles not unlike those of human hearts and livers and lungs. Long, sophisticated membranes were dotted with giant fusion reactors. And drifting on the surface were island-sized organs that spat out free-living entities—winged entities that would gather in huge flocks and sometimes rise en masse, millions and even billions of them soaring higher than any cloud.

Hatches, those events were called.

What Peregrine knew—what every person in his trade understood—was that each hatch was a unique event, and the great majority of them were worthless. Sending a fleet of raiders that returned with only a few thousand tons of winged muscle and odd enzymes was a waste of their limited power, and worse, a criminal squandering of lives. What mattered were those rare hatches that rose high enough to be reached cheaply, and even then it didn't pay to send raiders if there wasn't some respectable chance of acquiring hyperfiber or rare elements, or best of all, machines that could be harvested and tamed, then set to work in whatever role the city demanded.

Judging a hatch's value was three parts diagnosis, two parts art, and inevitably, ten parts good fortune. Telescopes tied into dimwitted machines did nothing but happily stuff data into shapes that brighter AIs could analyze. Whatever was promising or peculiar was sent to the raider leaders. The average day brought ten or fifteen events worthy of closer examination, and because of his service record, Peregrine was given first-glance at those candidates. But even with ripe pickings, he often did nothing. Other raiders flying their own ships would dive into the high atmosphere every few days, but sometimes weeks passed without Peregrine once being once tempted to sit in the pilot's padded chair.

"I want to grow old in this job," he confessed whenever his bravery was questioned. "Most souls can't do what I do. Most of you are too brave, and bravery is suicide. Fearlessness is a handicap. Chasing every million-wing flight of catabolites or sky-spinners is the quickest way to go bankrupt, if you're lucky. Or worse, die."

"That is one reasonable philosophy," his friend mentioned, speaking through the voice box sewn into a convenient neural center.

"I'm sorry," said Peregrine. "I wasn't talking to you. I was chatting with a woman friend."

The alien lifted one of his intricate limbs, signaling puzzlement. "And where is this woman?"

"Inside my skull." Peregrine gave his temple a few hard taps. "I met her last night. I thought she was pretty, and she was pleasant enough. But she said some critical words about raiders wasting too many resources, and I thought she was accusing me of being a coward."

"You listed your sensible insights, of course."

"Not all of them," he admitted.

"Why not?"

"I told you," said Peregrine. "I thought she was pretty. And if I acted like an unapologetic coward, I wouldn't get invited to her bedroom."

Hawking absorbed this tidbit about human spawning. Or he simply ignored it. Who could know what that creature was thinking beneath his thick carapace? Low-built and long, Hawking held a passing resemblance to an earthly trilobite. A trio of crystalline eyes pulled in light from all directions, delicate optical tissues teasing the meaning out of every photon. His armored body was carried on dozens of jointed legs. But where trilobites had three sections to their insect-like bodies, this alien had five. And where trilobites were dim-witted creatures haunting the floors of ancient seas, Hawking's ancestors evolved grasping limbs and large, intricate minds while scurrying across the lush surface of a low-gravity world.

Hawking was no social animal. And this was a blessing, since he was the only one of his kind in the city. Peregrine had studied the available files about his species, but the local data sinks were intended to help military operations, not educate any would-be xenologists. And likewise, after spending decades in close association with the creature, and despite liking as well as admiring him, there were moments when old Mr. Hawking was nothing but peculiar, standoffish and quite impossible to read.

But Peregrine had a taste for challenges.

"Anyway," he said, cutting into the silence. "I lied to that woman. I told her that I wasn't flying because I knew something big was coming. I had a feeling, and until that ripe moment, I was resting both my body and my ship."

"And she believed you?"

"Perhaps."

After a brief silence, Hawking said, "She sounds like a foolish young creature."

"And that's where you're wrong." Peregrine laughed and shrugged. "Just as I hoped, I climbed into her bed. And during one of our slow moments, she admitted who she was."

"And she was?"

"The woman was an engineer during the War. She was working in the repair yards while my mother served as a pilot. So like you, my new girlfriend is one of the original founders."

"Interesting," his friend responded.

"Fusilade is her name," he mentioned. "And she seems to know you."

"Yet I do not know her."

Then Peregrine added, "And by the way, she very clearly remembers your arrival here."

Fourteen moon-sized rocket nozzles stood upon the Great Ship's stern, and the center nozzle served as the gathering place for tired pilots and engineers during the War. Once the fighting ended, representatives of twenty different species found themselves trapped in this most unpromising location, utterly isolated, with few working machines, minimal data sinks, and no raw materials. Facing them was the daunting task of building some kind of workable society.

Hawking was a rarity—the rich passenger who had visited the hull before the comets began to fall, and who managed to outlive both his guides and fellow tourists. Alone, this solitary creature had scaled one of the outlying nozzles, and then his luck lasted long enough to find passage with a harum-scarum unit—the final group of refugees to make it to this poor but safe place.

"She feels sorry for you, Hawking."

"Why would she?"

"Because you're a species with a population of one."

The alien was unimpressed with that assessment. He cut the air with two limbs, his natural mouth rippling before leaking a disapproving click.

"I know better than that," Peregrine continued. "I told her that you're such a loner, it's difficult for you to share breathing space with me, and you know me and approve of me far more than you know and approve of anyone else."

The creature offered no reply.

"'Why call him Hawking?' she asked me. 'Nobody else does.'"

"Few others speak to me," his friend said.

"I explained that too," said Peregrine. "And I told her that your species are so peculiar, you never see reason for any permanent names. When two of you cross trails, each invents a new name for himself or herself. A private name blossoms, and it lasts only as long as that single perishable relationship."

The limbs gave the air an agreeable sweep.

"You picked Hawking, and I don't know why," Peregrine continued. "Except it's a solid sound humans can utter, unlike your own species' name, of course."

Quietly, with his natural mouth, Hawking made a sharp clicking sound followed by what sounded like, "Eech."

"!eech," the human tried to repeat.

As always, there was something intensely humorous about his clumsy attempt. Nothing changed in the creature's dome-like eyes or the rigid face, but suddenly all of the long legs wiggled together, signaling laughter, the ripples moving happily beneath his hard low unreadable body.

2

"And I remember your mother," the old woman had mentioned last night.

Like every citizen, Fusilade's apartment was tiny and cold; power had always been a scarce commodity in the city. But her furnishings were better than most, made from fancy plastics and cultured flesh, including a glass tub filled with spare water. Winking at her young lover, she added, "No, I doubt if your mother ever actually knew me. By name, I mean. But I was part of the team that kept those early raider ships flying. Without twenty ad lib repairs from me, that woman wouldn't be half the hero she is today."

Alopex was as famous as anyone in the city, and that despite being dead for dozens of centuries. She had defended these giant rockets during the Polypond War. But the alien eventually destroyed each of the Great Ship's engines, choking and plugging every vent, trying to keep reinforcements from reaching the hull. And at the same time, the captains below blocked every doorway, desperate to keep the Polypond from infiltrating the interior. Brutal fights were waged near the main ports, but none had lasted long. A barrage of tiny black holes was fired through the Ship's heart, but none delivered a killing blow. Then the final assault came, and despite long odds, a starship that was more ancient than any visible sun had endured a thorough beating but survived.

Afterwards, over the course of several months and then several years, the Polypond grew quieter, and by every credible measure less menacing.

Something was different. The alien was different, and maybe the Great Ship too. But those few thousand survivors could never be sure what had changed. With the clarity of the doomed, they had come here and built a refugee camp. Peregrine's mother proved a natural leader. Like her son, Alopex was a small person, dark as space, blessed with long limbs and a gymnast's perfect balance. And she was more than just an early raider. No, what made the woman precious was that she was first to realize that nobody was coming to rescue them. The giant engines remained dead and blocked. High-grade hyperfiber had plugged even the most obscure route through the armored hull. And worse still, the Great Ship was now undergoing some mysterious but undeniable acceleration. Without one working rocket, the world-sized machine was gaining velocity, hurrying its way along a course that would soon take it out of the Milky Way.

Alopex helped invent the raider's trade. In makeshift vehicles, she dove into the Polypond's atmosphere, stealing volatiles and rare earths, plus the occasional machine-encrusted body. Those treasures allowed them to build shelters and synthesize food. Every few days, she bravely led an expedition into the monster's body, stealing what was useful and accepting every danger.

Time and Fate ensured her death.

She left no body, save for a few useful bits of tissue that made up her meager estate. Her funeral was held ages ago, yet even today, whenever an important anniversary arrived, those rites and her name were repeated by thousands of thankful souls.

By contrast, Peregrine's father was neither heroic nor well regarded. But he was a prosperous fellow, and he was shrewd, and when one of the great woman's eggs came on the market, he spent a fortune to obtain it and a second fortune to build the first artificial womb in the city's history.

"I remember your mother," said the old woman, plainly proud of any casual association. Then with an important tone, she added, "That good woman would have been pleased with her young son. I'm sure."

Peregrine was almost three hundred years old, which made him young—particularly in the eyes of a much older lady who seemed to be happily feeding a fantasy. He offered nods and a polite smile, telling her, "Well, thank you."

"And I know your father fairly well," she continued.

"I never see the man," Peregrine replied with a sneer, warning her off the topic.

"I know," she said.

Then after a pause, she asked, "Did you mean it? Do you really feel that an especially large hatch is coming?"

"No," he said, finally admitting the truth.

Then before his honesty evaporated, he added, "There aren't any trends, and I don't have intuitions. And I never, ever see into the future."

Something in those words made the old woman laugh. Then she turned quiet and caring, and with sudden tenderness, she said, "Darling. Everybody sees some little part the future. Only the dead can't. And if you think about it, you'll realize…there's nothing more important that separates big-eyed us from poor cold blind them."

3

There was nothing to add after Peregrine's laughable attempt to say, "!eech." Hawking fell into perfect silence, indistinguishable from countless other silences; and Peregrine responded with his own purposeful quiet. He was sitting at one end of hanger, working with the latest data about hatches and general Polypond activity. His friend stood near the raider ship. Which was less animated, that sleeping machine or the alien? Hours and even days might pass, and the creature wouldn't move one antenna. Yet Hawking claimed to never feel lonely or bored. "A respectable mind always has fascinating tasks waiting in its neurons," he would say, which was perhaps why his very odd species lacked the words to describe painful solitude or empty time.

The day's hatches were distant and scarce.

Peregrine finally gave up the hunt. He sat at the end of the diamond blister, feeling the cold of deep space while studying the ever-changing scenery below. Clouds were gathering between their home nozzle and the next, the thinnest and lightest clouds shoved high above the others. This happened on occasion, and it meant nothing. But the result was a splotch of deep blackness, larger than a healthy continent and unpromising to the bare human eye.

Just to be sure, Peregrine played with infrared frequencies and flashes of laser light, making delicate measurements. Something inside that blackness was different, he noticed. Straight before him, something was beginning to happen, and that's why he wasn't particularly surprised when the clouds began to split, bleeding a strange golden light that was brighter than anything else in view.

Through his own telescope, he saw the vanguards of the rising hatch.

Moments later, on a shielded line, an AI expert contacted him. With a navigational code and simple words, the machine changed the complexion of Peregrine's day and week.

"This interests," it said with a flat, desiccated voice.

Peregrine found himself with a worthy topic. "I thought I was lying to that woman," he told Hawking. "About having intuitions, I mean. But look at this hatch. Look at the diversity. And that's without being able to see much of it yet." His heart was pounding, his voice quick and growing happy. "I don't know if anybody has seen, ever…a hatch as big and diverse as this one…"

Hawking did not move, but the hemispherical eyes absorbed the data in a few moments. Then the complicated mouth of tendrils and rasping teeth made a series of little motions—motions that Peregrine had never seen before, and chose to ignore for the moment.

"I'm leaving," the human announced.

Every raider with a working ship would be embarking now.

"It's going to be a rich day," he said, throwing himself into the first layer of his flight suit.

Finally, Hawking spoke.

"You are my friend," said the alien, nothing about his voice out of the ordinary. "And from all that is possible, I wish you the best.

4

Simplicity was the hallmark of a raider's ship. The hull was made from diamond scales bolstered with nanowhiskers, all laid across a flexible skeleton of salvaged hyperfiber. Resting in its berth, Peregrine's ship held a long, elegant shape reminiscent of the harpoons that populated ancient novels about fishermen and lost seas. But that narrow body swelled when liquid hydrogen was pushed into the fuel tanks. One inefficient fusion reactor fed a lone engine that was sloppy but powerful. The launch felt like the endless slap of a monster's paw, brutal enough to smash bone and pulverize the sternest living flesh. But like every citizen, Peregrine was functionally immortal, blessed with repair mechanisms that could take the stew inside a flight suit and remake the man who had been sitting there.

His body died, and time leaped across a string of uneventful minutes.

Opening new eyes, Peregrine found himself coasting, climbing away from the Great Ship. Six AIs of various temperaments and skills made up his crew. In his absence, they had continued studying the available data. One served as his pilot, and even when Peregrine reclaimed the helm, the machine waited at a nanosecond's distance, ready to correct any glaring mistakes.

Inside any large hatch, bodies came in different shapes, different species. The AI most familiar with mercantile matters pointed at the center of the hatch. "These gull-wands match those we saw fifteen years ago. Their wings had some good-grade hyperfiber, and nearly ten percent of the collected hearts were salvageable."

Gull-wands had tiny fusion reactors in their chests. One reactor was powerful enough to light and heat a modest home.

"How much could we make?" Peregrine asked.

An estimate was generated, followed by an impressed silence from every sentient entity.

But then Peregrine noticed a closer feature. "Over here…is that some kind of cloud?"

"No," was the best guess.

The mass was black along its surfaces, swirling in its interior, and through cracks that were tiny at any distance came glimmers of a fantastically bright blue-white light.

"Anything like it in the records?"

There was an optical similarity to clouds of tiny, extremely swift bodies observed only eight times in the past.

"In my past?"

"Not in your life, no," one voice replied. "During the city's life, I mean."

"Okay. What were those bodies made of?"

That was unknown, since none had ever been captured.

"So pretend that's what we're seeing," he said. "Estimate the numbers in that single gathering."

"The flock is enormous," another AI reported. "In the range of ten or eleven billion—"

"That's what we want!" Peregrine exclaimed.

Skeptical whispers buzzed in his ears.

But the human pointed out, "Everyone else is going to be harvesting gull-wands. Hearts and hyperfiber are going to be cheap for the next hundred years. But if we find something new and special…even gathering up just a few of them…we could pocket several fortunes, and maybe even upgrade our ship…"

His crew had to like the sound of that.

But the pilot warned, "Reaching the target will entail burning a large portion of our reserves."

"So do it now," Peregrine ordered, releasing the helm.

And for the second time in a very brief while, his fine young body was crushed into an anonymous jelly.

5

There was no perfect consensus about what the Polypond was—undiminished foe, mad psyche divided against itself, or the spectacular carcass of a once great foe. And in the same fashion, there were competing ideas about the place and purpose of the hatches. Since the rising bodies had mouths and were often seen feeding, maybe they were a favorite means of pruning old tissues and reviving what remained. Or they were infected with some new, improved genetics that had to be spread through the greater body. Maybe they had a punishing function, retraining regions that their Polypond master judged too independent. Unless of course hatches were exactly what they appeared to be: Biological storms. One or many species were enjoying a season of plenty, and working together, those countless bodies would rise into the highest atmosphere, spreading their precious seeds and spores as far as physically possible.

"Perhaps every answer is a little true," Hawking liked to caution. "Just as every answer is a little bit of lie, too."

Flying far above the hatch, Peregrine thought of his odd friend. But only briefly, and then he shoved the !eech out of his exceptionally busy mind.

"Projections," he demanded.

His ship was still plunging, its hull pulled into a teardrop configuration, the skin superheated and his sensors half-blinded by the plasmatic envelope. But his crew devised a simple picture showing him vectors and projections of a future that looked ready to end in the most miserable way.

"Our target is accelerating," his pilot announced. "I wish to abort before we collide with it."

The black mass, smooth-faced and distinctly iridescent, was punching its way through a scattering of high clouds. Some of those clouds were alive—vividly colored bodies as light as aerogel and easily shredded. Other clouds were water stained gray and red with salts and iron, dead cells and other detritus pushed skyward by the mayhem. Their target was tiny compared to the entire hatch, but it was already the tallest feature, and nothing like it had ever been seen before. Raiders bound for distant hunting grounds were noticing it. Even from two hundred kilometers overhead, the energies and wild violence were obvious. And even from inside a cocoon of superheated gas, two human eyes could appreciate the beauty of so many frantic bodies doing whatever it was they were doing.

"I want to abort," the pilot repeated.

Peregrine agreed. "But find the best way to hold us here, in its path. Can we do that?"

Instantly, the machine said, "Yes. But braking and circling will exhaust our reserves, and there won't be enough fuel for both cargo and the journey home."

Peregrine had guessed as much. "Let's compromise," he said. "Brake and assume a gliding shape. Where does that leave us?"

"Still dancing with the break-even point," the pilot warned.

"So make some calls." Peregrine named a few smart competitors approaching from more distant berths. "Pay them to wait above and share their spare fuel, when the time comes."

The teardrop flipped over, its engine throwing out a spectacular fire. Every raider knew: Ships larger and more powerful than theirs could trigger retribution. Was that an innate reflex or a Polypond strategy? Nobody knew. But Peregrine's ship was as close to the maximum size allowed, and if his plume exceeded the usual limits, even for a moment, a giant laser would pop to the surface on the unreachable sea below, evaporating his ship and then his body, and finally, his very worried skull.

But the burn went unnoticed apparently. Then the ship rested, pieces of its hull pulling away, forming dragonfly wings configured to work with the thickening winds. Each time they passed through one of the monomolecular skins, Peregrine felt a shudder. The vibrations worsened by the minute, growing violent and relentless, and after a point, numbing and nearly unnoticed.

Countless black bodies continued to rise.

At home, inside the city of refugees, an assortment of data sinks had survived from pre-war times. Even the best of them were incomplete. But inside the biological sections, Peregrine had found digitals of fish swimming in schools—a hypnotic set of images where tiny, almost mindless creatures managed to stay in formation, displaying grace and a singleness of purpose that never failed to astonish him.

This was the same, only infinitely more spectacular.

Those black bodies didn't ride meat and fins, but used tiny rockets and stubby metal wings. Perfect coordination had built a flawless hemisphere better than five hundred kilometers wide. Peregrine's best AI spotter singled out random bodies, carefully watching as they climbed to the outside edge of the school and then worked their way upwards, reaching the cloud's apex before doing a curious roll, each shucking off its little wings before firing a larger rocket, then diving back out of sight through gaps too tiny to see from above.

"Identify one of them and see when it emerges again," said Peregrine.

The spotter had already tried that, and failed. The bodies were too similar, and there were too many of them. But there was an easier, more elegant route. With the help of distant telescopes, the AI took a thorough census of the cloud, and then it let itself feel the gentle but precise tug made by that combined gravity. The precise size of the entire swarm could be measured, and with genuine astonishment, it admitted, "They are growing fewer, I think."

"Fewer?"

"Every minute, a million bodies vanish."

"Meaning what?" he asked. "The cloud is shrinking?"

"It grows, but its citizens are scarcer. And this has been happening from the outset, I would guess."

The pilot was managing their long fall while the ship's architect constantly adapted the shape and stiffness of wings, and the shape and color of the fuselage. To the best of its ability, the raider ship was trying to vanish inside the Polypond's enormous sky.

"Will any little guys be left when they reach us?" Peregrine asked.

Yes. Billions still.

"But what happens to the others? Where do they go?"

Data gave clues. Neutrinos and the character of escaping light implied a fierce heat, x-rays and even gamma rays seeping free. There was no way to be certain, but the black bodies could be simple machines—lead-doped hyperfiber shells wrapped around nuclear charges, for instance. If those bombs were detonating, then the interior of that cloud was hell: A spherical volume perhaps one hundred kilometers in diameter with an average temperature hotter than the guts of most suns.

What would anyone want with so much heat?

"The cloud is a weapon," Peregrine muttered, feeling horrible and sure. His first instinct was to glance at the rocket nozzle behind them, imagining the very worst: A bubble of superheated plasmas was being woven here, ready to be flung up and out into space. Like a child's ball, it could be aimed for a target several thousand kilometers wide—the rocket nozzle—and after one soundless flash, the city would cease to be.

But how would the Polypond launch the bubble?

The AIs were scrambling for answers. It was the ship's architect that imagined the next nightmare. What if the bubble wasn't going to be thrown, but instead it was dropped? If it was flung down onto the Great Ship's hull...the backside of the Ship, where the hyperfiber was thinnest...could it punch a hole into the hallways and habitats below?

Probably not, the majority decided.

But Peregrine and the architect wouldn't give up their nightmares. Since the War ended, no one had seen energies approaching what was being seen today. But of course the Polypond could have been patient since the war's end, silently gathering resources for this one spectacular attack.

Both solutions were possible and awful, and both were wrong.

The black cloud was still fifty kilometers below, and simulations were furiously working, and that was when a third, even stranger answer appeared with a withering flash of blue-white light.

In a blink, the top of that shimmering black mass parted.

Evaporated.

And from inside that carefully sculpted furnace sprang a shape at once familiar and wrong—a sphere of badly stressed, heavily eroded hyperfiber that was just a few kilometers across but rising fast on a withering plume of exhaust.

Making its frantic bid to escape: A starship.

"Reconfigure us now!" Peregrine shouted. "Whatever it takes, get us out of its way!"

6

On occasion, Peregrine and his inhuman friend discussed the Great Ship and what might or might be found within its unreachable interior. One despairing possibility was that the Polypond hadn't destroyed the ancient vessel, but it had managed to annihilate both crew and passengers, leaving no one beside a few souls clinging to life outside. On the opposite end of spectrum sat the most hopeful answer: Life onboard the Ship was exactly as it had always been, peaceful and orderly, and the captains were still in charge, and the Polypond had been defeated, or at least fought to a meaningful armistice. But if that was true, then for some host of perfectly fine reasons, nobody at the present was bothering to poke their heads out of the living ocean.

"But that doesn't explain this new acceleration," Peregrine would point out. "The engineers and captains…everybody everywhere…they assumed that these big rockets were the only engines. But plainly, they weren't. Obviously, they weren't even the most powerful thrusters available."

"It is quite the puzzle," Hawking conceded.

The acceleration was not huge, but making anything as massive as the Great Ship move faster…well, that was an impressive trick. "The captains found something new during the war," Peregrine suggested.

"A talent hidden until now," his friend added. "That notion has a delightful sourness about it, yes."

Sour was sweet to the !eech.

Peregrine would narrow his gaze, imagining captains standing in a crowded, desperate bridge. "They wanted to outmaneuver the Polypond. That's why they kicked the new motors awake, and now they can't stop them."

"That would be a compelling possibility, yes."

But Peregrine didn't believe his own words. "That still won't explain why the captains don't come out to get us. Even if they don't suspect anybody's here, they should send up teams to scout the situation…and even better, send messages home to the Milky Way…"

Long limbs acquired the questioning position. "Where would you expect the captains to appear?" Hawking asked.

"Inside one of the nozzles. I would."

Silence.

Peregrine offered his reasons as he thought of them. "Because the Polypond can't reach inside the nozzles. Because the captains could pretty easily work their way through the barricades and hyperfiber plugs. And because from the nozzle floor, they'd have an unobstructed view of the galaxy, and they would be able to measure our position and velocity—"

"The barricades are significant," the alien cautioned.

"To us, they are. We don't have the energy or tools to cut through the best grades of hyperfiber." Shaking his head, he said, "From what I've heard, whenever my mother's ship was damaged, she spent her free time trying to find some route to the interior. She explored at least a thousand of the old accessways leading down from here." Every tunnel, no matter how obscure, was blocked with hyperfiber too deep and stubborn to cut through. "But if there were captains below us and if only a fraction of the old reactors were working…they could still punch out in a matter of years…maybe weeks…"

Silence.

"So there are no captains," Peregrine would decide. Every time.

"Which implies what?"

"Somebody else is in charge of the Great Ship." That answer seemed obvious, and it was inevitable, and it made a good mind usefully worried. Yet that answer was a most frustrating creation, since it opened doors into an infinite range of possibilities, imaginable and otherwise.

"Who is in charge?" Hawking would ask, on occasion.

A few powerful species were obvious candidates. But each of them would have sent teams to the surface. They might be different species, but they would be drawn by the same reasons and needs that humans would feel.

"Perhaps the culprit is someone else," Hawking would propose. "An organism you haven't thought to consider."

Anything was possible, yes. Peregrine threw his ape arms into a posture that mimicked his friend's, underscoring the importance of his next words. "Nobody here is looking for a route down," he said. "What has it been? A thousand years since anyone has even tried."

The three hemispherical eyes were bright and still.

"Once I get enough savings in the bank," Peregrine said, "I'll take up my mother's other work. Just to see what I can see."

"That could be a reasonable plan," Hawking would say.

Most of the time, their conversation ended there. Peregrine often made that promise to himself, but he never had the resources or the simple will to invest in the luxury of a many-year search. Besides, he was the finest raider in the city, and raiders were essential. If he gave up his present work, the level of poverty everywhere would rise. Citizens would have to forego having children and new homes. At least that was his reliable excuse to wait for another decade or two, bidding time before setting out on what surely would be a useless adventure.

Hawking had never questioned Peregrine's lack of action. But then again, that creature was ancient and eerily patient, and who knew how many promises he had made to himself during the last aeons, all bound up inside his powerful mind, waiting to be fulfilled?

One day, Peregrine surprised himself; he imagined a fresh candidate and a compelling logic that would explain the mystery.

"It's the Great Ship," he offered.

The !eech was silent, but there was a different quality to his posture, and even the crystalline eyes looked brighter.

"The Ship itself has come to life," the young man proposed.

"And why would that be?"

"I don't know. Maybe it finally had enough of human beings at the helm, this damned Polypond trying to kill it, and all the rest of these unpleasant creatures running around inside it. So one day, it just woke up and said, 'Screw you. From here on, I'm in charge!'"

"Interesting," his friend said.

"And what if…?" Peregrine continued. Swallowing and then smiling, he asked, "What if we aren't just following some random line? Instead of heading out into nothingness, the Ship is actually steering us toward a genuine destination?" Then he laughed in a tight, nervous fashion. "What if our voyage has only just begun, Hawking?"

There was a momentary silence.

Then his friend replied, "Every voyage has just begun. If you consider those words in the proper way…"

7

Buried in those old data sinks were schematics for a host of impossible machines—devices too intricate or demanding to be built by refugees and their children. Included were wondrous starships like those that once brought passengers to the Great Ship. Peregrine had always dreamed of seeing vessels like those, and judging by the spectrums, that's what the apparition was: An armored starship equipped with a streakship drive, efficient and relentless, yet operating at some miniscule fraction of full-throttle. With just that whisper of thrust, the gap between him and it closed in an instant. Peregrine's ship was a tiny, toyish rocket that barely had time enough to fold its wings and kick itself out of the way. The rising starship missed Peregrine by less than ten kilometers. The silvered ball of hyperfiber stood on a plume of hard radiations, the exhaust narrow at the nozzle but widening as it drove downwards, scorching heat causing it to exploded outwards into an atmosphere that was cooked to a broth of softer plasmas, stark blue-white fire betraying only the coldest of the unfolding energies.

"Run!" he ordered.

His pilot had already made that panicked assessment. Using the last shreds of its wings, the raider ship tilted its nose and leaped toward space, not following the starship so much as simply trying to keep ahead of the awful fire. The black mass beneath them continued to churn and spin, and the living ocean below everything could see the starship. Defensive systems were triggered. The burning air suddenly filled with laser bursts and particle beams and a host of slow ballistic weapons that could never catch their target. Whatever the reason for fighting, hatred or simple instinct, the Polypond employed every trick in its bid to kill its opponent. And that's when Peregrine's tiny ship was kissed by one of the lasers, a portion of his hull and two entire wings turned to carbon ash and a telltale glow.

"Reconfigure!" he screamed.

The AIs began shuffling the surviving pieces, pulling their ship back into a rough shape that might remain whole for another few moments.

But the main fuel tank was pierced, leaking and unpatchable.

"We can't make it home," was the uniform verdict.

Peregrine had already come to that grim conclusion.

"Hunt for help," he said. "Who's close?"

"No one is," he heard.

The surviving portions of the black mass were still churning, a few billion fusion bombs riding little rockets. It was a useless gesture, Peregrine believed. But then he noticed how the cloud was changing as it moved, acquiring a distinct pancake-shaped base above which a tiny fraction of the bombs were gathering, pulling themselves into a dense, carefully stacked bundle.

In a shared instant, the pancake below ignited itself.

The resulting flash dwarfed every bolt of laser light, and even the stardrive faded from view. A hypersonic slap struck the last of those bombs, destroying most but throwing the rest of them skyward at a good fraction of light-speed. Then as the bombs passed into the last reaches of the atmosphere, they gave themselves one last shove, rockets carrying them close enough that the starship was forced to react, shifting its plume slightly, evaporating every last one of its pursuers.

But the pancake burst had launched more than just bombs. A fat portion of the atmosphere was being shoved upwards, and soon it would stand higher than Peregrine had ever seen. More out of instinct than calculation, he said, "Try wings again, and ride this updraft."

It wouldn't lift them much, no. But the soaring maneuver would keep them at a safer altitude for a little while longer.

"Now are there any raiders who can reach us?"

Several, maybe.

"Offer them anything," Peregrine told his mercantile AI. "Thanks. Money. My family name. Whatever works."

Moments later, a deal was secured.

The airborne wreckage of his ship continued to jump and lurch through the blazing atmosphere. Life support was close to failing, and once it did, his body would cook and temporarily die. Peregrine invested his last conscious moments looking up at the streakship, watching as it broke into true space, that relentless gorgeous engine throwing back a jet of plasma that grew even thinner and hotter as it began to find its strength.

"Yell at the ship," he ordered.

That brought confused silence.

"Assume there's a tribe of humans onboard," he instructed his AIs. "Curse at them and blame them for all our miseries. Say whatever you have to, but get them to talk back to us…"

"And then what?" asked his pilot.

"Remember everything they say," he muttered as his lips burned. "And everything they don't say…remember that too…!"

8

"You were once an engineer," he had whispered to Fusilade. "But not anymore, I have to believe."

"And why not?"

The arbitrary moment on the clock called 'morning' was approaching. The two humans were sleepy and physically spent. But Peregrine found the energy to explain, "I know every engineer. By face. By name. By skills. After all, I am a raider."

"You are."

"None of you founders are helping us fly. Your children and grandchildren, sure. But never you."

Silence.

"It's funny," he allowed. "I don't keep track of you. I mean humans and harum-scarums, the fef and all the others…those lucky ones who established our city. I doubt if I could attach ten faces to the right names, since most of you seem happy to keep close to each other…"

The only response was a smile, thin and wary.

Peregrine grew tired of this dance. "So what do you do with your time?" he finally asked.

The smile brightened. "I study."

"What subject?"

"Many matters." The woman was taller than Peregrine, and stronger. She pushed on his chest—pushed harder than necessary—and he felt his heart beating against the flat of her palm. Then very quietly, Fusilade asked, "What do you know about your half-brother?"

Peregrine offered a crisp, inadequate biography of a man who lived and died long ago.

"And your two sisters?"

There were three siblings in all. Two were raiders who eventually didn't return from their missions, while that final sister had followed their mother's other pursuit, hunting for a route back into the Great Ship. But a crude plasma drill exploded during testing, obliterating most of her mind along with her bones and meat.

With a shrug, Peregrine confessed, "I don't think about them too much. Different fathers and we never knew each other…and all that…"

His lover winked and said, "You know, he was their friend too."

"Who was?"

"You know who." The smile had been replaced by a genuinely cold expression, eyes weighing everything they saw—not unlike the !eech eyes. "He wore different names each time. But he was a companion to your sisters and your brother too. They weren't as good friends as you are to him, but he was always close. And when your mother had no living children, he would strike up a relationship with whoever seemed to be the best raider."

"I've heard that story before," Peregrine said. Then with a pride that took him a little by surprise, he added, "Yeah, everyone says that I've got some odd tie with Hawking, or whatever he wants to call himself…"

"What about Alopex?"

"What about her?"

"She and the alien knew each other. Not at first, no. At least, nobody in my circle remembers any relationship. But your mother invited your dear companion along when she went below, hunting for an open road to the Great Ship. I'm sure you can imagine why. That !eech could slip his way into some amazingly tiny crevices, if he had to…"

Peregrine was perfectly awake now.

Quietly, firmly, the ageless lover said, "I wouldn't want you to mention this to your good friend. What I'm sharing, I mean. Let's keep it between ourselves."

Again and again, the young man realized that he knew little about almost everything. Looking at the woman's stiff, unreadable face, he asked again, "What exactly do you do with your time?"

Her eyes narrowed.

"You're still an engineer, aren't you?"

"Do you think so?"

"The founders, and particularly the oldest of you…each of you has celebrated tens of thousands of birthdays. Minds like yours have habits, and habits don't easily change." Now he pushed sat up and pushed against her chest. The woman had an peculiar asymmetry—a giant black nipple tipped the small hard right breast, while its large and very soft neighbor wore a tiny silver cap. Between the breasts lay a heart beating faster than he expected. "So tell me: What kind of engineering do you do?"

"Mostly, I buy useless items in the markets."

"Which items?"

"Pieces of neural networks. You know, the little brains of those big corpses that you bring home…from gull-wands and clowners and the rest of the free-ranging bodies…"

Those brains were always tiny, simple of design, and often mangled or burnt. Generations of raiders had collected the trinkets, and not even the largest few had shown any hint of sentience.

"Maybe as individual fragments, they're simple." She pulled Peregrine's other hand over her chest, and smiled. "But if you splice them together, very carefully…if you spend a few thousand years doing little else…you'll cobble together something that captures a portion of one genuine soul. Maybe it's the Polypond's mind, maybe something else. Whatever it is, you find memories and images and ideas…and on occasion, you might even hear some timely, important news…"

"Such as?"

She refused to say.

"And what does this have to do with Hawking?"

"Maybe nothing," she replied with an agreeable tone. "But now that you mention it: What should we say about that very good friend of yours?"

9

In the end what was saved was too small and far too mutilated to reconstitute itself. Peregrine was a lump of caramelized tissue surrounding a fractured skull that held a bioceramic brain cut through by EM surges and furious rains of charged particles. The damage was so severe that every memory and tendency and each of his precious personal biases had to migrate into special shelters, and life had ceased completely for a timeless span covering almost eighteen days. Death held sway—longer than he had ever known, Nothingness ruled—and then after a series of quick tickling sensations and flashes of meaningless light, the raider found himself recovered enough that his soul migrated out of its hiding places and his newest eyes opened, gazing at a face that was not entirely unexpected.

"The streakship," he blurted with his new mouth. "Where?"

A limb touched his mouth and both cheeks, and then another limb touched his chest, feeling his heart. The limbs were soft strong and human—a woman's two hands—and then he heard her voice saying, "Gone," with finality. "Gone now. Gone."

"It got away safely?"

She said, "Yes," with a nod, then with her eyes, and finally with a whisper. And she leaned closer, adding, "The streakship has escaped, yes. Eighteen days, and it's still accelerating. Faster than you would ever guess, it is racing toward the Milky Way."

Peregrine tried to move, and failed. His legs and arms were only half-grown, wearing wraps filled with blood and amino acids. But he could breathe deeply, enjoying that sensation quite a lot. "What about my crew?"

"Degraded, but alive." The woman's face was pleased and a little astonished, telling him, "At the end, when you were rescued…when that other raider plucked you out of the mayhem…the AIs were flying what was really just a toy glider, barely as big as me, with one tenth of my mass…"

Peregrine tried to absorb his good fortune. How could you even calculate the long odds that he had crossed?

The ancient woman sat back, bidding her time.

"Did the streakship ever talk?" he asked.

"Yes." She nodded and smiled wistfully, and then with a matter-of-fact shrug, she added, "As soon as it got above us, we were hit with a narrow-beam broadcast. Yes."

"What did it say?"

"Life survives inside the Great Ship," she reported. "But our old leaders, the wise and powerful captains…they're gone now. All of them. Either dead or in hiding somewhere."

"Who is in charge?"

"Nobody."

"What does that mean?"

"From what the streakship told us, passengers are fending for themselves." The woman studied his new face. "However, there is one exceptionally obscure species that's come into some prominence. In fact, at the end of the Polypond War, they took control of the Great Ship's helm." She offered a flickering wink, and then added, "And oh…now that I mentioned that…guess who else has gone away…

"Somebody you know…

"Even before your body arrived home, he picked up his shell, and by the looks of it, scuttled away…"

10

Peregrine was perfectly healthy and profoundly poor. The raider who saved him had acquired most of his assets, while his debts to the hospital remained substantial, possibly eternal. He had no ship, and his crew was repaired and working with others. Several investors came forward, offering to pay for a new ship in return for a fat percentage of all future gains. But the only fair offer was a brief contract from his father, and for a variety of reasons, personal and otherwise, the young man decided to send it back unsigned and then follow an entirely new course.

If you live cheaply and patiently, it takes astonishingly little money to keep you breathing and content.

For most of a century, Peregrine stalked the deep tunnels and access ports that laced the Ship's central nozzle. Armed with maps left behind by his mother and sister, he hunted for routes they might have missed. He managed to find two or three every year, but each passageway was inevitably plugged with the high-grade hyperfiber. It was easy to see why no one kept up this kind of search for long. Yet Peregrine refused to quit, if only because the idea of failure gave his mouth such an awful taste.

New lovers drifted in and out of his life.

He occasionally saw the old lady engineer, meeting her for a meal and conversation. They hadn't slept together in decades, but they remained friendly enough. Besides, she had a sharp mind and important connections, and sometimes, when she was in the mood, she gave him special knowledge.

"You knew a big hatch was coming," Peregrine accused her. "That's why you seduced me when you did. Somehow, you and your founder friends pieced together clues that the rest of us don't ever get to see."

"Yet the hatch, big as it was, was only a secondary phenomena," she said. "Like blood from a fresh cut. I won't tell exactly how we knew, but we did. What was more important was that someone or something had emerged from one of the old ports. We had reasons to believe that an armored vessel was pushing through the Polypond ocean, heading our way…presumably to get into a useful position before jumping free of the Ship."

"And you suspected Hawking?"

"For thousands of years, I did. We did." Fusilade nodded, and then she said, "This isn't official. But in the final seconds of the War, a few messages arrived from the interior. They were heavily coded military broadcasts, which is why they aren't common knowledge. They describe the creatures that were taking over the battered Ship. The !eech, the broadcasts called them. And not wanting to alert the spy in our midst, we decided to keep those secrets to ourselves."

"But he's gone," Peregrine countered. "Why not make a public announcement?"

"Because we don't want to panic our children, of course."

"Am I panicking?"

"In slow motion, you are. Yes." The ancient engineer sat back in her chair, tapping at the heart nestled between her unequal breasts. "Spending your life searching for a way into the Ship, when we are as certain as we can be that there is no way inside…yes, I think that's genuinely panicked behavior…"

"Hawking disappeared, and that means there's at least one route out of this nozzle."

"If he did slip back into the Great Ship, perhaps. But for all we know, he's walking today across a living cloud off on some distant piece of the Polypond's body."

11

Peregrine had wasted decades haunting empty hallways and dangling from soft glass ropes. He could have wasted a thousand centuries before finding the relevant clue, but he was a lucky individual, and he had the good fortune of becoming lost at the proper moment. After two wrong turns, he found himself standing beside a tiny chute exactly like ten thousand other chutes. Except, that is, for the marks left behind by a delicate limb that had been dipped in paint. No, in blood. A blackish alien blood with a distinctive flavor, and the writing was a familiar script, showing the simple word, "HAWKING," followed by a simple yet elegant arrow pointing straight down.

The chute ended with a vast airless room built for no discernible purpose. Its walls were half a kilometer tall, and the floor was a circular plain covering perhaps ten square kilometers of featureless hyperfiber—stuff as old as the Ship, far better than any grade that could be chiseled through today. The only obvious doorway led out into the dormant rocket nozzle. Peregrine set up a torch in the room's center, and then he kneeled, searching that expanse with a powerful night scope. He should have missed the second doorway. If anyone else had ever visited this nameless place, they surely would have ignored what looked like a crevice, horizontal and brief. But someone was standing in front of the opening—a distinctive alien wearing a gossamer lifesuit, his long jointed legs locked into a comfortable position, the body motionless now and perhaps for a very long while.

Peregrine walked a few steps before breaking into a hard run.

On their private channel, Hawking said, "You look fit, my friend. And rather troubled too, I see."

"What are you doing here?" Peregrine asked.

"Waiting for you," was the reply.

"Why?"

"Because you are my friend."

"I don't particularly believe that," said the human. "From what I've heard, the !eech are my enemies…"

"I have injured you how many times?"

"Never," he thought, saying nothing.

"My friend," said Hawking. "What precise treacheries am I guilty of?"

"I don't know. You tell me."

Silence.

Peregrine had invested years wondering what he would say, should this moment arrive. "Why live with us?" seemed like a small, inadequate question, yet he asked it anyway. "Were you some kind of spy? Were you sent here to watch over us?"

There was a pause, then a cryptic comment. "You know, I saw you entering this place. I saw that quite easily."

"I've been climbing toward you for several hours," Peregrine complained. "Of course you saw me…"

Then he hesitated, rolling the alien's confession around in his head.

With relentless patience, Hawking waited.

Peregrine slowed his gait, asking, "How long have you been watching my approach?"

"Since your birth," the !eech said.

Peregrine stopped now.

After a few minutes of reflection, he said, "Those eyes of yours…they see into the future…?"

Silence.

"Do they see everything that's going to happen?"

"What eye absorbs everything there is to see?"

Peregrine shook his head. "A limited sight, is that it?"

One of the distant legs lifted high, signaling agreement.

"What else can you see, Hawking?"

"That I have never hurt you," the alien repeated.

"My half-sister…the one who died in the plasma blast…did you arrange that accident?"

"No."

"But did you see the accident approaching?"

Silence.

"And why did you come up on the hull, Hawking? The only reason I can think of is to spy on us."

"That is an obvious answer, and your imagination is richer than that, my friend."

Hard as it was to believe, the compliment forced Peregrine to smile. "Okay," he muttered. "You wanted to spy on our future. We're an independent society, free of the !eech, and maybe you're scared of us."

"That is an interesting assessment, but mistaken."

"I don't understand then."

"In time, you will," the !eech promised.

Then every one of its limbs was moving, carrying the creature backward into the narrow, almost invisible crevice. Peregrine began to run again, in a full sprint; but he was still half a kilometer from his goal when a warm gooey stew of fresh hyperfiber flowed into view, filling the crevice and pushing across the slick floor, glowing in the infrared as it swiftly and foever cured.

12

The final doorway had been opened just enough for a small human wearing a minimal lifesuit to slip through, and walking alone, he stepped onto a frigid, utterly flat plain. During the War, portions of the Polypond had splashed into the giant nozzle, dying here or at least freezing into a useless hibernation. Peregrine strode out to where he found a modest telescope as well as a set of telltale marks. His friend once stood here, those powerful eyes of his linked to the light-hungry mirror. By measuring the marks in the ice, and with conservative estimates of the heat lost by Hawking's lifesuit, Peregrine guessed that the creature had stood here for many years, pulling up his many feet when they had melted to uncomfortable depth and then dancing over to a fresh place before reclaiming his watchful pose.

Peregrine lay on his back now, slowly melting into the dead ice, and he fixed the same telescope to his eyes and purposefully stared at the sky.

The little city was barely visible—a sprinkling of tiny lights and heat signatures threatening to vanish against the vast bulk of the timeless, utterly useless nozzle. Millions of souls were up there, breeding and spreading out farther in a profoundly impoverished realm. Yet despite all of their successes, they seemed to have no impact on a scene that dwarfed all men and their small brief urges.

What wasn't the nozzle was the galaxy.

Here was what the !eech had been watching. Hawking had lived for thousands of years in a place that offered him comfort and the occasional companionship. But once the streakship had left, carrying its important news to the universe beyond, the creature's work had begun: Sitting on this bitter wasteland, those great eyes had been fixed on three hundred billion suns. Peregrine studied the maelstrom of stars and worlds, dust and busy minds; and perhaps for the first time in his life, he appreciated that this was something greater than any silly Polypond. Here lay an ocean beyond any other, and someday, in one fashion or another, a great hatch would rise from it—furious bodies riding upon a trillion, trillion wings, reaching for this prize that has been lost.

This Greatship.

www.ingramcontent.com/pod-product-compliance
Lightning Source LLC
Chambersburg PA
CBHW022032120726
47899CB00001BB/11